The
QUEEN'S
LADY

Part One

May Day

May 1517–June 1522

❧ 1 ❧

May Day

She would remember this forever after as the night she watched two men die, one at peace and one in terror. But now, seven years old and lost, Honor Larke knew only that she was out alone on a May Day night gone mad. She wedged herself into the shadows of a tavern doorway and prayed that the looters had not seen her. They were ransacking a house across the street, their torches flaring, and it seemed to Honor as though devils in a play had swarmed from the stage and hell blazed right before her.

She was trapped.

She could not go back to Cheapside. The London apprentices were rioting there. Their annual day of carousing had boiled into violence against the rich foreigners, especially the Italians, called Lombards, and Honor's chest still burned from tearing through a Cheapside mob pitching rocks at a goldsmith's shop while the women inside screamed in a strange tongue. But she could not go forward either, for thieves exploiting the night's chaos had joined some apprentices to lay waste this side street.

They were heaving booty out to their accomplices from windows in the three-storied merchant's house across from her. Bolts of silk billowed down in ribbons of crimson and jade. Wooden chests smashed onto the cobblestones, spilling papers and coins. A dozen thieves were scooping the spoils into sacks. One of them, a toothless old man squatting in the middle of the street, hummed as he picked through a scatter of Venetian silver spoons. A thief with a torch hustled by Honor's hiding place, and she gagged on the acrid smoke of the blazing tarred rags. She clamped her hand on her mouth to cover the sound.

"Will, catch this," a man called from a window. He tossed out a garnet-studded casket. "Careful. It'll fetch enough to buy a bishop's whore."

Above him, a voice crowed from the top floor. "I found me one!"

The knots of foraging men looked up. Under a gable, a hefty young apprentice stood at a smashed-out loading door. "Found me a Lombard!" he sang out. "Scribbling at his desk, he was!" He tugged a quill pen from his hair and waved it like a trophy. He darted inside, and for a moment the opening was empty, lit by the garish torchlight from within. Then a man was pushed into view. White-haired, he was dressed in a long, black gown. He stood still and quiet, his hands behind him. The boy took a fistful of the man's hair and jerked his head back, and the man twisted slightly, revealing a scarlet cord trussing his wrists.

Gaping up, Honor crammed herself against the tavern door until its latch gouged her shoulder.

"Can't see him," a man in the street groused.

The boy under the gable shoved the man, forcing him to step up onto the sill where he swayed unsteadily.

"No finery on him," the man below scoffed. "Where's his Lombard silks and jewels?"

"Hold on." The boy began draping necklaces over the head of his hostage and layering brightly coloured scarves around his neck. "There. Now he's a Turk."

This brought laughter from below. The boy giggled and piled on more trinkets. His sleeve snagged on one of the chains around the man's neck. Annoyed, the boy yanked free his sleeve, and the man scuffled forward to balance himself. His foot stubbed against an iron latch, and he fell. He plunged down, his gown rippling through the air. His body thudded onto the cobbles. He lay motionless. Silence, like a shroud cast out after him, settled over the watchers.

The toothless old man whined, "That's done it." He began raking in his bright spoons. "That boy'll hang, and the mayor's men'll be after us all."

"Shut your face," the boy snapped. "He's just a God-rotting Lombard." But within moments he and the others inside had sifted out into the street, joining the men who stood around the body. "Stupid old fart," the boy said. "If he'd just stood still . . ." He gave the body a savage kick.

Honor gasped. The boy caught the sound and wheeled. He squinted across at the murky tavern entrance. Honor wormed down the door, the back of her dress snagging on the rough wood. She squatted in the corner, heart pounding.

The boy motioned to a man with a torch. Together, they stalked to the tavern doorway. "Well, lookit here," the boy brayed over his shoulder. "A little spy." His grip burned Honor's wrist as he yanked her out. "Where'd you spring from, goblin?"

Though trembling, she dug in her heels. The boy grabbed her under the armpits, lifted her in the air and shook her roughly. "Speak up!" he said. She flinched at the blast of breath that stank of sour ale. He shook her again. "Be you English or a God-cursed foreigner?"

She didn't know how to answer. She wasn't sure what a foreigner was. Under the vise of his hands, her ribs felt on fire.

"Please, sir, I've only come to fetch home Ralph."

"And who the devil be Ralph?"

"My father's servant."

"A foreigner?"

"Aw, leave it," a man by the body called, preparing to leave.

Another said, "Gilbey's right. Mayor's men'll be coming. I'm off, too."

The boy set Honor down so harshly she staggered for balance. Wordlessly, men and boys gathered up their booty, leaving behind small piles of litter, and scuttled into the alleys. Their torchlight evaporated. Under the hiding moon the street went dark and cold. Papers fluttered. The faint, far-away bursts of shouts and shattering glass rolled over the rooftops then died in the air above Honor and the body. She looked across the street at it. It lay sprawled amongst the refuse, a black mound.

There was a moan. Honor's heart tightened. The sound had come from the body.

"*Per favoré . . . qualcuno . . . O! Per pietà!*"

Honor stood still, afraid, unsure. She heard a scrabbling on the cobbles. A dog was snuffling through the litter. It moved to the body and circled it.

The man did not move. "*Va! Va via!*" he gasped.

The dog seemed to sense his helplessness. It thrust its muzzle into the open neck of his gown.

"*Per pietà-à-à!*"

Without thinking, Honor sprang from the doorway. She snatched up a pewter goblet and hurled it. It struck the dog's hind leg. The dog yelped. She seized a pot and pitched it as well. The dog turned and bolted up the street.

"Who is there?" the man cried.

Honor came closer, cautiously, and stood over him. The moon sailed out from the cover of clouds, washing him with a cold, white light. Now she could see him clearly. He lay on his back on top of his bound arms. At his throat the scarves and necklaces were twined in a bright tangle. He did not move. His eyes were closed. His moans had stopped. Has he died? she wondered.

His eyelids sprang open. For a moment, man and child stared at one another.

"Thank you," he whispered. "The dog . . ." He stopped to cough.

"Do you hurt?" Honor asked.

A small smile tugged at his lips. "No hurt. Back is broken. Feel nothing . . ." His voice trailed. "*Muoro.* I am dying . . ."

If he's dying, she thought, how can he smile? But she realized what she must do. "Sir, I'll fetch a priest."

"No! No need!"

The sudden fierceness of his voice surprised her. She did not want to disobey him, but everyone knew that God would not allow a soul into heaven if it was filthy with unconfessed sin. "Sir," she said, marveling at his ignorance, "you must be shriven." She did not want him to burn in hell's fires forever.

"No," he insisted, faintly now. "Confession . . . priests . . . prayers to God . . . no good . . ."

She drew back. He was speaking blasphemy. Even a child knew that. But she noticed blood seeping from the corner of his mouth, dripping onto the cobbles like ink. Maybe dying is making him mad, she thought. Otherwise, how can he smile so? "Sir," she asked softly, "are you not afraid to die? And all alone?"

"You came to help me," he whispered. "When there was no one else, you came. What should I fear when I have *uno àngelo*—an angel—beside me?"

Honor stiffened at the sound of footsteps. The moon was masked again by clouds and she could not see far, but she could hear the low voices of men, their words indistinct.

The dying man heard them too. His body jerked once in a spasm. "Inside . . . my gown," he rasped. "*Piccolo àngelo* . . . take it." He was spitting blood. "Take it! Now!"

Honor kneeled and reached into his gown. She withdrew a slim book slightly larger than a man's hand.

"I wrote it," he said, his eyes glinting as if with joy, "for you."

"For me?" she asked, beguiled, though his comment made no sense, strangers as they were. She could not even read.

"But never . . . never show it to a priest!" He coughed. Honor winced as the warm mist of blood sprayed her hands. "You understand? Never . . . to a priest!"

"A secret?" she whispered.

Again, his lips formed a serene smile. "*Si, piccolo àngelo.* A secret . . ."

Blood bubbled out of his mouth. His head lolled. His dead eyes stared at her, wide open. But Honor felt no horror. Despite the violence done to him, his life had closed so peacefully.

"Somewhere 'round here . . ." It was a man's voice. Two dark forms were turning the corner of the ransacked house. Honor stuffed the book deep inside her wide sleeve and crouched. Looking across the body, she watched the men approach. They were kicking at the litter.

"You sure there was a purse on him?" one man muttered.

"I saw it at his belt," the other insisted. "When he fell."

"Well, find him and cut it. And let's be off."

"And his rings? Cut his rings, too?"

"Cut off his poxy balls, if you want, but get the purse."

The second man finally saw the body and shot out a finger. "There!"

They both hurried forward. A few paces from the body the second man stopped abruptly and held out his arm to stop the other. "Jesus, it's that sneaking girl."

Both men whipped out knives. They stepped toward her.

Honor jumped up, ready to bolt.

From behind her a thick arm swept around her waist and snatched her. Her body was jackknifed, facedown, and she could see only the heels of her abductor's boots. He bounded up the street, and she gasped for air, pinned against his thigh. She was joggled half a block before the man carrying her swung into an alley and halted. He hoisted her up roughly, his hands encircling her rib cage. Fierce with fear, she swung her fists at him with eyes closed, but he held her away easily.

"What do you think you're up to?" he cried.

Her eyes popped open. "Ralph!"

She threw her arms around his neck and pressed her face against the stubble of his cheek. "Oh, Ralph," she gulped, "they were smashing the houses! And they pushed the foreigner man out the window, and he fell, all broken! And those robbers were going to kill me, and—"

"Hush, little mistress, I've got you now." He cupped one beefy hand around the back of her head and hugged her with the other. "You be safe now. Hush." He began walking quickly.

She held tight, drinking in the familiar smell of his battered leather jerkin and feeling safe, indeed, in his embrace. Ralph Pepperton, at nineteen, was over six feet tall and built like a tree trunk. Honor had been told by her nurse, Margaret—with no little pride—that Ralph had never lost a fight. On Lady Day, when he had vaulted the neighbor's garden wall to visit the pretty scullery maid there, a brawl with two of that household's retainers had ensued, and the servants on both sides had bet money on Ralph. "An ox on two feet," Honor's father had called Ralph that day, and beamed as he pocketed his own winnings.

Ralph was heading up the dark alley, making for the glow of torches on the broad thoroughfare of Cheapside. "What a night," he growled, kicking through the garbage of dung and bones. "May Day's for fun, right enough, but this time the 'prentices have gone too far. They've burst Newgate jail and loosed the prisoners. And now they're off to fire the houses on Lombard Street. I watched some hound a Frenchman up the belfry of St. Mary's like a rat before they dragged him down and set on him."

He talked on as if to soothe her, though his voice was tight with indignation. "I grant the 'prentices have some cause to hate the strangers, but Sweet Jesu, there be some mighty sins committed this night. And they'll pay for it, sure as there's eel pie at Lent. But never fear, little mistress," he murmured, "you be safe with me."

She hugged him with all her might, but when he squeezed her in return she flinched, still tender from the apprentice's rough handling. Ralph stopped. Beneath a window where a candle flickered he pried her away from his neck and quickly examined her muddy face and arms. His voice was harsh with an anger she had never heard from him. "Whatever in God's good creation lured you out?" he said. "On this cursed night of all nights."

She pouted in silence and he hoisted her up as if to shake an answer from her.

"Stop that, Ralph Pepperton! I won't be shaken anymore!" Tears sprang to her eyes. "Let me go!"

Tenderly, he set her again in the crook of his arm. But his scowl remained firm. "Well?"

She glared at him, her arms folded over her chest. "I came out for *you*! And I don't see why you should be angry when I only came to save you."

"Save me?" he blustered.

"Yes. Master Ellsworth said he'd skin you alive if he found you'd left the house." Ellsworth was her father's chamberlain. After curfew, she had seen him prowling the house for absent servants, thwacking his stick ominously against his shin. "He was in a terrible fume. And I knew you'd left. I heard you at the kitchen door this afternoon, telling the baker's 'prentice you'd meet him later at the sign of the Ploughman's Rest."

"Do you mean you wriggled out of your bed, away from old Margaret, and came out to the Ploughman's . . . for *me*?"

"Yes. But I got lost." She bit her lip, remembering the fearful hours of wandering, then the mob, the flames, and the white-haired man falling to his death. "Oh, Ralph . . ." she said, fighting back tears, "it was only because of Master Ellsworth with his stick . . ."

Ralph's scowl had already softened, although he kept his voice stern. "Master Ellsworth and his stick be my lookout, mistress." He took her chin in his calloused hand and grinned. "But it be a kind little heart—and a brave one—that prompted you to do it."

She smiled back, loving him.

"Now," he said, stepping away from the wall, "we've got to get you back a-bed before Margaret wakes herself with her own snoring and finds you gone." He shook his head and whistled through his teeth. "Maybe dunk you in a bucket first, for I swear you're more mud than maid."

She followed his gaze toward Cheapside where bright torchlight was now spilling partway down the alley. She could hear shouting there, too.

Ralph looked back over his shoulder, then frowned as if rejecting that route. "The alleys will be crawling with lousels," he muttered. He looked forward again at Cheapside and set his jaw. Hugging Honor in one arm, he unsheathed his dagger and strode up toward the light. Just before they reached the wide street he ducked into the shadows and halted. Honor twisted in his arms to look.

Two bands were squared off like small armies on a battlefield. One, a mob of twenty-odd apprentices—young men from about fourteen to twenty—was jeering at the other, a city delegation. Above the street, half-open shutters revealed candles, and night-caps, and frightened faces.

The delegation was made up of three mounted aldermen— ineffectual-looking despite their fine velvets—who lurked behind a dozen foot-soldiers with pikes. In front of the soldiers, two more officials sat on horseback: a grizzled Sergeant of the Guard who wore half-armor, and a dark-haired man of middle age, unarmed and plainly dressed. The Sergeant's sword and steel breastplate glinted above the mob's torches.

"I warn you again," the Sergeant barked to the mob, "you are breaking the law."

"Pissing curfew," an apprentice yelled. "That's no real law."

Fuming, the Sergeant jerked a thumb at the simply dressed man beside him. "I'll take my instruction on the law from the Undersheriff here, Master Thomas More, not from rabble. Now, quit this place! Or end your days as gallows fruit."

A young man hefting a bloodied cudgel at the front of the mob strode up to the Sergeant's stallion. "And what about our grievance, then? What about the foreigners? There be hundreds of the buggers, snatching the crusts from our mouths."

"Aye," another bleated from the ranks. "And a God-cursed lender from Mantua bled my master with interest of fifteen percent."

"They infect the city with plague and palsy," the young man beside the stallion cried back to his mates. "Burn their kennels down, I say!"

The apprentices stamped. Torches bobbed.

The Sergeant swung up his sword above the young man's head. The air sighed with the sudden movement. "Sodden bastards," he shouted. "Quit this place!"

Thomas More's voice broke through. "Whoa, there!" His brown mare was dancing sideways. He jigged awkwardly at the reins, but the animal, apparently ignoring him, cut between the young man and the Sergeant, forcing them apart.

"Pardon me, Sergeant," More cried helplessly over his shoulder. "My horse is but green-broke."

The mare capered forward through the no-man's-land between the two camps, seemingly out of More's control. It veered into the front rank of apprentices, and several had to stagger backwards out of its way.

"You there. Jamie Oates," cried More. "Grab a-hold, boy."

A yellow-haired fifteen-year-old dashed out of the mob and grappled the bridle near the horse's bit. It settled instantly and stood still.

"I'm obliged to you, Jamie," More said, displaying relief. The boy beamed up and respectfully touched his cap.

More dismounted, turned, and shrugged a final apology. Then, before the bewildered eyes of both groups, he led his suddenly calm horse to a water trough at the mouth of the alley and allowed it to drink.

Honor craned her neck to see as she and Ralph watched from the shadows.

Above the horse's slurping Jamie let go a jittery giggle with a nod at the aldermen. "Master More, you'll have that mare pissing in their lordships' path."

Nervous laughter rippled through the mob. The Sergeant, the soldiers, and the aldermen kept a stony silence. Thomas More smiled indulgently at the boy. Then he eased himself up to stand on the rim of the trough. From this narrow platform he could be seen by all. "Young Jamie Oates here knows you can't keep a horse from pissing when it must," he called out with wry good humour. "Jamie, you're a quick, smart lad," he went on, still loud enough for all to hear. "You're apprenticed to Addison, are you not?"

"Aye, sir. Master Addison. Finest smith in Thames Street," the boy answered proudly.

More smiled. "Jamie's a credit to his master. He'll make a fine ironsmith himself one day." He paused for a moment while Jamie preened beside his friends.

"And when that day comes, Jamie," More continued courte-ously, "when you have apprentices of your own, what will you ask of them in return for the care you've given them? For their bed and board and instruction in a good trade, what's a fair return? Will you expect loyalty and diligence? Or faithlessness and insurrection?"

The boy's grin vanished.

A voice from the back of the mob shouted, "What good be his trade if foreigners take all the work?"

"Aye," cried another. "And you lawmen let them fleece us." Complaints rumbled.

More listened patiently, then held up his hands to ask for si-lence. "Jamie knows what kind of law I dispense. His master came before my court last month when a Flemish smelter claimed Addi-son had not paid him for a wagonload of iron. Jamie came to my court and gave testimony. Jamie, tell the men here what verdict I gave."

All eyes went to Jamie who was looking intently at the ground as if in search of a lost penny. More waited, his arms folded across his chest, his gray eyes gently fixed on the boy.

Jamie answered petulantly like an unwilling pupil. "Master More gave the victory to my master."

"And . . . ?" More coaxed.

"And he ordered the Fleming to pay my barge fare back to the workshop."

"And . . . ?"

Jamie's face reddened. "And ordered him to . . . to stand me and my master a pot of ale at the Golden Dog."

Waves of laughter broke out at the confession.

In the alley Ralph let out a snort of amusement. Honor had by this time wriggled out of his arms and clambered up onto his shoulder to get a better view, and she laughed as well, uncertain about what exactly had happened, but aware that, with nothing but his calm voice and words, Master More had made the rioters laugh and the soldiers smile. Even the fierce-looking Sergeant had lowered his sword.

"That lawyer's wind has cooled them," Ralph chuckled. He winced as Honor steadied herself with a handful of his hair, then he clasped her dangling ankles and whispered with a grin, "And if that mare of his be only green-broke, as he claims, then I'm the Duchess of Buckingham."

"My friends," More called out, suddenly earnest. "The Apostle urges obedience to authority. And I would not be in error if I told you that by raising arms tonight against the foreigners you have raised arms against God, and so endangered your immortal souls."

Several apprentices crossed themselves.

"God has lent His office here on earth to the King," More explained. "The foreigners dwell here with the King's goodwill. So when you rise against the foreigners, you rise against the King. And when you rise against the King,"—he pointed heavenward—"what are you doing but rising against God?"

He let this heavy question hang in the air. Honor had a sudden vision of the young King Henry, the eighth of that name, kneeling before a jeweled altar and forlornly praying for his erring subjects, his head bowed under the weight of his jeweled crown.

When More spoke again his voice was gentle, reasonable. "Now, let us suppose that the King is merciful with all of you tonight. Let us say he does no more than banish you from the realm."

Again he paused to let the full horror of such a sentence take hold.

"I ask you this: what country, after the disrespect for law that you have shown, would give you safe harbor? France? Flanders? Spain?" His eyebrows lifted in rhetorical expectation of an answer. "Say that some place *will* take you. Think now. In any land but England, it is you who would be called foreigners."

Several faces frowned at the dismaying paradox.

"Would you then want to find yourselves in a nation of such barbarity that the people would not allow you even a roof over your heads?" His voice rose to a crescendo of indignation. "A land where they whetted their knives against your throats, and spurned you like dogs?"

Honor looked over the top of Ralph's head at the subdued apprentices. They scratched their chins and glanced at one another, some ashamed, some bewildered. Again, she marveled at how Master More had worked such an astonishing change on them.

But the young man with the bloodied cudgel was unmoved. "Enough words," he shouted. He snatched up a large stone, and with a cry of, "God curse all poxy foreigners!" he pitched it. It struck the Sergeant's forehead. The Sergeant reeled back in his saddle, groping at the reins, blood trickling from the gash.

Both sides froze.

From a window a woman's voice shrilled, "You'll not murder the King's men!" She and her neighbors began pelting down a shower of boots and bones upon the apprentices. The Sergeant bellowed, "Down with them!" and led his men in a charge. Cudgels flew, splitting lips and noses. Thomas More, dismayed, stepped down and backed away.

Ralph's arm swung around Honor again. He toppled her over his shoulder like a bundle of cloth, edged around the fracas, and ran off down Cheapside.

* * *

By the time Ralph pushed through the gate of Christopher Larke's townhouse Honor was half asleep in his arms. Ralph hurried across the courtyard, and Honor stirred as he hushed the yapping dogs and headed for the kitchen door. There, under a hanging lantern, Ralph stopped to catch his breath. He lifted his face to let the breeze cool his sweat-dampened hair and shirt.

Honor winced at a pain in her side. She found its source, a hard corner of the little book inside her sleeve. She pulled the book out. Under the lamplight its blue leather cover swirled with gilt-tooled leaves and petals. The leather was spattered with dried droplets of blood. She looked up at Ralph. "The foreigner man gave me this," she whispered.

The book was fastened with two small brass clasps. She pried them up. Leaves of creamy, thick vellum fluttered, then settled open at the title page. Honor's eyes drifted below the incomprehensible letters to a drawing. It was a single, startlingly beautiful painting of a flower—a winding stem with toothed, oval leaves of spring green, and a blossom of four, joined petals. The petals burst out in glorious blue, a gay sky blue, bright and bold.

"Speedwell," Ralph whispered, smiling at the wildflower.

Honor's fingers traced over the elegant characters of the title as if she might absorb their meaning by touch. What mysteries did such a beautiful book have to tell? she wondered. *"Never show it to a priest!"* the foreign man had warned, and then he had smiled, though he knew he was dying. Did his book hold some secret that had made him smile like that? Her eyes were drawn back to the flower, so fresh and lifelike beneath her stare. "Speedwell," she repeated softly, and the blossom seemed almost to nod, as if trembling under her breath.

"Peppers," Honor declared suddenly, looking Ralph in the eye, "I'm going to learn to read."

He frowned. "Reading be for priests and clerks, not for ladies, mistress." He clamped her nose between his knuckles and whispered with mock anger, "And what's this 'Peppers,' if you please? That name was only for your lady mother to use, God rest her soul. Not wild little wenches like you." Honor squirmed, trying to pry her nose out from his grip, and she giggled when he finally pretended that she had beaten him and won free.

The kitchen door burst open. Honor's stout nurse, Margaret, gasped. "You're here!" She was disheveled and bleary-eyed. "Oh, little mistress, we've been looking everywhere. It's your father. Struck with the Sweat, he is."

Her voice came high and frightened as she crossed herself. "Blessed Jesu, Ralph, the master lies a-dying!"

Honor's father was writhing on his bed.

She stood near the doorway of the darkened chamber, Margaret on one side of her, Ralph on the other. Ralph tightly held her hand. Servants huddled along the walls. Some held apron corners or cloths to their noses to block the reek of putrid sweat.

Honor knew about the sweating sickness. It had killed her only other close relatives, two uncles. It frequently struck London in spring, and everyone dreaded it for the appalling swiftness of the death it usually brought. "Merry at dinner, dead at supper," she'd often heard the servants murmur. But they had meant the sweating sickness in other people's houses. Now, it was here, in hers.

On the pillow, her father's face was a stranger's face. His fair hair was dark with sweat. Red blotches mottled his cheeks. His eyes, which she had seen shed tears only when he laughed too hard, were seeping a milky discharge. He was moaning softly.

A priest she had never seen before stood by the bed. It was clear he was a muscular young man, but his broad back was to her and she could not see his face. On the table beside him a single candle guttered, and its light glinted in a crescent along the top of his bald crown, shaved to create his priest's tonsure. Below it, a fringe of black hair hung raggedly over his ears. The hem of his threadbare black cassock was crusted with mud. His scuffed boots had dropped clumps of horse dung onto the floor rushes.

"Who is he?" Ralph whispered to Margaret.

"Name's Father Bastwick," she whispered back. "The priest's new curate at Nettlecombe. Dog-poor, as you can see. He just rode in, out of the night," she said, wringing her hands. "He's been badgering the master for the corpse present."

Honor understood the fear in Margaret's voice. When Honor's mother had died ten months before at their manor of Nettlecombe in Somerset, the old parish priest had requested the embroidered coffin cloth for his mortuary fee—the "corpse present"—as was his right. Unreasonable in grief, her father had refused. The priest denounced him from the pulpit. Her father had remained stubborn, and the feud had festered all these months.

The young priest at the bedside suddenly said angrily, "By all the laws of custom and decree, you owe this debt to Holy Church."

Honor's fingers tightened into a ball inside Ralph's hand.

Larke's gaze wandered, unfocused. "Father," he said through labored breaths, "never mind . . . all that. I ask you only . . . hear my confession. Prepare me . . . to meet my God."

"I marvel at your blasphemous intransigence, man," the priest replied. "The amount is a trifle to you. The sapphire ring you wear would more than suffice. Pay the mortuary now. It is a surety against absolution of your sins."

"Never!" Larke cried with sudden violence. "No more grasping priests. You're vultures, all. Get out!" Sapped by his outburst, his head lolled on the sweat-stained pillow.

"Never?" Bastwick's voice was steel. "Never, Master Larke, is a very long time."

He snatched up the candle with a vehemence that made the flame shrink and twist as if in terror. He strode to the middle of the room and raised the candle high in his outstretched arm. He plucked the silver crucifix from his chest. Drawing its chain over his head, he thrust it up also so that his arms formed a V above his head. The servants sucked in horrified breath. They recognized the stance for excommunication.

"By the authority of the Father and of the Son and of the Holy Ghost," Bastwick intoned, "and of our Lady St. Mary, God's Mother in heaven, and of all the other virgins, and St. Michael and all the angels, and St. Peter and all the apostles, and St. Stephen and all the martyrs, and of all the holy saints of heaven, we accurse thee."

The servants dropped to their knees, crossing themselves.

"We ban and depart thee from all good deeds and prayers of Holy Church, and of all these saints, and damn thee unto the pain of hell."

"No!" Larke bolted upright.

"We curse thee by the authority of the court of Rome, within and without, sleeping or walking, going or sitting, standing or riding, lying above earth or under earth, speaking and crying and drinking, in wood, in water, in field, in town."

"No!" Larke was thrashing his way out of the sheets. He thudded onto the floor. He crawled towards Bastwick, whimpering. Honor lurched to go to him, but Ralph held her back. She thought his grip would crush her hand.

The V of Bastwick's outstretched arms glinted at either end with flame and silver. "Accurse him Father and Son and Holy Ghost. Accurse him, angels and archangels and all the nine orders of heaven. Accurse him, patriarchs and prophets and apostles and all God's holy disciples, and all holy innocents, martyrs, confessors, virgins, monks, canons and priests. Let him have no mass or matins, nor none other good prayers that be done in Holy Church."

Grunting across the floor, Larke reached Bastwick's feet. "No! I beg you . . ." Sobs choked him.

"Let the pains of hell be his mead with Judas that betrayed our Lord Jesus Christ. And let him be cast forever out of the book of life." Bastwick threw down the candle, extinguishing it, and spat on the ground beside Larke to complete the anathema. "Fiat. Fiat. Amen."

Larke moaned and clawed at the hem of the priest's cassock. Honor could not bear it. She broke free and ran to her father's bowed back and threw herself on it, her arms around his neck.

Larke's head snapped up. "The demons!" he screamed, delirious. "The demons are on me!" He clawed at the weight on his back to rid himself of the devils, and threw Honor to the floor. Gasping, she caught his eyes—yellow, bloodshot, wild with terror—and she saw he did not know her. He let out a harrowing yelp and grappled Bastwick's legs, weeping. His weeping turned to convulsive choking. He gasped. Breath would not come. His fingers clawed at his throat. Blood engorged his face. His mouth opened and closed in wordless horror. His fingers petrified into a sudden rigor and he fell to the floor, dead.

Bastwick looked down at the body. He bent over and lifted the lifeless hand. He pried off the sapphire ring, then said to the dead man, as if sealing a bargain agreeable to both parties, "This jewel, as I told you, will suffice." He closed his fist around the ring, turned, and walked toward the door.

Margaret ran forward and snatched up Honor and clutched her to her bosom. "Blessed Jesu, little mistress, what's to become of you now?"

Bastwick whirled around. "Who's this child?" he demanded.

"The master's only babe, Father," Margaret wailed. "And what's to become of her now?"

Bastwick did not answer. But he fixed his stare on Honor as if discovering a thing he had been searching for. She stared back, straight into the brilliant, black eyes that bored into hers.

Jerome Bastwick studied the sapphire ring on his finger and shut out the morning tavern voices around him. Outside the tavern, the city streets were uncharacteristically quiet; the night's rioting had been quelled by the Earl of Surrey who had marched troops into the city in the early hours. But Bastwick did not concern himself with the lull outside nor the voices inside that murmured over the night's events. He was absorbed by the ring. He twisted it on his finger, entranced by its beauty as pale sunlight from the window struck various hues of purple fire over the jewel's facets.

A yapping whippet bitch scrabbled past him. Bastwick lifted his head to reality: to the half-dozen men in the loft cursing over a cockfight; to the reek of the floor rushes, spongily matted with ale dregs and spittle, and rank with decaying fish and dog urine; to the scratch of fingernails against stubble coming from his broken-toothed companion across the table. Over the breakfast remains of beef and bread, Sir Guy Tyrell was considering the bargain Bastwick had just proposed. A dangerous bargain, but one that held sweet promise for them both.

"You're sure there's no boy?" Tyrell asked skeptically. Using the tip of the dagger that served as his eating knife, he picked a fragment of beef from between his chipped, yellow teeth. "No heir to spring up later and mar all?"

Bastwick shook his head confidently. "I assure you, the girl is sole heiress."

"And you really can hoodwink those poxy clerks at the Court of Wards? Confound 'em with papers in your Latin mumbo jumbo? The stewards too? It's a risk . . ." Tyrell broke off, his face darkening with mistrust over this area of expertise so far beyond his illiterate understanding. He lowered his voice, but his whisper was spiked with a threat. "Remember, priest, it's cheating the King you're talking of."

"*We* are talking of," Bastwick corrected him steadily.

The admonition brought bright red smudges of anger high on Tyrell's cheeks. "Aye," he snarled, "I mark my own hazard right clearly in this business. I mark which one of us will swing from the King's gibbet if we're found out. Not you. They can't hang a precious priest, can they?" With a sudden motion of menace he lifted his dagger and pressed its tip to the hollow of Bastwick's throat. Bastwick held his breath.

"But I swear to you now, man," Tyrell said, "blab of this to anyone, ever, and before I hang I'll have you praying and whimpering for such a tidy end."

Bastwick remained calm. He had known the cash-starved Tyrell for barely twenty-four hours; the day before, they had struck up a conversation in a Westminster corridor as each waited with the milling gentlemen who came daily to pick up any crumb of patronage that fell from the table of Cardinal Wolsey. Both had left empty-handed, and they parted. But though the acquaintance was slight, Bastwick prided himself on his swift judgment of men. And when the scheme came to him, he was certain this chance of quick cash—the revenues of an heiress's estates, to which a guardian was entitled—was one Tyrell could not resist.

"You say true, sir, about the risk—*my* risk—in managing the clerks, and the estate stewards," Bastwick said sternly. "You cannot do without me."

Tyrell's eyes hardened. He held the blade rigid at Bastwick's throat.

Bastwick did not flinch. His eyes locked with Tyrell's. "Therefore, my lord," he went on, "you must guarantee me the benefice."

Tyrell held the right to appoint a priest to a benefice in the west country parish where he was lord. The thought of it made Bastwick's heart race with joy despite Tyrell's dagger. His own benefice! With fat tithes, and rents from the glebe lands he would control! It was far beyond anything he could hope for from the miserly vicar of Nettlecombe. The old vicar lived high and dined with the Bishop, while he, Bastwick, scraped by on a pittance as his curate. He deserved better. He silently cursed his peasant background for keeping him in such servility. Still, he reminded himself, the abbot who had seen promise enough in him to educate him had schooled him well in what was possible: the Church was the one institution that cared more for a man's ability than his blood. Had not the great Cardinal Wolsey himself risen from his father's base butcher's shop? The cardinal—so rich, they said, he had fragrant imported herbs strewn over his palace floors twice a day. The cardinal—Chancellor of the realm, the second most powerful man in England, right hand to the King.

"Alright, priest," Tyrell growled, drawing back his dagger and sheathing it. "Profit's good. And we share the risk. We are agreed."

Bastwick relaxed. He noticed again the light dancing over the jewel on his finger. Yes, he thought jubilantly, a man of ability needs only the will to plant his foot firmly on the steps that will lead him up to glory.

The Larke household stumbled through the day following the master's death. Honor sat close to Ralph beside the laid-out body of her father and tried to listen to what Master Ellsworth was telling her, but his words were all a jumble to her. He spoke of her father's estates, of the King's Court of Wards at Westminster, of gentlemen who would soon be bidding there for her wardship. She understood little of it. In the hushed bedchamber that smelled of death, she hung onto Ralph's hand.

That evening, as she and Ralph crossed the courtyard to join the mourning household already at vespers in the family chapel, horsemen clattered through the gate. Honor saw Father Bastwick riding at the head of the band. He pointed to her. "That's the girl," he said.

The broken-toothed lord beside him ordered one of his men to seize her. The henchman dismounted.

Honor darted behind Ralph. Shielding her, Ralph called to Bastwick, "What's this about, Father?"

"Let her go. This is Sir Guy Tyrell. The girl is his ward now."

"What? Can the Court of Wards have judged so soon?"

"Do you question the King's justice, man?" Bastwick asked witheringly.

"Not I, Father," said Ralph. "If this *be* the King's justice."

"Ha," the lord snorted, "all will be legal enough once I marry her to my boy, eh, priest?"

Honor, pressing close to Ralph, could feel his muscles tense. He stepped backwards, pushing her back as well. He looked at the priest, "And what reward be in this unholy bargain for you, Father?"

Honor saw the priest's black eyes flash at Ralph with anger.

"I tire of this fellow's prating," Tyrell growled. He signaled to his other men. They dismounted and stalked toward Ralph.

Ralph fought, but he could not prevail over four men. They soon had him on his knees, his nose bleeding, his arms trussed.

The henchman did not find Honor easy to subdue. She kicked and bit and screamed for help. Bastwick glanced furtively around the empty courtyard. He jumped from his horse, pulled a knife from his boot and strode over to Ralph. He lifted Ralph's head by the hair and held the knife at his throat. Ralph sucked in a breath. "Come tamely, girl," Bastwick said, "or that breath will be his last."

Honor stopped struggling. Quietly, she stepped forward. The henchman hoisted her up onto the gelding brought for her.

"We should take the fellow, too," Bastwick said to Tyrell. "I believe there's a bond between them that might serve us."

Tyrell nodded, understanding. As his men pushed Ralph toward the gelding, Tyrell warned him, "Any trouble from you, we'll carve a finger off her."

So the two prisoners rode together out through Larke's gates, each as the other's reluctant jailer. Behind her, Honor heard the servants in the chapel singing prayers. And in the house, lying forgotten under the pillow on her bed, was the foreigner's little book.

The party passed under the city walls at Newgate where apprentices were being hanged in pairs. They reached the Great Western Road, and soon they had left London—and the King's justice—far behind.

❧ 2 ❧

Tyrell Court

On Honor's twelfth birthday it rained all day. The great hall of Tyrell Court stank of the damp wool and sour sweat of Sir Guy Tyrell's retainers, the armed band with which he intimidated the district. Having lounged and drunk their way through the enforced indolence of the soggy afternoon in the company of a few serving women of the household, they were waiting now for supper.

Honor sat in a corner. Bored, she watched rain dribble from the louvered vent in the middle of the roof of the archaic hall. Tyrell, chronically short of cash, had made no improvements to the dark, medieval house his father had left him years before. Raindrops hissed onto the fire in the central hearth. Its perimeter was littered with old charred bones beneath the spit. Its smoke hazed the hall.

Lady Philippa Tyrell, Sir Guy's wife, came in blowing her perpetually dripping nose on a rag. She took her seat at the head table. Boys began carrying in the supper—trenchers of beef and bread and turnips, along with pots of ale. The company noisily settled in at the benches along trestle tables abutting the head table.

Honor was approaching one of the tables when she saw Father Bastwick come through the arched doorway. She moved to a place farthest from the chair she knew he would take, the one beside

Lady Tyrell. Bastwick was a regular visitor at Tyrell Court, and often, in Sir Guy's absences, he took the lord's seat. This morning, Sir Guy had left for business in Exeter. Honor grabbed a second trencher for Ralph as the serving boy passed. She slapped some extra bread onto it and squeezed closer to the amply fleshed body of Mary, a friendly brew-house servant, to force a space for Ralph. He hadn't come into the hall yet. Probably still in the kitchen, Honor thought, telling jokes to the scullery maids.

Honor knew why Bastwick flattered and coddled Lady Philippa. The lady's cousin was an archdeacon in Exeter. Already, Bastwick had secured two more rich benefices through Lady Philippa's pressing of this cousin. Honor knew all about Bastwick's ambition. It glinted in his eyes, just like the jewel in her father's ring. Bastwick wore the ring always. Wore it like a trophy, Honor thought, the way a savage wears a necklace of his slain enemy's teeth. She hated him.

She turned her eyes from Bastwick and caught sight of another face she loathed. At the far table, across the central hearth, sat the heir of this bickering, noisome place. Hugh Tyrell. Her husband.

Father Bastwick himself had conducted the hasty wedding ceremony a week after he and Tyrell had abducted Honor. They had married her, at the age of seven, to eleven-year-old Hugh. That, she had soon come to understand, was her sole purpose here: Hugh would legally own all her property on the day their marriage was consummated. She understood the meaning of that word, too. The Tyrell Court servants, male and female, slept sprawled on the floor of the great hall, and no one living here could ignore the rutting that went on, day and night, in its grimy corners.

Honor's stomach tightened as she looked across at Hugh. He was now a pimpled sixteen-year-old who screamed at servants, lacerated his horses with whips in the hunt, and drank himself most nights into partial paralysis. Tonight, he was already close to stupefaction as he upended a leather wine bottle to his sucking mouth and drained its dregs.

The meal was almost over. Still, Ralph had not come in. Honor was wondering if he had gone to the dairy to visit the tousle-haired milkmaid whose smiles of invitation, whenever Ralph passed by, were unmistakable. Honor was feeling a pang of jealousy, when Lady Philippa rose, uncharacteristically, to speak.

Lady Philippa's voice was as thin and pinched as her face, and the diners did not immediately hush to listen. Above their noise, Honor, at the far end of the table, could not catch the lady's first faint words. But when grinning faces all along the tables turned Honor's way, and then snorts and guffaws arose, she realized with horror that Lady Philippa was speaking about her and Hugh.

". . . our son to consummate his wedding vows. It was the express direction of my lord before he left for Exeter. 'Make the girl a bride this night,' he commanded. And so, friends, join me now . . ."

Lady Philippa was raising her goblet in a toast. So was Bastwick. So were all the others. A toast to Hugh and his wife. That done, lewd words and laughter rolled from the company. Honor glanced over at Hugh. He was grinning like an idiot, trying to focus his glassy eyes on her. White spittle flecked the corners of his mouth. Honor's stomach lurched.

"No," she cried. "I won't."

The ribald din subsided. Lady Philippa stared at Honor stupidly. "What did you say?"

"I said no. I won't do it."

The company seemed so shocked that only one man's feeble jeer and another's obscene gesture greeted Honor's statement. But these infuriated her even more than the first boisterous outburst had done.

She jumped up. "I'd rather slit my own throat than lie with Hugh Tyrell."

Her shout echoed through the great hall.

Lady Philippa's face turned scarlet. She slammed her fist on the table. "We've fed and clothed you for five years, hussy. Now, by God, you'll do your part."

"Never!"

The company's silence gave way to a low rumble of delight at the anticipated battle. But Lady Philippa only stood rigid in anger, as if unable to speak or move.

Bastwick took control. Honor watched him stand and confer in whispers with Lady Philippa. Lady Philippa nodded curtly, obviously in agreement. Then, quickly and decisively, Bastwick ordered the company to disperse—all except Honor, Hugh, and one burly servant. The priest's words were an unequivocal command, and the men and women immediately, if reluctantly, pushed away from the tables. Bastwick beckoned the burly servant over and spoke with him. Honor could not hear Bastwick's words above the derisive laughter that burst from a pocket of people moving out into the passage, but something made her grab Mary's elbow and whisper, "Find Ralph."

Finally, the great hall was clear.

Honor remained where she stood, waiting for she knew not what. But her hands instinctively balled into defensive fists. In the silence Bastwick again said something into Lady Philippa's ear. Then, with one cold glance of scorn at Honor, Bastwick too walked out of the hall.

The burly henchman strode towards Honor. Lady Philippa did as well. Honor felt her pulse thudding in her throat. In one angry motion Lady Philippa swept away the debris of food from the table—knives and trenchers clattering to the floor—to clear a space behind Honor.

The man splayed his palm on Honor's chest. With a savage push he shoved her onto the table on her back. Her head thudded against a pewter bowl, hitting so hard that she saw purple and green fire swirl between her and the roof. The man held her down by her throat. She was choking, gasping for air. He hiked up her skirts, leaving her naked below the waist. He pried apart her legs. Then, still clamping her throat and one knee, he stood to one side of her.

From the corner of her eye she saw Hugh swaying forward between her legs, his mother behind him, pushing him. Hugh was tugging loose the strings of his codpiece. Fumbling, he pawed the codpiece aside, exposing his flaccid penis.

"Take a sniff of the girl," his mother hissed, "and be a man."

Honor kicked. Her foot hit Hugh's knee. He stumbled back, cursing. In the confusion, the burly servant lifted his hand from Honor's throat. She fought her way up. But the henchman was quicker. One of his fists cracked against her jaw, and the other slammed into her abdomen, throwing her back again, her bowels on fire.

She caught the lurid grin on Hugh's face. Her pain had excited him. He pulled the henchman aside, forced his way between Honor's legs, and thrust himself into her. Honor felt the violation like a jagged knife, stabbing, wounding, drawing blood.

And then, suddenly, Ralph was there. He sprang at Hugh and hauled him off. He grappled Hugh's head between both hands. Honor heard Hugh's neck snap. He crumpled to the floor on his belly, his face hideously twisted around to his back.

Lady Philippa screeched for help. Four men pounded in. The henchman pinned Honor down again while the others wrestled Ralph to the floor. Then, in anxious confusion, they looked to Lady Philippa for instructions. But she was shrieking, hysterical, pointing at the body of her son. One of the men hesitantly rolled Hugh over onto his back. He lay lifeless, his erection mocking death.

There was panic. The men shouted. Lady Philippa wailed. The henchman let go of Honor to throw his jerkin over Hugh's genitals. Someone cried, "To the well!" and two men lifted Hugh up and ran with him out towards the kitchen courtyard. Lady Philippa followed, staggering, clawing at Hugh's body while one of the men tried to restrain her. The other men shoved Ralph to his feet and pushed him out too. Honor stumbled after them into the drizzle.

In the courtyard they lowered Hugh onto the rain-slick cobbles by the well. The other men pushed Ralph down to his knees beside the body. Servants poured from the house, some carrying torches that hissed in the misty rain. The women stood huddled in fear, the men shouted, the children gaped. Frantically, the men sloshed buckets of water over Hugh. But he was dead. When the fact could no longer be denied, and Lady Philippa continued her uncontrolled shrieking, the frightened men began to kick Ralph. He curled into a ball and covered his head with his arms as boots thudded against his ribs, his shoulders, his back.

Bastwick came from the house, pushing his way past the servants. The men kicking Ralph stopped and looked at the priest.

Bastwick held up his hands, demanding order. He called for a couple of men to carry Hugh's body up to his bedchamber. He commanded several of the women to tend to Lady Philippa. The rest of the servants he ordered back inside, all except the two men guarding Ralph. Bastwick glared down at Ralph with a look so full of fury that Honor wondered if Bastwick himself would deliver a fatal kick. But he remained calm. "Clap the murderer in the pillory," he said.

The men dragged Ralph away. Everyone dispersed from the courtyard, Lady Philippa flailing her arms from inside the retreating knot of women and moaning, "Father, Father!" Bastwick strode after her to comfort her.

Honor was left alone. Everyone had forgotten her.

Hours later, she sat stiffly on the edge of her bed. For some time she had listened to the household uproar around her—men and women rushing up and down stairs with potions to calm Lady Philippa, with reports on carrying out Bastwick's instructions at the pillory, with cuffs and curses for the children who came to peep at the dead young lord. Then the clamor had dwindled, as if from exhaustion, and finally the house had quieted to silence.

Honor tried to ignore the pain of her bruised body, tried to ignore the humiliating blood on the inside of her thigh, still sticky with semen. She needed all her concentration to think about Ralph. Come morning, she knew, they would hang him. The King's law of arrest and trial did not penetrate this remote west country. She had often seen Tyrell hanging his own peasants whenever he saw fit. She knew she had to get Ralph away from here.

And get away herself. With Hugh dead her usefulness here was spent. Most likely Tyrell would cast her out alone and friendless into the world.

When she was certain the house slept she threw on a cape. She tiptoed to Hugh's chamber and went in. Hugh lay on the bed fully dressed, looking as though he had fallen into a drunken sleep at the end of a night's carousing. Honor reached out to the waist of his doublet. Deftly, she untied the strings of his purse and stashed the money into her pocket. Then, tugging on her hood against the drizzle, she slipped out into the night.

She heard Ralph's faint, tuneless whistle coming from the pillory beyond the orchard. She hurried past the shadowy fruit trees. She found Ralph by the garden wall. He stood beside the pillory post, his head and hands poking through the wooden framework's holes. He was whistling to block out the pain. His right ear was nailed to the wood.

For a moment Honor thought she would be sick. Then she scrambled to him. His eyes widened as he saw her. "Ralph," she said, "we're running away." She slid back the bolt on the framework and lifted the top board, freeing his hands.

"Right," he said grimly. Preparing himself, he sucked in a deep breath. Honor watched as he tore his ear from the nail.

They stole the big sorrel gelding that had carried them here five years before. With Ralph in front and Honor behind, the horse took them into the wooded track that led eastward away from Tyrell Court. As the night black boughs dripped rain on them, Honor glanced behind. No one was following them. We're going to make it, she told herself over and over, feigning more courage than she felt. They would get back to London. And once in London, she knew where she would seek justice.

Ralph shuddered silently, weak from his ordeal. Honor saw that his makeshift bandage—a strip she had torn from her cloak—was soaked with blood over the mangled ear. She did not know what to do to help him. She held tightly to his waist and pressed her cheek against his back, hoping to pass strength to him through her embrace.

And then she turned her eyes to the dark path ahead.

Part Two

Faith

July 1527–April 1529

❧ 3 ❧

Chelsea in Summer

Thwack! The arrow pierced the target and set the two shafts already embedded there a-quivering.

"Delta!" Honor shouted, jubilant.

"And after two epsilons," her guardian nodded. "Not bad. Care to try for an alpha before dinner?"

Honor held up her palm against the July sun and studied the target. Its concentric circles were boldly daubed with red letters of the Greek alphabet. She quickly fitted another arrow into her bow and fixed in her sights the *alpha* in the bull's-eye. "Homer, be with me," she murmured in invocation, and let the arrow fly.

It struck. "Alpha!" she cried in delight.

"Homer," he assured her, smiling sagely, "is always with us."

She laughed and eagerly reached for another arrow, but her guardian had already started toward the target to collect the shafts. "That's enough. Attempts to improve on perfection can only drive us mad," he called merrily over his shoulder. Halfway there he bent to pick up a stray arrow.

Honor slung her bow over her back and smiled. Her guardian was almost fifty and had never been a sportsman, and it was with a charming awkwardness that he wrestled the arrow from its tangle of low grass, his knee-length brown robe slipping askew on his shoulder. "You can't fool me," she called to his back. "You're just hungry. You smell Lady Alice's roasting beef."

His head jerked in a sudden laugh, and he cast his hands upward in a gesture of surrender and declared, "Another bull's-eye!"

She grinned. It was sweet to make Sir Thomas More laugh.

A young male servant popped over the brow of the low hill between the archery lawn and the house. "Pardon, Sir Thomas," he called as he began down towards them. "A visitor to see you."

More frowned. Honor could see he had forgotten the appointment. "The Vicar of Croydon, sir," she reminded him. "He wrote you. You agreed to see him today."

The lapse, she knew, was understandable; Sir Thomas managed a staggering workload. Over the last ten years he had held posts as Undertreasurer of the Exchequer, Speaker of the House of Commons and, most prestigiously, for three years, King Henry's sole private secretary—all while sitting on the King's Council too. For this outstanding service the King had knighted him. Sir Thomas had also found time to build up a literary reputation, one that even the King deferred to. Honor had been in awe when, soon after she had come into Sir Thomas's custody, the royal barge had docked at Chelsea, and from a window she had watched the tall, golden-haired King strolling the grounds with his arm around Sir Thomas's shoulder. He had come to give Sir Thomas the honor of writing an important public response to a tract by the wild German heretic, Luther. Besides his continuing duties on the Royal Council, Sir Thomas also heard the complaints of poor suitors in the Court of Requests and was a respected judge in Chancellor Wolsey's court of Star Chamber. But Honor knew that Sir Thomas relished all this labor, lightened as it was by his friendship with both King Henry and Queen Catherine. He often shared a private supper before the palace fires with one or both of them.

She also knew, however, that he cherished his rare, quiet days at Chelsea. And today he had only been home for a matter of hours.

The servant reached Sir Thomas and handed him a letter fastened, Honor noticed, with the Queen's seal. "This came for you as well, sir."

More broke the seal and quickly scanned the note. Honor saw

his brow crease, and his eyes flick to her face for a moment. Thoughtfully, he refolded the paper and put it inside his robe. "One thing at a time," he said. He looked at the servant and sighed with resignation. "Show the Vicar into the solar, Matthew. We're coming directly."

Matthew started to go, then called back as an afterthought, "Oh, and Lady Alice says dinner will be late. Maud has burned the beef."

More groaned. Honor laughed and took his arm to go in.

The Vicar pivoted in the oriel window as Honor and More entered. He was a stooped but wiry man in his sixties, floured with dust from the road. He bowed and wrung his hands with such suppressed excitement that it seemed to Honor as though he were winding up some inner spring. More strode forward to greet him and the Vicar pressed his eyes shut as if blinded by the sun.

"I'll tell my pupils of this for years to come, Sir Thomas," he wheezed, blinking. "The day I spoke with the author of *Utopia*."

More smiled, the gracious host, and offered a chair. The Vicar, never taking his eyes from More, groped for the seat.

More indicated Honor. "My ward, Mistress Larke, will join us if you have no objection, sir."

Honor bobbed a curtsy, then sat quietly at a far table to continue transcribing a list of petitioners to the Court of Requests.

"My secretary is ill with a flux," More went on, moving behind his cluttered desk. "Mistress Larke is assisting me in his absence." He laughed. "We two do our best, but still the claims of debts and the indictments and petitions seem to breed overnight like mushrooms."

The Vicar did not smile. He was regarding Honor with an expression of discomfort. "Most unusual," he muttered.

"My ward, sir, like my daughters, is an able scholar," More assured him. "They have always pursued their studies on an equal footing with my son."

The Vicar looked astonished.

More smiled. "Good learning, I'm sure you agree, leads to piety."

"Doubtless, Sir Thomas. But, in the case of *women* . . ." His face hinted at grave doubt indeed.

"The maxim is especially true in the case of women," More replied in good humor. Honor smiled over her writing; she knew this subject was one of his favorites. "For as women are by nature impure," he went on, "so learning cleanses them and sets them on the road to pious living."

The Vicar fell stonily silent, apparently unconvinced by this revolutionary manifesto.

"Honor Larke is an excellent case in point," More continued enthusiastically. "She came into this house several years ago, illiterate, ill-used, and with no more understanding of God's workings in this world or His glories in the next than has that poor, dumb creature there." He nodded at a pet monkey curled in sleep on the window ledge. "Indeed far less, I should say, for the monkey lives contented with its natural cycle of feeding and sleep and does not go in fear of my boot at its ribs. Whereas this girl, after five years under a brutal lord, arrived at my door unsure if there was any contentment at all for the wretched in a wicked world."

Honor blushed under the scrutiny of the two men and bent lower over her writing.

"Yet with education, sir," More summed up proudly, "this same girl now goes blithely to her bed, ears ringing with the conjugation of Latin verbs and the voice of Plato, and happy in the assurance that her life and mind, enriched by duty and service to God, will not be despised by Him at the final hour. And when she wakes up to our cook's burnt toast she can cut it into a right-angle triangle knowing that the square of the hypotenuse is equal to the sum of the square of the other two sides." He smiled at Honor. "Even her Greek improves."

"Greek!" the Vicar exclaimed. Honor understood his shock. Many in the theology-dominated educational institutions like Oxford considered Greek studies to be dangerously close to paganism.

The Vicar pulled himself together. "Well, girl, you were lucky Sir Thomas found you," he grunted. "I hope you are grateful."

"He did not find me, sir. I found him."

She had the satisfaction of seeing the Vicar's eyes widen at her mpertinent remark.

More strangled a laugh, then hastened to say with sober concern, "Pardon, sir, the fault is mine if the child speaks out of turn. I fear that, through contact with me, she has absorbed an annoying tendency of the lawyer's mind—the sometimes overscrupulous passion to have every fact correct." He cleared his throat and tugged at his robe with judgelike decorum, but finally was unable to hide his amusement. "Truth is, though, she's right. She came knocking at my gate because, as she made quite clear to me, I was the only lawyer whose name she knew!" He laughed.

The Vicar frowned.

It was obvious that Honor's presence would be an irritant to the meeting.

"Child," More said gravely, "wait for me in the New Building. I have some business for you there."

He turned his head to her and flashed a conspiratorial wink, and she rose and passed through the room with a controlled smile that she was sure even the Vicar could interpret as one of filial obedience.

In the dappled sunshine of the orchard she sang to herself under the fragrant vault of pear-tree boughs, then crossed the lawn that separated the large house and its gardens from the small New Building. Heat cradled the drowsing estate. The only sounds that drifted on the still air were the buzzing of bees and the faint tolling of the bell from the nearby parish church. Down at the foot of the rolling lawns the ribbon of the River Thames snapped stars of sunlight off its silver surface.

Reaching the New Building she stepped under the small porch gable, lifted the latch, and let herself in. She loved this place, for it reflected the quintessential Thomas More. It contained only three rooms: his library, a gallery for meditation, and a small, austere chapel. It was his habit to come here with his lantern at three in the morning for several hours of study and prayer before the household and the work-a-day world awoke.

She let the door swing shut and stood for a moment breathing in the cool, wood-paneled peace of the library. The furnishings were spartan. In front of the single window stood an oak desk and a plain, hard-backed chair. There was a small hearth. Cocooning the room, the walls were lined with bookshelves crammed with books.

Whenever she stood here, surrounded by books, memories tumbled back of the foreigner's strange gift on that May Day night ten years before—the little volume she and Ralph had opened together under the kitchen lantern to find the speedwell winking back at them. She had never seen the book again. At her abduction, Tyrell had turned her father's townhouse into a tenement, and all its contents had been bundled up and sold for quick cash. Where, she often wondered, had the foreigner's book gone? She had never forgotten its haunting, proud little flower, nor the unsettling serenity of the man's dying smile. And the more education she acquired, thanks to Sir Thomas's liberal instruction, the more her curiosity grew to know what had been written in that book. But, though she was always on the lookout for a copy of it, she feared that after so many years the search was hopeless.

She stepped up to More's desk. With eyes closed, she ran her finger reverently over its beeswaxed surface. "Gratias," she whispered, and touched her finger to her heart. It was a private ritual she had performed over a hundred times, though she was careful never to let Sir Thomas see her do it. He would have been dismayed—would have called her prayer blasphemous. And so it was, she knew, for it was not to God she gave her thanks, but to Sir Thomas himself.

She walked slowly alongside a bookshelf and bumped the knuckle of her finger lovingly over the spines. This was Sir Thomas's private world, and in it she felt close to him. So close that she blushed to remember how, when she was younger, she would sometimes let her mind wander into forbidden tracks. She used to imagine herself beside him, as his wife. She had sensed as soon as she came into the family that there was no bond of love between Sir Thomas and the blunt-faced Lady Alice who was, after all, seven years older than him; his four grown children were the issue of his first marriage. Lady Alice seemed to Honor to be more housekeeper than wife. What if, she used to ask herself, Lady Alice were to die, as Sir Thomas's first wife had? It was not uncommon for gentlemen to marry their wards, and she could bring to her husband a sizable fortune in her father's scattered estates.

She gazed out the window, shaking her head in embarrassment

at the recollection of such juvenile fantasies. The world looked quite different to her now. For one thing those estates, she had learned, had been in sad condition when she became Sir Thomas's ward. Tyrell had ravaged the land. He had sold acres of timber to a smelting interest that had razed the forests. He had stripped the mines of their treasure, then issued fraudulent—and worthless—mining licenses. Using violence and threats, he had extorted crippling rents from most of the tenant farmers, and thrown many others off their holdings to make room for destructive herds of sheep. Sir Thomas, as the administrator of her property now, was attempting, with her father's stewards, to repair the damage.

He had explained all this to her, and a great deal more. When, as a child, she had been married to Hugh Tyrell, she had only dimly understood her legal situation, though at twelve she had realized that if the marriage were consummated her property would go out of her hands. Much later, Sir Thomas had explained to her the nub of it.

An unmarried woman did not own property, though she could become the channel through which her father's property passed to her husband. Given this situation, Sir Thomas pointed out, abduction of heiresses was not an uncommon occurrence. There was even legislation, "Against the Taking Away of Women," but it was difficult to enforce, he said, and the attraction of an heiress's lands seized through an enforced marriage often seemed worth the risk to an unscrupulous man like Tyrell.

But Father Bastwick, too, Sir Thomas told her, had taken a huge risk in masterminding her abduction. He and Tyrell had cheated the King out of revenue in his Court of Wards, one of the most lucrative royal ministries. All orphans with significant property became, by feudal prerogative, wards of the King, who then sold the wardships. Gentlemen had to pay handsomely for the custody of wealthy wards, male and female. Indeed, since a guardian was entitled to pocket all the rents and revenues of the ward's estates until the young person's marriage, the bidding often was fiercely competitive.

But Bastwick had wielded forgery and fraud to help Tyrell snatch Honor's wardship and pay nothing for it. As Tyrell's payment, Bastwick had been well on his way to an archdeacon's post when Honor escaped with Ralph to London, found Sir Thomas, and brought her abductors to trial in Cardinal Wolsey's Court of Star Chamber.

Overnight Honor's world had changed. Wolsey awarded the custody of her and her property to More. Sir Guy Tyrell was sent to the Fleet prison. Bastwick, though immune from civil justice because of his clerical status, was nevertheless sent to a cell in the Bishop's prison for a period, his dreams of advancement in the Church shattered.

Honor had rejoiced that day in court, seeing Bastwick humbled. And yet, the image of his face at the trial still had the power to make her shiver. She did not think she would ever forget Bastwick's look of cold fury when More delivered his damning oration against him.

"Pity the Church," More had said under the court's star-spangled ceiling as he pointed to Bastwick. "Longing only to cure men's souls, she sometimes suffers disease herself in corrupt priests such as this."

Honor had caught the glint of pure hatred in Bastwick's black, hooded eyes—hatred for Sir Thomas and, especially, hatred for her.

The verdict was handed down, and Sir Thomas went victoriously to the bar to settle the custody. But as the clerks and officials rose and began to mill about, Honor saw Bastwick moving towards her. She could barely swallow, so parched was her throat, but she held her ground. Bastwick stopped in front of her. His body was completely still, his emotion controlled, but the muscles around his eyes twitched, betraying him. "You will live to regret this day," he said. The threat was no more than a whisper, but its malice seared her ears.

But Bastwick was wrong. She regretted nothing. Certainly not the news a year later that Tyrell had died in prison. Nor the fact that Bastwick had vanished from her life. Ever since the day of judgment she had been happy.

No, she thought, that was not quite true. One regret did nag— she had lost track of Ralph. He had thought it best, since the death of Hugh Tyrell at his hands, to stay clear of the law. So he had not come to the trial, had waited at an inn instead, and rejoiced with her when she ran to him to report the wonderful news. And then, as soon as she was securely settled with Sir Thomas, Ralph had left London. Honor had no doubt that he would merrily thrive in any place he found himself, but she often wondered where he was living and what he was doing, and who was laughing now at his jests and silly stories. She missed him. Dear Ralph, she thought, I owe him so much. How he suffered, that night at the pillory, for my sake . . .

There was laughter outside the New Building. Honor looked out the window. Sir Thomas was striding across the lawn toward her, laughing. She hurried to the door and stepped outside to meet him.

"Oh, child, I would you had stayed," he said. Reaching her, he placed a hand on her shoulder to steady himself. "Or, rather, it's well you did not, for I could not have kept a serious face if anyone had been there to hear."

"Why? What is it, sir?" she asked, smiling in anticipation.

"Oh, I would not have missed this Vicar's visit for the world! He wanted . . ." He broke off, shaken by another wave of laughter. Recovering, he set his face into a mask of zeal that parodied his earnest guest. "The Vicar came to ascertain from me the exact location of Utopia. He dreams of making a voyage there."

"What?" she cried. *Utopia* was More's popular book. Written in Latin, it was a lively account of his meeting with a traveler named Raphael who had made contact with an extraordinary island commonwealth in the New World. The book described the Utopians as a stable, highly organized and, though heathen, morally upright people who lived lives of monastic rigor. But it was a work of pure imagination; its title meant "no place" in Greek. "And does he really believe such an island exists?" she asked.

"Absolutely. His dream is to make a missionary expedition there! To bring to the ignorant Utopians the blessed civilization of the Church." He wiped tears of mirth from his eyes. "Ah, a most delicious fool."

"Well, sir, what he has taken from you in the ill-timing of his visit he has repaid in entertainment."

"True, true. Oh, child, I would not belittle a man for ignorance, for we are all born ignorant. But this was a self-blinkered, pompous fool. A dangerous one, too, for he has the teaching of boys under him."

He hooked his arm in hers and together they strolled toward a copse of oak trees that shaded the fish pond. By the time they reached the pond he was patting his pockets, searching for something. "By the way," he said, "I forgot, earlier. I have a gift for you." His hands stopped against his chest in midsearch, and he added gently, "I'm sorry I missed your birthday last week, child."

She blushed, pleased that he remembered. "No matter, sir. Though," she teased, "I call your excuse of the King's summoning you to Greenwich a feeble one."

"Ha! Perhaps I should have insisted he let me go. We were back in Westminster by then. 'I'm sorry, your Grace, the letters to the French King needs must wait and I must ride to Chelsea, for Honor Larke is seventeen years old today.' The King is a fond father himself. He might have given me Godspeed and one of his finest stallions to carry me."

"Or he might have had your head," she cried. "No, I'd rather see you past the date, and whole." They laughed together.

"We didn't get much work done that night in any case," More said, rummaging again inside his robe, "what with the music and the bonfires."

Honor could well imagine it. Her birthday was the twenty-fourth of June, Midsummer Eve, a holiday when bonfires were lighted in the streets and doors festooned with garlands, and people danced and sang through the city with drums and horns and pipes. "When I was little, in my father's house," she said with a soft smile, "my manservant, Ralph, told me that people danced around their fires at midsummer just to celebrate my birthday. And truly, sir, he assured me with such long-faced foolery that for many childish years I believed him."

"Charming," More chuckled. "Ah!" He had found the object of his search. From a deep pocket he withdrew it and held it out to her. It was a necklace, a delicately wrought string of coral and pearls, simple and exquisite.

"Oh, sir!" she stammered, delighted.

More looked baffled. "I fear you misunderstand. That is not my gift. No, no, that is only an ornament, a bauble, a toy for a child." Solemnly, he took her hand in his. "Put it away," he said quietly. She obeyed.

"My gift to you is something much more precious. More lasting. A reward for the great progress you have made. It's incredible, really, when you came here you couldn't even read, and now your Latin is as good as mine. Well," he winked, "almost. And you have excelled in mathematics, music, philosophy, even astronomy. In fact, your tutor tells me you are so far advanced in that science that you can point out not only the polar star and the dog star, but are also able—and this requires the skill of an absolute master—to distinguish the sun from the moon."

She laughed.

"Yes," he said, "your mind now rests on a rock solid foundation. And your heart," he smiled, "remains as soft as God could wish. Truly, child, you could not please me more."

Honor gazed at him, feeling too much happiness to hold inside. She threw her arms around his neck, her cheek against his. His hands went to her back and he pressed her to him. Then, suddenly, he pulled away. His face was flushed. Abruptly, he stepped toward the pond. For a moment he kept his back to her. She waited, fearing her impetuous show of affection had angered him.

He turned around to her briskly, and she was relieved to see that he was smiling again. "And now, Honor Larke," he declared, "my gift to you. It is . . . a name. A name in Greek, as befits a scholar of this little academy. '*Kale kai sophe.*' It means, 'Fair and wise.' What think you of it?"

Tears of happiness brimmed in her eyes. "A wonderful gift."

"And yours alone." Solemnity darkened his smile. "Remember, child, a thousand girls have necklaces."

A shout startled them. "Sir Thomas! Come quick!"

Across the grass Matthew stood where the lawn sloped down to the river. He was waving his arms. "Murder!" he cried.

More and Honor shared a horrified glance. They raced towards the breathless Matthew who pointed down at the reeds by the river's edge. On the bank, a man was bending over a girl, a maid in More's household. She was kneeling and looking up at the man. He held a knife at her throat.

"Stop!" More cried. "Villain!"

The man spun around in surprise. His knife glinted in the sun.

More scrambled down the slope, his robe flapping, his feet awkwardly thumping and slipping on the lush grass. He was running too fast and he lost his footing and skidded, then thudded onto his rear end. Following, Honor sailed past him, even more awkward in her long skirts. She windmilled down the hill out of control and crashed into the arms of the would-be assassin who dropped his knife under the force of the impact. The two stumbled back together as if locked in some heathen dance step. They finally came to a halt at the lip of the riverbank.

There was a moment of stunned silence. The maid wobbled to her feet and shyly looked at More still sitting at the base of the hillside. "Pardon, Your Worship," she stuttered, her hands patting at the cap that covered her ears. "A knot in my cap string. This gentleman offered to cut it for me."

More stared, uncomprehending. The girl cupped her hand beside her mouth and whispered loudly, "A foreigner, Your Worship. He speaks no English."

The man stepped around Honor and came shakily toward More, his hands uplifted like an apprehended criminal. He was young and of a stocky peasant build, with a moon face and wide, slate blue eyes. In serviceable Latin he made a nervous explanation. "I am an artist, sir. I was moved to sketch this young woman. I suggested she remove her cap. It was only the strings I wanted to cut."

"An artist?" More asked feebly.

"Hans Holbein is my name. A citizen of Basle. I come to you on the recommendation of our mutual friend, Erasmus."

A smile cracked across More's face. He slapped his green-stained hands together and bits of grass flew from his fingertips. "Master Holbein, on my backside I welcome you to England. Care for some burned roast beef?"

* * *

In the great hall, More leaned back pensively in his chair at the head of the main table. What he was hearing amused him, yet troubled him at the same time: his twenty-year-old daughter, Cecily, was reading aloud a letter Erasmus had sent with the young artist. It was clear to More that his extended family felt none of his own ambiguity. He could see they were all entertained by Erasmus's news. They sat beside him and at two long lower tables: his wife, his father, his son with his fiancée, his three daughters and their husbands, a clutch of grandchildren, assorted music masters, tutors and clerks. The kitchen maids had cleared away the first courses—the capon with apricots, the salvaged roast beef, the braised leeks—and everyone was listening to Erasmus's letter, their spoons clacking over bowls of excellent strawberry pudding from Lady Alice's kitchen. The renowned Dutch scholar had written to More:

"The arts are freezing here, so I have encouraged Holbein to come to you in England to pick up a few coins."

There was a murmur of approval and all heads turned to the red-faced artist. All except Alice, as usual, More noted; everyone except her and the very young children understood the Latin letter. His wife had rejected his every attempt to teach her to read, even in English. Cecily continued reading:

"As the firestorm rages here over Luther, I am condemned by both sides for my refusal to join either. I am told that a follower of Luther in Constance, a fellow who was once my student, has hung my portrait near the door merely to spit at it as often as he passes. My lot has become like St. Cassianus who was stabbed to death by his pupils with pencils."

Many at the table laughed. Sir Thomas More did not. How, he wondered, could Erasmus make jests about a man as dangerous as Luther? Disturbed, he fingered the rim of his goblet of watered wine as Cecily read on. The letter ranged over several more items of news in Basle. Then:

"Please convey my thanks to young Mistress Larke for the enjoyment her thoughtful essay on St. Augustine's *City of God* has given me. Or better yet, tell her that I will write my appreciation to her personally as soon as time permits."

More glanced at Honor with a proud smile, as did the rest of the family. Following the young artist, it was Honor's turn to blush.

Servants cleared the dishes and Honor and Cecily began a lute duet. Watching Honor, More remembered the letter inside his robe. He beckoned Matthew over and told him to ask Mistress Larke to come out to his library when she was finished playing. He excused himself from the table.

He passed through the sultry orchard, deep in thought. Though he walked slowly, the heat was oppressive, and sweat prickled his skin by the time he reached the New Building. The sweat made the coarse fibers of the hair shirt he always wore under his linen scratch even more uncomfortably than usual. Good, he thought with a chuckle at himself: a perfect, penitential complement to that second helping of beef.

The library was pleasantly cool. He laid the Queen's note on his desk and shifted a letter that was already lying there so that the two papers were lined up side by side. He regarded them for a moment, then turned to the window and looked out at the woods beyond the pond. What to do? To which request should he agree?

Which was best for the girl?

A smile crept to his lips as he recalled his laughter with her over the foolish Vicar. But the smile quickly faded. How the world has changed, he thought, since I wrote *Utopia*. When it was published no one had even heard of Martin Luther. Yet the very next year Luther nailed his wretched theses to the door of Wittenburg Church, and nothing had been the same since. That same year, Sulieman the Turk marshaled his dreadful army, too. And now? The pestilence of Luther's malice infects all Europe. The Turk has smashed the Hungarian army and casts his hungry eye westward on us. And in Rome . . .

Dear God, Rome . . .

Everywhere, Christendom quakes and crumbles. Can the old

bonds hold? Everything has degenerated. Even here. The King and Queen, who used to live together in such handfast companionship and never stooped to wrangle . . .

He did not let himself finish the thought. It did no good to stray down that path. Besides, he reassured himself, that particular crisis will be resolved once the King comes to his senses over the Boleyn girl, which must be soon.

He rubbed his eyes with his knuckles. He was tired, needed rest. It seemed he had not slept soundly since the news had reached England two weeks before of the catastrophe in Rome. So appalling. The civilized world had been stunned by it.

In May the Holy Roman Emperor Charles's troops, warring with France for years over pieces of the Italian peninsula, had fought their way to Rome. They were a mixed brew of Spanish, Italian, and German mercenaries. Unpaid for months and hungry for spoils, they mutinied. They burst the city walls and brought Rome to its knees with a reign of terror never before seen in Christendom. A third of the population was massacred. Cardinals were prodded through the streets and butchered. Nuns, auctioned to soldiers, were raped on their altars. The aisles of the Vatican were used as stables, and the precious manuscripts of its libraries shredded for horses' bedding. Pope Clement, with the jewels of his papal tiara sewn into the hem of his gown, fled the Vatican along a corridor connecting it to the Castel Sant' Angelo. While soldiers looted the Church's palaces, and stacked corpses rotted by the river, the Pope huddled in the Castel under siege. Finally, with Rome in ruins, the Emperor allowed the Pope to escape north of the city to Orvieto.

More shook his head, still hardly able to believe the enormity of the disaster.

There was a soft knock at the door. He turned to see his ward step into the room. He shook off his gloomy thoughts. "I have received a rather surprising communication from the Queen," he said as pleasantly as he could manage.

Honor stood waiting, and More saw by the slight wrinkling of her forehead that she could not imagine how the Queen's message could concern her.

He sat down at his desk. "It seems you have made a most favorable impression on Her Grace. Tell me, child, what passed between you and the Queen at Bridewell?"

He was referring to the glittering public ceremony some time before to which all the nobility of England had been summoned. The King had there enlarged his six-year-old illegitimate son, Henry Fitzroy, with the titles of Duke of Richmond and Somerset. It had been an extraordinary, symbolic declaration by the King, acknowledging, in the absence of a legitimate son, Fitzroy's right to some rank as a claimant to the throne. Sir Thomas, attending with all of his family, had read out the boy's new patents of nobility.

"Her Grace was ill with a headache, sir," Honor answered. "The day was very hot. She became so indisposed she had to leave the hall. I'm sure you remember, for everyone was most concerned."

More remembered it well. The Queen had stood stoically by her husband's side while he made a mistress's bastard eligible to inherit the throne. Not only was it an insult to the Queen, it also threw the claim of their daughter, the Princess Mary, into jeopardy. Watching his ward's open-faced reply, More wondered how much Honor had really seen that day. Had she understood anything of the humiliation the good Queen must have been suffering?

"Her Grace asked me to accompany her to her private chamber," Honor continued. "Perhaps it was only because I was near at hand. Though I did notice that Mistress Boleyn was nearer."

Did she really know nothing of the Boleyn girl's infamy? More was touched by the innocence of the statement. Gratified, too, for it was further vindication of his judgment to settle his family in Chelsea: city gossip was just far enough removed.

"In any case," Honor went on, "Her Grace asked only me. My heart ached to see her in such distress, and I offered to read to her. I read from Louis Vives and it seemed to calm her." Quickly, she added, as though to deny too much credit, "The chamber was cool and dark, sir, both good medicine, I do not doubt. Her Grace was wondrous kind to me."

More could not suppress a jolt of pride. Most of the Queen's ladies were vain, ignorant flirts. In fine weather they rode out hunting and hawking with their courtier admirers, and when it rained they turned to cards, cat's cradle, and gossip. Though they were all from prominent families, they had been sent to court only to make profitable marriages, and few of them were even literate, let alone able to soothe the nerves of this accomplished Queen by reading to her in learned Latin.

"Child," he said suddenly, "what say you to matrimony?"

Her mouth fell open. "Leave here? Leave *you?*" she blurted. A blush swept over her face and she looked down.

More was surprised. Had she really not thought about marriage yet? A girl so lovely, so aware? Perhaps not; the stricken look on her face told him that her heart was here, at Chelsea. He realized that it pleased him inordinately. The realization was unsettling.

With her head still lowered, Honor asked quietly, "Is it that fat doctor?"

More had to cover a smile with his hand. At Lent, a doctor friend of his father's, a portly widower, had come to court the girl. More had been passing the open solar door and overheard them talking. She was deftly cooling the doctor's ardor in a most original fashion—by grilling him rather mercilessly on the works of St. Jerome and St. Thomas Aquinas. The poor man fled without even staying to supper.

"No," More answered, amused. "The doctor has retreated from the field. But another hopeful has stepped into the breach." He waited for some response, but she stood stubbornly silent. "Are you not even curious to know who it is?"

"No," she said morosely. "But if my marriage is your desire, sir, my pleasure is naturally to obey you."

He frowned. "This is no answer, child. I will not sell you like a chattel to the highest bidder. But here," he said, poking at the letter on the desk beside the Queen's message, "here is Sir John Bremelcum writing to open a dialogue with me about you and young Geoffrey. You got along well with the lad when he was here at Christmas, despite his coughs and chills. Good family. And he's doing brilliantly at Cambridge. He'll make a first-rate lawyer one day."

He watched her for a promising sign, but she offered none.

Indeed, her obstinate expression suggested the opposite. More sighed heavily. He rose from his chair, turned his back to her, and gazed out the window. "I would like to have seen you safely and honorably married. The world is becoming a dangerous place." He added quietly, "Sometimes, I fear we may be standing on the brink of the very end." He could hear his own uneasiness hover in the stillness of the book-lined sanctuary.

He turned abruptly, suddenly all business. "Her Grace has need of new ladies-in-waiting. Two places have fallen vacant. She has asked that you fill one of them."

Honor's eyes grew large.

More frowned and added hastily, "I scruple to send a tender mind to court. Much vice breeds there. The Queen herself is the most virtuous of women—else nothing could make me even consider it—still, there is much vice. Had I given my word on you already to Sir John Bremelcum I would not hesitate to send my regrets to the Queen, for she well knows my promise is a thing I would not break, not for a world of court gold. Yet it is not so. There has been no such agreement with Sir John . . ."

His voice trailed. He had held off asking her inclination outright, hoping that, given a moment to consider, she might yet decline of her own free will. But he could put it off no longer. "What say you, child, to the Queen's request?"

She was staring at him, hope glowing on her face. "Are you giving me leave to choose for myself, sir?"

He hesitated, then answered, "Of course."

Suddenly, all her reticence was swept away by a huge, bright smile. More felt a pang of loss. How instantly the siren song of the court had severed her heartstrings from Chelsea—from him! And yet, her eyes were shining so clearly, so openly devoid of guile, that for a moment he could actually believe that she was making the right choice.

His eyes trailed down to the low-cut bodice of her gown. He noticed, for the first time, the coral and pearls of his gift glistening against the skin above her full, lifted breasts. And she had changed her dress since the morning, had she not? Yes, she had put on a silk one of a gleaming coral color. She must have picked it out especially, for he saw that it perfectly matched the necklace. Saw, too, that it gave fire to her lustrous dark hair and eyes.

He forced his eyes away. Blindly, he grabbed a sheaf of papers as if he meant to begin work. But it was no good. He turned back to her. "Oh, tread carefully, child," he said. "At court, many pretty necklaces are dangled before the eyes of the unwary."

❧ 4 ❧

At Court

"They're going to cut off his hand?" Honor asked, horrified. She turned to Margery Napier. The two girls were the same age, and for six months had shared duties among the Queen's two dozen ladies-in-waiting. They had stopped halfway across a colonnaded outdoor gallery at Greenwich Palace with bundles of the Queen's furs in their arms. "But why?" Honor asked. "What's he done?"

The gallery looked down on a cramped quadrangle where a crowd was forming. The quadrangle was hemmed in by the red brick walls of the scullery and spicery, and the gray stone walls of the granary, chandlery and brewhouse. This jumble of buildings huddled under the perimeter skyline of palace roofs serrated with gables and chimneys where the occasional flash of a gilded turret reflected the watery winter sun.

"It's the new penalty for brawling on the King's tennis courts," Margery answered blithely. Her eye was following a young lordling with a shapely leg as he and his wolfhound sauntered out of an alley. Man and dog left behind them a pattern of black hollows in the powdery snow as they joined the twenty or so people milling in front of a low scaffolding at the wall opposite the gallery.

Honor rested her bundle on the gallery railing. "But men quarrel round the palace all the time, then pay their fines and walk away. None has lost a hand for it."

"This one will," Margery said with quiet relish. "The King is in a fume. He says he is ill served by the pack of jackals at his court, and he's told the lord steward and the palace marshal that he'll have order."

It was the first Honor had heard of it. She studied the bright, bird eyes of her friend with a quizzical smile. "You don't miss a single flurry of the nonsense that goes on around here, do you?"

Margery tossed her head complacently. "I know that the gentleman who's to forfeit his hand wagered five pounds on a tennis match with Reginald Quince and that Quince lost the match, but would not pay. And I know that Quince got his ugly nose broken for his impudence. Which he heartily deserved, in my book. I'm sure he owes my brother five pounds and more for a night of cards last week."

"And who's the unfortunate young brawler?" Honor asked, scanning the crowd, though there was no sign yet of a prisoner.

Margery pouted her ignorance on this point. "One can't keep up with every wild fellow that roars into court," she said. "Although," she winked, "I have heard that he married into money, and while he sports and sparks here to his heart's content, his wife obligingly waits at home at Norfolk."

The hubbub below grew more raucous as courtier friends hailed one another and ladies swirled out of the palace in tittering knots. On men and women alike, brocades and silks and velvets in riotous shades of marigold, ladyblush, and popinjay blue set up a hum of color, as if a flock of exotic birds had fluttered down in place of the drab pigeons that regularly pecked here at the granary refuse. The scullery doors stood partway open, and the barefoot boys who scoured the cauldrons peeked out through clouds of steam and dared one another, giggling, to dart out into the throng.

Honor shook her head with a wondering smile. Even after six months with the Queen she was still astounded and appalled by the chaos of the King's court. As both a private household and a public organization it was a seething snarl of humanity surrounding the royal person. Bishops and peers; priests and prostitutes; astrologers, minstrels and falconers; vendors, wonder workers and sages—all were drawn to forage for the acorns of patronage under the royal oak. The place teemed with intrigue and violence, for every gentleman, nobleman, and churchman was attended by a throng of hangers-on, and this army of servants in various employs lounged and diced and quarreled through the crowded corridors, staircases, and courtyards. Up to a thousand people were fed each day at the King's table, where grooms armed with whips and bells patrolled the great hall to fend off scrounging dogs and rascals who tried to pass as servants. All men went armed, and daggers were drawn over every slight, real or imagined.

This tennis quarrel was no surprise to Honor; gambling was almost a religion here. Courtiers bet on everything from wrestling matches, to a lady's virtue, to the amount of wine a banqueting ambassador would consume, and both gentlemen and ladies were expected to play coolly, and for high stakes. The King himself often lost many pounds a day at dice. Tennis, the game most threatening to a man's purse, was not for the faint at heart.

There was the rumble of a single drum. Honor and Margery craned over the railing at a small procession snaking out under their gallery. Seven men emerged and started to walk across to the scaffold. Honor recognized their white-bearded leader as the royal surgeon. He supervised the maiming of state prisoners. She winced, thinking of the poor, quaking victim who had yet to appear. The grim band of officials filed up the five central platform steps. Margery displayed her skill by identifying them all: "The royal surgeon. Then, the sergeant surgeon—he'll be doing the deed. Next, the yeoman of the wood yard, with his man bringing up the block. Then the King's master cook with his cleaver. Then the farrier with his searing iron . . ."

She and Honor exchanged queasy glances at the thought of this instrument being used to cauterize a man's bloody wrist stump.

"I won't watch this," Honor declared. "No silly fool should have to suffer so." She hoisted her bundle off the railing. "And all for a tennis ball. It's barbaric." She started to go.

"Wait! They're bringing him in!"

Margery had caught Honor's elbow and was pulling her back, and Honor, submitting to a jolt of curiosity, leaned over the railing as the prisoner came out directly beneath them.

They looked down on the man's head, whose close-cropped, lazy auburn curls absorbed the pale sun and shot back gleams of amber. The head turned from side to side with a languid ease, as if the man were passing through a crowd of well-wishers, and, indeed, the people parted for him with a hush of fascination. His stride was long and loose and self-assured, despite a distinct pigeon-toed inclination of his right foot—or perhaps because of it, as if vanity were not at stake. It was the legacy of a broken bone mended awry, Honor supposed. But though it gave his walk an unmistakable peculiarity he seemed oblivious to the defect, as if it were a trifle that had no bearing on a man's power, just as a seasoned soldier ignores a battle scar.

He reached the base of the scaffold and stood for a moment with his back to the crowd. He wore a long-sleeved tunic of fine wool, of a green so dark it was nearer black, trimmed at the collar with marten but otherwise plain. Its skirt skimmed his knees where it met the tops of lived-in riding boots. A scratched leather belt as wide as a girl's wrist drew in the tunic just above his lean hips. A second belt sloped diagonally to an empty scabbard—he had been disarmed for his ordeal—and his left hand rested on the scabbard with a controlled tension as if to give warning that, though impotent of sword, this hand could yet do battle.

He started up the steps where the officials faced him in a line. When he reached the top, his broad shoulders eclipsed the shallow-chested old surgeon. He came to a halt, a head taller than every other man on the platform.

He turned slowly, deliberately, like a noble about to receive tribute. He scanned the faces before him, beginning with those at his feet, so that the bone ridge of his eyebrows obscured his eyes from the gallery. Between the red-brown hair and dark clothing, his clean-shaven face was bronzed as if by years of sun and wind, and the effect, in contrast to the gaiety of colour all around, was of a gilded antique carving in weathered wood. But when he tilted up his face, cobalt blue eyes snapped the carving into instant, vivid life.

He looked up to the gallery where Honor and Margery stood alone. His gaze traveled slowly over both of them, pausing for a moment on Honor. She felt warm blood stain her face and prick the roots of her hair. Then he looked away.

Margery, smitten, let out a puff of breath. "If I had a man like that about I'd want both his hands left on him," she purred. "Two hands, ready and able."

Honor studied the man warily. There was a mockery in those defiant blue eyes that shook loose from her heart all the pity she had wrought, in her fancy, for a contrite young hothead. This man was not contrite. And, apparently about thirty, he was not so young either.

The drum rumbled again. The officials shuffled to the sides of the scaffold. The sergeant put a hand on the prisoner's shoulder. "Richard Thornleigh," he intoned, "do you stand prepared?"

Thornleigh hesitated for a moment. He blinked at the sergeant like someone who had not fully heard, or had not understood, the question. Then, in reply, he slowly raised his arm above his head and brought it down in a flourish of a bow that was absurdly wide, absurdly dashing. The exaggerated gesture unbalanced him, and he stumbled forward. The sergeant had to snatch him by his collar to keep him from careening into the onlookers.

"He's drunk," Honor said, dismayed.

"So he is," Margery giggled.

The crowd shared Margery's outlook and laughter erupted.

Thornleigh righted himself and brushed the sergeant's hands away. He raised his arms to ask for quiet, and looked out over the faces until the laughter subsided.

"Gentlemen, ladies, forgive me." He spoke with grave deliberation, but in a tone that was a clear mockery of a famous, and pompous, preacher of the city. His hand flattened over his heart. "In contemplation of this moment, I have today drunk deep of sorrow. I only pray God that before the day is out He will not let my sorrow drown me. But," he added, listing dangerously to the left, and shuffling to a much wider stance to correct the imbalance, "I have also drunk deep of a bottle of sack." He smiled crookedly. "And a very good bottle it was, too. Perhaps God sent it me for a raft."

Another wave of laughter rocked the courtyard.

"Oh, Honor," Margery chuckled, poking her rib, "don't look so shocked. You can't begrudge the fellow a tumbler or two to ease his pain."

"I don't begrudge him anything," Honor answered sharply. "I know nothing of the man—except that he blasphemes at a singularly inopportune moment."

"And that he's a handsome dog," Margery murmured, "and brave enough to spit at the Devil."

Thornleigh was looking out across the people's heads with sudden soberness. "I have only one request," he said quietly. The people hushed.

"The penalty does not stipulate which limb is to be forfeit. I ask that my right be spared,"—he raised his right hand high—"that it may go on to do good service to my King." His hand swept down across his body and grappled the top of the empty scabbard as if to wield his absent sword.

A roar of approval went up from the crowd. Several women sighed. The royal surgeon nodded quick agreement. "Agreed, sir. Are you now prepared?"

Thornleigh drew himself upright. Although the chatter continued around him, his face slowly hardened, and Honor noticed, beneath the defiance that rode the surface of those bold, blue eyes, a deep-drowning flicker of despair. She saw that he feared this moment after all. Well, she asked herself as pity crept back, what rational man would not?

"Now," Thornleigh barked to the surgeon, "let's have done with it!"

The surgeon nodded to the farrier. The farrier plucked the red-hot sealing iron from its coals. The royal chef waddled forward and handed his cleaver to the sergeant.

Thornleigh strode up to the block. He scowled at it as if to steel himself for the ordeal. Then, quickly, he straddled the spot, stretched out his left arm, loosed the leather lacing at his cuff, and peeled back the sleeve. He thumped his fist onto the center of the block. Despite the cold, beads of sweat glistened on his brow. With teeth clenched and lips pressed thin together he sucked in a sharp breath that flattened his nostrils and filled his chest. His lip curled, and for an instant Honor thought she read in his face something disturbing—some fierce, aberrant desire that actually welcomed this punishment.

The sergeant raised the cleaver. It glinted in the sun. Honor turned away.

"Stop!" a woman's voice cried.

All heads in the courtyard turned to a door under the gallery. Honor and Margery looked down. A woman swathed in black sable strode out. Her yellow silk hem blazed below the fur, and rubies glittered on the yellow velvet hood that almost covered her dark hair. It was Anne Boleyn.

The sergeant lowered his cleaver. The crowd parted, whispering. Anne approached the scaffold. Thornleigh gaped at her in confusion. Anne handed up a paper to the Royal Surgeon. He scanned it quickly and raised his head to declare, "The King has issued a stay. The prisoner is released."

The crowd gasped. Thornleigh, half in a trance, walked stiffly to the edge of the platform. In front of Anne he dropped to one knee. She offered her hand. He stared at it a moment as if overcome with amazement, then he caught it up. She waited long enough to receive his prolonged kiss of gratitude on her fingers, then silently turned again and walked briskly back toward the palace. Snow swirled in the wake of her furred train.

An uproar broke out. Men swarmed the platform to congratulate the reprieved man. Dogs barked and ran in circles. A lady fainted. Thornleigh staggered under the crush of well-wishers.

Honor caught Anne's small smile of triumph just before she disappeared under the gallery. My God, Honor thought, she must have been watching and holding the King's pardon in her hand all along. Yet she had waited, letting the scene reach its horrifying climax before making her entrance as Lady Merciful.

"Well, there's proof of the hussy's power," Margery cried above the clamor. "As if we needed it. As if we weren't already sick to death of seeing fellows swarm around her, hoping to coast up to the King on the hem of her yellow skirts. This Thornleigh, I suppose, is her newest toy. Hmph!" she sneered. "She helps herself to men the way my lord Wolsey helps himself to pastries."

Honor was observing Thornleigh. Recovered, he was grinning now. His back absorbed the men's hearty slaps, but his eyes were narrowed in carnal appreciation as he allowed a buxom, cooing lady to lace up his sleeve while his precious, spared hand hovered over her white bosom.

"And the result of both gluttonies is the same," Honor muttered, watching him. "A swollen belly."

Margery tittered. Honor bit her lip, instantly regretting her lewd remark. The man had courage, she had to acknowledge that, even if it was strong drink that had fortified him. But there was an uneasiness tossing in her: she chafed with shame for her royal mistress's sake. Honor had learned a great deal in her few months in the Queen's service; she had not been at court one week before she knew all about the royal scandal involving Anne. And here was brazen proof indeed, as Margery said, of the strings that tugged this shabby King!

Her teeth were chattering in the cold. "I've seen enough," she said. She turned and left Margery ogling the carnival below.

When she entered the Queen's suite, free of her bundles and looking forward to settling before the warmth of the brazier, she found a half dozen girls gathered there, her fellow ladies-in-waiting. They were whispering in agitation. Several looked quite frightened. One quickly told Honor of the crisis. The Chancellor, Cardinal Wolsey himself, had just left in a great show of anger, she said. He had barged in and arrested the Queen's young secretary, Walter. "For spying on the King!" the girl breathed in horror. Wolsey's men, she said, had just taken Walter away. "Her Grace," another girl added with a nervous nod at the Queen's private chamber, "is quite beside herself."

A third girl was at the sideboard pouring wine to take to the Queen. Her hands were trembling. Honor came to a swift decision. Quickly she went to the sideboard. "Let me, Beth," she said. Beth relinquished the goblet, clearly relieved at the opportunity to steer clear of the storm.

Honor knocked gently on the Queen's door and opened it. The Queen's private chamber was empty. Honor stepped in and looked toward the far set of doors that stood open to the bedchamber.

There, Queen Catherine was on her knees in prayer before her prie-dieu. Its magnificent ivory carving glowed from the light of a rim of votive candles arching over the supplicant.

Honor went back and closed the door. Silently, she moved to a paper-strewn table near the bedchamber door and set the goblet down. But she did not leave.

Catherine's head turned slightly, sharply, as though in annoyance at Honor's continued presence, although her lips kept moving in her murmured prayer. Still, Honor did not go.

Catherine completed her orisons, crossed herself, and stood. Honor's resolve surged at the sight of the Queen's face. Strain had etched tiny lines at the corners of her eyes and mouth, and the votive candles' light glinted over the threads of gray in her light brown hair. Her squat figure appeared dowdy-looking despite her sumptuous purple brocade gown and costly amethysts. But there was a dignity and strength of will in her carriage, and in her calm eyes, that made Honor feel proud.

Catherine walked out of the bedchamber and glanced at the wine goblet. "Thank you," she said wearily, her thoughts elsewhere. "You may go." She closed her prayer missal and moved toward the fire that crackled in the hearth.

"Pray, give me leave to stay, my lady," Honor said. "I wish to help you."

From the corner of the hearth Catherine glanced over her shoulder at Honor. The smallest smile of indulgence came to her lips, colorless despite the fire's orange glow. "Help me?" she said softly, almost to herself. She looked back at the flames. "It's poor Walter who needs help now. And that I have just left in the merciful hands of God." A slight Spanish accent still clung to her speech, even after twenty-seven years in England; when she was fatigued it became pronounced.

"But that's just it," Honor blurted. "I know about Walter. That he carried your letters out."

Catherine's head turned slightly, again with that small, sharp movement of annoyance. "You mean, you know that the Cardinal claims it."

Honor took a deep breath. She would say what she had come to say. "More than that. I know Walter took your letters to Dr. de Athequa, who took them to Ambassador Mendoza. I know that this is how you correspond with the Emperor." She moved to the other corner of the hearth to be nearer the Queen. "My lady," she entreated, "let me take Walter's place. Let me help you!"

Catherine turned to her with an expression that was both surprised and wary. Honor watched the fire's shadows play unkindly over a face whose cares, like weights, had begun to sag the flesh. The Queen was forty-two, six years older than the King. She no longer danced, and rarely rode, and her waist had thickened from repeated pregnancies—six children born, five of them buried. It was a decade since her womb had quickened, and the only living child she had been able to give the husband she adored was a girl, not the male heir he craved.

Pity squeezed Honor's heart. How the Queen must have suffered through these past months. "The King's great matter," that's what everyone called it. Such a pompous phrase, Honor thought with scorn. What was so grand, she wanted to know, about a man in middle years infatuated to the point of irrationality? But the besotted King had actually asked the Pope to annul his marriage. Now, the Queen—everyone—was waiting for the decision from Rome.

Honor knew that if the Pope were to grant the King his wish the consequences for the Queen could be terrible: imprisonment in a convent, the bastardization of their twelve-year-old daughter, the Princess Mary—even, perhaps, the Queen's murder finessed by some overzealous minion of Wolsey.

And it had all begun, Honor realized with some wonder, while she was living at Chelsea, playing at archery and musing over Plato, blithely ignorant of the dark currents swirling at court and in Rome. After eighteen years with Catherine of Aragon as his wife, King Henry had privately commanded Cardinal Wolsey to dissolve the marriage. Wolsey had special authority, being a papal legate, and the King had apparently assumed that the Pope's agreement would be automatic; annulments of royal marriages were not uncommon.

The King had grounds, strange and shaky though they seemed to Honor. The marriage was the King's first, but it was the Queen's second, and that was the crux of his argument. When the King had married her Catherine had been the widow of his brother, Arthur. Scripture technically forbade matrimony with a brother's wife, so it had been necessary, all those years ago, to secure from the former Pope a dispensation to allow the union. Therefore, when the King decided he wanted his freedom, Cardinal Wolsey had called a secret tribunal and pronounced judgment that the Queen's second marriage—outlawed, after all, by scripture—had never been legal; that the King was, in the eyes of God, a bachelor. But then, before anyone—even the Queen—had been told the tribunal's extraordinary verdict, the unthinkable had happened in Rome. The Emperor Charles's mutinous troops had sacked the city, inflicting a massacre that had shaken Europe to its core. And Charles—Holy Roman Emperor of the vast German lands, ruler of Flanders, King of Spain, lord of the limitless New World—was Queen Catherine's nephew.

Overnight, King Henry's dream of a quick divorce had evaporated, for as soon as the Queen was told of his decision to cast her aside she dispatched an appeal to the Pope, a man now wholly under the domination of her invincible nephew. The English King's private matrimonial case had suddenly exploded into an international crisis. The dithering Pope, badgered by the King's envoys one day and threatened by the Emperor's the next, wrung his hands, it was said, and wept like a woman before all of them—and stalled. For nine months the King and Queen had remained at this impasse.

And Cardinal Wolsey's impatience with the Queen had grown thin. Everyone knew he chafed at what he saw as her intransigence against the King's wishes. Worse, he feared military intervention by the Emperor's forces. So he kept the Queen a virtual prisoner in her own palace. He maintained informants in her household, read every letter he could lay hands on that went from her desk, and refused to let her see the Emperor's ambassador in private. Nevertheless, Honor knew that the Queen had managed to eke out a fragile line of communication using her secretary, Walter, her confessor, Dr. de Athequa, and Ambassador Mendoza to get her letters across to Charles in Spain. But now, Wolsey had discovered at least one link of that lifeline, and had broken it.

"Please, allow me, my lady," Honor urged. "I can do everything Walter did. I can write your letters. You know my Latin is as good as his. And I could deliver them, too."

Catherine's wary expression had not changed. "Would you? Why?"

Honor hesitated, but only to search for the most concise words. She said simply, "You have been wronged."

Catherine's breath flew out of her as if she had been physically struck by the justice of the statement. "God knows!" she cried. Impulsively, she reached for Honor's hand in a gesture as filled with passion as her previous motions had been with caution. "I knew you were one to be trusted!" Quickly, she controlled herself. "But, my dear, there are grave risks. I am not at all sure it is right to ask such dangerous things of you."

"You are asking nothing, Your Grace. I am offering. And as for risk," she shrugged, "I have tasted of that before now."

Catherine's grasp on Honor's hand tightened. "Oh, I will thank Our Lord for sending you to me."

Honor's smile contained a glint of playfulness. "Do not forget to thank Sir Thomas, too, my lady, for my Latin. Had he not transformed the barbarian in me, I would be no good to you at all."

She was glad to see the warm smile that the Queen returned. "Indeed," Catherine replied with feeling. "A prayer will go, as well, for More, my dear friend." Her manner quickly sobered. "Can you begin at once, my dear?"

"Of course."

"Good. It is imperative that I tell Charles to send me lawyers. Ones experienced in dealing with the Roman court. The Cardinal has cowed the English advocates. I must have men from Charles's Flemish provinces, immune to Wolsey's threats. And I must have them now."

Honor quickly sat and took up pen and paper. She wrote at length, following the Queen's Latin dictation. With the plea to the Emperor completed, Honor folded the letter. "And now, my lady," she said, "where shall I find Dr. de Athequa?"

Catherine frowned. With a sudden movement she came to the table, took up the letter, and held it to her bosom. "No. I have changed my mind. You shall not endanger yourself for me. I'll find another way."

Honor bit her lip. She was not afraid; was ready to take the risk. But she knew, too, that she had no business contradicting a Queen. "How, my lady?" she asked gently. "There *is* no other way."

"One must be found. The Cardinal may have already squeezed poor Walter for de Athequa's name. I will not cast you, too, into such perilous seas."

Honor sat silent a moment. Suddenly, she brightened. "The masque," she said.

"Masque?"

"Tonight. At my lord Cardinal's. He is hosting a masque for the King and the Lady, and . . ." She saw the Queen flinch, and stopped. "The Lady" was the title that everyone at court, whatever their allegiance, applied to Anne Boleyn.

"Pardon, Your Grace," Honor went on, hating to give the Queen pain. "But you see, as Sir Thomas is invited to the masque, I am too. And Ambassador Mendoza is sure to be among the guests. I can take the letter directly to him. It will be so easy. No need to go through Dr. de Athequa at all."

Catherine appeared hopeful, but unconvinced.

"I promise," Honor smiled, "I shall take every care."

Catherine looked for a long moment into Honor's eyes. Then, with a small, grave nod, she gave her consent. She touched Honor's cheek with a gesture of motherly affection. "*Every* care," she said earnestly. "I'll have no ill befall you." Her warm smile broke through. "Else, how shall I answer to Sir Thomas?"

A hundred candles blazed in Cardinal Wolsey's great hall at Hampton Court. Wall-sized Flemish tapestries—miracles of artistry in gold, ruby, and sky blue threads—shimmered with larger-than-life-size scenes of the Virtues and the Vices. Many of the latter were being enacted with relish among the gaudily dressed crowd of ladies and gentlemen. Their laughing voices and the scuffle of their dancing feet all but drowned out the lusty efforts of thirty musicians in the minstrels' gallery. The pungency of spiced wine and roasted meats on side tables' mingled in the air with sweet herbs crushed underfoot, and with perfumed sweat. The King had disappeared soon after the dancing had begun. So had the Lady. But the revelers carried on.

Honor skirted the perimeter of dancers and moved toward the doors. She tried to keep her walk unhurried, tried not to show her excitement. She passed several groups, and could hardly believe that no one noticed her heightened color. Matrons gossiped and munched beside the food-laden tables. Gentlemen gambled noisily over dice in an alcove. Girls cooed around one of their number who had partnered a duke's son. In the distance, gray-haired statesmen conferring under the gallery surrounded the corpulent figure of Wolsey swathed in his red cardinal's robes. Honor's hands felt clammy as she thought of Wolsey, but she walked on. No one stopped her as she left the hall.

She was responding to the signal Ambassador Mendoza had given her. Upon her arrival an hour ago she had gone to him, and they had arranged the signal in a swift, whispered exchange. When he gave it, he told her, she was to wait a quarter hour, then meet him outside in the garden. So she had waited—had watched the dancers complete a galliard; had rejected two offers to dance; had been jostled by an angry gambler loudly searching for a man who owed him money. The wait had seemed endless.

The hardest trial had been keeping her secret from Sir Thomas. Seeing her, he had detached himself from the circle of statesmen around Wolsey, and, smiling, had come to speak to her. She knew that, councilor and friend to the King though he was, Sir Thomas sympathized with the Queen, and she could barely contain herself as he commented on the gathering and quipped about the young coxcombs. Her mission for the Queen had almost bubbled out of her.

Now, past all of these distractions, she made her way outside to the knot garden that overlooked the river.

Under moonlight, a dusting of undisturbed snow glinted over the frozen garden. The chill air bit Honor's throat as she hurried with quick breaths along a gravel walk. She hugged herself against the cold—she had left her cloak inside, for donning it might have aroused suspicion. She made for a latticed structure at the end of the walk. It was a kind of bower, three-sided, and covered over with cut holly boughs. A month before, Wolsey had ordered it erected for his comfort during a day of Christmas festivities when a choir of children sang for him and his household.

Honor saw a movement beside the bower—the swirl of a long robe—and recognized the shadowed silhouette of the Imperial ambassador. She reached the spot, and saw that he was shivering: he, too, had foreseen the imprudence of wearing his cloak. Don Inigo de Mendoza was a wiry, middle-aged Spaniard of high family and haughty disposition, and Honor could not suppress a smile at the sight of the proud gentleman clutching his robe's collar to his chin, shoulders hunched, teeth chattering.

"Ah! Mistress Larke," he whispered, taking her elbow, plainly anxious to get on with their business. Together, they stepped into the bower. Honor passed him the Queen's letter. She said, "Her Grace needs this in the Emperor's hands immediately." Mendoza nodded, then quickly left the bower. His footsteps crunched on the icy path, then faded to nothing. The mission had been accomplished in a moment.

Honor felt cheated: what an anticlimactic end to her hours of trepidation! She smiled at her own disappointment. What, after all, had she expected? That Cardinal Wolsey himself would spring up out of a garden urn? Shake snow off his great bulk and command her arrest? No. All was quiet. From windows in the hall, music reached her in faint pulses. She looked down at the River Thames. Lanterns bobbed among the clutter of ferries and barges tethered to the pier where bundled-up boatmen waited to carry guests back to the city. From the pier, blazing torches lined the way up to the palace terrace. No band of guards was marching toward her to take her off to prison. She shrugged with a smile.

She was freezing. She took a step to leave the bower. A man's voice startled her.

"A dangerous business, mistress."

Honor halted. The voice had come from inside the bower. She turned. A man was sitting on a bench tucked into the corner. He sat sideways, his feet on the bench, his knees drawn up under a heavy cloak. His face was completely in shadow under the holly boughs.

Honor took a wary step back. She and Mendoza had said little in their meeting, but it was enough.

"Yes," the man said quietly. "I heard." Three words only, but their sum was an unmistakable threat.

Honor swallowed. In the confined space she smelled brandy from his breath. She noticed a leather bottle lying on the bench beside him. Perhaps, she thought, he was nothing more than a drunkard, come out here to drink alone. Could she turn his intimidation around, use it against him? "What are you doing in the Cardinal's garden?" she asked sternly.

He gave a sharp nod toward the palace and snorted. "Avoiding a jackass inside. Claims I owe him dice money. And he's been known to rely on his sword to settle accounts." He chuckled. "No gentleman, I fear."

He had not moved. Lounging against the bower wall, he seemed to Honor harmless enough. "Good night, sir," she said firmly. She moved to go.

His sword scraped from its scabbard. The blade shot across the bower opening, blocking Honor's escape. She gasped.

"Oh, don't go yet, Mistress Larke," he said calmly.

"How do you know my name?" she asked, unnerved.

"Your tryst partner greeted you by it. As I said, I do have ears." In a sudden, clean movement, he swung his legs to the ground without lowering the sword. He looked up at her, his face now lit by a shaft of moonlight. Honor recognized him. This was the man who had almost lost his hand to the butcher's cleaver. The one Anne Boleyn had rescued. Thornleigh. And if he was Anne's confederate, Honor realized, his interest lay in discrediting the Queen. To Wolsey.

"You should also know," she said, pretending bravado, "that I am the ward of Sir Thomas More. He's just inside, sir, and he will not appreciate me being harassed in this fashion."

Thornleigh let out a short, mocking whistle. "You frighten me, mistress. *Two* adversaries inside. I may have to stay out here all night. So do take pity. Your company would be such a comfort while I'm marooned here. We could keep one another warm. You're shivering."

She saw that he was toying with her. Well, if that was all he intended, perhaps a little more bravado could get her out of this. She hugged herself and answered with disdain. "Thank you, no. Now, let me pass."

"Oh, come, come," he said pleasantly. "I'm agreeing to take on the heavy responsibility of your secret. Don't you think you owe me *something* for that service?" He lowered his sword, leaving her way clear to go. "You don't look stupid," he added meaningfully, laying the sword on the bench. "And my price is very reasonable."

So, she thought, he was threatening to inform on her after all. She accepted defeat. "How much do you want?"

Thornleigh scratched his chin thoughtfully. "Well, let's see. Moncton in there claims twenty pounds . . ."

"Twenty pounds!" she blurted. How could she ask Sir Thomas for even half that amount without arousing his suspicions? It was insufferable. She recalled Margery's earlier comment, and snapped, "I understood that your wife pays your gambling debts."

His face hardened. But he went on as if she had not spoken. ". . . but Moncton's a cheat, and I have no intention of satisfying him. So, all I'll ask of you, dear lady, is one kiss."

She was astonished. It was an idiotic request. He held her position at court—her very life, perhaps—in his hands. He could ask for anything. "You're brain-sick," she said scornfully.

"Only when I see a pretty face."

His amusement at her discomfort infuriated her. "And if I refuse?"

He chuckled. "You are not in a strong bargaining position here, mistress."

It was true. She imagined the consequences if he reported her to Wolsey. Walter, she knew, was already locked away in a prison cell. Being tortured? She shivered, and from more than just the cold.

He shrugged. "Only a kiss," he repeated reasonably.

She answered, as if uttering a curse, "Very well." She drew herself up and clenched her jaw. Her folded arms tightened into rigid armor. The iced air pinched her nostrils. "Let's get it over with."

He stood, and Honor's lips parted in surprise; she had forgotten how tall he was. He stepped close to her. He took her face between his hands and lifted it to his. His lips touched hers. She tasted the sweet residue of brandy. She felt his hand slide to her throat, felt her own pulse beat against his warm palm. His other arm went lower and drew her to him, his cloak almost engulfing her. He held her gently, yet she felt immobilized by his strength. As her every muscle softened, her mouth opened under his. Her arms dropped to her sides. She felt the heat of his body, his hands on her as if he owned her. And she knew that, for this moment, he did.

He drew his face away. She heard him laugh softly. "Open your eyes, mistress," he said. "The bargain was for just one kiss, no more. Sorry."

Her eyes flew open.

He chuckled. "You've never been kissed before, have you? But of course not. Not Sir Thomas More's ward. Oh, yes, I've heard the tales. Sir Thomas the Pious. I understand the man keeps such a chaste household, he actually segregates his servants so that male and female do not fraternize. Is it true?"

Honor wrenched herself from his arms. How dare this lecherous drunkard ridicule Sir Thomas! "This transaction is concluded, sir," she spat. "I trust I have now bought your silence?"

"Cheap, wasn't it?" He laughed. "But, I must be content," he said with mock resignation, "for the court, you know, is a buyer's market."

"And your skill in bartering, small," she retorted. "No wonder you need a rich wife."

His look at her darkened into one of scorn. "Well," he said, looking at her mouth, "all of us around here must sell whatever we can."

The insult was too plain. She raised her hand to strike him. He caught her wrist, held it a moment, then dropped it. He flopped down nonchalantly onto the bench and took up the bottle. "Go back inside, mistress," he said. "You're cold."

Honor turned on her heel and left him.

❧ 5 ❧

Smithfield

The small hunting party plodded over the drought-cracked road leading into London, and a parched breeze spiraled grit up into the eyes of Honor and Margery riding in the center. The two mounted gentlemen ahead of them were bickering over techniques of the day's kill, comparing it with other hunts, while three servant boys lazily brought up the rear, leading a pony laden with strings of bloody grouse and a fallow deer buck.

Honor peeled off a sweaty glove and picked the grit from her eye. Lord, she thought, how I hate hunting. The chase. The blood. The frenzy of the dogs—and the men—when they run down a wounded buck. Still, the wretched day has been worth it. I charmed all the information out of the Archbishop's nephew I'm likely to get for the Queen.

Margery glared ahead at the male conversation that excluded them, her eyes puffy in the heat. Honor offered her a look of sympathy. "Bridewell in twenty minutes," she said and smiled, "and the Venetian Ambassador's claret to cool us." But Margery remained grumpily silent.

The gentlemen's chatter had degenerated into a quarrel over who would be invited to hunt with the King's party the following week. Certainly not the Queen, Honor thought bitterly. The King only rode out now with Anne Boleyn; the Queen was not welcome.

Worse, if the loose talk Honor had coaxed from Archbishop Warham's nephew was correct, the Queen's prospects appeared grim; in the divorce battle, the Church, it seemed, was going to abandon her. Honor could almost hear the cautious old politician, Warham, murmuring to bishops in his archiepiscopal palace: *"Indignatio principis mors est."* The wrath of the King is death.

But still no answer had come from Rome. Winter had melted into spring, spring had dragged into summer, summer was almost at an end, and all nerves at court were in a jangle. The King fumed. The Queen endured. But the Pope would not act.

Honor stuffed her gloves into her pocket as the Jesus Bells of St. Paul's Cathedral clanged. Today was the Feast of Saint Michael. A short distance ahead the walls of London rose, and the city skyline—a square-mile thicket of steeples—wavered in the heat. As usual, several church bells were clamoring at once. Strange, Honor thought, how their discord is so familiar it sounds like harmony.

The party came up behind a cart piled with sides of beef, slowing their progress. Honor groaned with impatience. How she longed to be back in her room in a cool bath! The stacked carcasses shuddered over every pothole as if in some protracted death throe, and the carrion stink bled into the stench of the slaughterhouses and tanneries that were crowded, by law, outside the city walls. Their waste of entrails was daily slopped into the Fleet Ditch.

The smell was nauseating. Honor had had enough. "Margery," she said suddenly, "I'm off."

The other girl's eyes widened. "What, alone?"

But Honor was already trotting her mare towards an open lane. Laughing, she called over her shoulder, "See you back at Bridewell," and cantered away, happy at last to be free of dead things and dull companions.

The lane fed into the broad expanse of Smithfield fairground, and she reined the mare to a walk and threaded through the moving crowd. She was surprised at the number of people. She knew that horse markets were regularly held here—all ranks of people frequented its bawling grounds where packhorses and priests' mules were traded alongside finely bred destriers and hunters—but the usual market day was Saturday, two days away.

She squeezed around to the Augustinian priory church of St. Bartholomew the Great that fronted the square, and passed by as its bell peeled *nones*, the monks' three o'clock service. Beside the church was an empty flight of stands for dignitaries. Several idlers were lounging in the shade beneath its plank seating. Honor envied them the cool spot they had found. Definitely, she thought, a bath, first thing.

A gray-robed friar staggered out of the crowd straight toward her, his head bowed. Honor thought he must be drunk. As she jerked the reins to twist out of his way he collided with her horse's shoulder. The horse shied and Honor murmured soothing words to gentle it. The friar stared up at her. His red eyes were blurred with tears. His hands flew to his face in a gesture of misery, and then he dashed away.

There was a shout. Honor looked to her right. A procession was winding toward her. Probably a funeral, she thought. Maybe the dead man is someone the sad friar was close to. She coaxed her horse to one side, hoping to skirt the square and leave, but the crowd was swelling rapidly and the press of bodies forced her to stop.

A trio of mounted men-at-arms was followed by a workhorse dragging something, then by a half-dozen more men-at-arms on foot. The crowd had kicked up a lot of dust, and through this screen Honor could not make out what the horse had in tow. But as it neared her, the heads of two men became visible behind the horse's rump. Although she could not yet see their bodies it was clear they were strapped to a hurdle, the tilted wooden grill that was scraping over the ground.

This crowd hadn't come for a horse fair. They'd come to watch a burning.

"There he is!" someone said with a laugh. "Heywood the heretic."

People pushed to get closer, forcing Honor's horse forward too. The hurdle was now passing directly in front of her, and she saw the face of the prisoner nearest her. He was young and slight, his hair shaved in a priest's tonsure. He smiled winningly, like a child or a simpleton, at the people craning to see him. His arms were free above the ropes that bound him to the hurdle, and he offered the sign of the cross over and over.

An old man fell to his knees in front of the procession, halting it. "Brother Heywood, God take you to His rest," he croaked.

Honor was eager to leave this place of execution. She was about to kick her mare's flanks when her eyes were drawn to the other prisoner slumped on the far side of the hurdle. He was almost twice the size of the smiling friar. His face was turned away, and she could see only a mass of hair: a dirty blond tangle above and a full beard straggling below. Like the friar, he was barefoot and dressed only in shirt and hose. But unlike the friar he was smeared with the dried filth of long imprisonment, and the ropes around knees, waist and chest that strapped him to the wooden grill pinned his arms tightly to his sides.

"Look what you'll be missing, love," a young woman said, laughing. She sprang from the crowd to kiss him. Her companions whistled at her prank. As her mouth covered the prisoner's slack lips, her hand tousled his hair, revealing his cheek and ear. Or what was left of his ear. It had been mutilated, leaving a scarlet ruffle of cartilage.

Horror chilled Honor's scalp. Around the reins, her nails dug white crescents into her palms. "Ralph," she breathed.

The old man impeding the procession was dragged from the path. The horse and hurdle wallowed on. People rushed after it like gulls screeching in the wake of a ship.

The execution cortege stopped in front of Saint Bartholomew's Church. From inside came the dead chanting of monks.

Maybe it's not Ralph. Six years since I've seen him. An injured ear might be common. Among soldiers . . . or criminals . . .

She tried to move her horse forward but the crowd made it impossible. She slid off the saddle and abandoned the animal and fought her way on—shoving aside a woman hawking stick crosses, worming past a man with a child on his shoulders—until she burst into the front rank of onlookers. There, no more than five horse lengths from her, the hurdle had stopped. Still tilted off the ground, the prisoners lay stretched on it like gutted fish splayed in the sun to dry.

"Dear God," she whispered in despair. For it was no soldier, no criminal. It was Ralph Pepperton. Haggard and filthy, his bearded face a lifetime older, but the same man who had ripped his own flesh from the nail of the pillory to run with her from Tyrell Court and see her safely to London.

The last time she had spoken to him was just after the victorious trial that had made her Sir Thomas's ward. After bringing Ralph the judgment, she had gone with him to a wharf on the river near London Bridge. It was sunset, and Ralph was tossing his satchels into a barge bound for Oxford. They stood together on the water steps, unable to say good-bye.

"Oh stay, Ralph," she pleaded. "The news from Tyrell Court may never reach here. And even if it does and they accuse you, Sir Thomas is a wonderful, fair man. I know he'll forgive you. Come and meet him."

"Forgive murder?" Ralph shook his head with a smile. "If he does, he's not the clever lawman I took him for. No, mistress. Though you and me know the how and why of it—an evil mishap—the law sees things different. And maybe that's as it should be, for I swear I'd snap that lousel's neck again for your sake."

He had held her nose between his knuckles as he used to do to make her laugh when she was a child, but as a woman of twelve she had thought it undignified to respond. He let go and chucked her under the chin, then climbed into the barge. As he turned back to her he fished an apple from his pocket, shoved the whole thing between his jaws, and comically bulged his eyes. It had made her giggle like a child after all. The barge had pulled away. Ralph had popped out the apple and waved good-bye, grinning under the golden sunset.

Now, he lay lashed to the hurdle and his grin was the rictus of pain. His shirt, stripped off one shoulder, hung in shreds over his chest, now so lean that the white skin gleamed at the knobs of collarbone and rib. From plum-colored sockets he blinked at the people who jeered at him.

"Ralph!" Honor cried, but his eyes flickered over her, not seeing her.

She stared past him at the circular pit of sand. It was roped off and posted at intervals with guards. At the center, two ten-foot stakes stood ready. Heaped at the base of each stake was a three-foot pile of faggots and straw.

Her mind groped for bearings. *Some mistake . . . Some horrible mistake . . .*

There was a commotion beside the church. A group of dignitaries was mounting the stands. Fingers in the crowd pointed up at them: the velveted Lord Mayor and his aldermen; the Bishop of London's Chancellor and his attendant clerics.

The Mayor! He can stop this!

She barged back through the packed ranks and struck out for the Mayor's platform, treading on feet, deaf to people's curses. She was almost at the stands when laughter erupted. Three clowns had dashed into the pit, cavorting like monkeys, tumbling near the stakes. People had clambered onto the roofs of nearby houses to watch. Some sat, some ate. Others leaned out of windows. A woman suckled a baby. Beneath the dignitaries' stands a couple groped in the shadows, the woman fumbling at the strings of the man's codpiece while he kneaded her breasts. In the pit the clowns simulated a fistfight and the crowd's laughter crescendoed.

Honor glanced back at the hurdle. The guards were slitting the prisoners' bonds. The young friar sprang up instantly, erect, fresh-faced and smiling. Ralph slid down the hurdle on his back, dropped to his knees, then pitched forward. But when one hand groped in the sand to break his fall his back arched convulsively. Nausea curdled Honor's stomach as she saw the source of his agony: he had been brought here with one shoulder wrenched from its socket.

Guards flanked each prisoner and grappled their elbows. The friar walked tamely across the pit to the stake as if on his way to church. Ralph had to be hauled between the guards, his legs limp, his toes scraping a channel behind him in the sand. At the stake, they tied Ralph's hands behind his back. They bound his ankles with twine. They passed a chain around his chest to anchor him to the stake. Both tethered men now faced the stands where the Bishop's Chancellor was stepping down and striding out to deliver an address.

Honor tore her gaze from Ralph. The entrance to the stands lay to her right. There was only one central aisle and only one soldier guarding it, leaning on his pike. She lunged and reached the first step. The pike shot across her path and her hips thudded against its shaft as it locked on the far railing.

"Sorry, my lady. Only His Worship's party allowed."

Honor stood back. The guard, she saw, was no older than herself. "I bring a message from the Queen," she lied. "Let me pass."

The guard's eyes dropped to her silk sleeve. The embroidered badge there—the pomegranate of Aragon entwined with the Tudor rose—was the Queen's emblem. He gnawed his lip, hesitating.

"I beg you," she whispered.

At the desperation that flooded her face the guard relaxed. It was easy to deal with weakness. "Sorry, my lady. Orders."

Honor cast a look up to the Mayor on the middle bench surrounded by his aldermen. Recklessly, she shouted, "Your Worship!"

But the Mayor was listening with a scowl to a man standing before him, a middle-aged soldier who was holding up two head-sized sacks tied together with a short length of rope.

"With this gunpowder strung around the man's neck," the soldier was explaining, "the fire consumes him all the faster. I've seen it used in Lincoln, and I do recommend it."

"Why?" the Mayor asked. "We've never used gunpowder before. And what of the danger? The fire might spread. Up here."

"There is no danger, Your Worship. This only brings the man a quicker end. For mercy's sake."

The Mayor's concentration appeared to be wavering. His eyes flicked to a banner that drooped at the edge of the stands. Though gray clouds were beginning to roll in, the heat remained suffocating. A bead of sweat slid down his temple. "Mercy?" he asked vaguely.

"Mercy," a low voice interjected from the bench behind the

Mayor, "is the prerogative of God." The speaker lifted a hand to bat away a fly. On his finger a sapphire ring gleamed.

The Mayor brightened. "There's your answer, Lieutenant. We're here to carry out the law. The rest, as Father Bastwick says, we leave to God." His responsibility discharged, the Mayor turned away to chat with his aldermen. The Lieutenant bowed sadly and came down the steps. The guard lowered his pike to let him pass, then raised it to bar Honor again.

Her vision had darkened. Every face faded except the face behind the Mayor. Every object blurred except the sapphire ring and the brilliant black eyes above it.

He's behind this. Evil surfacing again . . . like scum . . . blighting everything he touches.

Fury overpowered her. Though the pike still barred her way, the guard had half turned to watch the Mayor. She lifted her foot and slammed it to the inside of his knee. His body buckled, his pike clattered to the ground.

She bounded up the stairs toward Bastwick. Aldermen cringed in astonishment. Bastwick turned and saw her coming. He stared for a moment, incredulous. Then hatred flooded his eyes. He leaped up and pointed at her. "Guard!"

She was three tiers from him—her fingers hooked to claw out those black eyes—before the guard was on her. Pain seared as he wrenched her arm and pinned her hand to the small of her back. Her eyes and Bastwick's locked. As she writhed under the guard's grip, Bastwick's mouth twitched into a private smile of victory.

Her arm was on fire, but the pangs finally shot reason back to her brain. *Attacking him is madness.* She sensed the guard's reluctance to bring all his strength to bear on a gentlewoman, and so she groaned loudly, as if faint, and went limp. His grip shifted immediately into an effort to support her. Just then a roar went up from the crowd. Honor's head snapped around. So did Bastwick's. All eyes in the stands looked out. The crowd fell silent.

The executioner had entered the pit. The dancing orange flame of his torch was the only movement in the square, and in the stillness Honor caught the Chancellor's final words droning from between the condemned men. The awful phrase crashed over her: ". . . second charge, for which the sentence is irrevocable . . ."

A steel band of terror tightened around her chest. No one convicted of a second charge of heresy could escape the fire. After a first conviction in the Church courts the accused could abjure, recant, and be released. But for anyone caught a second time there was no escape. That was the law.

No one . . . not the Mayor . . . not even the King . . . no one can save him now . . .

She turned and stumbled down the steps, Bastwick forgotten. The aldermen, settling for the spectacle, ignored her. The guard allowed her to go.

Honor forced her way again to the rope. Ralph's head rolled back and forth against the stake. His heaving chest, stripped bare in the struggle to tether him, glistened with grimy sweat. The anguish in his eyes ripped Honor's heart like a fishhook.

As the executioner stood by, the Bishop's Chancellor read out from a scroll the condemned men's heresies, beginning with the friar. "Divers and sundry times within the parish of St. Giles you have alleged that the sacrament of the altar is only bread, and not Christ's true body . . ."

"Stinking Lutheran!" a woman yelled.

". . . and you have alleged that no priest can absolve a man of sin; that tithes, mortuaries and oblations are not due to priests; that the pardons and blessings of bishops have no value . . ."

When he had finished the list, he looked at the friar. The crowd murmured, knowing the question that was to come. Would Friar Heywood, in terror of hell at this ultimate moment, recant and die in the bosom of the Church? There was no chance of pardon; both men, as second offenders, must burn. But by recanting and gaining absolution, the Church offered salvation for their souls. And so the Chancellor asked, "Do you abjure your heresies and return to the Church?"

Heywood smiled beatifically. "I trust I am not separate from the Church. I know that I am closer to God."

Amazement coursed through the crowd, most people condemning his wickedness, a few praising his steadfastness. No one seemed interested when the Chancellor crossed to the second man. On his way, he looked apprehensively at the bruised sky clamping down on the square. Rain clouds. He rattled through the second man's crimes: "You have on sundry occasions shown yourself to be of an erroneous opinion concerning the blessed sacraments . . ."

Honor strained at the rope to hear the charges, but she was too far away and the chattering people drowned out the Chancellor's words. They were interested only in the famous friar, not this unknown man. She caught only the phrase ". . . selling illegal Bibles in the English tongue . . ." and when the Chancellor impatiently asked if he would recant his heresies, Ralph only shut his eyes tightly. Whether it was a gesture of refusal or only of agony, Honor could not tell. The Chancellor waited only a moment before quickly striding away.

The pit was now clear except for the executioner standing between the two chained men. The air above the sand shimmered as if breathing back the absorbed heat of former fires. The crowd stilled. A dog barked in an alley. A far-off church bell clanged.

The Mayor rose and lifted his arms. "*Fiat justicia!*"

The executioner turned to the friar and thrust his torch into the faggots. Instantly, flames roared up. The executioner withdrew the torch, turned, and thrust it in below Ralph. The straw kindled, then flared. Ralph's body went rigid. Only his eyes moved, darting over the flames that licked his legs and hands and then subsided like the playful swats of torture a cat inflicts on a maimed bird.

There was now a wall of flame around the friar. All that could be seen was the top of his head. Clouds of gray smoke billowed over him. The hiss of the wood rose above the excited hiss of men and women who inched back from the blaze. Then, suddenly, it was over. His head slumped. The smoke had asphyxiated him.

The Lieutenant stepped forward. In a gesture of mercy he raised a sledgehammer and drove in the nail that held the chain at the back of the stake. The chain rippled away. The friar's body slid down the stake and melted into the fire.

There was a moment of utter silence. Then a groan of disappointment that the drama was so swiftly concluded. Then, all eyes turned to the second man. The flames around him were not so greedy. At the sides they only skimped along the damp wood, though in front they were leaping up in three-foot orange tongues.

Ralph was writhing under his chain. His abdomen pumped as if in spasm. But with his immense strength he was straining through the twine that bound his feet. It snapped. The two pieces sprang up like fighting snakes, then dropped into the flames. He lifted one freed leg and kicked wildly at the glowing wood. The chain gnawed his ribs, smearing skin away.

Honor gagged. Beyond the flickering screen of fire she saw a slime of excrement darkening his leg. She caught glimpses of his foot . . . kicking, recoiling, kicking again . . . the skin of his sole charred black. People shouted and cheered, excited by his primal struggle. Honor wailed as if the fire was consuming her own flesh.

Ralph's eyeballs bulged, dehydrated. Tears spilled, bubbled on his cheeks, evaporated. The tatters of his shirt curled and smoked. Sparks lighted in the bush of his beard. It flared like dry pine needles. Honor shrieked. Ralph shook his head wildly until the beard only smoldered.

The fire sputtered on endlessly, prolonging his agony. Not one merciful breath of wind rushed in to fan the flames. And Ralph's own vast strength kept him conscious and fighting long past the time when most men would have fainted.

Honor thought she would go mad. Like a wild animal, she sprang. As if infused with some of Ralph's strength, she clawed her way between two guards and under the rope. She tore across the open pit. As she neared Ralph the fist of heat punched her, scalding her throat, forcing shut her eyes, gagging her with the sweetish stink of his burning flesh.

She heard the rip of silk. A guard had snatched the back of her skirt. Without turning she bunched her fists and shot her elbows backwards into his ribs. His breath belched from him and he released her. Unbalanced, she toppled.

She scrambled onto her hands and knees. Two guards were racing toward her. She was almost at the holocaust beneath Ralph. She sprawled across the final two feet of scorched sand. Her brain flared a warning, but her hands, with a will of their own, pawed at the glowing logs.

She looked up. Ralph's red eyes, reflecting red flame, met hers. He recognized her. His crusted face expanded with joy—a joy that, for one instant, quenched the agony. Then his eyeballs rolled up, white inside the red rind of socket. His backbone arched. Sparks jumped to his head. His hair flared. Smoke boiled over him. Honor's ears were split by one harrowing scream from him. And then the fire engulfed him.

Both guards caught up with her at once. They lifted her arms above her head, twisted her limp body around, and dragged her facedown between them to the edge of the crowd the way Ralph had been dragged to the stake. At the rope barricade they pushed her underneath and dropped her on her knees. She knelt, stunned into immobility, and the guards decided it was safe to leave her. People near her, anxious to keep watching the man burn, shuffled in around her.

Her head slumped back. She was dimly conscious of a throbbing in her hands. They hung like bricks at the ends of her arms. She had not the strength to lift them. Nor to lift up her head. It hung back, so very heavy. The standing bodies around her restricted her vision to the shaft of sky above her upturned face. She blinked at the sparks drifting upward in this column of air—bright, spiraling stars that died to cinders against the gray sky.

The first, fat drops of rain splatted as warm as blood onto her forehead. Thunder crashed. The sky unleashed a deluge. People looked up. Several laughed, delighted at the relief the water brought. Then, suddenly, the wind rose. Rain began to lash them in whipping, stinging sheets. The mass of humanity around the pit began to crack apart. The water seemed to erode them into chunks, into small islands like the ones already forming on the baked roads leading into Smithfield. Men, women and squealing children scuttled away. Rain scythed across the stands, forcing the dignitaries from their seats. Hurrying down the stairs, they formed a current pushing through the eddying crowd. Running bodies swept out of the square like debris washed into a gutter.

As water pooled around her skirt, Honor opened her mouth and let the pins of rain sting and then die on her tongue. She gulped the drenched air, willing it to cleanse away the ash that clogged her throat and nostrils. She turned her head to the left. Across the pit, the weeping friar who had earlier collided with her horse kneeled too, in a silent anguish of his own. They were the only mourners.

The stake that had held the friar was demolished and rain pounded the hissing coals and washed the dead man's remains. The stake that held Ralph still stood, half eaten to charcoal. Under the chain, his twisted body hung, a black, shriveled lump.

Honor bent forward and vomited.

Something made her lift her head. Straight across the pit one other person, she saw, had remained behind. Father Bastwick. He stood under the gable of the dry church porch, watching her.

Above them all, the blind stone saints on St. Bartholomew's tower stood sentry in the sloping sheets of rain.

❧ 6 ❧

The Conscience of the King

King Henry sat with Anne Boleyn in the window seat of a gate-house in a manor near Oxford. His head hovered over her naked breast, but she was staring beyond him at the night sky, which was cut up by the mullioned windows into starry squares. The whiskers of his beard stung her as his lips and tongue worked around her nipple. "Ow," she murmured. He paused. Then he bit her.

"Ouch!" She clamped her hands firmly on both his bearded cheeks, lifted his head, and glared. His blue eyes looked up with all the apprehension of a child caught with a finger in the honey pot. He licked a dribble of saliva from the corner of his mouth and waited for his rebuke.

Anne's eyes narrowed, tugging together eyebrows as lustrous as black silk. She leaned back against the stone casement. Above her lowered bodice her black hair lay in stripes over her small breasts. The pink, erect nipples peeked out like berries through brambles. She turned her head and looked out at the night as if she were alone.

"Woman," he growled, "how long will you torture me?"

She watched a shooting star.

"Anne," he pleaded, "come to my bed."

"No."

"But why?"

"You've had my answer".

"But I don't understand," he whined.

Her tone was flat, businesslike, except for a note of weariness. "Your Grace cannot marry me, and the longer you single me out as you do, the more you jeopardize my chance of making a good match elsewhere."

"Marry you! God's wounds, am I not moving heaven and earth to do so?"

Her smile was disdainful. "Heaven is immovable, Your Grace, even by a prince as mighty as yourself. And as for earth, the patch beneath the Pope's feet shows little sign of yielding. Meanwhile, you already have a wife to share your bed."

She was forcing up the lemon yellow bodice of her gown, and he groaned at this signal that she was finished dispensing her favors for the evening. He grabbed her wrist to stop her. She stiffened in defiance.

Sudden, raw anger infused his face. He fought his way up from the undignified lover's sprawl in the window seat and stood over her, bulky with red velvet, gold silk, and precious stones. Henry Tudor was six feet tall, broad of shoulder and long of leg. He had been a skilled athlete all his life, and even at thirty-seven, and heavy with years of gluttony, his body still exuded an athlete's power. Behind him, the remains of the fire across the room illuminated his cropped, golden hair and seemed to make his huge form glow with majesty. But his lips, a small red bow in the broad face, pouted with indignation. "Have I not sworn to you that I no longer lie with the Queen? God's blood, what more would you have me do?"

Anne snorted. She rose and pushed past him. The room, lit only by the dying fire, was bare except for a bed, a table, and a scatter of cushions near the hearth. She kicked a tumbled coal into the fire. "If you were a Prince of Lombardy you would dispatch the barren old woman with a potion and marry whom you please."

Henry was genuinely shocked. Dignity crept back and inflated his chest. "I am, however, King of England. A Christian King. Such evils will not be countenanced in my realm."

Anne whirled around and glowered at him, her hands on her hips.

"And you would do well to remember," he went on, "that the lady you call 'old woman' is a Spanish Princess. Your great-grandfather rose from a mercer's shop, Mistress *Bullen*, but in Catherine's veins flows the blood of kings."

Anne flushed. Looking contrite, she dropped to her knees among the cushions, flung back her hair and looked up at him. "Forgive me, my good lord. For my presumption you must blame this plague of the sweating sickness that has kept us apart for so long. Your presence is so dear to me, and the separation from you, until today, has chafed me so, it drives me to say cruel things. Things I do not mean."

She lay back among the cushions, her hair spread across their gold brocade. Her long legs stretched sinuously under her skirt. Henry came to her and stood over her, fascinated. "Your Grace's displeasure is my abiding sorrow," Anne said softly. She extended her arms to him. "Forgive me?"

Instantly, he was on the floor beside her, kissing her mouth, groping inside her bodice, shoving it down to fondle her breast. She gently pushed him onto his back. She whispered in his ear, "Henry." She never dared to speak his Christian name except in passion, and he shuddered at the intimate thrill it gave. Her breath was moist. Her tongue probed his ear. Her hand crept down to his groin, and her fingernail scraped along the satin of his codpiece. "Henry," she murmured, "how I long to open my body to you. To discover *your* body . . ."

Suddenly, violently, she pulled away. She sat bolt upright and clamped her skirt around her knees. "But, of course, the Spanish Princess can do these things with you, for the Spanish Princess is your *wife*."

"Damn you, wanton!" He snatched her shoulders and wrenched her around so quickly that her hair whipped his face. She did not flinch from his anger, nor from his strength, but stared at him levelly, like an equal. But tears were brimming in her eyes, and her breath was harsh. Henry relaxed his grip and shook his head in bewilderment. No woman had ever refused him before.

The door swung open. Henry and Anne squinted up like trapped felons in the glare of the cresset lamps on the stairwell.

Sir Thomas More stepped through the doorway.

Seeing Anne—the wild hair, the naked breast—More froze. He was aware of a rustling sound and realized that he had stopped so abruptly the top papers on his armload of documents were spilling over his rigid grasp. A couple of scrolls fell at his feet, and papers kept fluttering down.

Henry began to chuckle. Anne, tugging up her bodice, giggled. They looked at one another, then fell back on the cushions together, laughing like children.

More lowered his head and sharply turned to leave.

"Thomas, wait," Henry sputtered. He was scuffling to his feet.

"I beg pardon, Your Grace," More said, his head still bowed to avert his eyes. He tried to purge his voice of emotion. "I believed Your Grace to be listening to the entertainment in the hall. Had I known . . ."

"No matter, Thomas, no matter," Henry said, still chuckling. He was helping Anne up as they both caught their breath. "The wretched fellows do not guard my door. It's Wentworth's blunder, not yours. Come in, come in. And close the door on that infernal light."

"Sadly, it is true, Your Grace," More said, bending for the fallen papers. "Sir James's people are in disarray at the sudden honor of your visit."

Henry swooped to help gather up the documents. "What's all this?" he laughed. "Have you brought this confounded paperwork all the way from Westminster?" He turned back to Anne, smiling.

"Just the backlog from Wolsey's desk," More said. He straightened and tried to regain his composure by shuffling the papers back into order in his arms. But, compounded with his shock, he was uncomfortably conscious of his own unkempt appearance. He had ridden from London that morning and knew the hours of travel showed in his bloodshot eyes, while the dark stubble that glinted with silver on his chin betrayed how many more hours he had been alone at work after joining the royal party; he had not expected to see the King before tomorrow morning. "The Hanse merchants are pressing for an answer about their lawsuit," he said as if to justify his earnestness, then added lamely, "but that can wait."

Henry was ignoring him. He was kissing Anne's fingers, lingering in her gaze. More watched. The lovers' eyes were locked in a silent, private communion. Henry led her around him in a stately sweep as if they danced to some music only they could hear. His lips brushed her fingertips in farewell. She sailed past More with a mocking smile. He forced his gaze to the ground until she was gone.

Henry moved to More's side, chuckling as he loaded the papers into his own arms in one unwieldy bundle. He dumped the lot onto the table. "No paperwork now, Thomas. Look at the night. The stars!" He gestured to the window as if the night sky were his private treasure hoard.

More smiled indulgently. "Your Grace is in a mood for stargazing?"

Henry was unlatching a door in the far wall. "I am, my friend, I am." He grinned over his shoulder. "And for your council, Thomas."

More sighed, then followed.

The door opened onto a stone staircase that wound up the octagonal tower of the gatehouse. After several turns it brought them to a door that opened onto the tower's flat roof. They stepped out into the night.

The waning moon was a paring of silver among the silver stars. The roof was rimmed with a shoulder-high wall, notched with crenellations that had been added for defense during the civil strife of sixty years before. From these battlements, archers had once rained down death on any foe who dared breach the moat to attempt entry at the main gates. The house sprawled around a central courtyard where a troop of men had spilled out from rooms crammed with Henry's entourage. They lounged at a campfire, tossing dice, and their laughter drifted up to the roof.

Henry sucked in a deep breath of the cool air, a relief after the hot day. Above his head a flag gorgeous with the Tudor arms rippled from a pole in the center of the roof. He looked up at it and frowned. "Can't get a clear view here."

He moved to the far wall where a bridge of wooden slats connected this gatehouse tower to a twin tower. Normal access to the other tower was along a guard walk topping the wall above the gate. But much of the masonry on the guard walk had crumbled dangerously away—its disrepair was a result of the long peace— and so the makeshift bridge had been strung out to span the thirty feet between the towers.

Henry stepped onto the rickety bridge and beckoned More to follow him. More tensed. "Your Grace, the bridge does not look strong . . ."

But Henry was already halfway across. The slats creaked underfoot. On the wall-walk fifteen feet directly below him, shards of jagged rubble glinted like fangs above the faint ground-floor torchlight. Henry stomped on. Safe on the other side, he turned and laughed. "It's fine. Come on!"

More followed, stepping gingerly. He slid his hands in jerks along the rough rope barriers on either side. Once across he breathed more freely.

Henry flopped down in the center of the tower. He stretched out on his back and bent one arm to cushion his head. "What a night." He pointed up. "Look, Thomas, the Pleiades dancing. There."

More sat beside him and drew up his knees and faced the stars. A feeling of contentment crept over him. A shared love of astronomy had been a bond between him and the King for years. He could recall many a balmy evening they had spent together on the lead roofs of Greenwich palace, pointing out constellations and discussing the movements of the sun and the planets through their crystal compartments that encapsulated the earth. "The seven daughters of Atlas," he mused. "But Electra, the 'lost Pleiad,' never among them."

"No need for Electra," Henry said. "Her sisters do a fine job, twinkling down at a man like ripe virgins."

More laughed softly. "Your Grace is merry tonight."

"I am, Thomas, I am. The air here is clean. Hunting's been superb. I'll say that for Wentworth. Best hunting all summer. And I've been on the move since Whitsuntide, you know, outrunning the cursed Sweat."

More sighed. He knew. He had followed the King through most of his panicked moves after the sweating sickness had broken out in Greenwich in June. Henry had fled the palace and ordered the poor of the town herded out in an attempt to halt the disease. While the Queen had stoically remained at Bridewell, Henry had shunted around the country from one friend's house to another, his host's purse invariably emptied by the honor of victualing the huge retinue of gentlemen, servants, clerks and musicians that crowded in after the King. He had kept his doctor at his elbow, hurried several times a day to Mass, and every evening confessed his sins. He feared sleeping alone, and had his friend, Francis Bryant, sleep on a straw pallet at the foot of his bed. More shook his head. What lengths we go to, he thought, to try to outfox death.

"At Hampton last night," Henry murmured, "Robert Wodehouse died."

"I heard," More said, lowering his voice in sympathy. He thought he read fear on the King's face: the dread of his own mortality.

Henry sat up. "We were boys together—Robert, Will Parr, and I. Trained together. Entered the jousting lists together." He managed a weak smile. "Robert even unseated me. Once." The smile crumbled. "He was two years younger than I." Absently, he fingered the walnut-sized emerald on a golden chain around his neck. The laughter from the men at the campfire sifted over the battlements.

"All quiet now, eh, Thomas?" Henry said, jerking his chin in the direction of the laughter. "But it was not always so. During the Troubles, Wentworth's grandfather was murdered below this very tower. Did you know? He'd betrayed York, you see. Fed information to the Lancastrians so they could ambush a Yorkist brigade on the road to St. Albans. A week later Edward of York marched into London and took the crown. But not before his knights had settled the score with old Wentworth. Hacked him to pieces on his own drawbridge." He shook his head. "My God, the bloody roses, Red and White. My mother told me all about the terrors of those days, Thomas."

"Terrors ended by your father, happily," More ventured. But he saw that Henry was not listening.

"The realm was virtually lawless then," Henry went on anxiously. "And all because the King was an imbecile. A pitiful half-wit who couldn't dress himself. Poor King Harry of Lancaster." He turned to More, his face pallid in the scant moonlight. "If I leave no heir, Thomas, will the horrors start again? The mighty factions my father hoped to curb are straining again at their leashes. Some have snapped them, and nip at my very heels. Look at Buckingham. True, I cut off his treasonous scheming along with his head, but what of Norfolk? And the grasping Percys? What of the villainous dogs in Scotland, panting for an empty English throne? I must leave an heir, Thomas. Without a son I consign my realm to bloody civil war."

"Princess Mary . . ."

"Bah! A woman's hand cannot rule this stubborn people. Even if she could, she must one day marry some prince of Spain or France or Portugal, and then her obedience to her husband would reduce England to a sniveling fiefdom, the vassal of a foreigner."

"I think not, Your Grace. Your subjects have been accustomed for too many generations to liberty and the rule of English law."

Henry suddenly roared, "I must have a son!"

More flinched. At the King's outburst the laughter below at the campfire hushed.

Henry hauled himself up and stalked to the wall and looked out over the dark valley.

More had stood when the King did, the ingrained habit of obedience. He watched the breeze tug the silken skirt of the King's gold tunic, and waited. The air was heavy with a melancholy smell of smoke and dying vegetation. Today's the Feast of St. Michael, More thought with a shiver. The end of summer.

The men's chatter from the courtyard slowly resumed.

Henry waved wearily behind his back. "Sit down, man," he said, staring out. "Sit down."

More sat. An owl hooted from the forest.

Henry's hand slapped irritably against the stone parapet. "How I detest this waiting for a judgment. God's wounds, I'll breathe easier when the thing is done, Thomas. The infernal waiting. It's enough to kill a man."

"Your Grace may not have to wait so very much longer," More said quietly.

Henry swung around. "What say you?" He moved in, wide-eyed with hope. "Thomas, what have you heard?"

"Only a rumor, sire," More said. He was far from happy to be the messenger of such news. Yet, he asked himself, how could he in conscience conceal it? "Just before supper your goldsmith arrived. He told me he had met a merchant on the road who'd come from Dover, having crossed from Calais. The merchant said he had seen Cardinal Campeggio's entourage arrive at Calais from Rome."

Henry smacked his hands together, exulting. For months he had been pressing the Pope to send Cardinal Campeggio as a special envoy to judge the divorce. "I knew it," he cried. "Knew it in my bones when Anne arrived today. Campeggio, soon in England! Ha! Making that Italian the Bishop of Salisbury was the best day's work I ever did." He laughed. "God smiles on me, Thomas."

"He always has, Your Grace." More made no attempt to hide the affection in his voice.

Henry smiled. He came and sat again beside his friend. "Thomas, I didn't bring you up here just to stargaze. I wanted to seek your council on this great matter. Until now I've not asked your opinion outright. And"—he chuckled—"God knows you've not been forward in voicing it."

More's palms prickled.

Henry went on. "Everyone else has had his say, ad infinitum. But you—you've kept mightily quiet. Well, I'm asking now. It's important. Give me your thoughts."

More tried to keep his face neutral but he feared the racing of his heart betrayed him. Fool! he chided himself. You knew the question would come one day.

Henry gently grasped the back of More's neck and leaned in to him as if to impart a confession. "I won't deny I dearly want you behind me in this, Thomas. In fact, there's no man's support I'd rather have."

The sincerity, the generosity, unbalanced More's shaky composure. He lowered his head to collect his thoughts. But his thoughts were in turmoil. Where did his duty lie? Should he march behind his King, right or wrong? Or leap in front to block him from this perilous false step? A pang of arthritis shot through his knee. He rubbed it. "These old bones bring news, too," he said, and offered an apologetic smile. "They tell me autumn nears."

"Don't change the subject, Thomas. Come, give me your council. Cannot you see God's hand in this? I do. I see so clearly that if I had done my duty to Him all those years ago, had obeyed His scriptural commandment, I'd have a son beside me now." His voice rose to indicate a quotation. 'If a man shall take his brother's wife, it is an unclean thing: he hath uncovered his brother's nakedness; they shall be childless.'"

More closed his eyes, sick of hearing yet again the scriptural passage from Leviticus. He had been appalled at how quickly the English bishops had jumped to mouth it back to the King. Bishop Fisher had been the only one to speak out for the sanctity of the marriage.

"It's as clear as the Dog Star above us," Henry concluded confidently. "I sinned in marrying Arthur's wife. As punishment, I am childless."

More cleared his throat softly. "But, Your Grace . . ." He hesitated. How to tell a king he's wrong? He lifted his finger in a debating gesture. "Leviticus is a lengthy catalogue of such injunctions. They are the harsh rules of a nomadic Hebrew tribe, a people living in the fractiousness of close confinement, in tents."

He knew it was a safe enough beginning, for the King was used to this sort of intellectual opposition from him; theological debates were a pastime with them, and both could quote long passages of Latin scripture by heart. "The Church," he went on, "has overruled many prohibitions in Leviticus, including the injunction against shaving off 'the corner of the beard,' and against eating the flesh of swine."

"Exactly, Thomas," Henry replied swiftly. "Overruled. The former Pope, in granting the dispensation, bent the law. God's law. The Pope was *wrong* to allow my marriage. He acted contrary to God's law in scripture."

More answered cautiously but firmly. "Acted on his authority as the Vicar of Christ on earth, Your Grace."

They were sitting face-to-face. More looked into the eyes of his King, eyes so hungry for approval. Were they hungry, too, for guidance? Was that his duty, after all? He felt a pang of devotion and longed to say something that would hold the King back from charging like a mad bull at the bright banner—the unspotted fabric—of Christ's Church. *The traditions of civilization over fifteen centuries are embodied in the authority of the Church,* he wanted to cry. *Your marriage with the Queen has lasted almost twenty years. Custom and tradition make it sacred. And the Church has spoken.*

As he thought this, hovering on the brink of speaking what was in his heart, he shook his head almost imperceptibly. It was not a gesture of defiance, merely of concentration, but it seemed to trip the spring of a trap in Henry's mind. His face darkened and bulged over his jeweled collar.

"By Christ's wounds," he cried, "I will have this annulment, for God tells me it is right! I'll not be thwarted!"

More felt his heart beat fast with fear. "Thwarted?" In the forest the owl's cry spiraled on the chill air. "Never by me, Your Grace." He shuddered. He knew that his moment of courage had ebbed, and was forever lost.

Henry was staring at his hands. "Thomas, I want you to understand something." He turned, calmer now. "God is speaking to me," he said. More listened uneasily, vaguely dizzy, for the crenellated walls around them blocked out the world, and shreds of cloud scudded overhead giving the illusion that the platform was moving. It seemed that he and the King were sitting alone, voyaging in some unearthly ship, adrift among the stars.

"He is speaking to me in three ways," Henry said with a low urgency. "First, through my intelligence, for canon law, as you know, is no mystery to me."

"All the world acknowledges that Your Grace is an accomplished theologian."

Henry hurried on. "Secondly, he speaks to me through my heart, for it has cracked with every babe that Catherine and I have buried."

Impulsively, More clasped Henry's forearm in a silent communion of sympathy; More was a man who loved his children.

"And now, Thomas, He is speaking to me through my blood."

His hand clamped down over More's. "There is a yearning, a hunger in my blood for Anne that inflames me in a way I've never known."

More winced. *Spare me this*, he thought. *As you are a merciful king, spare me this.*

"I have sinned in adultery before, Thomas."

"Please, Your Grace, I am no priest. These are matters for your Father Confessor, not for me. I beg you—"

"But you are my *friend*. A priest cannot understand this. He does not live as a man, like you and I do. No, all my previous sins of the flesh were mere acts of lust, Thomas. The lust that every man feels for a comely woman."

Every man. The words echoed in More's head like an indictment. In a flash, he saw Jane, his young first wife, lying naked before him. He cringed as if it had happened yesterday, remembering the lust that had consumed him on his wedding night. Another flash, and he saw Honor Larke running down to the water stairs to greet his barge, all smiles, her dark hair tumbled over the half-moons of her breasts swelling above her bodice. He clenched his fists in shame. Every man, indeed.

Henry grabbed More's collar. "No, Thomas, this is more than simple appetite. God has fired my blood for a holy purpose. He is telling me . . . commanding me . . . to beget a son."

More groaned inside. Such self-deception in a king!

The door of the other tower slammed open. Lantern light pooled over its roof as a man stepped out. Henry looked across at his friend, Francis Bryant.

"What is it, Francis?"

"It's . . . Sir William Parr," Bryant called, his voice dry. "He's dead . . . of the Sweat."

Henry's face went white. More understood instantly. Parr was the last of the King's boyhood mates.

Henry rose unsteadily and moved to the edge of the bridge. As he stepped out onto it his eyes lifted to the Tudor flag above Bryant's head. He blinked at it as if disoriented. His gait became an old man's shuffle, and he clung to the hip-high rope barriers of the bridge as if to a lifeline.

Alarmed, More hurried after him onto the bridge. They were moving across it together, More catching up, when a slat under More's foot snapped. A shard pitched to the crumbling wall walk below, bounced off the sharp rubble, and plunged down into the moat. More fought for balance, but his ankle was caught in the shredded slat and he stumbled onto the other knee. He flailed, trying to grab hold of the rope lines.

Henry whipped around. More was struggling to pull out his leg, but his weight splintered another rotting slat, enlarging the hole so that it swallowed his leg up to the knee. His outstretched arms wrapped around the rope behind him.

Henry came close. As he neared the hole the weakened neighbor slats squealed under the pressure and split. With a jolt More fell farther and his leg disappeared up to the thigh. Henry lurched back. Then he crouched. He opened his legs wide to spread his weight. He grasped both rope lines and inched his feet closer to More, his body hulking like a wrestler as he covered the last few feet. He leaned over and reached for More's chest and grabbed two fistfuls of his robe. But More clung desperately to the rope, his eyes fixed in terror on the jagged wall below.

"Let go, man!" Henry commanded, his voice fierce with strain.

More's knuckles whitened. His arms quivered with the effort of holding himself up, but his panicked grip did not slacken.

Henry's voice softened to the coaxing of a parent. "Thomas, you've got to let me take you. Look at me. And let go."

Their eyes met. Henry smiled. More let go.

Instantly, Henry's hands flipped under More's armpits. With a sudden, ferocious strength he grappled More to his chest. More's foot was sucked free. Henry shuffled backwards toward the flag tower like a bear dragging home its prey.

Safe on the roof, they leaned against the wall to catch their breath. Bryant, too, could breathe again, for the King was unharmed.

"Ha!" Henry laughed, and his eyes sparkled with the thrill of beaten danger as he bent to slap dirt off More's robe. More's hose were torn and his shin scraped, but he was not injured. Despite his protestations, however, Henry insisted on sending Bryant for the doctor. When they were alone again Henry chuckled, his pleasure vast. "You'll live, Thomas, but I'd advise a change of hose before you join the ladies."

More's heart still pounded. "Words, Your Grace, are insufficient to—"

Henry waved away the thanks. He looked down at his fingers and thoughtfully picked off flecks of hemp. "Thomas, before we go down, tell me, once and for all. In this great matter of my marriage, can you not see your way clear to come with me?"

More's face creased in a private torment.

Henry sighed. "No, I see that you cannot. Well, I would not put a man in ruffle with his conscience. And you said you have no wish to thwart me."

"Nor never will!" More blurted ardently.

"Then pledge me as much. Pledge your silence."

"I do, Your Grace, right willingly."

"Good. I'd not lose your council on other matters. Nor your friendship." He looked up at the stars, his voice heavy with sadness. "In these dark days, Thomas, a king must watch over every friend he has."

❧ 7 ❧

News

A pair of swifts skimmed over the placid surface of the pond at More's Chelsea estate. Honor sat on the bank under the oaks with her foot in the water and watched tiny ripples radiate away from her ankle. Cecily, More's daughter, sat on a bench behind her and rummaged inside a satchel. She lifted out scissors, balled linen strips, and a jar—all of which she laid beside her on the bench. Cecily's year-old baby was sprawled on the grass at his mother's feet, his mouth open in blissful sleep as bronzed leaves spiraled gently down around him from the oaks. Past the lawns that sloped to the Thames, the laughter of maidservants cutting rushes at the river bank drifted up on the late-afternoon air.

A trout sprang out of the pond for a fly. Its body twisted, flinging droplets like a shower of diamond chips. Cecily's hand jumped to her bulging belly. "Goodness!" she gasped. "One more hungry fish like that, Honor, and you may have to act the midwife!"

Honor glanced up and almost smiled. Absently, she pushed a loose lock of hair under her pearled headband, then turned back to her reverie.

Cecily's brow creased. "Now, enough daydreaming," she scolded. She patted the bench to coax Honor over. "Come. Let me dress those blisters." She pulled the stopper out of the jar and held the potion up, waiting with a stern expression as if Honor were a stubborn child refusing to come for its medicine.

Barefooted, Honor came and sat beside her.

Cecily took up one of Honor's listless hands and began smoothing a salve onto the palm. "They've healed very well, dear," she said. "And after just two weeks." When she had finished applying the ointment to both hands she cut fresh bandages from the linen strips. "Really, these are hardly necessary now," she declared.

She swathed Honor's hand, and sighed. "Ah, such pretty, tapering fingers. You know, if I were capable of envying anything in such a dear friend it would be the trimness of your body. 'Delicate' is the word that springs to mind. But no, that's not quite right. 'Delicate' suggests something rather passive, doesn't it? A kind of feminine passivity that isn't . . . well, it just isn't you, dear, is it?" She laughed. "There," she said cheerfully, finishing. She had wrapped the linen around both palms, leaving the thumb and fingers free.

Honor smiled her thanks, hating herself for the lie she had told: an accident in heating the Queen's wine at the fire. The Queen, for her part, had accepted that the "accident" had happened here at Chelsea. Honor loathed the deception. But Ralph's death was too painful even to think of; speaking of it would be unbearable. She had told no one.

"Will the Queen spare you to sit for the family portrait?" Cecily asked. "It's next Thursday, you know." She bent awkwardly to pick a crinkled leaf off her baby's forehead. "Little angel," she cooed. She straightened, then settled, and the exertion made her puff her cheeks with a laugh. "I fear Master Holbein will already need a larger canvas just to fit me in."

"I'll try to come," Honor said. She smiled. Cecily was her best friend and Honor loved her—when she'd lived here they had shared a bed, and all their secrets—but her matronly contentment rather amused Honor. After all, Cecily was only eighteen months older than herself. Today, though, she found Cecily's blanket of solicitude strangely soothing.

"Speaking of Holbein," Cecily said brightly, "let's hear the letter you said dear old Erasmus has sent you. Then I can give Hans the news from Basle when I sit for his sketch tomorrow. I know he hungers for tidings of his home."

Honor roused herself, and with stiff fingers drew a paper from her sleeve. Her letters from Erasmus were delights that she always shared with the More household. She had never met Erasmus—he had not visited England in over a decade—but following his gracious reply to the essay she had sent him, they had continued a lively correspondence. Honor was aware that it was a mark of some distinction to be one of a handful of females among the international body of colleagues with whom the scholar communicated. "Forgive me, Cecily," she said. "I meant to bring the letter before this."

"That's all right, dear, I'll hear it now," Cecily murmured good-naturedly. "Though heaven knows when I'll be able to pass the news along to Father," she sighed. "We haven't seen him for weeks. This latest epidemic of the Sweat has driven the King from Greenwich, first to Hunsden, then to Tittenhanger, and now I don't know where. And where His Grace goes, there must Father go as well. I'm so sorry you missed him."

Honor could hardly express how sorry she was, too. Her guardian was the one person to whom she felt she might unburden her heart, and she ached for a half hour of his wisdom to help her ease her sorrow. But, though hoping to find him home, she had hardly expected it.

She opened the letter and read:

"To Mistress Larke, and all alumni of the academy in the house of Thomas More: greetings.

Sad to say, the howling over Luther continues unabated. It rises to fever pitch when he attacks the trade in saints' relics, though there is no doubt the trade has become shameless. The Archbishop of Maintz boasts an exhibition of eight thousand items, including a clod of the earth from which Adam was created, a toenail of Saint Stephen's, a dollop of manna from the wilderness, a twig from the burning bush, and a drop of the Virgin's milk. And this goes on everywhere!

There are so many splinters of Our Lord's cross displayed in church reliquaries throughout Europe that a warship could not hold them all."

Cecily looked up wide-eyed. "He hasn't mellowed in his old age, has he?"

"He never hesitates to speak his rather formidable mind," Honor agreed, but her smile was weak, for Erasmus's faintly blasphemous satire brought echoes of the charges of heresy at Smithfield that chilled her. But then Erasmus, she knew, was an eclectic thinker; he always saw through cant. Though he was a priest, trained in the monastery, he had secured a special dispensation years ago that had released him from his vows of obedience to the Augustinian order.

She read on:

"People shriek at me because I do not denounce Luther. And, indeed, when he speaks the truth, I will not. Yet they should not worry; he speaks little enough of it. Lately he has fallen to raving about the 'German soul.' I fear he is the tree that bears the poison fruit of nationalism. Von Hutten has now joined in, urging 'we Germans' to stick together in the present danger. If things continue on like this I shall soon declare myself to be a Frenchman!

Certainly, one place that will never claim me again is Louvain. There, the selling of meat on Fridays or during Lent was punishable by law—unlike exploitation or war-mongering. I have been much happier here at Basle, where meat is always sold. Though my heart is Catholic, my stomach is Protestant."

Cecily and Honor exchanged smiles. Erasmus's notoriously finicky appetite was one of his more endearing quirks.

The gilded, late-afternoon sky was ripening into a rosy sunset. The maidservants ambled up from the riverbank with their bundles of reeds. From the kitchen, voices and the aromas of fresh bread and baking apples wafted across the lawn.

"But, tragically, even here in Basle [Honor read on] we are on the brink of civil war. The Lutheran Evangelicals have taken over the Council, expelling the Catholic leaders. There is talk of the University being suspended. I fear I must seek another home. But where? The lust for war boils over across Europe. Some people cry for a holy massacre of Luther's followers, some for a bloody crusade against the Turks. My essay, 'War Is Sweet to the Inexperienced' has infuriated all who do not want the world to come to its senses.

No, I cannot go with St. Bernard who praised soldiers, or St. Thomas Aquinas when he sanctioned the 'just war.' Why should we be moved by the arguments of these men more than by the words of Christ? Crusade, indeed! The Turks are clawing at the doors of Vienna, and all because Christians are too busy snarling at one another over Luther. I say to them: Do you wish to terrify the Turks? Then live in concord amongst yourselves.

But no one wants to hear me, though they love to hurl my tired old name, missilelike, into one another's camps. When I travel, people snatch up the stubs of candles I burn in the night, for souvenirs. I tell them they would do better to use my ideas as candles."

A bell chimed from the house.
"Goodness, so late," Cecily exclaimed. "Supper in an hour."
"That's really all there is, in any case," Honor said. She glanced again at the hastily written postscript, but kept it to herself:

"I have had no luck tracking down the book you asked me to seek. No title page with a single blue flower has passed under my nose. I promise, however, that I shall not abandon the search."

Honor felt a familiar pang of regret. She had thought that if anyone could find a copy of the foreigner's little volume, it would be Erasmus. Not only was he a renowned book collector, he was also in touch with all the ground-breaking authors in Europe. But his disappointing postscript deepened her conviction that she would never discover what mysteries had been written inside the foreigner's lost gift.

Cecily was pushing her bulk up from the bench to go inside. Honor picked up the baby and placed him in his mother's arms, then went back to the edge of the pond to put on her stockings and shoes.

"You'll stay, won't you, Honor?" Cecily asked. "Lady Alice has baked some apples. With honey, just the way you like them."

Honor was tying her shoelace. "I can't, Cecily. I must get back to Bridewell. The Queen likes me to read to her. The evenings are long for her these days." She did not raise her head as she spoke, for this was another lie. The Queen's comfort was not her reason for wanting to hurry away. It was something else, something gnawing inside her that frightened her.

She knew well the routine of the household. At supper one of More's daughters—Margaret or Cecily or Elizabeth—would read from Latin scripture. Afterwards would come family prayers in the chapel. Even when Sir Thomas was away he insisted on his family's strict observance of the practice. Now, Honor dreaded it. Since Ralph's death she had not been able to pray. She could not force herself into the meek and grateful state of mind required. Supplication, contrition, thanks: the prayers had always flowed so unconsciously. Now the words—the very thoughts—shriveled in her heart. She would not, could not, pray. It was terrifying.

Another manifestation of her grief shocked her, too. She had expected to feel grief as dullness, a dull ache. But instead, every sense throbbed with an acute awareness of life, of life's textures, of the vivid, simple joys that Ralph would never know again. The scent of new-mown hay. Crickets. The impossible yellow of sunflowers. Girl's laughter. Salt on the tongue. Every day, in mind and body, she was excruciatingly awake, tender as a bruise. If only she *could* feel dullness.

But that was not all. At night came something worse. At night, when Ralph's crusted face loomed, anger came. How could a just God inflict such horrors of body and soul on a man so good, so purely Christian, as Ralph Pepperton? The question had festered inside her into an indictment against God. And against His priest, Bastwick, for engineering the death.

Instead of prayers, her lips now formed a twofold vow, repeated every day. First, she vowed that she would never forget what Ralph had suffered. In her heart she whispered a solemn promise to him. "Every time I see a flame, I'll see your face, and remember." Then, she would pledge her oath that, somehow, she would discover how Ralph's murderer had worked his evil, and she would expose him. She was certain that if she scratched beneath the surface of Bastwick's new respectability she would uncover some criminal action. How else could he have risen from near ruin after her trial to a position of authority under the Bishop of London? How else could he have snared Ralph? She knew very little about Lutheranism or its adherents, but she did know Ralph. No contact with heretic sects, however pernicious, could have corrupted him into a bad man.

And she knew Bastwick. She recalled how, at Tyrell Court, his hunger for advancement was voracious. When he wasn't toadying to Lady Philippa, he was hounding Tyrell for another benefice with tithes and glebe lands, or insinuating himself into the affairs of the neighbor Abbot, helping to collect the Abbey's bridge tolls and court fines in order to connect with the Abbot's powerful Church connections in Exeter. Honor had come to understand what drove Bastwick. One day she had overheard an argument between him and Tyrell. Tyrell shouted that Bastwick's father had been a villein—a peasant bondsman—and Bastwick had stormed out without denying it. She realized then. It was dread of the poverty out of which he had crawled toward the Church that had been the crucible of his character. Now, even after the crushing setback she had inflicted on him at the Star Chamber trial, he had obviously clawed his way back up, all the way into the Bishop of London's staff.

But she had never doubted his will to revenge himself on her for that setback. And she realized now, with a bitterness she could almost taste, that Ralph's death neatly satisfied Bastwick's twin desires. What better way to rise even further in the Bishop's estimation than by delivering heretics to the stake? And what better way to slake his hatred of her than by burning someone she loved?

The bell chimed again. Honor glanced at the house. Though she could not face the family prayers, it seemed too rude to rush away without saying good-bye to Lady Alice. "I'll come in for a bit, Cecily," she said, and they walked up to the house, arm in arm.

Once inside, though, she could hardly refuse a goblet of wine from Margaret's husband, Will, or ignore their young son's eagerness to display to her his collection of chestnuts and pine cones. So it was almost an hour later, with Lady Alice insisting she carry a dish of baked apples back for the Queen, and the rest of the household drifting into the hall to eat, that she kissed Cecily good-bye and stepped out the front door to go down to the waiting barge.

Twilight was settling, cool and quiet. Above her, a scattering of only the boldest silver stars pulsed. With the warm dish cradled in her arm, she was almost at the gate that led to the lawn and the river when the solemn drone of Margaret's reading caught her through an open window of the hall: "Faith is the substance of things hoped for, the evidence of things not seen . . ."

She felt the hairs lift at the nape of her neck. She quickened her footsteps. But the words of St. Paul pursued her, insubstantial yet persistent, like the cloud of gnats darting around her ears. She hurried on until the sound of scripture died away behind her.

But as she crossed the lawn and came to the stairs that led down to the pier, other voices reached her, men's voices drifting up from the barge. She stopped, held in check by their tone, low and private, as though they dealt in secrets. There were two forms, mere silhouettes against the dying light on the river.

"Heretics. A filthy clutch of 'em," the boatman said. He was lounging in the middle of the barge, gnawing at a leg of the leftover Michaelmas goose that Matthew had brought him from the house. Matthew was squatting on the pier, listening. "Oh, my ears are always open, lad," the boatman added.

"And who's this merchant they suspect?" Matthew asked, excited.

"Sydenham? A skinner, so I hear. I warrant he's spent too much time peddling hides in the stinkpot heretic cities across the Narrow Sea."

"Tomorrow? That's when the raid's to be?"

"Aye. After curfew. Midnight, mayhap. Leastways, that's what I heard the Bishop's man to say." The boatman's lips slurped along a greasy tendon. "And you can see the cunning in it. If this Sydenham has called a gathering, and if the Bishop's man hopes to catch 'em all together, best to give 'em time to get their heathen antics underway."

There was a thrill of fear in the young man's next question. "And will they burn?"

The boatman belched philosophically. "Well, the devils're crafty, 'specially your foreigner heretics. They may forswear, and only suffer penance 'round St. Paul's. But, aye, if their prating be heretical, they'll burn. And if you ask me . . ."

"Boatman!"

At Honor's voice, Matthew sprang up and the boatman tossed his goose bone overboard.

"Matthew, go inside," she said. There was no mistaking her tone. Matthew touched his cap to her and was gone.

The boatman plied his oars and they glided downstream under the river of brightening stars. Honor sat rigid in the stern. The humped, black waves beat the hull in a chaotic rhythm, as if the thudding of her heart against her ribs was rendered audible, for the men's whispering had brought all the horror of Ralph's torture swarming back. She saw it again—Ralph writhing under his chain, and Bastwick smirking his twisted revenge. And, suddenly, she saw, like a ghost standing between them, a hunched man, shackled, waiting to be burned. A stranger named Sydenham.

Sweat scalded her palms under the bandages, scorching like the live sparks of coals. In a wave of revulsion she ripped the linen from her hands. The strips fluttered away behind the boat in pale streamers. She leaned over the side and plunged her hands into the cold water. And in that instant of relief, a relief that never shed its balm on Ralph, who writhed and burned forever in her nightmares, Honor knew what she must do. There was a warning she had to deliver.

❧ 8 ❧

The Conscience of the Queen

Honor's pen scratched over a sheet of parchment on the desk in Queen Catherine's suite at Bridewell palace. It was almost ten, and the Queen had been dictating letters to her for two hours. There was a pause in the stream of Latin dictation, and Honor glanced at the rain-streaked window beside the desk. If the Queen does not release me soon, she thought, I'll be too late to warn Sydenham. She had decided, after leaving Chelsea, that sending the merchant a message that could be traced back to her would be too dangerous. She must go herself. But the Queen had kept her all day by her side, first sorting a new shipment of books, then sewing and reading to keep her company, and finally dictating letters. There had been no chance to get away.

She watched the torch flames in the courtyard below as they buckled in the wind-swept rain. Beyond, the gray river heaved. She was under no illusions; it was a hazardous business she was about to undertake. She had discovered that Humphrey Sydenham lived on Coleman Street, but nothing more about him. But she knew, as everyone knew, that cornered heretics could be dangerous men. Many were criminals, outcasts: militant Lutherans, seditious Lollards, hysterical Anabaptists. And the thought of Bastwick finding her among them in the raid . . .

Should she wash her hands of this affair? Was it madness to risk herself? For outlaws?

She glanced at the low fire burning blue in the hearth. She recalled her vow, and instantly Ralph's face wavered in the flames. No, she thought, if there is even one innocent like Ralph at the meeting, I must go. To forsake this duty would be like forsaking Ralph himself.

The Queen's voice brought her back to her writing. The letter was to the Queen's nephew, the Emperor Charles.

"Therefore Charles, for the Pope to annul my marriage and undo what his predecessor has done . . ."

The Queen was pacing. As she moved from the fire to the window, then back to the fire again, she reminded Honor of the small wildcat, an ocelot, that Sir Thomas kept in his menagerie behind the house. The pacing, controlled yet urgent, was the same, and the eyes of the caged cat were glazed with the same desperation that she saw these days in the Queen's eyes.

". . . would bring grave discredit to the Apostolic See which should stand firmly on the rock which is Christ. Were the Pope to waver now . . ."

Catherine stopped. "Do your blisters cause you pain, sweetheart?"

Honor looked up hopefully. Should she jump at this chance to be dismissed? But the fatigue on the Queen's face checked her. The lady's situation was so pitiful.

"I am sorry to keep you, my dear," Catherine said warmly. "But the letter simply must go tonight. You understand."

"Of course, my lady," Honor answered. At least she would not have to deliver the letter; the Queen's physician, Dr. Vittoria, had become the new courier to Mendoza. "Please don't worry on my account," Honor added. "My hands are quite recovered. And it is always my pleasure to assist Your Grace." She reminded herself that the Queen had promised this would be the last letter tonight.

The Queen smiled her gratitude and resumed the dictation.

"Were the Pope to waver now, he might lead many into thinking that right and justice are not with him."

The words were unequivocal, and Honor looked up with a surge of awe for her mistress, a woman so unimpressive in voice and appearance, yet so firm in resolve.

"Now," the Queen mused aloud, "how to explain to Charles that Wolsey connives with France?"

Honor winced at the Queen's self-deception. The whole world knew that the reason behind the King's fever for a divorce was Anne Boleyn. But it was like Catherine to consider ranting about such a thing as beneath a Queen's dignity. In any case, it was clear she had convinced herself that it was Cardinal Wolsey's evil council—his desire to switch England's long allegiance with the Emperor in favor of one with France—which had corrupted the King.

"Well, leave that point for now," Catherine decided with a sigh. "There is even more distressing information I must send to Charles. The arrival of Cardinal Campeggio."

"His arrival, my lady?" Honor asked, surprised.

"Any day now."

"But last night you said the Pope's sending him was only a possibility."

"All that has changed, my dear. Though Wolsey would keep me in the dark, Ambassador Mendoza managed to get a message to me this morning. Cardinal Campeggio has left Rome. He is in France, awaiting only a fair wind to bring him over the Channel."

"Oh, my lady!" Honor said in sympathy. "And has the Pope empowered him as a papal legate?"

Catherine nodded grimly. "Yes. But with what precise commission, I know not. That is Campeggio's secret, and the Pope's."

"Do you mean it's possible, as you feared, that his mission is to judge the case here in England?"

"If so, it is a bitter blow for me. His Holiness has repeatedly assured both Mendoza and myself that the case, if it should come to trial, will be heard only in Rome. I tremble at Campeggio's coming. He holds a wealthy English bishopric. He is in Wolsey's camp."

Honor saw the danger. "And Wolsey is also a papal legate."

"Exactly. What justice could I hope for in an English court with these two as my judges?"

Honor noticed that the Queen was nervously fingering the rosary that hung at her waist. It was an exquisite work of ivory and turquoise, a gift the King had given her as solace after her final miscarried pregnancy ten years ago. She cherished it.

Together, they composed the warning to the Emperor about Cardinal Campeggio's arrival. Then Catherine closed with:

"Lastly, dear Charles, let me entreat your guidance. I am but a weak woman, ignorant and untrained in canon law. If, God forbid, this should come to trial in England, what is your advice? Should I present a defense, or might doing so jeopardize my claim that Rome, and Rome alone, has authority to judge?"

Honor looked up, eyes wide. "An ignorant woman? Untrained? My lady, you are more knowledgeable in matters of the law—of both church and state—than many who sit on the King's council."

Catherine stared out at the rain. Her fingertips drew small circles at her temples. "I fear that knowledge will count for little in this battle of wills, sweetheart," she sighed. She came to the desk to sign the letter. "But Charles is a chivalrous young man. The honor of his family weighs heavily with him. A plea from his helpless aunt may do more to rouse him to stiffen the Pope's back than all the law books I could throw at his head."

As Honor watched the small, plump hand write 'Katerina,' her heart beat faster, for her work here was finished. She could leave for Sydenham's. "Still," she said as she sprinkled sand on the wet ink and tried to conceal her uneasy excitement, "Your Grace seems an unlikely candidate for the role of the helpless female.

Your Spanish ladies have told me that in the dark days after Prince Arthur's death they marveled at your strength and ingenuity. What courage you showed, marching before the late King Henry to ask for wages for your maids."

Honor had heard all the old stories. Widowed at sixteen after a few months of marriage to the sickly teenage heir to the English throne, Catherine had become a diplomatic hostage to the slippery alliance between England and Spain. It was an alliance marked by the stinginess of the monarchs. King Henry VII, her father-in-law, had cut off her allowance while her parents, Ferdinand and Isabella, had insisted she was England's responsibility. For almost seven years she had waited in cold apartments beside the foggy Thames, fending off creditors, while her proud but threadbare Spanish entourage became the butt of English courtiers' jokes. Then, suddenly, everything had changed. King Henry had died. His handsome, eighteen-year-old son had mounted the throne as Henry the Eighth and, to make restitution to the shabbily treated Spanish princess, he had married her himself.

"You endured great hardship in those days, my lady," Honor said, "yet you triumphed. I do not doubt you will triumph again."

From the hearth, Catherine's sigh was private and intense. "To cross my lord is a triumph I have never sought."

She lifted her chin abruptly as if to banish self-pity. "Still, in the fight, knowledge and learning may be worth something after all, my dear, and I mean to defend myself with every weapon at hand." She marched toward the jumble of legal books on the desk and fingered their spines for the one she sought. She gave Honor a clear-eyed smile. "I have witnessed too many miracles to despair of victory in this particular battle."

Honor was intrigued. "Miracles, my lady?"

"When I was six, I saw the walls of Granada, held by the infidel for five hundred years, fall to my mother's modern guns and be reclaimed to Christ. When I was seven I saw the Admiral of the Ocean Sea, Columbus, return to Barcelona after finding a new world." She laughed lightly. "We watched this ragged Italian adventurer parade through the streets leading a string of wild men, naked except for their paint and feathers and golden ornaments.

Now, if heathen Granada can be brought to Christ, and new worlds be found, then surely I can triumph over one conniving Cardinal!"

Honor's smile was full of pride. May I find such resolve to do what I must tonight, she thought. She could leave it no longer. She stood. "Shall I take the letter to Dr. Vittoria as usual, my lady?"

"Yes. The Cardinal's web around me still holds fast."

The door creaked open. Both women turned startled faces. Margery crept in wringing her hands. "Pardon, Your Grace," she said. "My lord Ambassador . . ."

The Spaniard stalked past her. Dripping wet, he bowed to the Queen. Honor had to smile, seeing this impeccable gentleman standing in a small pool of water.

"Thank you, Margery," Catherine said, her voice charged with surprise and pleasure at the sight of Mendoza. "Now, off to bed."

Margery cast Honor a worried glance, then bobbed a curtsy and hurried out. Honor was about to make her own curtsy, thinking that the Queen's dismissal to Margery included her as well. But Mendoza, having peeled off his sodden cloak and hat, thrust them at her. She draped them on a high-backed chair, then was ready to go. Mendoza smoothed back his ruffled, silver hair with great dignity and eyed the decanter on the sideboard.

"A glass of wine, Don Inigo?" Catherine asked.

Frustrated though she was at more delay, Honor knew her duty. She crossed the room, poured wine, and brought it to Mendoza. He gulped it with uncharacteristic haste. "Madam," he said, answering the question in Catherine's eyes, "the Cardinal is ill. Some are whispering it is the deadly sweating sickness. He has hastened away from London's diseased air, to Hampton Court. His household is riddled with the sickness, and his staff is in a chaos of confusion. It offered an opportunity—which I judged worth the risk—to try, one more time, to come to you."

"I pray the Cardinal is not in mortal danger," Catherine said with a sincerity, Honor understood, that would astonish anyone who did not know her deeply pious character. "God keep him."

Mendoza grunted. "I am not sure my own Christian charity should be tested to stretch as far as Wolsey's obese body. But I hear he has weathered the worst and is busy in his bed, sifting the rush of requests for dead men's lands. Still,"—he jerked his head toward the door—"I dare not stay long lest I imperil you." A violent lashing of rain at the window rekindled his urgency. "I must tell you of the perilous events at Rome. Madam, the tide may be turning against us."

Catherine's flinch was almost imperceptible. She was staring at the Ambassador as if she had forgotten Honor's presence. Honor groaned inwardly. She could not interrupt, yet neither could she leave without a dismissal.

"His Holiness the Pope has returned from exile in Orvieto," Mendoza went on. "He finds Rome a pitiable and mangled corpse, he says, but at least he is home."

A smile flickered on Catherine's face. "From the moment the news arrived of Rome's capture I knew it was a sign to me from God. Did it not happen the very month Wolsey hatched his plot to destroy me?"

"God, of course, is on your side," Mendoza replied with diplomatic smoothness. "Certainly, as long as the Emperor's army was holding Rome the Pope has not dared to infuriate him by annulling your marriage. To do so would have been to sign his own death warrant."

Catherine nodded.

"However, at Orvieto," Mendoza continued, "His Holiness was desperate for help. I have been told he was camping under the dripping roof of the local bishop's derelict palace, shedding tears like a woman at his fate. King Henry's agents found him there. In his miserable condition he was looking anywhere for friends and money. And Wolsey was quick to supply him, you can be sure. Now that the Pope has returned to Rome, the King's agents throng him daily with petitions, and they hardly bother to veil their insinuations that he owes his English benefactors that much at least. Madam, they are poisoning the Pope's mind with tales of the Emperor's treacherousness. They are telling him that your nephew's ambition is to overrun all of Italy and swallow Rome whole. They sweeten these lies with offers to supply His Holiness with a handpicked English and French bodyguard to protect him against another assault. And now—"

"And now, Cardinal Campeggio is on his way," Catherine said grimly.

Mendoza nodded. "The situation is most grave."

Catherine began pacing again. Swiftly, she came to a decision. "Don Inigo, we must prepare our final defense. Immediately." She looked at him, one eyebrow raised in skepticism. "Have you heard who the government will allow me as council?"

Mendoza hesitated as if unwilling to burden her with more bad news. He tried to sound hopeful. "I understand there is a distinguished array of lawyers . . . Archbishop Warham, Bishop Fisher of Rochester, Bishop Tunstall of London, Dr. Standish, Bishop Clerk—"

Catherine held up her hand. "Distinguished these men may be, Don Inigo, but you know, as everyone knows, that they owe their livelihoods to the government. My lords Warham and Tunstall are good men, but timid and fearful. And Standish and Clerk are soft clay in Wolsey's hands. I know he has warned them all not to meddle against the King in this. Small comfort there." A trace of hope fluttered in her eyes. "Except, perhaps, for Fisher."

"The government, as you know, madam, will invoke Leviticus to show the marriage transgressed scriptural law. But we, too, have a good defense in scripture—in Deuteronomy. Besides our argument that the Pope did legally dispense with the injunction, we will rely heavily on the Deuteronomy passage. 'When brethren dwell together, and one of them dieth without children, the wife of the deceased shall not marry to another—' "

" 'But his brother shall take her, and raise up seed for his brother,' " Catherine murmured, completing the scriptural quotation. She paused a moment and stared again at the fire. "No, Don Inigo."

"Pardon, madam?"

She turned to him. "No. I will not put my faith solely in these legal and theological arguments. To me, the legality of the former Pope's dispensation is irrelevant, for I mean to rest my defense on the truth."

Mendoza looked perplexed. "The truth?"

"That I was never Arthur's wife, except in name. That I came to my lord a virgin, and he knows it. When this is made clear, in public, I do not doubt that God will move my lord to awaken to his duty. And then this nightmare will be over."

Even Honor was surprised. Her eyes and the Ambassador's met as if to ask one another if the Queen herself would awaken before it was too late.

Mendoza cleared his throat. "Madam, may we speak privately?"

"Of course." Catherine laid a gentle hand on Honor's shoulder. "Leave us, sweetheart," she said. She kissed Honor's forehead as if she were a favorite daughter. "You will be longing for your bed after these weary hours of toiling at my papers."

With relief, Honor curtsied and left the room. But after taking the letter to Dr. Vittoria, it was not to her bed she went, but out in the rain to Coleman Street.

🙖 9 🙖

The Brethren

Honor banged her fist against the merchant's door. Rain pummeled her head and shoulders and drenched her hooded cloak as she waited. A metal bolt scraped, the door swung open, and a young man stood before her. Behind his lantern, his narrow face glowed white against lank orange hair that hung to his shoulders.

"Master Humphrey Sydenham?" she asked.

He thrust the lantern out close to her face, examining her with fearful eyes. "No."

"I must see him." Her voice emerged with more strength than she felt. "His life is in danger."

"What?" The man looked frightened. "What's happened? Who are you?"

"I'll tell only Master Sydenham that. Is he here or not?"

The man gnawed his lip, hesitating, then pulled her in and shut the door. "Follow me."

He led her down a corridor and past a fine-looking great hall to a snug room bright with a fire and candles, though deserted. "Wait here," he said. He turned to go.

"But it's late and I—"

"Wait here!" He walked out and closed the door on her. His footfalls sounded down the corridor.

Honor threw off her hood and looked around. The room was paneled in fashionable linenfold-carved oak. Expensive silver plate gleamed in cupboards. The chairs were soft with velvet cushions. This was not at all what she had expected. She had steeled herself for a bleak, ascetic compound with a ring of zealots chanting in religious fervor. This room exuded nothing but domestic comfort.

She paced. Where was Sydenham? It was almost midnight. The Queen had kept her so long, there was no time left. If she waited any longer she would be in danger herself. She snatched up a candle and hurried to the door.

The corridor was empty. She started in the direction she had heard the man's footsteps take. She passed along a room-length of paneled hallway and came to a closed door. The latch lifted easily. Beyond the door, almost immediately, was an unlit flight of descending stone stairs. The hem of her sodden cloak slapped over the steps as she went down. The walls, too, were stone. The air was dank. A cloying smell—unpleasantly familiar, though she could not identify it—curled in her nostrils.

At the bottom the floor was beaten earth. A low, barrel-vaulted stone passageway hulked around her candle. She walked on. The passage led to another flight of steps, these ones going up. She heard voices, very faint, and she halted. The voices quieted. She climbed the stairs. At the top stood an arched, wooden door. She swept her candle over it and noticed a small opening at a man's eye level. It was a chink of less than a square inch, gouged out of the solid wood, a squint-hole for monitoring the identity of the person seeking entry.

She snuffed her candle and set it down. In the darkness she went up on her toes and pressed her eye to the hole. Her breath caught in her throat. She was looking into a huge warehouse, and near the rear wall thirty-five, perhaps forty people stood inside a ring of hand-held torches. Their faces were lifted towards a man who stood on the lip of a loft, his head raised and eyes closed as if in silent prayer. Honor felt the hairs at the back of her neck rise. This was a huge coven of heretics.

She was shocked to see so many women. Children, too. A couple of boys were rolling chestnuts on the dirt floor under a torch hitched to one of the loft-bearing posts. Stacks of animal hides were ranged along the windowless walls, and in the middle of the warehouse were three huge, round wooden vats, the kind she had seen used in ale brewing. Beside the loft on the far wall was a closed door as wide as a cart. She realized the warehouse must sprawl all the way back to the next street.

The man in the loft snapped from his trance and began to prowl along the edge. He was in his early twenties, Honor guessed, slight, and very fair. His white-blond hair, shaved in a monk's tonsure, stood out in short spikes over his ears, looking indeed like the thorns of Christ's crown that the tonsure was made to symbolize. Yet he wore no priest's cassock or friar's robe, only a laborer's faded tunic over sagging hose. He stopped and stared at the faces below him. The fervor in his eyes blazed all the way to the squint-hole at the back of the warehouse.

He slapped his hand on his chest. "Love of God!" he cried. "That is what should fill our hearts." He thrust out his other hand, palm up like a beggar. "Lust for gold! That is what drives our priests." Honor was struck by the vibrancy of his voice. It was a voice made for rallying men.

"The Church hoards one third of the landed wealth of this sovereign realm, my friends. Our rich Bishops send carts of gold to Rome, English gold from the sweat of English brows. They leech it from us in rents and tithes to finance the bawdy banquets and lascivious pleasures of the princes of the Church, and their wicked wars." He shook his head, then smiled grimly. "Glad I am of the spirituality's oath of celibacy, for if the Abbot of Glastonbury were to wed the Abbess of Shrewsbury, their heir would inherit more land than the demesne of the King."

There was soft laughter from the listeners. "If the priests have no heirs, Brother Frish," a man called up, "it's not for lack of fornicating."

Brother Frish laughed along with his audience. Then, suddenly, his arms shot up. "I say the priests are worse than Judas. He sold almighty God for thirty shillings but the priests will sell God for half a penny. They barter off their sacred wares like pork hocks at

a fair-stall. They sell the seven sacraments, they sell dispensations,"—he held out his palm again like a collection plate and
slammed his fist onto it with every transaction—"the chanting of
masses, prayers. And all this on top of their endless tithes and
fines, fees and mortuaries . . ."

Honor shivered at this last word. For a moment she was a child
again watching Bastwick wrench the sapphire from her father's
dead hand, the curse of excommunication still ringing. All for a
mortuary.

She shook her head to clear it of such visions of the past—and of
her unease at going among these criminals. I must finish this, she
told herself. Get inside, find Sydenham, and then get out again before it's too late. I've come this far. I'll see it through.

She lifted the latch and opened the door. A draught of stale air
rolled over her. She trembled, for the warehouse stank of an odor
that somehow dredged up the horror of Smithfield. A cold hand
grabbed her wrist. It was the orange-haired young man. He hauled
her into the warehouse and hustled her along the wall among the
stacked hides.

"I told you to wait," he whispered fiercely. He glanced nervously at the gathering, but the preacher talked on and the crowd
listened, apparently unaware of the intrusion.

"I tell you, I've got to see Master Sydenham," Honor whispered, equally insistent.

"Quiet!" He tightened his grip on her wrist until it was painful.

"But this cannot wait!"

He jerked a knife from his belt and held it at her rib. "You'll
wait until the sermon's done, and you'll be quiet."

Heart pounding, she stood still, a hostage witness to the heretical sermon.

"And let us not forget indulgences," Frish cried cynically. "The
priests will sell indulgence letters for fornication, for the breaking
of vows, for shunning confession, for ignoring fasts, and, of course,
for rescuing souls from purgatory. Purgatory," he repeated with a
sneer. "This dread place exists, the Church teaches, for the cleans-
ing of sinful man's soul after death, but the Church will gladly give
you remission of years of your soul's agony there—for a price.

Now, tell me this. If the Pope has the power to deliver a soul out of purgatory, why then can he not deliver it without money? And if he can deliver one soul, then why does he not deliver a thousand? Why not all? Let loose all the poor, tortured souls, and thus *destroy* purgatory." His fist punched the air. "I say the Pope is a tyrant if he keeps souls within purgatory's prison until men give him money!"

He wiped his brow with his sleeve, and then eased himself down onto the edge of the loft so that his legs dangled. His voice became gentle and warm. "Good friends," he said with a smile, "I am here to tell you that the Pope has no power to loose souls from purgatory because there *is* no purgatory. I am here to tell you that there are no priests, only God. That the painted images of saints the poor ignorant folk pray to for intercession in their worldly woes are only sticks and stones—and man must pray to God alone. That all the spells a priest may mumble over a piece of bread to conjure it into the body of our Lord cannot make it anything other than bread, for I have read in scripture that God made man, but nowhere have I read that man can make God."

Honor's mouth fell open at this litany of heresies, especially the last one. The miracle of transubstantiation—the bread of the Mass transformed into the living body of Christ—was the cornerstone of Catholic faith. Yet this preacher's words were full-blooded with conviction. His passion, so fearless, so generous, stunned her. It was as if, while she slept, someone had dashed her face with ice water.

Frish's voice rose again and his face was bright. "I come before you this night to bring you good news, my friends. We can cast off the chains of bondage to Rome. I have done it. I have been freed. How?" He reached over to a barrel beside him and lifted a black book that lay on top. He held it high. "With this. The word of Our Lord, Our Savior. His blessed word, illuminated by the sublime translation of Master William Tyndale into our own tongue." He waved the book slowly, like a banner over his head.

Honor shuddered as a voice from Smithfield echoed: ". . . *selling illegal Bibles in the English tongue . . .*"

This was the book for which Ralph had been burned.

"Not the word of Christ's desecrated Church," Frish cried,

"where the priests would have us grovel dumbly at their mystical Latin prayers, then shuffle home more ignorant than when we came. No! I have read Christ's message for myself." He clasped the book against his chest like a lover. His eyes gleamed with tears, and his voice was gentle as a song. "And scripture did so exhilarate my heart, being before almost in despair, that immediately I felt a marvelous comfort and quietness, and my weary bones leaped for joy. This is salvation, my friends. The shining, unadulterated word of God. Come! See!" He gestured to a large crate on the warehouse floor. "I have brought enough for all of you." He stood and climbed down the ladder from the loft, and people moved in around him with excited questions and comments.

Honor could restrain herself no longer. She wanted only to finish what she had come to do and then get out of this dangerous place. She glanced down at the knife at her rib. She sensed that the young man was more nervous than dangerous. "You're not going to use the knife," she said steadily. "Let me go."

He appeared startled by her sudden steeliness, and Honor seized his moment of indecision to wrench free of his grip. "I tell you," she said, "everyone here is in danger. Now, one last time, take me to Sydenham, or I'll leave you all to your miserable fate!"

He looked anxious but he said nothing. She took a few steps forward. He followed on her heels and grabbed her elbow. She was shaking him off when she saw a figure hurrying toward them: a portly, apple-cheeked man dressed in the rich, flowing clothing of a merchant. Behind him, the people carried on with their meeting. "What is it, Edward?" the man said in a menacing whisper. Under tufted gray eyebrows he was squinting at Honor in the way of the short-sighted. When he reached her his menacing look widened into surprise. "Who's this?"

"Wants to see you. I left her above, but she's come snooping."

Honor almost pounced, so great was her relief. "Master Sydenham?"

"Let her go, son," the merchant said. "Aye, I'm Sydenham. What be your business with me?" His voice was wary, but so gentle that it betrayed him; clearly he felt more curiosity than wrath at her presence.

"Sir, I bring a warning—" She stopped, surprised by the approach of a woman.

"Humphrey, what's the matter?" the woman asked. As she came to Sydenham's side her hand groped for his, and their fingers wove together in an unconscious gesture of comfort that told Honor the two were man and wife.

Mrs. Sydenham was a formidable-looking person, several inches taller than her husband and a startling contrast to him, for she was as gaunt as he was stout, and as pale as he was florid. Only their common gray hair unified them, but while his lay in short, springy curls, hers was stretched tightly back from a center part under a starched white cap. Her face was almost as sallow and bony as a cadaver, but the eye sockets blazed with life at their hazel cores. She was staring at Honor with a frown. Suddenly, she gasped and grabbed her husband's sleeve.

"What is it, Bridget?" he asked gently.

"I know this girl."

Honor was amazed at her effect on the woman. "Indeed, madam, I am surprised to hear it, for I know you not."

"You are Sir Thomas More's daughter."

"You are mistaken," Honor said.

"You lie! I've seen you with him at Paul's Cross. Sir Thomas More and all his family."

Honor bit back the anger rising within her. "If I had not known since childhood that lying is a sin, madam, my guardian would surely have instructed me, for Sir Thomas is known to all the world as the most upright, Christian teacher."

"Your guardian?" Sydenham blurted. "You are Sir Thomas More's ward?"

"Ward or daughter," his wife spat, "where's the difference?"

"The difference, madam, is that I do not lie!"

The eyes of the two women locked in animosity.

Sydenham held up his hands. "Now, now, Bridget. Let's hear what the girl has to say."

"Husband, do not trust her. She has come to harm us."

Sydenham removed his wife's hand from his elbow and held it

affectionately. He scrutinized Honor. "What is this warning you bring, girl?"

"Sir," Honor blurted, "the Bishop's men are on their way to raid this place. You must save yourselves."

Sydenham's mouth opened in dismay.

His wife intervened to ask coldly, "And how do you know this?"

"I overheard . . . some talk."

"Whose talk?" Mrs. Sydenham snapped in scorn. "The Bishop's? I suppose you are a frequent visitor at his palace?"

"No."

"Then whom did you overhear?"

"A boatman."

"A servant of the Bishop?"

"No. A Westminster boatman."

Mrs. Sydenham sneered. "Gossip?"

"What difference how or where I heard it? The danger is the same."

"The difference, mistress, is that I do not trust you."

Honor trembled with anger. An attack on her integrity was the last thing she had expected from this coven of criminals—criminals she was risking herself to save!

"But Bridget," Sydenham said gently, "why should she come to warn us if not as a friend?"

"Perhaps to spy us out. Make a list of names and faces. Perhaps only to confound and terrify us. Or perhaps both, and with this tale about a raid she could cause chaos enough and slip away in our confusion."

"But, my dear—"

"I know nothing of *why*!" Mrs. Sydenham's voice rasped, sharp with exasperation. "But I know that midnight raids are not Bishop Tunstall's method, and—"

"Not the Bishop," Honor broke in. "An evil man on his staff."

Unmoved, Mrs. Sydenham's eyes fell on her, burning with suspicion. "And I *know* this girl is attached to More."

Sydenham cast an anxious glance over his shoulder at the meeting, and Honor, appalled at the delay, saw that his wife's counsel had cut deeply into his own trusting instincts. When he turned back and reached out both his hands for hers she was not sure if it was in friendship or to take her captive.

"Thank you," he murmured simply. His grip was surprisingly firm. He let her hands go. "My dear," he said, smiling sadly at his wife, "friends of the Brethren are not so thick that we may cast one away when fate draws her to our door. Now, we have little time to move Brother Frish and all these good people out. Mistress," he said to Honor, "my son Edward here will escort you—"

"Wait." Mrs. Sydenham's arm swept toward the warehouse in an exaggerated gesture of invitation, and she asked Honor in a voice unctuous with disdain, "Mistress, will you fly to safety with us? *Are you one of us?*"

"No!" Honor's answer shot out too fast, an arrow loosed from her heart, and she took a step back, as fearful of contamination as if this were a gathering of lepers.

Mrs. Sydenham's smile was wry. "In this, at least, I believe you speak the truth." Her face hardened. "And if you are not with us, you must be against us."

Sydenham's eyes darted from one woman to the other. Sweat beaded his brow. He wrung his hands, trying to decide.

Honor's face flushed with rage. "This is madness! Madam, I came in good faith to save your husband from the flames of Smithfield. I see, however, that you are eager to embrace widowhood. Very well. I'll not stand between you and your heart's desire." She turned on her heel. Edward, suddenly bold, barred the door with crossed arms. She punched him on the shoulder. The blow was nothing, but he blinked in surprise and unfolded his arms. She stepped around him.

"Stay!" It was Mrs. Sydenham's voice again. Honor turned. The woman's face was stark with worry; her former hardness had vanished. "Please, tell my husband what you know," she said. "I will alert our friends."

Amazed though she was at this about-face, Honor sighed with relief.

Sydenham had already taken a step toward the meeting. "No,

THE QUEEN'S LADY   125

Humphrey," Mrs. Sydenham said brusquely, "if you speak you'll cause panic. I'll do it."

She hurried toward the gathering. The excited people, still unaware of any disturbance, were chattering and laughing around the preacher. Mrs. Sydenham pushed through to reach him. She bent to whisper in Frish's ear while the people babbled on. Frish shot a look back at Honor. Under his scrutiny she was uncomfortably conscious of the richness of her clothing in contrast to the drab group he stood with, and she turned her head away. As she did, she noticed, above the huge rear door, an odd movement in the air, as if dust were sifting from the roof, dislodged from the rafters to drift and sparkle down through the torchlight. The people sensed it too and hushed. Mrs. Sydenham looked up. Everyone turned breathlessly toward the wide, closed door.

There was a creaking, like giant wagon wheels beginning to move. For one frozen moment Honor saw the wooden door bulge. Then it burst. Huge splinters flew. Men-at-arms swarmed in. Cries of men and women pierced the rafters and ricocheted off the vats. The ragged ring of torches burst apart and their flames flared in the wind of rushing bodies. Honor turned to flee the way she had come, but an officer stood in the open door beckoning behind him to armed men running along the passage. She whirled around. Beyond the crush of people the splintered rear door lay open. If she could make it there she could escape. She dashed into the melee.

It was madness. Women snatched up children and were in turn snatched by officers. Men dropped under cudgel blows. Honor saw Sydenham running to reach his wife. Mrs. Sydenham stretched out her hand to him. As their fingers touched, a young officer lunged for Sydenham and hauled him sideways. He pinned Sydenham's belly against a vat, and scraped his cheek bloody along the surface. Mrs. Sydenham was engulfed by screeching people herding for the rear door. Honor glimpsed Edward among them, his orange hair flying. She could see that the first people outside were instantly trapped by officers in the alley, but a few who went after broke through and bolted into the night. It was the only way out. She groped her way around a vat, eyes on the door.

From behind, an arm locked around her head, covering her eyes. She was jerked backwards, lost her balance, and fell against her attacker. As he hauled her by the head, she had to clutch his sleeve to keep her neck from being wrenched. His other hand pushed brutally down on the top of her head, forcing her to the ground. She was dragged along the floor on her back, then bumped over a ridge that banged her backbone, then hauled into a narrow passage. Her captor crammed himself behind her and stopped. They lay together on their sides, her back against his chest. She felt his leg kick at something, then heard a sound like a metal door snapping shut.

His arm dropped from her forehead to her waist, pinning her arm. His other hand clamped her mouth. His palm was slippery with sweat. She sucked breaths through her nose. The smell of the place was foul, but she could see nothing in the pitch blackness around them. They lay with knees bent, as tightly packed as spoons, breathing together and sweating together in a grotesque parody of spent lovers. Honor could hear screams and scuffles outside their fetid cage.

The man's hand on her mouth lifted, but hovered as if ready to muzzle her again. "They'll leave soon," he breathed. "Hold on!" Even in a whisper the sterling voice was unmistakable. Frish, the preacher.

"Where . . ."—she coughed—". . . where are we?"

"Under the vat. Sydenham built a false bottom. For the Bibles."

Of course! The hides, the smell . . . it was animal fat, rendered for soap-making. This was the same stench that had drifted over Smithfield from the butchers' yards the day Ralph was burned. The rancid reek of death. Nausea swelled in her and she almost retched.

"Hold on," he urged. "Just hold on!"

Outside, the cool rain tasted delicious. Honor and Frish crouched in a muddy alley against a wall of the emptied warehouse. A lantern in the neighbor's stable yard cast the faintest of beams over them. The downpour had lightened, and Honor lifted her face with closed eyes to let it drizzle her skin and wash her clean.

"'As cold waters to a thirsty soul,'" Frish murmured, watching her.

"Proverbs," Honor said, and found herself smiling, for despite the cramps in her muscles and the residue of nausea and fear, she was aware of a light-headed clarity, an exhilaration that came with the joy of escape. She ran her tongue over salty lips. It was good to be alive!

She looked at Frish. Instantly, he lowered his eyes. It was the first time she had seen him close-up. His frame was very slight, his features small, his face fragile-looking. And every inch of it was cratered with pockmarks. Under her gaze he hunched into himself, and she realized that he was used to people shrinking from his ravaged face. Down from his makeshift pulpit, alone with her, all his sparkle and fire was snuffed out.

"Lady," he stammered, "I thank you. For the warning you brought. Mrs. Sydenham told me only that much. May I . . ."—he plucked at his frayed sleeve—"may I know your name?"

Honor hesitated. "Brother, it is I who must thank you," was all she could muster. But her gratitude was heartfelt, for she could imagine the consequences if she had been caught: at the very least, expulsion in disgrace from the Queen's employ and shame brought on Sir Thomas, and at the worst . . . she shuddered, thinking of the worst. "What happened to Master Sydenham?" she asked. "And his wife and son?"

"I saw Edward run out the back. Then I looked for you. In those clothes, you were not difficult to spot. I only hope the Sydenhams escaped, too, after Edward."

Honor watched him, wondering . . .

"Brother," she blurted, "did you know Ralph Pepperton?"

"Pepperton? No."

That was all.

"I must go," she declared suddenly. "I have been away too long. If Her Grace finds me gone—"

"Her Grace? Do you mean . . ? Have you a place at court?"

"Yes," she said, drawn by his stare. Despite his ugliness, his pale blue eyes shone with a power both mesmerizing and disturbing. "I wait on the Queen."

"I knew you were worth a risk!" Enthusiasm lit up his face, sweeping away all his shyness. "Lady, hear me. I have come from exile with Tyndale in Antwerp—"

"Exile?" she interrupted cautiously.

He shrugged as if to say that his personal situation was of no importance. "Arrested for preaching in Lincoln. I slipped the Bishop's bonds. But," he resumed in earnest, "I've returned to rouse support for the English Brethren. So many of us are poor—scholars, bookbinders, glaziers, bricklayers. Oh, we've attracted a sprinkling of well-to-do merchants like good Master Sydenham—God help him, now. But we need more friends, powerful friends. And with your ear at court you could do much to help us find them. No, do not draw back!" His small hands grabbed her shoulders. "I am not mad, I promise you. I know that there are men at court who would support us. You could sound them out. I have heard whispers that an influential gentleman sympathizes with us—a man on Cardinal Wolsey's staff, no less. A Master Cromwell. Alas, I cannot reach such men. But you can. And there are others. Even the Lady Anne Boleyn, so I have heard—"

"What?" She pulled out of his grasp. "You'd have me plot with my mistress's enemy? Brother," she said severely, "I was glad to bring a warning tonight for I would not see any of you burn. But I assure you I am not one of you. For God's sake, you are a heretic!"

Frish smiled as he would at a child, and murmured, "For God's sake, indeed." He cocked his head at her and asked in a matter-of-fact tone, "Mistress, did you never catch your father in a lie?"

Warily, she asked, "Your meaning, Brother?"

"I'll tell you a story," said Frish. "My father was a tenant farmer. I labored in his field from the day I could lift a load. When I was nine, the landlord stopped by our cottage to see my father, and when he left, my father told me the landlord had accused me of stealing some of his pears. I was desolate, not only because I was innocent, but also because the landlord had always been a friend to me, always told me I had promise. My father beat me for the theft. Years later I found out that the landlord, who had no son, had not come that day with any such accusation, but rather with an offer to pay for an education for me. My father, you see, preferred to retain my labor." He looked Honor in the eye. "The Church keeps us from God, mistress. It frightens us and punishes us in order to keep us enslaved. But I have caught the Church in its lie."

Again, she saw Bastwick standing over her own father, punishing him with the terror of hell, all for a mortuary.

"Are you so sure you are not one of us?" Frish asked gently.

She could find no words. Objections and denials withered under those fiercely pure eyes.

He lowered his head, disappointed by her silence. His body slumped again into meek self-consciousness. "Forgive me," he mumbled, "I've made a mistake. I'll go." He stood. "You will not want me to escort you. I would only endanger you further."

He flipped the hood of his tunic over his fair head. Instantly, it cut off the beam from his eyes. Without another word he left her side, his footsteps falling noiselessly. As he passed beyond the lantern's feeble halo, clouds blotted the moon, as if some massive hand in heaven covered it to shield him, allowing him to go in darkness.

But Honor heard his clear voice as he called back softly from the end of the alley, "God be with you!"

Chelsea in Autumn

"Is the litter for the Cardinal, Master DeVille?" Honor asked, looking down at the activity in the courtyard.

She was standing at a window of the library in the Bishop of London's palace. Cardinal Campeggio, the Pope's special envoy, had been a guest here since his arrival in London the week before. Now, his retinue was assembling for a move to quarters across the city. The palace was attached to St. Paul's, and in the shadow of the cathedral's spire servants and clerks jostled and shouted among horses, mules, and baggage carts, while at the center of the commotion the Cardinal's horse litter sat motionless. Honor glanced over her shoulder at the young cleric writing at a book-strewn table. "Is the Cardinal ill?"

"He suffers from gout," Percy DeVille answered without glancing up from his ledger. He was cataloging a shipment of books just arrived from Florence. DeVille was an assistant to the Bishop's librarian, and Honor had dealt with him on several occasions, borrowing rare books for the Queen. "It took him weeks to get here from Dover in that litter," he added.

Honor looked out again and caught a glimpse of the pale, balding man frowning out from the brocaded interior of the curtained couch. "Perhaps delay is his strategy," she said.

"Strategy?" DeVille asked, finally looking up.

"His best hope is that, given time, the King will change his mind about the divorce. Then the Pope would not have to act at all."

"Change his mind?" DeVille smirked over the rim of his eyeglasses. "Don't let affection for the Queen cloud your reason, Mistress Larke."

Honor turned from the window. "While your own affection bends toward the King?"

"Only toward the Church, mistress," he murmured, "only toward the Church." His pen scratched another entry.

Honor glanced at a far corner where a couple of priests, the only other people in the library, stood chatting. She was waiting for them to leave. A week ago she had paid DeVille to check the Bishop's records for information about Ralph's death, and she had come this afternoon to hear what he had discovered. But the priests were laughing softly, making no haste to go. She moved to DeVille's table and restlessly fingered the cover of a large, beautifully embossed volume of Cicero. "And in the King's 'great matter,' which way does the Church's affection bend?" she asked.

He raised an eyebrow. "Fishing, Mistress Larke?"

"Only for what will rise to the bait, Master DeVille."

He chuckled. "I'm afraid you'll take no great catch from these waters. Though I will say this much—under normal circumstances the King's case would be strong, based as it is on the scriptural injunction in Leviticus."

"But the Queen's case is surely stronger," Honor argued. "The former Pope dispensed with Leviticus in a papal bull that allowed the marriage. It's there in black and white."

"But the question is, can a Pope legally dispense with a scriptural injunction?"

"Come now, Master DeVille. Historically Popes have issued hundreds of such dispensations, and all sorts of royal marriages have been contracted on the strength of them. How can a papal dispensation be called illegal?"

"That," he murmured cryptically, "is the heart of the matter." He frowned at his dulled pen, took up a knife, and began to whittle the quill tip. "I understand from what one of the lawyers let drop that even the King is shrewdly skirting this issue. I hear he is planning to keep Leviticus in the background, and will argue to Cardinal Campeggio simply that the wording of the Pope's bull of dispensation was faulty, and therefore void."

Honor flipped through the Cicero to mask her excitement at the news of this legal twist; it would greatly interest the Queen. "You mean, then," she said, "that the King dares not attack the fundamental principle of papal authority."

"Not if he hopes to win."

"As you think he shall?"

DeVille smiled and examined the sharpened quill. "If I possessed the art of divination, Mistress Larke, I would not be a poor assistant librarian." He shrugged. "Who knows how Campeggio will rule in the name of Rome? As I suggested, normal arguments apply under normal circumstances, not the crisis we face today, what with the Emperor breathing down the Pope's neck. And look at it from the Pope's point of view. The King's demand for a divorce has led his Holiness into the jaws of a trap. He is being asked to declare that the judgment of a former Pope was wrong. If he admits that, he will be admitting to all Europe that a Pope has erred, and that is precisely what the arch-heretic Luther has been raving about, saying Popes have always subverted the eternal law of God and substituted their own corrupt judgments."

"How does Luther come into this?"

"Great heaven, mistress, look about you. The Emperor's German lands are awash with Lutheran heresy. That outlaw monk has brought the German people to the brink of anarchy. Luther and his followers threaten to tear Christendom apart. A false move now by Pope Clement could lead to a fatal rift."

"I cannot pretend to bewail such considerations if they help the Queen's cause," Honor said sincerely. Then she dismissed the idea with a flick of her hand. "But all that disorder is happening in the German lands. This divorce is an *English* wrangle."

"But it is a sticking point for the Church. On the one hand, to grant the divorce may rupture Christian unity. On the other hand, if the King's desire is not satisfied many are afraid he will create a rift *here*, between England and Rome, to the great harm of the English people. And then how quickly might the spread of Lutheran heresy infect our weakened island?"

"But that's absurd. The King is renowned for his orthodoxy. The Pope himself awarded him his title of Defender of the Faith."

"Ah, but that was before the Lady bewitched him. Now, who can say where this will lead us?" DeVille laid down the pen, peeled off his spectacles, and rubbed his eyes. "What a kettle the King has set to boiling. And all," he snorted, "for a woman. By the way, have you heard the people's name for her? The goggle-eyed whore. Though it is my belief she has not yet earned that epithet."

"Goggle-eyed, or whore?" Honor asked dryly.

"The latter. No, I believe she has kept her royal lover from proceeding to the ultimate conjunction. You look surprised, Mistress Larke," he said with satisfaction, "and I daresay most of the court, like you, accepts that the Lady shares the King's bed. But I think not. She is shrewd, if nothing else. She has learned from her sister's experience the value of soiled goods."

Honor considered this. Anne Boleyn's sister had once been the King's mistress, and when he had tired of her he had married her to one of his gaming cronies and shunted her off to a backwater. Honor knew Anne to be ambitious. DeVille, she realized, could be right. However, gossip about the King's private life was not what she had come here for. Impatiently, she glanced again at the two priests still talking in the corner.

But DeVille continued in a self-important whisper, "And I will tell you something else about the Lady. Many of the English bishops fear her."

"Why should they?"

"She has many admirers among the rogues at court, and several of them are tainted with suspicion of heresy. Seeing the Church has no love for her, she encourages these men. Now, if Queen Catherine were cast aside and this shrewish woman rises up in her place, what evil might she then brew against the Church?"

Honor was surprised. Two weeks before, in the alley of Sydenham's warehouse, Brother Frish had spoken of high-placed supporters of the Brethren, but she had dismissed it as wishful think-ing on his part. "But can a few mischief-makers really be such a threat?" she asked.

"More than a few, mistress. And they support others elsewhere in the city who are hard at work. My lord Bishop's agents recently uncovered a site of their trade in forbidden books. English Bibles, even."

Honor stiffened. "Really?" she asked. "Where?"

"Coleman Street, I believe. There was a raid, and the ringleader was arrested."

"What will happen to him?"

"He'll do penance round the cathedral if he abjures. If he gives trouble at his examination they'll hold him in the Lollard's Tower for a while." He jerked his head toward the southwest tower of St. Paul's.

Honor suffered a moment of alarm. Would Sydenham, under examination, implicate her? The thought was quickly subdued by a pang of shame; she knew enough of men to recognize one who could be trusted. About Sydenham's own safety she was not con-cerned: the soft-hearted, portly merchant was not the stuff of mar-tyrs. He would abjure, and hurry home.

She went to the window and looked out again. A chill fingered its way up her backbone: Bastwick had entered the courtyard. She knew that he worked in the Bishop's palace, but it was a large and crowded place and she had not really expected to see him. She watched him as he approached the litter with a large velvet cush-ion and offered it to Cardinal Campeggio, presumably for his gouty foot. The Cardinal reached out to accept the gift. Bastwick re-mained by his side, smiling and engaging him in conversation. Honor's eyes narrowed. Why this ingratiating behavior? It re-minded her of the way he used to minister to Lady Philippa. What web was he weaving now?

She heard a door close and turned. The two priests had finally left the library. "Now, Master DeVille," she said urgently. She hur-ried to a chair by his side and sat. "Tell me. What have you been able to discover?"

He glanced around to make sure they were alone. "Nothing," he said. "Sorry."

For a moment, she did not understand. "Nothing?"

"Nothing of what you were after. There is no entry, no mention whatever, of a Ralph Pepperton in the Bishop's records for September."

"But how can that be?" Could Bastwick have tampered with the records? she wondered. It was an action he might take if he had overstepped his power in persecuting Ralph. And he had committed forgery at least once before, in the documents concerning her wardship. "But did you check the date? What entry was made for the burnings at Smithfield on September twenty-second?"

DeVille was casually examining the lines on his palm. "You did not request that information. Only that I search for the name of Pepperton."

Honor bit back her anger. She dug for a coin in the purse at her waist and snapped it onto his palm. "I'm requesting it now. Find out."

The clatter of hooves from below brought her back to the window. Cardinal Campeggio's entourage was beginning to move out. And Bastwick, now mounted, was sticking close to the litter. But why was he going with the Cardinal when his post was here with the Bishop? Had his ministrations and flatteries brought such quick results? Had the Cardinal invited him along? "And what about Father Bastwick?" she asked DeVille, still looking out. "I hope my request was sufficiently clear on that score?"

"Quite clear," he replied pleasantly. "And in that I have had more success. Though, of course," he added with a sheepish smile, "since Pepperton's name does not appear . . ."

"You found no link between him and Bastwick," she finished for him, irritated. She would have to wait for days, maybe weeks, until he could look again into the records. "Well, what *have* you found out?"

DeVille leaned back in his chair and crossed his arms, ready to make his report. "Bastwick's a nobody. And seems to have come from nowhere. Though the deacon told me he'd seen Bastwick several years ago loitering in St. Paul's—begging gentlemen, apparently, for employment in their chapels."

Naturally, Honor thought. After the disgrace of his trial six years ago and his months in the Bishop's prison, Bastwick would have found it almost impossible to secure a benefice. But she did not say this to DeVille. She had told him nothing of her own connection with Bastwick.

"Eventually," DeVille went on, "he was hired as a miserable chantry priest in a hamlet in Norfolk. Hardly enough in that post to keep body and soul together. Then he became an apparitor in the Archdeacon's court, and finally an apparitor in Bishop Nix's court at Norwich."

It was a common enough pattern, Honor thought. Poor priests without benefices often took places in the Church courts which employed a host of petty officials. These courts dealt in moral delinquency, contested marriages, tithe disputes, and, of course, heresy. They were numerous, efficient, and constantly in session, and though most men and women in England would never see the inside of a civil courtroom, almost everyone at some time came into contact with the Church courts. Because the overwhelming number of cases dealt with sexual misconduct, people called them "bawdy courts," and they despised the apparitors, the officious inspectors whose job it was to watch the parish for lechery, adultery, and blasphemy.

"Eventually, Bishop Nix made Father Bastwick a proctor," DeVille said with a sneer.

"But he has no legal training," Honor protested.

"The rules are slack. A priest need only swear that he has read canon and civil law for three years. So, Father Bastwick arrived back in London last year with the high recommendation of Bishop Nix. Since then he has served Bishop Tunstall's Chancellor as a proctor. And in the past few days I've seen evidence that he's weaseling his way into Cardinal Campeggio's train. He'll probably end up a bishop one day," he sniffed. "Imagine. An utter nobody."

Honor watched Bastwick riding beside the Cardinal as the entourage wended through the churchyard, passing the cemetery cloister and the charnel chapel on the way to Cheapside.

DeVille, having finished with his report, fitted on his spectacles to begin cataloging a fresh stack of books. "I'll give Bastwick this much, however," he said. "He is energetic, and his keenness in rooting out corruption is remarkable."

"Remarkable," Honor agreed quietly, and took her leave.

At Chelsea, Honor could not sleep. It was the day after her disappointing interview with Percy DeVille. The day had been oppressively hot, a freak of late October, as if the desperate summer in one final, deranged assault had hurled all its resources at the desolation of oncoming winter. The night was sweltering, the room suffocating. She writhed on her narrow bed as on the rack.

She had come that afternoon to join the More household for the baptism of Cecily's new baby, another son. At evening prayers in the family chapel she had knelt with Sir Thomas and the others only by forcing her knees to bend, and had mumbled her prayers up to a God she feared was deaf. And now, as she tossed on her bed in a bleary semiconsciousness, her mind was riven by the twin specters that visited her nightly: Ralph's scorched body heaving against his chains and Bastwick's face, cold with vengeance.

She sat up. Her linen chemise was clammy with sweat. Enough, she thought. She threw her legs over the edge of the bed, whirled a light cloak around her shoulders, and padded softly down the stairs and out of the slumbering house.

The moon was full. On the lawn, the grass was already studded with pearls of dew that slid deliciously over her bare toes. She drank in the night air, pungent with the smells of damp earth. She looked down the slope. In the distance, moonlight glinted off the window of the New Building. The pond dreamed beneath the oak trees and beckoned her with stars of moonlight dancing on its placid surface.

She went down, settled on the pond bank, and dipped her foot in the water. The cold sent a shudder of delight through her, forcing her muscles to tense, then relax. Yielding to another impulse, she stood and let the cloak drop from her shoulders and waded out until the water was waist high. She stretched forth her arms and bent her body and gave herself to the pond like a bird trusting to the air.

Her chemise, buoyant with trapped air, billowed around her neck leaving her naked below the surface, and she laughed out loud at her own undignified state. She floated on her stomach and pulled away the water in long, languid strokes and let its velvet coolness tingle every inch of skin. This water-world was overwhelmingly physical. It prodded out the brambles of the nightmare stinging her mind and pushed them gently away like branches borne in the current of a stream. The relief was sweet. This was baptism, indeed! How odd it was, she thought, lulled in this calm pool, to recall the intensity of the afternoon's rite over Cecily's baby.

Family and friends had crammed around the baptismal font in the stifling parish church, everyone tightly buttoned and bound and encased in their finery. First, the priest had exorcised the devils from the child, and then, intoning the Latin prayers, immersed him. When he lifted the baby again, the little body was board-stiff, fists balled, eyes big as coins. The parents had fussed to calm him from the terror they thought he felt at this near-drowning. The others had crossed themselves with relief at the escape his soul had made, for had the baby perished before baptism his soul would have tumbled into limbo where he would be perpetually denied the sight of God—and even, some theologians said, suffer the torments of the damned.

Honor smoothed back her water-thick hair and wondered at the freight of fears and hopes a baptism was made to carry, through custom immemorial. Rebirth from the sink of original sin, salvation from the jaws of hell, entry into life eternal: so much was bound up in such a simple act. Yet she had marked the baby's face. It seemed to her his muscles had tensed not from fear—what did a newborn know of fear until it was *taught* to fear?—but rather from the thrill of sweat-sticky skin plunged into cold water, just as her own body had reacted moments ago. But in the baptistery, where the newborn creature was thrilling to the sensations of life, the adults had seen only death. They saw a battle for an invisible soul, and they gave their thanks to the victorious priest, and to God.

Honor flipped onto her back. The billowing shift was becoming a burden. She kicked her way to the shore, stood, and wrenched the sopping linen over her head. She heaved it towards the bank where it splatted onto the grass beside a thicket of bushes.

Now, she was completely free. On her back she glided out and sculled to the middle of the pond. Her hair floated over her neck, and she saw her breasts rise above the surface. They reflected the white light of the moon like polished, wet marble, black-tipped with ebony.

Looking at her own nakedness, she wondered what it would be like to marry—to lie with a man. At the thought, Richard Thornleigh surged, unbidden, into her mind. Or rather, into her body, as though his kiss of months ago—his embrace—had left its imprint in her very muscles. It was not the first time his image had returned uninvited. Whenever it did—when she daydreamed, or at night—the remembered heat of that kiss would overwhelm her, like an ambush. And always, her body responded the same way. Like now. The tug in her nipples, the melting warmth in her groin.

Abruptly, she splashed to a halt and treaded water. She ducked her face into the chill water and vigorously shook her head to clear it. A drunken swaggerer, that's all he was. And married, too. Good Lord, the last man she wanted to think about was Richard Thornleigh.

She waded back toward the bank, and stood in the thigh-deep water. She lifted a yellow oak leaf from the surface and sent it adrift again, like a tiny boat, with a flick of her finger. Richard Thornleigh, indeed, she scoffed to herself. A man of straw compared to Sir Thomas. Although she could now laugh at her earlier uncharitable fantasies about Lady Alice's demise, Sir Thomas nevertheless remained her ideal. What other man could match him? Oh, several had presented themselves since she had gone to court. There was always a young gallant or two anxious for her favors. But their incessant prattle of hunting and hawking, of who was in and who was out, had soon made her yawn. In any case, she was in no hurry to marry; she enjoyed serving the Queen.

There was a rustling on the grass. Honor turned her head. There, on the bank, was Sir Thomas. She lifted her hands to her navel, unaware, in her shock, that they offered no covering.

* * *

More froze on his way to the New Building and stared at the statue in the pond. Waterdrops bejeweled her body, gleamed in her hair, and trickled from her elbow. They slid over her moonlit breasts and dripped from her pointing nipples, like crystal drops of milk. They caressed the curve of her belly and settled on the triangle of curling hair that glistened like the dewed, night-black grass beneath his feet. Her eyes were round as a doe's hunted into the bracken, and the tips of her teeth sparkled behind lips that formed an "O" of surprise.

She splashed out of the water toward him, arms outstretched for her cloak by the bushes. It lay on the ground to his right, several feet behind him. She sprang up the slippery bank, and he turned as she passed him. She swooped for the cloak, unconsciously offering him her buttocks, as smooth and cool as a marble Madonna's breast, and almost close enough to lay a hand on.

She whirled around and fiercely clutched the cloak to her front, but the fabric was a stubborn, twisted bundle that would untangle itself no further than to barely cover her nakedness. She wrestled with it until one hand was splayed between her breasts, the cloth just covering them, while the other hand wrenched a corner of it down to shield herself below the belly. Her breathing was quick and shallow.

More tore his gaze away. He looked up with sightless eyes at the moon in the half-naked branches, his mind still fastened to her body.

She stammered, "The night is hot. I could not sleep."

"Myself as well," he said, still looking up—away from the rounded flair of her hips that swelled around that desperate patch of cloak. "I am on my way to prayer." He stepped past her stiffly, his face averted, then paused. "Go into the house, child. Cover yourself. And go in."

He strode away with great control. She watched his dark figure become fainter in the gloom, then heard his footsteps increasing in speed, like a man who waits until he is unseen before hurrying away from danger.

*   *   *

The next morning, under a cold, leaden sky, Honor stood inside the walled kitchen garden. Lady Alice was on her knees beside her, ferociously plucking out dead foliage among her neat rows of herbs. The last of the summer lay suddenly spent, dying in flower and leaf and departing bird, but despite the abrupt autumn chill Lady Alice's herb garden remained robust.

"Her Grace is fond of my sweet marjoram, so mind you cut plenty for her," Lady Alice commanded with gruff pride, and piled the tarragon she had cut into the basket on Honor's arm.

As their shears snipped, the morning stillness was jarred by a loud banging as of a heavy door slammed shut. It came from the direction of the New Building. Honor glanced back nervously at the doorway in the brick wall. She had hoped to be away on the river toward Greenwich, back to the Queen, before a chance meeting with Sir Thomas could take place. Still mortified, she could not face him without discomfort, and she flushed at the thought of seeing him open the garden door, coming up to the house after his hours of study and prayer. She had risen early just to avoid him, but Lady Alice had detained her, eager to send her off with gifts to impress the Queen with the bounty of her garden. Honor watched the door, her pulse drubbing against the basket-handle.

"It's only riffraff being brought from the lockup," Lady Alice grunted. She yanked out a weed by the root. "I swear, the lousels take up more of his time than the King's business does."

Honor relaxed. Of course, she thought, chiding herself with a smile. The slamming was not from Sir Thomas leaving the New Building. It was the lockup. As a Justice of the Peace he had always kept a jail for petty criminals. When she'd lived here she had heard the banging of its door often enough as drunkards and thieves were locked in or discharged. She almost laughed out loud at the timid state of her nerves. As she turned back to help Lady Alice, the barking voice of Holt, More's bailiff, scaled the garden wall as if to convince her. "Move along, now!" he ordered his prisoner.

Honor frowned. She loathed Holt. She knew he was detested by all the servants as well. He had once divulged to Sir Thomas a planned elopement of one of the laundry maids with a groom from a neighboring estate. Sir Thomas, naturally, had to scuttle the affair, but the girl was shy and secretive and had told no one of her pregnancy. Four months later they had found her shivering in a ditch beside the premature baby she had smothered in the mud. After that, Honor never trusted Holt. She often wondered why Sir Thomas kept him.

"One moment, I beg you," the other man outside the wall said weakly. "My ankle . . ."

For a moment Honor thought she recognized the prisoner's voice. Then she shook her head. This seemed to be a morning for odd fancies.

The men's feet crunched by on the gravel walk.

When Honor hurried a few minutes later down to the pier with Lady Alice's compliments to the Queen still droning in her ears, she was alarmed to see the Bishop of London's plush barge tethered beside hers. It was not his presence in the house that concerned her: Bishop Tunstall and Sir Thomas, she knew, were old friends. But several of his cleric-servants were taking their ease on the bank as they waited for him, and she scanned the faces, looking for Bastwick. He was not among them. Thank goodness, she thought. That's another encounter I would avoid this morning. There is much more I must discover before *that* meeting. Her boatman pushed away and strained at his oars, and she settled in the cushions, relieved to be gliding back to Greenwich and the Queen.

At three in the morning More rocked on his knees, alone before the altar of his stark, private chapel in the New Building. He was naked from the waist up. Flecks of blood had spattered the stone floor beneath him. A scourge lay limp in his sweaty hand. It was made of three knotted cords, each one ending in a tiny hook. He raised it again.

Slash! The cords whaled over his back. The barbed ends ripped his flesh. Welts split open.

He had awoken in his bed at two, horrified to feel the sticky proof of sin smeared over his thigh. It was no comfort that the Church did not call it sin, not if a man spilled his seed while sleep-

ing, unconscious of the devils in his body. But was I really asleep?
he agonized. Did I not, in that semiconsciousness, willfully beckon
forth the image of her naked body at the pond? Did my hands not
prickle with lechery?

Slash!

Why this degrading lust? Why, when I was sure that Jane's
death, so many years ago, would release me from its bonds? Oh,
God, even then, with Jane, I sinned most foully. I failed. St. Paul
forgive me, I used my wife as a whore. Even before I wed, I failed.
What a laughable attempt at piety, living with those good, Carthusian monks, yearning to be pure, like them. For two years among
them I strove for chastity, for that state which the Church has always revered above matrimony. But only the strong can hold to
such vows. The weak, like me, must marry . . .

Slash!

Sweet Lord, I did all I could to keep from sinning. When Jane
died, I took a wife older than myself. An ugly woman, a stupid
woman. A woman past child-bearing, so that intercourse with her
was forbidden. I cast temptation out of my bed, and I thought I
was safe in my constrained marriage. But the fire is always sparked
from somewhere else.

Slash!

The pain of flesh scraped from ribs threw him forward with a
strangled cry. He dropped the whip, and broke his fall with blood-
stained hands on the cold flagstones. He rested on all fours, panting, his head lolling. The hair shirt that he secretly wore every day
under his clothes lay on the floor nearby, mocking him in his failure. Soon he must rise and pull it on again, and the pulp of the raw
ruts on back and shoulder and rib would stick to its pin-prick
fibers, engorging it afresh with blood, reminding him throughout
the day of his abject unworthiness.

But even as he contemplated his baseness, the vision of his
ward's moonlit body bent before him, her parted buttocks tor-
menting him. Crouched on all fours, dog-like, he could not suppress the craving to enter her, dog-like. His erection throbbed and
made him weep in silent, wretched shame.

Slash!

Dear God, I suffer such agony of mind and body and soul! Suffer like Origen of Alexandria who finally castrated himself rather than befoul his body with lust. Suffer like St. Jerome who would beat his heart with stones, yet could not beat the maiden from his breast. No! Not like those blessed Fathers of our Church. To compare myself with them is abominable pride, the rankest of sins.

Slash!

The whip raged over his back. Blood speckled the floor. The single candle on the altar gasped, and More's head dropped to his sweating chest, bowed with the unbearable weight of guilt and shame.

𝕖⚬ 11 ⚬𝕖

Out with the Old, In with the New

Honor was still shaking snow from her hem when she entered the Queen's suite at Greenwich and found several clerics lounging in the antechamber. Apparently part of a small delegation come to see the Queen, these assistants were taking their ease with some of her ladies-in-waiting, bantering over mulled wine and roasted chestnuts. The door to the Queen's private chamber stood slightly ajar and male voices rumbled out. Inside, Catherine moved past the crack of the opened door. She glimpsed Honor and tensely beckoned her.

Honor went in. Catherine threw her a fleeting smile and a nod to close the door behind her. "Some wine, my lords?" Catherine suggested with obvious relief at the diversion Honor had brought.

Honor dutifully crossed to the sideboard to pour wine. In the silence, flames from the hearth leapt and crackled as if feeding on the fuel of tension between the three people she had interrupted. They formed a triangle: the Queen at the window, Cardinal Campeggio near the door, and the obese Cardinal Wolsey facing the fire. Both men were swathed from cap to shoe in the scarlet satin that blazoned the might of the Church.

"Your Grace is unkind," Campeggio protested to the Queen as if there had been no interruption in their talk. He shifted off his gouty foot, visibly in pain. "I am completely impartial in this sad business. My one goal has been to reconcile you and the King. To restore harmony. It is always the goal of the Church in such matters."

"Reconciliation. Bah!" Cardinal Wolsey grunted from the hearth. He kept his huge red back turned on the room, and as Honor offered him the goblet he waved it away with such vehemence that she stepped backwards too quickly and spilled some wine onto the Turkish carpet. "Can you reconcile the lion and the hyena?" Wolsey scoffed.

Catherine's lips twitched, but she said nothing.

Campeggio closed his eyes tightly as if to regain his composure. Honor could see from his gray face that two months of this English standoff had left him drained. He waited until Honor brought him wine, then gulped it down, and gave her back the goblet. "If, however, reconciliation is impossible," he went on doggedly, "then why, Your Grace, will you not agree to take the veil? Surely your retirement to a convent is the course that offers a blessed comfort to all. The King promises that your life in seclusion will be as rich and joyful as at any court. In whatever convent you choose, you shall keep state like a Queen."

"But not *be* a Queen," Catherine said witheringly.

Campeggio sighed. "No."

"And such a course would leave my lord free to marry again, would it not?" she asked.

Campeggio looked down.

"Am I not correct?" Catherine insisted. "That you have discretionary power to dissolve my earthly marriage in favor of a spiritual one in a nunnery?"

"There is a pious precedent," Campeggio urged. "The Queen of Louis XII of France took the veil—"

"Yes, my lord Cardinal," she cut him off bitterly. "So I have been told. Several times."

For a few moments the only sound above the fire's hiss was the click of the Queen's rosary beads slipping through her fingers, one by one.

Wolsey stamped his foot on a cinder. "By all that's holy," he growled, "you would lose nothing but the person of the King, and that you have lost already." The remark was all the more malicious for having been delivered to the fire, not to her face.

She addressed his back. "Have the courage to answer me at least. If I take the veil, would the Church consider my lord a widower?"

The monstrous bulk of Wolsey turned. He sneered, no longer even bothering to mask his contempt. "You know it to be so."

"As well as I know my duty!" Catherine flared. "Duty to God, who brought me to the vocation of marriage. Duty to our daughter, whom I will not desert. And duty to my lord, who, I doubt not, will presently shake off the wicked snares and vain councilors that beset him, and see where *his* duty lies. You spoke of lions, my lord Cardinal. Take care the royal one you serve, who seems to sleep, does not awake to maul you."

The folds of Wolsey's chins trembled in fury beneath his waxy face. Campeggio hobbled into the corridor of combat between the two adversaries, so ill-matched in stature, though equals in resolution. "Please, my lord. Please, my lady. We must remain calm." Wearily, he pinched the bridge of his nose. "Your Grace speaks of the Princess Mary. Now, we understand the strain on you in not having your daughter near—"

"In being mercilessly *kept* from her!" Catherine cried. "Cardinal Wolsey has forbidden me to see or contact her these many months. And," she added, her voice almost cracking, "you speak right. It goes hard, indeed."

"But, there!" Campeggio said brightly. "It is only a matter of agreeing to take the veil and you shall be reunited with your child. In making this slight sacrifice you would honor God, and honor the scruple of your conscience, too, without loss of any of your temporal goods or possessions, or those of your daughter. Take this offer, my lady, for your sake, and for hers."

"The scruple of my conscience do you call it?" Catherine stared at him, incredulous. "The holy state of matrimony is the state God called me to. Is that so little a thing? Shall I blaspheme against the sacrament of marriage? Shall I call myself a whore? My daughter a bastard? Call my union with one of God's anointed kings a sin that has defiled my honor—and his—for nineteen years? Endanger my very soul? Never! I long with all my mother's heart to see my child again, but never will I bargain for it at the cost of my immortal soul."

"I marvel at your obstinacy, madam," Wolsey sputtered. Campeggio, beaten, shuffled to a chair near Honor and slumped on its edge, apparently to ease the throbbing of his foot. Wolsey stalked to the center of the room with the breath wheezing out of him like wet moss squeezed underfoot. Honor instinctively backed up closer to the sideboard. She knew where Wolsey's fury sprang from. All of Europe was watching him, England's Chancellor, as this drama unfolded. His credibility with the King—his whole future perhaps—rested on securing the divorce. "You prate of the safety of your soul," he said to the Queen, "but what of the safety of this realm if His Grace is thwarted in his rights? Without an heir, you abandon it to bloody civil strife. Are these such 'little things'?"

"These things lie in God's hands," she said. "My soul's safety lies in mine." Straining for calm, she added tonelessly, in the manner of a catechism, "It is not necessary to be careful of many things, but only of the one thing needful."

"And what of the safety of the King himself?" Wolsey cried. "Foul designs are afoot. Plots on the King's very life. And be assured, madam, that if certain traitorous persons were to wreak their wicked plots, the blaming fingers would not fail to point your way."

Catherine gasped, truly shocked. "My lord's life is dearer to me than my own. I know nothing of such plots."

"Do you not?" he said with menace in his eyes.

"If it's murderers you seek," she cried, "then look no further than Bishop Fisher's door. That good man lies wracked on his bed, poisoned with soup from his own kitchen. Two of his household died of it—though, thank the Lord, the Bishop himself is out of danger now. Ask yourself, who would poison the one man of the Church who speaks up for my rights? Oh, I know his cook was blamed and boiled alive at Smithfield in his own kettle. But who forced the poor sinner's hand to do the deed? For a murderer, look to those who would profit by destroying my only champion. Look to those who serve the house of Boleyn."

"My lady! My lord!" Campeggio cried, his hands raised in despair at the pointless quarrel. Glowering, Wolsey held his tongue. Campeggio stood and smiled wanly at the Queen. "Your Grace, I see that your position is a lonely one. Would it not soothe your heart to see your loving daughter? It is easily arranged. Tell us only that your retirement to a convent is a possibility and she shall be brought to your side as fast as horse can carry her. To retire now is no more than dutiful obedience to the Church. Speak but the word, and let the Princess Mary come."

Catherine had to turn her face away, and Honor saw that her heart was breaking.

Wolsey appeared to sense the change: a crumbling, a chink in the Queen's defenses. "Accept this bargain," he rumbled as if to ram home his advantage, "or be banished from henceforth."

Honor's hand flew to her mouth to stifle a gasp. Campeggio groaned. But Catherine did not flinch.

"And take this thought for council," Wolsey plowed on. "Once banished from the court you will have no need of the large train you now enjoy, nor of your sumptuous household. These can, and will, be removed. But agree now, and you shall maintain all your state and dignity."

Catherine was looking deep into Honor's eyes, as if searching past their pitying warmth for an answer. She seemed to find it, for a small smile played on her lips. "My lord Cardinal, your threats of poverty hold no terror for me. I have been poor before, and friendless. I can live poor again." She gazed through the open doors of her bedchamber to the candle-gilded prie-dieu by her bed. Her eyes lingered on its carved ivory image of exquisite suffering nailed to a silver cross. "Leave me this one maid," she said with a nod to Honor, "and Dr. de Athequa, my confessor, and I can live out my days happy in my duty to God."

She turned to Campeggio. "My lord, I do wish to show myself an obedient daughter of the Church. I will live wherever my husband commands me. But in this one claim I shall not be shaken: I am the King's legal wife. If I were to be torn limb from limb for saying so, and then rise again from the dead, I would die a second time in defense of this truth."

"So be it!" Wolsey cried. "I have done!" He lumbered to the door and flung it open so that every wondering maid and cleric in the antechamber could hear him. He turned and pointed a bloated finger at the Queen.

"You have perverted many hearts," he said, "and who knows what deeds men will stoop to perform for your desperate cause? The King's Grace is not safe abiding near you. I am commanded by His Grace to tell you that he wishes no longer to be affronted by your presence."

For a moment he seemed to feed on the shock in her face. His final words were cruel with softness. "You are henceforth banished from the King's bed and board. And you are ordered to be gone this very night."

Two days later Honor again crossed the antechamber of the Queen's suite and came to the open doorway of the private chamber. The room buzzed with activity. Anne Boleyn's friends strolled, or lounged near the blazing morning fire. Servants bustled in and out, forcing Honor to step to one side. Some were carrying away the last bundles of the Queen's books and tapestries; some were struggling in under armloads of Anne's things: gowns, bird cages, sheet music, jewel boxes, a spaniel puppy. Anne herself sat on a chair in the center of the room looking bored. Hans Holbein was sketching her at his easel.

A snowball splatted against the window casement. Anne sprang up and ran to the window and flung the shutter wide. A second snowball struck. Shrieking with laughter, she skipped backwards to dodge the flying fragments, then instantly dashed back. She leaned over the snow-drifted ledge to shout down at the knot of horsemen below.

"You missed, Your Grace!" She scooped a wet clump of snow from the ledge, whacked it between her palms and, with a strong, practiced arm, pitched it down through the crystal air. She leaned out to watch its flight. "Winged him!" she cried, and hopped in place, clapping her hands like a child.

The King's laughter boomed up from below, buttressed by a cheerful round of his hawking comrades' comments. Then there was a thudding of horses' hooves over earth, gradually diminishing to a soft shudder, and finally to silence.

Anne's shoulders heaved in a happy sigh. She wiped her dripping hands on her skirt and turned back to the smiles of her friends. She winked at her brother, George, who was tuning the strings of his lute near a bright-cheeked young lady. Walking towards him, Anne made a small, funny pirouette in midstride that made George laugh out loud.

Holbein's voice barked from his easel across the room. "Lady! Sit! Be still!"

The command was so brazen, so barefaced rude, that one of the gentlemen almost choked on his wine, and several ladies giggled. Anne turned to the room with an acid smile. "Master Holbein's highly individual use of the English language has a charm all its own," she declared.

"Ah, but his paintings speak eloquently," said George.

"If he ever *gets* to the painting," Anne grumbled. "All this sitting—and just for a sketch." She flounced back onto the chair and presented the artist with her grumpily knitted brows. "Satisfied, Master Holbein?" she said, peering around a maidservant who was staggering by with a large mirror. Anne raised her voice and spoke with exaggerated clarity as if communicating with someone almost deaf. "Holbein see? Lady sits!"

This brought laughter from the guests, but Holbein only frowned in oblivious concentration as his hand whispered across the pink paper with his black chalk.

George Boleyn began to play a ballad, and Anne finally noticed Honor standing in the doorway. Her smile evaporated. "Yes, Mistress Larke?" she asked. "Surely the extra day has given you ample time for the removal of your mistress's articles. What is it? Some trinket she's forgotten?" Her hands flew up beside her face, mimicking a protestation of innocence. "Whatever it is, I swear it is unmolested! These ladies and gentlemen can vouch for me. I have not purloined any treasure of *hers*."

Honor kept her face civil but her heart raged against Anne's insolence. And all these preening camp followers too, she thought. Scavengers who've descended to share in the spoils. "Not something forgotten, my lady," she said politely. "Rather, something offered. Her Grace bids me ask if there is anything of hers you would like kept behind for your pleasure." Her eyes were fixed on Anne, but she sensed the dropping jaws and staring faces of the guests. George Boleyn's fingers stilled on the lute strings.

"She bids me say you are welcome to anything," Honor went on sweetly, "but she suggests, perhaps, the prie-dieu in the bedchamber? For your pious meditations? It is an exquisite work in silver and ivory crafted by a Spanish master. Though, of course, its commercial qualities will not be as important to you as its inestimable value as a channel to God."

In the hushed room Honor gloried at the successful double thrust of the Queen's parry; the offer not only displayed generosity, it sparkled with panache.

Anne recognized the ambush. Her eyes narrowed. "Tell your mistress," she said, "that I have no need of her prie-dieu. I do my praying in church and chapel as most good Christians do. More praying seems excessive. It leaves one sallow-faced and peevish." She picked irritably at gold filaments on her green brocade sleeve. "Well, don't just stand there, Mistress Larke," she almost spat, "come in. And take away the prie-dieu. I tell you, I have no need of it."

Honor smiled. She signaled to two heavily booted menservants behind her with satchels of tools, and pointed them to the adjoining bedchamber. George Boleyn then broke the silence with a ballad. Soon, his clear baritone was cresting above the music of his lute. Chatter began to percolate among the guests. Wine flowed again, along with the laughter of flirtation. Anne accepted a goblet and listened to George's song.

Everyone frostily ignored Honor, yet she knew she was caught in this hostile territory until her workmen had dismantled the prie-dieu. She looked at Holbein. He and his easel formed an island of stillness in the stream of bustle. She made her way toward the friendly ground. She had followed the moon-faced painter's success with great pleasure ever since he had arrived on the Chelsea riverbank a year and half ago. Sir Thomas had immediately commissioned him to paint portraits of the family, then had shown them to the King, who was enthralled by the artist's work. "Is there really such a marvel in England," the King had cried, "and can he be had for money?" Now, Holbein could hardly keep up with the demand for portraits from the lords and ladies of the court.

Honor touched his elbow, gently so as not to disturb his hand. He frowned up at the interruption, then instantly brightened at the sight of her face.

"How goes the work, Hans?" she asked. She leaned to whisper in his ear. "Can silk be made of a sow's ear after all?" His eyes twinkled and his shoulders lifted to contain a chuckle.

"Master Holbein seems able to make silk from thin air," a male voice murmured.

Honor looked up in surprise. On the other side of the easel a man was stooped, leafing through a standing portfolio of Holbein's drawings. The easel had obscured him from her view. She flushed crimson realizing he had overheard her remark.

As he lifted out two drawings and straightened to resume his examination of them, Honor's anxiety dissipated, for she sensed that he was somehow aloof from this gathering. For one thing, the slightly sagging cheeks and emerging double chin proclaimed that he was older than the others, perhaps in his early forties. Also, he was dressed in an ankle-length robe of black velvet with only a wide collar of sable to indicate his status, and this alone distinguished him from the bright plumage of Anne's friends. But there was something else that separated him and made him their superior—a look of sharp intelligence in his small, brown eyes, and a quickness there that devoured the details of Holbein's drawings, yet remained coolly detached. There was precision and resolution in his straight wide mouth.

"Remarkable," he murmured. He turned to study Holbein as if hoping to discover a link that connected the mastery of the artwork with the face of the master. He looked again at the drawings, then shook his head in admiration. "I do love to see reality in art, not fantasy. And here is reality—made more real. One almost expects these faces to open their mouths and complain about the weather." He replaced the sheets in the portfolio.

Holbein shrugged with an awkward smile, obviously pleased. Honor could not help laughing. "Hans, I've never seen you respond so warmly to praise."

He nodded and resumed his sketch of Anne, this time taking a pencil to scrawl a doodle in the corner of the large sheet. All four corners of the paper were figured with these doodles. Honor knew it was his way of noting details of the sitter's clothing: fabric texture, embroidery designs, jewelry. Later, he would refer to them when he came to paint the portrait. But she noticed that today the doodles were not all of clothing details. Among them, tiny animal faces and plants betrayed the artist's wandering mind. She realized, with some amusement, that he found drawing Anne as tedious as Anne found sitting for him.

"Master Cromwell has seen Rome and Florence," Holbein said as he worked. "Seen Leonardo da Vinci. Michelangelo's 'David'. Raphael. Master Cromwell knows genius. His praise is good."

Cromwell. The name struck a note in Honor's memory. But where had she heard it? She was sure they had never met.

Feeling her scrutiny, he introduced himself. "Thomas Cromwell. Your servant, mistress." He made a slight, stiff bow.

She smiled. "A traveler in Italy, yet surely a native of England, sir?"

"Of Putney, mistress," was the crisp reply, delivered with an ungarnished directness that would have made the young courtiers, in love with rhetoric, wince. "And my sojourns in Italy are long past. Though I trust some wisdom of the Florentines remains crammed in this skull of mine to do service yet to my lord Cardinal."

"And I am—"

"Mistress Larke," he filled in. "Sir Thomas More's ward."

Proudly, she acknowledged this with a small curtsy. Then: "You mentioned the Cardinal . . ."

"He is legal counsel to Cardinal Wolsey," Holbein volunteered as his chalk tapered Anne's nose, and he added, with the archness of the foreigner testing an unfamiliar idiom, "Wolsey's 'right hand.'"

Memory flashed. Honor saw again the officers boiling through Sydenham's warehouse, the foul vat, the scabbed face of Brother Frish. This Cromwell was the very man Frish had wanted her to sound out for the Brethren! She recalled Humphrey Sydenham's kind, worried face as he argued with his ramrod wife. What had become of Sydenham? She hoped he was safe at home after his misadventure, resolved to meddle no more in criminal activities. And what of Brother Frish? Had Bastwick caught up with him, or was he still at large? Had Frish, perhaps, even made contact with Cromwell on his own? Her heart suddenly twisted. Since Frish had held such hopes of Cromwell's interest in these underground affairs, could Cromwell possibly know something about Ralph? She had heard nothing more from Percy DeVille, for shortly after their meeting he had gone off to collect a manuscript from a monastery in Wales and would be away for weeks yet. She watched Cromwell's keen face as he murmured with Holbein over the sketch of Anne, Cromwell pointing his stubby finger at the expertly cross-hatched shading of the cheek. Should I hazard a question? she wondered. She was on the brink of forcing the conversation somehow in that direction, when Anne's voice lashed across at them.

"Master Cromwell, what are you and Holbein plotting over there? Is the rogue drawing me with horns? Or fangs perhaps?" Her friends laughed, for her tone was gay, but there was a note of stridency too, and her eyes darted among the trio of misfits at the easel and flashed mistrust when they lighted on Honor.

Cromwell spoke up stoutly. "Master Holbein's hand reproduces only reality, my lady," he said. His face remained blank, giving no hint that he was aware of the ambiguity of his statement, but Honor had to hide a smile: he had not categorically denied the existence of horns or fangs in the drawing, not if they reproduced reality. A legal mind indeed, she thought, eyeing him with amused respect. One to match the subtlety even of Sir Thomas.

"You must trust the artist, Anne," George Boleyn said. "He is the one with the skill to leave a copy of you to the world. When all of us poor devils are in our graves your face will live on, thanks to Master Holbein. A reminder of these happy days."

Anne had removed one of her rings and was playfully holding it up to her eye so that it framed the window. She squinted through it at the straight-falling snow. "I need no help from scribblers to leave my mark," she muttered. She moved her head around, the ring still at her eye, until Honor was in her sights. "But it's true, George, that these are happy days. Happy for England, don't you agree, Mistress Larke?"

"The realm does not groan under war or pestilence," Honor answered steadily. "And God keeps His Grace hale. I am content."

"Ha! His Grace is hale indeed. I have my hands full to keep him so!" Anne laughed, and her friends tittered. "Yet it is a joyful task," she went on in good humor, "for His Grace loves good pastime and merry company, and he has suffered for the want of both in his bedfellow these many years. A change was overdue."

There was a murmur as several ladies and gentlemen watched the Queen's trusted maid for signs that she would engage the enemy, but Honor only clenched her teeth.

Tasting blood, Anne plowed on. "It appears that Mistress Larke has no opinion on the subject. How unfortunate, for it is one that interests me mightily. Master Holbein, what have you to say? You must be an expert on change of many kinds, having changed your country for a better one, and changed your patron for a royal one. All you need to round out the new identity is a new religion. Tell us, have you made an alteration there as well? These mad upheavals in your native land must have left some mark? What exactly is going on among your countrymen?"

Holbein was gazing at her above the easel with a wide-eyed mixture of frustration at being once again interrupted in his work, and confusion at the questions, for Anne always spoke as rapidly as she moved, and with his faltering grasp of English he had only partly understood her.

Anne snorted a laugh. "Master Cromwell, can you answer for this poor, dumb creature?" She raised her goblet as if in a toast. "Your gift of claret is delicious, by the way. Now, answer for the speechless Master Holbein and you'll make yourself doubly welcome. Come, enlighten us."

"You speak true, Lady Anne," Cromwell said. "Vast changes there have been in the German lands."

"But explain them, if you please."

"Naturally, you are aware that several territories have officially adopted Martin Luther's new doctrine. The leaders of many cities—Master Holbein's own native Augsburg and his adopted city state of Basle among them—have embraced Luther's followers."

"Yes. What is that name they call themselves?"

"Evangelicals, my lady."

She smiled. "Fascinating. Go on."

"Well, the great centers of Nuremberg, Bern, Magdeburg, Strassburg, Zurich—all are now out of the orbit of the Holy Roman Church. And, naturally, these changes have altered institutions and the traditional patterns of commerce, too, producing even more change." Cromwell rocked on his heels with his fingers woven together over his stomach as if he was comfortably prepared to talk on in this way at some length. His voice carried clearly across the room, but Honor noted that his expressionless face still gave no hint of emotion. It was impossible to say whether he abhorred or applauded the Germans' religious experiments. He simply catalogued them.

"But how did it all happen so quickly, Master Cromwell?" Anne's question was serious, but she asked it with a tight, private smile, like a teacher who knows the answer and is laying a trap for the pupil. Honor found it disconcerting.

"Quickly, indeed," Cromwell went on. "You will recall the Edict of Worms issued by the Emperor only seven years ago. It excommunicated Luther and placed him in the Imperial ban. Since then, the formation of the Catholic League of Regensburg—which allied Ferdinand of Austria, Bavaria, and the south German Bishops, and was blessed by the Pope—has attempted to enforce the Edict. But many in England are not aware that this has brought about the Lutheran League of Torgau, which is attempting to *prevent* the enforcement of the Edict."

"And these Lutheran forces? Are they strong?"

"Strong but fragmented, my lady. There are conflicting elements, for the reformers are by no means agreed amongst themselves. Zwingli of Zurich, for instance, battles with Luther over points of reformed doctrine and, fearing an alliance between the Emperor's Hapsburg relations in the north and the Catholic cantons to the south, Zwingli is now preaching for an all-out evangelical war. Amid this great upheaval, power elites of both government and commerce are shifting daily."

"And where do the mass of the German people stand in all this?"

"There can be no doubt that many thousands of them support the new order, and some of their most powerful princes embrace it. Yes, vast change indeed. It is a new German reality we must all accept."

Having defined the point, Cromwell closed his mouth. Stares of unease met him all around, except from Honor, who was impressed with his grasp, and from Anne whose eyes shone with fresh interest.

"You are well informed, sir," Anne said, smiling at his cold-blooded dissertation.

"I try to keep abreast of all matters that affect His Grace's business."

"His Grace the Cardinal, or His Grace the King?" she asked pointedly.

"Both, my lady," was his bland reply. "Only if Cardinal Wolsey's servants keep him informed can the Cardinal properly serve the King."

"If he were properly serving the King," she said with sudden savagery, "he would by now have dissolved the King's illegal marriage!" Allowing her smile to brighten again, she added, "The King would do well to have such able servants about him as the Cardinal is blessed with, sir."

Cromwell only bobbed his stiff bow to acknowledge her compliment, but Honor was sure she had finally seen excitement flicker for a moment in his eyes. Was that his secret wish, then? she wondered. His reason for attending Anne, and bearing gifts of wine?

Was it proximity to the King he sought? If so, he was managing a fine balancing act; in a situation where everyone clung with tribal fierceness to one faction or the other—the Queen's party or the Lady's—it was still impossible to know in which camp he stood. And although he had spoken of the German heretics without a trace of disapproval, his loyalty to his master, a Cardinal of the Church, remained indisputable.

Anne carried on, warming to her subject. "Yes, the King would be well served indeed if everyone took the refreshing view of the Germans' reforms as Master Cromwell does. I confess I have a desire to investigate some of their new doctrine myself. It's a pity that reading their books is illegal here."

There was an audible intake of breath from several throats. Anne's eyes glinted as though she knew she was creeping out on a limb but enjoyed the view. "Yes, I've heard there is much wisdom in the works of some of these reformers," she said. "Men like William . . ." she frowned and appeared to falter in memory. "Oh, dear, what is that exiled Englishman's name, Master Cromwell?"

"Tyndale, my lady," was his clear reply.

"Ah, sir," she smiled. "You do not disappoint."

"But, my lady," Cromwell added calmly, "you are aware, of course, that these books are full of lies, obscenities, blasphemies. The Church has declared them so."

"Aware? Let me see. I am aware that the reformers preach the abolition of some of the seven sacraments. Of the seven—baptism, confirmation, holy orders, matrimony, confession, the Eucharist, and extreme unction—they declare they can find no sign in scripture."

"Clearly, this is heresy," Cromwell said mildly.

Anne raised an eyebrow. "Clearly, sir."

Honor watched them, fascinated. They were testing one another, she realized. Like two children on the bank of a swift-flowing river, each was daring the other to jump in first.

"But I am also aware," Anne went on, clearly relishing the roomful of stares, the danger in the air, "that Luther says the godly prince has a divine commission to reform the Church. For example, to rid it of grasping prelates. Now, this suggestion interests me, for there are some overmighty, odious priests, grown fat on the sweated labor of the people, who do the King no good, and whose demise would be a blessing to this realm. As for the Lutherans' disapproval of the Pope—"

"They call him Anti-Christ!" a shocked young lady murmured.

"Indeed," Anne said with withering scorn. "Touching on that, I, for one, can happily imagine a Church without a pope. For we must ask: is Christendom well served by a man who waffles and whimpers, who promises and then forswears, who cannot bring himself to grant the simplest and most deserved of requests concerning the marriage of one of Christendom's most loyal princes? Perhaps it is the Pope who is the heretic."

The room fell deathly quiet. "I am aware, too," Anne said, "that the reformers are calling for priests to marry, as Luther himself has done. Married a nun, no less." The imp of humor played over her lips. "Imagine. The monk and the nun. Will their children be born wearing habits, I wonder?"

A hollow, staccato laugh left one gentleman's lips and died on the air. Anne looked around her. Most heads were bowed or turned away. Suddenly, she clapped her hands to break the pall. "Enough philosophy! Come, George, let's have a tune. And where's my little spaniel? I'm sure I saw Eleanor bring him in. I long to hold him. Now, Lucy, pour some more of Master Cromwell's excellent claret . . ."

The room sprang to life in a flurry of relief.

Honor looked past Holbein's back at Cromwell. His shrewd eyes had not left Anne, but there was a shadow of a smile in them as he inclined his head to Honor and murmured, "The Lady Anne has an uncanny knowledge of the contents of illegal books she claims not to have read."

Honor wondered which of the two had won their dare. It seemed to her to be a standoff; that both had retreated from the bank unscathed and with renewed respect for the other's abilities. But Cromwell's face betrayed nothing. She longed to draw him out and make him declare himself. "Master Cromwell, have I understood the lady aright?" she asked with as much amazed innocence as she could feign. "Did she really express a desire for a Church without a pope?"

"She did, mistress," he answered. He brought his eyes around to Honor and added flatly and finally, though with a small smile, "And my son desires a school without a teacher. But we must all deal in reality, as our artist friend here does. My son may pine for freedom but he obediently takes his desk every day, for his teacher is still his master. For us, the Pope is still the Pope. And," he added meaningfully, "your mistress is still the Queen of England."

Holbein stepped back from his labor and wagged the black chalk in Cromwell's face to make a point. "Ah, but one day your son will graduate and then he will need a teacher no longer." His eyes twinkled at the surprise on the two faces beside him. "My English improves, I think!" he said coyly.

Cromwell and Honor blinked at one another. Then they laughed.

Boots thudded at the bedchamber doorway and Honor's workmen emerged hoisting boxes of the dismantled prie-dieu. They strode past her, nodding deferentially, then halted at the doorway to the antechamber to wait for her.

But Honor did not join them. Her eyes had been drawn to the upper left corner of Holbein's paper—to a flower among the doodles. Her heartbeat quickened. Sketched roughly but faithfully was the little blossom that had brightened the title page of the dying foreigner's book. Although naked of colour, every stroke—every vein of the four petals, every leaf-point—was the same. There was no mistake; the original flower was imprinted on her memory. Her very fingertips tingled at the remembered feel of paint on vellum that she had traced over as she sat in Ralph's arms under the kitchen lantern. "Speedwell," Ralph had said, identifying the flower. And for years, the book and the flower and Ralph had been entwined in her memory in an aching tangle of regret. Whenever she thought of him, she thought of the speedwell. But she had never guessed, had never known until this moment, that Holbein was its creator.

She lifted her face to him, hungry to find out, at last, about the contents of the book, about its author, about the extraordinary stranger who had given it to her that May Day night eleven years before. She opened her mouth—but which of a hundred questions should she ask first?

"Mistress Larke?" The steely impatience in Anne's voice snapped across the room. "I believe your task here is complete. We will not detain you longer."

All eyes were on Honor: the workmen waiting for her; Anne; the guests once more sniffing rivalry between the women; Cromwell. And Holbein, who had seen the colour leave her face as if drained by some ghost on his easel.

"Good-bye, mistress." Anne's dismissal clanged.

Honor had no choice but to leave.

❧ 12 ❧

The Brief

"A *second* papal bull? Great God in heaven, she has gone too far!"

Wolsey's fist crashed down on the table of Campeggio's private dining room where the two cardinals were sitting over the remains of their meal. His furious gesture set the Venetian crystal goblets trembling. He crushed between his hands the letter Campeggio had just passed to him. Minutes before, it had arrived for Campeggio from the Queen.

Across the table, the Italian cardinal shook his head and groaned in agreement. "More delay."

"Worse," said Wolsey. He flung the letter among the divorce documents they had been discussing in preparation for the court session to finally judge the case. "This utterly confounds us."

At Wolsey's first outburst, Jerome Bastwick had looked up from his writing at a desk in the corner. Now, he carefully watched the cardinals. They sat in dismayed silence for several moments. Bastwick cleared his throat softly, then spoke up across the room. "Pardon, my lords. But may I inquire what the problem is?"

"Problem?" Wolsey bellowed to the ceiling. "It's not a problem, it's a bloody rout!" He rubbed his forehead, eyes closed, as if overwhelmed by the disaster. He glanced at Campeggio. "We must speak privately. Dismiss your assistant."

"I'd rather he stayed."

"Bah," Wolsey growled. "His fawning irks me. You brought a phalanx of clerics from Rome, every one of them better trained than this fellow. Why do you keep him on?"

Campeggio stared disconsolately at his swollen foot elevated on a cushioned chair. "My Roman assistants have turned listless on this interminable posting," he said. "They long to return to civilization." He looked pointedly at Wolsey, making it clear he had intended the insult, and added with quiet bitterness, "And so, I must confess, do I."

Wolsey looked away, chastised.

"But though we Romans falter," Campeggio said, "Father Bastwick's energy does not. I've found him to be a tireless worker."

Wolsey waved his hand with an impatient gesture. "Suit yourself."

Campeggio looked over at Bastwick. "What was your question, Father?"

"I simply do not understand the Queen's disclosure, my lord," Bastwick said deferentially. "She says she has uncovered a *separate* papal bull of dispensation?"

"Not a bull technically," Campeggio explained. "A brief. But whatever it is called, the Queen is claiming that it has as much validity as Pope Julius's official bull of dispensation which allowed the King to marry her, his brother's widow. This brief was written by Pope Julius as well, she says, and was dated the same day as his bull. She says—"

"She *says*," Wolsey snarled, "that in Spain the Emperor's lawyers, in combing through evidence of the marriage treaty, uncovered this brief among the papers of Dr. de Puebla."

"Who is de Puebla?" Bastwick asked.

"Was," Campeggio answered. "The Spanish ambassador here at the time of the marriage. Dead now. The crux of the situation is that this brief also dispenses for the marriage, as the bull did, but with significant differences of phrasing."

"Fatal differences," Wolsey added blackly. He snatched up the vellum copy of the brief that the Queen had sent with the letter. Scanning it, he tapped a finger at his temple. "I have the official bull up here," he said. His finger stabbed at a word on the scroll. "It is this that sticks us. This phrase appears only in the brief: '*His et aliis causis animum nostrum moventibus*'—"moved by these and other reasons."

"*Aliis causis*, my lord?" Bastwick asked. "What 'other reasons'?"

"Unspecified," Wolsey answered with a grim glance at Campeggio.

"But the phrase changes everything," Campeggio said. "The canon law of dispensations is exact. Sufficient *causa*—adequate grounds—must always be listed why a waiver should be allowed."

"But," Bastwick pointed out, "the original bull *did* list them. First, that the marriage would confirm the friendship between England and Spain. Second, that it would prevent war between them."

"Exactly," Wolsey said quickly, trying to shore up the sand giving way beneath him. "And the King is attacking that sentence about the threat of war." Though he spoke now to Bastwick, his eyes betrayed him by darting hopefully to Campeggio. "The King argues that the former Pope was deceived about the situation since there was, at that time, no danger of war between England and Spain. Consequently, the bull was procured by obreption—by misrepresenting the reasons for applying for it—and must now be declared invalid."

"But," Campeggio said sternly, "if the Pope said he had been moved by 'other reasons' as well, although he did not list them, who can say how much the threat of war weighed with him? Perhaps he had private information that led him, and him alone, to fear such a war. There is no better *causa* known to canon law than the furtherance of good relations between states."

Wolsey's voice rose to an uncharacteristic plea. "But Pope Clement has *promised* the King—"

"He has promised nothing," Campeggio said firmly. "I am sorry, but this evidence cannot be ignored. It indicates that Pope Julius *knew* of other reasons, unstated but compelling reasons, to grant the dispensation."

"And took his reasons with him to the grave." Wolsey groaned. He threw up his hands, admitting the stark conclusion both of them had reached. "How can I fight a dead man? What defense can I mount against unknown motivations? By these '*aliis causa*,' the King's argument is shattered." He ran a hand over his sweating upper lip.

Campeggio heaved an exhausted sigh.

"Perhaps not, my lords," Bastwick said quietly. The cardinals looked at him.

Bastwick had stood. He was approaching their table. "This is only a copy the Queen has sent you, is it not?" he asked. "A copy of a copy? Well, how can we be sure the alleged brief even exists?"

Wolsey stared up at him. "What do you mean?"

"I mean, my lord, that the Queen is desperate."

A smile began to creep over Wolsey's face. "My lord Cardinal," he said, lifting his glass in a toast to Campeggio, "I congratulate you in the discovery of this most astute assistant." He lifted the glass in turn to Bastwick and studied him for a moment. "When all of this is behind us, Father, and Cardinal Campeggio has returned to his beloved Rome, you must come and see me. I can always make use of a good, sharp mind."

Wolsey settled back comfortably in his chair, and drank.

"Read."

Honor heard the distress in the Queen's voice. She looked up from the hearth where she was laying wood for a fire against the March chill.

Catherine was thrusting out a letter to her. "Cardinal Wolsey means to terrorize me," she said. "Yesterday, he announced that the legatine court, with him and Campeggio as my judges, will sit in June. And today, this. Oh, yes, he means to terrorize me. Read."

Honor rose from the cold hearth and took the letter. The small antechamber of the Queen's room at Richmond Palace was chilly, dark-paneled, and bare except for a bench under a single window, and her candle-studded prie-dieu in the corner. Here, Catherine spent hours praying after morning mass and before evening vespers. She and her reduced train were alone at Richmond. King and court did not come here anymore.

"What terrors can he threaten you with, my lady?" Honor asked as she began to read.

Catherine picked up her prayer missal from the bench and pressed it to her bosom as if for warmth. She began to pace. "Subtlety was never the Cardinal's virtue. How miraculous, he declares, that this brief should appear after twenty years when not a soul knew of its existence. Doubly miraculous, he says, that it should so conveniently support my position."

"He implies that you forged it?" Honor asked, incredulous. She had thought that Wolsey's tactics, so consistently brutal, no longer had the power to shock her. Forgery, in a case against the King, could be construed as treason. And treason meant death.

"More than imply it," Catherine said. "He threatens that no court of law will accept a mere copy of the brief, unattested as mine is. Only the original document, he says, can possibly be considered."

"But the original lies in the Emperor's treasury in Spain."

"Precisely. Wolsey is deliberately transparent. He makes no effort to mask his skepticism about the very existence of the brief. He recommends . . . how has he put it? . . . 'For your sake and your daughter's'—a clever touch of terror there, you'll agree . . . that I dismiss any intention of introducing the copy in court." She stopped in the center of the room and stared at the logs in the cold grate.

"If an agent could reach the Emperor for you . . ." Honor began, thinking.

Catherine shook her head. "Wolsey knows I am cut off from Spain. His spies watch my doors like jailers."

"Pardon, my lady," Honor said, "but is this new evidence really necessary to you? I had understood your defense to rest on the fact that you came to the King's bed a virgin, and therefore all quibbling over the legality of the bull of dispensation was irrelevant."

"And so my main thrust will remain," Catherine said. "But I am not such a simpleton as to arm myself with only one argument, and an unprovable one at that. As a supplementary line of defense, this discovered brief answers my prayers. Or so I had thought." Unnerved, she looked heavenward. "I thought God had sent me a weapon, but now . . ." A log on top of the stacked firewood slipped and crashed to the hearth, startling her. She hugged the missal as if it were a mast in a storm. She began to rock, unsteady on her feet, and the missal tumbled to the floor.

Honor dropped the letter and hurried over with arms outstretched to steady the Queen, but before she reached her, Catherine crumpled to her knees. Honor knelt beside her, embracing her. Catherine pulled back, trembling, blinking worry-smudged eyes up at Honor as if unsure of where she was.

"My lady, let me fetch Dr. De la Sa!"

"No! No!" Catherine whispered.

"But you are ill!"

Catherine shook her head in jerks, eyes shut. Slowly, with Honor's arm around her shoulders, she seemed to subdue her panic. Her rigid muscles slackened, her breathing quieted. They remained kneeling together, for Honor was unwilling to let her go, but Catherine raised a cold hand to Honor's face and stroked her cheek.

"Truly, sweetheart, I am not ill." She patted Honor's hand and started to rise, but again she faltered and clutched Honor's elbow, and rasped, "Though God knows how sick at heart!"

Honor winced at the tortured voice. The forty-three-year-old face before her looked fifty. Threads of graying hair had escaped the Queen's jeweled *chaperon*, and Honor noticed with a pang of alarm that her blue velvet bodice was sprinkled with crumbs of bread. Good God, Honor thought, does she hoard bread in this dark room to break her fasts? Munch it furtively during her solitary hours of prayer? This once-fastidious Queen?

Catherine turned her face to the flickering votive candles. She still held Honor's elbow tightly as if hoping to draw some of the younger woman's strength. "Wolsey means to strangle this evidence," she whispered. "He means to strangle my last hope. And I must do as he says. If I do not, the Privy Council threatens the most extreme consequences for my disobedience." She dropped her forehead onto Honor's shoulder. "Blessed Mother of God, what am I to do!"

"Madam," Honor said steadily, "let me go to the Emperor."

Catherine looked up, astonishment on her face. "What are you saying?"

"Send me to Spain. In Valladolid I can pour out to your nephew your plea to release this document from his treasury. I'll have it back here, safe in your possession, before Ascension Day. And with it you can confound these Cardinals in their legatine court."

Catherine stared at her. "Oh, but my dear!" she whispered. "Dare I hope . . . ? There is so little time. And . . . no, no, it is too dangerous."

"Not for a pilgrim," Honor smiled. "Don't you see? Easter is the perfect time for such a ruse. I'll be a pilgrim traveling to the shrine of Santiago de Compostela—just one among hundreds of English pilgrims."

"But Wolsey's spies . . ."

"I promise you I can evade them. Oh, my lady, let me do this for you!"

For a long moment Catherine searched Honor's face, marveling at the offer. Finally, she allowed herself to smile.

"How could I have doubted God's wisdom?" she said as tears blurred her eyes. "You are the tool He has sent me. With your help, I *shall* confound these Cardinals!"

Honor stood alone on the pier of Richmond Palace waiting for a barge. Her skirts flapped in the spring breeze as if they were as impatient as she to begin the first leg of her journey. She had brought no baggage to attract suspicion. She had arranged to spend this night at the London house of the Marchioness of Exeter, one of the Queen's oldest and most trusted friends. She recalled that the Marchioness had recently commissioned Holbein for a portrait. Poor Hans, she thought. She had overwhelmed him with her volley of questions when she found him alone after that morning in Anne's suite.

"I know nothing of the book, Mistress Honor," he had protested. "Yes, the drawing of the speedwell is mine. I remember doing it. But I never knew what book it was for. I made hundreds of woodcut drawings in those days." He had explained to her that most artists did not work in wood or metal. They provided the drawings, sometimes on the wood itself, and then the woodcutter did the rest. He had never known what volume the speedwell was destined for, he said, and never saw the final publication. He had even forgotten the name of the printer who had commissioned the drawing, "Because," he said with a shrug of apology, "I did it on a short visit to Lucerne." He had shaken his head. "I'm sorry."

Honor was sorry, too. Another dead end.

A barge was approaching the pier, still several boat lengths away. She raised her hand to hail it. But before she could wave, she felt a tug at her sleeve. She turned. It was the red-haired Edward Sydenham.

Furtively, he glanced back towards the palace, his face very pale. He thrust a paper into Honor's hand. Astonished, she opened her mouth to speak, but Edward held a finger warningly to his lips and shook his head. Then, as quickly as he had come, he hurried away.

The barge bumped alongside the pier. Honor climbed in and directed the boatman to Barnard's Castle wharf. As they glided out into the traffic of the river, she settled herself and unfolded the paper. She glanced down at the signature: "Bridget S."

Mistress,

I heartily recommend me unto you, not forgetting the courageous service you performed for me and mine, albeit in the end my untrusting heart did lead us all to ruin. Because I would not heed your warning, precious moments were lost and my lord was captured. He has lain these long months in the Lollard's Tower. But right glad I am his heart is ever cheerful in the love of the Lord, Our Savior.

Honor was shocked. She had not known that Sydenham was being held in the prison of St. Paul's. She had been so sure he would recant and be sent home.

Mistress, these trials are my lord's and mine and I will not trouble you with our woe. The meat of my dispatch is this. I have this day had talk with Brother F. He inquired after you. Speaking of the infamous night that has blighted the happiness of me and mine, he told me you had asked after one Ralph Pepperton. Naturally, Brother F. knew no such name. Indeed, there are perhaps only two persons who can satisfy you in this, each holding one piece of the puzzle. The first of those two is myself, for I know that the man you refer to once called himself Ralph Pepperton.

He came to my husband's notice three years ago in Coventry. He had come there years before as a masterless man fleeing some past crime that I know nothing of. He never spoke of those past days except to tell me once, in confidence, that his name had been Pepperton and that, for safety's sake against his former crime he had put on the name of Roger Pym. (Ever jesting, he told me that though his conscience cleared him, yet the magistrate might not.) He got his bread driving a dray for a skinner, and he wed a Coventry lass of our circle, and fathered two fine lads, and nowhere lived a better Christian soul than this good Roger Pym. His help in our humble efforts to gladden men's hearts with the word of Our Lord was always merrily offered. His ending will have made the angels weep.

For news of that dreadful ending you must seek the one other that I spoke of. More than this I dare not lay to paper. That other—the person with the shred of news that will fit mine—is your own guardian.

I tell you this, for I believe that those of us who live must bear witness for those who have suffered and died. Goodness must prevail.

Use this knowledge as you will. I have nothing but thanks in my heart for you for the help you tried to bring us. And I am safe assured that you will keep what I have told you unto yourself alone, except it be for the good purpose of breaking it unto your guardian.

And so I pray Jesu preserve you in long life to His pleasure.

From my London house, though I had liefer lie in filthy

straw so I might lie alongside my lord in his prison, I am ever your entire good friend,

Bridget S.

I beg you, destroy this paper.

Honor looked up, flushed with excitement. Now, she would learn the truth! Sir Thomas would lead her to her quarry. Bastwick was almost in her grasp. The erratic wind frisked across the waves and tugged at the letter in her hands.

"Boatman," she said, tearing the paper into pieces and scattering them on the river, "stop in at Chelsea first. At Sir Thomas More's."

❧ 13 ❧

The Menagerie

"Sir Thomas, mistress?" a servant in the house replied to Honor's question. "Why, he's out feeding his creatures."

Honor walked down to the menagerie, a stone shed that housed the two rows of caged exotic animals whose habits More delighted in observing. She stood in the doorway and found him stooped over a cage, obviously unaware of her presence. She watched with a smile as he coaxed a monkey to accept a scrap of meat he was poking through the bars.

"Sir!" she said severely, pretending disapproval. "Does this house not observe the Lenten fast?"

More looked up, startled. Then he straightened to greet her. "I believe," he said with a smile, indicating the forbidden meat in his hand, "we may absolve a heathen creature for clinging to some heathen ways."

"Oh, hunger is heathen indeed," she said with a laugh, and stepped into the dim shed. She bent to look into the monkey's cage and was shocked by what she saw. An emaciated figure was slumped in a corner among scattered bits of browning vegetables. Its fur was matted with filth, and a large bald patch, red and raw, festered on its shin. Its lusterless eyes followed her movements with only the barest glimmer of interest. "What's wrong with him?" she asked.

More sighed with concern as he held the meat again between the bars. "Cecily thinks he pines for his mother. I begin to believe she's right. He will not eat." He winked at her, adding, "Lenten fast or no."

The young monkey's head began to rock back and forth, mechanically, mindlessly. Its finger felt for its shin and picked at the raw wound. Honor turned her head, sickened by the animal's misery.

More abandoned his attempt to feed it. He dropped the meat inside the cage. "Most unnatural," he said.

A parrot's squawk mimicked him. "Unnatural! Unnatural!" it shrilled in absurd repetition. It made them laugh together, glad to be diverted from the monkey's wretchedness.

Farther along the row, under the parrot's hanging cage, a young wildcat, an ocelot, was scrabbling at its metal bars. They moved to it and stood on either side of the waist-high cage, admiring the beauty of the cat's spotted coat.

"Can you stay a few days?" More asked. "Until Good Friday at least?"

Honor shook her head. "I'm only passing, sir." She knew that Holy Week was his favorite time of year. He always tried to be home for it and loved having his family gathered together. "I'm sorry. My barge is waiting and I must be gone almost immediately," she said, then added, knowing it would make him happy, "On the Queen's business."

He beamed. "Good!" He threw up his hands as if to forestall her saying more, and protested, "No, no, I would not ask you on *what* business."

"And I would not tell you," she smiled.

He laughed. "That's right. Not me . . . not anyone." Suddenly, with a quick motion across the top of the cage he caught up her hand. "Child, it brings me joy to see you serve her Grace so faithfully. I know Richmond must be a dull place for you. So many of her giddy young ladies have been dismissed or have deserted her. But she has told me how she leans on you in this hard time, and finds comfort in your company. You make me very proud."

Honor blushed. Her devotion to the Queen was an act of love, and no hardship; she did not feel she merited such praise. Yet she drank it in, for nothing pleased her as much as the good opinion of Sir Thomas.

His face clouded. "Some of us are bound by other loyalties, and must needs keep silent in the King's great matter. But my heart is with your noble lady. We must all pray that she weathers this storm." The light in his eyes sharpened into alarm. "I shudder for the fate of the Church in this realm if the Queen should ever be usurped in title by the Lady Anne." Suddenly, he looked down at her hand. "You feel cold, child. Are you ill?"

She shook her head with an embarrassed smile, realizing how tightly wound up with anticipation she was. "No, sir, not ill." She withdrew her hand. "But I come with a question that concerns me mightily."

He seemed amused by her earnestness. "Then we must seek an answer. Mightily."

"Sir," she said, "what can you tell me of a man named Roger Pym?"

He looked mildly surprised. "I expected a rather different query," he said. "One about my note, perhaps. Did you receive it? About the latest candidate for your hand? A marquis's son—though the youngest—is not to be scoffed at, you know."

Again she shook her head, this time with impatience. "Later. But now, what do you know of Roger Pym?"

"Pym?" he mused. "The name does not—"

"He was burned at Smithfield the week before Michaelmas."

"A heretic?" This appeared to surprise him even more. "Let me see. September," he murmured, as if opening a file in his mind. "Yes, I recall the case. Pym. A drayman. From Coventry."

She barely waited for him to finish. "His burning was a mistake, wasn't it? A miscarriage of justice."

More frowned. "I certainly hope not. I am not aware of any."

She was taken aback. Was he sworn, as a Royal Councilor, not to divulge such details? She had not considered that. "Oh, sir, do tell me. It concerns me directly. Father Bastwick acted from the low-

est of personal motives in this, for revenge. He hates me for ruin-
ing him, hates everyone connected with me. But I know he went
too far and condemned an innocent man. Please, tell me how he
managed it."

More looked confused. "Who?"

"Father Bastwick."

"That accomplice in your abduction?"

"Yes. He serves now in Bishop Tunstall's court, but—"

"Does he? In Cuthbert's court?" More's frown of confusion
deepened into real concern. "I must put a word in Cuthbert's ear if
that is so. Bastwick's a bad priest and a bad man."

The parrot flapped and gurgled overhead. More smiled and
raised his hand to touch it.

Honor watched him stroke the bird's head. Did he know nothing
about Ralph's trial after all, then? Had Bridget Sydenham been
mistaken in directing her here? "Sir, are you not aware that Father
Bastwick arrested and interrogated Roger Pym?"

"No, he did not," More said, glancing over his shoulder at her.
"I did."

The parrot screeched, "I did!"

Honor blinked. "What?"

"I conducted both his interrogations, as a matter of fact. Alongside Bishop Tunstall, of course. Though,"—he held up a finger to
correct himself—"Cuthbert did excuse himself from some part of
the second session, ill with a headache as I recall. The job was left
to me and his archdeacon. We sent the wretch to the fire."

Honor's fingers curled around the cage bars at her hips in a con-
traction as involuntary as a cramp. "You?"

More's eyes ranged over a trio of birdcages beside the parrot.
"Yes," he said absently. "I remember I gave Holt a bonus after that
case. He did good work tracking the man." He looked at her, as
though suddenly curious. "Why do you ask? Did you know Pym?"

In Honor's grip the iron bars felt suddenly hot. "He was . . ."—
sweat pricked her in palm and groin—". . . my father's servant."

"You never spoke of him."

"I spoke of Ralph Pepperton." A fog was swirling in her head.
"That was his name . . . when I knew him."

More nodded. "Ah, yes. Your merry stories of 'Ralph.'" He shook his head sadly. "And he ended his days a heretic. Heavens, what a plague Luther has spawned. And somehow, I don't know why it is, servants seem the most easily infected. Why, even in this house—"

"Ralph was more than a servant. He was my friend."

"Ah, child, that is hard, I know," he said with feeling. "To watch a friend fall into such gross error is hard, indeed. I am truly sorry." He squeezed her elbow tenderly, and then, as if to put the unpleasantness behind them, beckoned her to follow him across the aisle to look at a new acquisition. "A hyena," he said, enthralled. "Gardiner sent it to me all the way from Tunis!"

But Honor did not move. The fog in her head seemed to be solidifying, pressing down on her brain like a slab of rock. She watched as he dipped a cup into a barrel of water, opened the hyena's cage and placed the cup inside. The animal shuffled closer in its chains.

"His arrest," she began. "How . . . ?" She had to stop to swallow. "How did it happen?"

More shrugged, watching the hyena drink. "How does it always happen? Sometimes it's drunkards whispering blasphemy in the alehouse, sometimes it's a grubby Lutheran pamphlet handed around at a brothel—"

"No," she interrupted, aware of the dullness of her voice, flat as axe-steel. "I mean, what cause did you have to arrest him?"

"Oh. Well, the first time, we intercepted him transporting contraband. Driving a dray out of the city onto the northern road at dusk."

"Contraband?"

"Bibles." He reached up to a peg for a satchel of meat scraps he had apparently brought from the house. "English translation by William Tyndale. Pym had hidden them under ox hides. I interrogated him the next day." He flipped open the satchel. The stench of decaying meat snaked up into Honor's nostrils. The chained ocelot, excited by the scent, circled and pawed at its door beside her.

"But you are a layman," she said. "Surely only the Church is empowered to interrogate."

"Oh, no. The law gives authority to lay officials to help interrogate suspects, in the company of clergymen of course. The anti-Lollard statutes are quite clear on the point."

"So," she said numbly. "You questioned him."

"And charged him."

"With what?"

More gave her a startled smile, as though the answer was obvious. "English Bibles? Heresy, of course." He fed the hyena. "His replies were shocking."

"You found him guilty?"

"Yes."

"And he recanted?"

More nodded. "Most of them do, you know." He crossed back to her side of the aisle, opened the ocelot's cage, and tossed in some meat. The frantic cat pounced on it. "They are not keen to die for their fantasies if they can escape the fire by perjuring themselves. Pym evaded us that time."

"What then?"

"Well, I had a feeling about that fellow," he said, watching the animal eat. "I've seen his kind before. A relapsed heretic is like a dog returning to its vomit. I knew he'd slip."

Honor felt the knot in her stomach tighten. She was piecing the story together. He had said a moment ago that he had given his bailiff a bonus. "So, you set Holt to track him," she said almost to herself.

He nodded. "And I was right. Not three weeks later Holt caught him in a dockside tavern rattling heresy to a rabble of lousels. Hectoring them, like a hag in her cups, that the miracle of transubstantiation is the Church's lie. Holt snatched his arm before the ale even reached his lips."

"And took him . . . to the Bishop's prison?" She dreaded to hear him contradict her.

"No, here." He gave a quick snort of satisfaction. "Sitting in my lockup he wasn't so keen to babble his blasphemies, I can tell you."

Honor had to force down a swell of nausea. Ralph had been chained here, at Chelsea! Mauled by Holt! She took a deep breath to steady herself. "What did he say at the second interrogation?"

"Nothing." The wry, good humor drained from More's face. "Pym was a hard man. Hard and stubborn. Absolutely refused to talk, though I kept him in my lockup for weeks. Oh, he muttered some insolence about his convictions belonging to himself alone. Then, not a word more."

"What more did you want?"

"Answers. About the printer of the Bibles. About his contacts in Coventry. About the hive of heretics—the so-called Brethren—that infest Coleman Street. But he uttered not a syllable."

"Not even in his own defense?"

More gave her a look of gentle admonishment. "Child, there *is* no defense. The Church, once struck, may turn her other cheek, but if that other cheek is smitten she must protect herself." He added pedantically, "On the penalty for a relapsed heretic the law of 1401, *De heretico comburendo*, is unequivocal."

"Death by burning," Honor whispered. Her heart had contracted in her chest, a cold ball of steel. "And Holt's testimony was all your proof?"

"Holt's and his brother's," More answered, scooping out the last scraps of fat to the gorging ocelot. "I would have preferred the corroboration of a more sober man than the brother, but it sufficed. In heresy cases the law requires two witnesses."

"The law," she whispered, trembling. Disgust was funneling up into her throat. It spewed out, uncontrolled. "How can you talk of a law that murders justice? You, who taught me to revere the law! You, who trumpet the goodness of equity, of the judge's duty to temper harsh laws with clemency. How can you praise the law when it is used to cut down good men and destroy them?"

More looked up, clearly astonished. "For heaven's sake, child, the man was a colporteur of banned books. True, in civil law where only handfuls of coins are at stake a judge may exercise clemency. But we talk here of *souls*. Pym was a heretic, far more dangerous than any thief or murderer."

"Dangerous?" she breathed, incredulous. "For encouraging people to read for themselves the word of God?"

Abruptly, he shut the ocelot's cage. His voice became stern.

"The word of William Tyndale, you mean—a clean contrary thing."

"But it is scripture still. How can you kill people for reading scripture?"

For several moments he only stared at her. "Naturally, after the death of a childhood friend," he said tightly, as if to remind himself, "you are distraught. Also, I must not forget that you, of course, are not familiar with Tyndale's wickedness." His voice became calm again, like that of a patient teacher. "Let me uncover to you some of his errors. His translation—"

"I don't care about that. It's *your* wickedness I have uncovered!" She took a step to leave, but he moved in front of her to block her way. She was trapped between the cages. "Let me pass," she cried.

But he would not. "I understand your grief," he said steadily, "but I cannot allow you to continue on in ignorance of the blasphemies of these men. Hear what abominations Tyndale has written, for God's sake. The Greek word 'presbyter' he has rendered not as 'priest' but as 'elder'—as if any old man may dispense the sacraments. With this alone he blasts away fifteen hundred years of the ascendancy of the priesthood. He translates 'ecclesia' not as 'church'—our Holy Mother Church—but as 'congregation.' As if Holy Communion were an idle gathering of friends. Worse, for 'penance' he substitutes mere 'repentance.' The church has always, everywhere, demanded that sinners *do penance*, but Tyndale tells us that if we will only repent in our hearts, God is satisfied. Don't you see? These are the lies that Pym was spreading."

"I see that you killed him for splitting hairs!" Her voice rose, shrill, choked with disbelief. "For quibbles over words." Again, she tried to push past him. His arms shot out, stretching to the cage tops of either side of her and pinning her to the spot.

"Quibbles?" he cried. "Girl, you know not what you say." He reined in his shock, but his arms still barred her way. "I grant that an English Bible may not be a bad thing in itself. But if such a book were someday to be made, it must be authorized by the Church, and its translation undertaken by learned men. This reckless, individual, headlong search for God in the maze of scripture lures men into appalling error. All the heretics, Lutheran and Lollard and Anabaptist alike, wail that salvation comes only from the Bible—'*sola scriptura,*' they cry—but it is a Bible interpreted by their own perverted minds."

"If interpretation is what this bloodshed is over," she snapped, "then who is to say which mind is perverted? Could it be your own?"

She saw that she had stunned him. She was glad.

"Look at Erasmus," she cried. "He is as learned a man as you, and he welcomes a vernacular Bible. He wishes learning were more common, so that scripture could be read by every fisherman and plowboy. Even by Turks and whores."

"My old Dutch friend is often swept away in his enthusiasms," More said sourly. "No. I tell you, it is Holy Church which instructs Christians how to live, not the Bible. Christians could be pure in their faith even if the Bible had never been written. Doctrine has passed *orally* from one generation to the next, through Holy Mother Church, God's instrument on earth. '*Quod semper, quod ubique, quod omnibus.*' 'What has been believed always, everywhere, and by all.' Tradition. Founded by the Apostles and continuing, unbroken, to the present day. Christ founded a church. He did not write a book!"

"Unbroken tradition?" she blinked. "Listen to yourself. The Church was in schism for decades, with three Popes at one time. The Greek Church, with millions of believers, is *still* schismatic. And doctrine *has* changed. The command for circumcision withdrawn ... dietary laws ... the formula of baptism ... even the teaching of the immaculate conception of the Virgin ... all modified."

More's smile was indulgent. "Your knowledge of the decrees of the Church's general councils does you credit. I am glad that your studies here were not in vain. And the supremacy of those councils is the very point I wish to impress on you. You see, the Church resolves her crises *internally*, in councils that represent all Christendom, just as in secular government Parliament decides for the realm. To let every individual decide changes in doctrine—or in law—is worse than madness."

Pinned between the cages she found she was shaking. She was furious at his power to hold her, furious at her own impotence to smash through his complacency.

But he seemed to read her silence as a sign that her hysteria was spent. "That's right," he said gently, "listen to reason." He removed his hands from the cage tops, though his body still blocked her way. He smiled. "Goodness, what would happen if I let every coarse fellow who grumbled against a judgment in the law courts traipse into my library and rummage through my legal books until he found a word or phrase to exonerate him from the law's penalties? Well, the heretics do just that. They catch at a word or a phrase from Holy Scripture, hoping it will release them from their duty to God. But the Church has ruled, and Christians must obey."

His eyes shone with a sincerity that she had seen countless times in the exuberant discussions that had been the joy of her life here, eyes that beckoned her to follow into the trimmed and sheltered lanes of accepted belief. But her mind screamed that these convincing words were spoken by the man who had murdered Ralph, and she bled inside as belief and rationality tore at each other, ravaging her heart. "Obey," she repeated hollowly.

"Yes," he smiled. "It is our duty."

"And if I dare to question, will you burn me too?"

His smile vanished. "Do not mock, child," he said with chilling firmness. "A great principle of authority is at stake here. If ignorant people root through the Bible for the answers they want, they call the Church false. They spark the fuse of sedition, for the Church is an essential pillar and prop of the social order. Never forget that without the Church, there is anarchy."

"And with the Church, apparently, there is carnage," she spat. "But have you not heard, sir? Christ told St. Peter to lay up his sword."

His mouth twitched. "I have no taste for this juvenile sermon. St. Augustine and St. Ambrose, as you well know, instruct us that Christian princes must punish heretics by terrible death, for the survival of the faith and for the preservation of peace among their subjects. Heretics are the enemies of law and order."

"But Christ bade us forgive our enemies! Are you more wise than Christ?"

"Christ," he answered evenly, "could not imagine the depths of sin and degradation to which our world would sink. He could not have foreseen the present crisis. If we now let the Church be torn to pieces by mad dogs like Luther and Tyndale we will all topple into chaos. And from chaos, straight into hell."

The fear kindling in his eyes dismayed her, frightened her. She wanted only to be away from him. Slowly, she took several shaky steps backwards between the cages. "I know nothing of what Luther has written," she said, "but surely even so lunatic a man could not desire the end of the world."

"He will wreak it nonetheless. He raves that people can be saved by faith alone—*sola fide*—even if they live wicked lives. What does this do but open the cave to let out roaring anarchy? What man will be constrained from doing wrong unless he dreads the punishments of hell? What man will strive to do right unless he hungers for the rewards of heaven? And who shall decide what is right and what is wrong? Shall a man refuse to obey the laws of Church and realm because of some paltry dictate of his individual conscience?"

Stepping backwards, she thudded against the wall. "But can there be no rational inquiry?" she gaped. "Is the Church assured in every detail?"

"We do not talk of *details*. Luther rants that man has no free will. And people in the thousands follow him. To negate free will is to blame God for man's sins." He had stepped after her into the narrow corridor between the cages and was moving toward her. Honor flattened her back against the wall. More stopped in front of her. They were standing almost breast to breast. "You must understand the gravity of this. If man has no free will to choose good over bad, piety over blasphemy, chastity over lewdness, then he is no better than the animals. But, of course, lewdness and licentiousness are Luther's gospel. What else can we expect from a lecherous monk who defiles his sacred vows of chastity to marry a nun? He makes Holy Church his brothel!"

He searched her face as though appealing to her to share in his horror. But the horror she felt was only for him. She could not mask it; did not want to mask it. She saw that it wounded him, and she was glad.

"I fear you are obsessed with this Pym," he said. "His death has twisted your heart. You must forget him. You say he was your friend, but you should know that he had other friends of the most evil sort. He was part of a criminal ring with cells in London, Coventry, Norwich, Lincoln. I myself led a raid on the warehouse of one of their leaders, a merchant in Coleman Street."

Her breath snagged in her throat. Sydenham. "You!"

"Heaped with tracts and banned Bibles the place was," More said, "and over them, men and women alike swooning like witches at Satan's own coventicle. And all led by a mad disciple of Tyndale's named Frish."

My God, she thought. *Brother Frish saved me that night . . . from you!*

"And this heretic merchant—friend of your beloved Pym, mind—is nothing but another of Luther's lecherous pimps. I kept him for some weeks in my lockup, and you would have been revolted had you heard his testimony."

Honor could scarcely believe it. Was Sydenham the prisoner she had heard Holt prodding along that morning after her swim? She'd heard them go by outside the garden wall. Had he been going to his interrogation in the house? She remembered that she had seen the Bishop's barge tethered at the pier. Had Sydenham's Church court judges been the Bishop . . . and Sir Thomas?

As if to confirm it, More said, "The wretch actually declared to Bishop Tunstall and me that God would be better served if priests were allowed to marry."

Honor saw in her mind the rotund Sydenham and his gaunt wife. She remembered the moment of high alarm during the raid when they had reached out to touch one another, a touch that both begged, and offered, comfort—a touch that symbolized their bond as man and wife. She felt tears welling, felt her vision blurring, her strength ebbing. "Perhaps," she murmured, "because he finds happiness in marriage . . ."

"Because he lusts! And rather than confess his sin, he mangles the words of Christ so that he may wallow in the filth of that lust!"

Honor could not tell if he was speaking now of Sydenham, or Luther, or all mankind, so strange was the gleam in his eye.

"And at this very moment," More said with disgust, "the heretic merchant lies in the Lollard's Tower, still refusing to recant. Well, we'll see how long he clings to his heresies when he smells the straw lit under him."

Her hand flew to her mouth to muffle her cry. The muscles of her legs dissolved. She had to grab his shoulder to keep from falling. He caught her by the elbows and held her up.

"You *are* ill! Oh, forgive me for speaking so crudely, child. I wish you could go through life knowing nothing of such people, such depravity."

She looked into his face. In his obvious anxiety for her welfare his gaze was ranging over her forehead, her cheek, her mouth, her throat. He was so close that she felt the heat of her own quick breaths reach his neck and then return to her. His fingers dug into the flesh of her arms. For a moment she had the irrational sensation that he was holding her this tightly in order to keep himself from falling.

He turned his head and stared for a moment at the shed's open doorway, as if in need of the fresh air beyond. He looked back at her sharply, struck with a thought. "Pym had changed his name, did you say? Oh, child," he warned, "beware any man who would hide behind a false name."

With a sudden rush of fierceness she wrenched her arms free. "Ralph never hid behind anything in his life!" she flared, the tears finally spilling.

"He hid behind heresy. Hid behind silence. But in the end, God found him out."

"It was not God who destroyed him, it was you! God would have seen Ralph's *heart*. You see only words. Doctrine. Contraband. Authority. Sedition. You are the one who hides. You use words to blind yourself to the carnage you do. But tear away the words and what do you see? What have you done? Murder! The brutal torture and murder of a good man!"

She pushed past him and ran towards the door. Her hip crashed against a stack of empty cages and they clattered to the ground, frightening the animals. She burst out into the sunlight and ran down to the barge on the river with the shrieks and yowls of More's creatures pursuing her.

❧ 14 ❧

The Rendezvous

Honor stood at a window of the long gallery in the Marchioness of Exeter's town house and watched the sun burn off the late morning mist above St. Paul's across the street. She was exhausted. Her sleep had been deranged by nightmares, as black and turbid as if she had been drugged. After rising with leaden limbs, dressing, and tugging a comb through her hair, she had wandered from her room, meaning to join the Marchioness downstairs. But as she passed the gallery, its quiet had lured her in. She gazed out at the bustle around the cathedral, and gradually her mind awoke.

The scene before her shocked her in its normality. Pigeons flapped onto the roof of Paul's Cross, the octagonal outdoor pulpit in the crook of the transept. Swallows wheeled around the great spire and the Lollard's Tower. Activity hummed through the village of church buildings inside the cathedral's walled enclosure: the Bishop's palace, assaulted this morning by glaziers on a scaffold; the cemetery cloister, with visitors strolling in to view its famous painting of the Dance of Death; St. Paul's school, where boys darted, as quick as fish, in and out of slamming doors. A gravedigger hustled his cart of bones over a path to the charnel house, and along Paul's Walk the usual stream of Londoners flowed through the cathedral itself. Inside it, she knew, merchants would already be haggling over exchange rates and lawyers drumming up trade, all of them jostling with the whores and beggars and dogs.

She watched in wonder. How could the world go on as blithely as before? How could people bustle into the great nave to gossip and buy and sell as if nothing had changed. For her, nothing would ever be the same.

How she had deceived herself! How blind she had been in her hunger for vengeance. And how wrong. Every night for months as Ralph writhed before her she had sworn her vow against his murderer, certain it was the same man who had terrorized her father on his deathbed and then abducted her. She had hoarded her hatred like so much rope, coiling it and laying it up with such confidence to snare Father Bastwick.

And then Sir Thomas stepped into the trap. What was she to do? Spring her hatred on the man who had opened his house and heart to her, and opened her mind to the world?

There was a screech of female laughter. A moment later the Marchioness, an elegant woman in her forties, breezed into the far end of the gallery. Three ladies skittered after her gasping in the throes of mirth.

"Oh, you're here!" the Marchioness called to Honor, still laughing. "No, no, don't leave on our account, dear. In fact join us, if Primero is to your liking. Take Nell's place," she said, nodding toward a green-eyed beauty. "You'll do the rest of us a favor—she's far too wicked for such an early hour. That's your ploy, isn't it, Nell?" she called gaily to her friend. "With your naughty tongue a-wagging we can't concentrate on our cards and you rake in your winnings."

The green-eyed lady sauntered to the middle of the gallery. "Maybe that's how the Earl's son I was telling you about raked his stepmother into his bed," she smiled. "I hear the fellow is possessed of a dexterous, cunning tongue, indeed." The ladies shrieked with laughter. The Marchioness's plump, younger sister had to hold onto her tall friend's arm to keep from falling over.

Servants scurried in with a table, chairs, and trays of cold partridge and capon. Pages followed with cards and wine. The Marchioness's friends, waiting out the bustle of assembly, strolled the gallery, chatting.

The Marchioness took Honor's elbow. "It's all arranged," she whispered, her eyes glinting with mischief. She hurried through the plan that she hoped would help the Queen, her dear friend of twenty years and more. "Tonight, you'll retire to the bedchamber next to mine, as you did last night, and in the morning I'll tell the servants that you've come down with a fever and must not be disturbed."

"And the doctor?"

"Yes, yes, his palm has been greased. He'll make daily visits to his 'patient,' so Wolsey's men—if they're still watching the house—will assume you're lying on your sickbed within."

Honor nodded. She had devised the scheme herself; only the doctor's acquiescence had been in question.

"Tonight," the Marchioness went on, "you can slip out amongst the musicians with my manservant, Owen. Under a cloak, and carrying a viol case, you'll look like one of them. Horses will be waiting at the Golden Dog, as you requested. You ride for Scotland at dawn. And take Owen. He's a quiet, stoic old thing but he's a fine swordsman."

Honor thanked her. She was satisfied that the Marchioness had believed her story about carrying the Queen's plea to the young Scottish King who was a staunch supporter of the papacy; it was safer for all that the Marchioness remain ignorant of her real mission. Now, everything was arranged. She was glad. She longed to be away from London. Away from England. Away from every sight connected with Sir Thomas More. Tomorrow's dawn could not come soon enough.

"Come, ladies, Primero!" the Marchioness called, clapping her hands. "Help yourselves to wine, my dears, and I'll begin the wagering with three crowns." She winked at Honor, adding, "I feel lucky this morning." And with much rustling of silk and clinking of glasses the ladies prepared to settle down to play.

Honor excused herself. There was still much to do to arrange the journey. She was passing the large, mullioned window when the rumble of a drum in the street made her turn. People were hurrying along Cheapside and crowding through Little Gate in the churchyard wall.

The green-eyed lady, curious, joined Honor at the corner of the window. "What is it, Mistress Larke? A robbery?"

"I know not, my lady," Honor said, pulling the louvered wooden shutter farther open.

The lady raised her glass in the direction of the pulpit, and said, "Some fuss over there at Paul's Cross." Around the pulpit people were jostling and squeezing each other for seats in the wooden galleries between the cathedral buttresses.

The other ladies crowded in behind Honor, pressing against her back to see. Each had a theory about the commotion. The tall one, still engrossed in sorting her cards, said it must be a proclamation for the Maundy Thursday ceremonies. The Marchioness wondered if it was to be the funeral oration for the Earl of Pembroke's mother who had died the week before of a flux. "No, look," the Marchioness's sister cried, pointing with a partridge wing.

A procession was turning the corner of the cathedral around the Lollard's Tower. Bishop Tunstall walked at its head, followed by several church officials and a trio of mounted men. Behind them came a mule-drawn cart loaded with a jumble of books. At the tail of the cart walked seven barefoot men and women, penitents who had abjured their heresies. The penitents stumbled on in their shame, bearing faggots on their shoulders as a symbol of the fire they had been spared.

The Marchioness's sister said brightly, "Oh, look, it's a burning, too. They're on their way to Smithfield."

But Honor had already seen. Behind the seven penitents came a black workhorse dragging a hurdle. A man was strapped to it, facedown. He was half naked and barefoot. He wrenched his face onto his cheek and Honor sucked in a breath. Even at this distance she recognized the face of Humphrey Sydenham.

How thin he was! And how gray. Gray skin sagged over his ribs. Gray strands of filthy hair jerked in the breeze. Gray sockets rimmed his eyes. Honor stared, stunned by the realization of what he had done. He had refused to abjure. Captured by Sir Thomas, abused by Holt in the Chelsea lockup, imprisoned for months in the Lollard's Tower, Sydenham had refused to give his tormentors the answers that would have saved him. He was going to burn for his beliefs.

The procession halted. Two of the Bishop's men clambered up with shovels onto the cart of books and began pitching them out. The other officials banked the books into a mound as high as the mule's neck. The crowd shuffled back to make room for the Bishop's Archdeacon who was coming forward with a torch. He tossed it up onto the top of the pile. The books smoked, then burst into orange flames. The black horse lurched with sudden panic and someone had to restrain it.

While the books burned, Bishop Tunstall, splendid in gold miter and embroidered robes, climbed the spiral steps of the pulpit and began a sermon. The crowd politely ignored him, for all necks were craned toward a burly officer striding forward with a whip. It hung from his hand and trailed along the ground like a pet viper. He took a wide-legged stand before Sydenham on the hurdle and cracked the whip high in the air. The crowd hummed with admiration at his expertise.

"Now that's a clever idea, to stop on the way," a lady's voice simpered over Honor's shoulder. "Lets the common people hereabouts see some of the punishment." She nibbled her partridge tidbit. "I mean, not every fellow can just drop his work and set off to Smithfield fairground."

"Oh, a vast improvement," the green-eyed lady laughed. "I'm sure the wretch who's about to be whipped would agree. Maybe you could have him brought into your servants' hall to provide a demonstration, Bess. A lesson in consequences for all sloppy maids and snot-nosed scullions."

Surrounded by the women's banter Honor lowered her head, unable to watch what was to come, unwilling to hear it. But their voices subsided, and the crowd across the street stilled, and when the sound came her ears could not escape it: the slash of leather raging over flesh. Once, twice, three times. She gritted her teeth until her jaws ached. Seven, eight, nine lashes. Ten!

"Well," the Marchioness declared when the whipping had

ceased, "the people had better get their fill of such sights now. If the goggle-eyed whore worms her way into the Queen's place there'll be no more punishments for heretics. The bitch is a Lutheran herself. All the more reason," she added archly to Honor, "to pray that she is routed by Her Grace."

Honor's head snapped up. Sir Thomas had said the same thing.

"Well, ladies," the green-eyed lady drawled, "the mummery's over."

Honor looked out. Bishop Tunstall had climbed down from the pulpit and was turning back to his palace. The penitents, their ceremony of humiliation concluded, were herded away around the cathedral where they would be released. Apart from the custodian beside the burning books, only the three mounted officials were left, and the black horse that would drag Sydenham to his death. The small procession began to move out into St. Martin le Grand, heading for Smithfield. Paul's Cross cleared, and the usual sounds of the churchyard—the hammers and shouting schoolboys, the birds and barking dogs—resumed. The ladies glided back to their cards.

Honor was left standing alone, watching the last of the street children skip after the hurdle. The Jesus bells of St. Paul's tolled. She flinched. The bells were so loud they seemed to be clanging inside her skull. They drowned out the human voices of the street. They obliterated the music of the birds. They gonged with a brazen, strident authority, as if proclaiming with sheer bombast their dominion over every living creature below. Dizzy, Honor rested her forehead against the shutter. She heard the wooden slats chatter slightly under her trembling head. As the last bell reverberated she remembered the words of Bridget Sydenham's letter:

. . . those of us who live must bear witness for those who have suffered and died. Goodness must prevail . . .

A little before midnight Honor left the house with the musicians. She was muffled under the hood of a pilgrim's homespun cloak beneath which her skirts were hoisted above riding boots. The Marchioness's servant, Owen, walked beside her. The yawning entertainers crossed the torchlit courtyard, strolled out through the main gate onto darkened Cheapside and, holding lanterns to light their various ways home, bid one another soft good nights. Tucked in among a trio of them, Honor lowered her head as they passed the pair of Wolsey's men lounging at dice under the sign of the Plowman's Rest. She knew the men had followed her the day before from Richmond and Chelsea, but as she strolled by them with the musicians they only glanced up before turning back to their dice.

Her "escape" had proved absurdly simple.

In the lee of London Bridge she sent Owen on ahead to the Golden Dog. Alone, with only a guttering lantern to light the dark, she stood for a moment, listening. Faint bursts of laughter echoed across the river from the brothels of Southwark. Reflections of torches on the bridge, the city's only viaduct, flashed off the black water under the twenty arched supports. The water around the arches formed a swirling rapids on the upstream side, a placid mirror on the downstream side.

Honor looked up. Lights in the houses and shops stacked across the bridge—some four stories high—winked in the darkness. Above the portcullis, two grizzled traitors' heads impaled on pikes grinned at the night-silvered clouds. Honor hurried away into the packed-earth lanes of the waterfront.

The sign of the Trident Inn whined on its hinges over the door as she entered. The landlord led her past the few morose customers in the tavern. He opened the door to a small back room and motioned her to enter. It was furnished with only a battered trestle table and some dusty barrels. The landlord bit the coin Honor offered, slipped it into his pocket, and shuffled out, closing the door behind him. Honor set her lantern on the table and moved to the unglazed window. She was staring out at the river, thinking, when the door creaked open again. She whirled around.

"A gentleman," the landlord announced.

Thomas Cromwell stepped into the room.

Uninquisitiveness was apparently the landlord's policy, and he waited only long enough to receive another coin from the visitor before closing the door a last time and leaving the couple alone.

Cromwell remained near the door. "A chilly night to be abroad, Mistress Larke," he said warily.

She hurried forward, throwing off her hood. "I believe the business I have to propose will be worth the inconvenience to you, sir."

"So your note promised." He stood still, gravely watching her. The table lay between them, and its smoking lantern.

Honor's mouth was dry. How to begin? Her pounding heart drowned out all rational thought. She twisted around and saw the black void of the river and felt suddenly trapped. From the tavern an old woman's mournful singing crept under the closed door, her voice sodden with drink and regret. Strangely, somewhere in the lost hope of the woman's song Honor found her courage. She turned back. Yet, still, how to begin?

By beginning.

"Master Cromwell, all the world knows how well and truly you serve Cardinal Wolsey."

His head jerked in a small bow, his smile pleasant and polite.

"But," she asked boldly, "what if I could pave the way for you to directly serve the King?"

The veil of his easy smile was torn away, and in his eyes she saw a flash of the hunger of ambition. She knew she had struck cleanly. Instantly, his veil of complacency dropped in place again. He took a step closer and was about to speak when she threw up her hands to stop him.

"Please, sir, no courtier's babble tonight. I am about an undertaking too large for such trifling currency. Rest easy; I know too little of you, and you of me, for either to bear the other any malice. Therefore, as neutral strangers, let us trust one another. I have asked you here to speak of goals that concern us, you and I. Though these goals lie in different territories, I believe the roads that lead to them cross on common ground. Trusting this, let us speak only the truth. You desire to serve the King." These last words were put as a statement of fact.

"There is," he said cautiously, "much honor in serving the King."

"And riches," she added.

His eyes were on her, unashamed, waiting. Finally, she caught what fed the hunger there. Like a small key turning in her head, understanding clicked. "There is also," she said, "power."

Cromwell's face darkened. "I am not fond of games, Mistress Larke. Why have you brought me here?"

She stepped up to the table and spread her fingertips on its top. "As the Cardinal's legal council you are no doubt aware of the brief written by the former Pope and recently discovered by the Queen."

"Naturally."

"With it, as you know, the Queen has evidence to shatter the King's case. He claims that defects in the dispensation make his marriage invalid, but the brief rectifies the defects, making the marriage legal."

"Indeed," he said impatiently. "Please, get to the point."

"The Cardinal is questioning the brief's authenticity, for the Queen has only a copy."

"I know that."

"I am on my way to Spain to ask the Emperor to release the brief to me, in the name of the Queen. The original. There can be no question then of its genuineness."

Now, Cromwell's eyes gleamed with interest. "Why do you tell me this?"

"I propose to hand over the document to you."

His mouth fell open. For a moment he only stared. "Hand it over to the Cardinal?"

"No. To you."

"What are you saying?"

"I am saying that I want you, secretly, to present the document to the King."

"Why would you want to do that?"

"I have reasons."

"But if the King has the brief he will, in all probability, suppress it. Holding it, he can pretend it does not exist."

"I am counting on that," she declared.

"I see," he said slowly, clearly perplexed.

"Do you?"

He stepped up to the table and his eyes narrowed as he studied her face above the lantern light. "Frankly, Mistress Larke, you astonish me. Why should you make me such an offer?"

"Let me answer by asking you a question. If the Lady Anne were to become Queen, she would welcome in the new religion, would she not?"

Cromwell's eyes grew wide. "Apparently, you are keen to see the advent of this so-called new religion."

"To see the rot in the old religion gouged out! The Church is a plague, with its power to hunt down and destroy men who seek only after truth. The realm must be cleansed of bloated priests and priest-ridden royal officials who persecute honest folk unto death." She looked away, conscious that she had revealed too much of her heart.

"I see," Cromwell said again, this time with a small smile. "The rhetoric is a trifle strained, but the sincerity most eloquent. Especially to these old ears. Fury is an emotion that only the young can muster, betrayed by the unjustness of an imperfect world. The old resign themselves; the young must rage."

She was disconcerted by the way he was studying her, as if she were a cipher. Sharply, she asked him, "Well, Master Cromwell, do you accept my offer?"

The perplexed look on his face creased into something close to derision. Derision tinged his voice as well. "And how do you propose that this extraordinary transaction be made? When you return, will you dine with me at Stepney while the court spies in my household watch us from a peephole in the gallery?"

"I have a plan."

"And what might that be?"

"I will collect the brief from the Emperor Charles at Valladolid, just as the Queen expects. I will set out to return to England with it. But the King's agents abroad are vigilant, I understand. How if I am attacked by one of them on the road? How if I should lose the document to him? After all, sir, I am a lone, weak woman, traveling with a single servant. Such a disaster could befall me."

When Cromwell spoke again there was no longer any trace of mockery. "Very tidy," he admitted.

"Now, will you accept my offer?"

He wove his fingers together over his ample stomach, contemplating her. "Mistress, farmers with cattle to sell cry down the Church for its plethora of fast days when we must eat fish. Fishmongers cry down the Church for its tithe on eels. And for all I know, eels may cry down the Church for blessing ships that sail upon the water. Now, you may have good cause to cry down the Church as well, but I mind that among the priest-ridden royal officials you just spat against is your own guardian, Sir Thomas More. A good and pious man, and known to all as a defender of the faith."

"A brutal man! Known to all as a defender of the Church's abuses!"

Cromwell seemed lost for words. Finally, he said, "Mistress, for the second time tonight you have surprised me." He ran a hand over his thinning hair, and chuckled, "And that is two times more than most people can surprise me." Again, he clasped his hands in front. "And so," he said thoughtfully, "you look for the day when the Church will be reformed. It is a goal that many good people share."

"Do you?"

He gave her his small, enigmatic smile, but no answer.

"Well, it matters not," she said. "If the Lady Anne becomes Queen, the goal will be realized. Now, will you accept my offer? I confess," she said with some warmth, "I had expected more thanks."

"Did you, indeed?"

"Your future will be made," she cried. "The King leans on men who deliver."

"Why do you not make this offer directly to my lord Cardinal?" he asked. "Or why not simply hand over the document to the King yourself? Why use me?"

"I do not wish to expose myself. But even without this consideration, I would never deal with the Cardinal. He represents all that people loath in the Church. His palaces and splendor, his bastard son elevated to high church office, his multiple benefices and bishoprics. Wolsey *personifies* the old Church. But you, sir, are a coming man. All the court speaks well of your temperance and your abilities. I have seen for myself your openness to change. And the Lady Anne trusts you. The way lies before you," she said, and added softly but sternly, like a warning, "to make or to mar."

Neither had moved. Across the table, they gauged one another.

"There is still a point that confounds me, mistress. Until this meeting you were a person known to me chiefly for your reputation as the Queen's most loved and loyal woman. And this papal document may be her last chance to salvage her marriage and her estate as Queen. Her last hope."

"There is no hope at all for hundreds of people who daily risk the wrath of the Church," Honor flared. "Under the Queen the wicked Church thrives. Under the Lady Anne I pray it may wither."

"Yet I know you love Her Grace. Are you really prepared to dash her happiness against your higher cause?"

He might as well have slapped her. She knew he had not meant it as a rebuke but she felt it as one. Stiffly, she rubbed the edge of the battered table in an effort to regain control. "Her Grace will be well treated," she said. "Whether she enters a convent, which would suit her temperament, or decides to live alone, she will be well treated. The King cannot abuse her. He would not dare insult the Emperor so. This way she will be reunited with the daughter she loves. And as for the King, she has lost him already. She deceives herself that it is not so, but he will never live with her again. That much is clear to all but her."

She gasped. She had rubbed the wood too hard and a splinter had rammed under her nail. Aware that Cromwell was studying her again, she ignored the pain. "Self-deception is our enemy," she declared. "I know. I once deceived myself about . . . someone." She heard the feebleness in her voice and was angered by it. "No," she said harshly, "the Queen should accept reality. As you once so wisely suggested we all do, sir. She should accept the world as it really is. She should go quietly, as common sense bids."

"Yet you do not," was his cool reply.

"I do not what?"

"Accept the world as it is."

She met his gaze, feeling calm for the first time since she had left Chelsea the day before. She answered simply, "I cannot."

Part Three

Hope

April 1529–April 1534

❧ 15 ❧

Spain

At an inn halfway between Santiago de Compostela and the Spanish coast Honor sat cross-legged on her bed with a book. She was bone weary, but repugnance at the mould on the wall inches from her back and the grime on the straw mattress kept her vigilantly upright. Ribald singing boomed up from the tavern downstairs. Her head ached from it. She rubbed her temple as her eyes wandered for the third time over the same passage in the book. She glanced at the rancid candle of tallow beside the bed. It had guttered down to a thin disk. In moments it would go out. She was too angry to concentrate on reading in any case. Cromwell's agent had failed to make the rendezvous. Whoever he was, he was supposed to have met her here by noon.

Her hand traveled up between her breasts. She felt through her chemise for the leather tube suspended from a thong around her neck. The precious paper, the papal brief, was rolled inside. She had hoped to have been free of its weight—and responsibility— long before this hour. She swatted a cockroach off the mattress. Curse this man of Cromwell's. What had gone wrong?

There was a drunken whoop of laughter from below, then a re- newed roar of singing. Honor slammed her book shut. Even if she could forget her worries, sleep would be impossible in the din.

And yet she longed for sleep. There had been precious little of it in the past few days.

The twenty-four hours she had spent at the Emperor's court in Valladolid—the fountains, the music, the perfumed feather beds—wavered behind her now like a mirage, a fantasy that had never really happened. On the return ride she had driven herself and Owen at a punishing pace. They had galloped into Santiago de Compostela and stopped there only long enough for Owen to offer up a prayer at the famous shrine of Saint James and spend his penny on one of its cockleshell souvenirs for his wife before they raced on to make the rendezvous in time. All for nothing.

The revelry below had been going on for hours. It had begun when a band of mounted mercenaries had thundered into the courtyard after supper, sending the handful of guests scurrying upstairs, Honor among them. She had heard all the hair-raising stories about mercenaries. They traveled in small companies, taking orders only from their own commander who hired the band to any prince or duke, bishop or banking house in Europe who could pay. On the field, they attacked in organized lethal formation with short swords and long pikes, and fought, as the Italians said, *"mala guerra"*—warfare without mercy. Between military engagements many companies split up into robber hoards to ravage the peasantry. Owen had knocked at Honor's door and whispered a warning to stay put and bolt herself in. "I'm about to do the same myself," he had said. "Anyone in his senses will keep clear of that lot. Just don't let them see you, my lady."

The candle sputtered and died. She sat for some time in the dark, furious, her head splitting. The vile room seemed like a prison. Even if she could not concentrate on reading, she wanted light. She had noticed extra candles in a cupboard along the landing that overlooked the tavern. Could I risk slipping out to fetch one? she wondered. Why not? The brutes were so drunk they probably wouldn't notice an earthquake. Cautiously, she slid the bolt on her door and crept down the dark corridor, then out to the landing. She crouched behind the railing and peered down through the posts.

The men—she counted twelve—looked like a flock of exotic

birds that had flown through a fusillade of gunshot: gaudy, ragged, and filthy. They wore brightly colored, baggy tunics and knee breeches slashed ostentatiously to appear cut to shreds in battle. The costume mimicked the infamous German mercenaries feared throughout Europe, the *Landsknechts*. Huge, tattered plumes swayed in their hats. Greasy but still vivid banners were bound diagonally across their chests, and strips of silk dangled at their knees as garters. Some wore short cloaks in brilliant colors. Most wore their hair shoulder length and wild.

Six of them sat bawling their song and guzzling ale around a table littered with scraps. One lay on his back on a soggy separate table droning his own melody, a profane version of a Lutheran hymn. The rest sat on the floor in corners, snoring, except for one who stood at the fireplace and spouted urine in spurts over the blazing logs.

Honor shook her head in disgust. It was true, she thought, that they were probably too drunk to be dangerous, but to get to the candle-cupboard she would have to move along the landing—it was farther away than she had remembered—and movement might draw their attention. It was not worth the risk. She stood to go back to her room, smarting at the self-imposed confinement decent folk always suffered in the presence of such louts. But as she straightened she noticed that a man sitting on the floor against the far corner was looking up in her direction. Instinctively, her hand went up to cover the hidden tube between her breasts. She took a quick step back into the shadows and stood perfectly still.

The man had slung back his blue cloak across his shoulder, and it covered his mouth so that between the cloak and his drooping hat not much of his face was visible. But Honor thought she read there a scowl of curiosity. He rubbed his eyes with the heels of his hands as if to clear a liquor-induced vision, then stared up again through the smoky air at the gloom of the landing. Honor held her breath. A dog came snuffling near the man's boot, and he looked down at it to deliver a half-hearted kick. The dog scuttled away, and when the man glanced up again at the landing it was with waning interest. Finally, he folded his arms and settled back against the wall to sleep. His head slumped onto his chest. Honor relaxed. She hurried back to her room, quietly closed the door, and bolted it. She sat again on the bed. She watched the fire-lit crack under the door until exhaustion claimed her and she slipped into a fitful sleep.

At dawn she paced her room. Below, the men awakened on the tavern floor, coughing, farting, moaning, and bickering. Finally, they shuffled out. Honor watched them from the edge of her window. By the stable, they stuffed their saddlebags with bottles, loaves, and sausages stolen from the wizened landlady who looked on in mute despair. Then, in a flurry of sudden military discipline they mounted and clattered out of the courtyard.

Honor waited until noon. But was clear that Cromwell's agent had utterly miscarried. Her plan to "lose" the brief had failed. It was impossible to remain in this ruin of an inn. The other guests had already fled. The larder had been stripped, and the landlady was slumped on a stool by the hearth, alternately moaning prayers and wheezing curses between pulls on the last jug of wine.

Honor and Owen rode their horses out at a walk. There was no hurry now. The port of La Coruna was only fifteen miles away, and the ship bound for England would not sail until the next morning. They ambled over flat, scrub land where farmers tilled the stony soil. The road descended to a valley where a village squatted in blank-eyed poverty. As they came up out of it, the country became hilly and the wind rose. Honor lowered her head against the dust. She gathered in the flapping, loose neck of her pilgrim's tunic that hid the leather case, and agonized over what to do next.

Carry the brief back to England? Wolsey would almost certainly have her searched as soon as she stepped ashore. The ruse of lying ill at the Marchioness's house had only bought her time, but by now he'd know she was gone and would most likely suspect her of dealing for the Queen. Dangerous. But she could somehow let him know that her intention was always to relinquish the brief; Cromwell would intercede for her. And certainly, if Wolsey's agents confiscated the brief, Wolsey would just hand it over to the King, so the outcome she hoped for would be the same. Curse it, though, the thought of relinquishing it to Wolsey rankled. If that was to be the result of all this trouble, she might just as well drop the brief into the ocean. It was Cromwell she wanted in her debt. In her debt, and in the King's good graces, and working, with Anne Boleyn, toward a new order.

Well, that grand scheme was obviously not to be. Should she drop the brief into the ocean after all, then, and declare that it *had* been stolen? That way, at least, the King would get his divorce.

Or would he? Might destroying the brief do more harm than good? The Queen was clinging to the hope it offered; she'd surely urge her lawyers to get her unattested copy allowed as evidence. It could drag on for months. No, only if the King had the original in his hands could he suppress it confidently—deny its existence or declare it a forgery. Otherwise, delay was inevitable. And every day the Church remained ascendant was another day for Sir Thomas to break the brave souls who opposed it. So. What to do?

She and Owen plodded down a hill in silence. Ahead about a quarter-mile she could see that the road narrowed into a bridge over a river. A shepherd was funneling his flock onto the bridge. Honor was despondently watching the sheep when she heard an odd sound in the distance behind her, like the flapping wings of a large bird.

She glanced over her shoulder. On the crest of the hill a man sat on horseback, motionless. His short blue cloak, whipped by the wind, rippled behind him with the sound of powerful, beating wings.

The mercenaries! Honor and Owen exchanged frightened looks. Quickly, she gauged her position. To the left, the road skirted a steep, rocky hill. Ahead lay the bridge—blocked by sheep. To the right, a thick woods sloped down to the river.

She looked back. The man on the hill was moving, descending at a trot. He spurred his horse and began to gallop toward them. Honor did not wait for the rest of the band to appear over the crest. She kicked her horse's flanks and lit out for the trees. The head start she and Owen had was slight, but she judged that their best hope was to lose themselves in the woods. Bent over her horse's neck she twisted her head to call to Owen. But Owen, apparently thinking only of following the road and assuming she would as well, was tearing for the bridge. Sheep were scattering before him in a frenzy of dust and bleating.

Honor galloped on alone toward the woods. A shower of stones spewed out behind her horse's feet. She heard the thunder of hooves pursuing her. She gripped a fistful of mane, and her legs squeezed the horse's sides. She broke into the first line of trees. Low branches scratched her face and hooked her skirt. She was forced to slow, though every nerve and muscle screamed for flight. Struggling to stifle her own sawing breath, she calmed the horse to a walk, then to a halt.

She listened. The thundering had stopped. And behind, through the tree trunks, she saw no movement. But the unmistakable rustle of underbrush told her that one man, at least, had followed her in. His horse snorted, and she knew that he was very close.

The urge to break out of the press of trees became overwhelming. She kicked her horse toward the blue sky glimmering through branches ahead. Soon she had broken free, and she was filled with relief to find that the woods opened onto a meadow. But fear squeezed again as she looked wildly around at the steep hills. They enclosed the meadow on three sides.

There was a crashing behind her. Without even looking back she plunged headlong into the middle of the meadow. At the foot of one of these hills, she told herself, there must be a path leading out. A cart track at least. She twisted to the left, but as the hill loomed and still she saw no route out of the meadow bowl she yanked the reins and veered to the right. Out of the corner of her eye she saw, with a flash of panic, how close her assailant was, his blue cloak snapping behind him.

A track! There, by a stand of poplars! But it lay even farther to the right, and she had to sharply wheel her horse around. She pulled too hard. She heard her horse's shocked wheeze as it stumbled beneath her. But she hung on, and righted the staggering animal, and was ready to gallop on to the poplars when she heard the other horse close behind her. A leather gauntlet scraped the back of her neck. It grappled her collar and wrenched her backwards and sideways, tearing her from the saddle. Her palms burned as the reins ripped through her grasp. She thudded painfully onto the grass on her side, the breath beaten from her.

She struggled to stand, but was too dizzy to get farther than to her knees. But she was aware that the horseman was wheeling in a circle back to her. Before she could turn she heard him, behind her, leap down from his mount. His gauntleted hands gripped the back of her pilgrim's habit and hauled her to her feet. With a violent tug he pulled her to him. The back of her head thumped against his chest. His leg snared hers at the knee, and the hilt of his sword bit into her hip. His arm shot around her waist and seized her opposite elbow, pinning both her arms to her sides. She heard him tear the gauntlet from his free hand with his teeth and spit it out. Slowly, he began a search of her body.

She squirmed. Deliberately, languidly even, his hand smoothed over her thighs, her hips, her belly. She gritted her teeth in silent rage knowing that a scream in this godforsaken spot would be useless, might even draw more of the villains. But if he attempted rape she was prepared to gouge with nails and teeth. If he would release her only an inch!

He grabbed the small purse hanging at her waist and jangled the coins. Abruptly, he abandoned it and continued to search up her rib cage. His hand moved between her breasts. It stopped when it reached the bulge of the hidden case. Quickly, he slipped his hand down inside the neck of her tunic. His fingertips brushed the skin of her breast. He clutched the case, lifted it out, and snapped it from its thong. Honor winced at the sting to her neck.

His leg uncoiled from hers. His arm withdrew. He swooped down to pick up his gauntlet, and then he stepped aside. For a moment Honor staggered at the sudden freedom. Then she whirled on him, nails raised to strike. But he was already striding away from her. She watched, dumbfounded. His back radiated satisfaction as he tossed the stolen prize in the air, caught it, and pocketed it inside the breast of his tunic. He whistled to his horse grazing across the meadow. As it trotted towards him he slung one edge of his cloak over his shoulder, and walked out to meet the horse. His easy, disdainful stride infuriated Honor.

And then she saw it. Recognized it in that sauntering walk: the unmistakable pigeon-toed inclination of the right foot. Richard Thornleigh. Her mind flashed associations: Anne Boleyn had prevented Thornleigh's maiming. And Anne Boleyn was wooing Cromwell to her side. Thornleigh must be Cromwell's agent!

"You!" she shouted. The word scythed across the drowsing meadow.

He turned. The edge of the cloak partially muffled his face. Furious, Honor ran at him and sprang up to tear it away. But he was quicker. His hands grappled her wrists, hard. She gasped. It was the first time he had inflicted pain, and she was suddenly aware of how useless her nails and teeth would be against his strength. As quickly as he had caught her, he let her go. His face was still half hidden, but as if to confirm her identification he settled his eyes, cobalt blue, on hers.

"Thornleigh," she spat, as if the name was an accusation. She scoffed at his brigand's cloak. "Not only late, but hiding like a coward."

His eyes narrowed at the insult. He slowly lowered the flap of material, revealing his face. And then he laughed.

She glared. "What amuses you, sir?"

"You. Accusing *me*. Intrigue and double-dealing are hardly the deeds of a proper little pilgrim."

"You were supposed to meet me at that vile inn yesterday at noon. That was the plan."

"So it was," he said casually.

"Well, what befell you?"

"Nothing worse than strong drink, so please don't fret for my health. The bout was not incapacitating." His smile was wry.

"Do you mean to tell me you missed the rendezvous . . . because you were *drinking*?"

"No. Because it was a stupid plan." He slapped the gauntlet against his thigh to remove bits of grass. "Was it yours?"

She fumed in silence.

He laughed again. "I see that it was."

"And so," she said witheringly, "afraid of the plan's slight uncertainties, you simply abandoned it."

He shrugged as if the topic bored him, then started again toward his horse.

She called to his back, taunting, "I had expected Master Cromwell to send a man who would not quake at a little risk."

He walked on.

"All right," she shouted, angry curiosity finally overcoming pride. "Why was it stupid?"

He stopped and turned. "Did you know the other people there?" he asked simply.

"What people?"

"At the inn."

"I have no idea. Travelers. Merchants. Who knows?"

"I know. One's a vintner from Madrid, name of Gomez. Sometimes trades at Greenwich Palace. Another's a Winchester clothier. And his wife traveling with him is the sister of Wolsey's chamberlain. All of you are bound for the same ship. Your meeting with me at the inn would have fueled their gossip for the whole journey home. You may be foolhardy enough to want Wolsey knowing enough against you to breathe down your neck from this day on, but I certainly don't. Dangerous. And stupid, because you should have known that that fleabag is the only hostel between Santiago and the coast. English travelers always stop there. As for the disguise, the landlady knows me. And I kept it up to pursue you because I saw no good reason to risk your manservant as a witness. As for maintaining it out here, that was for your own good. And mine. The less we know of one another the safer we both remain." He thrust his hand into the gauntlet and grunted in weary disgust. "Or would have, if you'd been able to suppress your heroics." He spread his hands as if to say that the litany of reasons should be sufficient. "Satisfied?"

Honor bit her lip, chastised. "Still," she said, "before you crow about your cleverness, sir, you'd best hope these same travelers you know so well do not recognize you, when you come aboard, as one of the brigands who terrorized them last night."

"I'll be returning on my own ship." His lips curled in a half smile. "No, my lady, thievery is not my usual occupation, though by your face I see you believe the calling suits me. But when I am not wrestling papal scrawls from foolish girls, I have a wool trading business to run. At a loss, at this point. And now, if you will excuse me, I have a cargo and crew to get safe home." He made a perfunctory bow and added, "pleasant though this chat has been."

He turned and covered the last few steps to his horse. As he caught up the dangling reins he glanced over at the trees. "Your old fellow will be thrashing through the woods by now, searching for you. Naturally, he'll assume you've been robbed." He threw her a frown of mistrust. "The mercenaries provided the perfect cover, so at least have the good sense to play along with the appearance of a robbery."

"Very neat, sir," she acknowledged tightly.

Ignoring her, he kicked his foot into the stirrup and swung himself easily up into the saddle. "Since I *did* rob you, you will be telling no less than the truth." He looked down at her. "Your fellow will probably assume that I have molested your body as well. That part of the story I leave to your discretion. Some ladies find such an experience lends piquancy to their past." He smiled. "Forgive me if I have not time today to oblige. Though," he added quietly as his eyes traveled over her body with obvious appreciation, "the temptation is sweet. I recall a kiss that augured well enough."

Honor could not subdue an indignant blush.

"But sadly," Thornleigh said in a tone of mock regret, "duty calls me away." He placed his hand on the prize within the breast of his tunic and lifted his chin with a long-suffering expression, like a knight leaving his lady for the battlefield. Then he snorted a laugh and lifted the reins.

Honor bristled. "Duty?" she said, glowering up at him. "As Cromwell's agent, or as the Lady Anne's lackey?"

His smile faded. He tugged at the reins and his horse danced back a few steps.

"Wait," she said. She walked up to the horse and took hold of the bridle, and asked, scowling with suspicion, "What will you do now with the brief?"

"Carry it to Cromwell, of course, and collect my gold. What else?"

"That's all this mission means to you? Gold?"

"It has its uses, mistress," he said dryly. "I own two ships that gobble gold."

She scoffed, "It's well, sir, that others have larger dreams than you. Dreams of the new order of justice this divorce may foster."

His face darkened. "Fantasies of justice are as easily shattered as conjured." Honor was surprised by the bitterness in his voice. "As for the Lady Anne," he added, his features resuming their lazy indifference, "I wish her well. She has bitten off a large mouthful. I only hope her cantankerous King proves digestible."

"But I'm sure you'll be on hand to comfort her should she require consolation. And will you pocket your cash for that task, too?"

His blue eyes flashed with quicksilver anger. Honor was glad. It eased some of her humiliation.

"You spout lofty words about justice, mistress," he said. "Pardon me if I question their worth when you come here to betray a noble mistress who trusts you with her life's blood."

Honor's heart was stung. She let go of the bridle.

Thornleigh snapped back the reins. The horse tossed its mane and Thornleigh wheeled away.

"Wait!" she cried. Halfway across the meadow he stopped, clearly annoyed.

"My horse has bolted," she called. "You can't leave me here alone."

"The victim and the bandit returning together? Even you can see the idiocy there. Your man will find you. Just be prepared for a bumpy ride behind him to the port."

His boots thwacked the horse's ribs, and as he bounded away he called back with a laugh, "Perfect penance for such a serious-faced pilgrim."

❧ 16 ❧

Blackfriars

"Henry, King of England, come into the court!"
Honor was so awed by the moment that her knees were trembling. She stood beside the Queen in the corridor outside the great hall of the Dominican monastery of Blackfriars. Inside, the court crier was calling in the King.

Nothing like it had ever been seen in England before—according to the French ambassador, Monsieur du Bellay, perhaps never in all Christendom: a reigning King and his Queen were obeying a summons to appear in a private court set up in their own land, to plead like common citizens. It seemed that King Henry, driven to distraction by Rome's interminable delays, did not care what admission he was making of the Pope's right to set up this legatine court in his kingdom. He cared only that the verdict was the one that for two years he had driven Wolsey and his frenzied agents at Rome to wring from the Pope. Divorce.

The crier called out, "Catherine, Queen of England, come into the court!"

Catherine stepped through the massive, arched doorway into the hall. "Here, my lords," came her clear reply.

Honor walked behind her. Once inside, they paused. The stone walls had been decked with costly tapestries, and sunlight from the high, lancet windows glinted off a million silver threads. On a dais at the far end of the hall the King sat on a throne under a gold canopy, shining in all his diamond and white satin magnificence. His dais had been placed to the right. Slightly lower sat the two judge-legates, Wolsey and Campeggio, splendid in their scarlet robes and tasseled, red Cardinal's hats. A little lower still, and to the left, was the Queen's chair. At its foot was ranged the whole bench of Bishops and, at the bar on either side, a rookery of lawyers.

Honor remained near the doorway. The eyes of a hundred and more faces followed the Queen as she swept across the stone floor. Bishop Fisher, her only real champion among her fearful councilors, watched her advance, his eagle eyes blazing loyalty from his skeletal face. The Queen took her chair. All eyes turned to the King.

The King smiled benignly at the Cardinal-judges, then leaned forward in his throne. Speaking with calmness and sincerity, he told the court of his great scruple. He said he believed that, in living with his brother's widow, a union expressly forbidden by Holy Scripture, he had been in mortal sin. He feared for his soul's salvation. He could bear it no longer. His conscience required judgment. Then, with a rustle of royal satin, he settled back and elegantly stretched out one shapely leg swathed in white silk and gartered with rubies.

There was a moment of stillness as men digested their monarch's speech, so pious, so reasonable. Bishops and lawyers turned to whisper to one another. Pages inched forward to slip documents into the hands of their masters. A recording clerk's pen scratched over parchment.

There was a flash of sunlight on blue velvet. The Queen had arisen, unbidden, breaking all proper procedure. With eyes fixed on the King she stepped forward, crossed around the judges, and mounted the steps to the King's canopied throne. She dropped to her knees at his feet and bowed her head. The court sucked in its breath. The King drew back, visibly shocked by her audacity, her proximity. His hands slid down the gilt arms of his throne and grasped the lion paws at the ends.

"My lord," the Queen said, "I beseech you, for the love that has been between us, let me have justice and right. Take of me some pity, for I am a friendless woman, a stranger, born out of your dominion. I kneel to you, the fount of justice within this realm, for I see around me no impartial tribunal. I do not recognize the authority of this court."

Her steady voice rang through the dumbfounded hall.

"I take all the world to witness that I have been a faithful, humble and obedient wife to Your Grace these twenty years, ever comfortable to your will and pleasure, being always well pleased and contented with all things wherein you took delight. And I take God to be my judge that when you had me first I was a pure maid, without touch of man. And whether this be truth or no, I put it to your conscience."

Not even a whisper could be heard in the stunned court. Honor, too, held her breath. The Queen had wagered all. She had confronted the King publicly with the one claim whose truth no living person but herself could swear to.

The King sat rigid, staring out squarely over the Queen's head. His hands still clenched the throne arms' lion paws and his bloodless fingertips seemed to form a second set of claws.

When he made no answer, the Queen spoke again. "My lord, I humbly beg you to spare me the extremity of this court."

Still, he said nothing. In the silence, the chirrups of birds fluted through the windows. "If you will not," the Queen concluded lifelessly, "to God alone do I commit my cause."

She stood, made a deep curtsy to her husband, and stepped off the dais. She did not give one look to the cardinal-judges or to the bishops, but moved slowly across the hall towards the open doors. Honor saw that her walk was as sedate as ever, but the light had gone out of her face, and all strength seemed to have ebbed from her body. Beneath the Queen's shoe an uneven flagstone tripped her and she stumbled. She quickly found her balance but stood still, as if unsure of which way to go, her hands fumbling oddly at her side. In a moment Honor was at her elbow, offering her arm and guiding her mistress away from the glaring mass of eyes. The court crier called the Queen back. But she walked on.

"Madame," Honor whispered as they neared the door, "you are called again."

"It matters not," Catherine said hollowly. "This is no impartial court for me. I will not tarry."

The crier called once more as the shadows of the doorway swallowed the Queen and her lady-in-waiting.

Weeks later the debate sputtered on all morning in Campeggio's packed, sweltering courtroom: had the young Prince Arthur, twenty-eight years ago, used the Spanish Princess Catherine as his wife or not? For hours the Cardinals and Bishops had probed old men's memories, dredging up their speculations about the Prince's sexual performance on that long-vanished bridal night. The groom had been fourteen, the bride fifteen.

Honor watched, disgusted, from the gallery. How this degrading spectacle dragged on! The judges had declared the Queen contumacious immediately after her extraordinary appeal on that first day, and the court sessions had slogged on for four more weeks without her. Now, as another ancient gentleman hobbled forward to give testimony pleasing to the King, Honor groaned. She pushed her way past the sweating bodies in the gallery and left the hall.

Outside Blackfriars she crossed the polluted Fleet Ditch over the bridge that connected the monastery precincts with Bridewell Palace. She went directly up to the Queen's private chamber. It lay in gloom, shrouded with heavy Flemish tapestries to shield its occupant from the noonday glare. Catherine sat alone in a corner, at work over her embroidery.

She looked up as Honor entered, and smiled. "What news, my dear?"

"Little to cheer you, my lady."

"Little cheer do I expect. Yet I must know it."

Honor took a chair near her. She picked up a spool of purple thread from the sewing basket and toyed with it. "Such a foolish business, Your Grace," she began. "One ancient lordling after another stepped forward with the most idiotic babble about your wedding night." She laughed, hoping to sound lighthearted, but the result was forced and spiritless. "Really, my lady, some told tales that stretched credulity so far, I wondered the speakers did not choke on their own nonsense."

"Let me hear it," Catherine said quietly.

Honor wound the purple thread. "First came the Marquis of Dorset. He said that following the marriage ceremony he had been among the lords and gentlemen who escorted Prince Arthur to your bedchamber, and he observed you lying in your bed under a coverlet. The Prince had a good complexion, 'ruddy and full of fire,' the Marquis said, and looked fit, he thought, to make any woman his wife. He finished by saying that he always *supposed* the Prince had used you as his wife, for—" she paused, recalling the courtroom sniggers, then went on softly—"for at the same age he had done so himself with his own bride."

Catherine was silent. She dipped her needle and tugged the thread.

"Truly, my lady," Honor urged, "the rest is all drivel to match this."

"Go on, my dear."

Honor looked down. "The Viscount Fitzwater gave testimony next. He recalled that the Prince had been wearing a nightshirt."

Catherine almost smiled. "Damning evidence, indeed. And to think that only last month I awarded Fitzwater's grandson the rights of forest to a manor I hold in Lancashire." She sighed. "Well, who was next?"

"Sir Charles Willoughby. He added something new. The morning after your bridal night, he said, the Prince had addressed him in front of several attendants, saying, 'Willoughby, bring me a cup of ale, for I have been all night in the midst of Spain!' "

Catherine shook her head with weary disgust.

"And that was all, Your Grace," Honor said, too quickly.

"What?" Catherine asked, amused. "No one else came forth to say he saw me actually in the same room with my husband? No more old men to swear that a worried boy's boast of manhood is absolute proof of a maiden's lost virginity?" Her smile faded into a look of infinite pity. "A frightened, sickly boy, who perished not five months later, too ill to withstand even the mild breezes of spring." She crossed herself. "May God, who knows the truth of this, rest Arthur's simple soul."

Honor wound her thread in silence.

"I can see that there is more, my dear," Catherine said, dipping the needle again. "Come, let me have it all."

This time, Honor could not even glance up. "Sir Andrew Talbot," she murmured. "He said his wife, now dead, had talked the next morning with her maid. The maid had spoken with a laundress. The laundress assured the maid, who told the wife . . . that the sheets of your bed were stained with blood."

Catherine's hand, poised with her needle, froze at the lie.

"And the last witness I heard," Honor said, rushing the words now, wanting it over and done with, "was Sir Joshua de Pencier. He testified that he saw Your Grace the next morning as you went to chapel. He said that your way of walking, your gait, was stiff. 'Like a woman who suffers in her nether regions,' he said, 'from having lain long with a man.'"

Catherine's hand flew to her lips as if to halt a retch, or perhaps a cry.

Impulsively, Honor bent forward to touch her mistress's trembling knee. Catherine clasped the hand, eyes closed. They sat together for several moments, Catherine walled up behind her humiliation, and Honor reaching out in pity.

And yet such chains hung about her own heart. Not chains of remorse. She saw the way too clearly for remorse; she did not repent what she had done. She believed, in the deepest, soundest part of herself, that she was fighting for right—that the strangling limbs of the Church must be amputated. Every day she shuddered for the unknown lives snuffed out by heretic hunters like Sir Thomas More. Bitterness shackled her heart. It was a rusty weight, and corrosive.

But every day, too, the sight of the Queen's private anguish forged a new link on a separate chain. Richard Thornleigh's accusation in Spain echoed: "You betray a noble mistress who trusts you with her life's blood."

The dissembling had been the worst. Apologizing on her knees to the Queen for the 'robbery' of the brief in Spain. Pretending to grieve at the theft, though the Queen assured her it could only have been arranged through Wolsey's treachery. Worst of all, accepting the Queen's tender kiss at having risked so much danger for her sake. It had been agony.

And then, the trial had carried on as if the brief had never existed. The Queen had sent Honor daily to monitor the court sessions, and neither side had even mentioned the brief. Honor knew that the King held the original document in secret under lock and key, and the Queen's lawyers, bullied by Wolsey into agreeing that the Queen's unattested copy was worthless, had dropped the matter. The Queen made no complaint. She declared again that she did not recognize the authority of the court and would obey only Rome. But Honor realized that the Queen had fallen back to this position in desperation after the one piece of evidence that might have saved her had been lost.

Trussed and loaded with these fetters, Honor could only hope that the verdict in the King's favor would arrive swiftly to release them both from the misery of waiting.

The afternoon crawled on.

Just before five o'clock, as Catherine was preparing to lay aside her sewing to go to Vespers in her chapel, the door swung open. Golden evening burst into the room, and the tapestries rippled in the gust of air. Margery stood in the doorway, out of breath and grinning.

"Madam!" she cried. "Great news! You are delivered!"

She rushed in and dropped to her knees. "Oh, madam, it is over! My lord Wolsey has thrown up his hands, admitting a quagmire of legal difficulties. And my lord Campeggio has declared the legates' court closed. Dismissed! Just this moment he said so. And my lord Wolsey, you know, must defer to him. Madam, Cardinal Campeggio has advoked the case to Rome! To *Rome*, just as you always demanded. Now, you will have justice. Is it not wonderful? You've won!"

Catherine's pale lips parted. She stared at Margery.

Margery laughed and clapped her hands. "Oh, I almost forgot the best part. When Cardinal Campeggio stood and made his dec-

laration there was a great commotion in the court, some men rushing out to spread the news and others rushing in to wonder at it,
and all men jabbering at once like a flock of nervous starlings. And
at that moment, my lord of Suffolk strode forward in a fume and
clapped his hand down on a table and shouted, 'By the Mass, I see
now that the old saw is true—that there was never legate nor cardinal that did good in England!' And at his words a great clamor
went up as some men huffed in agreement with him and others
puffed against him, and as I ran out to bring the news to you the
Bishops and lawyers and clerks were all shouting in confusion. Oh,
madam, I wish you had been there. Faith, you've never seen the
like!"

Catherine's hands slowly took up the embroidery once again.
The needle trembled in her fingers. "And my lord?" she said, her
voice a dry whisper, a thread.

Margery seemed unsure of what the Queen was asking. "Beg
pardon, my lady?"

Honor had hurried to the window at Margery's first words of victory, and had ripped aside a corner of the tapestry. Now she looked
out, seeing nothing. Her nails dug into the fabric as she struggled
to absorb the bitter news. The case advoked to Rome. More delay.
More endless wallowing in arguments by lawyers. More fires for
heretics while everyone waited. Perhaps for months. And the betrayal she had committed . . . all for nothing!

She turned and caught the Queen's stricken face. Compassion
flooded back, for she saw that the Queen was realizing her own
fatal miscalculation. This news did not mean that she had won; it
meant the King had lost. He had been slapped in the face in the
very act of bending his knee to the Pope. Whatever dying embers
of his love she had pitifully hoped might glow anew when all this
was behind them, Cardinal Campeggio had just stamped out. With
this fiat, the husband she adored was lost to her as surely as if he
had been struck dead.

Honor said to Margery, "Her Grace asks, how did the King respond?"

"Oh, truly, madam, I know not," Margery said blithely. "His
Grace was not there to hear. He had been watching earlier, but he

left the hall some two hours ago. Went to Greenwich, I understand, to arrange a masque for the Lady . . ." She checked herself before finishing the name.

But Honor saw the blood that suddenly stained the embroidery below the Queen's needle. She saw the tears escape the lowered eyelashes—the first tears she had ever seen this indomitable woman shed. The red stain bled in a widening circle, and Honor knew that the pricked finger weeping out that drop of the Queen's blood only hinted at the gash in her heart.

Henry, with Anne at his side, was singing lustily in the minstrels' gallery of the great hall at Greenwich—his musicians were rehearsing one of his own compositions for the evening's masque—when the news from Blackfriars arrived. The sheet of music fluttered from his hand.

His voice blasted through the hall. "Will no one rid me of this barren crone!"

The musicians' rebecs and shalms wheezed out a decaying spiral of sound. The smiles on the faces of the gentlemen around the King evaporated.

"Summoned as a witness to Rome?" Henry bellowed. "I'll see hell freeze over first!"

Thomas Cromwell, who had rowed from Blackfriars with the messenger, stood in the background, hands clasped over his stomach, waiting for the storm to spend itself.

Anne tugged at Henry's sleeve, trying to draw him out of the gallery. Her face was white, but she forced down her own rage. "Come, my lord," she whispered. "This is no fit place for a king to consider such matters. Look, here is good Master Cromwell ready to offer you council. Come away, my lord!" With glaring eyes she burned a path through the gentlemen and musicians and coaxed the King out of the gallery.

In his private chamber Henry prowled in front of the cold hearth, his wrath concentrated and ferocious. "Summoned! Like some sniveling shoemaker. To grovel before a foreign court. Me, a sovereign King anointed with holy oil!"

Anne stood thinking, silent and grave. Cromwell, by the door, never let his eyes stray from the King. "Obviously, Your Grace," he said, his voice deferential but calm, "it would be unwise to plead at Rome."

"Unwise? It would be suicide! The Pope licks Charles's boots! We know what the outcome of *that* hearing would be!" His fist smashed down on the mantel. "Just as we should have known the outcome of this farcical trial. All these grinding months and years, for failure! Wolsey should have known."

Anne's voice reached him. "You have been poorly served by your chancellor, my lord."

Henry's battered pride snatched at the suggestion. "So I have! I have been thwarted. By God's wounds, Wolsey will pay for fouling me with this shame."

Cromwell waited through a moment of ominous silence. Then, quietly, he ventured to the King's back, "Do you mean, then, to dismiss the Cardinal, Your Grace?"

Henry whirled around. "I mean to have his heart out!"

From the corridor beyond the closed doors came the muffled sound of a dog barking.

"In that case," Cromwell said evenly, "you will need a new Lord Chancellor."

Henry appeared to ignore him. Controlled now that he had a target for his rancor he sauntered across to Anne, though he continued to speak to Cromwell. "Why?" he asked caustically. "Do you imagine I am so fond of your council that you begin to sniff at the post for yourself? Is that it, Master Woolcarder?"

Cromwell did not bristle at this epithet the King enjoyed insulting him with. It had once been the truth; before he had taught himself the law he had been a merchant trading in woolen cloth. "Far from it, Your Grace," he answered. "But I am naturally concerned for the good government of your realm. Any successor to the post of Lord Chancellor must be a man of outstanding ability."

"Of *loyalty*," Henry said, turning to him. "I'll have no more self-serving parasites like Wolsey. All he ever looked to was his own magnificence."

"Indeed, Your Grace," Cromwell murmured. His mind was casting out a net over the likely candidates, quickly evaluating their potential usefulness to himself. "Able and loyal the man must be," he agreed, knowing that Wolsey had resoundingly been both. "My lord Bishop of Winchester is a most able man," he said, testing the water.

"No more priests. Must I be forever entangled with these Church puppets?"

"No, indeed, Your Grace. It is just that the post has customarily been held by a man of the Church."

"Then I'll change custom. I warrant I can be as well served by an honest layman. A man with no loyalties to foreign powers to thwart me."

"My lord Duke of Suffolk—"

"Would never be stomached by Norfolk," Henry said testily. "And the Duke of Norfolk, likewise, would be contested by Suffolk. No, no, forget both Brandon and Howard. They are like two bulldogs eyeing a bone that lies between them. Each would rather go hungry than let the other have it."

At his quip Anne let out a sharp, coarse laugh. It startled Henry, and he looked back at her with something like a frown. But her bright eyes remained smiling steadily into his as if inviting him to climb out onto the limb of defiance with her and mock the world below. Excited by her spirit he laughed too. He took her hand in his.

She brushed her lips over the back of his hand, then held it against her cheek. "My lord," she said, "you speak of foreign powers, but it is the foreign Church itself which thwarts you. Do without it, as your honor bids. You are a sovereign King."

Henry was staring at her mouth. "Sovereign," he said thoughtfully, as if appreciating the weight, the power, of the word for the first time. "Aye, so I am," he murmured. "Sovereign in my empire." He looked at Cromwell.

Cromwell did not miss the flame of triumph that glinted in the King's eyes. A spark of it seemed to arc through the air between them, like a brush fire jumping. It kindled an idea in Cromwell. Now, he saw the way ahead.

* * *

Two months later, on a drizzly day in early October, Honor burst into Cromwell's private chamber at Greenwich. Seated at his desk, he was just sending away a clerk with a sheaf of letters.

Honor threw off the hood of her cloak. "Is it true?" She held the back of a chair to keep her fury in check. "Sir Thomas as Lord Chancellor?"

"Not official yet," Cromwell said, laying down his pen, "but he should be sworn in towards the end of the month. Certainly by All Saints' Day. I made the recommendation myself."

"But why? How could you?"

"Calm yourself, Mistress Larke. Please, sit down. You look quite ill."

"Sick at heart, sir, at this news!" she said fiercely. "And sick to think I trusted you!"

"Mistress," he said with sudden coldness, "in politics one does not grab at what one wants like a peasant snatching sausages at a wedding feast. Now sit down, and I'll explain."

"Explain why you have raised that monster, that enemy of justice, to the highest judicial post in the land? Yes do, sir, if you can."

"Will you sit?" he snapped.

"No!"

He took in a deep, angry breath and held it a moment, but as it left his body it became a sigh of resignation, and the sigh ended in a chuckle. "You cannot be faulted on tenacity, mistress. And in politics that, too, is necessary."

She glared at him. "Well?"

"Well. Cardinal Wolsey, as you know, is in disgrace. He has already signed over his lands and palaces to the King in the hope of saving his neck."

Honor could not suppress a shiver. "You are quick to forget your former master, sir, now that the King cannot do without you."

"Are we going to speak of former loyalties or of Sir Thomas?" His small eyes gleamed at her like wet stones. "Or are they, in your case, the same thing?"

Honor smarted at the rebuke. "Forgive me," she said tightly. "Go on."

Cromwell leaned back in his chair and laced his fingers over his stomach. "The King demanded a laymen as his new Lord Chancellor. I suggested Sir Thomas because I believe he is the right choice. All the world knows him for a brilliant and honest judge, not puffed up by arrogance or ambition. His Grace was immediately taken with the suggestion of More. 'A man who's fonder of his family than of riches and high place,' he agreed. A man, he said, 'he was proud to call his friend.' The Lady Anne, by the way, was present at this conversation, and she asked whether so weighty a post could be entrusted to a man who had never spoken a word in favor of the divorce. 'He has not spoken a word against it, either,' said the King. 'Even in that he has shown his loyalty, for he swore to me he never would cross me.' Now that comment . . ."

"The confounded divorce!" Honor cried. "Is that all anyone can think of? What about the people Sir Thomas will burn?"

"It is the Church that condemns heretics. You know that."

"It is the state that burns them."

"Not if the Church is reformed and changes its rules. You had that goal clearly in mind when you summoned me to the Trident Inn six months ago. Keep to your original agenda, Mistress Larke. It is a sound one. New Queen, new Church. The divorce is the key. You want it. I want it. Because, most importantly, the King wants it. And I can get it for him."

"How?" she scoffed. "Wolsey could not. And since the adjournment, the case now rests in Rome."

"But the King's power rests here. King and Parliament are the forces at home. And Parliament convenes after All Saints' Day."

She threw up her hands. "Good Lord, what does Parliament have to do with this?"

He chuckled again. "His Grace said the same thing. Actually, when I specified that the Commons should be our target, his response was: 'What do I want with those blockheads?' "

To Honor none of this made sense. Exasperated, she leaned across the desk. "All I know is that Sir Thomas . . ."

"Forget Sir Thomas," Cromwell said. "His proven deference to authority is a bonus for us now. The point is he will not meddle, and that leaves me free to go to work." He leaned toward her with a cool, confident smile. "Have patience, Mistress Larke. Tenacity is necessary in this battle, yes, but if you are to see it through without tearing yourself apart you must develop patience. And trust me. Though the road ahead appears foggy, we are on track."

With a heaviness in the pit of her stomach, Honor straightened. Trust him? Have patience? She knew she had no choice.

The road into Cambridge was thick with winter mud. The wheels of the tanner's cart creaked over the sloppy ruts. Edward Sydenham nervously flicked the reins from the driver's seat. But the horse merely kept on at the same plodding pace it had maintained from London.

It was the supper hour in Cambridge, and getting dark. Most people were indoors. Chilly fog filled the quiet streets as if claiming a squatter's authority to the space the citizens had abandoned.

Edward looked at his two companions on the seat beside him, and tried to stifle his anxiety. Neither his mother nor Brother Frish seemed worried. They were engrossed in a private, murmured conversation. Edward looked past the back of Frish's head and watched the movements of his mother's thin mouth. She was discussing strategy, again. Again, only with Frish. Frish, the Great Man.

Frish was the reason for this trip. He, and the forbidden Antwerp books stacked under hides in the cart behind them: Tyndale's *Parable of the Wicked Mammon*, and Frish's own treatise against the doctrine of purgatory. They were bringing Frish to a meeting of the Cambridge Brethren. After that, he'd stay on to organize them. A sermon from him tonight, and distribution of the books, would go a long way towards heartening the dispirited Brethren here, Bridget Sydenham had decreed. And ever since her husband's burning, no one in their circle questioned Bridget Sydenham's decisions.

Edward watched the two conferring so earnestly. How could they remain calm? Under the new Chancellor's crackdown, scores of people were being arrested all over the country. But then, he thought with a touch of envy, their tasks here were important, and clear-cut. His mother was essential as the contact; her job was to introduce the preacher. The preacher's job was to inspire. *And me?* Edward wondered bitterly. Well, someone has to unload the books.

He caught his mother's sharp glance back at him.

"Watch where you're going, Edward." She frowned at the houses looming out of the fog. "Don't take a wrong turning. We're late as it is."

"Yes, Mother." Edward's head snapped back to his duty. Mustn't be late delivering the Great Man.

Edward saw the draper's bay window emerging from the mist, and said, "Master Price's is just up ahead, Mother." The house hadn't been difficult to find. He'd been there once before, helping his father. He wanted to point that out to his mother, but she was busy with Frish, tugging tight the hood around his face to mask him. Edward said nothing.

He stopped the horse in front of the draper's house. He glanced furtively up and down the foggy street, but the few pedestrians, intent on making their way home for supper, ignored the arrivals.

Bridget Sydenham climbed down. Frish followed her. "Keep an eye out, Edward," Bridget ordered. "I'll find where Master Price wants his load delivered. There's likely a back entrance."

Edward watched his mother and the preacher walk toward the draper's front door. Then the fog swallowed them.

He waited in the street. The gloomy mist closed in around him, chill and damp. He shivered and hugged himself, listening. In an alley someone was sawing wood. A baby bawled. Nearby, a dog's teeth clicked over a bone. He hated being alone with the books. He hoped Price would send out a man or two to help unload; the faster it was done, the sooner he and his mother could be on their way again.

The draper's door slammed. Edward stiffened. In a moment his mother was standing beside him—and with no one to help unload, he noticed.

"Master Price is jumpy," Bridget said in a stern whisper. "With the meeting going on, he refuses to have these goods on the premises." Edward recognized the irritation in her voice; his mother, he well knew, had no patience with cowardice. "The goods are to be taken to his storeroom around the block," she said, showing a padlock key.

"Dangerous for us," Edward growled. Instantly, he regretted this display of his anxiety, for his mother, scowling, climbed up onto the seat. Edward made no protest, knowing it would be futile, but his cheeks burned with humiliation: she didn't even trust him to manage the delivery. She motioned to him to take up the reins. "Go now."

Edward drove the cart around the corner, then into a mucky lane. He stopped at the storeroom doors and climbed down. Bridget unlocked the doors. "I'll stand watch," she said. "Be quick about this now." She marched back to the lane entrance, not even bothering to lift her skirt in the mud, and stopped at the corner as sentry.

Edward yanked off the hides that covered the books. After a quarter-hour of hauling out heavy armloads, squelching through the mud into the storeroom, and stacking the books inside, he was sweating. Grunting under the last load, he was halfway to the doors and raising his shoulder to swipe away the sweat that prickled his upper lip, when he heard his mother come running. He whirled around to face her. His foot slid in the muck. He lost his balance and fell, and the whole armload—twenty-odd books—tumbled around him.

Panting, Bridget reached the cart. Edward kicked aside a book and scrambled to his feet in dread. "What is it?"

"The Chancellor's men, I fear," Bridget whispered, grabbing the edge of the cart seat to climb up.

Edward froze. "They're coming here?"

"Coming down Poultry Street. Maybe heading for here. Or maybe for Price's house. That's worse."

Her resolution to flee energized Edward. He lunged for the cart to join her.

But Bridget held up her hand to stop him. "No. You've got to clear this evidence away. For Price's sake. For all our sakes!" She snatched up the reins.

Edward's mouth fell open. "You're leaving me?"

"I must reach Brother Frish before they do. Don't you see? We can't risk losing him!"

"But, Mother . . ."

"Finish here, Edward," she commanded. "Then run to the crossroads past the bridge. We'll pick you up there in the cart. Wait for us under the bridge."

She snapped the reins. The horse jolted into motion. The cart joggled up the lane, turned the corner, and was gone.

Edward swallowed. The metallic taste of fear was as bitter as his humiliation. Damn the preacher! Frantically, he began to scoop up the slimy books. But he was shaking so much that as quickly as he clutched them to his chest they slipped away like thrashing fish.

He heard a shout. He turned to face the lane entrance. A lantern swung into view and halted. It lighted the fog into a murky halo around the fist that held it. A second lantern joined the first one. Then another. And another.

Edward flung the last few books into the muck. He turned and ran. He didn't know where the lane led. He couldn't see. The fog was too thick. He heard his attackers' feet pounding behind him. He ran on, skidding in the mud. The lane narrowed. A wall of boards emerged dead ahead. Buildings rose on either side. There was no way out. Oh, God, to be trapped . . . !

He glanced behind him. Voices were shouting. The crowd of lanterns was bobbing closer, closer . . .

Edward turned to the boards. "Mother!" he cried. With arms raised and fingers clawing the air, he flung himself at the wall.

Snow was falling in London. Bridget Sydenham, sitting on the edge of her grandchildren's bed, glanced at the flakes drifting down outside the window. She looked back at little Jane and smoothed the dark curls away from the child's forehead. The boy beside Jane was already dreaming, eyes closed. These were the children of Bridget's older son.

"Grandmama," the girl asked sleepily, "must we always add Uncle Edward to our prayers? How long will the evil men keep him in jail?"

Bridget tried not to flinch as she looked into the girl's eyes. Edward had failed. Master Price was in prison and several others of the Cambridge Brethren too. All because of Edward. But she told herself daily that it must be God's plan. After all, God had allowed Brother Frish to reach the cart and return with her safely to London. And why? Because Brother Frish was essential to the cause. Could God also have a great task in store for her younger son, even if she could not see it? A glorious task? Every day, she prayed that it was so. And prayed that Edward would be able to meet it with courage. Just as dear Humphrey had.

"Yes, child, keep praying," Bridget answered. "God wants you to be very proud of your Uncle Edward." She looked out at the cold white flakes descending, straight and silent. "He is suffering in the name of the Lord."

❧ 17 ❧

The Devil's Hive

Hail clattered against the window like a handful of stones flung by a furious god. Honor put down her sewing and walked past the cradle where Cecily was tucking in her latest child, a daughter. At the window Honor hugged herself against the cold draft that whined in around the panes. She looked down at the gravel path that led from the house to More's wharf. Beyond, the swollen Thames heaved. No one was out in this weather. The path and the lawns lay deserted, bearing their backs to March's punishment.

"Sir Thomas cannot be traveling on the river this morning," Honor murmured. Both she and Cecily had been speaking in low voices, for the baby had just fallen asleep, but this remark came more softly still, and Honor knew she was trying to convince herself. She made her rare visits to Cecily only when she was certain Sir Thomas was far from home. Today, he was at Hampton Court.

"Gracious, no," Cecily whispered, tucking a shawl around the baby's feet. "He'd catch his death out in that bluster. You were lucky to make it here before it began." She beckoned Honor out of the room, a finger at her lips. Honor closed the door gently behind them. As she followed Cecily down the stairs she coughed. Cecily looked over her shoulder in alarm.

"You've had that cough since Candlemas, Honor." She shook

her head. "It's those drafty old chambers at Richmond, isn't it? I'm sure you're not given enough wood for fires. Come into the kitchen and I'll give you some Angel's Cup. My own recipe. Marigold and sowthistle in warmed ale with a pinch of white ginger. It did wonders for Lady Alice's hoarse throat."

They stepped into the hall and Cecily linked her arm in Honor's. "And I'm sure you've lost weight, dear, since I saw you last. Doesn't the Queen feed you? Though," she added quickly, "it suits you, to be sure." She laughed at herself. "I swear it's God's nudge at me to forestall vanity that I, who have everything a woman could want, look more like a pudding after each babe, while you shed flesh in that chill, lonely place, yet look more lovely every day." She glanced longingly at Honor's waist and sighed. "It's lucky I set little store by such things."

They were passing through the hall. At the far end, near the screened passage, Matthew was sweeping the flagstones with a rush broom. At the hearth two of More's grandsons were playing with chestnuts in front of a low fire. The boys' spaniel scrabbled across the floor to greet Honor. She crouched to pet it and closed her eyes as it licked her cheek.

"Matthew," Cecily called, "the fire here is dying and we're out of logs. Fetch some, would you?"

"Aye," Matthew murmured, and started toward the kitchen door.

"No, not from the kitchen," Cecily said. "That fellow's brought us green wood again. Get some from the malthouse store. It's seasoned." Matthew nodded and ambled out into the passage that led to the front door.

"Oh, while I think of it," Cecily continued to Honor, "I know I've given you the package of comfits and marchpane cakes for Her Grace, but don't let me forget to wrap some of last night's leg of venison, too, for yourself and her."

Honor laughed as she fondled the spaniel. "Her Grace may be out of the King's favor, Cecily, but he doesn't *starve* her. And I'm sorry to dispel your fantasy of me wasting away in her service, but we sup on beef and beer every evening, and sit before a fire hot enough to satisfy even you of my comfort."

The front door slammed and she jumped up. *Be calm*, she told herself, *it's only Matthew going out.* She bent again to the dog.

"Still," Cecily said, "the court is an unhealthy place these days." She picked up a boy's muddy shoe. "Dangerous, too. Look at poor Cardinal Wolsey. A warrant for treason out against him by order of the King. All his wealth forfeited. Then"—she snapped her fingers—"dead before they could bring him to the Tower."

"But I am no longer at court," Honor reminded her.

"No, and thank goodness for that," Cecily said with a vehemence that almost balanced the erratic logic. "But beef suppers or no, I hear it's not merry in the Queen's service, either, what with the King ordering even more of her ladies away. Not many of you left, are there?"

Honor shook her head sadly as she scratched the dog's ears. "Only a handful. Most of those who weren't sent packing by the King have deserted. Even Margery Napier finally gave in to the pleas of her family and left. Married Lord Sandys's son."

"That simpleton?" Cecily grimaced. "Ah, well," she sighed, "we all do what we must. But you, Honor, you're like a rock. Running and fetching for Her Grace. Straining your eyes to read to her day and night. Never stirring from her side."

Honor was about to dispute this hyperbolic picture of devotion.

"Yes," Cecily insisted, "I think your loyalty's quite wonderful. And I hope Her Grace appreciates it. Your sacrifice, I mean. You could have married two or three Earls' sons by now."

"I believe the Church still frowns on bigamy," Honor said with a smile.

Cecily laughed. "Oh, you know what I mean. It's been well over a year since the Blackfriars trial and you've stuck by the Queen through thick and thin—mostly thin—when you could have been well settled long before this. So, all I'm saying is, I hope she's grateful."

Honor asked herself, not for the first time, why *did* she work so hard to make the Queen comfortable? A penance for her betrayal?

Cecily came close and stroked Honor's cheek. "Don't think me a busybody, dear, but I worry about you. I believe this last twelve-month has been more of an ordeal for you than you let on. There's a sadness in your face I never used to see. And I cannot help thinking that marriage and motherhood are what's missing from your life. Goodness, most women of twenty have a husband snoring beside them and children scampering underfoot. But you spend your days in solitude with a grieving queen. It's not natural. It's not healthy."

Honor stood. She clasped her friend's hand and squeezed it affectionately. "Dear Cecily," she smiled. "Don't fret for my sake. I'm alright."

"Well, you must marry eventually," Cecily said matter-of-factly. "Woman's destiny, you know. You can't wait on the Queen forever." She started toward the kitchen door. "I'll just get that Angel's Cup for your cough." She disappeared into the kitchen.

Honor sighed. The dog rolled on its back, shamelessly begging more attention. Honor crouched again and stroked its warm belly. Its tongue lolled in voluptuous bliss. Was Cecily right? Honor wondered. Was marriage all she was good for? Was she useless, except as a channel through which her father's property could pass to a husband? Goodness knew she'd been useless enough up to now. The only thing her adventure in Spain had accomplished was to bring Cromwell what he wanted, the King's confidence. Cromwell said to have patience, but—curse his patronizing—she didn't understand what he was up to, and there was still no change in sight. She'd betrayed the Queen, and look at the results: Cromwell had advanced, Sir Thomas had risen to the chancellorship, and her grand scheme for a new order had crumbled to dust. What a botch she'd made. As the boys at the hearth burst into private laughter over their game, she looked over at them and could not help envying them their uncomplicated lives.

The door slammed again. Honor straightened and the spaniel bounded to its feet to keep near her, yapping and jumping up to paw her skirt. The boys called out to restrain it. Over the noise Honor hopped backwards, laughing, to get clear of the dog, and bumped into the arms of Sir Thomas.

"Steady, child," he said with a smile. "I'm mud from head to foot." From behind, he gently grasped her shoulders to hold her away from him.

She broke his grip and whirled around.

Three men walked in after More. All were soaked and their boots were caked with mud. Cuthbert Tunstall, Bishop of London, was wrapped in a drenched cloak. He headed straight for the fire, shaking water from his wide-brimmed hat. More's bailiff, Holt, came next with a chain in his hand. The third man was attached to the chain. He shuffled in, his wrists and ankles manacled. He and Holt stopped beside More.

Honor stared at the prisoner. She did not know him. He was a tall, reedy man, almost bald. His lips were purple from the cold. He wore no hat, no cloak, only thin wool breeches, a shirt plastered to his shivering skin, and a dripping leather jerkin. The sight of the jerkin unleashed a memory of Ralph that cut her heart.

"It's good to see you, child," More said peeling off his hat, "but where is everyone?" He nodded at the Bishop. "Our guest needs warm wine and dry clothing. Where's Lady Alice?"

Honor felt her throat tighten. She could not speak. In the silence, the Bishop glanced around at her from the fire. The spaniel sniffed the prisoner's legs.

Cecily burst out of the kitchen wiping her hands on a towel. "Father! My lord Bishop!" She bobbed a surprised curtsy. "Why, you're soaked to the skin! Oh, I'm so sorry no one was here to greet you. Lady Alice is stocking wine in the cellar with the vintner, and John and Anne are visiting Meg, and Elizabeth . . . oh dear, we simply didn't expect you."

"I dare say," More laughed, wriggling out of his cloak. "I didn't expect to *make* it here. You've never seen the roads from Hampton so thick with muck. Bishop Tunstall's horse dug in under shelter of a tree and for ten minutes refused to budge."

"French nag," Tunstall grumbled. "A gift from the Bishop of Orleans. I should have known."

"Well," More laughed, "Cecily will make you comfortable with a thick slice of English beef, eh?" He nodded to his bailiff. "Lock the prisoner away, Holt. Then get yourself dry and warm."

Holt shoved the prisoner toward the far end of the passage. His chains clanked on the flagstones. The boys, on their knees at the hearth, craned their necks, enthralled by the misery of the departing felon.

More frowned at the low fire. "Cuthbert, this won't do. Get you away to the hearth in the kitchen. And, Cecily, find our guest some dry clothes." He handed her his own wet things and took the towel from her hands. "And send in Matthew to stoke this poor excuse of a blaze."

"Yes, Father. He's just gone to fetch wood." Cecily gestured for the Bishop to follow her. "Do be careful, my lord, don't slip on that wet patch." They passed into the kitchen.

"I'll help . . ." Honor blurted, hurrying to follow.

"Stay, child," More said to stop her. "A word with you, first."

He stepped up to the hearth and smiled as his grandsons stood and bowed to him, then waved them on to return to their game. He faced the fire and rubbed the towel through his hair. "How goes it with Her Grace?" he asked over his shoulder.

"As well as can be expected," Honor said.

"And with you?" he asked, turning.

She was silent.

"How are you, child?" His voice was gentle, and warm with concern. "We never see you anymore."

"You are mightily busy in your new office, sir."

She could not hide the rancor in her voice, but he seemed not to notice it and only nodded wearily, agreeing. He shoved the towel onto the mantel and stared into the fire and slowly rubbed his hands together. She watched his back. The dark hair that hung just over his ears was still glossily wet, camouflaging the streaks of silver she knew to be there, and giving a false sheen of youth.

"This prisoner," she ventured carefully, keeping her voice disinterested. "What is his crime?"

"Selling illegal tracts. He's from Coventry. Came to visit his sister in Hampton and tried to peddle his stuff to the villagers." His sigh was heavy with fatigue. "Another cursed bookseller."

Honor had to force her eyes down lest he turn and catch on her face the contempt she could not mask, contempt for his rule by intimidation. Immediately upon taking office as Lord Chancellor he had declared publicly that the extermination of heresy would be his prime policy, and had issued two proclamations that clamped in place severe press censorship. The first commanded all civic authorities to identify persons possessing proscribed books, and they were to present the suspects not to a Bishop, as before, but to the Royal Council at Westminster. That was an innovation. Further, no scriptural books were to be printed in England unless examined by a Bishop, and all books approved were to include the name of the printer.

His second proclamation was a law and order measure for 're-sisting and withstanding heresy.' It denounced Lutheranism as sedition, commanded all officers—from peers to village constables—to be vigilant against heterodox sermons, and outlawed all unlicensed preaching.

Finally, he personally compiled an index of prohibited books and empowered himself to enforce it in Star Chamber by virtue of the Council's inherent, but seldom used, powers to punish breaches of proclamations. The proclamations had been followed by a bonfire of books at Paul's Cross.

Honor hated to think of this corruption of Star Chamber, the special court Wolsey had set up to bring quick justice to petitioners—the very court in which Sir Thomas had so eloquently defended her from Tyrell and Bastwick. Now, booksellers and pamphleteers were paraded under its star-gilded ceiling before the new Lord Chancellor who ordered them to do public penance, then threw them into the Fleet prison.

More turned around from the fire. "What is your interest in this bookseller?" A slight smile curved his lips. "Not another former servant lost to the Devil, I hope." Clearly, she saw, he meant the jibe to be droll. It could not have stung her more.

"I am interested in all men who suffer, as Christ bade us," she answered, head high.

More nodded, smiling. "You rebuke me, child. Indeed, I deserve rebuke if I act out of any motive other than Christian concern. But truly, these wretches are not worth your pity. They have cast themselves out of the community of Christian men. Their hearts are stone. They are lost. Unless we can prod them to recant. As, in the fire, some do."

"And then they are saved?"

"But of course," he said gently, as if reassuring a child that all was well. "Their souls may then go to God." He stepped up to her and lowered his voice. "I'll share some news with you, although it is not official yet. I have just received the results of a special inquiry into the death of one Friar Heywood, burned at Smithfield some time ago. People were whispering that Heywood did not recant at the end, but I now have proof that he did. You see? Documented proof of the good effects of punishment by fire. Besides protecting ignorant folk who might have been infected by his poison, the fire brought Heywood himself to die in the bosom of the Church. His soul was saved."

Honor stared. It was not so! Heywood was the young friar who had burned beside Ralph. But he had made no such abjuration at the stake. She remembered clearly. He had said only, "I trust I am not separate from the Church; I know that I am closer to God." That was all. She was sure of it. How could she forget one word, one gesture, of that horrible day? The awful realization flooded that, to prove a point, Sir Thomas was using the law to subvert the truth. Sir Thomas More was lying.

"A special inquiry?" she asked steadily. "Isn't that . . . irregular?"

His enthusiasm evaporated. "Well . . . yes. No bill of complaint or information was filed in proper form. I am sorry for that." He pulled his soggy collar away from his neck, obviously uneasy at her question. "I must change these wet clothes," he muttered. "But you see, the necessity of the situation forced me to act *ex officio*, using my authority . . . contrary to Star Chamber's due process . . ."

She looked away, disgusted.

He shook his head with a sigh. "It is dreadful, this epidemic of heresy. The Bishop and I can barely keep up with it. And there are so many tragic"—he seemed to be searching for the right words, aware of the pitfalls the wrong ones might create—"so many unforeseen consequences of its poison. Look at you and me. We have become strangers. Ever since . . . that day you asked about your former servant. Pym, wasn't that his name?"

Again she had to look down, unwilling to trust her tongue if their eyes should meet. But she felt him watching her.

"Child, I have missed your company."

She heard his heart reaching out to her in his voice, so tender, so full of good will. She had to fight to maintain a shield against its seduction as she looked up at him.

"You've grown thin," he said suddenly. Then, at her continuing silence, he added with a wink, "Does the Queen not feed you?"

Still she did not speak.

"I understand," he said. "I know your lot with your royal mistress is a hard one. You endure it with dignity."

Honor could bear his scrutiny, his presence, no longer. "Sir, if there is nothing else, I must be gone."

"So soon? I hoped we might talk . . . once I've changed . . ."

"Her Grace expects me."

"Even in this weather?"

She made no answer.

"Well, of course," he stammered, "if you must go . . ."

She curtsied with stiff politeness and hurried out of the hall.

She had just turned into the screened passage leading to the front door and was about to leave when Holt slipped in at the opposite end, wet from having locked up the bookseller. "All safe, your Lordship," he called into the hall.

More answered from around the corner, "Good."

Holt threw Honor a leering smile that made her shiver. He jangled his ring of keys. "Safe and sound and tucked up like a sleeping babe, eh, Mistress Honor?" He touched his sodden hat to her, then ambled into the hall to join More.

Honor lifted the front door latch to go. She heard More say to Holt, "I'll try for information this evening."

She stayed her hand.

"Got it already, your Lordship," Holt said proudly.

"Did you?" More sounded eager.

"I put the question to him in a manner so as to catch his undivided attention, you might say. The answer slipped out of him, smooth as a priest's prick from a whore's hole." He cleared his throat. "Beg pardon, your Lordship. I'm that pleased with the result, I'm forgetting your Lordship's tender ears."

"Forgiven," More grunted. "If you've really found out where we can track down Frish."

"That I did, your Lordship. Told me he was on his way to see Frish when we nabbed him. And to a house you'll be familiar with. Coleman Street again."

"The Devil's hive," More said. "Alright, get a few of your men together, and go."

"It'll take some time to harness the dogs, Your Worship. And, with the rain . . ."

"The rain is letting up, Master Holt. And there's five shillings for you if you bring Frish back here by nightfall."

"Consider it done!"

The front door slammed. More and Holt looked around from the hearth, startled by the violence of the sound.

She did not go upriver to Richmond. She went downriver to the city. She hurried north on Old Jewry, then north again up Coleman Street. The rain had stopped by the time she stood on the doorstep of Humphrey Sydenham's house. She banged a fist on the door and waited under the dripping eaves.

The courtyard was deserted. In front of the empty stable a cart robbed of three wheels sat lopsided and lame. It had been stripped for parts, and bits of wood and iron lay scattered around the skeleton, abandoned to rot and rust.

The front door creaked open. Expecting to see the red-haired Edward as before, Honor had to lower her gaze to a girl's small white face smudged with soot and framed by a tumble of dark curls. The child clung with both hands to the latch above her head. On the stone flags her feet were bare.

"I've come to see the mistress," Honor said gently.

The child only stared suspiciously, as if ready to bolt.

Honor drew from her pocket the package of honey comfits Cecily had given her for the Queen. The child's eyes widened at the gold ribbon, and as she watched Honor unwrap the silk her small

mouth opened in wonderment. Honor stretched out her hand, offering the candies. The child's grimy fingers instantly grabbed one
and popped it into her mouth. She beamed up, full of trust now,
and tugged Honor's sleeve. "I'll show you," she said.

Honor followed her to the great hall. The once fine room looked
like a soldier's encampment. Two long tables were upended and
shoved like blockades against the far doors. Ten or twelve straw
pallets lay in corners. On one, under a nest of dirty blankets, someone lay coughing. Heaps of clothing—more rags than clothes—
were ranged along the wall under the high windows. Beside the
hearth, jagged lengths of rich oak paneling lay in stacks, apparently to be used for fuel. Honor was shocked by the squalor. A
huge kettle was slung over the fire, and there a woman was bent,
stirring a ladle through a mess that stank of old cabbage. At her
feet two children were giggling over a basket of kittens.

"Mistress?" Honor said softly.

The woman at the hearth wheeled, brandishing her ladle like a
weapon. Her other hand tugged the closest child roughly to her
knee.

There was no mistaking the tall, strong body and fierce, bony
face of Bridget Sydenham. But how changed she was! The lady
Honor remembered had been a starched chatelaine, the well-
heeled wife of a merchant. This was the poor widow of a heretic.
Her dress was rough homespun, and her head covering, once so
crisp and white, was dingy and barely controlled the wiry tangle of
gray hair.

"Mistress Larke!" she cried. She moved the child aside and
stalked across the filthy floor straw. "I never thought to see you
again, not in this world at any rate. You are well met, lady!" Her
hands took Honor's in a firm clasp of friendship. To Honor, her
skin felt as dry as parchment.

"Jane, fetch a seat for our guest. Anthony, take her cloak." Bridget Sydenham's commands were instantly obeyed. Honor was led
to the fire. A stool was whisked under her and her sopping cloak
peeled away by small hands. Bridget Sydenham perched on a stool
beside her and gazed into her eyes as if searching for remnants of

the past. Honor glanced at Jane, the little girl who had greeted her, as the child struggled to drape the water-heavy cloak over the firedogs.

"My grandchildren," Mrs. Sydenham said, as if in answer. She spoke with neither pride nor displeasure, but she added with a rueful smile, "My elder son, my daughter, and their chicks have all come home to roost."

Honor did not have to ask why. As a heretic Humphrey Sydenham had died an excommunicate; his clan were outcasts. The Church forbade Christians all commercial dealings with excommunicated persons, and though the injunction did not officially extend to his dependents, cautious neighbors and business colleagues shunned a family tainted by heresy. Such consequence of error was a powerful incentive to ordinary folk not to stray from the paths of orthodoxy.

"You mentioned only your elder son," Honor said. "But what of Edward?"

Bridget looked down as if ashamed. "In prison. Tried for heresy."

Honor thought of Humphrey Sydenham, whipped on the way to his burning. "Good God," she breathed.

"Oh, do not fret for Edward's safety," Bridget said. "Leastwise, the safety of his body. He recanted. His prison sentence is for dealing in banned books. A mere three years."

She sounded disappointed. Honor did not know how to respond. "Is there anything I can do?" she finally asked. "Anything you need?"

Mrs. Sydenham let out a short, brusque laugh that was surprisingly free of bitterness. "Ha! Everything!"

"But have you enough . . . to eat?"

"We manage. My son sells these clothes." She pointed a nobbled finger at the heaps of rags. "My daughter-in-law does washing and sewing. We manage."

Little Jane leaned on her elbows across her grandmother's knee and happily sucked her sweet, staring with curiosity at the finely dressed lady who had come to call.

"These be our riches," said Mrs. Sydenham, nodding at Jane's head as the child nudged her grandmother's flat breast. Her tone was that of a clear-eyed businesswoman satisfied with the day's receipts, but her hand absently smoothed the child's dark curls in a gesture of infinite tenderness.

"The children are being trained up in the paths of righteousness. The older ones read from the Bible to our family circle. Even the youngest sit amongst us to hear the word of God. It is small suffering to live on cabbage and our wits when the reward is Christ in our hearts. What should we be doing, in any case, hoarding up coins and cramming our mouths with rich stuff as the sinful priests do?"

Jane stopped sucking her sweet and shot a guilty glance up at the stern face. Honor stifled a smile. Mrs. Sydenham continued talking to her guest, but Jane, taking no chances, flipped the candy under her tongue and smiled sweetly up at her grandmother, and Mrs. Sydenham went on in ignorance of the crime of gluttony being committed under her nose.

"This be God's will," the matriarch concluded. "We are content."

Coughs rasped from the straw pallet in the corner. A gust of damp air swirled in through a high, broken window. Content? Honor thought. No, I am not content that this family should suffer so!

It was midday. Holt and his men would be coming soon. "Mistress," Honor said, "I have come with a warning. Again."

"For us?" Mrs. Sydenham's arm wrapped protectively around her granddaughter's shoulder.

"Happily, no. But for one close to you. I have learned that my . . . that the Lord Chancellor means to search your house for Brother Frish. Is he here?"

Mrs. Sydenham's face closed in irritation. "Brother Frish is none of my kin. Why should they bother us about him?"

"A man just arrested by Sir Thomas, a bookseller, has informed. Under duress, I fear. If Brother Frish is with you, he must be warned." She searched Mrs. Sydenham's face for confirmation, but none was given. "Unless," Honor stammered, "he isn't here after all. Perhaps the bookseller was mistaken. Babbling to save himself. Delirious, even."

A man's voice across the room startled her. "No, Mistress Larke. Nicholson was not mistaken."

Honor jumped up. Jane scurried away. In the corner, Frish was getting to his feet beside the pallet. It was he who had been coughing in the dirty nest of blankets.

Honor's head snapped back to Mrs. Sydenham, accusing her with hurt eyes. "I thought you trusted me," she cried.

Mrs. Sydenham returned her gaze, unapologetic.

"Do not chide her, my lady," Frish said, shuffling towards them at the hearth as he hugged the blanket around his shoulders. "Loyalty sometimes demands evasion. Pray that your own friends, if pressed, maintain such closed mouths for your sake as this good lady does for mine."

Honor knew he was right. She accepted the reproof. And the warning. "Brother," she said, "you must go. Now. Sir Thomas's men are on their way."

"Go? Aye," he said. He gave a despairing shrug. "But where?"

"Have you not friends who will hide you?"

Frish and Mrs. Sydenham exchanged bleak looks. She said, "Our friends' charity has been stretched to the tearing point."

"The Lord Chancellor's crackdown has squeezed every family of the Brethren," said Frish. "His officers are so zealous, there are no safe houses left in London."

"But has there been no help from court as you once hoped?" Honor asked. "No support from Cromwell? Or the Lady Anne?"

Frish shook his head glumly. "Cromwell waits for the Lady. The Lady waits for the King. The King waits for Rome. No one at court will openly reach out a hand to us. Under More's vengeful eye none will risk it."

"Then you must go abroad," Honor said.

"How?" Frish dared her, his anger kindling. "Shall I swim to Flanders?"

His face had reddened, but the pockmarks that flecked his forehead, cheeks and neck remained dead white. She had forgotten how ugly he was. He coughed again. Under the slack blanket and threadbare tunic his slight frame seemed as starved of muscle as an old man's. His pale eyes were watery with exhaustion. It was clear that he was very ill.

"How, mistress?" he asked again, but quietly this time, contrite after his outburst. Honor had not forgotten that rich voice; it absolved what her eyes saw, and gave him beauty. "Even if I evaded More's hounds out of London," he said, "his officers watch all the ports. They know me. They smack their lips for the reward my trussed body would bring."

"Many of the Brethren have been caught trying to take passage to Flanders or Calais," Mrs. Sydenham said. "Pilots often turn them in." She added harshly, "for profit."

Honor looked from one to the other. Frish was hugging himself and staring blankly into the fire. Mrs. Sydenham had clasped her hands in her lap with sullen acceptance. Both looked tired, hungry, beaten. Honor swallowed. Frish's life, it seemed, lay in her hands.

She began to pace, thinking. Profit, Mrs. Sydenham had said. The word sounded a chime in her memory. Men would do much for profit. She stopped and looked back at them. "Thornleigh," she declared.

Both of them looked up, puzzled. "What?" Frish asked.

"Richard Thornleigh. A man with ships. A man who will use his ships for profit."

"Is he one of us?" Frish asked eagerly. "How is it we know nothing of him?"

"No, not one of you," Honor was quick to point out.

Mrs. Sydenham's eyes narrowed. "And you, mistress? Can you still not say, 'one of us'?"

"Madam, I am here to help," Honor flared, "and I will not be treated with such suspicion! No, I am not one of you. I cannot believe that this misery is God's will, as you do. I wish your good husband had abjured—yes, lied—and saved himself." She reined in her anger. "But I hate the Church and Sir Thomas More as much as you do. I have good reason. You, of all people, should understand that. You must trust me. There is no one else you *can* trust."

Mrs. Sydenham looked away. Honor feared she had gone too

far. How could she even think her provocation was as great as this starving widow's?

"What are you proposing?" Frish asked, eyes sharp with guarded hope.

"The man I speak of is"—she chose the words carefully—"a mercenary in this struggle. If I can find him, I believe he will do our bidding. But for a price."

Frish groaned. He steadied himself against the mantel, the hope knocked out of him. "I cannot pay."

"But I can," Honor said.

Both heads turned to her.

"Sir Thomas has always encouraged me to support certain charities—almshouses and the like. In making these donations I deal independently with the stewards of my father's estates, so they're accustomed to receiving my requests for cash." She laughed bitterly. "Saving a heretic from Sir Thomas will be my new charity."

Feeling strong now that her mind was firmly set on action she held out her hands in solidarity to the wondering pair. "This man Thornleigh may demand a king's ransom, but he is our best hope. Will you give me leave to seek him out?"

Frish nodded eagerly. After a moment Mrs. Sydenham said, "So be it." Each took one of Honor's hands. It was settled.

Quickly, Honor gathered up her cloak and turned back to Frish. "Come with me now, Brother, in my barge. I'll hide you in the outbuildings at Richmond somehow. It may take me a day or two to find Thornleigh."

Frish shook his head, smiling, and threw off his blanket. "I thank you, lady, but 'somehow' is not good enough." He was moving across the hall, picking up a cloak and satchel here, a crust of bread there. "I'll take my chances alone. When you've made the arrangements, send a message. Do you know the Blue Boar Inn, hard by London Bridge?" he asked as he reached the door. She nodded. "Good. Send word to me there. When it's time, I'll meet this Thornleigh wherever he says. God bless you!"

He was gone.

Mrs. Sydenham stood, her face grave. "You are wrong, Mistress Larke. I do trust you. I would I had trusted you sooner, that my husband might be with us still. I believe your heart to be true, and brave. But More's men have ways of splitting open even the stoutest heart."

She reached out and took Honor's hand firmly in hers. "This man, Thornleigh. He acts for money, you say? Take care the mercenary does not deliver you unto your enemy."

❧ 18 ❧

The First Rescue

Honor tracked down Thornleigh late that very evening. Her inquiries of him among clothiers at the Drapers Guild and the Merchant Adventurer's Company had led her, following his trail, to the cockpits and taverns that barnacled the precincts around Greenwich Palace. A tapster told her he'd served Thornleigh at about noon and sent her on to a noisy alehouse yard where a ring of bystanders stood yelling and whistling around a wrestling match. The proprietor, busy scribbling wagers, barely glanced up as Honor shouted her question in his ear. "Thornleigh?" he bawled to her above the uproar. "Left hours ago."

"Do you know where he went?" she asked, showing him a shilling.

The proprietor eyed her up and down, wiped his nose with his sleeve, and pocketed the coin. "You'll find him down by the oaks." He pointed toward the forest. "Taking money off the King's game-keeper."

In the gusty twilight she found the gamekeeper's lodging, a three-storied gatehouse on the edge of the forested deer park. She climbed the spiral stairs to the top floor and stepped through a doorless arch into a room hazed with smoke from a crackling log fire. Under the low, beamed ceiling the air hung heavy with the reek of sweat and the smell of cheap tallow from wall candles that spilled in gluts onto antler holders. A half dozen men sat gambling at a round table but Honor saw that Thornleigh was not among them. Beneath their table empty wine bottles littered the filthy floor straw along with dismembered capon carcasses, fly-blown evidence of the players' long encampment. As Honor approached, the men looked up from their cards. Their bleary, unshaven faces formed a circle of scowls. A wolfhound bitch lying in front of the hearth lifted its head, too, and growled at her through bared teeth.

Honor swallowed at the unwelcome reception. But she had come this far. She lifted her chin, pretending confidence. "Master Gamekeeper?" she asked.

A hook-nosed man with fat lips grunted, "Aye. What d'you want?"

"I was told I would find Master Thornleigh here."

The gamekeeper jabbed a thumb irritably in the direction of a closed door. "In there," he said.

Honor glanced at the door. She took it to be the entrance to a bedchamber. "It's urgent that I see him. Could you please wake him?"

The other men laughed. The gamekeeper did not. "No," he growled.

A man with a stringy beard snickered, "You'll have to wait your turn, wench."

"Wait?" she asked, uneasy in this company. "How long?"

The gamekeeper almost snarled. "Not bloody long, else he knows I'll have his guts for garters."

And so Honor stood in the middle of the fetid room, feeling like a petitioner come to some vagabond baron's court, waiting for him to emerge. The gamblers, ignoring her, went back to their cards. The greyhound yawned, stretched, and fell asleep.

Honor paced. It was already dark, and she still had to find decent lodging for the night. After leaving Bridget Sydenham's—and not knowing how long it would take to find Thornleigh and then get Frish safely away—she had sent a message to the Queen. There was sickness at Chelsea, she wrote; it was not serious, but the family needed her. Assuming the Queen's kind permission, she wrote, she would stay for a day or two. The Queen's communi-

cation with the world outside her chambers and chapel was so ten-
uous that Honor felt safe in the lie. With it she had bought herself
a little time, but there was still so much to arrange. And Frish was
wandering the streets of London, ill, hunted. She had to see
Thornleigh now.

She was about to march over and bang on the door when it suddenly flew open. From the dark interior Thornleigh's bare arm
shot out to still the door against the wall. His other arm, culminat-
ing in a bottle, was wrapped around a young woman, a plump,
peaches-and-cream beauty. Her yellow hair tumbled over a shoulder bare above her rumpled chemise. She clung to Thornleigh's
naked torso and together they staggered out a step or two, squinting at the light and laughing.

Thornleigh stopped, cupped the woman's chin, and bent to kiss
her. Her hand slid down his backbone until it reached the waist of
his breeches. Her fingers wriggled inside. He shivered. She went
up on her toes to whisper something in his ear. Thornleigh threw
back his head to laugh, and then he noticed Honor. He blinked in
surprise. He shut his eyes and shook his head as if to toss off an
hallucination. He looked at her again, raked fingers through his
tangled hair, and let out a laugh of amazement. "A pilgrim is come
among us!" he cried.

Honor glared at him.

Thornleigh turned to his companion with a look of mock piety.
"No one told me this ground was hallowed. Why, Mistress Farquhar, have you some holy relic secreted away that pilgrims travel
to touch? Some sacred treasure? Under your pillow, perhaps?" He
chuckled and massaged her buttocks through her chemise with
playful roughness. "Though God knows there's treasure sweet
enough right here."

The woman half-heartedly slapped his hand. "Pish!" she said
with a giggle. Thornleigh nuzzled her neck, then looked out
through the curtain of yellow hair at Honor's stormy face. He
straightened.

"I won her," he protested innocently. "At cards." He nodded toward the gamekeeper who sat moodily engrossed in the gambling.
Thornleigh grinned. "Her husband lost." He tugged his warm

winnings closer, and the gamekeeper's wife gazed up at him with heavy-lidded eyes, obviously satisfied with her husband's debt-paying arrangement.

Honor considered leaving then and there, but Thornleigh leaned out to her, suddenly serious, and whispered behind his hand, "It's not what you think, mistress. This is not a night of debauchery."

Honor looked at the woman nestling against his chest, then back at his face. Her eyebrows lifted in skepticism. "Oh?"

Straight-faced, he assured her, "Far from it." His stifled grin broke free. "The agreement with her husband was for one hour only." He laughed loudly at his own joke.

Honor turned on her heel.

"Wait," Thornleigh said, still chortling. "Do wait, Mistress Larke."

Honor kept walking. She was almost out of the room when Thornleigh called after her, "Come now, you're not going to leave just like that, are you? After you've come all this way to find me?"

She stopped. He was right. Infuriating though he was, it was pointless to go. Frish was depending on her. And who else could she approach?

"Do forgive me," Thornleigh said with exaggerated civility to her back. "Such bad manners."

She turned stiffly.

"And I haven't even offered you a glass of sack," Thornleigh said. He loosed the gamekeeper's wife and lifted the bottle he held towards Honor as if it were a peace offering. He brought it close to his eyes with a frown. "Empty," he muttered. He tossed it on the floor and looked around for another and spotted one beside the hearth. He strode past Honor, but before he reached the bottle his bare toe stubbed against the handle of a poker left on the hearth. Its tip nosed up red-hot out of the flames. Thornleigh hopped back, the handle apparently so hot it had almost burned him. With a soft curse he shoved his hand into a leather hearth glove, grasped the poker handle and picked it up. He studied the glowing prong for several moments, apparently forgetting both the bottle and Honor. She watched his face darken.

He looked back at her and said, as if their conversation had been unbroken, "That is, I assume it's me you've come searching for. Or"—he flashed her a conspiratorial smile that crinkled the skin around his eyes—"is it that you've fallen into depravity since we last met? Stalking midnight revels now, are you? Well, mistress, you've found the right place." He bent to pick up the bottle and held it toward her, then spread his arms as if offering himself as well. "Join me?"

Honor simmered at his insolence. She was provoked, too, by the smirk on the face of the gamekeeper's wife who was leaning against the door jamb, watching. Honor stepped up to Thornleigh and pushed away the proffered bottle. "Save your bawdy offers for your strumpets," she said. "I have other business with you. Where can we speak privately?"

"Oh, this is privacy enough," he said with a laugh. Still holding the hot poker and the bottle, he stepped over the wolfhound bitch and flopped into a chair. He set the bottle on the floor. The dog continued to snore at his feet. He stretched his long legs across her back as if she were a footstool. "Don't worry about them," he said, jerking his head toward the gamblers. "They wouldn't hear the crack of doom. Not unless it was followed by God in person, come to sit in on the game." He scratched his lean belly absently as he chuckled. "The presence of the Lord might raise the stakes, though, eh?" He looked up at Honor. "Now. What can you possibly want of me?"

She stepped closer, unwilling to be overheard despite his assurances. He made no move to rise.

She crouched at his side. "I want your ship," she said.

"Ha! You, and all my creditors." He smoothed one bare foot along the dog's fur, making her shiver in her sleep.

"Hear me, sir," Honor said. "A man's life is in peril. I must arrange his passage to Flanders. Immediately. Can you take him? Have you a ship near London?"

"'Immediately!'" he mimicked her. "What," he said, scratching his stubbled chin, "have I not time to shave and throw on a shirt?"

"Then you do have a ship nearby."

"Snug and safe at anchor in the estuary. And I mean for her to remain so."

"I am willing to pay. Handsomely. In gold."

"You'd better be, mistress, for passage 'immediately.' The channel's a cauldron of spring storms, fouler than an old maid jilted at the altar." He studied her face with suspicion. "And who's this mysterious cargo? Don't tell me you're still sneaking around, stirring the pot behind your kind mistress's back?"

She stood, furious. "Look who talks of sneaking!" she snapped, tossing a glance at the gamekeeper's wife. The woman stood braiding her hair in the bedchamber doorway.

"I had her with her husband's blessing," Thornleigh protested, amused. He craned his neck to look past Honor at the gamblers, and raised his voice. "Isn't that right, Farquhar."

Without looking up from his cards the gamekeeper stabbed the air with his finger obscenely. "Pox on you, Thornleigh!"

Thornleigh grinned and spread his arms to Honor in a gesture of triumph. "You see?"

"I see a drunken sot," Honor flared. "A lousel not fit to entrust this mission to."

The light of enjoyment died in Thornleigh's eyes. He bent for the bottle and took a long pull from it, then wiped his mouth with the back of his arm. "An accurate assessment, mistress" he murmured to the bottle. His eyes flicked up to her, hard with scorn. "So find some other fool."

He put down the bottle and turned his attention grimly back to the hot poker. He was holding the handle so that the glowing tip pointed directly between his eyes, and he glared at it, absorbed, shutting out the room. He seemed locked in a contest to stare it down, Honor thought, as if it were a living creature that was challenging him. Slowly, deliberately, he lowered it until it pointed at his breastbone. Both hands were grasping the handle, and the tip was poised inches from his skin. It was as if he intended to brand himself.

Honor watched, appalled. What was this perverse game he was playing? Was he daring himself to suffer pain? She recalled seeing the same steely challenge in his eyes that day at Greenwich when he had finally dropped all bravado and thudded his fist onto the

block, ready to let his hand be severed. She remembered thinking
then that he seemed somehow to be welcoming the punishment.

"There is no time to find help elsewhere," she said fiercely.
"The friar's life rests in your hands."

Thornleigh blinked. He looked up at her. "Friar?"

She knew she should not have said so much, but at least her declaration had broken his malevolent trance. "His name is Brother
Frish," she answered, hazarding all. "The Lord Chancellor is on
his heels for heresy. He was convicted once before and escaped
the Bishop of Lincoln's prison. A second conviction will send him
to the stake. Brother Frish does no man harm, but the Chancellor
will burn him unless you carry him to safety."

For a moment she thought she saw real interest glinting in the
blue depths of his eyes.

"You're risking a lot for a raving friar, my lady," he said. But the
interest quickly drowned, and mockery again washed shallowly in
his eyes. "The Lord Chancellor, you say? The mighty Sir Thomas?"
He whistled softly through his teeth. "You seem to make a habit of
biting hands that feed you."

Honor felt like slapping him. "If it's money you need to stiffen
your backbone, I've told you I will reward you well."

"Let's see it."

"See what?"

"Your gold, woman," he growled.

She was taken aback—by the request and by the bitterness that
fueled it. "I haven't brought it here," she stammered. "I need time
to—"

"A pity," he cut in. "Good night." It was a clear termination of
the interview.

He again moved the poker tip toward his chest. He stared down
at it as if mesmerized, slowly drawing it closer until it was only a
finger's breadth away. She knew he was going to sear himself.

It was exasperation that made her strike. She kicked the poker,
knocking it sideways from his grasp. It clattered to the floor. With
a yelp the dog sprang to its feet. The men at the table looked up.

Thornleigh sat stunned, mouth open, hands still uplifted as

though the object he had been holding had inexplicably vanished. He gaped at Honor, his face as clear and wondering as a child's.

With a jolt of energy concentrated in one fluid movement he rose and stood over her. He stared into her eyes with a naked intensity that could have been fury, or contempt, but which Honor somehow knew was nothing more than astonished curiosity. It charged his face, his body, his breathing.

She stared back at him, as unnerved by his sudden proximity as he had been by her action. He loomed over her, but she stood rigid, her curiosity equal to his.

She spoke first.

"Why do you seek to hurt yourself?"

"Why do you seek to risk yourself?"

She heard his breathing slowly becoming steady. As his chest heaved and settled, she was aware of firelight gleaming off his skin. She felt warm blood sting her cheeks. She dragged her eyes away from him, but it was only to catch the smirk of the gamekeeper's wife at the bedchamber doorway. The woman winked at her as if in understanding that they appreciated at least one thing in common.

"Thornleigh!" one of the gamblers shouted.

Honor and Thornleigh turned. The gambler was pointing at them. "Behind you!"

Thornleigh looked behind his feet. Smoke was curling up from the floor. The fallen poker had set the floor rushes alight, and small teeth of flames were eating a widening circle across the stone.

Thornleigh swooped for the sack bottle, upended it, and sloshed the wine over the fire. Instantly, the flames died. The damp rushes at the edge of the blackened circle smoldered. The men at the table went back to their game.

Thornleigh picked up the poker and replaced it safely on the hearth, then turned to Honor. He folded his arms across his chest and studied her. Honor had the unnerving sensation that it was she who had now become his challenge.

"This is my proposal, mistress," he said. "I'll tell you my price. Then you tell me if this friar's skin is worth saving after all."

Her comment to Frish had been well founded. Thornleigh did want a king's ransom.

Honor stood alone, hugging herself outside the doorway of the Blue Boar Inn near Botolph's wharf. The fog around her glowed with a sickly phosphorescence, made murky in patches by lights on London Bridge, though it was only three by the clock. No, more like four, she realized. It must be an hour she'd been waiting.

The tavern door opened and a customer ambled out. Honor turned her face away. The customer padded off homeward and was swallowed by the fog. His footfalls faded. All was silent again.

Her ears picked up a soft scuffling of feet, then a scraping along the stone wall of the alley. Then a cough. She stepped around the corner and peered into the gloom. A man's face emerged. It was Frish.

Relief converted her tension into a steam of anger. "Where have you been?"

He shuffled up to her and she gasped at the sight. His face was as white and damp as raw pastry. His eyes were black smudges. His white-blond hair, ragged with bits of straw, was matted to his skull. His hand was bandaged with a strip torn from the hem of his tunic, the strip grimed with dried blood. A ripped sandal clung to one foot. The other foot was naked and bleeding.

He read the shock in her eyes. "London is a dangerous place for fugitives," he murmured.

"Your foot . . ." she whispered.

He shrugged. "A contest with a dog over a bone. The dog won." He slumped back against the wall, eyes closed, as if this slight effort at speech had sapped him.

"My God," she said, "you haven't rested since leaving Mrs. Sydenham's, have you?"

"Who can rest and stay one step ahead of More's men, and alive?" His eyes sprang open showing pinpoints of fear. "Why have *you* come?" he asked. "I said, send a message. Has the plan foundered? Has Thornleigh refused? Is it—"

"All's well," she quickly assured him. "I simply thought it was safer to see the thing through by myself. I'm my own messenger."

"Then . . . it's really arranged?" he whispered, trembling.

"Yes. Thornleigh's ship, the *Vixen*, waits for you off Gravesend. You ride there now and sail for Bruges tomorrow with the tide. Take my horse. She's tethered at the end of the alley. No, don't worry, I'll hire a barge to carry me back to Richmond." She handed him a purse of coins. "Give Thornleigh this."

The purse held only a quarter of the amount Thornleigh had demanded, but it was all she had been able to raise that morning by selling the jewelry she was wearing to a Cheapside goldsmith. She could only hope that the promissory note she had tucked inside the purse would satisfy Thornleigh until she could write to the stewards of her father's estates for the balance. "Now, listen," she said. "The instructions Thornleigh gave me are these. When you arrive at the wharf, the signal—" She saw him shiver. Her first thought was that it was from joy. Then she realized it was fever. "Brother, it's at least a two hour ride. Can you make it?"

There was faint barking in the distance.

"I can," he rasped, pushing himself from the wall in a show of resolve. "More's bailiff and his dogs are not far behind. I *must*." He swayed. The purse dropped from his fingers. Honor caught him under both arms and held him up. He weighed no more than a girl.

He pushed out of her embrace and bent to retrieve the purse. He stood up straight, but she saw the effort it required. Sweat was crawling down his cheeks. "I thank you, good lady, with all my heart," he whispered. "And now, I'll trouble you no more . . . but say farewell." He tried to smile, but his fever-blurred eyes could not focus on her face.

Honor grabbed the purse from him. "No, Brother. You'll not say it yet."

She threw her arm around his waist. Half dragging him, she staggered down the alley to the waiting horse. She propped Frish against its flank, then braced her legs and bent with hands buckled together, like a knight's groom, to lift him into the saddle.

Frish hesitated, ashamed.

"There's no time for this," she ordered. "Let me help you up!"

With a groan of humiliation he slipped his bloody foot into her cupped hands. She held herself stiff until he had struggled up onto the horse's back. She mounted in front of him and jigged the reins. Too weak to protest, Frish could not prevent his forehead from slumping onto her back as they started down the street.

The fog lifted shortly after they passed London's wall. "Small mercies," Honor muttered as she strained to see signposts in the dusk.

They reached Gravesend harbor three hours later, in darkness.

By the time Honor had tethered the horse, helped Frish down, and hauled him to the wharf, she was chilled with sweat and her legs trembled with exhaustion. She sat Frish gently on a coiled heap of wet rope and looked around. The wharf appeared deserted. Another small mercy. She gazed at the black void of the river. Somewhere out there Thornleigh said the *Vixen* lay at anchor. "I must leave you for a moment, Brother," she whispered.

She hurried into a nearby tavern and returned with a lantern. Panting, she sat beside Frish on the heap of rope and tried to calm herself with several deep breaths. Frish's head slumped onto her shoulder. She threw a large handkerchief over the lantern, held it toward the water, and flapped the cloth up and down five times.

She peered out into the blackness for several minutes, then repeated the signal. Could Thornleigh see it? She sat watching, listening to the slap of water against the wharf and to Frish's ragged breathing. A feeling of dread gathered around her heart. Was Thornleigh out there at all? Or did he lie drunk in some London brothel, a man not fit to pledge his word?

She signaled again. Again, no response.

Frish was shivering horribly. She took his head upon her breast and stroked the blotched face. He was babbling, falling into delirium. "Hold on, Brother," she murmured. "Hold on."

But hold on for what? she asked herself with rising panic. What was she to do next? The inn where she had borrowed the lantern was full, and even if she could find another inn they must go back to London eventually if Thornleigh had deserted them. Take Frish back to London now? He would never be able to sit the horse. Even if she tied him to her and they made it back through the pitch of night, where could they hide? A tavern? Holed up inside like rats? Waiting for More's men and dogs to sniff them out?

A lantern burst of light. Dead ahead. Another, and another. Five of them!

"The signal, Brother! Thornleigh's on his way!"

She grabbed his tunic collar and jerked him forward to get him to his feet. He was limp in her arms. Together they lurched down to the water steps and there Honor stood holding him upright, tottering with the strain, waiting. She heard oars lapping through the water, and relief flooded her when she saw a winking lantern light bobbing closer like some lost, drunken star. The pointed prow of a skiff broke through the gloom and the boat skimmed alongside the water steps.

The rower had his back to her. A scrawny man with gray hair sprouting below an oily red cap. Not Thornleigh. Honor's heart thudded. It was a trap! Thornleigh had informed. This was an agent of More's, come to arrest both Frish and her!

With a soft cry of panic she hauled the semiconscious Frish around and began to stumble with him back up the steps.

"Halt there!" the rower said.

Terrified, Honor staggered on.

"Mistress Larke!" the man called in a forced whisper.

She reached the top stair, gasping under Frish's weight.

"Stop, mistress! I'm from the *Vixen*!"

Honor lurched to a halt, desperate to flee but utterly unable to carry her burden farther. "You're not! You're from Sir Thomas! How else could you know my name?"

The man stared up at her, confused. "Know your . . ? But Master said—"

"What master?"

"Master Thornleigh."

"But he didn't know I'd come!"

This appeared to baffle the man even more. He scratched his head, knocking his cap askew. "Master said he gave you his instructions, my lady. Who else would come but you?"

Honor let out a huge breath of relief. It was not a trap after all. This was Thornleigh's man. Fear, she realized, had blinded her. Though her original intention had been to send Frish here alone, only she had known that. Obviously, Thornleigh had assumed she would accompany Frish.

"Jinner's the name," the scrawny man said, setting down his lantern. "Samuel Jinner. At your service, m'lady." He dragged off his oily cap, but he did not smile. Rather, his mouth drooped. His eyes drooped, too, and his nose, and his mustache. His very beard, a scraggly gray patch in the middle of his chin, drooped in two forlorn wings. But he stood in the skiff, bandy-legged but stalwart, with an arm outstretched for duty. Honor trusted him instantly.

"Master Jinner, you are well met," she sighed, for the burden in her arms was too much to carry even one step more. "This is Brother Frish."

Jinner flopped his cap back on. "I'll take him aboard, my lady," he muttered, shaking his head as he reached for Frish, "though he don't look fit to me." He laid the moaning man in the bow.

"He's very ill," she agreed, "but his fate will be far worse if he tarries longer in England. Please, tell your master to give him every care."

"Don't you fret," Jinner assured her solemnly. "I've found that several leagues of sea water put between a man and the law does wondrous things for a man's health."

Honor smiled. She wiped sweat from her face and was aware of a light-headed exhilaration. She recognized the feeling. It was the same buoyant sense of well-being she had felt the night of the raid at Sydenham's when she and Frish had crouched in the alley under the soft rain, so keenly alive after the danger—and free. *I did it*, she thought, exulting. *I got Frish away from Sir Thomas. It worked!*

Jinner hobbled toward his oars, then touched his cap to her. "I'll be off, m'lady. A betting man wouldn't lay down a farthing for my fate either if I tarry longer from the *Vixen*."

"Is Thornleigh such a hard master?"

Jinner made a vinegar face. "Let's just say the Devil himself could take a lesson from the master when the mood's upon him." He grappled the oars.

"Wait!" she said. She drew the purse from her cloak. "The

mood will be on him soon enough if you take him the man without the money." She knelt on the bottom step and leaned over the gunnel, offering the purse.

Jinner nodded, a gloomy gesture he apparently used instead of a smile. He shipped the oars. "I'm obliged, m'lady. I'd clean forgot." He took the purse. But instead of tucking it away, he opened it.

Honor held her breath. Would he know how much money Thornleigh was expecting? Could she bluff her way through this? "It's all there, Master Jinner," she assured him stoutly, "except for a small—"

"I don't doubt it, m'lady," he interrupted. He drew out a single coin. "And now it's all there but for this. Master asked it, for the service." He slipped the coin into his pocket, then tugged tight the purse strings and tossed the purse back onto the steps where it thudded at Honor's feet. He looked up at her wondering face.

"And master bade me give you this message. The price named, he says, was but to establish value. As to the form of payment, he says . . ." Jinner stopped. He let out a deflated sigh and scratched the back of his neck. "Curse the Turk's mother for a whore, I swear the blasted speech was in my head when I set out." He leaned over his oars and puckered his face, puzzling to remember. Suddenly he cried, "That's it!" He closed his eyes and squeezed out the remnant of the message in rapid, concentrated spurts. "As to the form of payment, he suggests that you . . . find a more imaginative method . . . of discharging the debt . . . and . . . he looks forward to settling accounts . . . when next you meet."

His eyes popped open in relief. "And now I'm lightened of that ballast I'll say farewell in earnest, m'lady."

He pulled on the oars, and the skiff nosed out into the river.

Honor stared after it for a long moment, amazed. Thornleigh did not want money after all. He wanted her. With a snort at his insulting suggestion, she snatched up the purse. Did he think she was an object to be bargained for, stamped with a price like the gamekeeper's blowsy wife? And yet, as Jinner's lantern faded and darkness cloaked her face, she felt her stiff mask of indignation slip. For imagination tugged like a restless child hand-held by its mother at the fair. What might it be like to settle this account Thornleigh-style.

❧ 19 ❧

Master Cromwell

"Five pounds. That's all I need," Honor implored. "Just enough to transport this cargo to safety. It's urgent, or I wouldn't be asking."

"Nor accepting my invitation to dine," Thomas Cromwell added dryly across the table. They were eating alone in his office in the King's palace of Whitehall.

"Don't think I'm ungrateful for the help you've given us," Honor said. "The intelligence at the harbors, the small checks against the Lord Chancellor's agents—all these have been a blessed relief. But you can't imagine the expense of the missions. Wages for the crews. Accommodation in Flanders for the refugees. Citizens' papers to make up. And all the palms to be gilded along the way. It's endless."

"You'll manage. You always do. Another glass of burgundy?"

Cromwell's ink-stained fingers reached across the remains of his meal for the decanter. The dishes of stewed beef, leeks, partridge, figs, and sweetmeats were shadowed by stacks of ledgers and papers which, here and on other tables, crammed his small office. "Or I have a fine malmsey if you'd prefer," he said. "A gift from Lady Hales."

"How good of her," Honor murmured. Her politeness was strained, for she was biting back the urge to continue pressing for the money. But Cromwell, she had learned, could not be rushed. She had organized four escapes since Frish's flight to Bruges six months ago—eleven people dispatched to safety on Thornleigh's ships so far—and Cromwell had often been an asset, even if his pace of doing things was never quick enough to satisfy Honor. She held up her hand to refuse the wine. "And what's the attorney-general's wife angling for these days?"

"Tin mining license," Cromwell said, cutting himself a slice of cheese. "On land I own in Devon."

"Formerly Cardinal Wolsey's?"

He grunted assent as he savored a mouthful of the cheese. Honor could not help smiling, intrigued as always by the man's coolness. At the mention of his profit from his former master's fall he showed no sign of remorse—nor, indeed, of triumph, although Wolsey's death had been Cromwell's making. He had organized the disposal of the Cardinal's vast lands to the great financial benefit of the King—the re-named Whitehall Palace had been Wolsey's York Place—and Cromwell had proceeded to put on the dead Cardinal's status and power like a discarded cloak. But he wore it with indifference. Honor knew his gratification lay elsewhere. Wolsey and Cromwell were utterly different men.

Wolsey had reveled in pomp, in display of his magnificence; some said he had even hankered to be Pope. His obsession had been the maneuvering of England's interests in Europe, and he had left the domestic administrative institutions of the realm as he had found them, stultified in the medieval web that radiated out from the King's household core. Cromwell, on the other hand, cared little for display. Somber in dress and deportment, his genius was for organization—intensely detailed, intensely personal. Honor had been amazed at how quickly he had acquired control of the financial machinery of government. She knew that his sights were now set on the three powerful royal secretariats. She had watched his steady workmanlike ascendancy, and did not doubt his ability to achieve his goal: he itched to remold the realm. "A backward nation, England is," he had once grumbled to her after an old knight in Parliament had pined for another invasion of France even though King Henry, earlier in his reign, had swallowed two humiliating defeats there. "What business have we," Cromwell had asked Honor, "squandering men and resources to try to capture some ungracious dog-holes in France, or shaking our swords at Flanders? Look at the facts. In commerce our merchants would sink without the Flanders wool trade. In industry we cannot even satisfy the domestic demand for pins. Our military might is not much greater than the papacy's. Invasions, indeed!" Then, as now, Honor admired his clear-eyed perspective.

She pushed aside her plate. "I'll join you in a glass of Lady Hales' malmsey another day, sir," she said. "For now, I am quite sated." She leaned across the table. "But my hunger for your assistance remains sharp. Can you not manage even five pounds? It's not much."

"Not much? It's what my clerk makes in a year."

"Your clerk can be thankful he has his post and his liberty," she shot back. "Others must flee for their lives."

Cromwell chuckled. "I've said it before, Mistress Larke. You are nothing if not tenacious."

"Sir, it would make such a difference," she pressed. "In the case of this cargo bound for Amsterdam, five pounds means the difference between a safe hostel or a ditch in the rain with the dogs. And one of the men is over sixty."

"What of your own resources?"

"I dare not draw again on my funds for another month. I've already stretched my credibility with the stewards of my father's properties. If they should write to Sir Thomas about it . . ." She did not need to finish. She was still legally More's ward—management of her property would remain in his hands until she married, when it would become her husband's—and both she and Cromwell knew that More must be kept from discovering the real use of the large allowances she was drawing for "charity."

"Well, what about Thornleigh?" Cromwell asked. "After each of your missions, as you call them, his ships' holds come home crammed with goods for sale. He must be turning a fair profit."

She shook her head. "His ships gobble money, as he is forever reminding me. Right now, it happens to be true since he's just built a third one, a new carrack. Besides, he's paying masons and carpenters on a new fulling mill he's putting up at Norwich, and his fleece barn at Aylsham suffered a fire and needs a new roof. All his capital is tied up."

"But surely he can cover the amount you need until next month."

"No," she said quickly. She lowered her eyes. "I already owe him too much." Although he'd never demanded settlement, she thought—in any form. Nor complained about covering the rising costs of the missions. Her debt with him had burgeoned, and she knew she could never come up with such an amount in gold should he suddenly demand repayment. Yet he never did. She often wondered why. Sometimes it seemed to her that he was operating from some private grudge against the Church, though he never spoke of it. But lately she had come to believe it was something else. During Frish's escape Thornleigh's only concern had been for payment—in one form or another. Now, he acted quite differently, and she felt it must be the dangerous work itself that had subtly wrought this change in him. Oh, he was as abrasive as ever—indeed, more so whenever he thought she was acting recklessly. But the work required cleverness and steady nerves, and Thornleigh, she had to admit, had plenty of both. It was as though he thrived on the danger.

But the missions were wholly Honor's creation; Thornleigh, they both understood, acted only as her agent. And so her mounting debt to him festered in her mind. Every day she was more aware that his magnanimous deferral of repayment actually strengthened his claim on her. She sensed that a reckoning would someday be expected, after all. And she wondered—not for the first time—what she would do when that reckoning came. For if the perilous work had wrought a change in him, it had done no less in her. She had come to trust and value his judgment. To rely on his skill at hammering solutions out of crises. Even to relax in his company, happy when a mission had gone smoothly. And, she could no longer deny to herself his powerful attraction

She realized Cromwell was speaking. ". . . your fine efforts, and you know I'd like to help, Mistress Larke. It's just that my position here . . ." He spread his hands to indicate his office.

"Yes, of course. I understand," she said, trying to sound indifferent, though it rankled; she would have to ask Thornleigh to cover the expense again. But she knew better than to coerce Cromwell. Besides, he had not absolutely refused. He might yet come around. Before she left, she would ask one more time.

She pushed away from the table and walked to the window. It overlooked a terrace frilled with orange trees set in tubs. Under the greenery two of Anne Boleyn's maids were taking turns tossing a ball to a laughing, beribboned gentleman. Honor shook her head at the folly of the place. Anne now lived at Whitehall like a Queen. For her, the King had ordered a massive expansion and redecoration of Wolsey's old palace. Engineers had supervised the razing of hundreds of neighboring houses, clearing twenty-four acres. Shifts of workmen had built tilt yards, tennis courts, bowling alleys. In the galleries, Holbein had painted magnificent figured ceilings. So much has changed, Honor thought, yet so much remains infuriatingly the same. She felt weariness creep into her bones, and her spirit. The last few days spent organizing the current mission had been exhausting, and there would be little rest for several days yet. But it was not the tense nature of the work that discouraged her; it was the growing conviction that *real* change would never come.

"By the way," Cromwell was saying, "I heard Thornleigh ran into some trouble at Bruges. I'm sorry. But I gather you've found a new, safe harbor?"

She turned and nodded. "Amsterdam is serving for the present. We have three men there now to assist us."

"Trustworthy?"

"Thornleigh's satisfied they are. I only handle this side, you know. I'm told that one, a German Lutheran, was once a mercenary. Imagine. Frish brought him into the fold in Antwerp, then sent him to us. Another's an Anabaptist."

"Good Lord, those fanatics? Deliriums about the communal holding of property and all that?"

Her smile was wry. "Yes, all that," she said. "He's a gentle, quiet soul, apparently. How he reconciles his involvement with us, given the Anabaptists' rule of nonresistance, I don't know."

"Dangerous folk, Anabaptists," Cromwell warned. "They refuse military service, and the taking of all oaths. Mind this fellow's madness does not infect your crews."

She shrugged. "The only madness I see is the obsession men have for killing other men whose ideas differ from their own."

Cromwell let the matter drop. "Brother Frish is well in Amsterdam?"

"As hale as a man can be who eats little and sleeps less and survives on nothing but scripture." She smiled. "Thornleigh saw him in Haarlem just after Candlemas, happily preaching to a group of fishmongers."

"Thornleigh was unhurt at Bruges, then?"

"Yes."

"What exactly happened?"

"As he sailed in, the port officials were on the quay, waiting. They're anxious these days, you know, to appease the Lord Chancellor."

"Naturally," Cromwell nodded. "In the interests of good commercial relations with England."

"Whatever their reasons," she said angrily, "they work hand in glove with the Chancellor's agents. He sends them to sniff out heresy among the Englishmen trading there. In any case," she said, forcing back her enmity against Sir Thomas, "our Anabaptist contact rowed out to warn Thornleigh. He put about, but the officials sailed after him. They tried to board. In the skirmish, a man of Thornleigh's was wounded and fell overboard and drowned before Thornleigh finally caught the wind and sailed free."

Cromwell shook his head in commiseration.

"He hugged the coast in bad weather for a few days," Honor went on, "but finally had to put in at a fishing village near the French border. Our two refugees slipped ashore. Thornleigh had a rough time back home in Norwich. Bishop Nix's chancellor, Dr. Pelle, had been informed about the incident and interrogated him. Thornleigh had to talk his way out of it."

"How? Pelle is no fool."

"Thornleigh told him he'd thought the Flemings were pirates. Pure bluster." A small smile curved her lips. "He's good at that."

"And what happened to the refugees?"

Honor's smile disappeared. "Arrested by the French authorities and sent to prison. We've had no more word."

"Dear me," Cromwell sighed.

Honor shrugged off the pall of defeat. "We ran a good mission two weeks later, though. Not a snag. And on top of that, I believe I've finally convinced a poor nervous chandler who's been hiding out for months to let me send him to safety on the voyage next month."

"Excellent." Cromwell's face was keen with interest. "I heard of a chandler who made a stir at Moorfields sermonizing on Lammas Day. Is it the same one? What's your fellow's name?"

Honor hesitated. She did not like to divulge information to anyone who did not absolutely need to know. But then, Cromwell knew everything already—about her seditious activities at any rate. If he'd wanted to destroy her and the people who relied on her he already had enough evidence to fill a prison ward.

"Master Rivers," she answered.

"Ah. Rivers."

Honor smiled. "He's agreed to emigrate on one condition. That we supply enough grog to keep him too drunk to see the Channel's waves."

Cromwell chuckled, then shook his head in admiration. "You do excellent work, Mistress Larke. I take my hat off to you." He slapped the table with sudden resolution. "In fact, I'll go one better than that. I'd like to give you that five pounds you need."

"Oh, sir!"

"No need for thanks," he said, scribbling a note. "After all, we're in this battle together." He handed her the paper. "Take this to Eustace on your way out. He'll give you the cash."

She thanked him profusely, then rose to leave.

"Oh, must you go?"

"Truly, sir, I must hurry if I'm to reach Yarmouth by tomorrow."

"Delivering cargo to Thornleigh?"

"Yes." She gathered up her cloak, lost in thoughts of the immediate difficulties ahead. "The Queen believes I'm buying books

for her library, and I must return to her by the end of the week."
She was suddenly aware that this abrupt departure might appear
rude. "But, sir," she hastened to add, "I have enjoyed your hospi-
tality."

"I'm glad," he said dryly. "Else one might think you'd come to
me only for my money."

❧ 20 ❧

Speedwell

"Boat off starboard bow!" the bosun shouted.

Richard Thornleigh looked up from his charts spread out in the sterncastle cabin of his new ship. He pushed away from the table so suddenly it made the chair legs screech on the floor and the horn lantern beside his charts tremble. He strode to the door and pulled it. It stuck. Curse fresh carpentry, he thought, and kicked its base to loosen it. He stomped down the four stairs to the main deck. As he crossed to starboard, several crewmen backed out of his way.

At the railing Thornleigh glowered out at the skiff skimming toward the ship through the twilight. Honor stood in the bow, obscuring Jinner at the oars. One corner of her emerald green cloak fluttered behind her like some great butterfly's wing. Thornleigh clenched his teeth. Damn! You'd think she'd have learned by now to keep low. He glanced back across the deck and frowned at the shore. Lights were glinting in the towers of Yarmouth's medieval wall and in a couple of the windmills scattered on the beach. And three ships—a pair of Dutch carracks and an English coaster—lay at anchor not far from his own stern. Anyone could be watching. He looked back at the skiff and saw why Honor was standing. A low hump covered the space between her and Jinner. Well, at least she'd had the sense to cover the old man with a tarpaulin.

The skiff bumped alongside the ship. Thornleigh jerked his head at a crewman to throw the rope ladder over the side. Honor scampered up it. Thornleigh strode over to her and asked in a furious whisper, "What in the name of the fornicating Devil have you been up to?"

"Collecting your cargo," she whispered back. "Better late than never, they say."

"Who says it?" he boomed. Then, whispering again, "Curse you for a Turk, woman, this crew of mine would not be likely to say it. Not with their necks stretched under a gibbet! Where have you—"

But she had turned away and was signaling down to the skiff. Thornleigh looked down at a wizened face peering out from under the tarpaulin. The fugitive crawled out and stood—a stooped, wrinkled old man. He cautiously peeled back the tarpaulin, revealing three curled figures: a boy of about four and a pale young woman with a baby in her arms. Thornleigh was shocked into silence.

Honor beckoned the fugitives to hurry up the ladder. She pulled them the last few feet and pushed them gently on deck one after another, like a cat moving her kittens. They huddled together. Thornleigh could see that they were limp with fear, seeing his glaring face. Jinner came up last.

Honor wrapped her arm around the little boy's shivering shoulders. She reassured him with a gentle voice, even as her eyes struck sparks of defiance off Thornleigh's. "Master Thornleigh means no harm, lad" she said. "He's just very careful of his ship."

Thornleigh wanted to shake her, but he swallowed his anger. Madness to wrangle out here in the open. "Jinner," he growled. "Get these people out of sight."

The fugitive trio scurried after Jinner across the deck to the companionway, and went below. Honor began to follow. Thornleigh grabbed her elbow and turned her around. "You," he said. "In my cabin."

Once inside, he swung the door behind them. Again it stuck, refusing to close completely. With a curse he kicked it shut. "Now," he said, coming up to her, "what's going on?"

"What do you mean? Master Paycocke—"

"Paycocke's welcome. I expected him. But who are the others?"

"His granddaughter, Alwyn, and her children."

"Come to see him off, have they?" Thornleigh asked with all the sarcasm he could muster. He knew what was coming.

"No," Honor said firmly. "They sail with you tomorrow."

Thornleigh groaned. But before he could protest she declared, "I couldn't leave them behind. Richard, they have no other family."

"Good Christ! How can we settle them all over there? Have you even *thought* of the expense?"

"I knew you'd be concerned for their welfare," she said, invoking sarcasm in her turn. She opened her cloak and pulled out a purse and tossed it onto the table. "Five pounds. From Cromwell. And Alwyn has a little money of her own, too, to get them started. And they won't need papers because they're Paycocke's dependents. Satisfied?"

Thornleigh scowled at her and shook his head. It was useless to argue. What was done was done. It would be more dangerous to send the woman and children ashore than to keep them on board.

"Well, if that's settled . . ." Honor murmured. She was tugging her cloak back in place, avoiding his eyes. "It was a long ride. If I may, I'll stay the night." She added quickly, as if to forestall argument, "I'll be gone in the morning before you see me. Alright?"

Thornleigh walked to the small high window beside his table and looked out. *No, damn it, none of this was alright.*

Honor waited. In the silence, the wooden ship creaked.

Thornleigh's exasperation finally exploded. "A day late! A whole, bloody day!" He whirled around. "Woman, you take too many risks."

"You take risks too," she flared.

"That's different."

"Why?"

He brushed aside the question and jabbed a thumb at the window where a scatter of ships could be seen lying between them and the shore. With sails furled, they were skeletal shadows in the gathering dusk. "It's bad enough we have to lie here, exposed to all the world. Bad enough we can't take on cargo from the cove as we used to, what with Bishop Nix and that blasted Dr. Pelle watching my every move. But, my God, to bob here for an endless day . . . with two fugitives already aboard. Two more, I remind you, than we agreed was safe, with Paycocke coming. To bob here . . . watched . . . such easy prey. And now, *five* of them for God's sake. And one a woman. Six, if you count the blasted baby!"

Honor said nothing. Thornleigh turned back to the window tight-lipped, damming up harsher words. He slapped his hand hard against the wall. Then he wheeled around again and spat out a final grievance, making it an accusation: "And not knowing if you were alive or dead!"

"Obviously, I would have made it on time if I could," she said indignantly. "Hunted people can't always meet your rigid schedules."

They stood staring at one another, both defiant.

Honor was the first to relent. "I'm too tired to fight," she sighed. Softly, reasonably, she explained. "I went to pick up Paycocke as planned, but he was distracted about his granddaughter's safety. A few months ago her husband was convicted of heresy. He abjured, but the Chancellor gave him a two year sentence. He died a week ago in the Marshalsea prison. The old man and his granddaughter have only each other now. He was so upset, I offered to take her and the children as well. But it was twenty miles out of our way to reach her, and Paycocke is so frail and, with the children, the ride was so slow . . ." Her voice trailed off. She added, with a quiet desperation that Thornleigh rarely saw in her, "The Chancellor's net spreads farther every day."

He noticed for the first time the shadows under her eyes. The trip had obviously been an ordeal for her. Well, it had not been much less so for him. A sleepless night, trying to beat from his mind the images that had swarmed when she'd failed to arrive— images of her on a stone cell floor, squirming naked beneath a grunting jailer. Or stretched in agony on the bishop's rack. "Better late, you say?" he muttered. "If all unravels, you might think you were better dead."

She lifted her chin high. "At least that would make your life easier, wouldn't it." She turned on her heel to leave.

She struggled with the stuck door. Thornleigh had to smile. She finally yanked it open, gathered her dignity again, and flounced out.

Two hours later Thornleigh sat at the end of the table watching Honor, at the opposite end, tell an amusing story. Between them, all the passengers were crowded on benches, drinking Thornleigh's ale and laughing. On one side sat old Paycocke and his granddaughter—she cradling the sleeping baby in her arms, he with the boy on his lap, the drooping young eyelids fighting to stay open. On the other side sat two young men who had already been aboard for a night and day—a bespectacled bookbinder and a stocky, bearded wheelwright.

The mood in the cabin was jovial. But Thornleigh was aware that his passengers' merriment was more frantic than relaxed, tinged as it was with fears of an uncertain future—and more than a little nervousness in his company. Nevertheless, they were enjoying Honor's boisterous accounts of his victorious skirmishes with the authorities. The tale she was telling now was of his recent coup against the Bishop of London.

"And so," she said, "Master Thornleigh assured the Bishop in his most honeyed, most *lying* merchant's voice"—her audience laughed and stole furtive glances down the table at Thornleigh— "'Nothing easier, Your Grace!'" she said, lowering her voice to mimic Thornleigh, and doing it so abominably that even he had to smile. "'I'll act as your agent and gather in the filthy books for you to burn. Next cargo of wool cloth I carry to Antwerp I'll root out this wicked new edition of Tyndale's—'"

"I know the book!" old Paycocke piped up enthusiastically. "Tyndale's *Answer To Sir Thomas More's Dialogue*. He's written it to refute More's *Dialogue Concerning Heresies*."

"The very one, Master Paycocke," Honor confirmed. "But what the Bishop didn't know, sir, and Master Thornleigh did, was that Tyndale's new edition had been ill made, botched at the printer's, and Tyndale longed to reprint it. "'Aye, my lord,' says Thornleigh to the old Church fox. 'Give me the means, and a fair commission, and I'll go and buy up every last book and deliver them home to you.' Well, he did get the money and he bought them all. And he sailed back from Antwerp, his hold crammed with Bruges silk, licorice, and thimbles, and twenty crates of Tyndale's *Answer*. So, the Bishop got his books to burn, Master Thornleigh got a generous commission, and William Tyndale got the Bishop's gold . . . enough to print a beautiful new edition!"

Old Paycocke threw his head back with a hearty laugh that belied his frail constitution. The other men banged their mugs on the table, hunched over it, wheezing in helpless mirth. "It's sheer poetry, mistress," Paycocke cried. "Listen.

> The bishop got the books to burn,
> Our man got his commission,
> And Tyndale got the Bishop's gold,
> To . . ."

Other voices chimed in,

> ". . . print a new edition!"

There were waves of laughter.

Thornleigh leaned back in his chair with an indulgent smile at the hilarity. He lifted his hand to signal the cabin boy to pour more ale all around. But the boy, he saw, was slumped in a corner, asleep. Honor apparently noticed it too, for she reached for the pitcher and started around the table to serve the ale.

Thornleigh's eyes followed her. Her face was bright, all her weariness melted away by her own warm energy. That energy had thawed the fears of these timid people, too, he realized. She could do that so easily. When she wanted to. What an amazing woman. In fury, she'd kicked a red hot poker from his hands to get his attention, but she could be as soothing as a mother's embrace to these people in distress.

He watched her move, turn her head and bend, pouring ale. He loved looking at her. The colors of her silk dress gleamed in the lantern light—the skirt, pale green like a shiny new apple; the top, a shade like the apple's first blush. The pearls of her headband shone in her dark hair like dew. She glowed, he thought. Especially amid the browns and grays of these drab Protesters. Wasn't that what they were calling themselves these days? No, Protestants, that was it. But then, she'd stand out anywhere, even without fine clothes. With that face—that body—what man could fail to notice her?

He remembered how he'd glibly talked her into that midnight kiss in the Cardinal's wintry garden—a quick, stupid victory that he'd forgotten as soon as he'd won. So much had changed since then. The Cardinal was dead. Tonight was warm summer. And no one was likely to talk Honor Larke into anything these days. But—the biggest change of all—he'd give the earth to be able to kiss her again.

"As satisfying a tale as I've heard in many a month, Mistress Larke," Paycocke was saying, dabbing tears of laughter with his sleeve. Honor smiled and topped up his mug. "And you, Master Thornleigh," the old man went on. He got to his feet and his face became solemn. "I salute you, and I thank you, sir, as well. For despite these hearty tales, I know you are taking great risk to give me and my family hope—and these other friends here, too. Yes, I'm sure every heart here thanks you." He lifted his cup. "To Master Thornleigh, and his bonny new ship!"

The others murmured, "Aye!" and raised their cups in a toast.

Uncomfortable, Thornleigh waved away the thanks. "She is a beauty, though, isn't she?" he said. He was immensely proud of the ship.

"And is it true what I have heard, Master Thornleigh?" the young woman, Alwyn, shyly asked. "That tomorrow, with us, your ship takes her maiden voyage?"

"It is, mistress." Thornleigh sensed her uneasiness and knew the others shared it; none of them had ever been on the sea. "And a grand crossing it will be, I promise you. She's sound as an oak. I've never seen a carrack better built."

"There now, Mistress Alwyn, it must be so," Honor smiled as she reached Thornleigh's side with the pitcher. "Only perfection could make him stop grumbling about the cost of building her."

The others laughed. Thornleigh hid his smile in a sip of ale.

"And what have you called her, sir?" the bookbinder asked.

"To tell you true," Thornleigh said, wiping his mouth, "she hasn't yet been named." He looked around at the whole company. "Any suggestions? Offer me a good one and I'll name her here and now."

"How about the 'Thomas More'?" the wheelwright put in cynically. "As a tribute for sending us off to see the world."

"Or 'More Trouble'," the bookbinder punned.

There were groans.

"Or 'More's Nemesis'," Honor muttered. Thornleigh frowned at the hardness in her voice. He'd noticed that it tainted her, in face and speech, whenever she mentioned More. Why she hated the man so, he couldn't fathom.

"Have you no thoughts yourself, Master Thornleigh?" Paycocke asked.

"None so far. But I'll have a good name only, mind. A singing name. One to make her happy and speed well."

The others chattered on, discussing the challenge.

"That's it!" Honor cried softly.

She was standing at Thornleigh's elbow. He looked up, and was surprised at the sudden pallor of her face.

"You said 'speed well'," she said. She set the pitcher on the table and dropped to her knees at his side. "Oh, let *Speedwell* be her name."

He saw the eagerness in her eyes, big as a child's. As she gazed up at him, her hand rested artlessly on his knee, light as a lamb's fleece, and warm. He felt his body respond. "Please, Richard," she whispered. The entreaty—so hopeful, so devoid of guile—tugged at his heart and brought a smile to his lips.

She withdrew her hand and stiffened. "Don't mock this," she said. "I have my reasons for wanting it." She stood, her face hardening. "Private reasons. You wouldn't understand."

His smile vanished. Once again, it was Mistress Larke with her private hurts and hates. Brusquely, he called above the chatter, "Well, we cannot understand everything, can we, Master Paycocke? Presumptuous of mere men to think so."

"Indeed, sir," Paycocke answered amiably, having heard only

the question and none of what went before. "Omniscience we must leave to God."

Honor took up the pitcher again. She moved around behind Thornleigh to serve ale to the other side of the table. As she passed him he caught her wrist. "All right," he said quietly. "If it means that much to you. *Speedwell* she shall be."

Her eyes met his in a silent thanks so eloquent, he wished it was in his power to give her such happiness again and again, just to be rewarded with that look. Then she moved away.

The others were delighted with the name. Toasts to the ship erupted. Everyone smiled and chattered. The christening—the sweet, English familiarity of the name itself—seemed to bind up their frayed nerves with a comforting ribbon of security.

The company began to stifle yawns. Everyone was tired, and the gathering soon broke up. Paycocke and his granddaughter, each carrying a sleeping child, drifted to the door, followed by the bookbinder and the wheelwright. They left for their quarters, everyone chuckling over choice parts of Honor's tale of Thornleigh and the Bishop.

Honor trailed after them. Thornleigh's voice stopped her at the door.

"Sleep here tonight," he said.

She turned to face him. He saw her eyes dart to his lantern-lit bed tucked in its berth. She had misunderstood him. And her look was not one of happy anticipation. He noted it wryly; yet it stung him. "Don't fret, mistress," he said. "I'll be spending the night with the crew."

He saw blood rush to her cheeks at her error.

He brushed past her. "Be up at first light," he ordered, and went out.

Brooding, he walked across the main deck under the stars. He drank a ladle of water from the rain barrel near the main mast. He tugged at a rope's knot to test it. Damn, but it was like his heart was on a seesaw, dealing with the woman. Up when he could see her smile, down whenever they wrangled. Which was often enough, God knew, with these rescues of hers. Constantly hurling herself into danger.

He turned to look in on the men in the fo'c'sle. At least he could feel pleased with the new crew. Of course, he'd hand picked them. And, to ensure loyalty, paid them double the usual fifteen shillings for a return trip to the Low Countries.

He didn't notice the figure at the railing gazing ashore until he'd reached the fo'c'sle door. It was the breeze rippling her skirt that caught his attention. Then he heard her soft sobbing. Honor? Needing comfort? He hurried to her side. He'd take her in his arms this time. No more hesitating.

She turned, startled. It was the old man's granddaughter, Alwyn.

"Oh, don't be angry, Master Thornleigh," she said, brushing tears from her cheeks. "I know your orders were not to come on deck. But since it's so dark I thought I might be allowed, just for a moment. I simply had to have a last look." Her voice wavered as though she was trying not to cry. "One last glimpse of England."

He looked at the sky. With no moon, the night was as black as pitch, and the only lantern was far aft, up on the sterncastle deck. He hadn't even seen her himself at first. "Alright," he agreed. "For a moment." He looked out at the black water to give her time to recover.

"Little ones a-bed?" he finally asked.

She nodded silently. Together, they stared out for several moments. From the fo'c'sle came the sweet-sad tune of a sailor's tabor pipe. Suddenly, a sob escaped her. "I know nothing of Dutch or Flemish, Master Thornleigh," she blurted. "Nothing of strange, foreign ways!"

He leaned on his elbows across the railing and watched the pin-prick light of a night watchman's lantern creep along Yarmouth's town wall. "Do you like cheese, mistress?"

She looked at him, surprised.

"They have an uncommon fine cheese in Amsterdam," he said. "Delicious with a good ripe apple or a thick trencher of rye bread. 'Gouda' they call it." He turned his head to her. "Can you say it?"

"Gouda?" she stammered.

"There. Now you know some Dutch."

She almost smiled.

"It's that simple, mistress. Your boy'll be jabbering it soon enough, you'll see. 'Gouda' may even be your little girl's first word."

Her face clouded again with worry. "They'll grow up more foreign than English, won't they?"

"They'll have two tongues to speak, double the tools most people have for understanding the world. That can't be an ill thing, now can it?" He smiled gently at her. "There's good and bad folk abroad, same as everywhere. Same as in England. Same as in your own village, I warrant."

She nodded, calmed, and this time she managed a small smile.

He watched the pale, anxious, young face. She looked about the same age as Honor, he thought, yet so different, so adrift. In fact, she reminded him a little of Ellen. "I'm sorry about your husband, mistress."

"He's with God," she said simply. After a moment she looked up at him. "You're very kind, sir. Not at all what Mistress Larke—" She stopped herself, her fingertips at her lips.

Thornleigh grunted, straightening. "Mistress Larke and I sometimes see things differently. Doesn't mean she's always right."

The ship's bell rang to mark the watch.

"You'd best get below now," Thornleigh said. "Your children will need you rested, come morning."

"True enough. Good night, sir," she said, and turned to go. She was several steps from him when she looked back and whispered shyly. "And thank you."

He leaned again on the railing and looked out. A game young woman despite her fears, he thought. Not so much like Ellen after all. Ellen. Last time he went home he'd found her curled up in a soiled shift, lost in a stupor of sadness that had lasted for four days, according to his sister, Joan. Four days in which Ellen had not dressed, nor bathed, nor even risen from the bed. When Honor's message had come asking him to run a second escape voyage, he'd jumped at the chance to get clear of home.

He looked down at the black water, thinking of home. How

many times over the past few years had he spurred his horse out of the courtyard of his manor, Great Ashwold, barely getting past the gate before he kicked into a gallop and raced away from the place, away from his wife? His clinging, incomprehensible wife.

And away from his responsibilities. Adam was running wild. Ellen couldn't control the boy, a rambunctious eight-year-old, curious as a young wolf. The task of seeing that he stayed out of trouble and stuck to his lessons had fallen to Joan. But Joan deserved a house of her own, a family of her own. If Giles Tremont ever got up the courage to ask for her, Thornleigh knew Joan would be keen to accept. He had no right to hold her there, minding his household like a servant. He must let her marry.

But Ellen was utterly incompetent at running a large manor. Thornleigh's jaw tightened in anger as he thought of her. Yet he knew his anger was better directed at himself. After all, who had rushed into marriage with a seventeen-year-old girl he barely knew? Even Ellen's father, though eager for the match, had warned him. "She's a good girl, but somewhat . . . queer," the old knight had confided just before the wedding. But Thornleigh had found Ellen comely enough, a quiet little thing, soft of voice. He'd have settled for far less to get hold of the large dowry her grateful father offered. *That* was very attractive, indeed. The thriving manor of Great Ashwold. With its paying tenants and flocks of sheep, the manor was a bracing step up for a young clothier with his way to make.

But Thornleigh had had no idea then of the bottomless melancholy which, without warning, could drag his new wife into some private hell and chain her there in torment for days. Joan believed, as did the neighbors and the parish priest, that a devil had bored into Ellen's skull and lived there, sometimes at work, sometimes asleep. After nine years with Ellen, Thornleigh had come to think of it more as a disease. Still, much good his theories did her. A way to help her—that he'd never found.

Except the babies. She loved babies. She had been good with Adam when he was small: tender and watchful. Mothering had made her happy. But then there had been a series of miscarriages, and that little fiasco at the bishop's court. And the black moods had crept back. Then, little Mary had been born, and . . . His hands involuntarily balled into fists.

No. There would be no more babies.

He quickly turned from the railing with an urge to escape thoughts of home—the same urge that made him gallop back out through his gates after every brief visit there. He wasn't proud of it. But, God help him, that's the way it was.

He cast his eyes up over *Speedwell*'s furled sails. What *had* made him proud was that second voyage he'd run for Honor. And the ones that had followed. Real accomplishments. Even the trouble with the harbor officials in Bruges; it could have gone far worse. The fact was, he'd never felt so alive. The work was unpredictable, challenging, exhilarating. And there was Honor.

He looked up at his cabin on the forecastle deck. She was there, inside, behind his door. He felt like a dolt for leaving her in such a stupid way, like some pouting love-starved pup. She'd be gone in the morning. He wouldn't see her again for at least a month.

A wand of light glowed under the door. He stared at it, and imagined her bare feet moving along the floor. Her hair loosened from its band. Her body loosened from its silken cocoon. He pushed off from the railing, strode to the door, and knocked.

She opened it. Still dressed. What excuse could he muster? "I forgot to lock away the charts," he said, walking in.

He rolled up the parchments, stashed them into a trunk and locked it. It was done in a moment. Nothing else to keep him here. At the door again, he turned. "I'm sorry. All that shouting when you arrived, I mean."

She nodded. He saw that weariness had crept back to her face. "I'm sorry too," she said. "You were right. Sometimes I am . . . reckless."

She had never admitted so much. It was a thread of intimacy, of connection, and he wanted to spin it out, wanted to wrap it around them both, wrap her close to him. He could not leave. Not yet. "The ship," he said. "Why does naming her *Speedwell* mean so much to you?"

She sighed. She went to the corner of the window. It's sill was at the height of her chin. He came and stood beside her. She looked out at the blackness, and told him her story. The book. Ralph. Sir Thomas's perfidy.

By the time she had finished, Thornleigh was leaning his shoulder against the wall, his arms crossed, watching her. "So that's why you can't forgive More," he said.

"Never." Again, he thought, that chilling voice, hard as an undertaker's spade. "Well then," he said, "I'm glad you forgive *me*."

"You?" She looked unsettled, surfacing from her trance of spite.

"For my earlier bluster."

Her mouth began to curve in a smile. Mentally, he ran his thumb over the soft lips. "Nothing to forgive," she said. "Indeed, I should thank you. For so much, over these past months."

"Oh? For insulting you in the Cardinal's garden? For molesting you in Spain, and deserting you there? For constantly opposing your wild schemes?"

Her smiled ripened. "Naturally, for all that," she said with mock seriousness. "But also," she added softly, "for saving me from the worst of my . . . wild schemes."

"There's a lot there worth saving," he said seriously. God knew he meant it.

A puzzled look flitted over her face. "You're so different from . . . well, from that time in the Cardinal's garden."

"So are you."

She lowered her eyes for a moment. "In any case," she said, "it's you who must forgive me. I was wrong about you. I took you at first for a drunk and a wastrel, but you're neither."

He cocked an eyebrow at the backhanded compliment. "Thanks."

She was studying him. "And Anne Boleyn. I was wrong about her, too, wasn't I? I mean, about you having a . . . a friendship with her?"

"Yes," he smiled. "Wrong again."

He caught a glitter in her eyes. Mischievousnesss? "Not wrong, though," she added, "in deducing that was exactly what Anne wanted from you."

He shrugged. "Hard to believe, eh?"

"No," she said steadily, looking into his eyes. "Not at all."

The sheer sincerity of it startled him, thrilled him. God, what a

woman. He reached out for her. He slipped his arms around her
waist, bent his head to kiss her.

She suddenly drew back. "No." But her palms were warm on
his chest. There was no strength in their pressure. Gently, he
pulled her to him. "Honor . . ."

"No, Richard." This time she tried to jerk free. But he read desire in her eyes. Unmistakable. So he held her. And felt her muscles soften.

"Unless . . ." she began.

"Unless?" Anything!

"Unless I'm wrong about something else too. Your wife."

Thornleigh felt the last word like a slap. Ellen. Till death us do
part.

They looked hard at one another. From somewhere across the
deck, a sailor began to sing a ditty.

"But," Honor said softly, "I see that I am not wrong."

"No," he answered. Disappointment and desire surged in warring waves. "I have a wife. I can't change that."

He let her go. She stepped away and turned from him. He felt
the thread of intimacy snap. Not looking at him, she said, very low,
"I will not be a married man's dalliance."

He walked to the door, opened it, and left.

Alone, Honor doused the lantern. She unfastened the lacings of
her clothes and let the heavy garments drop to the floor. She
pulled back the coverlet of Thornleigh's bed and crawled naked
inside. She lay with eyes open in the dark, aware of the smell of
him on the sheets. From across the deck came the sweet-sad
music of a sailor's pipe.

I have a wife, he'd said.

And I? Honor thought. *I envy her.*

She yielded her weary body to the rocking *Speedwell,* and to
sleep.

She was on deck at dawn. Crewmen jogged by her to their sta-
tions, some still rubbing sleep from their eyes. From the forecastle
deck Samuel Jinner barked orders. The bosun's whistle shrilled.

Boys, monkey-quick in the rigging, readied to set free the great, cocoon-like shrouds. One unfurled above her, stirring and rippling in the morning breeze as if it, too, was just awakening. The first rays of the sun sparked the red and white banners that snapped above the crow's nest, and suddenly the whole ship basked in soft morning sunlight. Her oiled oak timbers glowed. The gay designs of stripes, chevrons and stars on the outside of her hull flashed off the water in bright ripples of red, green, white and gold. Honor took it all in, along with a swallow of sweet, salt air. The *Speedwell* was indeed a beauty!

On the sterncastle deck Thornleigh stood under the gold wash of the sky calling commands, preparing his ship to sail. Honor took a deep breath and came up beside him.

Thornleigh was shouting angrily to Jinner. "Who's bowsprit lookout?"

"Rawlings," Jinner shouted back.

"He's half asleep there! Tell him to sit up smart or I'll have him lashed."

"Aye, sir!" Jinner said, on the run.

Thornleigh looked overhead, mentally checking lanyards that tendrilled the masts as he said to Honor, "Thought you'd be ashore by now."

"I'm just going."

He glanced at her face. "Don't fret. I'll get them all safe over."

"No, it's not that. I have a favor to ask."

"Well?" He turned away to watch a crewman securing a sheet.

"You see, there's a rather desperate case. A chandler named Rivers."

"Master Wade!" Thornleigh called. "Send up the carpenter to see about these parrels. Two are cracked."

"Aye, sir!"

Thornleigh looked back at her. "Yes?"

"And, well, I'll need to run another mission before you get back."

Thornleigh was watching the quartermaster roll a barrel past them. "Stonor," Thornleigh growled, "I hope for your sake this grog's better than the swill we had last crossing." He moved to a ledge to pick up a chart.

Honor followed him. "So," she said, as boldly as she could, "can you spare the *Vixen?*"

He turned to her and let out a snort of incredulity. "You want *all* my ships?"

"Not quite. I've no need for the poor old *Dorothy Beale.*"

"Not yet," he scoffed. He looked at her hard. "On credit again, I suppose? Crew's wages and all?"

She returned his look steadily, and nodded.

"And," he added softly, "with collateral security I apparently cannot seize."

The reined-in regret in his voice forced her to look away. She was afraid that if she gazed too long into his eyes, she would be lost. She said coldly. "This must remain a business arrangement."

"I see. Well, in a business arrangement it's customary for both parties to get something they want."

His sharpness stung her. And irritated her. A man's life was at stake and all Thornleigh could think of was his own hurt pride. "Look," she said, "you won't have to deal with me for much longer. Cromwell assures me the King will soon get the divorce, and when Mistress Boleyn is Queen this persecution of the reformers will stop. But until then, I need access to two ships."

"And to my capital."

"Richard, if our work founders, men will die. You know that. Already there are too many we can't reach."

"Some of them don't want to be reached. Some are lunatics."

"And some," she shot back, "have been reduced to such pitiful husks by the Chancellor they can no longer react like men!"

"It always comes down to the Chancellor for you, doesn't it? The man doesn't act alone, you know. He's not the Devil incarnate."

"Close enough."

"Honor, you can't save the whole world."

"I can save enough to make a difference."

He watched her, frowning, but said nothing more.

"I know," she began, eyes down, "I know I owe you . . . a great deal of money for what you've done already. And I'll keep my promise to pay it all . . . one day. But for now, think of what must be done. Think of Paycocke and Alwyn. Can we leave people like that to the clutches of the Chancellor?"

Around them, the bustle of embarkation continued.

"Jinner!" Thornleigh called, his eyes still locked on Honor's. "Lower the skiff. Mistress Larke is going ashore."

He took her elbow and hustled her down to the main deck and across to the railing as if he were escorting a mischief-maker off his ship. The skiff splashed into the water and the rope ladder was tossed over the side for her. Her hands were on the ropes and she had taken the first step down when Thornleigh said, "Tate."

Honor looked up with a question in her eyes.

"I've a good pilot named Tate," Thornleigh said. "I'll leave orders for him. Meet him at St. Nicholas's here two weeks from Sunday at noon. Tate's yours, and the *Vixen*."

She beamed. "Thank you." She started down.

He leaned over the railing and called after her, "And God help you if you're late again!"

❧ 21 ❧

The Hold

Several months later, at ten o'clock on a gusty May morning, Honor and Jinner stood on Pinnacle Tower in Yarmouth's town wall and nervously looked out at the masts of carracks and coasters beyond the beach. The *Dorothy Beale*, Thornleigh's oldest ship of his three, still lay at anchor. Piloted in Thornleigh's absence by Master Tate, the ship was supposed to have sailed hours ago.

Honor hugged herself as she thought of the jittery fugitive she had sent aboard the night before. Edward Sydenham. He'd found courage enough to escape the Bishop's prison a week ago, but he had none of his father's gentle forbearance nor his mother's fierce stoicism. This delay, she knew, would be gnawing at his belly.

It was her fault. She knew it. Thornleigh had warned her that the *Dorothy Beale* was sorely in need of refitting. They had not yet sent her out with the *Speedwell* and the *Vixen* in the missions. But when Edward, on the run, had come to Honor begging for help, she had decided to press the old hulk into service. She had not realized the extent of the problem, however, until seven that morning, the hour that the ship should have been underway. As she was rising from her bed at Thornleigh's Yarmouth townhouse, Jinner had banged on the door.

"Rat-eaten rigging and piss-bloated bilges," he'd reported,

scrubbing in the matted hair under his red cap. "She's a tub, m'lady. It'll take some hours more."

Then, she and Jinner had just sat down to a silent, tense breakfast when a messenger arrived from the Bishop of Norwich's Chancellor. Dr. Pelle, she was told, wanted her to present the ship's bills of lading for examination at the Tolhouse within the hour. She and Jinner had immediately rushed to Pinnacle Tower for a look out at the *Dorothy Beale*, and breathed a little easier to see that no officials' boats were alongside her.

At least, she thought now, *not yet*. Exchanging anxious glances, she and Jinner climbed down to the street and made their way to the Tolhouse.

Pelle sat in his high-backed chair framed against an arched window in the Tolhouse hall. His impeccable black velvet robe emphasized his white hair and parchment-white skin as he leafed carefully through Honor's papers. Finally, he looked up at her. "A profitable cargo of wool cloth, Mistress Larke. Your partner flourishes."

"Yes, sir. Thank you, sir." She gave him a vapid smile. The story she and Thornleigh had circulated was that she had invested substantially in his wool trading business. It was uncommon for a woman to be so personally involved in trade, but not unheard of. It explained her frequent trips to Yarmouth, and her presence around Thornleigh's ships. As for Queen Catherine, she was gone on a pilgrimage to humble herself before the Holy Blood of Hales, and Honor would not be needed again for at least a week. But even when the Queen was home, her joyless days were spent in a trance of prayer; she hardly seemed to notice Honor's absences.

Pelle checked the destination on the papers. "Amsterdam. And who sees to Thornleigh's shipment there?"

"Oh, dear, it's"—she made a show of struggling for the name— "I believe it's . . ."

"Deurvorst?"

Honor felt a rush of panic. Klaus Deurvorst was the young Anabaptist who settled the refugees she and Thornleigh sent to Amsterdam. "No, it starts with an 'S'," she said, still pretending to search her memory. "I'm sorry, sir, but it's so hard to keep straight all these foreigners Master Thornleigh deals with." Suddenly, she brightened. "Spreckles! That's it. His factor in Amsterdam is Mineheer Spreckles. Queer name, isn't it?"

"Where is he now?"

"Spreckles?"

"Thornleigh," Pelle said evenly.

"Homeward bound on the *Speedwell*, sir. From the Antwerp spring fair. And I do hope he's remembered the Bruges lace I ordered. Why, last time—"

"And your other ship?" he interrupted.

"The *Vixen*? Oh, her mizzenmast snapped in a gale off Calais, sir. She's in for repairs. Such expense! You'd scarcely believe the price of—"

"Indeed. Well, I'm sure you are anxious to get the *Dorothy Beale* underway as soon as she is ready." Pleasantly, he added, "I hope the delay has not upset your passengers?"

Honor's heart missed a beat. "Passengers! Bless me, Dr. Pelle, we'd have to *pay* a person to take passage on the *Dorothy Beale*, she's that bad! But, you're right," she smiled. "I would like to get her underway."

Pelle was studying her face. "Forgive the inconvenience," he said with a thin smile, "but hard times call for hard measures."

"Oh, the times are evil, just as Your Good Worship says," Honor burbled. "But the honest people of Norfolk are safe assured of your very best efforts in keeping our harbors safe." If I'm boring enough, she was thinking, he may excuse me without more questions. "We should all be doing more to assist you is how I see it, and I know I would if I could but, bless me, it's all I can do to keep an eye on Master Thornleigh's shipments. Why, I recall one time when a lame-brained apprentice mixed up several bales of good worsted . . ."

As she prattled on with a silly story of arithmetical errors Pelle's face twitched with irritation. His harbor-agents—a dozen men lounging in the room—idly listened in.

"Lord!" Honor finished. "How these loutish 'prentices do try us! It's a burden, I can tell you, for a poor, helpless woman." She sighed, then bestowed on Pelle a luscious, almost carnal smile. He jerked back his head as if physically threatened by it. Honor knew that Pelle, unlike many of his fellow churchmen, was revolted by the ways of women. She had discovered she could cut short these interrogations by provoking his aversion.

"Master Thornleigh rails at me something awful. I must be vigilant with the 'prentices, he says, else we'll lose a pretty penny. Oh, he does get wild. But," she shrugged, letting her green cloak fall open to expose the naked top of her bosom, "I soon calm him." She winked at a weathered soldier at Pelle's elbow. "After all, he's a man like any other and can be led, can't he, Captain? Once a woman's been shown a man's leash, she soon learns how to tug it."

There were sniggers from the officers. Honor was almost ashamed of her performance, and of the lie it inferred, yet she knew by the film of distaste clouding Pelle's eyes that the stratagem had been effective; he wanted only to see her gone.

He leaned forward and handed her back the papers, and dusted off his fingers as if they had dirtied him.

She masked her relief. "If that is all, Doctor Pelle . . ?" she asked sweetly.

"Yes, yes," he said, waving her away.

She bobbed a curtsy.

"But please," he added, rising, "convey my respects to Sir Thomas More. A worthy gentleman, well-beloved of the Church."

Honor felt her simpering smile congeal. She was afraid Pelle had noted it, and she cursed herself for her transparent face. If he knew her connection to Sir Thomas, how much else did he know?

"Good day, mistress," he said darkly.

She curtsied again, then turned. Jinner trotted after her through the room. Pelle's men watched her pass with looks of lazy appreciation of her beauty.

Outside on the steps Honor gratefully gulped down a breath of the cool morning air. "One for us, Sam. Now, let's check on the ship. Maybe Tate can make the second tide."

They said nothing more as a trio of Pelle's officers sauntered past them up the steps. Honor glanced at the leaden sky, then hurried down to South Quay, Jinner marching at her side with his bandy-legged gait.

They were climbing into their skiff when a greasy little fishing boat, coming in too fast, crunched against theirs.

"Steady on, Claypole," Jinner cried to the rower, a wiry, long-haired old man whose clothes, as greasy as his boat, were shaggy with peeling patches that jerked in the breeze.

Claypole shot Jinner a scornful glance and muttered something under his breath. He scrambled forward to the bow, then hopped out and hastily tethered his boat. Eyes down, he hustled off along the quay with patches twitching.

"Crazy old scavenger," Jinner muttered, and lifted the oars.

Honor sat in the bow and watched the town wall slide by as Jinner rowed them through the harbor entrance, then out toward the moored ships. Her heart tightened at the thought of Edward Sydenham. She knew his nerves were raw from a week of evading the authorities. Even worse, he had served much of his sentence in a tiny cell of the Bishop of Ely's coal house, manacled there for months without a beam of sunlight or a candle.

Poor Edward. His imprisonment and escape had been torture enough, but Honor did not think they had scarred him as much as the reunion with his mother. He'd scrounged his way to London just to see her. But, according to Edward, Bridget's disapproval at his arrival was only too obvious. "I was supposed to die a martyr, and make her proud," Edward had growled to Honor. So he had grabbed a few belongings, ready to leave her house for good. And his mother's only comment, he said, was to grant him permission to take his father's Bible. Then, he'd slammed the door on her, and run.

Jinner's voice broke into her thoughts. "M'lady!" His raised oars were frozen in the air.

Honor looked past his shoulder. Three boats were funneling out of the harbor entrance. In one, she could just make out the form of the leather-faced captain from the Tolhouse. She slapped the gunnel, cursing Pelle for his suspicions. "Hurry, Sam," she cried. "If they're coming to search the *Dorothy Beale* we've got to hide Edward."

Jinner strained at the oars. Minutes late they were clambering up the *Dorothy Beale*'s fraying rope ladder. Honor hopped on deck and looked back at the captain's boats. They were heading straight for the ship. She sent Jinner to alert Pilot Tate, then ran across the deck and hurried below. She found Edward in the carpenter's cabin reading from his father's large English Bible to the spellbound carpenter's apprentice. As Edward looked up at her he slammed the book shut, the instinct of the hunted, and pushed his limp orange hair back from his face.

"The Bishop's men are about to board us," Honor said. "You've got to hide. Follow me!"

Edward's face drained. Stunned by the crisis, he did not move. Honor snatched the Bible from him. In her haste she fumbled it, and it crashed to the floor between them, splayed open by its very weight. Its pages fanned, and Honor saw a row of names neatly written on the fly leaf. She recognized several of them, and Edward's handwriting, and realized with a jolt of horror that it was a list of his fellow Brethren.

"Fool!" she cried. She checked herself, and stifled her anger. "Edward, we have no time. Hurry!"

Still he did not move. Honor bent and swept up the Bible and hauled Edward by the elbow out of the cabin.

They dashed past empty hammocks that stank of the ghosts of two generations of crewmen living close-packed, then went down the lower companionway. Here, in the gut of the ship, was the hold.

Honor stumbled forward in the gloom. The hold reeked of seeping bilge water. The plank floor was slippery with a mucous film. Stray crates and barrels bruised her shins. She grunted, pushing them out of her way, one arm hampered by the heavy Bible. She hiked her skirt to get over the step for the mainmast in the center of the keelson, and made her way past the brick galley and its cold cauldrons. Just beyond it, a low ramp led to a platform that covered two bays for firewood and ballast.

She hurried up the ramp. Between the bays she dropped to her knees and put down the Bible. She felt with her fingertips along the platform floor until she hit upon a depression the size of a knothole. She flashed a smile of triumph at Edward. He had remained on the stairs. Standing to straddle the spot, Honor hooked her finger into the depression and yanked. A two-foot-square hatch shuddered loose. She lifted it, revealing a narrow pit—a yawning square blacker than the blackness of the unlit hold. She jerked back her head at the stomach-curdling foulness that rolled out.

"Come," she said to Edward.

But Edward had frozen on the stairs. His hand flew to his throat. The putrid air seemed to be suffocating him.

"You'll be safe in here," she said. "They'll not find you, I promise."

His glassy eyes were locked on the pit. He shook his head in jerks. "No . . . not . . . again . . ." He would not, could not, move.

"It won't be for long, Edward. An hour at most. Then they'll go. Hurry, now!"

"No! They'll stay till they find me! They know I'm here!"

"Of course they don't," she reassured him. She realized that his phobia was magnifying the danger. "Pelle orders these snap searches all the time, of us and others. For him it's routine. You have only to hide here quietly for an hour, probably less. Then they'll go, and you can come out."

"Don't you understand? They *know*!"

She felt a chill. "Edward, what are you saying?"

"Your pilot was taking forever . . . rigging and nonsense . . . we should have sailed hours ago. I was going mad . . . waiting below . . . I couldn't breathe. I had to get on deck. Just before you came, I went up. I stood at the railing. It was only for a moment, I swear! Oh, God . . . how could I know Claypole would be rowing by? He saw me. He knows me!"

Honor blanched. Claypole. The harbor scavenger who had collided with her and Jinner. He must have tipped Pelle.

"Damn you! I told you to stay below!"

"I couldn't help it! It was Satan . . . working his worst on me!"

She stalked toward him. "No, it wasn't. You've made this mess yourself. Well, you can damned well deal with it yourself!" She pointed a stiff arm behind her at the pit. "Now swallow your fear and climb down there while I try to get rid of Pelle's men. Move!"

"No!" In a burst of panic to be gone he twisted on the stair and slipped. His fingers clawed at the slimy wood above him. He found a hand-hold and bolted up the steps.

She ran after him. She caught up with him outside the carpenter's cabin. Though he was taller than Honor, she grappled the shoulders of his shirt and wrenched him against the closed doorway and pinned him there, her fists bunched beneath his chin. He blinked at her impotently, stunned with terror.

"Listen to me!" she said. "If you're found, you put me and every man on this ship in peril, and many ashore as well. I will not let that happen. You *must* go below. There's no place else that's safe. I promise you I'll get rid of these men."

Under her fists his body twitched as though in convulsions, wracked by dry sobs. He let out a thin wail. Appalled, she released him. He slid down the door and fell to his knees, weeping out of control.

He'll never go below, she realized. Even if we drag him into the hole and cover it, he'll scream from within and draw them to him.

She looked up. Frightened crewmen stood silently on the companionway. The iron-faced Pilot Tate watched her, waiting. Jinner gnawed the edge of his mustache and watched her, waiting. From the upper deck, the bosun's shout told them that Pelle's men were nearing. Sweat trickled down her ribs . . . her heavy cloak was stifling her . . .

The cloak!

She whirled it from her shoulders and crouched. "Edward, listen. You shall not go to the hold. Can you hear me? You shall not go down there. Can you walk?"

He lifted his tear-stained face and nodded.

She beckoned the pilot and two other men to help him to his feet. "Put this on," she said to Edward as she threw the cloak over his shoulders. "The officers will see you, but they'll think you're me. They know I'd be leaving the ship before she sails. Jinner will take you ashore. Just hold the hood tightly around your face, do as Jinner says, and you'll be safe. Do you understand?"

Edward nodded shakily, wiping his eyes.

"Sam," Honor said, stopping Jinner on the companionway as

the men hustled Edward to the upper deck, "take him to the far side of the quay. Get a fast horse of Thornleigh's and send him off to Lynn. Master Ives of the *Falcon* might give him passage. Tell Edward to give Ives this." She shoved a purse into Jinner's hands, then clutched his arm. "And be careful, Sam. That scavenger Claypole has betrayed us."

Jinner's face hardened. "Bastard!"

"Go now."

"But my lady, what will you . . . ?"

"Go!" she cried, and shoved him up the last two steps.

Minutes later she peered out a crack in a lidded gunport and watched as Jinner helped the shrouded figure down into the skiff. The captain's three boats were closing in. They could not fail to notice the skiff pulling away from the ship, but Edward was tightly clutching the hood of the cloak, and Jinner was rowing in a wide arc around the boats. Honor slumped with relief to see that the captain was ignoring the retreating green-cloaked "lady." If Sam made it to shore, she told herself, Pelle might not ask to see her immediately. He wouldn't expect Thornleigh's wanton, ignorant little "partner" to know anything. Later, when the search proved fruitless, he might ask for her at the house, but Sam could put them off the trail. And by then Edward would be gone.

The three boats banged alongside. Honor ran across to the hiding place and snatched up the incriminating Bible. She crouched on the platform and swung her legs down into the pit. She took a deep breath. *They'll be thorough*, she thought, *but they'll be leaving empty-handed.*

Pelle's men stomped through the hold shoving barrels, kicking crates, clanging around the galley cauldrons, poking into the firewood bays. After twenty minutes the captain barked the order to withdraw above deck. Honor heard the shuffle of many boots ascending the stairs. Then, there was no sound except the rhythmic low squeaking of ropes against wood, and wood against wood . . . and the thudding of her heart.

Could she come out now? Was it safe? She only had to lift the hatch and climb out. No, she'd be a fool to come out. They couldn't possibly have left the ship yet. She must be patient. With any luck they'd soon start to think that Claypole had been mistaken. They'd give up and go. Pilot Tate would come for her. *Be patient.*

But it was so vile! So black . . . she couldn't even see her own hand. And no room. She couldn't keep standing like this . . . with the hatch pressing down on her neck.

As she hugged the Bible her fingers drummed its cover. Her fingertips felt the stark, embossed gold cross. In a flash of grim humor she saw herself standing like some pilgrim lost in prayer, with head bowed and the Bible clasped to her bosom.

Couldn't keep standing . . . but this scum on the floor . . . oh, God, it was on the walls, too! *Stop this*, she commanded herself. *Stay calm. Put the Bible down. There, now . . . sit on the Bible. Alright. Better . . .*

There was only enough room to sit with her knees drawn up. Even then, her toes touched the far wall. In the corner she felt something soft against her foot. She did not know what it was. And then, with a shudder, she did know. A dead rat.

Oh, please, please *let them leave soon!*

"Steady, boy!"

Behind the stable at Thornleigh's house Jinner was still fastening the horse's cinch as Edward clawed up into the saddle and glanced over his shoulder with hunted eyes. He had thrown off Honor's cloak—it lay at Jinner's feet—but had covered his telltale orange hair with a black cap from the stable.

"Don't fret, sir," Jinner said, grunting as he tightened the strap. "Star is Master Thornleigh's fleetest gelding. He'll carry you to Lynn quick as a jackrabbit. Remember, now, it's Master Ives on Salter Street. He's across from—"

"Where's the purse?" Edward cried in a strangled whisper.

"In the saddlebag," Jinner said. He gave a sharp tug to the cinch.

"That's good enough! Let go!" Edward said, and shoved Jinner away.

"Good luck to you, sir," Jinner growled through his teeth, and slapped the horse's rump hard. It galloped down the lane belching breaths under Edward's furious kicks.

A few minutes later, still puffing from the dash up from the stable, Jinner peered out a corner of Thornleigh's front room window. A knot of officers was marching down the street toward the house, a sergeant and five men, all armed with swords. Jinner kneaded the green cloak bunched in his hands.

A fist banged the door. Jinner balled up the cloak and thrust it into a chest. He caught a servant boy watching him from the entrance to the kitchen. With a finger to his lips he motioned the boy to keep quiet, then illustrated the consequences of disobeying by jerking the finger across his throat like a knife. The boy shrank back into the kitchen.

Jinner answered the door.

Honor arched her back. Fire flared up from her buttocks. Thirst thickened her throat.

Toes numb now . . . she almost wished her legs were, too, instead of these needle pains. And stomach cramps. What she'd give to stretch . . . just stretch this one leg . . . it was on fire . . .

Forget the leg! She could endure this. She *could!* But what could be happening up on deck? It had been hours . . .

There'd been a skirmish. That was it. Tate had fought back. Been killed. All the crew were dead and no one knew she was here!

Stop it! There was no reason for Tate to fight. Soon he'd come. But, oh, how much longer? Was it day or was it night?

In her ears the washing of the ocean swelled and sighed as if a monstrous living seashell breathed inside her skull, and that brought even wilder fantasies . . .

Tate had confessed to Pelle! Told him everything. They were both up there, sitting on deck, smiling together like two toads slimy with the scum of this pit, smiling and waiting for her to perish below in this tomb!

Violently, she beat her forehead on her knees, smashing the hallucination.

How much longer . . . ?

* * *

Jinner sat in the deserted tavern staring into his mug of ale. From the neighboring precinct of the Benedictine priory came the unhurried chanting of monks at Compline, their eight o'clock service to God. Jinner buried his face in his hands. Ten hours she'd been in the hold.

The sergeant who had come to the house had accepted his story that she had ridden off to Norwich. "After that, it's back to London," Jinner had said. Then he had asked, feigning surprise, "What's this all about, Sergeant?"

"*Dorothy Beale*'s impounded."

"What? Why?"

"Dr. Pelle's got his reasons. Crew's been brought ashore, too."

Jinner had waited a moment. "When can they go back aboard?"

"You ask too many questions, mate."

At least the crew had not been arrested. The cabin boy of the *Dorothy Beale* had skulked by Thornleigh's back door to deliver that news. Pelle suspected a stowaway, the boy had told Jinner, but didn't have enough evidence for arrests.

Over his ale Jinner rubbed his face with both hands, cursing Pelle, cursing Edward Sydenham. "And curse that harbor rat, Claypole, to the hottest coals in hell!"

Honor heard a sound overhead. A man, cursing softly. Very close. Tate had come! No, wait! She must be sure!

She was so tense that her teeth ripped off a piece of the inside of her cheek, and she had to clamp her knees to keep her quivering muscles still. She craned her neck to see a sliver of lantern light sifting down the crack at the hatch edge, and strained to hear.

"Just my rotten, God-cursed, pissing luck," the voice whined.

Her heart plunged. Not Tate.

"Aw, leave off," a second voice said, this one deep and rumbling. "The faster we get through this lot, the faster we'll be above deck." The timbre of his voice was so low that Honor imagined the wall at her back was reverberating, and though he spoke of hurrying, his words rolled out slowly, with deliberation.

"And out of this pissing dungeon," the first voice whined. "Christ, I hate a hold."

"Leave off, I said."

"But it's such a pissing waste of time. There's no poxy stowaway. What're we looking for anyway?"

"There might be printed Lutheran smut. Tuppence if we find any."

"Just tuppence? Christ, Legge, I swear you'd step into the jaws of the Devil if a penny lay on his tongue."

"Look, I've got six mouths to feed," the bass voice said, "so shut yours and help me shift this lot. Captain said look round the galley."

Honor heard more thudding, more grumbling. The men's voices became indistinct as they moved to another part of the hold. The sliver of light died. Then, from farther off—at the top of the stairway?—a shout. "Hoy! Legge! Captain says come up."

"Right," the bass voice answered.

"About time," the whiner said. Boots clomped toward the steps. The bass voice called up, "Do we go ashore then?"

"No luck," the voice at the top of the stairs answered. "Captain says we bunk down in shifts. Keep a watch on every deck, and search regular as long as it takes to find the bugger. Dobson, you're to stay below here."

"Me?" the whiner cried. "Christ, how long?"

"Till you're relieved, man," said the voice on the stair. Then he laughed. "Never mind. Can't take us more'n a few days. We'll either see him . . . or smell him."

The others' boots clomped off.

The whiner's voice was faint, as if he were slumping down alone on the stair. "Aw, piss on this."

Silence.

. . . a few days!

She felt the insects of panic crawl over her skin. She had to come out now! Smash the hatch up and crawl out of this hell-hole. He'd seize her. They'd question her. But they'd be lenient with a gentlewoman. Yes, that was it! She'd invent a tale—she'd done it before. Spew out some excuse, spin some lie, confuse them with enough female-flabby babble to save herself . . . *save herself!*

Suddenly, as though an icy wind had blasted her, all her mind's motion froze. Only one word howled on inside her brain, desolate, alone. *Myself.* It moaned like a grieving soul lost in barren wastes. *Herself* . . . abandon the others . . . *save herself* . . .

If she saved herself, the Bible would be found, with its names. Others would suffer. Some would die.

And she knew she could not do it, whatever the cost. She could not snuff out a score of lives, not for just *herself* . . .

And if the cost was her own life?

She swallowed.

But they'll leave before it comes to that . . .

Leonard Legge emerged on deck into the blustery twilight.

A guard with teeth like moldy cheese ambled toward him shoveling food from a wooden plate into his mouth. "Cold beans and grog in the fo'c'sle," he mumbled through a mouthful. "Find anything down there?"

"Nothing," Legge answered. Irritated, he ran a hand through his long black hair lined with streaks of silver and swept back from his forehead like a mane. His only vanity, it did little to balance his coarse, red face. Legge scowled. "Seems we're staying."

"Aye. Plenty of grog, anyway," the guard said, and shuffled on.

Legge walked to the railing, rested his elbows on it, and looked out, thinking. He'd been working Pelle's harbor patrol for only a month and didn't know what to make of the sight he had caught that morning. He had been rowing the captain's boat, and they had approached the ship just as Mistress Larke's skiff was pulling away. As he watched her go he was sure he'd seen a bright orange lock of hair lick out from her hood before her hand swiped it back under. A large hand. And her form . . . the hunched shoulders, the bowed head, the stiff neck . . . those couldn't belong to the little flirt—the dark-haired flirt—who had amused him and the other men in the Tolhouse hall. And why hadn't she even looked back when they had boarded her ship?

He pried up a splinter of wood from the parched railing and used it to pick his teeth. *Dobson's right*, he thought. *Piss on this.*

. . . Was it day or was it night? How many days? Or nights?

The ship swayed and her head rolled back and forth along the wall like a doll's. Slime clumped her hair. Vomit-flecked spittle caked her mouth. She retched, but there was no liquid left in her squeezed-out stomach . . .

The guards were relieved regularly. There was always one on watch. Not even a breath of air above the hatch was possible.

The first time she had felt the warm trickle of urine seep between her legs she had cried tears of shame. The grimace of weeping had split her cracked lips and she'd tasted the metal bite of blood. But that was the first time. Now . . . now, she hardly felt the trickle . . . her drawn up legs were slumped apart and felt nothing . . . her foot crunched the rodent bones and felt nothing . . . her cracked lips bled, and she felt nothing . . .

Shortly after eleven o'clock on the second night Jinner and Tate stood on the town wall, as still as stone monuments. Rain lashed their faces as they gazed at the lantern lights—mere sparks—on the far-off *Dorothy Beale*. Beyond the dunes, white-crested waves stood up as furious as fighting cocks, battering the beach, battering the anchored ships, and battering the rolling *Dorothy Beale*.

"Think they've found her?" Tate asked.

"They'd have brought her ashore."

"Not in this storm."

They looked out in silence.

"She must've come out," Tate said. "No one could stay down there this long."

Jinner gnawed the end of his mustache. "You don't know her."

"Jesu," Tate muttered, "how can she bear it?"

Rain trickled around Jinner's drooping, bloodshot eyes. "Curse this storm for a witch's spell, a skiff can't get out in it."

"Even if we could, we'd never get aboard past Pelle's men."

"Think I don't know that?" Jinner snapped. "But, Mother of

God, how much longer can she last?" He watched the ship. Finally, he said quietly. "Let's shove off."

They turned and walked away.

They were trudging up a dark street when a door opened not far ahead, spilling candle light. A man tottered out to the doorstep. Claypole. Tate and Jinner stopped. They watched him as he turned back to a blowzy, half-dressed woman in the doorway. He squeezed both of her massive breasts, then slapped her buttock in farewell. She closed the door. The wet street went dark and cold again. Claypole tugged his hat down to fend off the rain and started up the street, whistling.

Jinner and Tate exchanged glances, then followed him. At the intersection of an alley, they struck. Jinner gagged him from behind, ripped his arm back, and hauled him off the street. While Jinner held him, Tate smashed his nose, then plowed a boot into his groin. Claypole fell and writhed in the muck, gasping and spitting blood. Jinner drew a knife. Tate crouched, took a fistful of Claypole's hair and yanked his head, face up, to stretch the scrawny neck across his knee.

Claypole's eyes gleamed with terror as Tate pried apart his jaws. Jinner straddled his chest. With the tip of his knife, Jinner hooked out the informer's tongue, grabbed it, and sliced it off.

"Point a finger at us again, rat," Jinner said, "and next time it'll be your throat."

. . . Was it day or was it night? How many days . . . or nights? Were her eyes shut . . . or open? Was it black . . . everywhere? Everywhere . . . *ubique. Quod semper, quod ubique, quod omnibus* . . . "What has been believed always, everywhere, by everyone." But it wasn't dark everywhere . . . was it? Didn't the sun shine . . . somewhere? On lakes . . . waterfalls . . . sparkling cool water . . . water . . .

In her pain-fogged mind only one bright thread—the merest filament—still glimmered: she had kept faith. She had only to come out, but she had not done it. She had decided to die rather than send others to death. Against every urging of her body, she had kept faith.

But that body was no longer under her command. She could not restrain the feeble sobs that struggled up from deep in her belly. They reached her ears as if they came from somewhere else, someone else . . . some forgotten prisoner whose mind wandered in madness . . . from a living grave by the mainmast that sang in the keelson . . . sang of captivity, chained to a coffin that rolled on the fathomless sea . . .

And there were other voices . . .

. . . the siren song that coaxed ceaselessly, "Come out! Confess, and be saved!"

. . . *Kyrie eleison* . . . *Kyrie* . . . "*Father, have mercy upon us* . . ."

Father! . . . "*Christopher Larke, we damn thee unto the pain of Hell. We curse thee* . . . *within and without, sleeping or waking* . . . *lying above earth or under earth* . . . *in wood, in water, in field, in town* . . ."

Ralph! . . . "*selling illegal Bibles in the English tongue* . . ."

Richard!

Suddenly, she knew she was dying. She had been clinging to a precipice, but it was crumbling away. She could hold on no longer. There was one moment of sheer, insane terror—a crimson explosion inside her brain.

She let go.

But death did not snarl at her from the pit as she fell. It did not open its fangs to savage her. It enveloped her, tenderly, quietly. Then she knew. Death was no more than a gentle stopping of all the motions of her body. It was like a strong warm wind on a summer hilltop, a wind that streams so powerfully on the face, it closes the eyes and stops the breath. She gave herself to it, to this overwhelming summer wind, and as she allowed herself to fall into it, it cradled her in its comforting embrace.

She had chosen this death. She had battled the pain and the terror for three days. She had succeeded. And this was peace.

On the evening of the third day the *Speedwell*'s banners frisked in the breeze as she slipped through the lightly frothed waves toward Yarmouth harbor. Thornleigh took the stairs up to the sterncastle deck two at a time and strode along the starboard railing, filling his chest with the sweet tang of the evening. He stopped by the hanging bronze bell he was bringing back from Antwerp was a beautiful object, cast by Peter van den Ghein of Mechlin. He spread his hands around the gleaming metal. Its engraving felt new-minted sharp beneath his callused palms. *Cost a fortune*, he thought, *but what a piece of work. She'll love it.* And he let his finger fly against it just to hear its brassy ping.

They were close enough to see the lazily turning windmills on Yarmouth's beach when the bowsprit lookout yelled, "Boat off port bow!"

Thornleigh crossed and gazed out. A skiff was bobbing through the low waves toward the ship. He saw the red cap on the man hauling at the oars. Jinner. The skiff came alongside.

"What's amiss, Sam?" Thornleigh called down.

Jinner lifted his face, showing gray skin around hollow eyes.

"Christ," Thornleigh said, "you look like you've walked with the Devil himself. What's happened?"

"Let me aboard. You'll hear it all." Jinner tethered his boat to the ship and stood to come aboard, but as the ladder was thrown down for him he did not move forward. He lowered his head and wept.

☙ 22 ☙

The Bible

Thornleigh's face burst above the water, his teeth clenched around a knife. He sucked breath, desperate for air, but he saw with relief that he had surfaced less than ten feet from the *Dorothy Beale*'s bow. Panting, he glanced back. Under gathering storm clouds that blotted the moon, Jinner, in the skiff, was almost invisible.

Thornleigh swam to the anchor line and grabbed hold. From under the bulge of the hull he could see nothing up on deck, but he knew there were sentries. He and Jinner had spotted two on lackadaisical patrol, one fore and one aft. He doubted there were more; they wouldn't be expecting attack. He adjusted the tightly bound, oiled leather bag slung over his bare back, pulled in a last deep breath, and began to grapple his way up.

Just below the upper deck he braced his foot on the shelf-like plate that spread the chains to the shrouds. He swung himself, hand over hand, along the plate until he was past the forecastle. Groping for a handhold, he peered up over the deck. A sentry clomped by only feet away from the top of his head. He waited, straining to keep his grip on the slippery oak. When the sentry was halfway to the main mast there was a long rumble of thunder. The noise cover gave Thornleigh his chance. He heaved himself aboard, darted up the forecastle ladder to the forward mast, and crouched behind it.

At that moment Jinner's voice burst out of the blackness, bawling a tavern song. Right on cue. Both sentries idly moved to the port railing and joined one another to look out. Thornleigh wrenched the leather bag from his shoulder and dug out the tinder box. He sparked the flint on the steel. Instantly, the linen strip caught fire. He dropped it onto a coil of rope under the mast. As soon as the rope flared, Jinner's voice swelled into a lewd and highly original chorus of the song. The sentries laughed at the invisible drunkard's increasingly obscene interpolations. They didn't see Thornleigh cut off a flaming length of rope and dash with it toward the main mast where he tossed it into an open keg of pitch. And they didn't hear him, over Jinner's caterwauling, as he dove off the starboard side.

A sleepy guard emerged on deck from the companionway and halted abruptly. Before him, flames were leaping up the forward mast. "Fire!" he yelled.

The sentries whirled around. The bases of both masts, and all their lower rigging, were alight. One sentry sprinted to the sterncastle to ring the bell.

"Fire!"

In the water Thornleigh listened to the bell clanging and the sentries shouting. He felt his way along the hull to a battened gunport just above the water line, and waited. He heard guards begin to scramble up on deck, but he held himself back, giving time for all of them to come up. When their noise on deck had become a din he smashed his knife against the gunport hatch until it splintered away. He swung one leg over, heaved himself through, scraping his ribs along the jagged opening, and tumbled inside.

He whipped the knife from his mouth and crouched, ready to fight any stragglers. But he had timed it well—there was no one, only abandoned hammocks and the bedroll litter of encampment. He headed for the companionway down to the hold. He could only hope that no guards had remained below.

He went down the final steps into the silence of the hold. In the gloom, his chest pounded with relief as he sensed that all was clear.

He made his way towards the ramp, bare feet slipping on the cold slime of the floor, then up to the platform between the bays. His fingers, still numb from the water, fumbled for the recessed opening. He found it. He sheathed his knife in his belt, and was about to pry the hatch loose when he heard, beneath the muffled frenzy of the crew above him, a sound—eerie, low—a sound that scraped a claw of dread over his heart: the mournful song of the mainmast in the keelson.

He shook off the premonition. Bending, he pried up the hatch and laid it aside. A blast of foulness struck his face. He looked into the pit. A shape was slumped in the shadows, motionless. A corpse.

His fists clenched in rage. He refused to believe it—even to believe the overwhelming odor of death. He dropped to his knees and thrust his hands out for her, and wrenched her up by the fabric on her back. He hauled her out of the pit and dragged her along the platform, and laid her on her back. He took her face between his hands. It was cold. Cold and still. He slapped her cheek, hard. Nothing. He laid his ear on her breast and tried to hear—to feel— some throb of life. Nothing. He took up her hand and crushed it inside both his hands as if with his strength he would crush life back into her. But her hand lay cold and still.

He caught the first whiff of smoke. He knew he had only moments, but he could not bring himself to let go of her hand, to give her up to death. Yet he knew he must. The ship was burning. He had to get out—and get her body out. He forced himself to loosen his grip on her. His fingers slid over her palm. And then he felt it. A tremor in the vein at her wrist. A faint pulse.

Sweet Christ, she was alive.

He gathered her into his arms and hurried up the companionway and headed back through the main deck toward the smashed gunport. The shouting on the upper deck was now a chorus of panic. The smell of smoke was intense. As he passed the companionway that led up he turned his back to shield Honor from flames that were licking down the stairs. He reached the gunport and stopped. He saw that the shattered gunport was far too narrow to get through with her in his arms. He'd have to push her out first, then dive after. There was no other way.

He lifted her unconscious body into the opening and let go. His heart contracted as she slid from his arms with a gentle rush like a dead child he'd once seen buried at sea. He heard the faint splash of her body. He grabbed the sides of the opening and was about to dive out when he remembered: the hatch to the pit! He'd left it aside! If Pelle found the hiding place all of them would be suspect. Run back and put it back in place? My God, no, she'd drown. For one agonized moment his eyes strained back over his shoulder at the stairwell leading to the hold. But for him there was no choice. He looked down at the water for her. His last thought as he grappled the sides of the gunport was: once the fire had destroyed the ship, they'd never know.

He dove out.

Leonard Legge stumbled toward the companionway through the litter of empty hammocks and bed rolls. He had slunk away from the pandemonium on deck and rushed back down to rescue the gambling winnings he had left with his gear. He'd grabbed the money, but now he had to get out. His eyes were stinging in the smoke, and by the time he reached the stairs again the top two were on fire. He looked around for something to smother the flames, and saw, in the gloom at the gunports, a shape—a man?—dive out.

It was only a glimpse, and between the fog of drink in his head and the thickening smoke all around he wasn't exactly sure what he had seen. The heat behind him snapped him back to the danger. He snatched up a blanket and beat at the flames on the stairwell. Men above were sloshing buckets of water on it too, and soon the blaze died. Legge started up the dripping steps, then looked back to the spot where he had seen the figure. Curiosity reclaimed him. He hurried down again.

He stuck his head out the gunport. He could see nothing in the black water below. A flaming spar from the deck plunged by his head and he ducked back in. As he did, eyes down, he noticed that water was pooled on the floor at his feet. His own boots from the stairs weren't that wet. He saw that the pool was at the end of a trail of water. His eyes followed it to the companionway that led down to the hold. He hesitated. The fire was bad; he should get out. But if there was something down there . . .

He grabbed a lantern from above a hammock and rushed down to the hold. In the darkness he had to crouch to see the wet footprints, but he was able to follow them up the ramp. He tripped over a stray hatch. Cursing, he fell forward. One leg slipped into a hole. He stopped himself just before he toppled all the way in. He lowered the lantern partway down the hole. From the depths, the feeble gleam of a golden, embossed cross glinted up at him. A Bible.

Honor's eyelids twitched open. She saw only gloom. Not an oppressive gloom. More like the inside of the tithe barn near Nettlecombe where she had played as a child, where the golden dust of winnowed grain floated in the air. From the softness where she lay she turned her head. The room wasn't large. The high, single window was shuttered, its edges leaking golden light. She was aware of a smell, a comforting blend of leather and fresh-sawn wood and sweat. She sat up with a start. She was in Thornleigh's berth in his cabin on the *Speedwell*.

From the jolt of sitting, a hammer pounded in her head. She had to drop her forehead onto her drawn-up knees to ease the blows. The curled posture took her back inside a hideous, indefinable nightmare. To break free of it she hauled her legs over the side of the bed. She sat hunched, her breathing shallow, and tried to stitch together the dark fragments that lay shredded in her mind. She remembered . . . dying? Yet how could that be if she was here? Her memory was a blur, and each fragment dissolved when she tried to grasp it, like night-time shadows that slink away at the rising sun. Only one thing was certain: she was not dead.

Suddenly, she was overwhelmed by a hunger for the sight of the world. She pushed herself from the bed. As she stood, her legs buckled and she clutched the table for support. She shuffled toward the closed door. As she reached for the handle her sleeve drooped over her hand. She looked down at herself. She was dressed only in a man's linen shirt. She knew she should not show herself this way, for although the shirt was far too large for her its hem came only to her knees. But the craving to be outside blotted modesty. She pulled the door open. Light poured over her. The *Speedwell*, at anchor off Yarmouth, was basking under a sunset of molten gold in a red and limitless sky.

"M'lady!" Jinner lurched from his post on a stool near her door. But halfway to his feet he halted in amazement at the sight of her bare legs and he dropped the hunk of elm he was whittling. Honor ignored this crouch in which she had locked him like some fairy spell. Squinting, she shambled forward to the edge of the sterncastle deck.

Jinner snapped from his trance and sheathed his knife. "Cloak," he said, and hobbled off behind her into the cabin.

Honor stood blinking at the bold brightness all around her. Radiant sunset. Blue sea. And everywhere, heady sparkles of white. White gulls wheeled overhead. White-bronze stars of light snapped off the water. Sun-bleached linen gleamed on her own body. And beyond this bedazzle of white lay mile-wide ribbons of gold, unfurled across the red vault of sky. She shut her eyes and saw the red-gold glory still, dyed crimson on her eyelids.

The sun-warmed plank beneath her feet infused its heat into her. She felt its energy, the original fire of sun in living oak, an energy that raced up every vein, through every tendon, until it reached her arms and seemed to lift them without her volition. She spread them wide, eyes still closed, and felt the soft fabric of the shirt sleeves slide like tepid water off her forearms, exposing more skin to sun. A breeze rose to hug her, caressing the curves of thigh, belly, breast and shoulder, and luffing gently through her hair. She inhaled the salt tang, then let out a huge and grateful sigh. It was good to be alive!

Her eyes sprang open and she saw Thornleigh. He stood high on the forecastle directly across the length of open deck. He was leaning over the railing, watching her with a smile.

She slowly waved her arm to hail him. The sun kissed the vein at her wrist. Thornleigh's hand went up in a matching silent salute.

A flash of green swamped her vision. Jinner was bundling her cloak around her. Memory exploded: the cloak, Edward, the hold. She whirled on Jinner.

"Where's Sydenham?" she asked, afraid to hear what danger Edward might have exposed them to.

"Safe away," Jinner assured her. Honor relaxed.

Jinner shook his head. "Though why your first word should be for a lousel with cold porridge for guts," he grumbled, "I'm sure I don't know."

She laughed, lightheaded with the happiness of waking up alive. Even the tug of bruised stomach muscles felt delightful. "Having just experienced what he declined, Sam, I'd say he showed great judgment."

Jinner's familiar, morose shrug enchanted her. She flung her arms around his scrawny neck and kissed him hard on the mouth. He wavered, dumbstruck.

She heard Thornleigh's laugh roll across the deck.

Suddenly, in the middle of laughter herself, her lightheadedness spun into dizziness. Her legs softened into willow saplings. Her hands slipped down Jinner's skinny chest and she slid to the deck and landed, loose as a puppet, on her backside.

Jinner sprang to fetch his stool. Laughing again, Honor let him help her onto it. "Why, you're as weak as a kitten," he said, chastising her. "Now, you sit here, and I'll fetch vittles. It's bread and grog you need."

She felt for his hand to stop him. "No, Sam, it's a friend beside me I need. And some answers." Questions were bubbling up inside her. It was clear everyone was safe, yet how had it been managed?

Jinner grunted happily and lowered himself to sit cross-legged at her feet. He picked up the hunk of elm and unsheathed his knife. Somewhere across the deck, a sailor's tabor tweedled a jig. "I'm carving you an angel," he said, gouging a chip of wood. "I reckon it's the one who watched over you. 'Course, once we had you aboard I knew you'd make it through."

"We?"

"Me and the master." Jinner twitched a horny thumb in the direction of the forecastle, and they both looked across the deck.

Thornleigh was frowning. Jinner made an exaggerated nod to assure him of Honor's safety after her tumble. Apparently satisfied, Thornleigh turned to his pilot who was waiting at his elbow, obviously wanting his attention. Both of them stepped back to resume work at a table where various brass instruments of navigation lay among scrolls and charts.

Jinner cocked an eye up at Honor. "He did the swimming, for I never did learn the art of it. But it were lucky for you both that I fought to keep the poxy skiff in line. And who d'ye think's been ladling broth into you for the last two days?"

Her eyes widened, and she waited to hear the story. Jinner obliged. He told her how, in the small hours of yesterday morning, he and Thornleigh had fired the *Dorothy Beale.*

"What? You set fire to her while I was in the hold?"

"Aye. A right beautiful blaze, too. Worked like a charm. But after we had you safe out and back aboard *Speedwell*—Pelle was watching the house, you see—well, then the master was in as foul a mood as ever I've beheld him. For when we looked back, damned if Pelle's men hadn't doused that fire."

"Why should that make him angry?"

"Well, in getting you out seems he'd left the hatch off the hiding place. He was afeared they'd find it—open, when it was closed in their searching, see?—and there'd be questions."

Honor was struggling to remember something of the rescue, some glimmer, but it was still all blackness.

"He stalked this deck till dawn," Jinner continued. "Then he decided to strike."

"Strike?"

Jinner closed his eyes as if to savor the recollection. "You'll hardly credit it, m'lady. He's done some fool things before, and I've seen most of 'em, but this beats all. He barged into Pelle's own house—I was right behind him—and shook his fist in Pelle's poxy face, and demanded an apology!"

"What?"

"Aye! For impounding his ship unlawfully, and letting her burn while in his custody! Oh, it was rare. Master stomped and fumed and swore, and Pelle had to listen, all the while twiddling his thumbs like a grubby priest who'd been caught with his hand in the alms box. And what d'ye think? Master not only got the *Dorothy Beale* released, he demanded payment for damages. And what's more, he got it! So that's the upshot of the whole blessed foofaraw, m'lady. Which is to say, nothing at all."

Honor's wondering gaze was drawn to Thornleigh on the forecastle. What a gamble he'd taken! She had to smile, for she could well imagine his performance with Pelle, a fine display of ruffled Thornleigh feathers with much noise and fury. Yet all the while he must have been wondering if the manacles would be clamped on him before he got the last oath out. A gamble, indeed!

She watched him at his calculations as he checked a steering compass, unfurled a chart. He wore a loose white shirt and coppery breeches, and the ruddy-gold sun burnished his auburn hair. He was the incarnation of this very light.

He stepped aside to put away the chart, revealing the table's far end, and Honor was startled to see there a child—a well-dressed boy, perhaps nine years old. He stood over the table and pushed a tangle of brown hair from his eyes as he worked a pair of dividers over a map.

"Who's the boy, Sam?" she asked.

Jinner glanced up. "Master's son." He went back to his whittling.

She had known of the boy's existence. He lived, though, at Thornleigh's manor of Great Ashwold near Norwich, and Honor's work on the missions had brought her only to Thornleigh's townhouse in Yarmouth. This was the first she had seen of his son. A handsome lad, she thought, watching him. Tall and straight and easy-moving, like his father. But there was also a shyness in the face, a doe-eyed quality that made her curious about what other strains made up the mettle of such a fine-looking young creature.

No, she thought, it was more than curiosity. She had never imagined Thornleigh's wife as being attractive. Stately, perhaps, and dourly conscious of the wealth and status she had brought her husband; a haughty woman who might well drive a warm-blooded man into other, kinder, arms. That was the picture that had made sense to Honor. But the boy's face spoke of gentleness, not pride.

Honor felt a stab of jealousy. Was there more to keep Thornleigh at home than she had believed?

"Tell me Sam, what's the boy's mother like?"

Jinner frowned down at the angel's face emerging from his chunk of wood. "Master doesn't speak of her. Bade me not as well."

An odd answer, Honor thought. She drew up her dignity. "Perhaps not to other, common ears," she said, "but surely you may to me." Her voice was tinged with authority, as she had intended, and she winced to hear the hardness in it. It was a craven ruse. Yet her curiosity burned.

Jinner nodded, accepting her command like fate. "Mistress Ellen. A simple lass. Oh, she be my better, I do mind, being a great knight's daughter, and me bred out of the lead mines of Swaledale. But she be of a simple *nature*, if you catch my meaning. Quiet-like. Sometimes singing all to herself. I've known the lass many a year."

No stone-faced matron, clearly enough. Here was a startling new picture. "But why does he not speak of her?" Honor asked. The question was hardly out of her mouth when a companion question hovered in her mind: was Thornleigh so fond of his wife that he hated even to bandy her name? Hesitantly, she added, "Does he love her so very much?" She wanted with all her heart to hear it was not so. She knew she had no right; knew that, after refusing him herself, the wish was petty. Still, she longed to hear Jinner contradict her.

He shrugged. "Love? That I couldn't say. They don't talk much. She sometimes seems more child than wife."

"Then why his silence? Tell me, Sam."

Jinner was mute a moment, and kept whittling. Then: "A while back the master was called to the Bishop's bawdy court. His lady was being held there."

Stranger and stranger. "What was the charge?"

"No charge. A whispering neighbor had led the 'paritor to suspect her of reading heretical tracts." He shook the wood chips from his sleeves. "Oh, she be no madwoman, no raving witch like some I've seen. The suspicion were all nothing. It seems a trifle now. She'd got a bit of writing at a scribbler's stall, and the neighbor who saw it thought it strange she should be meddling with books."

"But it *is* a trifle. They don't usually harass for so little cause. Especially a knight's daughter with a respectable clothier husband."

"But the father was dead and the husband was not about, m'lady. And, like I said, she be a simple soul. Felt the shame of being called to court right keenly, poor thing. Well, the master went and argued there, for they had no right to keep her. She was let go, and went home with him, and all was well again."

Honor nodded. But the explanation unsettled her. Thornleigh, she now saw, had his own grievance against the Church, his own private reason for involving himself in these dangerous missions. It meant he was not acting just for the payment she was promising to make one day. The realization surprised her, as did her own reaction: she felt it like a kind of loss.

Still, she thought, his wife's incident at the Church court did not seem so dreadful. She sensed that there was more behind Jinner's reticence. "Sam," she said sternly, "what else?"

"Oftimes," he said, "Mistress Ellen sinks into a powerful sadness."

Honor shrugged. "So do we all, sometimes."

"Not like her," Jinner said darkly. "A demon sometimes steals inside her and sucks her happiness away. I've known her since before the master married her, and that cursed demon's always been with her. But one day . . . one day was the worst." His gaze drifted up to the furled sails above their heads. The angel carving lay forgotten in his lap. "All Saints Day if I recall aright—'twas four year gone, for I recall the lad yonder was just turned six—the master and me rode home to his manor hard by Norwich. We'd just sailed back from Flanders on *Vixen*. Her hold was fairly bursting with damask and oranges and spice. I can still smell that cinnamy-bark if I close my eyes tight."

He did so, and Honor smiled indulgently, waiting.

"We rode into the master's courtyard, and all was quiet as the grave. Master said to me then and there he wondered if his lady'd been taken by one of her strange, sad fits. But then he thought it couldn't be so, for his lady was then nursing a baby daughter, and the wee ones always made her merry. Well, the grooms in the courtyard said not a word, but slunk away into the stable. Master caught up with a maid and asked her what was what. At first she wouldn't speak. And then, when the master shook her, then she *couldn't* speak for weeping. But soon it all came out.

"Things was bad, the chit said. Very bad. Days before, Mistress Ellen had wandered into the cow byre with the babe and sat down there to suckle it. But the black mood was upon her. The devil, you see, had stolen her wits, and when she wandered out of the byre she left the wee thing in the straw. Alone it was, all the night. The milkmaids came in the morning. The babe was dead—chewed all over by rats."

Honor's mouth opened, but no sound came.

"The master came before the coffin, his face as white as the babe's winding sheet. And when the mistress, weeping there, saw him, she shrieked as if she was in pain, a terrible sound, like a marten I saw once strangling in a snare. Mistress Ellen jumped up and ran for a knife and sliced at her wrists, one after the other, till the blood fairly gushed. The master slapped her face to stop her. He had the maids bandage her wounds. Then Mistress Ellen slept and slept and slept."

"Merciful Jesus," Honor whispered.

"Amen to that," was Jinner's low reply.

Overhead, the pipe tune twined with the screeling of gulls. The sky's radiance was fading. The sun was a sinking red ball.

"Master took it hard," Jinner summed up. "For a long while after, I thought he was goading the Devil to take him. Gone to seed, he was, with drinking and dicing and carousing. Once, he got into an evil scrape at the King's palace, no less."

"Brawling on the tennis court," Honor murmured, piecing together the past.

"Aye, and almost got his hand chopped off at the King's command."

Honor was recalling the glimpses she had caught in days past of

Thornleigh's self-destructive bent. Had grief driven him to act that way?

"And this much more I can tell you," Jinner said. "When he found that babe dead, 'twas himself he blamed. Said if he'd got home sooner he could have stopped it." He spat on the deck. "Aye, that were an evil time."

Vigorously, as though to dispel such unwelcome reminiscences, Jinner attacked his carving afresh. "He's better these days, though," he said. "And I credit it to the good work you've snagged him into, m'lady. Less of drink and dice, and a lot less wenching." He caught himself and looked away with a blush. "Lord, now I've said too much."

Honor's thoughts were a jumble. Thornleigh grieving. Thornleigh wracked by self-doubt. These were new images, indeed. And they engendered such new feelings of tenderness in her. Every time she thought she knew this man, he proved her wrong. And lured her closer to him.

Uncomfortable with her own thoughts, eager to dispel them, she bent to examine Jinner's handiwork. The angel looked more like an exhausted whore. Its haggard face was a flat, sorry lump. "Samuel Jinner," she said and laughed, "you're an honest creature, and I'd trust you with my life, but you're no artist, man."

"You should value your life more than to trust it to Jinner."

It was Thornleigh's voice. He stood before her, eclipsing the red sun. The boy was beside him.

Honor pulled the cloak tighter around her shoulders.

Jinner jumped up. "Be you cold, m'lady? High time you were back in your warm bed. I'll fetch some broth for you and light a candle inside." He hustled away.

Thornleigh placed a formal hand on the boy's shoulder. "My son asked to meet you. Adam, this is Mistress Larke."

The boy bowed gravely. Honor tried to match his gravity but a smile escaped her, for the velvet shyness in his brown eyes was bewitching.

"I'm happy to meet you, Master Adam," she said. "Is this your first time aboard the *Speedwell*?"

"It is, madam."

"And how do you find her?" Having seen his rapt effort over the map she made a guess at his passion. "Would you like to be master of her one day?"

Adam's seriousness dissolved and his face glowed. "I *will* be! My father says he will put me as 'prentice to Master Fulford, and Master Fulford has sailed all the way to Prussia." He glanced up at his father with an expression that knew nothing of fear.

"Not till you're thirteen, boy," Thornleigh said.

Adam's face fell, though he absorbed the fiat with a stoic nod. His eyes darted to Honor as if afraid he had betrayed himself by showing too juvenile a disappointment. Then, bravado surfaced. "That's alright," he said stoutly to her. "By then I'll know even more than Master Fulford's pilot, for my father is teaching me, both sea and stars."

"Then I have no doubt you'll surpass even Master Fulford himself," she said warmly. Adam smiled, his cockiness melting into a relaxed confidence that she thought suited him well.

Honor was aware that Thornleigh was watching her. His expression was not unlike Adam's earlier gravity. "Go on, now," he said to his son. "Pack away the charts. We've done for the day."

Adam bowed again to Honor, but this time with ease, already a friend. She and Thornleigh watched him slip down the stairs and cross the upper deck. For a moment neither spoke.

"Thank you," she said softly, smiling up at him. "For my life."

Thornleigh looked hard into her eyes. "I've said it before. You take too many risks."

She turned away, stung.

Jinner was approaching the stairs with a bowl of soup. They waited through another silence as he carefully climbed, shuffled past them into the cabin, and began to clatter around inside.

Thornleigh began awkwardly, "In the hold . . . that was . . . an ordeal. How are you?"

Honor turned back, all business. "Very well, thank you. Shaky, but well."

She looked up as a trio of curlews careened over the mainmast. She watched them head for home. "I wonder when this will end," she said with a sigh. "The hiding, the persecutions. The deaths.

And all because people want to read the Bible. You'd think . . ." She gasped. "The Bible!" In the happy haze of recovery she had forgotten it. Words began to tumble out. "Richard, when you brought me out of the pit did you retrieve the Bible too?"

"Bible?"

"Edward's. I took it with me down there. He'd written names in it."

"Jesus."

"You mean you didn't bring it out?"

"No."

"Then it must still be there."

He shook his head. "No, as soon as we had the ship back I went down myself to replace the hatch. There was nothing inside. I'm sure."

Honor was confused. "Then what happened to it?"

He thought for a moment. "Who knew you had it?"

She tried to remember the tense scene on the *Dorothy Beale* before Edward had escaped. "Some of the crew did. We were in the carpenter's cabin when I took it from Edward."

"Could have been Timothy, then."

"Who's Timothy?"

"Carpenter's apprentice on the *Dorothy Beale*. Tate said he was chums with Sydenham."

"But how . . . ?"

"Most of the crew went back on board when I did, to collect their gear. He could have gone down to the hold just before I did. Fished the Bible out."

"Where is he now? Can we ask him?"

Again, Thornleigh shook his head. "He took off. Came to tell me he'd had enough, wanted a quieter job. He was a good lad. I paid him and let him go. He didn't say anything about a Bible, though."

They looked at one another, puzzling the clues. "Timothy must have taken it," Thornleigh said finally. "None of Pelle's men could have."

"Why not?" she asked. "Sam said you didn't go to Pelle and get the ship back until morning, so there was plenty of time after the fire for one of his men to find the open hatch. And they were thorough. I heard them when they searched."

"But if they'd found the Bible we wouldn't be standing here talking. We'd all be in Bishop Nix's prison."

"Unless . . ." She hesitated, turning around an idea in her mind.

"Unless?"

"I wonder if we have an unknown friend among the enemy."

The thought, it seemed, had not occurred to him. "It's possible. If so, there's no danger. He'll probably make himself known to us sooner or later." He paused, considering it again. "But I doubt that's what's happened. It's far more likely that in the crisis with the fire they never found the open hatch. Then Pelle returned the ship, and Timothy fished out the Bible and left." He shrugged, done with the mystery. "Whatever. You're alive. We're not in Nix's prison. I have the *Dorothy Beale* back. All's well."

"Yes," she said. "You have her back, and Pelle's money to rebuild her, too, I hear. It worked out well for you."

He nodded with a self-satisfied look that she thought was forgivable under the circumstances. "Still," he said, "burning my own ship is not the method I'd normally choose to turn a profit."

"No." Honor could not resist a saucy smile. "And I am glad it was only the tired old *Dorothy Beale* I was hiding in. You might have had second thoughts about a fire if it had been your beloved *Speedwell*."

He laughed.

In Yarmouth a bell chimed faintly from St. Nicholas's spire. Thornleigh looked out at the last rays of sun disappearing beyond the town. "About the boy," he said suddenly. "I'm sorry to bother you with him."

"It's no bother. I'm glad to meet him. He's a fine lad."

Thornleigh's proud smile was quick. But a frown followed just as quickly. Abruptly, he looked down and kicked half-heartedly at an invisible clump of earth. "I'd planned to keep him away from you. It's awkward. Explaining our relationship, I mean. But once he saw you, he insisted on meeting you. And now . . . well, it's obvious he's taken a liking to you."

Honor stiffened. "I understand," she said frostily. "Don't worry. I shan't bind his heartstrings to me."

"No, I didn't mean—"

"It doesn't matter." She looked out at the now cold-looking ocean. Fatigue was claiming her like the darkling shadows that were claiming the deck. "I'm very tired," she muttered, getting up from the stool.

On her feet she found she was wobbly again. Thornleigh's arm rushed around her waist to steady her. The cloak slipped from her shoulders to the deck. His grip around her tightened.

She looked up into his face. "No, I'm perfectly fine," she said quickly.

Jinner rattled out of the cabin door. He hurried up to Honor and snatched her elbow. "Alright, sir, I've got her now," he said helpfully.

She had no choice but to let herself be taken from Thornleigh.

"Come along, m'lady," Jinner coaxed, bending for the cloak. "A little broth and a good sleep'll do you wonders." He led her toward the cabin. She dared not glance back over her shoulder at Thornleigh as she stepped inside. Yet she felt his eyes on her.

She sat on the bed. She watched the open doorway as Jinner fussed with soup bowl and spoon, hung up her cloak, adjusted the lantern. Finally, he touched his cap to her, said good night, and went out. He closed the door. She wished he had not. She watched it for Thornleigh, sitting still.

It was wrong to want him to come. Wrong and selfish and impossible. She told herself as much, over and over. She got up, and paced, and told herself again. Wrong. Selfish. Impossible. And clearly, she thought with a wry smile at her own folly, it was not going to happen.

She pulled back the cover of his bed. She heard the door latch lift. She turned.

He stepped inside and stopped. He looked at her for a long moment. "You said you were perfectly fine," he said. "Well, I'm not. When I pulled you out of the hold I thought you were dead. It was the worst moment of my life."

Her breath caught in her throat. "I thought I *was* dying. And Richard, the last thing I remember thinking was your name." She knew she had just told him, "yes." She didn't care. It was what she wanted.

He shut the door and came to her. He took her in his arms. He murmured, "Don't ever die on me again." He bent and kissed her. Her legs turned again into willow saplings, but this time not from fatigue. Her arms went round his neck, and she returned his kiss with passion. His hands smoothed up her back, her shoulders, rucking up the linen shirt, then down her throat, her breasts. She could not catch her breath.

There was a sound at the door. Thornleigh whirled around, shielding Honor with his body. The door opened. It was Adam. "Ready to study the stars, Father?" he asked brightly.

Honor stepped away, head down, cheeks on fire.

Thornleigh glanced back at her, his face tight with need. Quickly, he regained control. He strode toward his son. He did not look back at Honor. "Good night," he said gruffly, and left.

Thornleigh stopped at the top of the stairs to the deck and looked back. Adam, about to go down, stopped too. His eyes followed Thornleigh's to the cabin door. "I like Mistress Larke," he said. "She's pretty."

"Very pretty," Thornleigh murmured. "And very brave."

The band of light under the door went dark.

He put his arm around his son's shoulders, and together they turned away.

Leonard Legge was standing alone, nervous. He smoothed back his long hair with both hands, uncomfortable in this gilded chamber of Hampton Court. He hated the way the palace made him feel. Like a peasant. Cardinal Wolsey had built it, he knew, but it belonged now to the King. Strains of music from the King's entertainment down the corridor filtered in around the closed room. Legge picked up his hat from the table and began turning it around in his sweaty hands.

The door opened suddenly and Legge twisted around like a

caught criminal. He jerked a bow to the priest in the doorway. "Afternoon, Father."

Jerome Bastwick strode past him to a desk neatly piled with papers. Bastwick had put on weight in his new-found prosperity—his sterling work with Cardinal Campeggio had brought him the reward of a Royal Chaplaincy—but his compact body still exuded the energy that had taken him from his father's hovel, where he had fed the pigs, to the private Chapel Royal, where he offered up Christ's blood before the King.

"Well, Master Legge?" he asked without interest. He shuffled through some papers and lifted a letter to read. "What have you for me today?"

Legge reached for a burlap sack on the floor. He loosened the strings and lifted it tantalizingly over the desk. "You said to watch her whenever my duties with Dr. Pelle don't interfere. Well, it so happened that the two crossed-like."

He upended the sack. A large, brown leather book slid out.

Bastwick put down his letter. He reached out to touch the book. His finger traced the stark gold cross embossed on the cover. A Bible. "Hers?" he asked.

"Hers."

"Excellent, Master Legge. Excellent."

"Do we nab her now, Father?"

"No. Not yet." The Bible, Bastwick knew, was not quite enough evidence. Also, if he waited, she might lead him to net a larger catch, a whole coven of heretics. A success like that, even the King would notice. He could wait a little longer.

Besides, she had Cromwell's protection at the moment. But one day that could change. She'd be friendless then. Exposed. Just as he had been that long-ago day in Star Chamber when her accusations had stripped him of every thing he had striven to attain. Exposed—just as he had been for a whole year in the Bishop's cell, haggardly watching the red-eyed rats watch *him* from the corners. The nightmare still had the power to throttle his sleep. All because of Honor Larke.

"Later," he said. "When she slips. And then, Master Legge, we shall be ready."

❧ 23 ❧

Dismissal and Despair

"It's late, Master Cromwell," Honor said with a sigh. "And I must deliver an anxious couple to Yarmouth, then hurry back to join the Queen in her new lodging."

She stood looking out the window in Cromwell's office at Whitehall. Once again, Cromwell had entertained her with a fine dinner. Again, Anne Boleyn's maids were amusing themselves tossing a ball on the terrace below. And again, Honor wondered how long she would be able to control the unraveling threads of her dangerous work. Recent failures and frights had exhausted her. The poor chandler, Rivers, had been caught and burned. There had been her own close brush with death. The constant, frantic rushing to and from the Queen's residence had frayed her nerves. And then there was Thornleigh. Her humiliation had been keen the night his son had broken in on their moment of passion; she had resolved afterward to stifle her feelings for him. But the result was that time spent with him was agony, so hard was the knowledge of all she could not have with him. She felt she was balancing on a precipice.

There was a shrill of giggling from the maids on the terrace. Honor hugged herself with a shiver of exasperation. "Is all of this really leading us anywhere, Master Cromwell?" she asked, looking out. "To a new Queen? A new order? Sometimes I wonder. So

327 THE QUEEN'S LADY

many people risking so much. Yet, what exactly have we accomplished?"

"Patience, mistress."

Patience. Cromwell's eternal panacea. She was about to snap back at him but she held her tongue. "You know, it's strange," she murmured, watching the game below, "but Her Grace's spirit is a constant example to me. She made a comment yesterday when my Lord of Suffolk came to threaten her with this latest move, even more desolately far from London than she is now at Rickmansworth. She said that she would go wherever her husband ordered her, but she would prefer the Tower, since the people of England would then know what had become of her and would keep her in their prayers."

"Ah, yes, your mistress," Cromwell groaned. "How quickly any mention of the Dowager Princess sours a good meal and pleasant conversation."

Honor turned, her lips pursed in annoyance at the insulting title the King was insisting be applied to the Queen. "His Grace may call my lady by what new name he will, but while Rome refuses to act, she is still his wife, and Queen of England. And the pitiably reduced state she lives in is nothing less than a disgrace. Will you not speak to the King, sir, and entreat him to restore some of her ladies and household?"

"Her predicament is her own doing. You know she refuses any servants about her who will not call her 'Queen.'"

"She *is* Queen."

"Your devotion to her is touching, but—forgive me—confusing."

Honor shrugged. She didn't expect him to understand. How could he, when she hardly understood it herself. "My position with her is the perfect cover," she said wearily. "Even you have said so."

Cromwell grunted, conceding the point. "Lord, what a bulldog she's turned out to be. Nature wronged her in not making her a man."

Honor was surprised. "You think her steadfastness admirable, then."

"I think she may well get her wish of residence in the Tower," he answered gruffly. "Now, enough talk of her." He rose and came to her. As he approached, he withdrew a folded paper from his gown. He snapped it open and held it inches from her face. "Seen this?"

It was a printed white page, a pamphlet. Honor glanced at the title: *A Dialogue Concerning the Evil Abuses of the Church*. A chill contracted her backbone but she returned his gaze. "Yes," she said steadily.

"Is it yours?"

"The author's name is printed below." She pointed to it. "'Ephos.'"

"So I have noted. Odd name. My question stands. Is it yours?" He was watching her intently.

Honor hesitated. The pamphlet was wildly heretical, and therefore seditious, and Cromwell was the King's most trusted councilor. But she reminded herself once again that had he wanted to harm her he had far more damning evidence of her work than this. "It is," she answered, head high. She felt a grim satisfaction at the sight of the pseudonym, part of the Greek name Sir Thomas had given her, spelled backwards.

Watching her, Cromwell folded the pamphlet and stuffed it back inside his gown. He beamed. "Fine work, Mistress Larke. I did not know you were such an eloquent word smith. Your style is spare yet passionate. Utterly compelling."

Honor relaxed. "I had the best of writing teachers," she said with quiet bitterness. "Sir Thomas More."

"Ha! Exactly so." He strolled away, clearly amused by the irony.

She did not share his mirth. "Is that why you wanted to see me?"

"As a matter of fact, it is." He walked around the table, picking up an apple on the way. As he settled back in his chair he tossed the apple from hand to hand. "I could use more of this sort of writing. Powerful, clear broadsides to bring the message home to the literate among our countrymen. What do you say? Can you do more of this kind of thing?"

Honor heard some inner voice whisper caution. "I could," she said.

"Printed in quantity?"

"Yes."

"Here, or abroad?"

"Abroad is safer."

"But possible here? Hopkin's press, perhaps?"

"Too small. But I know others. It's possible."

"Delivered at my instructions to a safe depot?"

"Certainly."

"Good. Then it's settled." He picked up a silver knife and began to peel the apple.

She watched him, searching for clues to his thoughts, but his face, enigmatic as always, was devoid of any emotion. Though their words of heresy and treason hung in the air his eyes were calmly fixed in concentration on peeling the apple skin in one long, unbroken strip.

"No, sir," she said firmly. "It is not settled."

He glanced up, surprised.

"I wrote that pamphlet in anger," she said. "I am not at all convinced it is a course I should pursue."

"Why ever not?"

"I have no time for such indulgences. The missions take up every available hour, and . . . well, to be blunt . . ." She hesitated.

"Oh, do be blunt, Mistress Larke."

"It's just that your other schemes make no sense to me. I see no sign of progress."

"Nonsense. All is proceeding exactly as we want."

"We?" she flared. "Master Cromwell, four men have just been burned! Thomas Bilney, Richard Bayfield, John Tewkesbury, Thomas Benet—all dead at the hands of the Chancellor before I could get to them. And poor James Bainham likely to be the next. It is not what *they* wanted, sir. And I assure you it is not what I want!"

She saw by his frown that her outburst had finally disturbed him. Good.

"It is all a question of stages, mistress," he said calmly.

"And what stage are we in now, pray? A retrogressive stage? All part of the plan, is it, Master Cromwell?"

"Perhaps I was wrong not to have explained my strategy to you. May I do so now?"

She shrugged, weary with wrangling. "Is there a purpose? I really should be going."

"There is a purpose, yes. I'd like those pamphlets done, you see. So far, the printed word has not been used to influence the popular will. An oversight, I believe. In the coming battle, I intend to use humble ordnance like your broadsheet to great advantage. May I explain?"

She sighed, but she came and sat again, ready to listen.

"After the Blackfriars fiasco," he began, "the King said something that put everything squarely into place for me. He said, in his anger, that he was sovereign in his own empire. Now, if the King is an *emperor*, I reasoned, he cannot be subservient to Rome. He can act independently from Rome. He could, for example, stop the flow of Englishmen's gold to Rome. It seemed to me that just such a—I won't say threat—but such a sober piece of persuasion might be used to prod the Pope into signing the divorce."

"But it hasn't."

"I also knew," he said, overriding her objection, "that caution must be taken. A stand bold enough to frighten Rome could also frighten our pious countrymen. To most of them the Pope's place at the head of the Universal Church seems as constant as the rising sun. Fear can cause unrest, and unrest undermines a king's security. We have the unfortunate example of Henry II and Archbishop Becket to instruct us, to say nothing of the papal interdict under King John when all Church administration was halted and English commerce stymied. No. It would not do to have the people mumbling against *this* king. He must not appear a tyrant. The cry against Rome's domination must come from the people themselves."

Honor was becoming impatient with the lecture. "But you just said the people are pious and fear change."

"I speak, in the second instance, of the people as a political entity. Parliament. If Parliament passed a bill to withhold Church monies, I reasoned, the threat to Rome would be just as flagrant, but the King could not be called a tyrant, for Parliament is, by definition, the people."

"Yes, it's been a clever plan," Honor agreed irritably. Over her plate she was idly crumbling a crust of bread into fragments. "The King, I'm sure, is delighted. You've engineered Parliament to do the dirty deed, and the King and his burgesses are pocketing much of the Pope's gold. But this threat, this sober persuasion, as you call it, of drastically reducing Rome's English income has accomplished exactly nothing. All the legislation you've pushed through your precious Parliament—the reform of mortuaries and plural benefices, checks on the Church's commercial operations—all of these are excellent, but what is the result? No scream of pain has yet been heard from the Pope. The Bishops' courts remain intact. And Sir Thomas continues to send men to the stake."

"That is why the time has come to move into the second stage."

"Second stage?"

He smiled. "Politicians, like battle commanders, are only as good as their tactics." He munched a slice of apple. "True, our course so far has made little discernible progress with the Pope. But look at what we have gained at home. A field newly drawn up, and all to our advantage. The King behind me. The men of Parliament savoring their first real taste of power—and seeing what gold rolls back to them for exercising it. And the Church here trembling, on the defensive. Now is the time to attack."

"Attack?"

"To really threaten Rome."

"With what?"

"The Imperial autonomy of England. Immune to papal judgments. And once again it is essential that the impetus is seen to come from Parliament. The challenge now is to get their support."

"Support for what? What in heaven's name would you have Parliament do?"

"Declare the King to be the supreme head of the Church in England."

She stared, dumbfounded. The King? Supreme head of the

Church? The idea was shocking in its brazen originality. Stunning in its simplicity. If the King was supreme he could write his own divorce, sweep clean his own Church. It was masterful.

Her thoughts suddenly snagged. "But doesn't this current impasse in Parliament defeat you? I know you've maneuvered your latest batch of anti-clerical bills through the Commons, but the bills are mired in the Lords, aren't they? If the old guard there of Bishops and Abbots is balking at reform legislation, how can you possibly expect them to go even further?"

"Exactly so. The Lords' bombastic reaction is ideal. Better, in fact, than I had hoped." He picked a piece of apple pulp from between his teeth.

Honor was baffled. "You *hoped* for the Lords' opposition?"

He nodded. "All perfectly predictable. Just as is the Commons' wrath against the Lords for impeding progress."

Honor whispered, "Good heavens." Understanding crept over her, bringing with it a huge smile. "Master Cromwell, I owe you an apology. I have underestimated you." She laughed at the brilliance of the scheme. "Let me see if I have it. The more obstinately the clergy cling to their old ways, with no attempt at reform, the more spiteful is the people's wrath. Pious they are, to be sure, but God is one thing, and greedy priests quite another. Now, you will use the fury of the Commons as a battering ram to beat down the walls of the Lords. And all without you lifting a finger in the attack. It's wonderful! But can it really work? Are the people angry enough?"

"They will be," he said. "If Sir Thomas More's policies of ferocious protection of Church privilege continue to enrage them."

"But of course," she cried, understanding it all now. "Oh, that this plan might snare the monster!"

"And," Cromwell added pointedly, "if there are hundreds of your pamphlets out there to inflame them."

She smiled. "I see."

"I thought you might. Then you agree to write them?"

"Willingly."

"Excellent." He stood. "We can discuss the details later."

Dismissal. "Of course," she said, rising to leave.

"By the way," Cromwell said, "I've heard something rather distressing. I'm afraid Sir Thomas may have gotten wind of Master Hopkin's little press."

Honor stiffened. "How?"

"I don't know. But it might be best to warn him."

"I shall. Thank you."

Cromwell was leading her to the door. "If you'd like, I could send the message to Hopkin myself. You're so busy just now."

"Would you?"

"Certainly. Still at his old lodging, is he?"

"No. He's moved to Milk Street. Beside Montgomery's. Oh, Master Cromwell," she said, touching his arm, "do urge him to contact me. Tell him I'm ready to help if he needs me."

He patted her hand. "Indeed."

They were at the door. Honor drew aside the brown velvet curtain that hung over it.

"Mistress Larke," Cromwell said, "there is one thing more. Your worries about having to rush back to the Dowager Princess are finally at an end. The King has decided to terminate your employment with her."

Honor whirled around, mouth open. "What? But why?"

"His Grace is highly displeased with the Dowager Princess's insistence on styling herself as Queen. He has declared her staff must be cut back even further. He singled you out especially."

"Me?" She was shocked. Why had Cromwell waited to tell her this? "But Her Grace relies on me."

"Exactly so. I'm afraid the King can be vindictive when crossed."

"Good Lord," Honor muttered. "What shall I do?"

"I thought you'd be pleased. A fortuitous development, I'd say. Now, without raising suspicions by quitting her, you are free to do as you like."

"Free to see my work founder," she cried.

"Nonsense. You can accomplish everything from Chelsea. Sir Thomas is always at Westminster."

"I will never go back to his house."

"Well, go to another man's house, then. Marry."

"Marry?" she parroted.

"Thousands do, you know," he said dryly. "And you can't live alone." Honor knew he was right. Municipal ordinances forbade single women living alone, clear evidence, city fathers feared, of a bawdy house. If Honor flouted the regulation she would only draw suspicion.

"Why not accept one of the suitors Sir Thomas is urging," Cromwell suggested. "Or perhaps that old Baron from Yorkshire. Duncombe. Been panting after you for months. Even asked *me* about you."

"And lose control of my property to him? Jeopardize all my work?"

"Oh come, come. The Baron's in his dotage. You could carry on right under his dripping nose. He'd never notice."

Knuckles rapped the other side of the door. A gangly young clerk opened it.

Cromwell fixed Honor with sober eyes. "Marry, mistress. Marry a quiet man, away from all of this. One day, you may be glad of a safe haven." He nodded at the clerk. "Come in, Andrew. Mistress Larke is just leaving."

Alone with his clerk Cromwell dictated a note: a name, an accusation.

"Is that all, sir?" Andrew asked.

"Yes. No, wait. There may be another Hopkin in Foster's Lane. Better add a notation that it's the one on Milk Street. Next to Montgomery's."

"Yes, sir," Andrew said, writing. "To the Lord Chancellor again, sir?"

Cromwell nodded. "And anonymous again."

The clerk pocketed the note and hurried out.

Alone, Cromwell moved to the window and looked down at the young people tossing the ball under the leafy branches. Would Mistress Larke call one in five a fair ratio? he wondered. One of her unfortunates dropped in Sir Thomas's path now and then? After all, the more the dragon devoured, the sooner the people would rush out to slay him.

❧ 24 ❧

Shearing Time

In Yarmouth harbor Honor heard the news. She was delivering the latest refugees, a Protestant couple, to the *Vixen* for transport, and was surprised to find Pilot Tate, not Thornleigh, in charge of the ship. Thornleigh, Tate said, was too busy to leave home.

"With wool business?" she asked, recalling it was shearing season.

"Aye. And with settling his wife's affairs."

"His wife?"

"Did you not know, mistress? She's dead."

Honor was abashed at how happy—how instantly happy—the news made her feel. She tried to enforce onto her mind a proper respect for the dead. But it was no use. She had never even known the woman. She was glad. Shamelessly, girlishly glad.

She knew that Thornleigh's manor of Great Ashwold was only fifteen miles away. If she set out now, she would see him by nightfall.

It was late afternoon when she dismounted in the courtyard of Great Ashwold. She gave her mare to the groom with instructions to brush and feed her carefully; there was no hurry.

With a pleasurable flutter of uncertainty in her stomach, she knocked on the big front door. A bearded, shuffling servant opened it. Honor asked immediately for the master. The man showed her to the great hall, then shuffled away. Not even an offer of refreshment, Honor thought, with some amusement at the laconic fellow. Well, no matter. Richard's face would refresh her enough. She stepped into the hall.

Thornleigh was alone there. He sat on a stool before the hearth. His back was to her, but she saw that he held a poker, and with it he was absently prodding a piece of charcoal in the dying fire.

"Richard," she said, coming to him.

He looked up at her. His chin was stubbled, his eyes bloodshot. His face was expressionless. "Ah," he said quietly.

Her heart twisted. He looked exhausted. She dropped to her knees beside him. "Richard, I'm . . . so sorry." Moments ago it would have been a lie, but the sight of his haggard face changed everything.

"Then you've heard," he said flatly, turning back to face the fire.

"Yes." She looked around the hall. There was dust on the table, and a smell of decaying fruit drifted from a corner. The floor rushes, crushed and dry, looked as though they had not been changed in weeks. And the house seemed very quiet. "Where's Adam?" she asked.

"With my sister. Joan got married last month." He looked at Honor. "About Ellen . . . did you hear how?"

"No."

"The God-rotting apparitor told her a pack of lies. Frightened her to death." He smiled bitterly. "No, that's not quite right. I accomplished that all by myself."

"An apparitor? What do you mean? What happened?"

"They hauled her into Nix's prison. For heresy. She was awaiting trial when the apparitor came around, sniffing for more business. Told her if she didn't give the names of her accomplices she would be burned, I would be excommunicated, and Adam would be called a bastard. A beggar woman in the same cell told me about it . . . after." He shook his head. "All Ellen had to do was abjure, and they'd have had to let her go. But she didn't know that. She believed the lies. She hanged herself."

Honor's hand flew to her mouth. "Oh, Richard!"

He did not look at her. "And do you know what evidence those jackals cited to arrest her? One of our good neighbors, it seems, reported hearing her say a Paternoster in English to our son. That was all. A bloody prayer. In bloody English. Oh, yes, very suspicious. Christ, she picked up such things like a parrot—songs, rhymes. It didn't mean anything to her. I could have *told* the bastards that." He glared at the fire and added, "But, of course, I wasn't there."

She shivered at the tone of his voice. She didn't know what to say. "Can I get you anything? Some wine?"

He ignored her. "No burial in consecrated ground, of course. They pitted her at the crossroads outside the village. But first, because she'd done away with herself . . ." He shook his head and did not finish.

He did not have to. Honor knew, as everyone knew, the regimen that the Church inflicted on a suicide's corpse. It was foul with unabsolved sin, the Church taught, and its ghost would never rest unless a stake was driven through its heart. That was the law.

Honor bowed her head. If she had lacked feelings before for Ellen Thornleigh, she made up for it now with a swell of pity. But, she told herself, what was done was done. Her real sympathy was with the living.

She leaned close to Thornleigh and lay her arm across his shoulders. "Richard," she murmured.

He looked at her hand on his shoulder. He rested his cheek against it and closed his eyes. His eyelids trembled. Honor sensed a battle going on inside him. A battle not to weep? It tugged forth her pity again, but with tenfold the tenderness she felt for the sad, dead woman. She stroked his hair, his cheek. She said his name quietly, over and over.

He kissed her hand. He turned his face to hers. His pain moved her more than she could say. She nudged closer and brushed her lips over his, softly. She had meant only to give comfort, but the touch of him immediately kindled her. She craved more. She pressed her lips on his.

His response was instant. His hand cupped the back of her

head, holding her to him. He kissed her again, harder, longer. She felt his need.

She pulled free only long enough to stand and move in front of him, between his legs. He looked up at her, his breathing becoming ragged. She bent and kissed the warm skin at his throat. Her fingers pulled at the lacings of his shirt, opening it so that her mouth could move down to his chest. He groaned. His arms went around her waist and he pulled her to him, making her arch her back. He pressed his face against her breasts.

She wanted more. She slid down against him and knelt between his legs. She kissed his forehead, his cheek—her mouth burned by the rough stubble—his mouth. He held her shoulders tightly, and his kisses covered her throat, then the exposed skin of her breasts.

"Richard," she breathed. "Marry me."

He stopped. He looked bewildered. "What?"

"There's nothing to keep us apart now," she said eagerly.

He blinked at her as if trying to comprehend. His breathing was still uneven. "But—"

"You want me, don't you?"

"God, yes."

"Well, now we can be together. Marry me."

He shook his head as if to clear it. He looked at her, his expression eloquent with desire and uncertainty in equal parts. "My wife's been dead only two days, and you—"

"That's right," she broke in. "Your wife is dead. And I'm alive."

His hands lay motionless on her hips. "Honor, you don't understand what's happened here. I—"

"Of course I do, and I'm sorry. It's tragic. But it's done. It can't be changed." She was reaching for him again, longing for him. "And I can't change how I feel for you."

His arms stiffened, holding her at arms' length. "No. You don't see it," he said sternly. "I killed her. As surely as if I'd tightened the noose. I killed her."

"That's nonsense, Richard. She was unstable. Sam, told me. She was that way when you married her, he said. It had nothing to do with you."

"It had everything to do with me. I was never home. Couldn't stand being here. Her endless melancholia. I left her alone. All the time. And then, when she needed me most—"

"You can't blame yourself. There was nothing you could do for her."

He shook his head. "Maybe there was." He stared again into the fire as if facing an inquisitor there. "Children. She loved babies. Maybe if I'd . . ." He paused.

"She had Adam," Honor offered weakly.

But Thornleigh was dealing now only with the interrogator within the glowing coals. "We had a baby daughter. Ellen . . . neglected her. The baby . . . died."

"I know, Richard. Sam told me. Don't torture yourself."

"After that," he went on bleakly, "I wouldn't . . . be a husband to Ellen. I couldn't trust her, you see? I'd think of her abandoning another child, so I didn't . . . I wouldn't . . . take her to bed."

Honor said nothing. When he looked back into her eyes, she was afraid he could read the surprise there. She did not want to show it, did not want to hurt him more than he already had been hurt. But she saw that it was too late.

With a groan of humiliation he twisted away from her. He got up and walked quickly to the door. He half turned to her, avoiding her eyes. "I'm needed at Aylsham for the shearing. Stay if you want."

He left the hall. Within moments she heard his horse's hooves clatter out of the courtyard.

"Careful, Master Thornleigh," a shearer called. "That ewe can nip right smart."

Thornleigh's mind had been straying. He bent again to apply the shears to the ewe's leg. Already, he was up to his knees in fleece. He finished the job, let the ewe go, and straightened. He wiped the sweat from his face with his sleeve, and looked around. The shed, hot and dusty, was full of bleating sheep and grunting shearers, the men's blades flying over the animals' backs.

The shearers were an itinerant band; once they'd got through Thornleigh's flock here at Aylsham they'd set out for his neighbor's pens. They were skilled laborers, and he knew they did not need his help; he could not match the speed of even the least experienced of them. But he had thrown himself into the work to keep his mind occupied. Ellen's awful death he had accepted. He hoped her spirit might now find peace. But for the two days he'd been here he'd been able to think of nothing but Honor.

He stepped out of the shed, rubbing at a knot in the muscles of his back. A child ran to him with a foaming tankard from her mother's nearby table, a makeshift alehouse set up for the shearers. Thornleigh gave the child a penny for the ale and quickly quaffed it down.

Wiping the foam from his lip, he walked across the dusty path to a field and stopped to watch the activity. This was his tenting yard. A half-dozen men and women were busy spreading wide swaths of cloth, wet from the fuller's, over two twenty-foot wooden frames. The broadcloth, stretched on tenterhooks across these frames, would be left in the sun to dry.

Thornleigh was pleased with the success of setting up the tenting yard next to his shearing shed. With them close together, and with his new fulling mill operating on the stream nearby—he could faintly hear the men's mallets pummeling the cloth there— he'd been able to reduce the time he used to spend riding the shire to supervise the various craftsmen with whom he dealt.

Still, he thought ruefully as he stretched his back to ease the stubborn muscle knot, the amount of work for him in overseeing the enterprise seemed to end up the same, if not more. Every important decision remained his.

He shook his head at the conundrum: there wasn't enough work to keep his mind off Honor, but too much to let him get away and ride back to her. He ached to see her.

What an idiot he'd been. What a blinkered, self-wallowing, fog-brained fool. He'd been groping in the darkness of self-blame for so long, had thought of himself as cold-blooded for so long, that when the woman whose love he wanted most in the world had knelt and offered herself to him—offered him a chance at genuine happiness—what had he done? Refused her. Shrank away like some addle-brained wretch let out after years in prison and frightened by the sunlight. *Refused* her. Fool!

But her—she was magnificent. Bold and obstinate and generous. Unbending in her purposes. Yielding in his arms. God in heaven, he loved the woman.

Restless, thinking of her, he watched the tenting. All was going smoothly here. And the fulling mill was operating trouble-free. And the shearers certainly didn't need his clumsy pair of hands. Could he leave now? Go to her? Was there any point? Would she still be there? Would she understand that he was ready to put his many failures with Ellen behind him, and be happy?

"Master Thornleigh!" a man's voice called from the office near the shearing shed. "Can you come, sir? There's a Yarmouth waggoner in confusion about which bales of worsted he's to take. And the dyer's asking payment for his woad."

Thornleigh closed his eyes, hoping to savor in his mind, for one last moment, the image of Honor smiling up at him. Did he have any right on God's green earth to expect that she'd still care? No. In his mind she was sadly turning from him. He had missed his chance. With a feeling of loss more hollow than he had ever known, he let her slip away.

He walked back to work.

In the stable, Honor stood stroking her mare's nose, lost in thought as the groom finished buckling the saddle.

"All set, mistress," the lad said shyly.

Honor looked up from her reverie. "I'll walk her out myself, Harry. Thank you. Now, off with you to the hall. They won't wait dinner for you, you know." She gave him a coin.

"Thank *you*, mistress!" he said with a grin. "Safe journey." He touched his cap to her and hurried away.

Honor took the bridle and led the mare out through the open stable doors. She walked slowly. She was in no hurry to leave Great Ashwold. She had come to like the manor very much. But she had stretched out her time here as long as she reasonably could. Three days of walking the grounds, talking to the tenants, introducing herself to Thornleigh's sister, Joan, and her new husband, Giles, at their house in the village, exploring on horseback the summer countryside, visiting the steward's lodging to discuss the wool trade—just as if she truly were Thornleigh's business partner. Or wife. Waiting. Hoping he would come back. But he had not come back. Now, her excuses to tarry had run out. She must leave.

The mare's hooves clacked on the courtyard cobbles. It was noon, hot and still. Honor passed a maid on her way to join the household at dinner, though the girl was ambling, apparently in no hurry to get there. Harry, the groom, had stopped near the front door of the house. Red-faced, he went to the maid and they fell into whispered conversation. Honor smiled. So that was why the girl was in no hurry to rush inside. Her horse moved on lazily toward the open main gate. When it began to wander toward some tufts of sweet grass growing by the fleece shed, Honor allowed it to go there, to stop, and nibble. She stroked its neck and thought of Thornleigh.

Why had she acted like such a fool? Barging in on his sorrow. Demanding a return of the love that had overpowered her. She blushed to recall her impetuous behavior. Three days here had cooled her brain, at least, if not her heart. Her feelings for him had not changed. But she saw that her declaration had been wretchedly ill-timed. He had been shocked. And who could blame him? What a selfish creature she had been. What a brazen performance. What a fool.

She sighed and rested her forehead on the horse's warm, smooth neck. And she wondered again, as she had for the past three days, where she would go. To London, of course. But which of her limited options there was preferable? Which would allow the most scope to carry on her work? For nothing, nothing in the world, would keep her from fighting Sir Thomas. The Marchioness of Exeter would be glad to see her, and have her stay. But Honor's heart sank at the thought of the marchioness and her idle, gabbling, heartless friends. What a barren life. Besides, might not the work be jeopardized there? Could she safely operate from such a household, so open to public scrutiny? But if not to the Marchioness's, where? Go to the wizened old Yorkshire baron at his townhouse? Accept his proposal of marriage? The horse's neck shuddered to shift a fly, and Honor had to smile—a shudder was exactly her own response to any thought of the doddering old baron.

Beyond the barrier of horseflesh she heard a cart horse clatter through the gate. For the last two days carts had been arriving from Aylsham, Thornleigh's other manor, bringing sacks of the overflow of the fleece here for storage. Honor sighed. Aylsham, where Thornleigh was. London, where she must go. She straightened, resolved to wish away no more of this fine afternoon. The marchioness it would be. And now, she and her mare could dawdle no longer.

She reached down to the mare's cheek to tug the bridle. Munching grass, the horse stubbornly refused to budge. "Come on, old thing," Honor coaxed. "Time for us to go."

The clack of hooves on cobbles came nearer. Honor looked around. It was Thornleigh on horseback. He alone had come through the gate.

Their eyes met. He seemed surprised. "You're still here," he said.

Honor looked down, her cheeks on fire. He could *tell* she had stayed for him . . . it was so clear on his face. He thought her wanton. She should have left hours ago, days ago—fool!

Thornleigh dismounted. Honor looked up. He was holding the reins distractedly, looking at her, and his horse made the most of the loose tether, dropping its head to join Honor's mare at nibbling the grass.

Honor swallowed. "I was just leaving."

"I see."

"I stayed . . . to see Adam," she said idiotically. "He seems very happy at your sister's."

"You met Joan, then."

"Yes."

He nodded, his thoughts obviously elsewhere, though he was watching her intently. "Good."

She dragged her eyes from the sun-coppered skin at his throat where he had loosened his doublet and shirt in the heat. "Well . . . I'd best be going." She bent to reach for the bridle.

"Honor, I know I have no right, but . . ." He did not finish the thought.

She looked up. His face was clouded with uncertainty. "No

right?" she asked quietly. At her heart, hope was clamoring to be let in.

He took a deep breath. "To ask you to stay. The other day, when you came . . ." Again, he stopped himself. He frowned and looked down. "God, I was a blockhead to leave you."

Honor felt happiness flood her. "But you've . . . come back."

He looked up quickly. Seeing her smile, he let out an astonished breath. He caught her hand. "Honor—" Suddenly, he was aware of the groom and the maid watching them from the house doorway. "Can't talk out here," he muttered. He glanced at the fleece shed beside the horses. Its door stood open. "Come," he said, pulling her.

The shed was packed with huge, stuffed sacks of fleece—some stacked almost to the roof, some piled on either side of the door to form soft pillars, some mounded up around the small window like a pillowy casement. Honor moved to the center of the small available space. Thornleigh closed the door. They were alone.

She turned. He came to her. Looking into her eyes, he still seemed hesitant, as though not sure he had interpreted her smile outside aright. But Honor *was* sure. She could barely keep herself from flinging her arms around his neck. She touched his lips with her fingertips. She could not stop her fingers from caressing his cheek, and then again his mouth. Abruptly, he took hold of her shoulders. There was amazement on his face. "My God, you really are mine, aren't you?"

She smiled. "I've been yours since the first time you held me—in the Cardinal's garden, in the snow."

Outside, a farmer on a donkey clomped by the window and the man peered in as he passed. Instinctively, both Honor and Thornleigh ducked and went down on their knees. They were facing each other, their bodies just inches apart. He had kept hold of her shoulders as though to pull her down from the farmer's curious eyes, and now his grip on her tightened. All his former hesitancy had vanished. The look in his eyes was pure desire.

He reached for the band that held back her loose hair, lifted it and dropped it on the floor. He took her face between his hands and kissed her. He brought his body closer to hers. Trembling, she held onto his arms, reveling in his tautness, his unmistakable strength. Still kissing her he unfastened the front lacing of her bodice and spread it to reveal the loose fabric of her chemise. His mouth traveled down to her throat. She felt her tumbled hair catch at his lips. His breathing had become rough. Kissing her neck again and again he undid the chemise tie between her breasts and started to tug the fabric down. Honor froze. She pulled back. Suddenly, she was the one who was hesitant, unsure. She had never lain with a man. The dark memory of Hugh Tyrell's violent penetration brought a pang of confusion. "I've . . . I've never . . ." she stammered.

He stopped. He looked into her eyes, his breathing still ragged. But a small smile of understanding crept to his lips, and with both hands he gently smoothed back her hair from her forehead in a gesture of pure tenderness. It quite disarmed her. She smiled too.

Suddenly he let go of her. He pulled his dagger from its sheath. He leaned sideways toward a bulging, ram-sized sack of fleece and plunged the blade in and wrenched it down, ripping open the sack. Fleece tumbled out, spilling around their legs in a pillowy snowdrift that reached halfway to their hips. Honor laughed in delight. Thornleigh grinned. His arms went around her and he pulled her over with him into the downy bed.

On her back she let herself sink into the fleece's soft embrace as it frothed over her shoulders. Lying beside her, Thornleigh leaned over and kissed her gently. His hand slipped into the froth and slowly spread open her chemise. His kiss became insistent. His palm smoothed over her naked breasts. Wanting him, her mouth opened under his. She fumbled with his doublet, wanting to feel his skin. He wrestled out of the doublet and wrenched off his shirt, then pressed his body against hers. She felt his warmth, his hardness, his need. His mouth went to her breast, his tongue to her nipple. She could barely catch her breath as he slid her skirt up, beneath the fleece. His hand molded up her thigh, and as his fingers touched the warm, wet cleft she gasped at the startling pulses of heat his touch ignited inside her. He groaned and wrenched aside his codpiece and pushed her legs apart. He hesitated. She sensed he was afraid of hurting her. She pulled him on top of her

and held him tightly. "Yes," she breathed. He entered her, and
when she moaned with pleasure he plunged. Again and again. The
pulses of heat became waves. *She* was a wave, cresting in ecstasy.
He exploded inside her. Her back arched. She was the wave . . .
she was the heat . . . she was him . . .

She lay with her head on his chest, loving the way the rise and
fall of his chest matched her own recovering breaths. She thought:
From this moment forward, I am changed. The world is changed.

Thornleigh gently rolled her onto her back in the fleece. His
hand moved languidly over her breasts, her belly where her skirt
was bunched up, her naked thigh, then back up again to her
throat. His callused palm, his gaze on her body, made her shiver
anew.

He smiled. "Honor," he whispered. His expression turned serious. He looked into her eyes. "Stay," he said. "Marry me, and stay
forever."

❧ 25 ❧

Resignation

Thomas More sat on a stone bench in the royal garden at White-hall, waiting for the King. The alcove in which he sat was quiet, insulated by tall clipped hedges on three sides. Beyond, he could hear faint, raucous laughter from men and women bowling on the green; but here, inside the alcove, bees hummed peacefully among the roses, red and white. The flowers, he noticed, were now past their best. A few brown-tinged petals fluttered to the ground even as he watched. He glanced uneasily at the white leather pouch that lay on the bench beside him. It contained the Great Seal of the Realm, the emblem of the authority of the Lord Chancellor. Today, he would relinquish it to the King.

More was glad of the peace of this spot. He needed it to compose himself. The strain of his position had become almost unbearable. For months he had longed to resign. He had even begged his old friend the Duke of Norfolk to intervene with the King for permission to retire. But the King had kept him dangling like a worm on a hook. Expected him, like everyone else, to bow and scrape before his strumpet, the Boleyn woman. Asked him to read out in Parliament the opinions of foreign universities, all favorable to this abominable divorce, and all purchased at great expense by Secretary Cromwell. And then the dreadful climax to Cromwell's maneuvering: the total submission of the English clergy to the King's demands. The bishops, almost to a man—except, God be praised, old John Fisher—had finally, meekly, signed away their sacred, age-old rights of autonomy. From now on the King would tell the bishops when to convene, what laws to pass, and who could sit on a commission to regulate them. Regulate! Vile word. A Cromwellian word. Would he regulate, like the commerce of cobblers or fishmongers, the earthly representatives of God?

It had been horrible. A complete rout. And More could only accept defeat. His entire policy since this wretched affair had begun had been to protect the Church in Her hour of need until the King's lust abated and his piety returned. But More knew now that he had failed. The strumpet ruled, and the Church lay wounded, gasping.

How could the King allow a woman to wreak such infernal harm?

A woman. He watched a bee lift from a blossom, its body dusted with golden pollen, and he thought of Honor Larke. Married. Her note informing him of the event had been terse to the point of incivility. Married to a Norwich clothier. A man whom More had never heard of. The news had made him suffer. Why had she done this in private? Oh, certainly it was her right; he could not prevent her. Not unless the match were grossly below her rank, which this was not. But why had she not come to him, consulted him? Her hurt feelings over that dead servant could not possibly have festered all this time. Why had she avoided him for so long?

The offense of it all cramped his heart. The news, her method, her grudge—and something more. She had chosen for herself. She had refused to accept any of the suitors he had approved, refused to settle into a quiet, Christian marriage. Instead, she had taken a man for herself. A union of love. A coupling of passion.

His palms were moist. He thought of the man, the one to whom she had given herself. Who was he? Who had made a wanton of the girl? He rubbed his sweaty palms on his gown. He must investigate this. He would send Holt. Yes, Holt would find out. All of it.

"Ah, Thomas!"

More looked up. King Henry stood at the entrance to the garden alcove, feet planted wide apart in his characteristic stance of power. More immediately rose.

"Glad you could make it," Henry said pleasantly. He made an apologetic gesture that took in More and the bench and then, wiping the sheen of sweat from his florid face, he grinned. "The ladies would not let me leave the bowls, you see." His jolly attitude almost calmed More's nerves, though they both knew why More was here: the King had summoned him—with the Great Seal. He could cast More into prison, or strike off his head. And yet, More thought, he sounded like a satisfied merchant welcoming an associate to dinner. What charm this king could wield, when he wanted to.

Henry strode to the bench and sat. He let out a quick puff of breath, settling his bulk after the exertion at sport. He glanced at the white pouch, then ignored it. "You should exercise more, Thomas. You look wan. Join the young people in their games, as I do. Does wonders for the constitution. Although," he chuckled, "Anne always beats me. What an arm the woman has!"

More could not even muster a smile.

"And she's full of vim today, I can tell you. I'm taking her with me to Boulogne for this meeting with King Francis, and she's gay as a child let out of school, what with ordering her clothes and jewels. Gay as a child!"

More had heard all about it. Henry had sent a messenger to Queen Catherine with an order that she must relinquish the royal jewels to the Boleyn woman. The Queen had refused to do so without a written command from her husband. Henry had furiously scrawled the order, and in the end, Catherine had been stripped of every piece of jewelry, except, at her insistence, her wedding ring.

"Ah, yes," Henry finished happily, "my Anne must sparkle. She'll look a treat beside that faded old woman of Francis's."

More looked away. This was torture.

"What's the matter, Thomas? Don't care for my speaking of Anne?" The bite in the King's voice startled More, unnerved him. And when he looked back, the King was watching him, his eyes narrowed in naked suspicion.

Henry suddenly pushed himself to his feet. "Well, you won't have to listen to much of anything I have to say from now on," he said, almost growling. "You're finished here, man. Finished! I won't have ingrates around me, bruiting it about that I'm a lusting tyrant."

The words, though said in anger, had been controlled. But now, Henry moved to the Great Seal and with a sudden motion of fury swatted it from the bench as though he were annihilating all opposition to his wishes. The seal tumbled into the grass between them.

"Your Grace," More said, bowing in fear, hardly knowing where his voice was coming from, "never have I said such evil things. Never would I. You are my lord and sovereign."

"But not your friend, eh, Thomas?"

More looked up. The King's eyes brimmed with hurt, the accusing hurt of an abandoned boy. More could not help but feel pity. "Your Grace did me great honor in accepting my humble friendship," he said with feeling. "It has ever been a sacred trust with me. And one that I have held most dear. If I have been lacking, it has not been for want of love."

Henry stretched out his arm and laid his hand gently on More's shoulder. There were tears in his eyes. "No," he said sadly, "that I do believe." He removed his hand and drew himself to his full height. "But you've failed me, Thomas. And that I cannot let go."

More felt a coldness in his legs, a dread of what was coming. He wished he could sit down.

"As your sovereign," Henry said with formal detachment, "I dismiss you from your office." He nodded toward the pouch in the grass. "Give me that."

More ducked for the pouch and picked it up with trembling fingers. He offered it to the King.

Henry took it. "Go home to Chelsea, man. Live quietly with your family. And never come my way again."

More's legs almost gave way in relief.

Henry turned his back on him and walked away.

Thornleigh stood on London's Billingsgate wharf, a busy unloading site between the Bridge and the Tower, and shook hands with his London agent, saying good-bye. Thornleigh was on his way across the Channel with the *Speedwell* to sell cloth at the big November fair in Bergen-op-Zoom. But he'd come into London the night before to off-load a portion of the shipment for his agent to sell at Blackwell Hall, the national woolcloth market. These last minute arrangements had just been completed. Carters, with the London cloth, were rolling away under the agent's supervision. Thornleigh was ready to row back out to the *Speedwell* anchored in midstream. But Honor still had not come to see him off as she had promised. Late again, he thought.

He wished that she were going with him. He knew she'd love the international fair. And he wanted her beside him. The timing was perfect, with Adam off visiting Joan and Giles for a few weeks. But she'd said she couldn't leave; too much to see to at the printer's. This damned pamphlet work she was doing for Cromwell, he thought, annoyed—it kept her in London for weeks on end. He hadn't seen her since Michaelmas. Well, not until last night. He smiled a little, remembering. At least they'd had last night.

And, he reminded himself, at least the wild escapes were finished, now that Sir Thomas More had resigned. They could say farewell publicly now, like a reasonable man and wife, not skulk around hiding stowaways. He was glad that was over. Although the recollection of her response to More's resignation still chilled him. "What?" she had said angrily on hearing the news. "You mean the King is just going to let him go home? No humiliation for opposing his policies? No disgrace?" The King, it seemed, was more merciful than Honor would have been.

But the rescues were over, thank God. Now, if only she would finish this nonsense with the printing. It, too, was dangerous work; the heresy laws had not changed. He wanted her home, and safe.

It struck him that maybe she was late because of discussions with Cromwell at Whitehall. If so, maybe he could catch her there. Say good-bye, at least. There was plenty of time before high tide, when he must set sail.

He walked down the wharf to hail a ferry, dodging the lightermen who were unloading cargoes ferried in from the ships at anchor. Apprentices passed him, rolling barrels of fish and wine, hefting sacks of grain and salt, packing mules with glass from

Venice, rope from Sweden, armor from Germany, pepper and ginger from the Levant.

A ferry banged alongside the watersteps and Thornleigh climbed aboard. The river was calm, at the turn of the tide. It was the best time to shoot the bridge. The water there was compressed by the twenty piers into twenty-one small rapids, and there could sometimes be a difference of five feet in the levels on the two sides.

The ferry approached the bridge and Thornleigh looked up at a small commotion on it, a knot of people leaning out a gap between two of the shops, shouting and pointing down at the river. Thornleigh shook his head. Animals were forever falling into the water and drowning. Sometimes, people too. The animals became the property of the constable of the tower, a perquisite. This time, it appeared to be a cow. But only last month a serving girl had tumbled in and was rescued by an apprentice. Thornleigh wondered, with a smile, if the constable got the girls, too.

He looked westward at the bend in the river where Whitehall lay. He wished he could have a week with Honor.

"Misplaced your wife, have you, Thornleigh?" Cromwell, behind his desk, looked mildly amused.

Thornleigh bristled, but he let the remark pass. "Any idea where she might be?"

"Prodding Hopkin at his press, I'd imagine," Cromwell said, dipping his pen to resume his work. "The pamphlets are long overdue. The man's a snail."

Thornleigh quickly looked around, irritated that Cromwell would speak so unguardedly. They were alone, but when the clerk had ushered Thornleigh into the office, they'd left behind a corridor noisy with milling men, all waiting to bring Secretary Cromwell requests, complaints, gifts. Even a spy or two, Thornleigh did not doubt, waiting to make a report. Anyone might be listening.

"Don't worry, man," Cromwell said tartly, writing. "I do know what I'm about."

Yes, but to whose advantage, Thornleigh wondered. If the walls had ears, talk of presses and pamphlets could easily place Honor under suspicion.

Cromwell paused in his writing and looked up. "More to the point," he said, "your wife knows what she's about too. You should have more faith in her. She's very capable. Leave her be."

"I believe I appreciate sufficiently my wife's good qualities, sir," Thornleigh said, not bothering to mask his anger. Curse the man's condescension! "And I won't waste any more of your valuable time. Good day."

"Thornleigh," Cromwell called to stop him. At the door Thornleigh turned stiffly. Cromwell put down his pen and gestured apologetically with both hands at the messy piles of papers on his desk. "The day has been chaotic. It has shortened my temper. Forgive me."

Thornleigh gave a curt, barely polite nod. He waited.

"I really am pleased about your marriage, you know," Cromwell said in a friendly way. "A very fine thing for Mistress Larke." He smiled. "Sorry, I should say Mistress Thornleigh." He settled back in his chair. "I actually feel I can take some credit for it, too," he said expansively. "I'm the one who urged her to marry. Did she tell you?"

"No. But I'm glad you did," Thornleigh conceded.

"So am I. And I wish you both joy."

Thornleigh only nodded, uncomfortable. Things were clearer, he felt, when he could mistrust the man. Still, there was no good reason to make an enemy of him. "Well," he said awkwardly, "I'll be off."

"To Hopkin's?"

"No. Too far out of my way. I must sail with the tide." He hesitated. "Thank you, sir," he said sincerely. "For your good wishes."

"Oh, no," Cromwell said with a mild wave of his hand. "Thank *you*. For giving Mistress Larke a roof over her head when she needed one. She is important to me. And when she was dismissed, I do confess I suffered a moment of alarm about her future."

"Dismissed?"

"Yes. From the Dowager Princess's suite."

"Oh?" Thornleigh felt a pinprick of anxiety. Honor had never mentioned that she had been dismissed. "And when was that?" he asked.

"Hmm?" Cromwell was already back at work, writing. "Oh, in July, wasn't it?" he said, half distractedly. "Yes, I recall the day—St. Mary Magdalene's day—and the King so vexed with the Dowager Princess for still styling herself Queen. Demanded a further reduction in the number of her ladies. I immediately informed Mistress Larke. She was quite upset about the fate of her work." He looked up and smiled, terminating the interview. "Yes, a fine arrangement for her, Thornleigh. Fine indeed." He brusquely wished his visitor Godspeed and called for his clerk to bring in the next petitioner.

The Feast of St. Mary Magdalene, Thornleigh thought as he closed the office door and pushed out through the crowded corridor. That was the twenty-second of July. And Honor had come to him at Great Ashwold not a week later. She'd found him a widower. And her first words, almost, had been, "Marry me."

Was that all their marriage was about? A cover for her work? How had Cromwell put it—an 'arrangement'?

Nonsense. He shook off the thought. It was an insult even to imagine it of Honor. She was so warm. So happy when they were together. And in their lovemaking she gave him every proof of her satisfaction a man could hope for.

When they were together. Yet she was so often away, on this wretched work. Suspicion followed him down the corridor like one of Cromwell's sneaking spies.

He stepped outside into the bright sunshine and walked quickly away from the palace. That was the problem, he told himself—the murmuring, claustrophobic court. He was glad to be leaving it behind. He took in a deep breath and lengthened his stride toward the river, and the dark imaginings Cromwell's words had invoked began to slink from his mind and evaporate.

He climbed into the ferry, hoping Honor might already be waiting for him back on Billingsgate wharf. Yes, he would put the nonsense completely out of his mind. He'd kiss her good-bye, and he would not even mention it.

It was hot in the printer's room behind the kitchen, and Honor's dress was damp with sweat. The air was stale, too, for the shutters had been closed against curious neighbors; Honor and Hopkin, the printer, had been working in candlelight for most of the day. As Honor used both hands to roll inking pads over the metal letters wedged into the press bed, a bead of sweat tickled her upper lip. She lifted her shoulder to wipe it away, transferring yet another smudge of ink from her face to her sleeve.

Her legs and arms ached. Around noon the wooden frame of the frisket had cracked, completely shutting down the work, and for hours she and Hopkin had been wrestling to reassemble the screw mechanism. Now, however, they had got the press operating again, and were turning out a printed page every few minutes.

"I'm not satisfied with these new letters the foundryman has sent," Hopkin was grousing as he carefully laid a sheet of virgin paper on the tympan. "He's not filed the edges properly. Look at that. Just like sand. I'm going to return half of them tomorrow."

Honor groaned inwardly at Hopkin's perfectionism, a constant trial. But she stifled the urge to argue; she would deal with his concerns tomorrow, after they had the pamphlets done.

The door opened and Hopkin's wife poked her head inside the room. "Come for supper now, Jonathan. And Mistress Thornleigh, you're most welcome to stay, of course."

"Supper!" Honor gasped. She had no idea it was so late. She ran to the shuttered window and opened it a crack. Outside, it was dark. Her shoulders slumped, and she closed her eyes and let out a deep sigh of disappointment. Richard would already have sailed. She had missed saying good-bye.

❧ 26 ❧

Midsummer Eve

It was June twenty-fourth—Midsummer Eve, the Festival of St. John the Baptist, and Honor's birthday. She jostled her way through the crowd in Yarmouth's market square as bonfires blazed and men and women danced around the flames to the music of pipes. Up and down the street people were milling past garlanded tables of cakes and ale that the town's wealthy citizens had set out. Girls wearing crowns of wildflowers flirted with young men in fantastic costumes and masks. It was a balmy, starry night, and the whole town was celebrating.

Honor was looking for Thornleigh. He had sailed into Yarmouth this afternoon after a month away at the Antwerp spring fair, and had immediately sent her word that he was coming home to Great Ashwold as soon as the cargo was unloaded. But Honor, impatient to see him, had hurried to the port, for this latest separation had been a long one; before he had sailed, her work had once again kept her in London for several weeks. Her excitement tonight was tinged with regret, however. They were going to have so little time together.

She pushed doggedly past the knots of revelers. A boy chasing a squealing piglet cannoned into her stomach with a thud that hurt, then ran off without a word. Honor glared after him.

She walked on, nearing the church of St. Nicholas, and skirted a fat, tipsy couple who were dancing, clumsy as bears. Suddenly, a man—or a fiend—swooped into her path as if he had plunged from the sky. She halted with a gasp. He was bearded, tall, and powerfully built, dressed all in black, and his lifted arms arched over her like the wings of a bird of prey. His eyes leered down into hers from a black wolf's face, lurid with streaks of paint—gold, red and green—and fringed all around with lustrous, quivering black feathers. A low growl threatened from his throat.

The eyes blinked. A blue-eyed wolf. Honor reached for the mask's snout and wrenched it up. A sharp intake of breath underneath it told her she had scraped his nose.

She laughed.

Thornleigh massaged his nose. "So glad I didn't frighten you, madam," he grumbled, and shoved the mask up onto his forehead where it rested, instantly inanimate.

"You've grown a beard," she said, frowning at the short, trim growth.

He turned his profile and waggled his head in a parody of a courtly coxcomb. "Like it?"

"No."

He laughed. "Ever truthful! Some things never change. Thank God."

"You do make a breathtaking monster, though," Honor said, caressing his cheek. She smiled up into his eyes. "Welcome home."

He took her in his arms and was about to kiss her, then stopped and looked beyond her. A man cross-eyed with drink was weaving straight toward them, his hands fumbling below his belt. Thornleigh saw the glinting spout of urine just in time and drew Honor away from the approaching fountain. The drunkard lurched on and the crowd skittered apart for him. Thornleigh laughed. "Effective way to clear a path!"

"But intrusive," Honor said, pulling him back and folding her arms around his neck. "Now, what were you saying before?"

"Just this," he murmured, bending to her.

Their kiss was long and hungry.

"Oh, Richard," she sighed, drawing back only far enough to look at him, "it's wonderful to see you."

"And you," he said with feeling. "Eight weeks is eight weeks too many." He studied her face, smiling. "I'm so glad you came tonight." He pulled her close again. His voice was low and urgent. "Let's go home."

"In a bit," Honor said, looking away, hoping it would be easier to tell him out here in the crowd, rather than at home, that she was going. "Let's walk a little first."

She took his arm and they began to stroll among the revelers.

"How's Adam?" he asked. "Giving you any trouble?"

"Not at all. I've set him to study Erasmus's *Adages*." She added with a smile, "That is, when I can get him away from the skiff he's building at the millrace." She looked at him. "Profitable trip?"

"Very." He cocked an eyebrow. "And blessedly dull."

Honor half smiled. She knew he was glad the rescue missions were over. But her work was not, despite the softening of government policy. The new Chancellor, Thomas Audeley, a compliant officeholder, had his hands full dealing with the government's continuing anti-Church policies, and the bishops were busy battling those policies in order to save their own livelihoods; in the anxious new political atmosphere, no one was inclined to care much about heretics. Except Sir Thomas More, Honor thought grimly. Although in retirement, he had been feverishly busy with his pen.

To counter the diatribes More was turning out, Honor was spending more and more time composing pamphlets and overseeing their printing in London. She was now writing as furiously as More, though anonymously. It kept her away from home far more than she liked. And more, she knew, than Thornleigh liked.

"There's news," she said brightly.

"Oh?"

"Oh, yes. For one thing, a coronation."

"*That* much I've heard. Queen Anne. Were you there for it?"

She nodded. "Along with half of London. Three days of folly. Bannered flotillas on the river. Cannon booming from the Tower. A procession through the streets with the new Queen sitting in her litter, her hair streaming free like a virgin . . . and her belly out to here."

Thornleigh laughed. "Five months' pregnant, they say."

"Apparently it did the trick, though no one seems to know exactly when or where the King married her. But this is his chance to have a legitimate son, so his new puppy archbishop cleared the way to the altar." At Archbishop Warham's death Honor had been amused at how quickly the Boleyn family's chaplain, Thomas Cranmer, had been elevated to the primacy of Canterbury and had immediately declared that the King was without doubt, in the eyes of God, a bachelor.

"What of Queen Catherine?" Thornleigh asked, and then corrected himself. "The Princess Dowager, I mean."

"The Pope, it seems, has refused to recognize the new marriage, and he's ordered the King to take Queen Catherine back. The King became so furious he's packed her off to the fens of Buckden with only her father confessor, her doctor, and a skeleton staff."

Thornleigh let out a low whistle of sympathy.

Honor looked down. She was not proud of the part she had played, however ineffectual, in bringing the Queen to her present wretchedness.

"Did you see Cromwell while you were there?" Thornleigh asked.

"Yes." She could not suppress a smile. "I went to congratulate him, since the new Queen's rise has happened exactly as he said it would. But when we met he was wincing at the drain the coronation banquet had made on the royal purse. He said the King went absolutely mad on his wardrobe. He fairly dripped gold. But then, from what I saw for myself at the procession, every gentleman and peer in England had done the same. Some must have been wearing half their fortunes on their backs. And they came out in full force, vying with one another to show the King their loyalty to his new Queen."

Thornleigh smiled. "I wonder who was left at home to tend the sheep."

"Sir Thomas More was."

"Not invited?"

"Oh, he was invited—and was conspicuously absent."

"Silently brooding in his library, no doubt. This new order of things is far from his liking."

"Brooding, perhaps, but hardly silent," she said harshly. "He's writing reams of trash. Huge, vitriolic tomes. While you were in Flanders the latest volume of his *Confutation of Tyndale's Answer* came out—that's five volumes so far! And other books too, all drearily laced with his malice for heretics. Listen," she said, closing her eyes to recite, "'. . . *these heretics of our time that go busily about to heap up to the sky their foul, filthy dunghill of all old and new false, stinking heresies, gathered up together against the true Catholic faith of Christ . . .'* He scribbles on like that ad nauseam. He also carries on at some length about whether demons are taking the form of beautiful, wicked women these days, and if so, that young men must beware their lures, et cetera, et cetera. All very tiresome."

"Who reads the stuff, though? The man is out of power. No one listens to him. Besides, the new English Church, severed from Rome, will soon be entrenched."

"It's not yet."

Their walk had brought them to the stone enclosure around St. Nicholas's. Thornleigh stopped under a lantern jutting from the wall and turned to Honor. "The work is done," he said steadily. "You've accomplished what you wanted. It's time to get back to living a normal life." He looked soberly into her eyes. "Honor, it's all over."

"Not for me," she said with quiet bitterness. "I'll fight Sir Thomas, as long as I can."

Thornleigh frowned. Honor knew that she had disturbed him. She looked away, wanting to deflect his displeasure. She scanned the square and brightened. "Look," she said, pointing. At the far side of the square a crowd had gathered at a huge wagon, a two-storied, moveable stage flanked by blazing torches. Laughter rolled from the people standing in front of it.

"Let's go see," Honor said, grateful for the diversion. She took Thornleigh's elbow.

But he would not be moved from his discontent. "It's only the baker's guild doing the Last Judgment," he said testily.

"Oh, come on." She pulled him across the square and they stood at the back of the crowd and looked at the stage. Gradually, watching the lively play, Thornleigh's dour expression softened.

Two baker-actors stood on the wagon's top platform. One, dressed as a fat monk, was piteously begging the other, a stern-faced St. Peter, to let him through heaven's gates which were painted in yellow stripes on a blue cloth. But St. Peter remained unmoved. The monk began to whimper about his blameless life. "He's lying!" eager voices shouted from the crowd. As the monk's pleas became more desperate, angels—dressed as ordinary bakers and millwrights and watermen—filed behind him. Every time he told a lie one of them kicked him, and with each kick the watchers whistled and stamped their approval.

A curtain swept open on the lower level where a backdrop painted with orange flames depicted hell. There was a low, admiring "Aah" from the audience as a huge wooden serpent, green and scaled, glided forward on rollers, and eerie music of pipes and tambourines sounded from behind the doors. A baker playing Satan stalked on stage brandishing a sword. He was horned and almost naked, his body painted red. With a menacing leer he climbed aboard the serpent. Above, the angels led the quaking monk to the edge of a staircase connecting Heaven and Hell, and forced him to look down and behold Satan. Fascinated, the crowd stood quiet.

Thornleigh leaned over to Honor. "This'll up the stakes with the brewers."

"What?"

"It's a yearly feud here. Bakers' guild against the brewers'. They try to outdo one another with their plays. But," he added with a chuckle, "unless the brewers' Great Flood has sharpened up since last year, they can't touch this."

There was a loud roll of thunder. Satan swung his sword overhead and the serpent's jaws opened wide, showing a garish red maw. Gasps were heard in the crowd. An explosion erupted from the beast's throat. It vomited fire. Several women screamed. One threw her apron over her head. A child began to wail. Honor saw an old man cross himself.

Thornleigh had folded his arms across his chest and was studying the fire-breathing viper. "Gunpowder," he muttered, sniffing the air. "Sulfur."

Honor shook her head, watching the frightened faces around

her. "And sticks pounded on kettles for thunder. How can they be afraid of sparks and paint and noise?"

Thornleigh shrugged. "People see what they want to see."

"Or what they're told to see."

"Or what they fear to see," he added.

"Blind," she said in disgust, "and what's worse, content to be blind."

Satan was by this time displaying his evil fury with fine gusto, pumping his sword arm up and down, and with every pump the serpent he rode bellowed fire. Suddenly, a head of cabbage thrown from the audience thumped Satan on his horned temple. He lurched sideways, then tumbled from his mount and thudded to the stage on his backside. He sat up scowling. With his legs straight out before him he looked more like a furious, red-faced baby than the Lord of Darkness.

A great peal of laughter burst from the audience. More vegetables pelted the actors, more loud delight rose from the crowd. Then, quick as a sneeze, a fistfight broke out near the front. It seemed to light a fuse that burned through the throng, igniting bursts of shoving and punching among the young men. Within moments the whole crowd was scuffling and shouting.

"It's the brewers getting even," Thornleigh said with a laugh above the noise. A man with blood streaming from his nose reeled backwards towards Honor and stopped only feet away from her. He straightened and plowed headlong again into the fracas. Thornleigh whisked his arm around Honor's waist. "Let's get out of here."

They made their way through the square until the brawl was well behind them, then walked on among the quieter revelers. They passed a bonfire where three men were dancing a jig. Children ran past, squealing. They walked by a couple kissing in a doorway. Thornleigh glanced at the lovers, then smiled at Honor. "Those two have the right idea," he said, stopping to put his arms around her. Honor gave herself to his kiss. "How about we go out to the *Speedwell?*" Thornleigh said, nuzzling her neck. "The crew are all ashore. We'd be alone." He looked into her eyes and mur-

mured, "I'd like to lock the cabin door and make love to you for
about three days."

Reluctantly, Honor pulled out of his embrace. She could put off
her announcement no longer. "Richard, I've got to leave for London in the morning."

He straightened abruptly. He looked away, clearly angry.

"Richard, please listen . . ."

A braying interrupted her, and she and Thornleigh were forced
to part as a priest on a donkey ambled between them. A trio of giggling children hopped after the donkey, tying flowers to its tail.
One of them, a bright-eyed girl, stopped to stare up at Thornleigh's mask. He pulled it off his forehead and bent to place it on
her small face. She ran after her friends, growling in savage delight.

Once they had gone, Thornleigh still did not look at Honor.
"How long away this time?" he said.

"Two weeks. Maybe three."

"Or four. Or five."

"No. I promise."

"You promised once before."

"You mean about seeing you off at Billingsgate? I told you what
happened at the printer's. I told you I was sorry."

"I'm sorry too." Finally, he looked at her. His eyes were hard
and cold. "This isn't working out very well, is it?"

Honor shivered. "What do you mean?"

"This marriage. If you can call it that. Maybe there's another
word for it. An 'arrangement'?"

"Richard, don't talk like—"

A ball of fire swamped her vision. A boy was dashing by with a
torch. Its heat blasted the side of her face, and the wind-like rush
of the flame roared by her ear. In a flash of horrified memory she
saw again the executioner's torch at Smithfield as it plunged into
the faggots beneath Ralph. Her eyes followed the moving flame.
The boy reached a man-sized mound of logs and sticks, and with a
primitive yelp of joy he thrust in the torch. The fuel burst into
flame. Honor went rigid, fists clenched, eyes wide.

Thornleigh was watching her. "What is it?" he asked. "What's the matter?"

She stared at the blaze. Her breathing was shallow. "I can't see him," she whispered, frightened.

Thornleigh glanced at the bonfire. "See who?"

Her hands flew to her cheeks, and she cringed, shaking her head, still staring.

Alarmed, Thornleigh grabbed her wrists and jerked her around, away from the fire, to face him. "Tell me. What's wrong?"

"I swore!" she cried. "Swore I'd never forget. Never look into a fire without seeing Ralph's face. But . . . he's not there anymore!"

"Good," Thornleigh said steadily. "If he's gone, let him go."

"No!" She pulled out of his grasp and whirled around to look at the blaze. She beat her fists against her temples. "I promised to see him . . . always. To never forget his pain."

"Stop this!" He caught her again, this time by the shoulders, and wrenched her back to him.

She struggled, trying to free herself. "You don't understand!" she cried. "You've never understood. Or cared."

He held her firmly. "I do understand. If you can't see death in the flames anymore it's time to look again at life."

"What are you talking about? Can't you understand? *I am sworn.* To keep faith. To—"

"You've kept faith enough to save a hundred blasted sinners. Whatever you owed, you owe no more."

"I won't abandon Ralph!"

"Ralph is *dead*!"

She shook her head to shield herself from his words, and strained, though he still held her, to look over her shoulder at the bonfire. Tears welled in her eyes. "If I try . . . if I only look harder . . . I know I'll see him."

Thornleigh suddenly flung her around to face the fire. "Go on, then, look at it!" he said. He gripped her shoulders, hard. "What do you see? You belittle people for seeing devils on a slapped-up stage—you scorn them for willingly blinding themselves to what's real—but you're no better. You want to see ghosts. Well, look hard. What's *really* there?"

A ragged circle of people had drifted in around the bonfire and stood, talking and drinking. The blaze crackled as someone tossed on a splintered board. Honor looked deep into the flames but, try as she might, she could not conjure up Ralph's face. Instead, strangely, she heard his laughing voice, telling her, as he used to do when she was a child, that people set fires on Midsummer Eve to celebrate her birthday. Other words echoed—was it Ralph's voice still?—"You owe no more!" She began to feel it might be true. Slowly, one by one, the chains that hung around her—chains of guilt, of sorrow, of regret—began to fall away. She felt oddly lightened. But then she hugged herself, suddenly afraid that without the familiar weight of the chains she would be adrift, and she searched the fire again. But there was no writhing specter. Only flames leaping on wood. Reality. Tears spilled onto her cheeks, the molten waste of her struggle.

She was trembling, and Thornleigh slackened his grip. "Look there," he said gently, pointing. "Not death. Life." He gave a soft laugh, and Honor saw why. At the side of the fire a mumbling old crone had lifted her skirt to warm her withered buttocks, as if it were a winter twilight and not a sultry summer eve. Across from the crone a young man was helping a buxom girl toss roasted chestnuts in a pan. The young man took the opportunity to brush his arm against the girl's breast, and she shot an elbow into his ribs. Farther around the circle a boy, crouching with a stick, was singing to himself as he dreamily drew goslings in the ashes.

Honor felt a smile begin. Then she caught herself, and the smile vanished. She turned slowly back to Thornleigh, wiping her tears away with the back of her hand. He took her by her shoulders again, but gently this time. "You're right, of course," Honor said quietly, dully. "Now, let me go."

But he did not. "Promise me you'll put this obsession behind you?"

"I promise . . . to deal only in reality," she said. "And one reality is that I am sworn. Let me go. I have important work to do. Tracts to write. Lies to set straight—"

"My God, listen to yourself! You mumble it like a catechism."

"What do you know about it?" she flared.

"Everything. I once thrashed about in the same ditch of guilt. And I'd dug it for myself, just as you have done. I know what it's like to have venom eating inside you."

"Then let me be!"

"No. Listen to me. This anger is a poison only to yourself. It has no power to change what's done. It can only corrode your own spirit."

She opened her mouth to fling fighting words, but none would come. Her mind could not seem to grasp hold of any. "I . . . I must . . ."

"*Why* must you?"

She blinked, confused. It was difficult to remember *why*. "But . . ."

He tightened his grip. "Honor, you know what I say is true. Let this hatred go."

"But how can I? As long as Sir Thomas hurls his poisoned arrows I must—"

"Oh, Christ, Sir Thomas!" Thornleigh groaned. "Always Sir Thomas." He threw up his hands. "Usually a man's rival is someone the lady *loves*, not hates!"

Honor felt slightly dizzy. The fire-sparked darkness seemed to be humming. "What do you mean?"

He shook his head at her as if at a stupid child. "I mean that I've been fighting Sir Thomas for you since the day you kicked that poker from my hands. The day you woke *me* up to life. Well, the time has come for you to choose between us. You can spend your life with me—a *real* life with me, mind—or you can run with your vendetta against More. One or the other. It can't be both."

She blinked at him, astonished. "An ultimatum?"

"God, Honor, what else can I do?" He spoke as though exasperated to the point of helplessness. "Look at me," he said, thumping a palm on his chest. "What reality do you see *here*? What kind of man?"

She knew the answer in every fiber of her body. He was the standard against which she judged every other man and found all wanting.

Tenderly, he took her face between his hands. "If you see anything but a man who loves you," he said, "who's been waiting for you to work this fever of spite out of your blood, then you are blind indeed."

He was staring into her eyes. His hands were hot on her face.

"Honor," he groaned, "I can't wait any longer. Choose. Which will it be?"

You, of course! she wanted to cry. And yet, must she forsake the work that could bring about so much good?

"Do I have to ask you again to marry me," Thornleigh asked. "To truly be my wife?"

His need was irresistible. Honor could find no breath to speak.

"In law, you know," he said cautiously, "silence is construed as consent." He bent and, tentatively, kissed her. Heat swept through her. He drew back his head. He was smiling.

Her mouth opened, hungry for the feel of him, the taste of him, again.

There was a jangle of tambourines and a skreeling of pipes as musicians and tumblers capered into the square, surrounding them.

"Honor," Thornleigh whispered, but before he could say another word she thrust her fingers into the red-gold tangle of his hair and stopped his mouth with hers.

❧ 27 ❧

Cromwell's Summons

Honor rested back in warm bathwater sprinkled with lavender buds, took in a long, deep breath of the lavender perfume, and smiled. Buttery March sunshine was beginning to stream through the oriel window in the bedchamber at Great Ashwold, but despite the sun's radiance the early hour had called for more warmth, and behind the pool of her blue silk robe that she had dropped on the floorboards, the flames of a newly laid fire danced in the hearth, banishing the morning chill.

She reached out to a stool beside the tub for three unopened letters that lay beside the pouch of lavender. The letters, just delivered by Honor's maid, made up a flurry of communication from the larger world outside Great Ashwold that Honor found most exciting.

But she was glad Thornleigh had not seen them delivered; he had left her sleeping, and by now he would be saddled up for the two hour ride into Norwich. Honor had instructed her maid to give her such letters only in private. She regretted the subterfuge with Thornleigh but felt justified in using it, for she had kept her promise to him—on the whole. Since Midsummer Eve, through a quiet autumn and winter, she had not seen London—had strayed no further than to accompany him now and then when business took him to Aylsham or Yarmouth, for he always asked her to join him.

And she had been happy. She was absorbed in learning the intricacies of the woolcloth business. She had forged a delightful friendship with young Adam. She was deeply in love with her husband. What more could she want?

She looked guiltily at the letters. No, she thought defensively, she would not give up the innocent stimulation of outside correspondence. Nor give up the writing she still managed to do, though she was no longer involved with any printing. The writing was only for herself now—a calmer, and at the same time more intensely focused channel for her ideas about the justice that still had not come to England's Church courts, for the King, having got his new Queen, had done nothing to change the old laws. However, she indulged these private interests only when Thornleigh was away. Harmless though they were, they represented to him a preoccupation he insisted was dangerous for her. If he knew, he would chafe. They would quarrel. It was better this way.

She shuffled the letters, examining them. One, with a plain exterior, gave no hint about its author, but the two others Honor quickly recognized. There could not have been more contrast in the appearance of the pair. The first was a creased and battered brown paper, its brown blob of sealing wax cracked, and the ink of its outer direction smeared with grease; all were marks, she guessed, of the letter's long and tortured journey to reach her. The second was crisp and white, fastidiously sealed with red wax into which an imprint—the head of the Roman god Terminus—stood out in sleek relief. But even before she saw this well-known device of the writer, Honor recognized the elegant handwriting on the outside as Erasmus's.

She placed Erasmus's letter and the unknown one back onto the stool and tore open the bedraggled, brown one. It was unsigned, but its first words confirmed her assumption: Brother Frish. As she unfolded the paper she heard a walking horse's hooves clack over the cobbles in the courtyard. That would be Richard, on his way, she thought. She settled herself happily against the tub's back, sending lavender buds swirling around her, and read.

Frish was full of excitement. He had married! He spoke tenderly of his German, country-bred wife, and scathingly of the celibacy the Church required of priests and monks—"a mockery of God's love," he wrote. He was finally a whole man, he said, using body and heart and mind as God had made them to be used, for he was certain that the love between man and woman was pleasant to God, "implanted in us by Him."

Honor smiled, understanding. She looked out at the budding chestnut boughs, their ripe tips crowded against the second-story window pane as if nestling close for fellowship. How beautiful the world was this morning. In the distance beyond the chestnut tree and the courtyard wall, the last shreds of silvery mist were lifting from the woods, and the strengthening sun struck gold on her arm, reminding her of the first yellow celandines and marsh marigolds she and Adam had seen the day before blooming across the woodland floor. Yes, she thought, how beautiful the world, and how sweet and powerful Frish's words. "A whole man," he had written. His eloquence moved her this morning more than she could say, for she was almost sure that she was pregnant. She had kept the discovery to herself, not wanting to speak of it until she was quite certain. Now, holding the knowledge with the delight of holding a gift in readiness, she wondered: when would be the perfect time to tell Richard?

She felt a tug of pity for two other women, two unhappy Queens. Anne Boleyn had been delivered of her first child, a girl, not the son the King craved. The princess had been christened Elizabeth, but Honor had heard that the King, foul-tempered with disappointment, had stayed away from the ceremony. And Honor thought of Queen Catherine. The fearful, dithering Pope had finally declared his verdict in the divorce, seven long years after the King had first requested it. And when it came, it seemed like some cruel jest on all concerned: the Pope had pronounced in favor of Catherine. Much good it did the lady now, Honor thought, locked away with her rosary, her prie-dieu, and her confessor in her bleak house on the fens.

She shrugged off these gloomy thoughts and turned back to Frish's news. He rambled on in high spirits about his absorbing work in Antwerp with William Tyndale. They were embarked, he wrote, on learning Hebrew in order to tackle a translation of the Old Testament, one that he hoped would match Erasmus's ground-breaking translation fourteen years before of the New Testament from the original Greek. The task would take years, Frish said, but he had never been happier. He closed, sending her his love and benediction. She folded the paper. Brother Frish, it was quite clear, was hale and hearty.

She picked up Erasmus's letter and tore open the seal, eager to hear his witty version of the news from Freiburg where he now lived. But his familiar, gently mocking voice was now strained with discouragement. Religious battles, he wrote, had sunk the German territories into ghastly bloodshed. She had known, of course, that the Lutheran Evangelicals had taken many German cities and Swiss cantons from the Catholic authorities with the force of arms; she knew, too, that in the fighting, both sides had brandished Erasmus's writings as moral ammunition. He wrote her now that, had he known an age like theirs was coming, he would never have written many of the things he had.

This saddened her. Erasmus had been one of the first and certainly the most eminent to accuse the old Church of decadence and decay. Years ago he had even congratulated Luther for "seizing the Pope by his tiara and the priests by their paunches," and had hoped that much good would come of the German monk's radical ideas.

But, [he wrote to Honor now] just look at the Evangelical people. Have they become any better? Show me a man among them whom their Gospel has changed from a drunkard to a temperate man, from a brute to a gentle creature, from a miser to a liberal person. There are few. Many have actually degenerated. I have never been in their churches, but I have seen them return from hearing the sermon, as if inspired by an evil spirit, the faces of all showing a curious wrath and ferocity.

Honor hurriedly scanned the rest of the dispiriting letter, barely taking it in. She had no desire to think of bloodshed and religious hatred, not on this bright morning. Besides, there was no time to loll about any longer; a full day lay ahead. Adam would soon be in the hall waiting for his Latin lesson with her, and there were arrangements to be made for the upcoming visit of Thornleigh's sister and her husband. And, if enough time could be snatched for herself, Honor thought, she might make some headway today on a treatise she was writing, calling for reform of England's still unchanged heresy laws. She went up on her knees to quickly finish washing, and then she remembered the third letter. She reached for it. It was plain, white, with no distinguishing marks.

Madam,
  After my right hearty commendations, and trusting this intrusion on your quietness which you bade me not disturb will be forgiven when you know the cause, I am enforced to write my mind plainly unto you.
  A grave matter has arisen touching the King's Grace. It requires your immediate presence here. Forgive the silence of this letter, but more cannot be said until it be said unto your face, that I may therein know your mind.
  Therefore come, madam, and come posthaste. I urge this of you, both in the discharge of my duty to the King's Grace and in the manifestation of my hearty good will which I bear unto you.
  From London, this 10th day of March,
  Thos. Cromwell

Honor heard boots thud in the passage—a man's heavy tread, approaching. Cromwell's letter fluttered to the floor as Honor instinctively folded her arms across her breasts. Only then did she think of the letters. Quickly, she leaned over the tub, grabbed the two pages on the stool and shoved them, with Cromwell's letter, underneath the stool. She dropped the lavender pouch on top to cover them.

The door swung open. Thornleigh was several strides into the room, absently sorting a handful of papers, when he noticed her. "Oh. Sorry," he said, stopping. "Left a receipt in here."

Honor relaxed. Still kneeling, she sat back on her heels, and her hands splashed softly into the hip-high water to pick up the soap. A smile crept over her lips; she loved the way his presence overpowered any room he entered. She watched him now as he scratched his cheek. The beard had long gone. A rush of warmth swept her as she remembered waking up in bed in Yarmouth the morning after Midsummer Eve to see him standing at the window, shaving.

Thornleigh hadn't moved. His fistful of papers was forgotten as he watched her lather her neck, and all his thoughts of business, apparently, blurred.

She loved that, too—the way he always beheld her body with such straightforward, uncomplicated pleasure.

And he did behold her. Sunlight glinted on her hair, tied up loosely with a blue ribbon whose tips, water-dipped and dripping, clung to the nape of her neck. Her wet breasts glistened, the nipples tightening under his gaze.

He cleared his throat. "I'll just get the book I wanted. The receipt, I mean."

He went to a table, quickly found the paper he was looking for, and crammed it into his tunic. He turned back to her, his task completed, and slapped the belt at his hips. "Must go," he said, rooted to the spot.

She smiled. "Safe journey."

"Thanks." He watched a milky patch of foam slide down from her neck and slip over her breast, curving around the red nipple. She raised the cake of soap and bent her arm to reach her back.

"Let me," he said, striding forward. He tugged off his loose cloak and tossed it on the floor. He knelt at the side of the tub and took the soap from her, dipped it, and lathered it in his hands.

A sigh escaped her as he massaged her shoulder blades in small, then widening, circles. Her head slowly bent forward, her neck like a wax taper melting. With eyes closed she felt with both hands for the rim of the tub to steady herself as his pressure increased.

His palms smoothed down her back and over the flare of her hips, molding her shape down to the water, then back up to her shoulders.

But instead of starting down her back again one hand moved around to the hollow of her throat. It went downward with the sliding foam and smoothed over her taut breast. She sensed that her nipple was hard against his palm, like a pebble. Behind her his other hand gripped the far rim, and she leaned back against the tensed muscles of his arm.

From the courtyard a young groom's breaking voice cried out, "Mistress Agnes, where's the master? Am I to keep holding Tess here, saddled up for him?"

But the boy's question, and the answer if one came, neither Honor nor Thornleigh heard. As she parted her lips for his mouth his hand smoothed soap froth over her belly at the water line. Kissing her, he lifted her forward with his arm at her back, and she stood on her knees, water dripping from the triangle thicket of curling hair.

Slowly, gently, his fingers slid into the warm cleft that was slippery with foam and desire. She cast her arms around his neck with a moan, and pressed her cheek against his chest, her lips brushing the rough wool tunic. She shuddered against him, then pulled his head down by his hair to kiss his mouth again.

He scooped water and poured it over her shoulders and then gathered her in his arms. He lifted her from the tub and laid her down on the spread silk robe before the hearth and sat back on his heels to unbuckle his belt.

Honor opened her arms to the joy of him, the losing of herself, the finding of herself, the joy of him.

As they uncoiled, the young groom's whine again breached the bedchamber. "Shall I take Tess in, then? Where's the master gone to?"

This, Honor and Thornleigh heard. "To heaven," he murmured into the softness of her neck. He rose and went to the window, stumbling on his scattered clothes, and called down to the boy. "I'll be right there!"

He dressed quickly, and Honor propped herself up on an elbow and laughed out loud as he hopped in place with one boot on and a foot halfway into the other. He grinned, picked up his cloak and moved toward the door.

"Richard," she said suddenly. "I need to go to London tomorrow."

Halfway across the room he turned, still smiling, for her tone had been light.

"I want to buy some silver candlesticks for Joan," Honor said, not really lying, since this gift for her sister-in-law was one she had given some thought to. "She's been so kind. I'd like to make the purchase in person."

"I'll take you," Thornleigh said simply, and started again to leave.

"No. I mean, well . . . you'll be in Norwich till tomorrow afternoon, and I'd like to leave first thing in the morning."

"No trouble. I'll ride back from Fowler's after supper this evening. In the morning, I'll take you."

"Ride back in the dark?" she protested. "No, it's not necessary. Sam will come with me. I'll be all right."

"I'll *take* you," he said, emphatically closing the discussion.

Despite her consternation, she had to smile at the sheer grit of his will. "I think, my love," she said with gentle wryness, "you just did."

He laughed. He started again for the door, then turned back to kiss the air in Honor's direction, still moving backwards. He bumped against the stool by the tub, knocking it over and inadvertently kicking the pouch of lavender. With a sheepish smile he bent to right the stool, and his boot scuffed over the letters. He stooped to pick one up. Honor groaned inwardly, for she saw that the letter was Cromwell's. Thornleigh's eyes darted first to the signature, then to Honor.

"Read it," she said quietly.

Thornleigh did so. For a moment he said nothing. He dropped the letter onto the stool. "When were you going to tell me? Or were you just going to sneak out the silversmith's back door?"

"Of course not," Honor said. Kneeling, she was pulling on the silk robe.

"But you are going to see Cromwell?"

"I must. Richard, we owe him. He was always a friend. Anyway," she added lamely, "it's probably nothing."

Thornleigh snorted. "He'll have you up to your neck in illicit folly. He uses you, Honor. You're not stupid. Why can't you see that he uses you?"

She was stung. "He does make use of me, yes," she said defensively. "He uses what I gladly offer. And I will offer to help him now, if it's in my power."

"Christ," he growled. He looked away from her, shaking his head. Sharply, he turned back. "And if I refuse to let you go?"

She was taken aback. But she forced wryness into her voice. "What will you do, my love? Lock me up?"

"This is no jest, Honor." He looked deadly earnest. "I'll refuse you if I must. For your own good."

She shivered. Why was he hacking open this chasm between them? She said steadily, "I would hope you won't do such a foolish thing."

He said nothing, but the look of angry resolution still darkened his face.

How she hated this quarrel! She stood and came to him. "Richard, please listen to me. I've got to do what I think is right. Let me use my judgment."

"That's just it. You *don't* use judgment. You barge into things. I know you." He was pacing now. "And one of these days it's going to get you killed. Well, I won't let that happen. I won't let you *make* it happen. Not anymore." Abruptly, he stopped and stood rock still. "I forbid you to go."

She felt indignation fire her cheeks. She faced him. "You think you know me? You don't know anything about me. You don't know what I think. Or what I feel is important. Or what I need to do."

"Important? To run around playing at intrigue? To let Cromwell jerk your strings like a puppet?"

"To be part of something bigger than myself," she cried. "My God, can't you understand that?"

"Oh, I understand. I understand that you value this nonsense above everything else. You love intrigue for the bloody thrill of it!"

She threw up her hands. "You see?" Her breathing was hard and shallow with anger. "You *deny* me your understanding. You deny me your trust. Is that your whim with wives? To refuse them what they need most? You refused her your body. You refuse me everything *but!*"

His face tightened as if she had struck him.

They stared at one another for a long moment.

Finally, Thornleigh said, with great control. "I can't live like this. If you go to London, don't bother to come back."

He strode to the door, and was gone.

"But, it's incredible!" Honor said.

Cromwell, looking pleased, leaned back in the chair behind his littered desk at Whitehall. He laced his fingers together over his stomach. "Incredible," he said, "but true."

"The King really wants to welcome Frish home?" Honor asked. She was standing in front of the desk, her eyes bright with hope. She wanted, needed, this mission to be of huge significance. Significant enough to justify her awful quarrel with Thornleigh, and the hateful thing she had said. Significant enough to make him accept that, about this work at least, she had been right. He would have to take her back, then . . . would he not? After all, there was the coming baby. "Has the new Queen wrought such a miraculous change?"

Cromwell held up his hands to check her enthusiasm. "The Queen I cannot answer for," he said. "This is the King's desire. At my suggestion, I might add. And 'welcome' may be too strong a word."

Honor's face clouded. "But Frish would be quite safe, wouldn't he? I could not possibly agree without absolute assurances of his safety."

Cromwell lifted his hands higher, this time to fire up in her the enthusiasm he had just dampened. "Safe, aye, have no fear. The King wishes personally to meet with him. If you can persuade Frish to return, he'll travel with a written safe-conduct guaranteed and signed by me."

She knew this was as good as the King's word. Master Secretary Cromwell had made himself the most powerful man in the realm after the King. But the first bubble of her excitement had already burst, and she was now full of skepticism. She *would* show judgment! "So. Brought back to meet with the King. And all—do I understand you aright?—all for show?" she asked warily.

"I prefer to say, for the sake of persuasion."

"Just who's to be persuaded?"

"His Grace is anxious to seek out foreign approval for his marriage."

Honor could not help thinking that foreign approval was the only approval the King was likely to get. The common people of England apparently thought of the new Queen as an upstart at best, a whore at worst. Honor had heard stories that everywhere, on Sundays, when priests asked for worshippers to join in a prayer for Queen Anne, people walked out of the churches en masse.

"The King," Cromwell was saying, "wishes to forge new friendships, new alliances, with some of the more powerful German princes. The Protestant princes, that is. He hopes to find open minds amongst them, and feels that the English exiles could be the perfect link between him and them. Showing his goodwill to the exiles will prove his goodwill to those princes."

"But why Frish? Tyndale is far better known."

"Tyndale is a spiteful and hostile man. I doubt if he would budge to aid the King. But Frish might well be glad to come home."

Honor was shaking her head. "I don't like it. It's only another political stratagem to you. But if anything were to go wrong it's Frish who would pay the forfeit. And I shudder to think how."

"I'm surprised you hesitate," he said coolly. "I'm surprised you think so little of what the man himself would want. Ask him. A chance to turn the King of England Protestant? I warrant he'll hop the first ship and be practicing his sermons on the cabin-boys, Bible in hand. It's the chance he's dreamed of."

She knew he was right.

Cromwell leaned forward. "And you, Mistress Thornleigh, are the key. You are perhaps the only person Frish would trust to follow back to England. Also, you know where to find him quickly."

She gave him a doubting smile. "And you cannot? Why, Master

Secretary, I understand your network of agents is so thick, a man may not kick his neighbor's cat without you know of it."

"Spies?" He waved the suggestion away like a dish of too-rich sauce. "I find no need for such hole-in-corner antics. I simply keep in touch with a great many men in a great number of localities. Why pay spies when people will gladly whisper to you, of their own accord, what neighbor is kicking whom?"

Honor found little to placate her in Cromwell's cold-blooded view. She moved to the window and looked out. Oddly, his words had ignited a memory, a story Sir Thomas used to enjoy telling. There was once a man, Sir Thomas would say, who moved into a new village and wanted to know what his neighbors were like. In the middle of the night he pretended to beat his wife to see if they would come and reprove him. But though he loudly whipped a sheepskin while his wife, playing her part, wailed and screamed, no one came. And so the next morning the man and his wife left the village to seek a decent place to live.

How strange, she thought, to recall Sir Thomas's gentle fable at this moment, and so fondly. Yet as she felt Cromwell's penetrating stare on her back she was struck by the gulf between the two mens' views of community. Sir Thomas's ideal of conformity as the cement of a harmonious, ordered society was worlds apart from Cromwell's stark understanding of human motives.

"I can offer you a large cash incentive," Cromwell said.

She turned to him sharply. "If I do it, I'll do it for the justice of it."

"As you wish."

The derision that tinged his smile chafed her, and she could not resist adding, "Though such *unsolicited* generosity would have been blessedly welcome once, when men were hunted by dogs."

He dropped the smile. "Let us deal with the present, shall we? I have legislation pending in Parliament that is going to remap the face of the realm. I offer you a chance to make a small but vital contribution to that remapping. However, if you prefer to decline, to live in the past and sigh for what might have been, then I will take no more of your time." He rose irritably and looked at her, waiting, as near to anger as she has ever seen him.

"Of course I'll do it," she said evenly, trying to push Thornleigh to the back of her mind. "I consider it a duty, and a privilege." And a chance to see her work vindicated. To—how had Cromwell put it?—turn the King of England Protestant. This could shatter forever the very concept of "heresy."

"Good," Cromwell said pleasantly. His vexation instantly vanished and Honor had the uneasy feeling that he had never really doubted her consent.

He came around the desk to her. "I'd like you to leave immediately. Within a day or two, if you can."

"That's no problem."

"Will your husband accompany you?"

"No." She offered no explanation.

"Then you'll need an escort. Shall I send a couple of my servants round to your lodging?"

"Thank you, but Sam Jinner's here with me. I'll take him, and one of our London apprentices."

"Well, let me know if you need anything else. I'll have the letters of safe-conduct sent to you right away. And now, you must excuse me. I'd ask you to stay to dine—Lord Lisle this morning sent me a haunch of venison—but I've already invited a few recalcitrant members of Parliament and I fear our discussions would be tedious to you."

"Politics are making a courtier of you, Master Secretary. This dismissal is positively gallant."

He shrugged, and she knew he had missed her jest.

She smiled. "Well then, I'll leave you to your dreary stratagems." She had heard the talk, even in Norfolk, about Cromwell's heavy-handed tactics with Parliamentarians. He was badgering and bribing friendly members and threatening hostile ones, apparently taking no chances with the new slew of bills he had steered before the Commons. "But tell me," she said as she gathered up her cloak. "This session of Parliament is dragging on so. When can we hope to see your great *pièce de résistance*?" Though the King had smashed the privileges of the bishops, he still had not taken the ultimate, revolutionary step of naming himself head of the Church.

For the first time in their conversation Cromwell's eyes kindled, fired by the issue dearest to his heart. "You've heard of the King's twelve great cannon?" he asked. "The Apostles, they're called. Drawn by a dozen draft horses and able to blast a hole through fourteen feet of castle wall. Well, the bills now before Parliament, though only half as many, are my Apostles. With them, the castle of papal jurisdiction in England will finally be razed."

He explained, counting the bills off on his fingers. The first five, which he called his bombardment, provided that all citations from Rome would be nullified; that the English clergy would give allegiance solely to the Crown; that revenues formerly paid to the Pope by English bishops on appointment to their sees would now be paid to the King; that the royal succession would be settled on the King's male heirs by Queen Anne; and that it would no longer be heresy to deny the papal primacy.

"With this barrage," he said, "we breach the walls. The sixth and final step, the taking of the castle keep—the *pièce de résistance*, as you call it—will be an Act to make the King Supreme Head of the Church in England. I hope to have it a *fait accompli* by Christmas."

"You have labored mightily, sir." She laughed. "I am exhausted hearing of it."

He was not amused. "The molding of a new order, mistress, does require some sweat."

She hardly knew herself why the victory seemed somewhat anticlimactic. It was a victory she had striven for, and yet her months of quiet at Great Ashwold—and, yes, of contentment—had given her an appreciation of the deep satisfactions of hearth and home. Cromwell's single-mindedness now seemed faintly obsessive.

"And you are quite certain of the passage of these bills?" she asked.

"A few laggards here, a few snarling bulldogs there. We'll round them up and bring them to heel."

"I see. And what about Sir Thomas?"

Cromwell looked mildly surprised at the question.

"Though out of office," Honor explained, "I know he has influence still. Do you ever see him?"

Cromwell grunted. "Sir Thomas is a stubborn man."

"That he is," she said with a smile, glad that she could do so now when thinking of her former guardian. This softening, she knew, she owed to Thornleigh. It was he who had swept her heart clean of rancor. But the thought of him now, of their quarrel, brought pain. Again, she forced his image away. She concentrated on Sir Thomas. "What's the problem?"

"More still will not declare for the marriage."

"But he does not actively oppose it, does he?"

"Not publicly. Not verbally. But he is loud with his pen. Every denunciation of heresy he writes—and he's been writing a whirl-wind—is a denunciation of the restructured English Church, and therefore of the King's marriage. Oh, he's careful never to mention the marriage, he's too clever for that. Too much so for the King's taste, I can tell you."

"Well, you're clever, too," Honor said. "Why not match him? These new bills of yours—for example, this statute settling the royal succession on the new Queen's issue—why not call in Sir Thomas and ask him to swear an oath to uphold it. He can hardly fail to agree once it's the law of the land."

Cromwell blinked at her.

Perhaps, she thought, he didn't see the point. "It's really very simple," she said. "Sir Thomas has balked at attacks on the Church's authority because the way was open to do so. But if Parliament passes the new statutes, and if you insist that as a loyal subject he conform, then that way is blocked. Sir Thomas reveres the law, especially when it is made with the communal voice of Parliament. The law, English law, is his lodestar."

He continued to stare at her. "An oath?"

"Yes. Have him swear. Then you can send him home, declawed, harmless."

A light broke over Cromwell's frozen features. "My God, woman, what an idea. It *is* simple. How could I not have seen it?"

"You are too close to the problem, sir," she said lightly. "I have a little distance now." For Sir Thomas's sake, she thought, pleased with herself, this solution was ideal. It would save him from Cromwell's antagonism, from the King's wrath, possibly from great harm. Yes, she told herself, there is satisfaction in *true* charity. And for that she knew she must give Thornleigh credit. Must give him credit for so much. Suddenly, the thought of not seeing him again—not loving him again, not sharing her life with him—brought a sickening wave of misery. But she shook it off. This mission must be done. It was right. And he would see that it was right!

At the door she turned. "Enjoy your venison, Master Secretary. If I make haste to Antwerp, perhaps the next haunch Lord Lisle sends you, you'll serve to Brother Frish, for I undertake to have him on your doorstep within the month. Good day!"

❧ 28 ❧

"Heresy!"

The girl was a redhead, freckled, wide of hip, and seventeen. In a cramped withdrawing room at Windsor Palace she sauntered past a knot of idle courtiers and moved toward the King who sat ensconced in a window seat. Little red plums on the plate of partridge she was bringing him rolled like loose ship's barrels above her swaying walk. A bleary-eyed gentleman stood saying something to the King, but the pounding of rain on the window, and the nearby plunk of lute-strings, tinny against the din of nature outside, combined to drown out his words. In any case, the King ignored him. With hands on his spread knees, he was watching the girl approach.

A plum teetered off the rim of her plate, rolled along the floor, and stopped between the King's beefy legs. The girl went down on her knees to fetch it. She lifted the fruit between her plump thumb and forefinger and popped it between his puckered lips. He munched; she giggled.

Across the room Anne stood watching the girl. She shouldered her way past the guests and came before the King. The window behind him was opaque from the heat of pent-up bodies.

"Won't you favor us with a song, mistress?" Anne said, tugging the girl up to her feet. "My brother awaits with his lute to accompany your sweet voice." She dug her nails into the girl's arm and shoved her into the room. Faces nearby turned aside, trained not to notice.

Anne's head snapped around to Henry. In a tight whisper she said, "You mock me, sir!"

"You mock yourself with these fishwife antics. Be content."

"Content? When you take your pleasure with every flouncing strumpet before my very eyes?"

"Then shut your eyes! Shut them and endure, as your betters have done before you."

Anne's mouth dropped open at the insult.

Henry heaved himself to his feet. "I grow weary of this place," he growled. He pushed past her, clipping her shoulder as if she were a beggar in a crowd. She glared after him, then hurried out. A flurry of her women followed in her wake.

Henry stalked across the room, as restless as a bear on a chain. Pages hopped out of his way as he approached the table of refreshments. It was laden with slabs of cold venison, half-picked carcasses of quail and partridge, bowls of Spanish oranges, and spotted winter apples.

Father Jerome Bastwick offered up to him a dish of honeyed apricots. "A sweet, Your Majesty?" Bastwick was always careful to use the title the King had lately come to prefer.

Henry shoved an apricot in his mouth and licked his fingers gloomily. "You're kinder than my wife, Father."

"A Royal Almoner's duty and privilege, Your Majesty," Bastwick said, still thrilled with his recent appointment. He had used the names listed in the Bible from the *Dorothy Beale*, brought to him by Legge, to catapult himself into this post, stretching out the arrests of the heretics to give himself maximum glory in the eyes of the bishops. "You are my great good lord," he concluded, bowing deeply to the King.

"Ah," Henry groaned, "this place is like a prison, Father. No galleries, no gardens, no tennis." He lowered his head to rub the back of his neck. "And no riding in this interminable rain."

"To be sure," Bastwick commiserated, "Windsor is not Whitehall."

"Even the inducements here," Henry said with a glance at the freckled girl, "begin to pale after three days of rain."

Three days before, the court—a small army of gentlemen, officers, servants, horses, mules and dogs—had snaked through the
countryside to the bleak old castle of Windsor which had remained
untouched by Henry's passion for rebuilding. They had arrived in
a downpour, and it had rained ever since, though no amount of rain
seemed to cool the unnaturally sultry air. Life in the castle had
slowed to a groggy torpor. Servants slumped with ale in shadowed
corners, and throughout the place there was an odor of damp wool
and steaming boredom. Men and women, their nerves unstable,
crackled at one another and wandered through airless corridors.

Henry motioned Bastwick to follow him to the far window.
They stood side by side staring out at the twisting gray sheets of
rain. "News?" Henry asked.

"No more than I communicated to Your Majesty yesterday,"
Bastwick said. "One moment, word of the Emperor's troops massing at Rotterdam or on the Spanish coast. The next moment, a
confirmation that all was only malicious rumor."

"May God keep it so."

"Amen to that, Your Majesty. And yet we must be vigilant."

Henry nodded grimly. "Imperial invasion. Dear God . . ." he
murmured with a shudder. "Cromwell does not keep me as informed as he should. His woolcarder's mind is locked on Parliament."

Behind them the girl's thin singing wobbled above George Boleyn's lute. Henry winced, his musician's ear offended by her
pitch. He stared out the mullioned window. Soggy black leaves
slapped up against the panes and quivered beside the lead bars
like hunted men begging sanctuary at a rich man's gate.

Henry leaned sideways to Bastwick and whispered. "This excommunication the Pope has hurled at me, Father. I have bared
my teeth at Rome for it, for the Pope had no right. No right! But
something in my soul trembles, for all that. Something that will
not let me sleep. Excommunication. My God, any foreign power
now has the blessing of the Church to take possession of my realm,
if they can. And excommunication cancels all vows of allegiance
ever made to me."

"In no true subject's mind, sire."

"No true subject, aye. But what of traitors lurking in dark holes throughout the land? What of their plots against me, eh?"

"They will be crushed," Bastwick said quietly.

Henry was not listening. "Sometimes I ask myself, What is Charles waiting for? A signal from some pack of disaffected nobles here? But who? Who will the traitors be? So many enemies . . . here, abroad . . ." He sighed heavily, then managed a wan smile. "Forgive me, Father. I babble. It is this wretched place. That, and my wife's loss at Candlemas. A son . . ." He stopped himself. A son born dead.

"But the Queen will conceive again, Your Majesty. Soon she will give you the lusty prince we all pray God for."

"Think you so?" Henry asked shakily.

"God will not desert you, sire."

"Sometimes, Father"—he dropped a hand like meat on Bastwick's chest—"I swear I don't know what God is telling me. These lost children . . ." Eyes moist, he searched the priest's face for sympathy.

"A blessing it perished," Bastwick assured him with brutal bluntness, "shrunk and misshapen as it was." He did not notice Henry flinch.

"I've taken you from the pudding, Father," Henry said flatly. He made a vague gesture behind him towards the table, giving his royal chaplain leave to go.

But Bastwick did not go. He glanced over his shoulder, assuring himself that no one was near enough to listen. "Your Majesty, there is something I think you should see." He pulled from his cassock a small leather-bound book.

"What's this?" Henry asked.

"I take a great liberty which I pray Your Majesty will pardon. This," Bastwick said, lifting the book, "is the work of an English friar, an exile living in Antwerp. His name is Frish."

"Why, I believe that's the man Cromwell wants me to meet," Henry said, interested. "He's on his way home, apparently. It's rather intriguing, you know. Cromwell says several of these exiles hold some surprisingly sound theories. For example, the divine commission of the godly prince to reform the Church. Also, the duty of citizens to give total obedience to their King." Gingerly, he took the volume from Bastwick. "Do you know, I've never actually read any of the stuff Tyndale and these fellows have written." He bounced the book on his palm like a merchant testing the heft of a bag of some exotic spice, wondering if there was profit or loss in such a novelty.

"Perhaps you should, sire, before you meet the man."

"Might as well," Henry said, and added glumly, "there'll be no riding today."

"I hope I have not offended . . . ?"

"Not at all."

"I felt it was my duty. That Your Grace should be aware . . ."

"Of course. You've done well, Father," Henry said expansively. As Bastwick backed away, bowing, Henry cracked a schoolboy smile. "Better keep nigh, though, Father. I may cry out if I feel my soul in danger."

He ambled to the window seat and thudded down to peruse the book, settling back as if he had taken up a fable of King Arthur to while away the rainy afternoon. Gradually, the buzz of voices in the room faded from his consciousness, and Henry immersed himself in Frish's *A Christian Vision*.

The bored men and women around him strolled, and stifled yawns, and picked at their food. George Boleyn finished his strained duet with the girl, then sang, alone, through two melancholy ballads. A greyhound under the table woofed softly in its sleep.

Suddenly, the King's voice roared from the window seat, "Heresy!"

White lightning illuminated the room. It froze bodies in the act of whirling around to face the King. Henry lunged up from the seat and hurled the book as if it were a snarling creature gnawing his hand. It skittered across the floorboards and stopped at Bastwick's feet. Bastwick stiffened. Panic flooded his eyes.

"Blessed Mother of God!" Henry sputtered. "He claims God's grace can be had by faith alone! He claims the body of Christ is not present in the bread of the Mass! He calls the veneration of saints *idolatry*!"

Bastwick relaxed. He bent to pick up the book, careful to hide his satisfaction. "Forgive me, Your Majesty, for inflicting such pain. But now you see the filth that some wish to insinuate into your realm. Can you allow such slanders to taint your new Church?"

"By all that's holy, no! Abominable, wicked heresy." Purpling, Henry bellowed again. "Bring me Cromwell! Bring me that miserable woolcarder!"

Honor and Jinner had ridden hard all day. When they arrived at the gate of Cromwell's Stepney house in the early evening, Honor was parched and aching. With a blistered fist she pounded to be admitted.

The gate clattered open. Honor left Jinner with the horses and ran ahead of the porter. The main door was opened for her, but she had not taken five steps toward the hall when Cromwell's chamberlain glided out to stop her. He was a pale, aloof man who wore a constant sneer. The Lord Secretary, he told Honor, was entertaining important guests at supper in his hall. It was, the chamberlain said pointedly, a private gathering.

"Tell him I must see him," she said.

"If you will wait in the solar—"

"No," she cut him off. She could not risk being seen by any of Cromwell's guests. "Tell him to come out to me in the garden. And tell him it's urgent!"

For half an hour she waited, pacing the paths under an ancient yew tree in the twilight shadows. She could not be still. She was brimful of rage and disbelief at what she had found out. What had gone wrong? Again and again, she went over in her mind the events of the past weeks.

The mission to fetch Frish had begun uneventfully. She had left with Sam Jinner and Jeremy, apprentice to Thornleigh's London agent, sure that it would go well. And she had been right. All had been smooth sailing: the trip to Antwerp, the enlistment of the joyous Frish, and the voyage with him back to Harwich. It had not taken four weeks.

She had intended to accompany Frish all the way to Cromwell's door, but at Colchester Frish had insisted she leave him. "Go home," he had said, smiling, "for I can see your heart is there. You've done enough. Go home and be happy."

"Take Sam with you, at least," she had urged. Frish had agreed to that. He had kissed her cheek, and said good-bye, and he and Jinner had ridden south.

Honor had started north with Jeremy, her mind full of nothing but overrehearsed speeches she hoped would bring a reconciliation with Thornleigh. She had stopped overnight at a well-known inn at Ipswich. After breakfast Jeremy was feeling ill, and Honor was strolling the innyard and pondering whether to ride home alone or stay the day or two until the lad could travel comfortably, when Jinner had galloped in on a lathered horse.

Gulping breaths, he told her the awful news. He and Frish had got as far as Chelmsford, he said. They had stopped to water the horses and find a bite to eat. Frish had started talking scripture with the groom, and Jinner had told him he'd meet him in the tavern across the street. He'd just picked up his mug, he said, and had walked to the open door to stretch his legs when he saw three men dragging Frish down the street.

"The magistrate's men they were, m'lady. Tapster told me so. I followed, thinking if there's trouble I'd be better able to help if I stayed nimble. Well, damned if they didn't clap the good Brother in the stocks in the market square. Folks began pitching dung at him like he was a common lousel. I hustled over to the magistrate to see what could be done, but he only threw up his hands. Said some officials had come from London for Brother Frish. Wouldn't say more. By the time I got back to the square—mayhap an hour later—the good Brother was gone. They'd taken him, you see? But where or why, or even who's done it, that I know not, m'lady."

In fury, Honor had swung back to London with Jinner.

Where, in God's name, is Cromwell? she agonized. The arched window at the end of his hall glowed with the candlelight of his supper table, and a faint wash of his guests' laughter drifted across the garden. Honor kicked at the gravel and beat her fist into her palm. It was all to show herself her anger, all to keep from facing the premonition that hulked at the back of her mind: had she delivered up her friend to death? Around her, smells of damp earth and musk-roses floated up like shy spirits set free by night. She found that she was shivering.

A rustle in the grass startled her. She swiveled, and stumbled on the yew tree's exposed roots. She peered into the shadows. The path she stood on led through squat, regimented fruit trees to a wicket gate, dim in the far wall. But on the path nothing moved. All was still.

Above her an owl hooted in the branches of the yew. She looked up through boughs shaggy with night-dark leaves. The owl sat frozen like some stone image on a pagan tomb.

The rustling sounded again. A figure—a man—slipped out from the line of fruit trees and halted. "My lady, get you gone!" he whispered. "You are not safe abiding here!"

Though he stood in darkness, his face obscured, Honor recognized the gangly form. Cromwell's clerk. "Andrew?" she asked the shadows. "What's wrong? What's happened?"

"There's men abroad this night to track you down!"

Fear clogged like cloth in her throat. "What do you mean? What men?"

"I cannot say more. Only . . ." He stopped as a laugh went up in the hall. "Oh, you are in danger, my lady. Get yourself away, while you can."

"But what's happened to . . . ?" A loud snap of a branch made her look up. The owl was lifting from its perch with a movement of broad wings that was eerily slow and soundless.

She looked back. Andrew was gone.

Footsteps crunched from the opposite direction and she whirled around. A swinging lantern was approaching the iron main gate. She could not see the face of the man holding the lantern out before him, but the footsteps, she was sure, came from not just one man, but from others behind him as well.

She ran down the path to the wicket gate and dashed back to Jinner at the stable. They grabbed their horses from the startled groom, and fled.

* * *

It was hot noon. Sir Thomas More pressed his palm against the window casement. The stone was cold, refreshingly cold. It helped a little; the trembling of his hand lessened.

He was standing alone in a dim second-story room of the Archbishop of Canterbury's palace of Lambeth and looking down on a large garden where twenty or thirty clerics were milling—bishops and abbots, their chaplains and clerks. Some had already been inside to stand before the commissioners, then had returned to the garden to chat with colleagues awaiting their turn. All had been summoned here, like him, to swear the Oath.

More watched the churchmen, faintly sickened by their behavior. They strolled the paths arm-in-arm. They gossiped on benches. They laughed under apple trees and hailed one another at intersections in the hedges. To him, standing above them, their faint chatter sounded both flat and frantic, like so many bumble-bees droning in the heated, garish foliage. He had to narrow his eyes at the glaring sunlight that seemed to throb off the scarlet flowers and glossy emerald leaves, off the blinding brass of the sun-dial and the hectic clerical silks. Finally, he drew his head back into the cool gloom. No. He felt no impulse to join that sweaty, grinning throng.

He knew the commissioners downstairs had hoped he would. "Why not walk a while and think," Audeley had suggested. Audeley, his dull-witted successor as Lord Chancellor. Oh, yes, More thought, the commissioners' expectations had been obvious: once in the garden and bantering with the others, my resolution would surely falter.

The others. He wondered again why he had been called in with this body of clergy. He was the only layman among them. Already, commissioners had sped out to every shire in the realm, marshaling justices of the peace to administer the Oath to every Englishman. Cromwell, with characteristic thoroughness, had organized the unprecedented action. Why, then, have they brought me in with these illustrious churchmen, he asked himself, when I could just as easily have been approached at home in Chelsea? Did Cromwell intend it as an honor? Or a threat?

"Walk and think," Audeley had said.

But More had done with thinking, and had come instead to this cool stone chamber.

He looked at his hand. It still trembled on the casement. Around his fingers he could make out, on the stone, traces of the fire that had threatened the palace years ago. Faint smears of soot, mere shadows, curled in crevices between the blocks. That fire had been long ago, he thought, and yet, like skin that has been scalded, the scars remain, though on skin they would show tough and white, and on this stone, a ghostly black. He felt the shudder leap inside him again, beginning at his heart and trembling down into his bowels where a primordial panic squirmed. Would violence done to his body leave indelible scars like this? The shudder increased the tremor of his hand and again he flattened it against the stone to stop it. But the fear in his bowels would not be quelled.

He closed his eyes and forced himself to re-examine the scene he had just played out with the commissioners. Had he made any slip?

"May I see a copy of the Oath?" he had asked them. Refusing a chair, he had stood before their table: Audeley, Cromwell, Archbishop Cranmer, William Benson, Abbot of Westminster, and a few others. More's skin had prickled at the sight of the last face at the table: Jerome Bastwick, the King's new almoner.

Politely, they had showed him the printed Oath with the Great Seal of the Realm affixed, and a copy of the Act of Succession. Politely, they had let him read in silence.

The Oath made reference to the Act of Succession which stated that the swearer would "bear faithful obedience to King Henry's heirs by his most dear and entirely beloved lawful wife, Queen Anne." More had felt a jolt of hope. Would they be satisfied if he swore simply to the royal succession as decreed by Parliament? With that he had no quarrel. Succession was a temporal matter, and Parliament was well within its rights to fix it on whatever heir it chose. It had done so many times, over several hundred years.

He read on: "Ye shall observe, maintain and defend this Act and all the whole contents and effects thereof, and all other Acts and

Statutes made since the beginning of this present Parliament."
His stomach tightened. Here was the quicksand. ". . . *all other Acts
and Statutes . . .*" The lengthy preamble of the Act of Succession itself declared that the King's marriage with the former Queen
Catherine had been invalid from the beginning since it had been
made against the laws of God. For More to accept the Act of Succession, then, was to accept that the Church had erred. Worse,
other Acts of this Parliament recognized the King as Supreme
Head of the Church in England, and for him to accept that was . . .
impossible.

For a moment, standing before the commissioners, he shut his
eyes to subdue the shudder and in that moment a high-pitched
laugh from the garden pierced the room, a laugh rich and ribald.
More raised his head, eyes open. "My lords," he said, "I cannot
swear this Oath."

Along the table the commissioners glanced at one another as if
unsure of what they had heard.

"Cannot?" asked Cromwell.

"My conscience will not allow of it."

"The law of the land requires it," Cromwell said.

"Then must I refuse the law."

There was silence. A bumblebee trapped inside a window
thumped against the glass.

Chancellor Audeley cleared his throat. "Sir Thomas, all the
learned, honorable men in the garden—bishops and abbots—all
have sworn."

"Not all in the realm will, I think."

"All will who value their heads!" came Cromwell's stern reply.

More had been about to correct him, for the threat was not
strictly accurate. The charge for refusal to swear the Oath was misprision of treason which was not a capital offense as was high treason. But the penalty was still terrible: forfeiture of all possessions
and imprisonment at the King's pleasure, perhaps for life. But
More said nothing.

Archbishop Cranmer asked, as if to clarify a point, "Sir Thomas,
these learned prelates who have already sworn—do you say that
they were wrong to take the Oath?"

"My lords, I do not say any of these gentlemen is wrong to swear. I leave every man to his own conscience and think it not unreasonable that every man should leave me to mine."

The commissioners buzzed together for a moment. Then Bastwick spoke. The puckered smile of victory on his lips was so controlled, so subtle, that only More was conscious of it. "Sir Thomas, is it that you do not approve the Royal Succession?"

The other commissioners quieted for the answer.

"My lords," said More, "I am right willing and ready to swear to the succession as it is decreed by Parliament." But no farther, he thought.

"Then why will you not swear the Oath?" Audeley asked with a perplexed frown. "For what cause?"

"The cause of obstinacy," Cromwell growled. "The King will not tolerate this, sir."

"If the King will grant me immunity I will gladly give my reasons."

"Immunity?" Cromwell scoffed. "Impossible."

"Then, if I may not declare the causes without peril, to leave them undeclared is no obstinacy."

"Tell this commission why you will not swear," Cromwell demanded.

"My lord," said More, "I will not."

Archbishop Cranmer made a small, conciliatory laugh. "But if—oh, do let us find our way happily out of this thicket, Sir Thomas—if you will not swear, yet you do not say that those who do so are wrong, then you must be in some doubt as to whether to swear or no. And one thing you will agree as certain is that a subject's duty is to obey his Prince. The King has ordered you to take the Oath. The certainty of your duty should prevail over your doubt."

More suppressed the smile of derision that rose to his lips. He said only, "Were that so, my lord Archbishop, then might we say that if a man had any doubts about what his conscience required of him, an order from the King would settle all."

"And so it should," cried Cromwell.

"Unless a man sets himself up above the King," Bastwick said pointedly.

"I have never," More quickly declared, "set myself above the statutes of the King in Parliament, nor never will. Well I know there are times when the edicts of the state must overrule a citizen's right to private judgment. But the moral authority of the state is delegated to it by the community of all Christian souls—" He stopped abruptly, afraid of saying too much.

The Abbot of Westminster sputtered, "Surely, Sir Thomas, you must know yourself in error when you see that the Parliament and the King's whole council of the realm stand on the other side, and you stand alone in this refusal!"

"My lord Abbot, if I believed that I stood utterly alone, indeed I would tremble to set my mind against so many. But I am not alone. I have on my side as great a council, and greater: the general council of Christendom. I will not swear."

Cromwell threw up his hands. "And will not say why not!"

"And *must* not say why not."

They stared at him.

"Why not walk a while and think?" Audeley had suggested.

At the window of the burned chamber More rested his forehead against the stone casement and tried to will the shudder to subside. As he did, the babble of the churchmen in the garden faded. The gray, barren space behind him hummed with the holy silence of sanctuary. When he lifted his forehead, he saw that his sweat had left a smudge, dark like the traces of smoke beside it.

Soon, he told himself, *I must go and stand before the commissioners again. And this time they will ask only once. I must hold the course of silence. Silence, in law, cannot be construed as an admission of guilt. Silence will be my sanctuary.* He closed his eyes and realized that the shudder, and the trembling of his hands, had finally stopped. He had conquered his body. He had beaten its craven urge to capitulate.

"Thank the Lord," he whispered. "The field is won."

🙂 29 🙂

The Petitioner

There was a faint creak outside the door of the attic room, and Honor whirled around from the window. A dagger lay on a barrel beside the single candle. She lunged for it, raised it, and stood watching the door. Silence returned. She relaxed. The Sydenham's once-great house was now a bleak, dilapidated tenement, and although its rooms below her were crammed, the inmates slept the exhausted sleep of poverty. Still, she tensed at every scrape and thud that echoed through the barren corridors and crept up the rickety stairs to the attic. She was hollow-eyed from lack of sleep. Since bolting from Cromwell's, she had been hiding in this garret.

"I think I've been followed," she had whispered to Bridget Sydenham at the front door. Even as she had spoken, the gaunt, wasted face before her had made her regret her decision to come. "I've endangered you," Honor had said, turning. "I'll go."

But the bony hand had pulled her across the threshold. "If God has set your footsteps toward me, who am I to question His wisdom?"

That had been two days ago.

In the garret, Honor walked back to the window and looked out at London's skyline thrusting into the cold moonlight—the spire of St. Paul's, the jagged roofs on London Bridge, the fortress of the

Tower. Her mind still swam with confusion. Nothing made sense. Except that everything had unraveled. That much was terrifyingly clear.

There was a clatter outside the door. Honor snuffed the candle, pressed herself into the shadows against the wall, and lifted the dagger. From the window a shaft of silver-blue moonlight bisected the small room and fell just short of the doorway.

The door swung halfway open. Bridget Sydenham leaned in, her hand cupped around a candle. Honor sighed her relief. Suddenly, a man's body obscured the flame. Honor flattened against the wall again, her dagger lifted, her heart thudding. There was nowhere to run to, but she would fight before she would let them take her.

The man kicked the door fully open and stepped into the darkness. His knee thumped the barrel. "Curse it!" he muttered. "Where is she?"

"Richard!" Honor sprang out and flung her arms around his neck, knocking him backwards a step. "You came!"

Bridget Sydenham turned away with her candle and softly closed the door.

In the darkness, Thornleigh pulled Honor away from him. He had seen the glint of metal as her arms went around his neck. He disarmed her and tossed the dagger onto the barrel.

They looked at one another. To Honor, Thornleigh's face in the shadows appeared expressionless. But he had come to her!

"Are you alright?" he asked.

"I am now."

"Honor, I—"

"Oh, Richard, I'm so sorry. For the dreadful things I said."

"No, it was my fault. I acted like an idiot."

"But you were right! I should never have left. I don't even know what's happening anymore. You were so very right."

"No. I was wrong to demand . . . to say what I did. I should have helped you, not tried to stop you. God knows I don't want you to change. And I will from now on. Help you, I mean. Whatever you want to do."

"I only want to be with you. All this . . . it's madness. I'm finished with it. Forever."

He gathered her to him and kissed her long and hard. As they caught their breath, she hugged him, pressing her cheek against his chest. He smelled of horses and sweat, and she could taste salt from his kiss. She drew back and pulled him into the shaft of moonlight to look at him. His clothes were spattered with muck. On his chin grime was smeared over stubble. His eyes were red-rimmed with fatigue. She calculated the speed with which he must have made the journey. She had sent Jinner galloping north with the news as soon as Mrs. Sydenham had taken her in, but Jinner could not possibly have reached Great Ashwold much before noon. "My God," she said, "you must have ridden without a stop." She caressed his cheek. "My love," she whispered.

He grabbed her hand and kissed it. His face betrayed his worry, and when he spoke his voice was low and urgent. "We're leaving England. At first light."

"What?" Her eyes widened. "What have you heard?"

He held her hand between his, as if to steady her. "I stopped to change horses in Chelmsford. I saw . . ." He looked down for a moment. "Honor, they burned Frish."

The tendons in her knees dissolved. Thornleigh caught her by the elbows and held her up. She buried her face in her hands. "My God," she whispered. "What have I done?"

He drew her to him and held her and stroked her hair. "You have done nothing. Others, though, have done nothing less than murder."

She looked up into his eyes. She was suddenly so cold that her head shivered and her teeth began to chatter. "It was I who delivered him up to them!"

"No. You could not have known." He tightened his hold on her arms. "It's not your fault. Frish wanted to come. He knew the dangers. He's always known the dangers."

The injustice of it, the pure, black evil of the atrocity swept her. She beat her fists on Thornleigh's chest. "Bastards! I'll find them! I swear, whoever is responsible—"

Thornleigh shook her. "No!" He held her steadily. "Honor, this is not the hill to die on. There's nothing we can do now for Frish. We've got to leave."

Fury and remorse tore at her heart, but she knew that he was right. Frish was gone. Nothing could change that. And screaming at the man who loved her and had rushed to her side was a waspish child's response. A solution to their crisis was what was needed. She swallowed her rage, and nodded to show him she was rational again. "But leave England? How can we?"

"How can we not? They've killed Frish and they're after you. We can't stay."

"What about Adam?"

"He's safe with my sister for now. We can send for him. When all's calm."

"But what if I'm being watched? Richard, I think I was followed from Cromwell's."

"If you were, you must have given them the slip before you reached this door. Otherwise, what could they be waiting for?"

"I don't know. I don't even know who's after me. Or why. I've done nothing illegal in months."

"Except bring Frish back. An arch-heretic," he grimly reminded her.

"Brought him at the King's command! No, it makes no sense. Who could possibly be behind this?"

"It has to be a man of the Church. You and Frish have no other enemies. The Bishop of London?"

"Why would he bother now? He's capitulated to the new order along with all the other churchmen."

"Archbishop Cranmer?"

She shook her head. "He lives to oblige the King, and I was acting for the King."

"Well it can't be Cromwell. Why would he betray you when you were only following his orders? Unless," he scratched his chin, thinking, "unless his own orders were changed."

"Changed? How?"

"Do you think the King could have had second thoughts?

About Frish? If so, maybe he and Cromwell had some kind of falling out."

"But when I went to Cromwell's I heard laughter from his hall, and music. A strange way to carry on if he'd fallen foul of the King."

"Cromwell's a man who'd land on his feet no matter what the fall."

"You mean, if something happened to turn the King against Frish, then—"

"Then Cromwell would cut you off as neatly as the bishops have cut off the Pope. Their bread is buttered by the King, and so is Cromwell's. He'd sacrifice you."

"But to whom? The King? Oh, Richard, can the King be so vindictive?"

Thornleigh shook his head as if to clear his mind of everything but essential facts. "Look, we can't wait to find out any of this. Our best chance is to get out now. I've sent a message to an old friend, a merchant of the Hanse. He's sailing to Rotterdam tomorrow."

"From the Steelyard?" She felt a surge of hope. The Hanse merchants of the Baltic enjoyed special privileges, including their own autonomously controlled riverfront territory with warehouses and wharf called the Steelyard. Because of the invaluable trade they brought, the government was always loath to harass them, even when they had sometimes illegally imported heretical books. If she and Thornleigh could make it to the Steelyard, Honor realized, it would be a kind of sanctuary from which they could embark to safety.

"We must be there at dawn," Thornleigh said. "And trust that my friend Guttman has received my message."

"But do you think he—"

She stopped, hearing a noise outside the attic door. They both stood still and listened. Feet shuffled on the stairs. A fist knocked on the door. Bridget Sydenham opened it and entered with her candle.

"Master Thornleigh," she said, "it may be nothing, but I've been watching a man outside the gate. He's been lurking there for some time."

Thornleigh strode to the door. "Stay here," he told Honor.

He went out with Mrs. Sydenham and closed the door.

Honor waited in the silence. She paced until she could stand it no longer. She had to know what was happening.

Softly, she went down one flight of stairs. She heard the crash of the front door slamming. She ran to the landing and looked down. Thornleigh was hauling in a man by the collar. The man turned, tossing back long black hair streaked with silver, and Honor saw his face. He was a stranger to her.

"I tell you, sir," the man protested, "I was only looking for a haven! I was told—" He stopped abruptly, as if afraid he had said too much.

"Told what?" Thornleigh demanded.

The man hesitated, then closed his eyes and blurted, as if to hazard all, "Told this was a safe house."

"Who said so?" Thornleigh shoved the man hard, making him stumble back against the wall, cringing. Bridget Sydenham stood at the front door to block his escape.

"Oh, please, sir, it was at a secret meeting, and he didn't give his name. But he told me, if ever I had need, this house would hide me."

Something in the man's voice caught Honor off guard. It was a low, rumbling voice, unhurried even in his extreme agitation, and it tugged at some string of memory. Yet his face, coarse and red, meant nothing to her.

Thornleigh was watching the intruder with clear suspicion. "Why have you picked tonight to come?"

"Oh, sir, as God is my witness, I have need of a haven now!"

That's it! Honor thought. This was the voice from the hold of the *Dorothy Beale*—the guard who had searched with his whining mate while she crouched in the pit.

As if he had heard her thoughts, the man glanced up at the landing where Honor stood and she realized that he had seen her; it was useless to hang back any longer. She started down the steps.

"My lady!" the man cried. His face lit up, as if with recognition. The surprise of it made Honor stop.

The man bounded over to the foot of the stairs and threw himself on his knees below Honor. Steel scraped as Thornleigh drew his sword from its scabbard and lunged. The man's hands flew into the air like a caught felon. Thornleigh halted his sword point an inch from his throat.

Though the man held his head rigid above Thornleigh's blade, the black hair that flowed to his shoulders quivered with tension. "I beg you, my lady, save a drowning man!"

"Who are you?" she asked warily. "How do you know me?"

"From Yarmouth, my lady," he cried happily. "No, you don't know me, but I've seen you. And you do know my master. Dr. Pelle. I'm with his harbor patrol."

Honor and Thornleigh exchanged tense glances.

"Yes," the man cried, "I know of your secret work."

He flinched as Thornleigh's sword jerked to his throat and the tip pricked his skin. "Please, my lady!" he cried, "I am one of you! For months I've kept my true heart hidden from Dr. Pelle!"

"And kept on working for him?" Thornleigh growled.

"It was wrong, I warrant, to dissemble and still do his bidding." His face creased with the strain of his guilt. "Wrong to do—" he paused and looked at Honor with intense contrition "—to do many of the bad things I've done. I'm heartily sorry for it. But, you see, I'm a poor fellow, my lady, and a father. I pray God will forgive a sinner with a wife and five babes to feed. For since the blessed day when I first heard the Word of God at that secret meeting—"

"Get to the point," Thornleigh said, letting the cold steel prod again, "or you'll feel an inch more of mine."

The man continued to speak directly up to Honor. "I don't know how it happened, but somehow Dr. Pelle suspects me. He knows! I've run off . . . brought my family to London. But I'm sure he's on my heels. I came searching for this house where I was told I would find help. And now, praise be to God, I have found *you*!"

While he spoke, Honor had cautiously come down to the bottom of the stairs. Thornleigh had also drawn back his blade a little, and the man took the opportunity to snatch up the hem of Honor's skirt and kiss it. "It's like a miracle," he cried. "Oh, my lady, I must get away across the Narrow Sea. You can do it. I know you can. Please, do not forsake me. You are my only hope!"

"You expect a great deal of me, sir," she said, eyeing him, still wary.

Thornleigh had not sheathed his sword. "Any man of Pelle's could come up with a story like this," he scoffed.

"Please, sir, you must believe me!"

"Give me one good reason why."

The man's eyes flicked between Thornleigh and Honor several times. He swallowed. "Because of the Bible," he said evenly.

"Bible?" Honor asked, on guard. "What do you mean?"

"That day Dr. Pelle had us search your ship, the *Dorothy Beale*, I knew you were hiding in the hold."

Honor stiffened.

"I knew it wasn't you that left in the skiff under that cloak of yours. I knew it, because I saw orange hair fly out from under the hood."

"My God," Honor whispered.

"And later, during the fire, I found your Bible. Full of names, it was."

She looked at him with a mixture of astonishment and delight. "*You* found it? I always wondered—"

"So you found it," Thornleigh cut in. He was not so easily swayed. "Why haven't you contacted us before this? You've had months."

"I was afraid, sir. I have a family to think of."

"What did you do with the Bible?"

"Got rid of it, sir."

"How?"

"Burned it." The man looked back to Honor. His deep voice became a plea. "I ask you, my lady, would I have done all that if I meant you harm?"

Honor was moved. "I am right glad to know you, sir." She held out her hand to him with a disarming smile. Thornleigh allowed the man to take her hand and kiss it.

"And," Honor said, "I'd like to help you in return for what you did for us. If you can be ready to leave in the mor—"

Pain flared up her arm as Thornleigh jerked her by the elbow. He pulled her aside.

"Don't do this," he whispered roughly. "Even if he's telling the truth, we don't need this now. Let me get rid of him."

"Richard," she said, "we owe him for keeping that evidence hidden. He saved us from Pelle. He's proved he's a friend. Now Pelle's after him. And I would not let a dog who had bitten me fall into the hands of Pelle, let alone have it happen to a friend. Besides," she said, so softly it was almost to herself, "we've already lost one friend today."

Thornleigh rubbed the back of his neck. "I don't like it."

"But would you call him a liar? The facts are too plain."

Thornleigh only shrugged.

It was enough for Honor. "Richard," she said fervently, "if you insist, I'll turn this man away. I'll not go against your will again. But I truly believe he needs us. Can't we help?"

Thornleigh, though looking far from convinced, finally said, "I told you I would. I meant it."

She smiled. "It's the last time. I promise."

He nodded.

Honor went back to the petitioner. He was still on his knees. "Master . . ."

"Legge," he said quickly, gratefully. "Leonard Legge."

"Master Legge. Come at dawn to the Steelyard wharf. If you don't mind traveling as our servant," she smiled, "we'll get you across to Rotterdam."

Thornleigh groaned as he came beside her. "At least," he urged her in a tense whisper, "let me hold him in this house overnight."

Legge heard this. For a moment the eyes of the two men met and reckoned one another.

Legge's eyes darted back to Honor. "I beg you, my lady, let me say farewell to my family. God alone knows when I may clap eyes on them again. And my wife's expecting our sixth any day."

Honor glanced at Thornleigh. He continued to glare down at Legge. But she could not help thinking: what if it was Richard pleading with some stranger, afraid he would never see his own unborn child? And she could tell that he did not really mistrust Legge any longer; if he did, he would not even consider letting him go. She turned back to Legge and nodded her assent. Thornleigh moved away shaking his head.

Legge grabbed the hem of Honor's skirt again and sputtered out his thanks. Bridget Sydenham helped the grateful man to his feet and showed him out.

Thornleigh sheathed his sword and took a few steps toward the closed door. "I'm surprised you didn't hand over to him all our money, too," he said. "To buy gruel for his dying mother and twenty destitute cousins."

Honor came up behind him and rested her cheek on his back. "Don't be angry, my love," she said. "Brother Frish is lost, but this man we can save. All will be well. I feel it."

He grunted. "You *still* take too many risks."

She drew him around. "But this is the last one." With her hands on his shoulders she kissed him softly. "Let's not waste time quarreling. We have only a few hours before dawn."

Hand in hand, they walked back up to the attic.

They undressed one another and gazed at one another in the moonlight, neither speaking a word. They drank each other in, asking and answering with eyes, hands, mouths, bodies. Their lovemaking had never been so abandoned, so generous, as both of them reveled in pledging a commitment too deep for words to convey.

After, Thornleigh lay naked on his back on the fresh floor straw. His eyes were closed. Honor, naked as well, was on her knees, straddling his hips.

She watched his face, loving him, loving the moment. A gentle rain pattered on the roof, and in the moist air of the spring night the straw around them breathed back a scent of summer meadows. "Go home, and be happy," Brother Frish had told her. Good advice, she thought. And though Frish was gone, and everything had changed and she could not go home, she knew that as long as she had this man she would be happy anywhere. Should she tell him about the baby now? No. Tomorrow. When they were away from all this, and safely on the water. He was leaving everything behind because of her. She would save this news as a gift to cheer him. A gift that only she could give.

She ran her fingertips over his belly and watched the muscles tighten in response. She lowered herself so that her nipples grazed his chest and her hair fell in curtains on either side of his face. His hands smoothed down her back and over her spread buttocks and she felt him harden inside her again.

She whispered a taunt into his neck: "Nothing at all?"

He laughed. It had been a joke between them ever since the time when he had said it first. It had been on the evening after they had first made love in the fleece shed. They were standing with the rest of the household in the great hall, everyone noisily dispersing after supper. Honor had caught Thornleigh watching her across the room, and read the desire in his eyes. She had left the hall first.

She had waited for him in her bedchamber, sitting on the edge of the bed. Thornleigh had come in, stood before her and kissed her, then pulled off his doublet so that he stood in shirt and hose. Impatient for him, her hands had gone up to his throat and tugged at his shirt lacings to loosen them, but with the fumbling fingers of inexperience and desire she had only succeeded in tightening the strings into a knot. While he, as impatient as she, had turned his attention to unfastening the knot, her eyes had traveled down his body to the bulge of his erection. Her hand had moved to touch it. He had flinched in surprise. She had drawn back, afraid she had done something wrong, for she new little of the ways of men. "You don't like it?" she had asked.

He had let out a short bark of a laugh. "I like it! Believe me, I like it." He had fixed her with a look that was filled as much with tenderness as with desire. "Honor, there's nothing you can do that I won't like. Nothing at all."

Timidly at first, her fingers had touched him again. Her touch became firmer, and she had watched him close his eyes as if in pain. Abandoning his shirt altogether he had fought to unlace his codpiece, and Honor had time to do no more than kick off her shoes before he was on her, and they tumbled together on the bed, eager for one another.

Now, lying in the moonlight, Thornleigh chuckled again at the reminder. He rolled her over onto her back. She looked up into his eyes, their blaze of blue now sea-black in the shadows.

"There's nothing you can do that I won't like," he whispered. He smoothed her hair back from her forehead and his face became suddenly grave. "Except leave me."

"Then," she said, as tears of love clouded her vision, "There is nothing at all."

❧ 30 ❧

London Bridge

Thornleigh's chestnut stallion trotted down Coleman Street snorting steam into the morning chill, frisky to canter despite the double load it carried. Honor rode pillion, her arms snug around Thornleigh's waist. No one had followed them. Richard was right, she thought. If anyone had come after her from Cromwell's, she must have given them the slip. As she nestled against the warmth of his jostling back she felt the fear of the last two days and the sadness for Frish lift from her heart like the morning mist rising above the gabled houses. They were leaving behind everything they knew, but somehow the future did not frighten her. They had each other, there was money enough for the short term—she had tucked most of it into her underskirt— and she had a vague but firm conviction that somehow all would be well.

The cobbles glistened after the rain that had washed the city clean. A cloud of sparrows wheeled above the church of St. Thomas of Acon, and its lead roofs glinted in the first lemony beams of the sun. Honor smiled. They were less than half a mile from the Steelyard and the waiting barge that would take them out to the German ship.

The stallion's hooves clattered into Old Jewry as the street awoke. Shutters banged open. Aproned housewives were sweeping thresholds, shooing away the lean, scavenging dogs and the even leaner cripples who had spent the night huddled in dry doorways. Yawning apprentices opened the doors to shops, hefted sacks, rolled barrels. A carter cursed his stalled nag.

Honor and Thornleigh continued down Bucklersbury Street and Budge Row. The strengthening river sounds—lightermen's shouts and boat whistles—clashed with peeling church bells. The stallion's nostrils quivered at the fish-pungent air.

On Candlewick Street a farm family was setting up a vegetable stall, and a yellow-haired girl, no more than five it seemed to Honor, left her parents and brothers to scamper after the stallion. Skipping alongside the horse, the child offered up a fistful of violets. Honor took the flowers with a smile and quickly fished out a penny for the small, bobbing palm. The little girl romped back to her family.

Honor tucked the nosegay into her bodice and hugged Thornleigh. In six months, she thought, we'll have a child of our own. She was bursting to tell him. And they were so near the river now. Through a slit between buildings she even caught a glimpse of the Steelyard's lifting crane. They turned the corner. Here the crowd was thick. Thames Street and the Steelyard lay dead ahead. Honor could contain the news no longer. "Richard—" She broke off as a rooster flapped in front of the horse.

"Mmm?" Thornleigh murmured, eyes still front. He was searching among the pedestrians. "You realize," he said, "if Legge's not at the wharf we don't wait for him."

Honor understood. "Richard," she blurted, "I'm pregnant."

Thornleigh jerked the reins. The horse halted abruptly. They were in the middle of the intersection, and foot traffic swirled around them. Thornleigh's head snapped to the left to look back at her. His profile showed the open mouth and wide eyes of surprise, but Honor could not tell if it sprang from pleasure or dismay. Still looking left, Thornleigh's eyes lengthened their focus, fixing on something across the intersection. His face hardened. Honor felt his muscles tense.

"Where'd he get a mount like that?" Thornleigh muttered.

Honor followed his gaze. Under the archway of an inn courtyard

Legge sat astride a fine-boned, gray Arab—a very expensive horse. He was looking away, preoccupied with edging to one side of the arch to let a cart pass. Then, glancing behind him, Legge jerked his head in a beckoning gesture. Four mounted men, blank-faced like mercenaries and wearing swords, eased their horses forward and stopped, forming a "U" behind him. All five sat watching the street.

"Richard, you were right!" Honor cried under her breath. "What a fool I was to trust him. His master must be behind this. Pelle, and Bishop Nix."

"No time for that now." Keeping his eyes glued to Legge's small company, Thornleigh tugged the reins, making the stallion dance backwards so that more foot traffic flowed between them and Legge.

"Can we go back and circle?" Honor asked. "They might not spot us if we come from the west."

Thornleigh shook his head, then nodded toward the opposite corner. "Look."

Across the street another mounted band of three men lay in wait, these with bows slung on their backs. They scanned the crowd like suspicious jailers. There was no way Honor and Thornleigh could enter the Steelyard without passing between these two armed groups.

"But none of them are wearing Nix's livery," Honor whispered. "Who in God's name are they?"

"Swords and bows are livery enough," Thornleigh muttered. Cautiously, slowly, he turned the stallion. "They haven't seen us. We'll go back, then head west for Ludgate, and get out of the city at least." He quickly checked his sword hilt, then pulled out his dagger and slipped it back to Honor. "I'll navigate, you handle the armaments aft." As Honor tucked the dagger into her belt Thornleigh's hand pressed her knee. "Sorry, my love," he said, "no sea voyage today."

He had just lifted his heels to nudge the horse's flanks when a portly priest hustled out of the crowd and hooked his fingers in the bridle. "Good morning, sir," he greeted Thornleigh, all smiles. "Is this the way to St. Martin's? I'm in a muddle, what with—"

"Not now, Father," Thornleigh said through clenched teeth. He jerked the reins to free the bridle and the priest's arm flew up. His sleeve flapped over the horse's eye. Frightened, the horse reared. A woman, seeing her child near the lifted hooves, let out a shriek.

The heads of the men with Legge in the archway snapped in the direction of the cry. The archers' on the other corner did too. Honor looked back at the archers. Another rider had emerged beside them, a man in a black cloak. Honor felt a fist of fear slam into her stomach. *Bastwick*. Her eyes met his.

"Hold on!" cried Thornleigh. His heels thwacked the stallion's ribs. The horse bounded forward.

Honor saw only blurs of colors, heard only a roar of voices as the stallion careened around carts and children on Thames Street, dodged stalls and barking dogs. Men and women lurched out of the way of the horse, then moments later had to shield their eyes from flying mud as Bastwick and his pack pounded after in pursuit.

Thornleigh swerved north, then galloped along a clear stretch of Old Fish Street, down an alley, and into a trash-strewn lane. They were nearing Ludgate Hill. Honor knew he meant to get past the city walls, tear across the open fields, and try to lose Bastwick in the woods beyond.

But as they broke out of Carter Lane below St. Paul's and cannoned up Creed Lane, minutes from Ludgate, she saw with horror that an oncoming funeral procession choked their route. Thornleigh hauled on the reins. The stallion skidded in the mud, then stopped. Above its bellows-breaths Thornleigh and Honor gazed in desperation at the river of black-draped mourners funneling into the street toward St. Paul's.

Thornleigh cursed. "To pick this morning of all mornings to be buried." He had to shout above the clamor of the Jesus bells of St. Paul's peeling so near that they drowned out all other noise of the street, even the tramping of the mourners.

Thornleigh wheeled the horse around. Honor gasped as she glimpsed Bastwick's flying black robe. He and his riders were closing the gap.

Thornleigh looked frantically for a way out. To the west, the funeral. To the south, Bastwick. To the east the reverberating fortress of St. Paul's. He tugged the horse's head to face north, but there a curious crowd was moving toward them to gape at the magnificent funeral. It would be impossible to make headway through that crush.

"Honor, I'm going to try to shake them off, then race for the bridge. Can you hang on?"

Her tightening grip around his waist was answer enough.

She shut her eyes as they bolted forward again. But suddenly she felt the horse tilt upwards beneath her. She heard a grating from its hooves. Her eyes sprang open. They were bounding up the steps of the cathedral!

At the top, where the huge doors to the nave stood open to welcome the dead man's cortege, knots of startled priests and lawyers dashed out of the horse's way. At the foot of the steps Bastwick and his pack, cursing in frustration, were reining in their mounts.

The stallion clanged into the cathedral. Honor felt darkness close in as the sun was blotted out. Gossiping merchants stood mute, and whores hovering at pillars crossed themselves as the apparition crashed up the length of the nave. Dogs crouched and snarled. At the crossing, where the great altar's gold and silverwork shimmered in candlelight, Thornleigh wheeled to the left, spurring the horse past a jeweled saint whose uplifted arms seemed frozen in horror.

As they barreled straight for a cluster of priests at the open north door Honor shut her eyes again. She heard the priests flutter apart. She felt the sunlight hit her face, felt the horse tilt downwards as they catapulted down the steps. By the time she looked again they were crossing the churchyard and tucking through Little Gate, leaving the cathedral's walled enclosure.

After that, the race east along Cheapside was easy going. The thoroughfare was crowded, but wide enough that the stallion could gallop. They turned south. Honor could see ahead the flags fluttering from the rooftops of London Bridge. Her heart pounded with hope. In minutes, with luck, they would be across, in Southwark. The boundary of London was fixed at the stone posts at the Southwark end of the bridge, and anyone escaping beyond the posts from the authority of the city could easily lose themselves in Southwark's warren of alleys, cockpits and brothels. She glanced over her shoulder. She saw no closing pack, no Bastwick.

"You've done it!" she cried in Thornleigh's ear. "We've lost them!"

Then, dead ahead, Bastwick shot out of a side street. But he was looking toward the bridge, apparently thinking they had passed him. Thornleigh blazed right by him. Honor looked back. Bastwick was whipping his mount after them, bent like galloping Death over the horse's neck, his black robe streaming. His men poured out of the side street and followed him, Legge in front.

Honor pushed against Thornleigh as if to help force them up to the massive arched entrance of the bridge. It was so close! She could see the last of the rainwater dripping from the saw-toothed bottom of the raised portcullis. But Legge on his fast Arab was tearing up the gap between them. He was almost upon them.

Thornleigh's stallion thundered onto the wooden timbers of the bridge. Light dimmed as they entered the tunnel-like space formed by the shops that crowded both sides, the upper stories almost touching. The air hummed with the rush of the river churning around the stone supports. An ox cart halfway across the bridge was slowly rumbling toward them.

Thornleigh slowed to zig-zag around pedestrians. Legge sped past them. Suddenly, ahead of them, the ox cart lumbered sideways. It stopped. The beast and wagon, turned in this way, effectively sealed off the bridge. Legge had done it; riding to the ox's head, he had forced the cart into a blockade. Thornleigh had no choice but to haul the stallion to a stop.

Behind, at the bridge's arch, Bastwick gave a signal. His horsemen fanned out, closing off the entrance. One of them galloped forward to join Legge. Seeing this array, the terrified driver of the ox cart leaped down and ran off toward Southwark. Two workmen on a scaffolding clambered down their ladder and bolted into a doorway, leaving the ladder quivering in their wake. Frightened pedestrians fled, and Bastwick's men allowed them to squeeze out. Shop doors slammed.

In the emptied space between the ox cart and the attackers, Thornleigh and Honor were trapped. Bastwick's three archers jumped from their horses and whipped the bows from their backs. They fixed their arrows. Bastwick pointed. "The woman," he commanded.

Thornleigh let out a blood-curdling battle cry. Head bent, he kicked the horse and plunged straight for the archers. They stumbled backwards in surprise. Thornleigh immediately wheeled around and began to gallop back toward the ox cart. Honor knew he was going to try to jump the short gap of harness between the cart and the ox.

She clung fast. From behind, two arrows whizzed by her ear. One thudded into the cart's side. She saw the cart loom up, felt the stallion tense for the jump. But before it could leave the ground there was a *whack!* as a third arrow stabbed into the horse's rump. The horse staggered. Honor swayed, lost balance, and thudded to the ground. She scrambled to crawl free of the flailing hooves.

Thornleigh looked back at Honor, and in that moment the terrified stallion, blindly following Thornleigh's original command, rallied and leapt. Thornleigh sailed over the harness gap and clattered onto the other side, safe.

Alone on the battlefield Honor reeled to her feet. Her skirt was ripped, her palms scraped and bloody. She looked back. The archers were fitting fresh arrows. In an act of sheer instinct, Honor flattened her bleeding hands over her belly to protect the life inside.

Thornleigh saw the gesture. There was agony in his eyes as he watched her standing helpless in the line of arrow fire while he fought to calm his panicked horse.

Legge, at the ox's head, saw the gesture too. He scowled. "Why, the woman's with child," he said to the man beside him.

The man barely heard. "What?"

"Five babes I have, and don't you think I've seen my Mary hug her swollen belly just like that?" He cursed. The poxy priest had said nab the woman, not murder her. They could easily have nabbed her in the night, but when he'd told Bastwick the couple's plan to involve the Steelyard Germans, the priest had decided to wait and swoop down on all of them at once. "The priest's a greedy fool," he muttered.

Thornleigh had finally turned the stallion in a wide sweep, and was preparing to jump back across the cart harness to rescue Honor. He kicked the horse's flanks. The hooves thudded in approach. The horse flew into the air just as the archers' bows twanged again. The horse screamed as one shaft ripped into its chest, another into its throat. It dropped onto the harness, iron bolts flaying its skin, blood spurting. Thornleigh was thrown backwards to the ground, still separated from Honor by the cart.

Honor heard another arrow sing through the air. It ripped across her upper arm, stinging. Blood oozed, but the tip had only grazed her flesh.

"Christ," Legge growled. "Murdering a pregnant woman's not to my taste."

Honor scrambled up onto the wagon-seat to get across. She stood in clear view of the archers.

"Lady!" Legge shouted. He was riding toward her. "Lady, take my horse," he cried, and slipped from the saddle.

Honor looked at him, amazement in her eyes.

"Never fear," Legge cried with a grin as he let go the horse, "I'm a good swimmer!"

The archers were running forward. Honor did not hesitate. She hiked up her skirts and sprang down onto the Arab. At last, both she and Thornleigh were on the far side of the cart. Legge, having sprinted past them halfway across the bridge, veered into a gap between buildings on the downstream side where the water was calm, and dove off.

Honor kicked the Arab toward Thornleigh. He was trying to stand, but his left ankle buckled under him, broken in his fall. She circled him and stretched out her hand for him. One of the archers had by this time made it up onto the wagon. He stood on the seat and drew his bow string.

Thornleigh was hobbling toward Honor when the arrow pierced his shoulder blade. He swiped back at it like a man scratching.

Bastwick cried to the archer, "Not him! The woman!"

At Bastwick's command Thornleigh's eyes flashed back to Honor with sudden understanding. He slapped the Arab's rump. It bounded forward. "Over the bridge!" he shouted after her.

She hauled on the reins. "Not without you!" She was trying to turn, but the horse was used to a firmer hand and it scudded sideways, out of her control.

Thornleigh was limping to the workmen's ladder on the upstream side of the bridge. Clumsy with his injured foot, and the arrow still quivering in his shoulder, he pulled himself up onto the scaffold and grabbed a carpenter's mallet. Honor watched as he clawed his way from the scaffold up onto a narrow roof gable and straddled its ridge.

At that moment Bastwick on his horse plunged over the harness gap.

"Honor!" Thornleigh yelled. "Run! Now!" He hurled down the mallet at Bastwick. It struck Bastwick's horse on the shoulder and the horse shied.

Bastwick pointed up to the roof in fury. "Get him!" he shouted.

The archers took aim at Thornleigh.

"Richard!"

He crouched on the roof tiles as their arrows flew. They missed him. They whipped out new arrows and trained them on him again.

"No!" Honor screamed.

Wildly, she kicked the horse and lunged toward Bastwick. "Make them stop!" She skidded beside him. He snatched the Arab's bridle. She saw the red flame of hate burning at the core of his black eyes. She fumbled for Thornleigh's dagger at her belt, lifted it, and plunged it into Bastwick's knee. He recoiled with a scream.

She looked up at the roof just as an archer snapped his bow string. The arrow plowed into Thornleigh's thigh. His foot slipped on the roof slates, and he had to stand straighter to get a foothold. The second archer took aim. The bow string twanged. The arrow blazed, glinting sunlight, flashing feather colors. It plunged into Thornleigh's eye. His hands flew to his bloody face. Bristling with three arrows he staggered backwards along the spine of the roof. Then he fell. Honor's heart stopped. In a sliver of blue daylight between walls she saw his body plunge down toward the rapids that smashed against the stone arches.

She could not move. She could not think. The horse sensed her impotence. Feeling riderless, panicked by the smell of blood, it cannoned across the bridge into Southwark.

The pursuers could not catch it. Bastwick had rewarded Legge well. The gray Arab was a very fast horse.

Part Four

Charity

June 1534–July 1535

❧ 31 ❧

The New Jerusalem

The wagon behind the nag was piled high with spindly furniture, and it crept across the treeless Westphalian plain like a miniature castle in tow—upended chair legs were its battlements, a standing clock its turret, and a limp linen towel wound around a broomstick its sorry flag.

The afternoon was hot and windless, and the scraggy dray horse plodding at the head of this migrating residence slowed as it approached a bald incline. On the wagon seat, Hermann Deurvorst, master tailor of the city of Amsterdam, clicked his tongue in encouragement to his old mare. Hermann never used the whip. He murmured soft words, and soon the animal grudgingly strained up the low hill. Hermann's pudgy, sunburned face relaxed into a smile at this proof of the power of persuasion over coercion. For the hundredth time he rejoiced inwardly that he and his wife were moving to a city where, true to Anabaptist doctrine, violence was a thing of the past.

Not like Amsterdam. It had become a perilous place for Anabaptist families like the Deurvorsts. Their belief that infant baptism permanently enslaved the child to the Church, and their insistence that grown men and women be re-baptized, choosing God with adult eyes, had made Catholics and Lutherans alike turn on them savagely. The Emperor Charles had ordered that Anabaptists throughout his domains be drowned. Hermann had heard that at Salzburg three had been thrust alive into a burning house. His wife's brother had been in Zutphen when several were nailed by their tongues to a pulpit, and Hermann had seen with his own eyes the heads of Anabaptists on long poles spiking the shores near Amsterdam.

He had watched and despaired. Then, one morning he had read a letter, cautiously circulated, from an Anabaptist preacher in Münster. It told of the wonders that had occurred in that city. A group of Anabaptists led by a Dutchman named Matthias—called The Prophet by his followers, the letter said—had won the people's support over both the Catholic overlords and the rich Lutheran merchants. Christian brothers and sisters in Münster were now free to follow the Inner Word. Equals in the sight of the Lord, they shared all things communally. Violence and enslavement to priests and princes were mere memories of the barbarous Old Ways. In the letter the preacher had invited all believers to join them:

He who seeketh his everlasting salvation, let him forsake all worldly goods, and let him with wife and with children come unto us here to the New Jerusalem.

Hermann had thrilled to the words as if to a call from God himself.

The wagon lumbered up the mound and Hermann turned to the compact, sharp-featured woman on the seat beside him, his wife, Alma. She was squinting at a plume of thick smoke rising straight ahead beyond the hill.

"Of course, she may want to go on," Hermann said, picking up the conversation with his wife that had been interrupted by the horse's reluctance. "To Cologne, or Strassburg."

The couple had been talking, as they often did, about the quiet young Englishwoman who rode behind in the covered part of the wagon. She had arrived on their doorstep a month ago asking for Klaus, their grown-up son. Klaus had once helped fleeing English Protestants settle in Amsterdam, and Hermann discovered from the lady through cautious questioning—he had learned to be very careful when speaking about religion—that she had organized those escapes. A remarkable accomplishment.

"Klaus lives in Deventer now," Hermann had told her, proud of his son. "He married and moved there a year ago." Hermann had spoken to the young lady in English, a tongue he had mastered well enough from conversing with the immigrants Klaus used to bring around for a meal; the lady seemed to know only a smattering of Dutch and German.

The news about Klaus had appeared to bewilder her.

"Have you no other friends here?" Hermann had asked, concerned, for she had looked very pale and adrift. But Klaus, it seemed, was the only name she knew in Amsterdam. "I wish I could help you," Hermann had said, "but my wife and I are just about to leave the city ourselves."

The young lady had nodded silently and turned away from their door. Hermann and Alma had watched her wander like a lost child into the busy street, a horseman cursing her as she drifted across his path. Alma had run after her, and when the Deurvorsts left Amsterdam they took the young Englishwoman with them.

"But I hope she'll stay with us," Hermann said as he watched the horse's tail swish flies off its bony rump. "I'm afraid she couldn't look after herself."

"I've told her she's welcome as long as she wants," Alma said. "Heaven knows she's no trouble. She eats almost nothing. And her needlework will fetch good money in Münster. I've never seen such fine handiwork as she turns out day and night. Though I've told her over and over, 'Don't strain your eyes.' But she says she's contented working. Poor soul. With a baby coming, too."

Hermann shrugged philosophically. Both he and his wife had given up trying to encourage the young woman to speak of herself. She sewed in silence and helped Alma with the household tasks without complaint, but she also spent long periods staring into candle flames, and Hermann knew her heart was weighed down with some secret sorrow. "Well, whatever her trials," he said brightening, "she accepts them with meekness. That pleases God. She'll be alright."

His wife nodded, but absently, for she was peering again at the far-off black smoke. It rose in an undisturbed column into the blazing blue sky.

"What could it be?" she muttered. It was too thick to be the smoke of a household chimney, and though they had passed a few stumps of burned-out castles hulking on hillsides, the legacy of the savage Peasant's War nine years before, they had seen no recent signs of violence. Nor had they heard any reports of trouble. But, then, they heard no news at all, for they passed through villages without stopping, and camped alone; it was the wish of the Prophet Matthias, stated in the letter, that God's Elect should distance themselves from the heathen world.

The wagon continued to creak up the incline. When it reached the top, Hermann's eyes widened. He stopped the horse. Alma held her breath at the sight.

"Praise God," Hermann whispered.

On the plain before them the walls of Münster stood shining under the noonday sun. The black column of smoke rose up from behind the city. A scout was galloping toward them, enveloped in a swirling cloud of white dust.

The young scout led the wagon to the closed western gate, and Hermann and Alma gazed up with open mouths. The city walls were lined with hundreds of people crowding and craning down at them. Some clutched scythes and pitchforks. There seemed to be many more women than men. Despite the large number of people there was an eerie, overwhelming silence.

"Who goes there?" a voice shouted from a tower.

"Brethren from Amsterdam, so they claim," the scout shouted back.

The thousand eyes stared down. No one moved.

The scout, waiting, nervous, whispered to Hermann from the corner of his mouth, "God must be watching over you, Brother. Incredible that the enemy didn't see you."

"Enemy?" Hermann asked, astounded. He wasn't sure he had heard correctly. The scout's dialect was difficult to follow.

"The Prince-Bishop's army," the scout said.

"But we saw no soldiers," Hermann protested. "We saw no one!"

"I believe you. The question is"—he nodded to the staring multitude on the walls—"will they?"

Someone called out, "Here comes The Prophet!"

The crowd shuffled and parted. A wizened man dressed in gray robes limped to the edge of the wall. His long beard was striped black and gray, his face sour as a crab-apple. At his side walked a lean, handsome young man with yellow hair. He was clothed in sky blue silk, and rings sparkled on his fingers. He was smiling. But the old man glowered down at the wagon as if ready to hurl thunderbolts upon it.

As the throng waited for the Prophet's response, Honor stepped down from the back of the wagon. She wore a simple white dress of Alma's, and sunlight glinted off her loosened hair. She looked up at the walls and blinked in the sun's glare after the gloom of the wagon.

At that moment the pounding of hooves made the thousand watching eyes snap up. A white horse, saddled but riderless, plunged across the mound in the distance behind Honor, then disappeared. The old man on the wall clutched his chest and lurched backwards. "It is a sign!" he croaked. "The Heavenly Father speaks to His Prophet! 'Behold a pale horse; and his name that sat on him was Death.'"

He stared down at the intruders. "The Heavenly Father will have none but the Pure, none but the Elect, in His city!" His skeletal finger homed in on Honor.

The thousand eyes narrowed.

"She is our sister!" the Prophet cried. "The Lord has led her through the valley of the shadow of death! Let them enter!"

The gate rumbled open.

Honor walked into the city after the wagon and looked up, dumbfounded. People were cheering from the walls as if for a conquering hero. Laughing men and women swarmed the wagon and pulled it forward. There were shouts of, "Welcome, Sisters! Welcome, Brother!" A girl tossed down a garland.

Honor heard Hermann breathlessly call to the scout who rode alongside. "Was that really the great Prophet Matthias?"

"In the flesh," said the scout exultantly. "He brought us our miracle."

"Miracle?"

As the wagon was led through the cheering streets the scout explained. For months, he said, Prince-Bishop Franz von Waldeck, overlord of the territory before the righteous revolution, had been massing an army of mercenaries several miles from the city. That very morning the Prince-Bishop had finally attacked the eastern gates. The Münsterites had swarmed out and, with God on their side, the scout said, had inflicted dreadful casualties. They had beaten back the soldiers, and the Prince-Bishop's armored knights had thundered away in humiliating retreat, leaving scores of their men writhing and dying on the plain at the eastern side of the city. To the west, though, where the Deurvorsts had come from, there was no sign of the carnage. All this had happened not more than two hours before.

Amid the clamor Hermann strained sideways to follow the fantastic story. "You fought?" he asked, as though trying to grasp it. Honor wondered, as well. Anabaptists were forbidden to bear the sword.

"And won!" the scout grinned, kicking his horse forward.

Everywhere, people rushed out of doorways with greetings, gifts of sausages, wineskins. Men, women and children danced around the wagon, singing psalms, ecstatic at their deliverance from the might of the enemy and thrilled at the sign of God's favor embodied in the innocent newcomers.

The Deurvorsts' wagon was brought to the broad market square. The square was flanked by the cathedral and the former Prince-Bishop's palace. Hermann and Alma climbed down from the wagon and joined Honor in acknowledging the onion-breath embraces of women. The horse and wagon were led away.

A lieutenant in an iron helmet stalked over. His crooked nose appeared to have been broken more than once. "Brother, are you and your family re-baptized?" He looked Honor up and down, skeptically.

"Of course!" Hermann declared, beaming.

"Well," the lieutenant grunted, "the preachers will check your story. Meanwhile," he jerked a thumb at the cathedral, "your family will be billeted there."

"Billeted?" Hermann asked, startled. "In a church?"

"We've had hundreds of you refugees tramp here. Dutch, German, even some Spaniards. There's more of you than us. Now," he said gruffly, "you must give over your purse. All goods are held in common here. The Elders"—he pointed across the square to a dozen well-dressed men standing at the door of the palace, the sour-faced Prophet and the yellow-haired young man among them—"they hold the treasury in trust until God can claim His own." He held out a dirty palm, waiting.

"Gladly, gladly, Brother," Hermann laughed. Quickly, he pulled three small purses of coins from his clothes. His face was flushed with excitement as he dropped the money into the lieutenant's hand. He smiled at his wife. "All goods held in common, Alma. Isn't it wonderful? The New Jerusalem. It's all we hoped it would be."

Alma did not answer. She was watching their savings disappear into the lieutenant's tunic. His grunt was the only receipt he offered before marching away.

Honor distractedly felt for the small bulge of coins tucked inside her underskirt. The brothel owner who had hidden her in Southwark and the ship's master who had carried her to Amsterdam had both demanded exorbitant sums, and although the Deurvorsts had refused any payment from her, this small purse was the last of her money. She must hold on to it.

Hermann looked around them, his smile undimmed, then said to Alma, "The scout who brought us in, my dear, his dialect was so thick, and what with all this noise I must have misunderstood what he said. These good people rejoicing cannot be fighters."

Horns blasted. Drums rattled. Honor and the Deurvorsts joined the excited people higher on the cathedral steps and looked out, unsure of what was happening. A bent old woman poked Honor's rib and cackled, "The victory celebration. You interrupted it."

There were shouts and cheers as grimy but smiling soldiers marched into the square. They were followed by a black clump of preachers, then a procession of rowdy, costumed actors. At the palace doors the twelve elders stood in a line and looked on approvingly.

The actors cavorting at the rear of the parade were parodying the princes of the Church. One, dressed as the Pope, was strapped at the waist to a hurdle, and a long carrot was jammed in his mouth. Then came a wheeled platform carrying fat cardinals counting money bags, and leering saints who swiped at women's breasts. The crowd roared with laughter. The platform was hauled by six sweating, manacled prisoners in harness.

Hermann was distressed by the obvious misery of the prisoners. He plucked the sleeve of the cheering old woman, "Who are they?" he asked, pointing.

"Captives?" Alma asked anxiously.

"No," the old woman said. She spat into the dust. "They're the scum among us. Drunkards. Fornicators. Filth."

A band of teenage boys burst through the crowd. With ropes they were dragging a life-sized, painted wooden image of a saint. In the distance behind them the black column of smoke that Alma had noticed earlier could still be seen billowing outside the walls.

"That's St. Mauritz's," the old woman winked, following Alma's gaze. "Up in smoke!" She laughed.

The boys dragged their church booty facedown like a prisoner, making its rigid feet carve channels in the white dust. People formed a circle around them. One of the boys straddled the statue, raised his dagger, plunged it into the saint's eye and gouged out wood pulp.

Honor shuddered. Her vision blurred. She closed her eyes and saw the narrow roof on London Bridge again, saw the arrow ripping into Thornleigh's eyesocket, saw him fall. His blood pooled crimson on the backs of her eyelids. She felt for the step and sat, shivering.

From the crowd two men rushed forward with swords to attack the statue. They hewed off its arms, then its head. A woman scurried out clutching a kitchen knife and hacked at the trunk in a frenzy to destroy the hidden genitals. The crowd clapped and stomped.

"Good God," Hermann whispered.

There was a thunder of moving feet. Honor opened her eyes. The crowd was rushing to the edge of the cathedral close where the six manacled prisoners were being tied to the lime trees.

"Sinners!" a woman shrilled.

As a dozen guards armed with muskets filed in front of the prisoners, the Prophet Matthias climbed the cathedral steps. His arms flew up. The guards aimed at the captives. The crowd hushed.

"'And all the sinners of my people shall die by the sword,'" the Prophet intoned. "God will have nothing unclean in his city. He will have a holy people to praise His name!" He dropped one arm in a chopping signal. The guards fired. The prisoners slumped dead over their ropes. The people cheered.

Hermann Deurvorst's face drained to the color of the dust.

✌ 32 ✌

The Elect

The Festival of Victory lasted for three days.

The market square was the nerve center of the red-eyed, delirious city. By day, under banners that proclaimed THE COMING OF THE LORD IS NIGH thousands ate at communal tables, and in the open air the preachers conducted mass baptisms, the blessed symbol of personal freedom. Several young people killed themselves immediately after the rite, inflamed by the ancient teaching that promised everlasting glory to those in a state of innocence following holy immersion. By night, the square flickered with the watch fires of the freelances who had deserted from the Prince-Bishop's troops.

All day, Honor wandered the streets. Isolation was unbearable, for every thought of Thornleigh brought waves of grief that made her almost physically sick. So she plodded through the city to numb herself, dazed by the shocking sights. When evening finally stalked in from the plain, exhaustion would force her back to the cathedral, a stone hulk stripped of its treasures. Months before, the citizens had pried open its tombs in the nave. They had shattered the stained glass windows, smeared the wall paintings with lime, shoveled dung into the font. Honor would pick her way through the smoky cooking fires of the camped refugees to get to the niche the Deurvorsts had settled into, a small chapel in the north transept. The chapel was the tomb of a crusader Baron, and his sleeping marble effigy took up most of the space. There, Honor would eat a little bread and cheese, sip some water, then fall into a black and dreamless sleep.

In her sorties she saw ransacked Catholic houses and the shells of looted churches. Church towers had been broken down and turned into platforms for ordnance. Church bells and the coating of steeples had been melted down for bullets. Priceless carved altars and ancient tombstones had been rammed up against the bolted city gates.

Packs of grubby boys—the people sneeringly called them Angels—roamed from dawn to dusk, foraging. One evening Honor saw the Deurvorst's wagon overturned in an alley. The chairs had been pilfered, the clock was gone, and Angels scrabbled over the box like mice, scuffling through the broken remnants of Alma's pots and ladles. Another morning, stopping by a waste lot embroidered with wildflowers, she noticed a couple of Angels trying to trap a cat behind a privy, and her eye was caught by a richly painted church panel depicting the Virgin. She recognized the style of the magnificent work as Hans Holbein's. The painting had been propped up as a makeshift wall for the privy.

Honor noticed that the homespun clothing on many of the people she passed was oddly adorned—velvet sleeves on a woman collecting dung in the square, a feathered silk cap on a grimy watercarrier—and she gradually realized they were wearing the abandoned goods of long-fled Catholic burghers. And there was a strangely disproportionate number of women. The young scout, meeting her one day by the well, had explained—for Honor understood more German than she could speak—that most of the Catholic citizens had left the city early in the revolution and had left their households in the care of wives or daughters until they could return. But six months later they had not returned, and women now outnumbered men three to one. He also told her how the Elders had set a day the previous February for the banishment of all the remaining unbelievers—all those who had refused to be re-baptized. Hundreds had been forced out of the gates into the driving sleet of a vicious winter night. Those who had not perished in the cold were massacred the next day by the Prince-Bishop's knights. After that, no one had dared to leave the city.

Into these troubling surroundings Honor and the Deurvorsts settled as well as they could.

About two weeks after their arrival, Honor was carrying water back to the cathedral late in the afternoon. She trudged with her bucket past the citizens who were setting supper on the communal tables, and had reached the lane that ran down the side of the cathedral when she heard angry shouts. She looked over her shoulder. A couple of women were beating a little girl away from a supper table in the square. One woman threw a clump of manure at the child. The child broke into a run. Several women chased her. The girl sprinted down the cathedral lane, her long golden hair flying as a half-dozen women pursued her, hurling stones at her back. The girl ducked into a chapel porch. The women stopped in a cluster, still jeering and pelting the open porch door with stones. Honor could not understand the volley of German words, but the abusive nature of them was clear enough. Then, having vented their anger, the women turned back to the square. They stomped past Honor, still muttering their indignation. Curious, she set down her bucket and started down the lane.

She looked into the porch. In a dark corner the girl, perhaps seven or eight years old, Honor guessed, sat on the floor hugging her drawn-up legs with her head lowered between her arms. Poking from her tattered dress, her legs and arms gleamed white and thin, like peeled sticks.

Honor wondered what the child had done to provoke such fury from the women. She held out her hand. "Are you hurt?" she asked.

The child's head snapped up. With a snarl she lunged for Honor and bit her hand. Honor jumped back. The child, too, retreated as quickly as she had sprung, and cowered in the corner again. They stared at one another. Honor was more astonished than hurt; the bite had been no more than a nip, and the teeth had not broken the skin. But what kind of terror could have prompted such an attack?

Huge green eyes took up half the child's grime-streaked face, and her hair, falling in long, golden curls, was spiked with dried leaves and twigs. Despite the dirt, Honor was struck by the child's beauty. She moved a step closer. The child flinched and cowered further into the corner.

A man was lounging at the inner door, cleaning his teeth with a toothpick, and he leaned around and stuck his head into the porch. "Don't worry, sister," he chuckled, "that one's got no real bite left."

"Who is she?" Honor asked, staring at the lovely face.

"She! Ha! Well you might say so. That's a God-boy. A little priest tart. Left behind when his keepers were sent packing. At first he tried to run with the Angels, but they kicked him off." He mouthed the toothpick to one side and grinned. "He's a filthy little turd, but he won't hurt you."

Honor now understood why the women had chased the child from the communal tables. The righteous citizens, she knew, would not tolerate such refuse of the priests near them. She crouched before the boy—she saw now that the "dress" he wore was actually a small cassock that he had outgrown—and held out her hand again, cautiously, as she would to a wounded dog that might bite again. "Don't be afraid," she said in her halting German. The man at the door snorted his disapproval and pushed off, back into the cathedral.

Honor waited for some response from the boy. Suspicion glinted in his enormous eyes. His fists were balled. His teeth were chattering. She wondered how to convince him of her goodwill. If the priests had kept him, she reasoned, he may have known no other life than the cathedral. She decided to try another tack. In Latin she asked, "Are you hungry?"

The boy's mouth dropped open in amazement. His eyes grew even larger.

Again in Latin, she asked, "How many days since you've eaten?"

"I . . . don't know. I ate some carrots . . . one day." The soft voice was unsteady, but the Latin was flawless.

Something in Honor's breast swelled at this small victory. "Come," she said, gently taking his hand. "My friends have bread and soup for you."

Alma and Hermann were resting in the chapel after their day's labor. They sat on the floor with their backs against the marble tomb as Hermann read aloud in Dutch from his Bible. They smiled at Honor as she came in. She walked by them softly so as not to disturb Hermann's reading which he kept up even as he and Alma glanced with curiosity at the boy.

Honor could see, beneath their kind smiles, the exhaustion in both their faces. The past weeks had been a trial for the Deurvorsts. Hermann spent his days sweating in the municipal cloth works, while Alma often stood for a whole morning among the milling petitioners in the palace ante-chambers, waiting to request a house from the Elders who ruled the city. When she was not there she and Honor sewed for hours in the chapel; the Elders' wives paid well for their fine embroidery, and the payment, in the form of cheese or eggs, or even salt, was a welcome addition to the communally doled-out fatty pork, bread and cabbage.

The boy had crouched near a corner of the chapel. He shot occasional glances out at the camped refugees in the nave, but he was intently watching Honor as she cut a slice of creamy yellow cheese and laid it on a thick slab of rye bread. His whole body trembled at the pungent smells. She offered it to him with a smile, and he grabbed it with both hands and brought it to his open mouth. Then his eyes darted to her with a shy look, as if he knew he was guilty of bad manners. With a gesture of restraint that touched her heart, he lowered the food, made a quick sign of the cross, and murmured a Latin prayer of thanks.

Hermann abruptly stopped his Bible reading. "What's he doing?"

"Something he hasn't done for days," Honor said with a smile. "Eating." She was glad Hermann's English was as good as it was. It was exhausting trying to keep up with the couples' Dutch and the Münsterites' German.

"No, I mean what's that papist mumbo-jumbo?" Hermann said. "Tell him to stop it!"

The boy, not understanding the English words, finished his prayer in a rush to get to the food. He rapidly crossed himself again.

"Stop that!" Hermann shouted. He thudded shut the Bible. His body had tensed and his face was red. Alma, too, was scowling at the boy.

The boy chomped down on the bread and cheese. Without chewing he gulped the mouthful, then tore off another.

"God-cursed little bugger," a voice murmured in German. Honor saw that it was the man with the toothpick again. He was leaning against the chapel arch. "Priest's bum-boy," he explained to Hermann, with a nod toward the child, and made an obscene gesture with his finger at his backside.

"Mind your own business," Honor snapped.

But Hermann and Alma leapt up as if they had been told a rabid animal was loose. "Get him out!" Hermann cried.

Honor was stunned by his reaction. "But, Herr Deurvorst, he's starving. And we have plenty."

"I won't have such filth here!"

"What are you talking about?"

"He's a sinner!"

"He's a child."

"He has not repented!"

"What has he to repent?"

"Abominable sodomy! Get him out! Only the pure, the Elect, may remain in the new Jerusalem." He kicked the boy's small foot as if it were a snake slinking toward him. The boy hunkered further into the corner.

Honor was appalled. "Herr Deurvorst, what are you doing? Anabaptists have always stood against violence."

"Primitive Anabaptists. Now, I know that to smite the heathen is no crime. Only the sinless shall remain."

"The sinless? Good God, in the victory celebrations I saw them hunt whores into alleys and strangle them."

"It was necessary. Through re-baptism and submission to the Elders, the Elect can do no sin."

"Submission to priests was what you were *escaping*!"

"The Elect only *seem* to rule. They are vessels for God's will. Priests are usurpers of the Word." He held up his Bible. "All that is necessary for salvation is the Word."

Honor heard an echo of Sir Thomas's equally passionate declaration: "All that is necessary for salvation is the *Church*."

"The usurpers of the Word are out *there*," she cried, pointing in the direction of the square. "They've shut down the institutions of law and medicine as blasphemous. Denounced mathematics as a black art. Forbidden all books except the Bible."

She was shouting now, in English, and Hermann, in his anger, began to shout back in Dutch. The boy, gulping mouthfuls and watching the argument with huge, frightened eyes, was muttering a Latin prayer. Some refugees from the nave had begun to gather behind the man with the toothpick, and he was answering their questions in German. No one was listening to anyone. It was all confusion.

Hermann snatched the remnant of bread from the boy's hands and pitched it to the floor as if it were contaminated. The boy flinched. Stiff-armed, Hermann pointed across the cathedral. "Out! Get out!"

Honor, afraid now for the boy's safety, grabbed his elbow and pulled him to his feet. She tugged him, though he strained to reach back for the crust, and pulled him from the chapel. She had to push through the knot of people. She heard someone hiss, "Papist!" A woman spat on her neck. Stunned, she halted, feeling the woman's spittle scald her skin. As she wiped it away there was silence.

"Fornicating scum!" a man yelled, and hurled a boot. It struck the boy on the head. The boy pressed closer to Honor. She wrapped her arms around him. They started to walk. The refugees followed them. Honor and the boy quickened their pace as people began shouting insults and taunts at their backs. By the time they reached the other side of the cathedral they were almost running, and under a hail of shoes and bones they burst out the porch door.

Honor glanced up the lane at the citizens milling in the square for supper. She couldn't take the boy there. That crowd would be worse than the one in the cathedral.

The boy was tugging her sleeve. "No, this way!" he said. She followed him, and they ran down the lane to the lime trees in the cathedral close where the bodies of the executed prisoners still hung in their chains around the tree trunks, putrefying.

They ran past burned buildings—the canons' college, the cloister, the library, the charnel house—all empty. The whole cathedral enclosure was as deserted as if plague had swept through it. The boy pulled her down a tree-lined path. They reached a two-story house and stopped in front of it. It was a good-sized stone structure, but it was blackened from fire, and appeared empty and gutted like all the rest. The boy looked around to make sure they had not been followed. "Come," he said.

Inside the ravaged main room Honor stood looking at the staircase. Or what was left of the staircase. It had a beginning—one charred step. And it had an end—two steps suspended from the upper floor. But it had no middle. Fire had obviously eaten it away, then had died before it had reached the second floor.

A rope dangled from the railing of the landing. The boy grabbed hold and shimmied up. Honor watched his agility, fascinated; for the first time he really looked to her like a boy.

He jumped onto the landing and stared down at her. Clearly, he expected her to climb the rope as well, but in her skirts, and pregnant, it was impossible. She shrugged her incompetence. He slipped down the rope again. "Wait," he said, and disappeared around the corner. She heard a scraping and banging, and when he returned he was hauling a ladder. Together, they lifted it and leaned it against the landing. He scurried up, and she climbed after.

He led her to the main bedchamber. She stood in the doorway, amazed. The room had been stripped of everything valuable except for one item: a huge, pillowy feather mattress in its carved four-poster frame. Its covers and hangings were gone. The room's chairs, tables, bookcases, wall sconces—even the window shutters—had all been taken, but this small meadow of luxury remained. Perhaps the bed's sheer size had discouraged the looters; perhaps the fire had forced them out before they could remove it or destroy it. In any case, it sat magnificent and solitary in the barren room.

The boy smiled up at Honor. "You are welcome to my home, madam," he said. The Latin was as elegant as an Abbot's.

Honor and the boy sat together cross-legged on the deanery's big feather bed. They glanced out the naked window every now and then when a soldier's shout or a laugh arose from Münster's square. Night was skulking closer to the house like an undertaker summoned to a death. But Honor and the boy were absorbed in talk. He was telling her his story.

His name was Pieter. He had been left as a foundling at the small monastery of St. Stephen's-in-the-Woods about an hour's walk along the riverbank from Münster, and had been raised there by the monks, which explained his fluent Latin. A year ago he had been brought to the cathedral to assist the Dean, a Father Mueller, whose house this was. Pieter had lived here, and Father Mueller had been teaching him—two hours every day, Pieter said proudly, "no matter how busy Father was." Then, Pieter said, the barbarians had come. The priests had begun to leave. At Epiphany the last ones, including Father Mueller, had been chased out of the city gates with pitchforks. Pieter had hidden in a woodpile, and when the mob was through he moved into the floating second floor of the ruined deanery. He had been living on stores in the kitchen the citizens had not found, but lately the food had run out and now he snatched what he could from the square when the citizens weren't looking. "They don't scare me," he said stoutly. "Father told me God will punish them."

Honor had no wish to press him about this Father Mueller, the man, she imagined, who had sodomized him. And so she said, as brightly as she could, "I'm grateful the monks taught you so well. It's good to have someone to talk to. I know so little German."

Pieter grimaced. "The peasants' tongue."

"Don't you speak it?"

He shook his head.

"Not at all?"

"Why should I? I'm not a peasant."

She almost laughed. He might as well have been holding his nose in the air.

"When Father Mueller comes back and we finish my schooling he's going to send me to the university in Cologne. He says I'm going to be a bishop."

She managed a small smile, then looked out the window where a quarter-moon was trying to shine above the glow of the watch fires in the square. She hadn't the heart to tell this child that as long as the Anabaptist mob ruled here no priest was coming back. Nor did she want to face the fear that was creeping into the corners of her mind. "It's late," she said. "You should go to sleep."

Pieter stretched out his legs as if to lie down, then looked unsure. "You'll stay, won't you?"

She nodded, smiling.

"And may I sleep beside you?" he asked.

"Of course. It's your bed."

"No," he said, looking a little guilty. "It's Father's." He pointed to a corner. "I used to sleep over there. Except on Saturdays. On Saturdays I slept here."

"I see," she murmured.

Pieter lowered his head. "I hope he won't be angry."

"Pieter," Honor said softly, "you don't need to fear him any more."

"Who?"

"Father Mueller."

Pieter looked confused. "But I love Father Mueller," he said simply. "I miss him. On Sunday mornings he always gave me candied apricots or sugared almonds. I like the apricots best. He told funny stories, too." He looked at her again with the sheepish expression. "But I don't think Father will mind that I've been using his bed while he's away, do you? And, after all, you are a guest."

So that was all his guilty worry amounted to, Honor realized. He was only concerned about their using the priest's bed. "I'm sure it's alright," she said.

Reassured, Pieter lay down beside her. She continued to sit and look out the window, thinking.

After a few moments Pieter asked cautiously, "My lady?"

"Yes?"

"Are you . . . are you like the other barbarians?"

"What do you mean?"

"Are you a heretic?"

She smiled down at him and stroked the golden curls. "I'm just a human creature, Pieter, as hungry and confused as you."

"Oh, I'm not so hungry now. Thank you for the bread and cheese. And you shouldn't worry. God will fix everything soon." He flipped over on his side to sleep. "I knew you couldn't be one," he murmured, satisfied. "None of the barbarians know Latin."

Honor rested her head on the wall. The room was dark, but the feeble moonlight cast a patina over the cobwebs in the corners and over the dust on the window sill. Mice scrabbled and squeaked behind the walls.

She had to smile at the boy's assuredness, at his happy delusions, but it was a smile heavy with uncertainty and self-doubt. She had been wrong about so much, and here, in this child whom she had cast as a victim, she saw that she had been wrong again. Pieter did not see himself as helpless and exploited. He recalled only good things about the priest who had kept him—the fondness, the teaching, the stories, the treats.

Yet the child was living inside a bubble of dreams.

Just like me, she thought bitterly.

Never had she felt so alone, never so wretched. She had misread, misjudged everyone. Nothing was as it seemed. This starving, delicate-looking boy, it turned out, felt superior and invincible. Herr Deurvorst's kindness was all veneer. She saw now that she had been wrong about everything and everyone—and from the very beginning. When Ralph had been burned she had been so sure it was Bastwick who had hounded him to the stake, then had discovered it was Sir Thomas. She had revered Sir Thomas, the witty scholar, the loving father, and had found that his heart was pitted with hatred: the man of letters who burned books and men. She had betrayed the Queen in the hope that the King, with a new wife, would curb the Church's abuses, and then found that the King had no such intention. She had been wrong to trust Cromwell's assurances, and wrong, so very wrong—her greatest mistake—to carry Frish back to England, to his death. Even Richard, she told herself—and at the thought of him grief stabbed mercilessly—

even there I deceived myself. Richard the selfish, unable to un-derstand her important work, that was how she had thought of him for so long, and so obstinately. And she, tunneling ever deeper into her private spite against Sir Thomas, was unable to see the light of Richard's love until he pulled her up and shook her eyes open. In the end, he risked everything for her. Because of her great mis-take, he lost everything for her . . . died for her . . .

She rocked her head from side to side, sickened by the horrible results of her blunders, wretched with the knowledge of her errors, her willful blindness. Even so, she thought as tears stung, all the dreadful loss might at least have meant something if it had brought about a shred of good. But it had not been so, for, worst of all, she knew now that she had been wrong to believe in the reformers. She had thought they were going to create a new world, but all they had created was a new Church. Here, it was as fear-wracked, as vicious, as brutally tribal as the old one. Good God, what was this hell she had landed in, where children were stoned in the name of Christ and left to starve?

She felt her spirit spiraling down into hopelessness. Everything beloved lost; everything innocent despoiled. And was this hell-on-earth to be her punishment for her great offenses? Why not? she thought. For sheer, wicked wrong-headedness who deserved it more? And how masterfully ironic that she should be cast out as a heathen for consorting with a Catholic child!

Despair was seeping like ice-water into her heart. She heard again in her mind Hermann Deurvorst's words: *Only the sinless shall remain.* What was to become of this child? What was to become of her? Of her baby? Were they fated to perish here, throttled by the frenzy of a city, a world, gone mad? She slumped back against the wall, unable to prod her mind to action, unable to think of how she was going to survive against the mob of Münster. How long until she and Pieter were found and . . . exterminated?

She whispered to the darkness, "I don't know what to do . . ."

"My lady?" Pieter murmured. He turned to her.

Still speaking to the air she said, "I'm so afraid . . ."

"I know what to do," Pieter said. He jumped off the bed and pulled her by the hand. "I'll show you. Then you'll know, too."

He led her down the dark corridor to a door and opened it. In the blackness she could see nothing, but she sensed that the room was small; she smelled its stuffiness. Pieter let go her hand and hurried forward and scratched around. She saw the flare of a piece of tinder, Pieter's hand cupped around it and glowing with its light. She looked up. They were standing in a chapel.

All its treasures were gone. There was no altar, no carved saint, no crucifix, no chalice, no paten. But she knew, in her bones, that it had been a chapel, and when she looked at the wall above where the altar must have once stood, she noticed a lightened pattern on the stone in the form of a cross. A crucifix had hung there.

Pieter was reaching into a shallow cupboard. He brought out a small, stubby votive candle which he lit with the tinder then placed on the floor. He reached in again and carefully lifted out a heavy, golden crucifix. He crouched down and placed the foot of the crucifix on the floor beside the candle, and let it tilt back so that the wrought golden Christ on the cross seemed to slump in agony against the wall. He stepped back beside Honor, crossed himself, and kneeled.

"This is what to do, my lady," he said, pressing his palms together and smiling up at her. "God will hear us."

The light of the small flame glimmered over the golden image of sacrifice, the sacred wellspring of Christianity. The tiny room glowed with the comforting light. "Will He?" she whispered.

"I'll pray for a miracle," Pieter said. He stared intently at the cross, his green eyes gleaming. "And you," he whispered to her, "you pray, too."

Is that the answer? she asked herself. Pray? Was that what she must do? She'd been wrong about everything else . . .

She lowered herself and kneeled beside Pieter and folded her hands in supplication like his. She gazed at the golden cross, at the twisted body of the God, made man, who was dying, forever, to atone for the sins of humankind. She felt the hypnotic pull of its authority. Its power was mesmerizing. Old phrases of contrition and beseeching that had not passed her lips in years began to creep back into her mind and take hold. *My sinful pride has led to abominable errors. There is no strength in me. Lord, have mercy upon me.*

"At St. Mauritz's once," Pieter whispered, "at Corpus Christi, I saw the priest lift out the blessed Saint's bone from the reliquary. His leg bone. Some of the flesh was still on it."

Honor's concentration was broken. She frowned at Pieter.

"It's true, my lady. I saw it! And that day a man with a withered foot who had not walked a step for ten years prayed over the Saint's bone and then jumped from his cot and danced off down the nave. A miracle! And I heard that a dumb woman who prayed over the bone was later praying at a chapel crucifix and she saw the wounds of Our Lord bleeding afresh, and she touched the blood and put a drop on her tongue and suddenly she could speak. Another miracle! And we'll get one as well if we just pray hard enough, my lady." He closed his eyes, but then he, too, frowned. "Too bad we don't have the blessed Saint Mauritz's bone now," he said. "That would bring us a miracle for sure."

She laughed. She knew it was wrong, but the image of her and this extraordinary boy mumbling for a miracle over a rotting piece of meat on a bone was too much, and she laughed. And at that moment, she felt a flutter in her belly. Then a tight tug. It was so unexpected, so strange a sensation—like a heavy wave of water lapping on itself deep within her—that she gasped. The baby had quickened. There was a life inside her. For the first time she understood it, really understood it, in her very blood: a life!

She sat back on her heels. "I'm going to have a baby," she exclaimed.

"Now?" Pieter asked.

He was gazing at her mouth as if he expected a small, bald head to slither out. It made her laugh again.

Again, she felt the flutter inside. Another laugh escaped her, so wonderful was the sensation.

She was suddenly, overwhelmingly, aware. Aware that a moment before she had let a fanciful child talk her into kneeling to beg help from a piece of hammered gold. Aware that they had been doing it because they were powerless. Aware most of all that, somehow, she must find power—real power—and she must find it within herself. Nothing else, no one else, could protect this life that she was carrying. Richard's child.

God could not help her. Only she could help herself. Only she could act, and to act she had to think. And all these religious motions—begging exemption from punishment, beseeching reward, carefully cultivating the delusion of being in God's care—all of these were just impediments to clear thinking.

Clear thinking, she told herself. That's what was required now.

Her eyes locked onto the image of torture on the cross. Now that she felt life stir inside her, the image suddenly disgusted her. Its message was of sin and punishment and, above all, of death. This was the icon of a cult of death. But life must be her concern now—her own life, Pieter's life, the life of her baby. Wrong she may have been about many things, and terrible had been the consequences of her folly, but, thinking clearly, she knew there had been much right on her side, too. The missions—the rescue of over two dozen people—that had been right. And there was still some good she could do, and must do.

From an open window at the end of the corridor she heard the smash of glass from the square, then a peal of wild laughter. She placed her hand on her belly and made a silent vow. As she had once rescued lives from the fury of the Catholic state, now she promised that, whatever it required from her, her child would not be born in this Protestant hell.

In Amsterdam, Leonard Legge kindly thanked the Dutch housewife for her time, touched his hat to her, and stepped away from her threshold. As soon as the woman had closed the door, Legge dropped his smile and spat on the ground. "Bugger all foreigners," he growled. He wondered if the stupid woman had even understood his questions.

He'd asked the questions so many times, they now seemed meaningless even to him. "Had the lady or gentleman seen an Englishwoman named Mistress Thornleigh in these parts? Did the lady or gentleman have any information of any person who had seen such a woman?"

Legge glanced down the street. A half-block away, on the far side of the street, his master stood asking the same questions of a tousle-haired housemaid. Legge saw the maid shake her head. No luck there either, it seemed. As usual. Legge wondered how long his master would continue this useless search. Last month, they had knocked on half the doors of Antwerp. And now, thanks to the hazy recollection of a half-drunk Antwerp sailor, they were disturbing the fat housewives of Amsterdam. It seemed to Legge that they might as well be searching for a special grain of sand upon the seashore.

Legge watched his master turn away from the house—with every rebuff his shoulders seemed to slump a fraction more—and trudge on to the next door. He was exhausted, that was plain. And the Lord knew he was not yet fully recovered to health. After Legge had fished him out of the Thames and carried him to his home, Legge and his wife had been sure the man would die of his arrow wounds. But he had not died. He'd lost an eye, and hadn't been able to stand for some weeks, but he had clung to life. Just as Legge, very much in need of a new master, had clung to the chance to leave England for a while in this man's service.

Legge sighed at the futility of it all as he knocked on the next door. An old man answered and scowled at the strange face. Legge launched again into his round of questions in execrable Dutch. The old man shook his head irritably and made to shut the door.

Then a woman, younger and far more curious, came to the man's side. Legge repeated his questions. Oh yes, the woman said brightly, wiping her hands on her apron. A young Englishwoman had come to her neighbors, the Deurvorsts. Eagerly, she pointed next door.

Legge, energized by the discovery, begged her to wait. He ran the half block to fetch his master. Together, they hurried back to speak to the woman. She repeated what she had told Legge.

Richard Thornleigh's one good eye opened wide with hope. He thanked the woman, and started to run to the house next door. But the woman called after him, "She's not there now, sir. Gracious, no. She went with the Deurvorsts when they left Amsterdam. Oh, two months ago at least. And where they went, only the good Lord knows."

❧ 33 ❧

Immortality

Honor and Pieter continued to live as outcasts in the ruined deanery, but Honor set her mind to finding a way to escape. She made cautious, regular excursions to reconnoiter the city wall. If she and Pieter were to get out, the wall would be their first obstacle. All the gates were barricaded, and the Elders' lieutenants constantly patrolled the perimeter for signs of treachery within, lest some Judas throw open a gate to the enemy. Meanwhile, outside the walls, the Prince-Bishop's troops were camped, ready to murder any Münsterite who dared emerge. That, Honor knew, would be their second obstacle.

On one such outing she discovered a sally port near the western gate. She found that this small door, obscured by the piled rubble of the barricades, had been left unbarred. Apparently, it hadn't been thought necessary; Münsterites had not exactly been rushing out to meet the enemy's fire. This, she thought, might be the door to freedom.

She also befriended the scout who had escorted the Deurvorst's wagon into the city that first day. He lived far from the cathedral and knew nothing of her changed, outcast state. In the long, still afternoons, she chatted with him at his post below the eastern gate. Once, though he was not supposed to, he took her up on the wall for a look out at the Prince-Bishop's troops camped in the distance. During these encounters she casually probed him for information about the movements of the soldiers who patrolled the wall. Somehow, she hoped, if given enough information, she could devise a plan of escape.

The parched July weeks crept by.

Usually, Honor and Pieter spent the cool of the day in the deanery, for no citizens went out among the derelict cathedral buildings. When night fell, the two of them would slip out into the market square. There, they joined the dogs and the few other shadows—other "heathen," Honor surmised—who emerged from God-knew-where to scavenge in the mounds of refuse left after the communal meals. Water, at least, was not a problem. There was a well in the cathedral precincts.

When they did venture out in the day, Honor found she could pass without notice if she moved quickly and was alone. Pieter had to be more careful. Honor had cut his long curls, then had successfully begged a rag picker for some not-too-tattered breeches and shirt to replace the small cassock. Pieter looked like a boy now, but it was not enough; his golden hair, green eyes and sweet face were too well known by too many of the citizens. But since he was better at scavenging—nimbler with his hands, and faster on his feet—he often took the chance of going to find food. At such times, he always brought home more than Honor did, though usually his return route involved some imaginative detours through the side streets to shake off an irate citizen or two before he could double back to the cathedral close.

But even the communal cooking pots were daily rendering less and less. Choked by the ring of enemy troops, Münster was beginning to feel hunger. Some of the city's dogs and cats were going into the huge kettles now. "Well," Honor had muttered as she and Pieter sat on the bed one night reluctantly examining a suspicious-looking bone, hungry though they were, "at least when we forage now there'll be less competition from dogs." Pieter had laughed. But the situation had not seemed funny to Honor the next day when, watching from the bedchamber window, she saw a crowd assemble in the square and heard a preacher shout out the penalty for hoarding food: execution.

One morning she heard a noise downstairs. She tiptoed to the landing, but saw no one below. She climbed down the ladder and went to the front door. On the threshold lay a small bundle, an embroidered linen kerchief knotted around some lumps. She unfastened the cloth and found a stick of cured sausage the length of her forearm, a fist-sized chunk of cheese, and a half a loaf of rye bread.

"It's a miracle," Pieter said, his mouth watering at the treasure trove. "God sent it."

Honor looked down the path. The squat figure of a woman was hurrying away between the trees. "No," she said, with a small smile. "Frau Deurvorst brought it."

"Yes," Pieter agreed, and added triumphantly, "but who sent *her?*"

Honor laughed. "Little theologian."

She put away half of the cured sausage. The rest of the food she and Pieter gobbled then and there.

After that, things got slowly worse.

One evening after a day when the city had seemed strangely quiet, Honor was stooping to pick up crusts under a table in the square when she heard two other scavengers, an old couple, whispering. It seemed that the night before, the Prophet Matthias had beheld a sign of crossed swords in the evening sky. Fired with holy zeal he had ridden out with a small band to smite the enemy. He had failed. The Prince-Bishop's troops were now displaying his severed head on a pike below the walls. Honor imagined the head, shriveled and crusted with flies after a day in the baking July sun.

Leaderless, the city seemed to shrink into a stupor of fear. People whispered in shuttered houses. Münster was waiting—for deliverance or destruction. Finally, the nervous preachers called an assembly. Citizens shuffled into the square, like frightened cattle, Honor thought, watching from the deanery window.

There was a shout. Matthias's disciple, the handsome, yellow-haired young man, strode out of the palace dressed in billowing blue silks. Since the day she had arrived with the Deurvorsts, Honor had discovered who he was: Jan Bockelson, a twenty-four-year-old actor-poet from Leyden. His smile was radiant as he stood on the palace steps and addressed the people. He declared that he was taking up the Prophet's mantle. From henceforward, he said, he would guide the Elect. Relief rippled through the crowd. Calm was restored. Women fell to their knees, sighing.

Jan of Leyden threw his arms wide, rings sparkling, and issued a proclamation. In view of the excessive number of single women in the city, he said, and in light of the Elders' detestation of fornication, the Elect were commanded from that day forward to take several wives each.

"Adultery?" someone in the crowd gasped.

"By no means," Jan of Leyden said with a laugh. "Polygamy."

There were murmurs of disbelief. A man giggled.

Jan smiled. "We will follow the example set by the Old Testament patriarchs, by Abraham, by Isaac, and by Jacob. In this way we will stamp out harlotry and increase the Elect."

There was a heavy silence. Someone cried, "Sin!"

Jan of Leyden's sunny smile hardened to a diamond brilliance. "It is the will of the Lord that the Elect shall multiply as the sands of the sea. All who refuse shall incur the wrath of God, which will sweep them from the earth!" He turned on his heel and disappeared inside the palace.

For days, preachers in pulpits throughout the city expounded the new Edict. Every woman, they declared, must marry one of the Elect. Adulterers would be executed. Any woman with two husbands would be beheaded. Jan of Leyden himself immediately married the beautiful young widow of the Prophet, and ten other women.

When Honor heard of it she shook her head in disgust. Another manifestation of the sickness gnawing at this deranged place, she thought. But not long after, the Edict was brought personally home to her. She was on her knees picking dandelion leaves at the edge of the waste patch where the privy was adorned with Holbein's Virgin, when her wrist was grabbed and she was wrenched to her feet by a burly man. She twisted under his grasp. Shielding her eyes from the sun, she looked at his face. She recognized him. He was one of the thick-necked peasants from the Harz Mountains who camped in the nave of the cathedral. Often, when she had lived there with the Deurvorsts, she had seen this man watching her as she passed.

"I marry you," he said. The declaration was only a string of grunts, and Honor stared, not comprehending the dialect.

"Marry!" he barked, as if to someone deaf.

Now she understood. "No!" she cried. She tried to pull away. His grip tightened, and he scowled as though he meant to strike her. Frantically, she looked around. There was no one in sight.

With her free hand she tugged at her dress, stretching it taut over her belly. "Look!" she protested, English words tumbling out in desperation, "You don't want me, I'm five months pregnant!" But her slender body was lithe with the hard living, and the mound below her navel still small. The man's face slackened with lust at the sight of her breasts, swollen by pregnancy, under the light fabric. Instead of discouraging him she had inflamed him.

He started to drag her away. She dug in her heels, but he jerked her hard, and pain flared up her arm. Suddenly, a high-pitched wail stopped them both. From behind, Pieter came flying at the man and butted him in the small of his back. Without releasing Honor the man swung a massive fist. It smashed into Pieter's face and he sprawled back, blood dripping from his lip. The peasant yanked Honor again. Again, she heard the high-pitched cry. This time Pieter chomped down on the beefy wrist. The man yelled in pain and let go. Honor and Pieter ran. They didn't stop running until they reached the deanery.

After that, Honor didn't dare go out in daylight for fear that the peasant would see her again and claim her. She was under no illusions about the Elders' will to invoke the penalty for disobeying the Edict. *"All who refuse shall incur the wrath of God which will sweep them from the earth."*

But it turned out that many of the Münsterites felt an equal dismay over the Edict. A few days after the incident with the peasant, Honor awoke to drumrolls. She hurried to the window. People were rushing into the square. They seemed to be forming into two distinct parties. There was shouting and, from a side street, the dull popping of gunfire. She hurried outside and down the path to the edge of the close. Two cannon were rumbling across the square towards the Town Hall. The people were running now. One part of the crowd, the larger part, was swarming toward the smaller one. Honor did not dare go any nearer, but she could see that the larger group was engulfing the smaller one. Down the street the canon boomed. The crowd cheered. Honor caught the arm of a young man limping by her and holding a rag to his temple. "What's happening?" she cried.

A coup had been attempted, he told her breathlessly. A disgruntled ex-alderman named Mollenbecke had gathered a bunch of hotheads and at midnight they had broken into the homes of Jan Bockelson and the Elders. They'd taken them as prisoners to the Town Hall. The ringleaders were holed up there. But, he grinned, the citizens were rallying. "Have to stand together now," he said, "and beat back the Devil Bishop."

It was all over in an hour. Under bombardment the rebels were driven out. Jan Bockelson and the other captives were freed to the cheers and embraces of the crowd. Honor hurried back to the deanery.

She watched as Mollenbecke and seven co-conspirators were tied to the lime trees. A judgment seat was carried out for Jan Bockelson. The people crowded around him as he sat smiling, the huge sword of justice resting across his knees. He passed the sentence of death, then asked if any good citizen, as a service to God, would fire the first shot. Two young men rushed forward, eager for the privilege. When the eight ringleaders slumped, dead, the crowd cheered again.

Fifty-eight other rebels were then brought forward. Jan and the Elders dispatched them personally with the sword of justice, beheading the fifty-eight, one after another. The corpses were hauled away. The people went home, satisfied.

The next morning Honor awoke and heard no birdsong. She realized there had been none for days. All the birds had been killed and eaten. She knew that the time for planning had run out.

Something the man had mentioned during the coup stuck in her mind. "Beat back the Devil Bishop," he had said.

She left Pieter sleeping, shoved into her pocket the leftover piece of Alma's cured sausage, and went out of the house. She walked across the city to the eastern gate and saw the scout trudging up the stairs to the wall. She hailed him and asked if she could come up for a look. She drew from her pocket the piece of sausage and offered it. He looked around. It was noon, hot and quiet, and most of the other guards were sitting or lounging in what shade they could find along the wall. No one seemed to be watching him. He shrugged. "Why not?" he said, and jerked his head for her to follow.

What she saw from the wall made her heart beat fast with hope. A month before, she had looked out on this same view of the plain. The besieging army had then been camped a couple of miles away. Now, their camps had crept closer. They were digging trenches. They had moved cannon into position. There was, in general, an unmistakable increase in activity. The Prince-Bishop was preparing to attack.

She turned and said as much to the scout. He was furtively munching the sausage with his back to the other guards. He swallowed and wiped his mouth and said to her with grim confidence, "We're ready for them."

Honor knew this was her chance. If the Münsterites succeeded in repelling an attack on the eastern gate, she reasoned, the Prince-Bishop's troops might fall back in the confusion of defeat just as they had done on the strange day she and the Deurvorsts had arrived. That would leave the other gate, the western gate, clear of outside troops.

She thanked the scout and hurried back to the deanery. Now, it was just a matter of waiting.

The attack came the very next day. Late in the afternoon Honor heard shouts and gunfire and the noise of hundreds of feet running through the square.

The scout had been right; the Münsterites were well prepared for the attack. They swarmed out the eastern gate and, incredibly, against all odds, beat back the Prince-Bishop's army for the second time. The city erupted in victory celebrations.

Honor had already told Pieter that they must wait an hour or so for darkness, because if her calculations were wrong they would need the cover of night for any hope of surviving outside the walls. They watched the celebrations from the cathedral close.

People capered through the streets, sang psalms, gleefully fired the already gutted houses in the Catholic quarters and left them to smolder. At dusk Jan of Leyden, laughing, swept out of his palace with his eleven wives. He treated the people to an outdoor feast for which the Elders' private stores and cellars had been opened. Thousands of people choked the square. Tables were squeezed in. Bonfires roared. Musicians and actors piped and sang, and Jan and the Elders moved among the dazzled throng and served them with food and wine from their own hands. The people stuffed their sunken cheeks and danced in the firelight, intoxicated with the almost forgotten belly-heat of wine. Honor and Pieter watched from the cathedral shadows beyond the bonfires ringing the square. As the people became more drunk, Honor frowned; she and Pieter would have to make their way through this throng to get to the sally port.

At the height of the celebrations a preacher climbed the palace steps and threw up his arms. "Brothers! Sisters!" The musicians quieted. "The Heavenly Father has revealed His commandment!" cried the preacher. "It is God's wish that His holy servant, Jan of Leyden, prophet of God, defender of the New Jerusalem, shall reign among us as King of this holy city. King of the New Zion!"

Jan of Leyden sprang up the steps, splendid in silk as orange as the flames lighting him from the square. His eleven wives followed and shuffled into a horseshoe behind him. "Brethren," he called out, smiling, "God has appointed me King of the whole world. His will be done!"

There was a cheer, and underneath it the whimpering sigh of women. An Elder placed a golden crown on the new King's head and two pages hurried forward to flank him, one bearing the Old Testament, the other the jeweled Sword of Justice. From his row of wives Jan beckoned forth the former widow of the Prophet, called her his Queen, kissed her, then laughed like a child. The people stamped, ecstatic.

Thunder rumbled. Honor looked up. A storm was brewing.

"Now. We go," she whispered to Pieter. She took his hand firmly, and together they emerged from the shadows.

Her idea was to skirt the edge of the square then dash for the western gate, but the throng was so dense that the revelers had spilled down into the side streets as well, and Honor and Pieter found they had to push their way through the crush of bodies. Nevertheless, they made good progress and had got three-quarters of the way around the square when they came up against a long table. People were standing and sitting, laughing and eating all along its length. Honor tugged Pieter. "This way," she whispered.

But Pieter's eyes were feasting on an aromatic roasted hind end of piglet on the table. He stopped and leaned over to it, ready to tear off a handful. "Forget it," Honor said, pulling him back.

A woman's voice sang out, "Aw, let the little one have it, dearie. Why not?" Her laughing red face was slick with sweat.

"That's right," a man beside her said. "Plenty for all." He slapped the table. "Up with you, lad, and help yourself."

The woman slipped her hands under Pieter's arms and lifted him against her withered bosom and set him down on the table. "Why, it's the little God-boy!" she cried. "Look, Hans."

"So," the man snorted, "the little piggy wants a taste of piggy, eh? Alright." He tore off a chunk of the pork and dangled it in front of Pieter's mouth. "Let's hear some of that papist piggy talk, boy. Here you go. Let's hear you pray for it."

Pieter looked at the succulent piece of meat and licked his lips. Honor stood to one side, unable to do anything. If she created a scene it might prevent her and Pieter from getting away. Pieter didn't understand the peasants' German, and she could see that he didn't know what they were asking of him, though he looked ready to do anything for a bite of the meat.

"That's right, give us some of your heathen mumbo jumbo," the woman said with a laugh. "Sing for your supper, boy." She made an extravagant sign of the cross over Pieter's chest, ending with a swipe at his crotch. Suddenly, Pieter seemed to understand. He crossed himself to placate them, then grabbed for the meat.

The man snatched it away. "Where's your manners, bum-boy?

The lady asked for some mumbo-jumbo." He made a whining, sing-song parody of a priest saying mass. "Like that."

Pieter understood. With eyes fixed on the chunk of pork he began to sing a *Kyrie Eleison* in his sweet soprano voice. The man let him have the bite.

Pieter chewed and swallowed and sang again, louder. The couple slapped their thighs and laughed. Others beside them joined in the merriment, and soon Pieter was singing the mass and gulping mouthfuls and frantically crossing himself like a puppet whose handler was pulling too many strings at once.

Honor was sickened. If only they would tire of it and let him go!

Suddenly, a strained voice rose above the clamor. It came from the far side of the square. It was a male voice, loud, and raw with anger. "The King laughs, but tomorrow my children will still be starving!"

At the long tables the people hushed. The sparking of the bonfires was the only sound.

"Brother"—the King smiled across at the man as friend to friend—"this hardship we are undergoing is merely God's test. The Elect must be proved fit to ascend to His side in heaven."

There was fevered grinning at the tables as each citizen reamed his heart, desperate to be sure that he was fit.

The King turned to a movement near him. One of his wives, a thin, pale young woman in white, had come forward and was standing at his side. "The man is right," she said simply to him. "How can we and the Elders live in plenty when the people starve?"

Jan's face turned livid above the fire glow. He reached behind him for the Sword of Justice. He swung it up, flashing fire, and brought it whistling down on his wife's neck. Her head was sliced off and rolled down the steps.

There was appalled silence. Honor reached out to cover Pieter's eyes.

The King wiped his glistening face with his sleeve. The corners of his mouth jerked up. His actor's voice rang out, clear and irresistible. "'And power was given unto them over the fourth part of the earth, to kill with the sword!' Only the sinless shall prevail!"

Silence.

Then, a thin voice wailed, "Praise the King!"

A wild, deafening roar of approval went up. Music surged back to life. The young woman's bloody head and body were carted away. Dwarfs tumbled. People ate in greasy, frantic handfuls, laughing, electrified by the glory of their exalted status. God's Elect.

Honor was pulling Pieter off the table when someone yelled, "And death to the sinners!"

The couple who had been laughing a moment ago at Pieter now turned and glowered at him. The man repeated in a growl, "Death to the sinners."

Honor yanked Pieter to her side. She turned, ready to run, but she saw, only paces away, the thick-necked peasant from the cathedral staring at her. He took a step toward her. She wrenched Pieter's thin shoulders around in the opposite direction and pushed him past the scowling couple.

She heard the man's voice behind them, "Don't let the sinners escape!"

She and Pieter fought forward through the packed bodies. They reached the edge of the square and broke into a run.

With the knot of citizens on their heels they bolted down the dark side streets, hand in hand, toward the sally port.

They ran past small fires still flickering in former Catholic houses, and past Angels scurrying like rats over rubble-heaps. They were almost at the sally port—it was just around the next corner—when they came up to a burning shop front, and suddenly its whole facade came crashing down in their path. Honor snatched Pieter back, away from the flaming debris. She looked behind them. The voices of the citizens and the glow of their torches above the rooftops were getting closer.

She turned back to gauge the best way around the fiery obstacle. The facade had fallen out into the street, but between the burning building and the burning debris there was a path that was clear. She thought they could get through it. She glanced inside and it registered in her mind that the place was a bookseller's shop—or had been; it had been stripped of books. In its front room the flames that were creeping forward along the walls were eating empty bookcases and barren lecterns. Then, at the wall before her, something caught her eye. Her heart thudded heavily once, and then it seemed to stop.

An empty bookcase had been partly pulled out and stood at an angle to the wall. Behind it, gouged into the masonry, a niche held several sagging shelves. They were crammed haphazardly with books, and on the top shelf was a book that Honor had never expected to see again. It stood facing her. Its cover had been ripped away, perhaps in some violence before the owner managed to heap his treasure into this hiding place, and on the exposed title page, winking at her through the firelight, was Holbein's bright blue speedwell. It stood there, only paces away from her.

Unthinking, she stepped forward to reach for it. Pain seared her wrist. She lurched back, beating the sparks on her sleeve against her body. Flames were now sweeping up the sides of the book-case, cutting her off from the books behind. On the lower shelves of the niche some volumes were already blackening and smoking. One burst alight. She knew that within minutes the whole cache would be on fire. It was madness to risk herself for this book. Madness even to consider it. And impossible not to.

"Pieter!" she shouted. "Run! Get to the sally port, and get out!"

Obeying, he tore along the path, but once past the fire he stopped and turned. "You must come too!" he cried.

There's no time, Honor thought. The citizens were coming . . . she had to get out with Pieter. Yet . . . if she acted quickly . . .

She snatched up the hem of her skirt, and with her teeth ripped off a strip and wrapped it several times around her hand. She was coughing in the black smoke boiling around her. The heat was intense. She thrust her hand into the flames and grabbed the book-case and pulled. It toppled. She pawed at the fire in the wall. Smoking books tumbled down around her. She caught the one she wanted in her arms and stepped back, slapping sparks from its cover, and hugged it like a rescued child. She turned and dodged the blaze along the path and grabbed Pieter's arm. As the fire billowed forward in a sudden sheet behind her, she and Pieter jumped away and raced around the corner.

"There it is!" cried Pieter, pointing.

The sally-port lay dead ahead.

He spurted forward to open it. Honor staggered on, her strength suddenly spent, her body heavy with its inner burden. The door swung open and she saw the black, yawning square of night beyond. She stepped outside. She was conscious of the ringing blackness of the starless sky. And then, of stumbling endlessly over a pitted moonscape. The rain finally fell. Within an hour they were drenched. But Pieter knew the way to the river bank path that would take them to St. Stephen's-in-the-Woods.

Honor let herself be led.

She awoke because of the singing.

Still half asleep, she was aware that she was nestled in straw in a warm corner of the monks' cow byre. Daylight sifted in through cracks in the wattle-and-daub walls. A light rain whispered on the thatch roof. She closed her eyes and stretched, and the straw released a fragrance of summer meadows. A memory drifted back of the straw in Mrs. Sydenham's attic where she and Thornleigh had last lain together, and an ache to lie again in his embrace, engulfed by the warmth and strength of his body, flooded through her. The shock of reality stabbed—never would she see him again!—and she was overwhelmed with misery.

Then the baby in her belly kicked. She realized she was ravenous.

Around the corner of the cow-stall the singing continued. It was Pieter's solo, sweet, soprano voice blithely caroling a *Kyrie Eleison*. Sharp scrapes of his knife whittling a stick accompanied the tune and kept strict tempo. "*Father, have mercy upon us . . .*"

Honor smiled. The plan had worked. They had met no soldiers, and the monks at the small monastery had been glad to take them in, though, as the Abbot had apologized, their guest house had recently burned, and women, of course, were not allowed in the infirmary. Honor hadn't cared. The Abbot had handed them dry clothing, the byre was warm and snug, and she and Pieter had slid into sleep the moment their weary bodies had collapsed into the straw.

Yes, she smiled to herself: together, she and Pieter had done it.

"The book," she cried, remembering, and sat bolt upright. She pawed the straw, searching for it. It wasn't there. Had she only dreamed she had found it?

Pieter came skidding around the corner. He tossed aside his knife and stick. "I have it, my lady!" He pulled the book out of his shirt and thrust it at her. "See? I kept it safe for you. And I have these for you, too." From his pockets he fished out two small red apples and an egg-sized mound of soft white cheese wrapped in a cabbage leaf.

Honor's eyes darted with longing between the food and the book. Hunger and curiosity battled inside her. Hunger won. She laid the book in her lap and gobbled the cheese, then an apple. Pieter knelt beside her, his face bright.

"The storm is over, my lady," he said, looking at the roof. "It's only a sprinkle now. And Brother Karl is just harnessing his cart to go to Hagen. He says we may go with him, if we will. Shall we?"

By the time they met Brother Karl outside, the rain had completely stopped. Honor thanked the blushing young friar for his offer of transportation. She and Pieter climbed into the back of the cart among a dozen hat-sized rounds of goat cheese tucked into straw. The cart joggled out of the monastery gates and into the dripping woods, and Pieter curled beside Honor and began to doze. Honor watched the monk's back until it jostled along with the easy rhythm of the horse's chinging harness.

Then, with excitement fluttering in her breast, she took up the book. There was no doubt about it: whether it was the original or a copy she did not know, but it was certainly the same book the dying foreigner had thrust into her hands—the hands of a lost, illiterate child—that May Day night seventeen years before. Above Holbein's blue speedwell were the black printed shapes of words that had stared back at her, obstinately hiding their meaning. Now, they proclaimed themselves in bold Latin:

A Treatise on the Immortality of the Soul
By Giulio della Montagna
Doctor of Philosophy
University of Bologna

It was not a long essay. Within an hour she had read it all. Its thesis was simple but—although couched in calm, philosophical logic—wildly heretical. Mankind would do well, this della Montagna was suggesting, to abandon the fairy tale of life after death.

Honor's hand rested gently on the final page. Her heart was racing. Immortality a fairy tale? Something simply made up to placate the human heart, like Pieter's fantasies of saint's bones and miracles? Yes, she thought, immortality is something people desperately want to be true. And, yes, the desire for something to be real does not make it real.

Her mind leaped ahead, charged with the energy of discovery. If immortality was a dream fabricated by man, then, she asked herself, might it be possible that all the other so-called laws of religion were mere fabrications as well? For belief in immortality was the foundation of religion, whether the believer was Catholic or Protestant, or even a Turk. And if that foundation was no more than a mirage—a wish, a hope—then the whole creaking edifice must come crumbling down.

Suddenly, nothing seemed so clear to her, so utterly knowable, than that the childish craving to live eternally in heaven had led mankind to live inside a web of lies on earth.

She *knew* this. She felt that she had always known it.

Had she known it as long ago as the day of Ralph's death? She had blamed an uncaring God and could not pray, but she had realized even then—had she not?—that it was men, not God, who demanded the killing. And when she was so desolate in Münster, her grief and guilt weighing her down so that she had fallen to her knees beside Pieter, ready to pray, at that moment, yes, she had come face-to-face with the truth that she alone could act in her life— could work with or work against the lives around her—and that God, whatever God was, had no part to play. But had she known the *whole* truth that night? The extraordinary, dizzying truth that della Montagna's essay was leading her to see?

Her past beliefs were breaking apart and dispersing like the spores of torn puffballs on the wind; they now seemed just as insubstantial. And as new thoughts tugged the dead roots of superstition and dogma from her mind, clearing space, she saw that she knew the whole truth now. All the fairy-tales—immortality of the soul, heaven and hell, Satan and sin—God himself?—all stood naked and quaking, unmasked as the paltry human fears and desires they had always been. They were fables of reward and punishment to make children obey; to make adults into children.

The realization was exhilarating. It was liberation.

The cart broke out of the woods into sunshine, and Honor let her head fall back, eyes closed, and felt the sun's warmth kiss her eyelids and cheeks. Slowly, a laugh began to bubble up from deep inside her, for the irony was sweet. For seventeen years she had wondered what strange and powerful mystery lay inside the lost little book, but now that she had found the book she saw that she had already discovered its mystery—discovered it all by herself the night she had kneeled in the deanery chapel beside Pieter: life is all.

She turned the final page to close the book and exposed the inside of the back cover. Running diagonally, and marred with several ink blots, were three scrawled lines of text that her child's eyes had comprehended only as three unraveling strings.

I write in haste. They have broken into the house. If any should find this work of mine, I beg you, deliver it to the one who has inspired so much in so many. To Erasmus of Rotterdam.

Her fingertips touched the lines in wonder. So the dying foreigner had been the book's author, della Montagna himself! Of course! Now she recalled his words, so strange sounding at the time: "*I wrote it . . . for you!*" Finally, she understood why he had been able to smile at her that May Day night, though he was dying. It was because he could die in peace, undisturbed by the terrors of a manmade God. Hours later her father had died, too, but deranged with fear at the Church's curse of eternal torment in hell. If only her father could have seen that it was all just words!

The sharp new relief into which those two May Day deaths were now re-cast suddenly overwhelmed her. Understanding took hold of her brain and shook it, like a great spring wind bearing down on a tree to shake loose last year's clutch of shriveled leaves until only the branches remain, clean, stark, ready to bud out into new life. It was a gift of far greater value than della Montagna could ever have imagined he was handing to a child.

Or had he?

"I wrote it . . . for you."

The young monk driving the cart looked over his shoulder at Honor and said shyly, "Hagen is some forty miles off. I hope the journey will not tire the lady?"

"Not at all, Brother," Honor assured him. "A good time for contemplation. And," she added quietly, "it seems it is only the beginning of our journey."

The odd vibrancy in her voice made Pieter turn his head. He flopped onto his back, slapping bits of straw from his bright hair. "A journey?" he asked. "Where are we going, my lady?"

She had not known until a moment ago. She looked out at the grain fields basking in sunshine all around them. They seemed to push the cart onward with their radiance. "We're going to see a priest," she said, smiling with delight at the paradox. "The wisest priest of all. Desiderius Erasmus."

❦ 34 ❦

The Garden at Freiburg

"No! It is not fit for human consumption!"

For most of his seventy years the renowned scholar Desiderius Erasmus had battled parochialism, intolerance, tyranny, and salt fish. Why, Honor thought with a sigh across the supper table, should today be different?

"No better than the slop they used to poison us with at the monastery!" Erasmus cried, his Latin vivid as always. He poked the plate away from him using one finger as if to protect the other digits from contamination.

His housekeeper, a thick-waisted, formidable daughter of the Black Forest with a face like a pork chop, stood glaring over him, the mortal sin of murder simmering in her eyes. "That's good pike, you old fart. A whole pfennig I saved on it! Anyway, what can you expect with the pittance you give me for marketing?" Her German, while every bit as vivid as her master's Latin, was wasted on him. For four years the two had lived in the same house as if in some cell of the Tower of Babel; neither understood a word the other said.

"You thought you could hoodwink me, didn't you? Hide the putrid stuff under one of your noxious sauces. Woman, you underestimate *this*!" he crowed, tapping his nose as he thrust it triumphantly in the air. It was a long, pointed nose, a sharp triangle, and Honor had to laugh at the way it transformed his pale, up-turned face into a sundial.

"It's alright, Marthe," Honor intervened, lifting the offensive dish from Erasmus's place. "We'll send it over to the Frobens. Pieter will love it."

Honor sympathized with Erasmus, for Marthe's cooking was abysmal and her housekeeping just a step above slovenly. Her continued employment with him was a testament to his generous nature; she had come with the house and had no place else to go. "Like you and me," Erasmus had once told Honor with the sigh of self-pity he had perfected to elegance, "the woman is a refugee. From different cities each of us fled to Freiburg, seeking sanctuary from the savagery of the Protestants."

"Though I doubt, sir," Honor had teased him then, "that she had first rejected invitations from the King of France, Mary of Hungary, and Sigismund of Poland, all begging her to make her home with them."

He had fluttered a hand disdainfully. "To be a puppet at their courts, you mean." Pretentiousness was not among Erasmus's many foibles. He had finally accepted the modest house in Freiburg, placed at his disposal by his friend King Ferdinand, the Emperor Charles's brother, mainly because the climate agreed with his delicate health.

Marthe snatched up the plate of fish. "Starve, then, you miserly bag of bones!" she shouted in German.

Not understanding, Erasmus huffed in Latin, "I'll *starve* before I eat such dregs!"

Honor looked from frazzled housekeeper to pouting academic. It was difficult to know to which unlikely creature she owed more. Though he had known Honor only through her letters, the fastidious old bachelor had taken her in, a penniless, pregnant woman with a hungry boy in tow, and had asked no questions. And when she finally came to explain that she had been hunted out of England as a criminal against church and state, Erasmus, who had made non-partisanship an iron principle of his life, merely nodded, offering no recriminations. But Marthe had a strong claim on her too, for it was thanks to her calm midwifery six months ago that

Honor, after a difficult labor, had been safely delivered of a healthy daughter.

"Just bring fruit, please, Marthe," she said, entreating peace. "We'll have it in the garden. And bring Isabel out too, if she's awake." Grudgingly, Marthe accepted Honor's arbitration and flounced into the kitchen.

"Did you really have to eat slop in the monastery?" Honor asked with a smile as she and Erasmus rose. They spoke in Latin, for although Erasmus had once taught at Cambridge—a stint, he assured her, that he had barely endured, aghast as he was at the filth of English houses, and depressed as he became at the backwardness of English letters—Erasmus knew no more than a smattering of the English language.

"Gray salt fish, day in, day out," he answered. "And around us, moldy walls and stinking privies. And a flogging for any infringement of the myriad rules." He shuddered. "Thus are those of callow and tender years disfigured under the pretext of religion."

"Whyever did you stay?"

"As an orphan I was shunted into the monastic life. Once there, and finding a friend or two to lighten my misery, I made the hideous mistake of taking the vows. It was a coarse and frigid life," he concluded mournfully, and tugged his heavy furred robe closer to his throat, though the evening was balmy.

They were strolling arm in arm into the small walled garden, moving slowly, the pace ordained both by Erasmus's arthritic joints and by a mutual wish to savor the golden, early evening light. It gilded everything—the broad leaves of the chestnut tree, the cherry blossoms floating down from frothed branches, the fiery red flowers on the climbing beans.

"Ah," Erasmus smiled as they came to a table where a canvas pouch lay, "Pieter has been feeding the birds again."

"And left the seed out. Again."

"No matter. See? They have come for their supper." He tugged open the pouch's drawstring and scattered a handful of seed. Birds fluttered out of branches and drifted down around their feet. "Is he staying at Froben's again tonight?"

"Yes." Honor smiled. Pieter, now fluent in German, had become entranced with the printing press at the home of Erasmus's publisher and his wife. "And it gets harder to scrub the ink off him each time he comes home. Oh, I haven't told you yet. They've offered to take him on as an apprentice." `

"Ah, that's good," Erasmus said. "He's happy there."

"Happy? He's ecstatic. He talks of nothing but tympans and friskets. And he's positively poetic when he sighs to me of half Gothic and Italic type styles."

Erasmus chuckled. "Just like young Froben's father. Revolutionized the trade. If I did not love that man for introducing Roman type, I positively bless his memory for making my books small and inexpensive. Even a baker's son can afford them. Do you know, when I was a boy—before the printing press—it took twenty-five sheepskins to make enough parchment for a two hundred page text. A fortune! And a scribe needed five months to copy it out."

They sat down together on a bench under the cherry tree. Erasmus flung out another handful of seed.

Honor watched the birds peck in the grass between the flat stones. "You love this place, don't you? This garden where cardinals and princes and learned men come to visit you."

"Most of them strangers, and too many of them fools," he said, eyes twinkling. "But yes, this garden is my blessing. My favorite spot on earth."

"And mine," she said softly. "An island of sanity in a world gone mad." She stretched her legs and her neck, cramped after the afternoon spent at the desk where she was helping Erasmus compile a new edition of his Latin *Adages*. She took a deep breath of the blossom-fragrant air. She had found contentment here. Isabel was her joy. Pieter was thriving. And the sorrow over Thornleigh's death she was trying with all her will to put away, as friends here told her she must. She tried to imagine grief one day coming to an end, like a wound finally run dry of blood. But still, some nights, the flow was impossible to stanch, and came in hemorrhaging tears. However, she was trying to force herself to think of the future for her daughter's sake. To imagine, one day, even going back to England. So far, she had not even written home. Adam, she knew, would be well taken care of by his aunt. For now, it was safer for him, for everyone, if they knew nothing of her whereabouts. Yes, here she'd found security and comfort and, in assisting Erasmus, fulfilling work. Why not peace, then? She rubbed her neck, evading her own question, for she knew that, quite apart from missing Thornleigh every hour of every day, the answer had to do with Sir Thomas. And she did not want to think about Sir Thomas.

"Epicurus would have us spend all our days in gardens," Erasmus was saying.

Honor smiled. "But only with friends. And definitely no fools."

"Then on both scores I am blessed, my dear, since your arrival," he said, patting her hand.

She was moved. "Sir, you honor me."

"Most fitting," he chuckled, "since you are Honor itself."

She leaned back against the tree trunk. Somewhere, far beyond the ivied walls, a woman was singing a lullaby. "Your Garden of Eden," she murmured.

He frowned. "Oh, I hope not. That garden of the Old Testament is a terrifying place. A scene of suspicion and dread, of deceit and fury. And of no turning back. It makes me quite nervous," he said seriously, and Honor laughed. "No," Erasmus said with a smile, "I prefer a quieter garden. Something like More's setting for his *Utopia* is the ideal. His affable storyteller, Raphael, sat on a bench much like this one, I imagine."

Honor ran her fingers along the stone seat. Memories flooded back, despite her will to dam them. "And I first read that tale sitting on a bench under Sir Thomas's own oak trees by his pond," she said.

"That is charming." But Erasmus's smile had already faded at his own inadvertent injection of More's name. These days, they both avoided speaking of him. The news from England was too distressing.

For thirteen months More had been a prisoner in the Tower of London. The day after Honor had arrived in Freiburg, Erasmus had told her all he knew about it. They had been sitting over dinner in this very garden.

"More has refused to swear some reprehensible oath," Erasmus had explained. "The King is calling himself Supreme Head of the Church in England—vanity of vanities!—and Secretary Cromwell has decreed that every man in the kingdom must swear to acknowledge him as such. But More will not do it." He had irritably batted away a fruit fly as if it represented the tyranny of monarchs. "Now More and Bishop Fisher are being held without trial, and accused of misprision of treason, whatever that odious phrase means."

Honor had tried to clamp down her shock at the news. "It means criminal resistance to the government short of conspiracy or rebellion," she had explained, as steadily as she could. "The penalty is imprisonment at the pleasure of the King."

"A shameful king!" Erasmus had said with feeling. "More has served that prideful man for almost twenty years."

Honor had struggled to grasp the scope of Cromwell's gambit. She had suggested this oath to him only as a means of quieting Sir Thomas. But the whole realm made to swear?—it was extraordinary. No, she thought, she should have anticipated Cromwell's thoroughness, she who knew his zeal for efficiency. But Sir Thomas's response had been even more extraordinary. Who could have foreseen it? Indignation had risen in her, sudden and sharp, but unlike Erasmus's hers was not directed at the King. "Why would he take such a reckless stand?" she had said. "How can he be so foolish?"

Erasmus had shrugged. "More is a man of passions."

And then, one drizzly day in November just after Isabel was born, the house in Freiburg had received a further shocking report. Cromwell and King Henry had pushed another Act through Parliament, a new Treason Act. In a stroke, this statute made it high treason to deny the King any of his titles, or to speak or write a word against him. And the penalty for high treason was death.

"How can Englishmen allow it?" Honor had cried. "Making treason out of words alone."

"Still, such words must be *written or spoken* for a man to be in jeopardy, and if I understand this correctly," Erasmus had said, tapping the letter from a former student in England, "More has refused to say *why* he will not take the Oath. As long as he says nothing, it seems he is safe. They cannot execute a man for silence."

After that, they had heard no further news from England until two weeks ago, the first of May. Four Carthusian monks had been executed for refusing the Oath. And Sir Thomas More still lay in the Tower.

From the kitchen came the clang of pots, and the birds foraging in the garden rose in a cloud and hovered in an undulating layer like a shaken blanket, waiting for what would follow, crisis or calm. The blanket broke apart, some birds fluttering again to the ground and some, too timid, spiraling into the cherry tree. Petals drifted down on Honor and Erasmus.

Erasmus spoke up brightly as if to dispel the gloom he had invoked with More's name. "Epicurus's school in Athens was called The Garden, you know. And unlike Plato's Academy and Aristotle's Lyceum he admitted women students. Yes," he said, brushing petals from his lap, "Epicurus's vision is a fine one."

Honor spelled out that vision with mock earnestness, like a pupil reciting a lesson. "Practice of all the virtues, from which pleasure is inseparable. A simple life, quiet and withdrawn, where philosophy becomes the art of living, and where human relationships find their highest expression in friendship."

He smiled. "You have been reading your Lucretius."

"*Your* Lucretius, sir, for I never read his philosophy until now. Your library holds treasures that Sir Thomas's and the Queen's did not."

Erasmus folded his arms contentedly and closed his eyes against the slanting, golden rays. "Epicurus is a perfect example of the immortality men enjoy through books. For what would we know of Epicurus's thought without his student Lucretius's great poem, *On the Nature of Things*?"

"That's the only immortality available, according to Lucretius," Honor teased. From the bench she picked up a cherry blossom, freckled with decay, and twirled it in her fingers, musing. "That dread of God's wrath in Eden that you spoke of—it's really the dread of death, it seems to me."

"Hmmm," he murmured, considering the idea.

"A hard punishment, don't you think, that God should turn his wrath on man simply for tasting of the tree of knowledge? Lucretius suggests that knowledge can dispel the fear of death. If we can understand that the soul dissolves with the body, he says, and that nothing of us exists after, then death is nothing to us."

"So he did," Erasmus nodded dreamily, the master mildly encouraging the student. "The very idea of *not existing* instills the fear that he considered to be the cause of all the passions that disorder men's lives."

"And so," Honor said thoughtfully, intent on the blossom, "we comfort ourselves with the fantasy of immortality."

Erasmus's eyes popped opened. He shifted on the bench. "You cite your Niccolo della Montagna. Again. Forgive me," he grumbled, "I cannot share your enthusiasm for that man's thesis."

She tossed away the blossom. "You must at least admit that the journey his little volume made to find you was a brave one."

"I admit no such thing," he huffed. "Nor can I imagine why della Montagna was so eager, all those years ago, to gift me with such a strange treatise."

"Because, sir," she smiled, "you have been, and are, the beacon of goodwill to those who stalk the lonely frontiers of unconventionality. You champion mankind's ability to reason."

"Ah, the ancient battle: reason over faith," Erasmus sighed, clearly exasperated. "As if God has not given us challenge enough just to live together in harmony. And look how miserably the whole world fails at it!"

Honor was silent for a moment. "Sir Thomas used to tell me that faith is stronger than reason. That since the Church has taught immortality of the soul for so many hundreds of years, and it is believed by so many millions of people, custom bestows truth on the belief, just as custom bestows truth in the law. He used to quote Aquinas's dictum that the natural desire of everyone for immortality proves that the soul is immortal, just as the innate desire of a child to eat proves that there is food."

"Codifying the unknown is a futile pursuit. I, for one, am fully occupied in trying to live *this* life as Christ bade us."

"And I," she said somberly, "am now a long way from Aquinas."

Erasmus looked at her with concern. "My dear," he said, "the immortality of the soul is God's promise to us. The sweet certainty that, with His grace, we will one day dwell with Him."

"Being certain of something does not make it true," was her steady answer. "Take this Polish man who has written you with his extraordinary proofs that the earth revolves around the sun. Copernicus? Is that his name?"

"A mathematical theorem only."

"But what if it is true? Then all those people who are *certain* that the sun revolves around the earth are wrong. Have been wrong for centuries. And we may have deluded ourselves about the life of the soul in just the same way. Della Montagna says that, like the mule who has all the instruments of generation but cannot attain it, man yearns for immortality but cannot attain it. Della Montagna says—"

"'*Della Montagna says*' . . . Are you a parrot?" he cried. "Can you not think for yourself?"

"Indeed I can, sir," she said with quiet fierceness. "But to speak truly of where my thinking has brought me would be to grieve you more than I already have, and that I am loath to do."

For a few moments they sat in strained silence.

"Where is that wretched woman with our wine?" Erasmus said testily.

"Sir," Honor blurted, "consider this. If man has created the concept of immortality simply to ease his fears of death, then surely we must ask whether other beliefs are not mere fabrications as well. Whether the fables of Heaven and Hell have been plumped up by generations of churchmen and legislators merely to keep citizens on the straight path. Even whether—"

"No!" He threw up his hands and turned away. "Do not say it. Over that precipice I can never follow you." He looked back at her, his face drawn as if with pity. "A godless universe? How can you bear to imagine it? How could we live on in such darkness? How find any structure for morality?"

"But should we allow fear to create untruths?"

"Some things are unknowable. They *must* be taken on faith."

"What you call faith Epicurus calls conjecture. Man can only conjecture whatever does not appear, he says, and he warns that when man does so, thought moves into a sphere where error is possible."

"Good heavens, child, Epicurus lived before God revealed the truth of Christianity!"

"But men continue to tear one another's throats for conjecturing—and in the name of God."

"I have always taught that it is madness to do so."

"And I revere you for that. Yet you remain loyal to a Church that burns people for questioning. For tasting of the tree of knowledge."

"For years I have begged the Church—popes and cardinals—to desist from such violence. Inquisitions and heresy-hunting are abominable to me."

"But the Church teaches—"

"The Church, like every other institution, is flawed by the nature of human desires. By abuses and wicked practices. But these are not reflections of true Christian behavior. We must all advance in faith and love, and leave the unknowable to God." He sighed heavily. "But my voice is drowned out in the cacophony of the age."

She held her tongue, for she saw that she had distressed him. He was an old soldier in the battle against intolerance, one of the first, and armed only with his eloquence. When all around him howled down his pacifism as cowardice, or as a lack of Christian steadfastness, he remained the only leader unwilling to kill for his beliefs. Tolerance remained his obsession, and his despair.

"The hope," Erasmus said with a strength of will that belied his weary face, "lies in all of us rejecting the *externalities* of religion. We must focus on its substance, on the desire for peace and brotherhood that is the truest imitation of Christ. No—" he shook his head—"I cannot repudiate a Church that has endured for fifteen hundred years, has brought the light of education and hope to millions, and still teaches at its core the blessed message of love for one another that Christ bequeathed us. The Church has been my mother, and until a better way is shown me, I will remain with Her."

Honor was moved by his conviction, ashamed at having aggravated him. He was not the enemy. It was pettiness to harass him. She touched his arm, offering peace, and there was a twinkle in her eye. "You remain with her but will not accept elevation in her ranks?" Upon Pope Clement's death eight months before, the new Pope Paul III had immediately offered Erasmus the red hat of a cardinal.

"No," Erasmus smiled, relaxing, charmed by her finesse. "Not that. When God calls me from this raving world, I intend to die as I have lived. A free man."

The garden gate clattered. Again the birds on the ground lifted and hovered. "Pears and wine!" Marthe called as if she were hawking her wares.

"Pears and wine," Honor translated gently to Erasmus.

He made a vinegar face and muttered, "The latter, no doubt, abominably watered. It *was* a splendid Burgundy, sent me by the Bishop of Cracow. Thank the Lord there's nothing she can do to destroy a pear."

"Now, now," Marthe cooed to the baby straddling her hip. "Enough of that, my pet. Not for you, my little darling." She was waddling towards them with the dessert on a tray, and the baby was reaching across her ample bosom for the fruit. Marthe clattered the tray onto the table.

"There she is," Erasmus cried, rising. "Little Isabel!" He bent like a doting grandfather to tickle the baby's chin.

Marthe slapped his hand. "Don't strangle the poor child!" She pivoted sharply to disengage him from the baby.

"Witch!" Erasmus sputtered. "You'll snap her neck doing that!"

"Keep your claws off her!" Marthe warned.

"I'll take her," Honor said with a laugh. She held out her arms, and the other two capitulated to her superior claim. She took Isabel onto her knee, kissed the soft cheek, and smiled into the bright, round eyes—as speedwell-blue as Richard Thornleigh's.

Marthe and Erasmus crowded in, prattling and cooing. The baby crowed with delight. Honor could not help laughing. "And to think, little one, that I worried you'd grow up without a family."

"A child cannot have family enough," Erasmus said definitively. "I never knew my own father. My poor parents—did I tell you? . . ."

Marthe groaned, sensing he was beginning a long-winded, incomprehensible story, and turned and waddled back to the house. Erasmus, triumphant, lifted the baby into his arms. "My poor parents," he continued to Honor, "had desperately wanted to marry, but my mother's family forced them apart as soon as her condition became apparent, and then spread the evil lie to my father that his beloved had died. In grief, he took priest's vows."

Honor had to smile. Erasmus had recited this romantic tale for so many years, he had convinced himself of its authenticity. But Johannes Froben had told her the facts. Erasmus, it seemed, had conveniently forgotten both that his father was already a priest when his parents had met, and that the couple's long-standing relationship had also produced a brother for Erasmus—one three years his senior.

Erasmus plumped the baby back on Honor's lap and sat with a deep, self-pitying sigh. "And I, orphaned, and dumped into a foul monastery."

Honor wrapped her arms loosely around her daughter and nuzzled her neck. She brushed her lips absently over the silken head. Above the garden, the light was fading. "Monasteries," she mused, her thoughts dragged again by the tide of memory. "You hated the experience, yet Sir Thomas always spoke fondly of his years with the Carthusian monks."

"Ah, the Carthusians," Erasmus murmured with a shiver. He and Honor exchanged glances. At the beginning of May, the latest report from England had deeply shaken them both. The four Carthusian monks who had also refused to take the Oath had been dragged out of the Tower on hurdles. At Tyburn, before a great crowd, they were butchered—first hanged until they choked, then cut down still living and, one by one in front of the others, castrated, disemboweled, and beheaded. The monks had been the only other men in England besides Sir Thomas More and Bishop Fisher who had refused the Oath. The barbarous method of their execution was the standard penalty for traitors.

The baby whimpered. Erasmus was pulling himself slowly to his feet. Lost in thought, he tugged his heavy robe about him as Honor loosened her bodice to feed the baby. "I wish," Erasmus said, "that More had never meddled in this dangerous business. It is perilous striving with princes!" He sighed heavily. "I feel the chill. I shall go in."

He heard the baby's sucking and looked back at the contented child and mother. "Ah, the picture of peace," he said, smiling fondly. "Yes, stay, my dear. Enjoy the last of the light. I want to check a reference in Cicero before I retire." As he padded across the flagstones the birds fluttered up again in a mass and finally made their exodus over the garden wall.

For some time Honor remained in the garden. The baby lay dreaming in her arms, the rosebud mouth still sucking gently in sleep. The sky glowed darkly, as blue as a cave of sapphires, and it made black lace of the ivy that tendriled the tops of the walls.

No, she thought, Erasmus was wrong. She was not the picture of peace. Her thoughts did not bring peace. When she lay down, the finger of guilt that pressed on her forehead throughout the night would not bring peace. And her bold rhetoric to Erasmus? What good was all her fearless prattle about the universe when she could not even resolve the turmoil in her own breast? Confusion, anger, guilt. The King and Cromwell had lured Sir Thomas into their prison. But she had given them the key.

❧ 35 ❧

The Cardinal's Hat

King Henry stood with arms outstretched like a crucified man as the tailor's apprentice tugged at the measuring tape around his waist. "What do you mean, adjustments?" Henry growled. He glared down, and the flesh of his neck folded upon itself. "You mean I am grown fat?"

The nervous master tailor snatched the tape from his apprentice. "Pardon, Your Majesty! My idiot boy here must have made an error." He cuffed the apprentice on the back of the head, then personally measured the King. The tape read fifty-four inches: a mammoth gain since Christmas. Sweat erupted on the tailor's forehead. Twenty years ago, when he had been an apprentice himself, the King's waist had been a trim thirty-four inches. An inch for every year since! He swallowed and shot a grin up at the flabby royal jowls. "In any case, sire, what is an inch or two to your expert craftsmen? A mere nothing." He shuffled backwards, flicking his hands at his two apprentices, the order to pack up. "I promise Your Majesty the new armor will look splendid."

Henry's grunt was sour with self-pity. "Body of God, they used to call *me* splendid, not my armor." He looked forlornly around the room, begging comfort, but Anne was staring out the window and Bastwick, writing at a desk, seemed not to have heard the conversation.

"Splendid, indeed, Your Majesty," the tailor agreed, herding his underlings on ahead. He crept backwards out of the bedchamber, bowing and murmuring. "Thank you, Your Majesty. Good day, Your Majesty . . ." His voice finally dwindled away.

Anne turned to Henry and burst out in anger. "Well? Is it true? About Mary?" Moments ago she had stormed in with the question boiling in her mouth but had bitten it back until the tailor had gone. "Tell me!"

Henry clenched his teeth.

"The whole palace is whispering of it, you know," Anne said. "That you actually went crawling to your daughter. That she's refused to take the Oath. Again."

"Madam, this is not the time to indulge your spleen. I am to meet the new papal envoy any moment now, and—"

"Just tell me if it's true."

Henry mustered what cold civility he could. "It is."

"By all that's holy!" Anne exploded. "If I had a child that obstinate I'd bash her head against the wall till it was soft as a baked apple. How can you grovel so before her insults?"

"Good heavens," Henry said, nonplused, "Mary is of my blood."

"You have another daughter. Elizabeth is of *our* blood. And *she* is not a bastard."

Henry's voice roared out, "But still, madam, *I have no son!*"

The room seemed to buckle at his sudden fury. Bastwick's fingers involuntarily squeezed his pen. Anne's face turned pale as chaff. She crossed to the door, her brocaded skirt hissing over the carpet, and swept out.

"Bah!" Henry flopped into the chair across from Bastwick and clawed at the pearl-crusted collar that chafed him. For the audience with the new Pope's envoy he was dressed very finely in a ruby-studded, white satin doublet and gold-embroidered, red taffeta gown. "You are fortunate in your celibacy, Father." He sighed gloomily. "I was intended for the Church, you know. Sometimes I think it is a life I should have preferred, had my brother Arthur lived to rule."

Bastwick murmured over his writing, "God had more glorious plans for you, Your Majesty."

Henry toyed with a quill, as fidgety as a schoolboy. "That I would not know," he grumbled. "God keeps His plans secret from me." He tossed the quill aside. "Curse the woman, she goes too far with Mary! She's stripped her of her household, you know. Forced her to act as lady-in-waiting to Elizabeth, too. Mary, a Princess of nineteen, waiting on a baby. Anne hopes to break her." He chewed his lip for a moment, brooding. "And people are whispering. They're saying Mary's sickness last month was the result of poison from Anne's hand."

Calmly, Bastwick dipped his quill. "The people are cattle, sire. They also say," he added contemptuously, "that the Queen is a witch."

Henry was gazing at his hand. His eyes, between puffy lids above and puffy pouches below, were slits like those of a lizard. "She does have a sixth finger, you know. A pulpy, half-formed thing. She's clever and hides it with her long sleeves." He looked up. Fear glinted in the eyes caged behind the flesh. "Is that not a sign of Satan, Father?"

Bastwick cleared his throat diplomatically. "The Queen is not unwise to fear your many enemies."

"But is my daughter really my enemy?" Henry whined.

"Your Majesty," Bastwick said patiently, "I have *told* you of the plots that the Emperor's ambassador is breeding, and all his evil hopes are founded on the Dowager Princess and the Lady Mary. Those two are the lightning rods through which the Emperor's might will strike at you."

Henry slumped lower in the chair.

"In the North," Bastwick continued, "we know Thomas Dacre of Greystock has pledged support for the Dowager Princess. Now, we suspect the Earl of Northumberland and the barons Lord Hussey and Thomas Darcy as well."

"How the nest of vipers grows."

"Daily, I fear. In the West George Neville, Lord Abergavenny—"

"Neville? Body of God, I beheaded his father-in-law Bucking-ham fourteen years ago. Is this another of the family come to hound me?" Henry sighed, suddenly marooned in the past. "I can't recall . . . what was it Buckingham did, all those years ago? Treason, of course, but what exactly was the plot Wolsey uncovered? Strange how the details blur."

"In the Southeast," Bastwick plowed on, "there is a formidable array whispering against you, Your Majesty, led by Sir Thomas Burgoyne and the Earl of Rutland. And Lord Edmund Bray, I have heard, has reported to the Imperial ambassador that at least twenty great gentlemen and over a hundred knights are eager to take up defense for the old Queen and the old religion. Then there's the Earl of Shrewsbury, and the Marquis of Exeter, and the Poles— both Henry Lord Montague and Sir Geoffrey—and even, in exile Reginald—"

"I know, I know. Catherine always hoped for a marriage there, Reginald Pole and Mary."

"You must never allow that, Your Majesty. As things stand, these men grumble treason in separate corners of the realm, but behind an alliance of Pole, with his Plantagenet royal blood, and the Lady Mary, whom many feel to be your true heir, your enemies would swiftly unite."

Henry groaned. "It's true. Inside my very realm enemies surround me. And outside, England stands in such weak isolation. The French have walked away from talks for a marriage between Mary and the Dauphin. The Scots are seeking an alliance with the Emperor. Where are the allies I need? Where are the friends? And now," he cried, "my own daughter cannot be trusted."

"No more than the Dowager Princess," Bastwick warned.

Henry wagged a finger. "Now there, Father, you are in error. The old woman is a trial, to be sure, with her whimpering letters from her sickbed, but she has never evaded my authority. Nor ever will, not even to save her life. That," he said with a sneer, "is why the people love her." He pointed to a paper on the table lying apart from Bastwick's tidy sheaves. "Just look at that, you'll see what I mean."

Bastwick quickly read the letter. Catherine was again begging her husband's permission that Mary be allowed to live with her. She concluded with:

For my part, I pardon you everything, and devoutly pray God that he will pardon you also. For the rest, I commend you unto our daughter Mary, beseeching you to be a good father unto her. Lastly, I make this vow, that mine eyes desire you above all things.

Henry snorted. "Pitiful, is it not?"

"Oh, take heed, Your Majesty," Bastwick said warmly. "The lady Catherine is a proud, stubborn woman of very high courage. If she took it into her head to take her daughter's part she could with little effort muster a great array and wage a war against you as fierce as any her mother, Isabella, ever waged in Spain."

Henry's eyes narrowed. The war Isabella had waged in Spain had overturned the throne of Castile.

"With or without her outright encouragement," Bastwick urged, "these rebel lords are prepared to rally around her standard, confident that under her they can consolidate their gains, confident of a leader whose views about the old religion are their own, and whose personal popularity is their best link to the masses. And if these lords do rise up against you in her name, the Emperor can do no other than send support for his aunt. The Bishop of Rome as well."

At the mention of the Pope, under whose edict he remained an excommunicate, Henry's fingers curled around the arms of his chair as if to throttle them. He looked at Bastwick with a flash of irritation and disbelief. "But how could Catherine manage it, marooned out in the fens at Kimbolton? God's blood, she's more closely watched than a virgin. And since my officers replaced her staff, she refuses even to leave her private rooms. She's more strictly imprisoned by her own pride than by any order of mine."

"I beg Your Majesty to look about you with more care," Bastwick pleaded. "The Dowager Princess may not lead, but in her name others will."

Henry frowned like a man reaching a sturdy-looking bridge he has been told is rotten: he was cautious, yet unwilling to yield to a danger so invisible. "But who? I know the men you mention. Northumberland. George Talbot. Edmund Bray. Courtney of Exeter. I know their natures. Without a rallying call from Catherine, which I tell you she will never give, none of these lords would dare to move."

"And the men who are not lords?"

"You mean the drunkards in the taverns? All that tap talk about the bad harvests since I put away the old Queen?" Henry waved a heavy hand, dismissing the threat. "Cromwell is dealing with that. Hanged men say no slander."

"No, sire, I mean the men you hold in your Tower. Fisher and More. The whole realm knows of their opposition to your will, and of their love for the old Queen. The potential rebel lords at least have sworn the Oath, but Fisher and More have not. A word from either one, and the rebels will cease to merely grumble. They will muster."

Henry squirmed, then hauled himself from the chair. He moved to the window and looked out, his hands balled on either side of the casement.

Bastwick spoke to the massive back. "And of the two, sire, Sir Thomas More is the one you must fear. Bishop Fisher is old and has little fight left in him, and the people have no love for such a prince of the old Church. Indeed, he has shouted so long against your policies that many feel he has led himself into the Tower. But More is a layman. And well liked. And his silence has moved many hearts."

Henry's voice was very low. "Thomas could always do that. Could always move people with that gifted tongue of his. Now, with his silence, he moves them still."

His fist thudded on the wall. "Moves them against *me*! God's body, all have turned against me." Rhythmically, his fist pounded the stone. "Wife. Daughter. Friend. All turned into enemies."

There was a soft knock. The door opened. The royal chamberlain swept in, smiling with excitement. "The papal envoy is arrived, Your Majesty. He waits in your Presence chamber."

Henry's shoulders shivered as if to shake Thomas More from his back. He shunted himself around and stood with feet wide apart. "Well? What's he like?"

"Most cordial, Your Majesty. An elderly, courtly gentleman. And, he says he is eager to give you great news."

Henry's eyebrows shot up. "Is he now?" He thrust his thumbs into his sash and pulled himself up to his full height, and his lungs inflated with the vigor of kingship. He glanced at Bastwick. "Well, Father, shall we see this eager pigeon from Rome? Perhaps he brings a clean slate with him. Come!"

Following the chamberlain, they strode together across the private chamber, then through the withdrawing room. A guard opened the door to the audience chamber, and a plump of gentlemen chatting near the canopied throne quieted for the King's entrance. Henry stopped for a moment in the doorway. He cast a small royal smile on the Roman envoy whose ingratiating bow took his white head lower than the silver knob of his walking stick.

At this show of deference, Henry beamed. He leaned to Bastwick and whispered, "Perhaps God has heard my prayers, Father. This new Pope may be ready to bargain after all."

"I'll get it yet!" Honor laughed. She was panting from the exercise. "You can't run away!" She was straddling the path to the gate in Erasmus's garden, her arms stretched out to her sides to cut off Pieter's route of escape.

Pieter was grinning and panting, too, from the game. He had just come with the Frobens from their house, and Johannes Froben, master printer, had proudly announced to Honor that Pieter had brought her a sample of his first solo work at the press. But Pieter, red-faced as he pulled the paper from his pocket, had been shy to present it; too many mistakes in it, he said. Honor had laughed and reached for it, but Pieter had jumped back, and soon the thing had become a contest. She had already chased him three times around the vegetable patch where Marthe was on her knees ruthlessly thinning a riot of carrot seedlings.

Honor wiped sweat from her upper lip. "Oho, you're in trouble now!" Her grin was full of exuberant menace as she began a predatory stalk toward him.

"To the tree, boy!" Froben shouted through his laughter. He

THE QUEEN'S LADY 483

and his wife had been watching the chase from the bench under the cherry tree. Baby Isabel was solemnly watching, too, sitting on the grass between their feet. "Get behind the chestnut tree!" Froben urged.

Pieter darted sideways toward the thick trunk. Honor sprang after him, almost on his heels. She swiped his shoulder, but he zigzagged out of her grasp. She lost her balance and lurched forward in an ungainly stumble, her arms windmilling to regain her balance.

The baby gurgled with delight and clapped tiny hands that were stiff with glee. That made Katerina Froben laugh so hard she had to lean against her husband's shoulder.

Honor was laughing, too, and she was bending over with her hands on her knees to catch her breath when she heard the garden gate close behind her. A moment later she felt Erasmus's bony hand grasp her elbow. She turned and was about to laughingly explain the mayhem in his garden, but he interrupted her.

"News," he blurted.

She looked at his haggard eyes. This news could only be bad. "From England?"

Erasmus nodded, swallowing. He was out of breath as well. It appeared he had hurried to get home. Honor led him to a chair under an awning that stretched out beneath his upstairs study. As they both caught their breath, she glanced back at the others. Pieter had run up to the trio at the bench holding a huge sunflower in front of his face like a mask, and he was creating great hilarity as he ran around them in circles making lionlike roars.

Erasmus sat shaking his head in bewilderment. "So strange. So unaccountable. Is this new Pope bloody-minded or simply an imbecile?"

"The Pope? What do you mean, sir? What has happened?"

"The Pope has named Bishop Fisher a cardinal!"

"You mean, King Henry has released Fisher?" A spark of hope flared in her breast. If one prisoner had been freed, she thought, why not the other? "Released Sir Thomas, too?"

Erasmus groaned. "I mean no such thing."

"Then how —?"

"The Pope, whether utterly blind to the events in England or simply wanting to terrify the King—who knows to what purpose?—sent his envoy to London to declare the appointment of Fisher as Cardinal. I just bumped into Hendrich in the square. His factor was doing business at the London court when it happened. He said the King was in a rage as never before."

A hand tightened around Honor's heart. "Why, what has he done?"

Erasmus pulled off his velvet cap and distractedly raked long fingers through his gray hair. He went on as if trying to make sense of the disaster. "Apparently, at the announcement, the King strode up to the envoy, a frail old gentleman, and snatched his walking stick from him and cracked it in two across his knee. He pointed a jagged end into the envoy's face and shouted that very gladly would he see his bishop tricked out in a new, red hat—and to be sure of a proper fit, he would send Bishop Fisher's head to Rome!"

Honor closed her eyes.

"And then the King stormed off, and several heard him say that he would not rest until he saw both the traitors' heads impaled on London Bridge. He'd have it done, he swore, before the Feast of St. John."

Erasmus threw up his hands in a gesture of helplessness. "Ah!" he sighed, "what a chaos of misfortune my old friend More has brought on himself. Truly, it is perilous striving with princes."

He edged from the chair. "I must go and send a message to our Bishop. Perhaps something can yet be done . . . a letter to the Pope . . . a plea to the King. Though," he murmured, moving toward the house, "I fear that there is little hope." At the door he glanced back at Honor. "Gracious Savior, what a world!" He hurried inside.

Alone in the shade of the awning Honor stared out at the garden. Its sun-hot colors felt suddenly blinding. Sir Thomas was about to die. Within the month. She would be sitting in this quiet garden, and across the Channel the ax would clang, severing his head from his body. And that would be the end of it. The end of the man who murdered Ralph Pepperton. Who gleefully sent

Humphrey Sydenham to the stake, and loosed his dogs to run down Brother Frish. The end of his hold on her. And would she then rejoice? Rejoice to know that Sir Thomas More was dead?

Slightly dizzy, she turned her head. Beside the kitchen window two lean dragon-flies were dancing their silent courtship in midair. They alighted on the window sill, their bodies joined and trembling together in the sun.

She realized that Pieter was standing in front of her. Smiling shyly, he held out the exercise he had printed on Froben's press. He thrust the paper into her hand, then dashed back to join the others.

Honor's eyes strayed down to the Latin words. The text Pieter had used for practice was St. Paul's letter to the Corinthians.

> Though I speak with the tongues of men and of angels and have not charity, I am become as sounding brass, or a tinkling cymbal.
>
> And though I have the gift of prophecy and understand all mysteries and all knowledge; and though I have all faith, so that I could remove mountains, and have not charity, I am nothing . . .
>
> When I was a child I spake as a child, I understood as a child. But when I became a man I put away childish things . . .
>
> And now abideth faith, hope, charity, these three; but the greatest of these is charity.

Honor stared at the paper. Some of the letters were slightly crooked. The last line was imprinted too faintly, and there was an error in the spelling of *'fides'*—faith. Yet . . . *Out of the mouths of babes*, she thought. Pieter. Despite all that has been done to him he lives without rancor. In his prayers he still remembers the priest who used and abandoned him. Pieter lives in charity.

She lowered the page. Slowly, an answer began to lap at the edges of her mind. The restlessness of weeks, the ambivalent anger of months washed away. All that was left was the knowledge that Sir Thomas was part of her. To imagine him dying was to die a little herself.

He had taught her to read. Taught her to think. "A book is like an acorn," he had once told her on the bench under the oaks. "Just as the acorn holds within itself a colossal tree, a book holds within itself whole other worlds." She saw that everything that had come to her in the years that had followed—the wrestlings of her conscience, the striving for some better social order, the fulfillment of love and the despair at its loss, the disillusionment at the self-deception of the world and the hunger to know why men craved such self-deception—all this turmoil was nothing less than life itself. And the turmoil, the sweet, exasperating search—consciousness, in fact—had begun at Sir Thomas's side. If consciousness was life, then life was what she owed him.

She looked across the garden. Pieter stood grinning over Isabel and gently waving the sunflower, as large and as sunny as his face. He swept it like a sorcerer's wand over the baby's head as if he were invoking some shield of safe-keeping to surround her. Isabel's arms shot up to touch it. Pieter flopped to his knees with a disarming smile, as if to say she had vanquished him, and he handed her the flower. The Frobens laughed gently.

Honor felt tears spring, yet she was smiling. What a circle her search had led her in! Strengthened by Della Montagna's little book, she had cleared her mind to ask the most forbidden question of all: had man created God? But St. Paul—and Pieter—had cleared her heart to ask the only question worth asking. What did it matter if God existed or not when love and duty on earth required all of one's self, both heart and mind?

It had taken only moments to realize that she did not want Sir Thomas to die. It took only a heartbeat more to realize that she could not *allow* him to die.

The Feast of St. John the Baptist, the King had threatened. Midsummer Day. Little more than three weeks off. Twenty-four days to race from Freiburg to London.

She heard Isabel's cry. Her breasts tightened, the need in her baby's voice tugging forth her milk. She looked at the child and felt the stab of separation. Heavens, was she mad? Abandon her child? Return to England? No, no, the risks were too great! If Bastwick should catch her . . . Erasmus was right. Sir Thomas had brought this crisis on himself. What had she been thinking of?

She hurried toward the bench where the crying child sat with the Frobens. Just then Pieter lifted Isabel up in his arms. Isabel kept crying and stretched out both hands to the couple who stood and crowded in, concerned. Marthe, too, was on her feet, slapping dirt off her apron and hobbling closer. Honor stopped at the scene before her. Anxious, generous faces encircled her baby. Even Erasmus's white face had poked out from the open window of his study to look down. Pieter hugged Isabel and rocked her. Isabel stopped crying. Then, she snatched a fistful of Pieter's golden hair. "Ouch! Isabel!" he cried, wincing, and the others laughed, even the baby.

Honor saw that she was not needed. Again, Sir Thomas's crisis returned to her mind. But, she agonized, if she went, what would become of her child? The hollowness of losing Richard was still agony enough, but to lose Isabel, too . . .

Losing Richard. The cutting fact loomed larger than all others, still. It flayed her, still. She bled, still. And felt drained. Did it really matter, she asked herself, if Bastwick caught her? If Bastwick killed her? Life without Richard was a drab thing. And if, in hazarding that life, she could save Sir Thomas . . . if she could act one last time, act boldly out of love, not hate . . .

Honor watched the happy faces before her, feeling frozen, as if her body had disappeared from their view. Yet her spirit seemed to be floating above them all, just as Pieter's giant sunflower had floated over Isabel. She had no choice, she realized. Life beckoned to Isabel with outstretched arms, and whether her life's beginning was spent with her mother or with others, her bright future was undimmed as long as there was love. And, looking at these friends around her, who could doubt that there was love?

But for Sir Thomas all that beckoned was death.

She realized she was trembling. She closed her eyes. "Forgive me, Richard," she whispered. "For this one, last risk, forgive me. It is a debt I owe."

* * *

Thornleigh let himself be pulled up the dark nave of Münster cathedral, though he feared what the child might be taking him to see.

"Deurvorsts," the boy repeated eagerly, tugging Thornleigh's sleeve and pointing toward a chapel in the north transept. Deurvorst was the name Thornleigh had asked about as he had wandered for hours around the smoking city piled with emaciated corpses. This filthy boy had seemed to know the name, and, for a handful of coins which Thornleigh had gratefully poured into his small grimy hand, he was now leading Thornleigh to the end of the nave. Thornleigh felt light-headed from the mixture of dread and hope, for this could be the end of his search. But would it be an end that he could bear to see?

The search—months of dejected slogging punctuated by moments of optimism—had brought him this morning to the outskirts of Münster where an inn-keeper had sworn that Honor, with the Dutch couple, had entered the city just before the siege had begun. And so, before Münster's walls, all Thornleigh's hopes had stood ready to be fulfilled or blasted. The latter—he tried to face the fact—was by far the more likely, for he had arrived the morning after the Prince-Bishop von Waldeck's troops had finally smashed into the city and taken their awful vengeance.

He and Legge had pushed their way past the others sifting through the gates in the wake of the destruction—camp followers; frantic people seeking relatives; looters and foragers—and Thornleigh had seen sights he would never forget, though he knew he would try all his life to do so. Ten-year-old girls had been raped and strangled. Old men—the Anabaptist "Elders"—had been flayed, some left to swing in chains from the town hall, some pushed from church towers to be dashed onto the cobbles below. The erstwhile leader of these people, "King" Jan of Leyden, had been strapped naked to a sizzling-hot iron throne in the market square, and a sizzling crown lowered to sear his skull. His twisted, enthroned, putrefying corpse still sat upright in a mockery of kingship. The foragers skirted it, crossing themselves.

And the inhabitants had been put to the sword. Only a handful of scrawny boys—Angels, they called themselves—had been nimble enough to evade the soldiers in the onslaught. Now, the soldier's blood-lust had been slaked, and the boys felt bold enough to emerge. Thornleigh's guide was one of these. But they appeared to be the only survivors. Most of the inhabitants, in fact, had died of starvation before the attack.

If Honor was alive in this cathedral, Thornleigh knew, it would be a miracle.

The child tugged him into a small chapel. "Deurvorsts," he said again, and again he pointed, triumphantly.

Thornleigh froze. Spread-eagled on top of the marble tomb of a crusader baron was the naked corpse of a middle-aged woman, dried blood clotted between her thighs. Below her feet a man's headless body sat slumped against the tomb, a Dutch Bible stuffed into the bloodied cavity of his neck. The chapel held only these two dead people. No living being.

Thornleigh staggered out of the cathedral into the light. Afraid he might retch, he lowered himself onto the stone steps. The corpse-putrefied air of the street sickened him further. He lowered his head between his knees.

If she was in this city, somewhere among the mutilated dead, he did not want to know it.

"Sir?"

Thornleigh looked up. Legge stood before him. Even he had been made white-faced by hideous Münster.

"Place is a bloody charnel house," Legge murmured, sitting with a thud beside Thornleigh.

Thornleigh looked out at the city square. A company of soldiers on horseback clattered arrogantly through, sending the knots of scavengers scuttling aside. Thornleigh watched a woman at the bottom of the cathedral steps as she tugged the boots off a dead man and handed them to a child with a sack of booty larger than himself.

"Sir," Legge said, not without sympathy. "It'd be a miracle if she'd lived through this."

Thornleigh flinched at this echo of his own desolate thoughts. He nodded slowly. In long-besieged Münster, where most had starved to death, the rest now lay massacred.

Could he hope for a miracle?

Thornleigh buried his face in his hands. He had never believed in miracles.

❧ 36 ❧

The Bell Tower

Summer thunder rumbled above the Tower of London.
It was dusk. Honor walked behind a guard up to the portcullis
of the Lion Tower, the first of the three gate towers that defended
the entrance across the moat. Like an executioner's drumroll, the
thunder accompanied her all along the route into the ancient
fortress. She passed over the moat bridge, her eyes fixed on the
stone nest of fortifications that loomed ahead. Royal garrison and
arsenal for four hundred and fifty years, the Tower's layers of en-
compassing walls had been added by generations of medieval
kings to protect their palace and armories, treasury and mint.
Though surrendered more than once by the garrison in civil wars,
the fortress had never been taken by force.

Rising at its center was the gleaming cube of the White Tower
built by the Conqueror, its four, capped turrets flaring under flashes
of dry lightning high in the iron clouds. The White Tower stood
impregnable inside two square curtain walls, one wall enclosing
the other, both muscled with towers. On the wharf the King's ordnance bristled towards the river.

Once over the moat bridge Honor followed the guard through
the Byward Tower in the first curtain wall. To her right, Traitor's
Gate yawned over the river. To her left, at the corner of the inner
curtain wall, rose the Bell Tower. It was named for the bell on its

round roof that had sounded curfew for over three hundred years. The Bell Tower contained only two chambers. The lower one was Sir Thomas More's cell.

In the inner ward they entered the house of the Lieutenant, Sir Edmund Walsingham.

"Ten minutes, mistress," Walsingham said, scraping his key into the iron-barred door of the Bell Tower. They stood at the end of a corridor in his residence. It was the only entrance to More's cell.

"Ten minutes!" Honor protested. She pointed to the paper he held, which she had just given him. "But Sir William included no such order." Sir William Kingston, Walsingham's superior, was the Constable of the Tower and a long-time friend of both Sir Thomas More and Queen Catherine. Gambling on his loyalty to these old friendships, and that he would be ignorant of her criminal status in the eyes of the Church, Honor had visited Sir William's London house that morning. The visit had been a huge risk, but as soon as Sir William received her, smiling, she knew she had guessed right: Bastwick's vendetta against her was a personal one that had not involved officers of the state. Sir William had amiably asked what he could do for her. She had begged one interview with More.

Walsingham crushed the paper in his fist. "The Constable may have given you leave, mistress," he said, "but Secretary Cromwell gives orders, too. And when Master Secretary is displeased he's been known to stretch a man's neck longer than is good for his health. Ten minutes."

He swung open the iron door. Honor looked onto a spiral staircase. Lit by one narrow window slit higher up, the staircase appeared dim and cold in the sickly light of the approaching storm. Behind Honor, lightning streaked the corridor.

She stepped in. The door clanged. Walsingham's retreating steps faded. Honor went down. The staircase coiled once into darkness. At the bottom, candlelight groped out across the stairwell. Honor's stomach tightened with dread. Sir Thomas had been in prison for fourteen months. Would she come upon him in rags, slumped in a corner, babbling? She stepped off the last stair and stopped. More was standing in the center of a small room, straight and calm. His body blocked the single flame guttering on a table behind him. His face was in shadow, for he was looking directly at her.

"Is that . . . ?" He hesitated and peered through the gloom.

Honor stared back. He was very thin. Lank clumps of gray hair reached for his shoulders like blind men's fingers. She had never seen his face anything but clean-shaven; now his beard, also gray, crept halfway down his chest. At the sides of the collar of his dusty gown the wirelike threads of his hair shirt needled out.

"It is!" More cried softly. A small laugh escaped him. "Had I known I need only be cast into prison to entice you to visit, child, I would have contrived to fall afoul of the law much sooner."

Honor relaxed as two fears dissolved: his wits had not deserted him, and clearly he knew nothing of her former work. Either case would have made her mission here almost impossible.

"Come in, come in!" he said brightly.

Honor took a step into the stone cell. It stank of mousy straw, damp masonry, and urine. Two windows, long slits deep in the stone, allowed in the murky twilight. In front of the table, bare but for the candle, there was a stool and a chair. A straw pallet lay in one corner; in another, an empty grate.

"Please, sit," More beckoned, indicating the chair. "My servant—you remember John a Wood?—is gone to buy an egg or two from the captain's wife for our dinner. Several fine hens she keeps, though their eggs are somewhat tough." He was dusting the chair for her with a fold of his gown. "But an egg's an egg," he laughed. "I survived far worse fare as an undergraduate at Oxford. Sit, please. I am so glad to see you, child! But how came you here? They allow me no visitors."

His heartiness astonished her. Whatever she had expected, it was not this. He seemed contented, happy almost. "The Constable . . ." she stammered. "He remembered me from my days with Her Grace . . ."

"Ah, good old Sir William. Always a friend to the Queen."

A shout from a ferry on the Thames, faint but sharp, penetrated the cell.

"Sir, I have only a few minutes with you, and—"

"Then you must use them to tell me how you are," he said with pleasant authority. He perched on the stool and gestured again for her to take the chair. Stiffly, she sat. Their knees almost touched.

"Now," he said as if her coming was as commonplace as the visits she used to make to Chelsea in the first year she lived with the Queen, "tell me all. You have a husband I have never seen." He wagged a finger at her. "You should have broached to me your plans to marry, you know. But never mind that now." He looked down suddenly, as if the recollection made him uncomfortable. "I actually sent a man to Norfolk at the time to make inquiries, for I was concerned about your welfare. But," he shrugged philosophically, "I had just resigned from office and could ill afford such retainers. The man absconded from my service without giving his account."

Honor felt a chill up her spine, for the man he had sent had probably been his bailiff, Holt. Holt was a man who would have uncovered information about her work if he had set to it; she was grateful now that he was also a man who would only serve a well-paying master.

"In any case," More went on, "general reports satisfied me of this Richard Thornleigh's worth. So, now, tell me of him. Does life in Norfolk suit you? And children? Has God blessed you yet with children? They brought me here over a year ago and I get no news, you know."

At Thornleigh's name Honor stifled the pang that leapt to her heart. "Sir, I have not come to . . . It is of *you* we must speak. Of how to get you away from this place."

More folded his hands calmly in his lap. She saw that the nails were chipped and packed with dirt. "I understand the King already has some such plan for me. Though," he chuckled, "the destination he has in mind would not be my first choice." He looked up at the window. "But a man may lose his head and still come to no harm," he said quietly. "The *final* destination, please God, will make up for all."

He leaned to touch her hand. "No, don't worry. This is not such a bad place. I am sure I am as near God in this cell as ever I was in my fine house. Nearer, maybe. And the regimen is not unpleasant.

Rather like the time I spent in the Charterhouse monastery. That is," he sighed, "it was so until a few days ago when Master Riche fetched all my books and paper away. He came, like all the others, to try to pry from me . . . a thing I would not give. He failed. And so, like a peevish child he took away my books."

"A thing you would not give?" Honor grasped at this opening. "Do you mean acceptance of the Oath?"

More took in a long breath and smiled, and Honor knew he would evade the question. "Do you know, before Master Riche came I wrote a book here. I called it, *A Dialogue of Comfort Against Tribulation*. In scratching it out I thought how very much like a prison is this earthly life. Men are mistaken to presume that they wander free in the world. It is not so. God incarcerates us here on earth in a prison so subtly built that, although it lies open on every side without any wall in the world, and though we wander as far as we may within it, the way to get out we shall never find. And—is it not strange?—upon this prison men build another prison. They garnish it with gold. In it they buy and sell, brawl and chide, dice and gamble, and breed sin in its dark corners. And God is angry at us that we, amid all this folly, forget ourselves and our jail, even forget our chief jailer, God. But God does not forget us. He sees all the while the wicked rule we keep in prison. And so he sends the hangman Death to do his executions."

"No, do not shudder, child. Prisoners like me are blessed, for we have the time to think of these follies, of the bondage of sin. Time to see that all our worldly goods are well lost—they were but added fetters. Time to prepare for true freedom in God's eternity." He added, very softly, "Bishop Fisher is with Him already."

Honor looked down. The Bishop had been beheaded two days before. "Yes," she said. "I arrived back the day they . . . the day he was executed."

More nodded. "A most brave man. And the King, to do him justice, was kind to let him face the ax. No traitor's death after all."

"Kind?" she asked, incredulous. Even at the isolated inn where she had spent the night she had heard the reports. Fisher had been executed at nine in the morning and his headless body had been stripped and left naked to the flies on the scaffold until eight in the evening, then tumbled into a shallow grave at All Hallows Church, in Barking. His head had been parboiled and set on a pike on London Bridge. "If this King is kind, may we never see a tyrant."

More's eyes sparkled with amusement. "The last time I spoke with Bishop Fisher—it was the day we were interrogated by the commissioners at Lambeth—I passed him in the garden, and in the tension of the moment, for we both knew where that day's decisions might lead us, I jested that I hoped we would meet again in heaven. And he observed that the way we had chosen was certainly straight and narrow enough to be the heavenly route!" He laughed.

Honor did not. She was losing patience with his composure, and his jesting. She went to a window and looked out over the city that was celebrating Midsummer Eve. Faint waves of raucous laughter from across the moat scaled the curtain walls. On the horizon, the small glows of bonfires looked puny under the vast, illuminating flashes of lightning. But still the rain held off. "Midsummer madness," she murmured. She turned back sharply. "Sir Thomas, there is not much time left. I have come to—"

"That's right," he said pleasantly. "You said you'd arrived two days ago. From Norfolk was it?"

Exasperation flared in her. Why did he insist on this chatter? "No, sir. From Germany."

"Germany?" His eyes narrowed as if he were bracing himself for unpleasant news. "You left England? Why?"

Honor dropped to her knees before him in the straw and took his hand. "There is no time to explain, sir. Let me say only that for almost a year I have been living in Freiburg as a guest of your old friend, Erasmus. His house is quiet and comfortable and full of your friends, and I have come to take you there."

"Erasmus!" he whispered. She saw that she had surprised him, and there was a smile of relief in his voice. But she noticed, for the first time, the gray hollows of bone around his eyes, and the bloodshot whites within.

"Listen to me," she urged. "They cannot condemn you without a trial. Bishop Fisher signed his own death warrant with his open declaration against the King, but against you they have no evi-

dence. They must give you a trial, and when they do, take the
Oath. Confound them all. Walk away from this wretched place a
free man. Bring away your family and come to Freiburg!"

The corners of his mouth trembled. "No." The single word
rang with finality.

But Honor had seen the tremor that betrayed him, a crack in his
pleasant mask of control. She seized on it. "Sir, you would be so
happy with us in Freiburg. I have been helping Erasmus with his
Ecclesiastes. A forest of a work he calls it, and so it is. Four volumes
already. And many's the time he's wished aloud he had you close
by to offer advice on its progress. His study looks out over a dreaming garden. It is just the place for you. You could write there to
your heart's content. Scholars visit us. Johannes Froben lives
nearby, transforming manuscripts from Florence and Paris on his
new press, and . . . and I have a daughter there. Her name is Isabel. Oh, sir, nothing would please me more than to see her grow
and learn, as I did, under your tutelage."

He was watching her with glistening eyes. Her heart beat faster;
she knew she was winning him! "Erasmus speaks so fondly of the
times you spent together," she pressed on. "'More's Academy' he
always calls your home. And when he does, such happy memories
stir in me. I think of the days when you and I talked of Pliny and
Virgil under the oaks by your pond. I think of our stargazing
nights, and of the laughter we shared over *Utopia*. Do you remember the foolish Vicar of Croydon, sir, who dreamed of voyaging
there? I remember all of it. My life has run along a very different
path since then, but I always—"

"Enough!" The command came from him in a strangled whisper. He pulled free his hand. "The King is more merciful than
you. He does not stoop to torture."

"The King is planning to kill you! I am trying to save you! Sir,
take the Oath and come out. These quibbles of dogma, in both
church and state, are not worth dying for. Take the Oath, and live."

"'Quibbles in dogma'?" Warily, he drew back his head. "So you
phrased it once before. We were in the menagerie, do you remember? You questioned me about Pym. Pepperton, you called him.
We quarreled."

She lowered her eyes. "I remember." She looked up again to find that his gaze at her now smoldered with suspicion.

"Constantly, you know, they send interrogators to me here," he said. "Cromwell, Audeley, Thomas Boleyn. Master Richard Riche. Even," his lip curled, "Father Bastwick." He wielded Bastwick's name suddenly, malevolently, like a knife, and Honor felt a moment of alarm; she had not known Bastwick was one of the commissioners in this case. "They come," More went on, "and they all echo the same refrain. 'Take the Oath and come out!'" His eyes bored into hers. "Have they now sent you?"

"No! How can you think it? I abhor what they have done to you."

"Yet you demand what they demand."

"For your own good."

"So Cromwell tells me."

"To ensure your safety."

"And what of the safety of my soul? How can a lie ensure the safety of my soul?"

"It is no lie to take this oath. It is a miserable oath, a miserable piece of work." She rose from the straw, indignant, her anger fueled by the dreadful knowledge that it was she who had suggested the idea to Cromwell—but not with such a penalty attached! "What kind of promise is it that must be wrenched from a man under fear of death? Which of the King's subjects will be more loyal for having sworn it in the shadow of the ax? What kind of King would demand it under such conditions?"

"It is the law."

"Very well, then," she said, "let us speak of the law. The Oath asks for compliance with the law. And the law is a thing you have always cherished and obeyed. Obey this one!"

"It asks for something else *above* the law. Above God's law. My conscience cannot go so far."

"Yet your conscience would send your body to be destroyed?"

"My body is a poor thing. I marvel so many fight over it."

"This is no jest, sir!" she flared. "You called the King kind in sparing Bishop Fisher the horrors of a traitor's death, but his kindness may not extend to you."

More shuddered. "I know," he said, the light in his eyes withdrawing into the caverns of sockets. Honor saw terror thrashing there. "Father Bastwick often paints the picture for me . . . the agony of the Carthusian monks . . . slowly dismembered. He enjoys telling me of these things, and—" he looked straight at her— "and of other things even more dreadful."

Again, Honor felt suspicion aimed at her in his stare. It startled and unnerved her.

"But I endure it," More concluded. He stood and moved to the window, done with arguing.

But Honor could not give up so easily. "And what of your family? Have you no pity for them, living in penury, your property forfeited to the Crown? I have heard that Lady Alice is now selling her clothes to pay for your upkeep here, yet all of your family have taken the Oath."

"I do not quarrel with anyone whose conscience leads them to do so. Mine will not."

"But what of their safety? Your silence puts your family in danger, though I imagine they are as ignorant as everyone else what your real motives are."

He whirled around on her. "My silence keeps them *out* of danger! Don't you see? If they have sworn the Oath in genuine ignorance of its true meaning they can still be saved in heaven. But if I tell them why the Oath is damnable, why I refuse to swear it, then they are no longer saved by a clear conscience before God."

"Damnable?" she asked quietly.

He stepped back. His face closed. "I have declared again and again: I will not take the Oath; I will not say why." His shoulders heaved with a sigh of infinite weariness. "I do nobody harm. I say none harm. I think none harm, but wish everybody good. And if this is not enough to keep a man alive, in good faith, I long not to live."

"If you are so anxious to die," she said mercilessly, hoping to shock him to his senses, "then why this coy silence? Why not speak out against the statutes and have done?"

He gave her a mirthless smile. "Now you sound like my interrogators, indeed." He looked out the window. "No. I have not been a man of such holy living as to be bold enough to offer myself to death, lest God, for my presumption, desert me."

She watched him, overwhelmed with sadness. She had hoped that she could somehow charm him, or shock him, or beg him into relenting. But she saw that the hope had been a mirage. He had always lived by his principles; now, he was prepared to die by them. "You need not be coy to me about the reasons for your stand, and your silence," she said, halfheartedly batting straw from her skirt. "I know them."

Interest glinted in his eyes.

With some irritation, she intoned what she believed to be his reasoning: "If you do not believe the King to be Supreme head of the English Church—"

"And I do not *say* whether I do or no," he quickly pointed out.

"Quite," she agreed tightly. "But *if* you do not believe it, then by swearing you do believe it you perjure your immortal soul. However, if you declare your reasons for refusing to swear, you forfeit your life. And so you are threatened by a double-edged sword. It is a sword made sharper by the Church's teaching that, since life is a gift from God, to forfeit it is a sin."

His smile was small but proud. "I taught you well."

Somewhere above them, an iron door clanged. "Yet, apparently," More sighed, "the King will settle for nothing less than my total submission."

"Your recantation," she said softly.

He looked sidelong at her. She saw that her use of the word had prickled him. It sparked an idea. Could she *shame* him to his senses? "You have been just as merciless to other men," she said harshly. "To so-called heretics."

The accusation sizzled in the air between them.

"Admit it," she said. "As Chancellor of England you forced men suspected of heresy to answer whether or not they believed the Pope was head of the Church, knowing they would violate their conscience if they said 'yes' and would be burned if they said 'no'. Why should you balk at being forced to make the same impossible choice?"

"There is a difference. When I examined heretics, the law of every country in Christendom laid down that the Pope was head of the Church. The doctrine that the King is Supreme head of the English Church is accepted only here, and rejected in every other country in Christendom."

"But you burned men for holding to their conscience! You argued that it was seditious for a Protestant to refuse to burn a Bible when commanded to do so by the King. But now, you refuse a command of loyalty from that same King."

"Protestants?" He spat out the word. "You call these vermin 'Protestants'?"

"They protest arbitrary authority. As you are doing. The oath you demanded of them, with all the deadly might of the Church behind you, was intolerable. Just as the King's demand for this oath, with all the might of the state behind him, is intolerable."

"The heretics condemned themselves with actions. I do nothing. I simply maintain silence."

"You burned Ralph Pepperton for his silence!"

His face darkened. "That name again. Should I have guessed your true heart that day? The day we quarreled over Pepperton? You turned cold, and afterwards avoided me. Well, tell me now, what do you 'protest'? Do you protest authority so much that you would snatch felons from the law? Carry them away in ships and deposit them abroad to infect the innocent people of other lands? Is that your protest?"

She stared, dumbfounded. Then, suddenly, she understood. "Bastwick told you this."

"Then you do not deny it!" A thin cry came from his throat. "My God. Until this very moment I did not believe it. I thought Bastwick poured such poison in my ears only to wound me. To weaken me. And I resisted!" He held his head, appalled. "I was so sure he lied." He staggered to the stool, clutched for it and thudded onto it. "This is a place for reckoning truth indeed! Honor Larke, the viper in my bosom. Honor Larke, the heretic!"

Honor's heart seemed to stop. He knew everything! And, knowing it, he hated her. All bonds between them now were severed.

The chasm that separated them roared with emptiness, as vast as any imagined pit in hell.

"I thought I had taught my children so carefully. You, who were so quick to learn—I thought I had taught you so well." Blank-eyed, he swiveled on the stool so that his back was to her. "What a cesspool we have made of God's creation!" he moaned.

He was talking to himself, to the walls, cutting her off completely. He lifted his eyes to a crucifix on the wall. "Lord, we defile Your blessed sacrifice. Everything we love on earth turns rank. In truth, I long to leave it!"

Honor tried to take a step toward him, but she could not move. It was as though she stood on the edge of the chasm, and on the far side he was wandering away from her, drifting off toward the mists of death, fading from her view. She burned to call him back. Could she make a bridge with words—the bright, strong words of her newfound understanding? Could she then grasp his hand and haul him back to her side, the side of life?

With a surge of anger at the delusions that stunned his mind, she wanted to shout across to him, *These are hallucinations. I have seen every kind of self-deception forged into every kind of faith in God. I have watched you all kill one another for faith, and I watch you now begging for death, begging at the feet of a man bleeding to death on a cross. Your religion is a cult of death!* She wanted to shout, *Why do you long to leave life for a mirage of heaven? Why, when we have wild musk roses, and swallows, and love between man and woman, and work, and learning, and watching children grow? Are these not heaven enough?*

But she said none of these things. Something held her back. She could neither speak nor move.

More, oblivious to her, heaved a shuddering sigh. "The light in the cathedral is a heavenly light. The gold of saints' halos . . . ivory of their bones . . . red of their blood on the stones . . . stones where Saint Thomas was slain by his king."

He was staring at the gray wall as if he saw such colors emblazoned there, and Honor realized he was lost in a time forty-five years ago, a time when he served as a page-boy in the house of the Archbishop of Canterbury. Days spent in the cathedral that enshrined the bones of Archbishop Thomas à Becket, murdered by a jealous king, and made a saint.

"I long for peace, Lord," More murmured. "I long for sanctuary from the moil of men, the grasping for gold, the lusting, and the vile desires. Once, in the monastery, You gave me that sanctuary, Lord. I was not worthy then. But soon . . . soon, God willing, I will stand among the choiring of angels, and the blessed community of apostles and saints and martyrs that throng the skies . . ."

He rose, lost in his vision, his back still to her. He stretched his arms stiffly at his sides, palms up, so that with his body he formed an arrow, a man offering himself to his God, and intoned:

> "Give me the grace, good Lord
> To set the world at nought;
> To set my mind fast upon thee,
> And not to hang upon the blast of men's mouths;
> To be content to be solitary;
> Not to long for worldly company . . ."

Now, Honor understood what held her back. Now she knew that, finally, she was looking at the real man. Not his thin shield of jests and wit. Not even the beaten armor of his hatred of heretics. But the man who stood naked in his faith. A man in whose huge imagination the heaven-scapes were so peopled with centuries of noble saints and martyrs that any human touch would shatter the magnificent dream.

> "To know my own vileness and wretchedness,
> To humble and meeken myself
> under the mighty hand of God . . ."

And suddenly, she knew what she must do. He had chosen his destiny. Death was his choice. And she must let him die. Equally emphatic was an echo of the truth that had just burst upon her. *Heaven enough, right here on earth? Yes! I want the roses and the swallows. I want to go back to my child. I want to help her grow. What a shift is here! Sir Thomas must be allowed to die, and I can see again why I want to live!* Anger toward him drained out of her, and in its place flowed a sensation of pure love. He chanted on:

> "To bear the cross with Christ;
> To have the last thing in remembrance,
> And to have ever before mine eye my death
> that is ever at hand . . ."

Finally, Honor could move. She almost fell toward him. "Sir Thomas, you *did* teach me well. All the understanding in my heart is thanks to you, and all the tools to search for truth."

She was standing before him, face-to-face, and the impulse of tenderness was so strong in her that she flung her arms around his neck. She held his body tightly against hers and kissed his cheek.

He shivered. In a sudden, violent motion like a spasm his hand plowed into her hair. The other hand swept down her back and groped at her buttock. His lips burned her forehead.

He pulled back. Fear blazed over his face. "Satan!" he cried. "I *knew* you would one day come to me in this guise! Come with soft words and soft flesh, tempting me to abandon God!"

He grabbed two handfuls of her hair and wrenched her head backwards. Honor gasped in pain. "Now I see you, what you are, woman! It is Satan who has tumbled you into heresy. Satan had taken your body as his host." He shouted into her open mouth, "I know what you desire, devil! But my immortal soul you shall never seize!"

His hands ripped free of her hair and instantly manacled her wrists. He twisted her arms behind her, bending them and pinning them against her back with such a savage jolt that she cried out.

"How long have you inhabited this soft body, Satan?" he cried. "Have you been sucking this girl's blood these many years, tempting me to wallow in the muck?" He crushed her to him, pressing her breasts hard against his chest. "Has that been your sport? Have you danced her into a travesty of Christian marriage with another devil, to delight in filthy fornication?" He breathed on her neck,

"And has that devil-husband fed here, amongst these limbs?" His open mouth pressed her throat.

Suddenly, he gasped in horror at his own actions. He released her as if her flesh had scalded his palms.

Honor stood before him, panting, stunned. "You're mad!"

"Leave me, Satan!" he shouted. With the back of his hand he slapped her cheekbone so hard it almost stunned her. "Leave me!"

He raised his arm again to strike. But she caught his wrist with both hands, stopping him. Their arms locked overhead like two warriors.

From the stairwell came a short, sharp laugh. More and Honor twisted.

Jerome Bastwick stood at the cell's entrance.

"What's this?" Bastwick said, and clucked his tongue. "Disharmony in the More household?"

Walsingham came down the final step and waited at Bastwick's side.

"Well," Bastwick went on pleasantly, "perhaps, through this meeting, we can salvage some harmony after all. Do you both remember the last time we were all together? Star Chamber, twelve years ago? We only need gold spangles on this ceiling to make us believe we are in that court again, do we not? We lack only our august judge. But let us take his absence as a cue for a further alteration."

He gave a sharp nod to Walsingham who moved toward Honor.

"The verdict, for instance," Bastwick said. "That verdict never suited me. This time, to see justice done, let us snuff out the *real* criminals. The traitor, and the heretic."

As Walsingham grabbed Honor's arm, Bastwick smiled. "*Fiat justicia.*"

The King's Good Servant

The crowd came early to watch Sir Thomas More die.

He was not yet in sight, but around the roped-off scaffold on Tower Hill the people pressed close: common men and women, lords on horseback, soldiers with staves, courtiers and their ladies. One rising gentleman of the court, however, Master Richard Riche was not present.

Riche had stood as the Crown's witness at More's trial in Westminster Hall on the first day of July. He had been asked by one of the eighteen judges—Cromwell, Audeley, and Thomas Boleyn among them—to tell the court of the conversation that had passed between him and Sir Thomas on the day he had been sent to remove the prisoner's books.

"As I was leaving," Riche had testified, "I put a hypothetical case to the prisoner. 'Say that an act of Parliament made me King,' said I. 'Would not you then take me for King, Sir Thomas?' 'Yes, sir,' replied the prisoner. 'That I would.' 'And say that a further act of Parliament made me Pope,' said I. 'Would you, then, take me for Pope?' 'For answer to that,' the prisoner said, 'let me put a case to you. Suppose the Parliament made a law that God should not be God. Would you, then, Master Riche, say that God were not God?' 'No, sir,' said I, 'for no Parliament may make such a law.'"

"And what said the prisoner to that?" a judge had asked.

"He said, 'No more, Master Riche, than Parliament can make the King Supreme Head of the Church.'"

More had groaned at the charade. Defending himself, he had protested, "My lords, can you really believe that after so carefully denying answer to your subtle questions day in and day out for over a year, I would have babbled the secrets of my conscience to such a man as this?"

But only one witness was required for a conviction of high treason. Riche's perjured testimony sufficed. After fifteen minutes of deliberation the judges sentenced More to death. Mercifully, the barbarous sentence for a traitor was commuted to beheading.

Then, More had finally broken his long silence about his motives.

"My lords," he said, rising before the judges. "This indictment is grounded upon an act of Parliament directly repugnant to the laws of God and His Holy Church, the supreme government of which no temporal prince may presume by law to take upon himself."

Murmurs of astonishment had rippled through the packed court. "This realm of England," More had continued, "may no more refuse obedience to the See of Rome than a child may refuse obedience to a father. England, being but one member and small part of the Church, may not make a particular law disagreeable with the general law of Christ's universal Catholic Church any more than the City of London, being but one poor member in respect of the whole realm, might make a law against an act of Parliament to bind the whole realm. This statute is contrary to the laws and statutes of our own land as laid down in Magna Carta, 'that the English church may be free and that it may exist with all its laws uncorrupted and its liberties unviolated,' and further it is contrary to the sacred oath which the King's highness made at his coronation, swearing to defend the Church."

"And," he had said with rising fervor, "as for my lords' marveling that I so stiffly stand against all the bishops, universities and learned men of the realm, I say that for every bishop who stands with this statute, a hundred stand against it, not in this realm, but in the rest of Christendom. And not only bishops, but a great majority of the living and the dead, and all the holy saints in heaven, too, and all the general councils of Christendom for a thousand years."

"I have no more to say, my lords, except that, as the blessed apostle St. Paul consented to the death of St. Stephen by stoning, and as those two holy saints now are both friends in heaven, so I trust that, though your lordships have been my judges here on earth to my condemnation, we may yet meet merrily in heaven to our everlasting salvation."

Walking now toward Tower Hill, More heard the crowd hush as the first people saw him approach with his escort. He tried to walk steadily. He held tight with both hands to a small red cross. He beat back the thought that red was for martyrs. Pride, the worst of sins.

A woman reached out and touched his shoulder. He heard her fingernails scrape on his robe as she was pulled away. He looked straight ahead.

He saw dust hovering above the straw on the scaffold. The sheriff and the executioner stood there already, waiting. Flies were buzzing over the polished wood of the block. The block itself was very low; he saw that he would have to lie on his stomach to stretch his head across it.

The stairs to the scaffold creaked under his step. For a moment he had to lean on the lieutenant's arm to steady himself as he went up. The executioner walked forward to meet him and, as tradition demanded, went down on his knee for forgiveness. More raised him up and embraced him, and gave his blessing. Then, he looked out across the circle of upturned faces.

The sheriff strode quickly to his side, hands raised. "Forgive me, Sir Thomas. The King's Grace has ordered that you make no lengthy oration."

More squinted up at the bright July sun, then down again at the expectant faces.

"Good people . . ." He was surprised by the thin sound of his voice. Thin and dry. But people were leaning forward. They wanted to hear him. He cleared his throat to begin again. He could smell the sawdust in the bucket that would hold his severed head.

"Good people," he said, "I entreat you to pray for me here on earth, and I shall pray for you in heaven."

He caught the sheriff's frown. The sheriff looked as if he feared he would have to stop a speech after all. But More had only one last thing to say. He looked above the faces, to a band of white clouds on the horizon. His voice came strong and clear.

"I die the King's good servant . . . but God's first!"

Bridget Sydenham had firmly taken her granddaughter's hand and turned the child away from the scaffold as soon as Sir Thomas More mounted the steps. They were leaving. Bridget had no desire to hear More's words, and she was not a woman who thrilled to see her enemy's blood spilled. She had wanted only to satisfy herself that justice was done. To bear witness. For her husband Humphrey's sake.

Pulling the child away from the crowd, Bridget walked with her towards Cheapside. Little Jane had difficulty keeping up with her grandmother's smart pace. As they neared the shops, a cheer went up in the distance behind them. Bridget looked back at Tower Hill. There was silence at the scaffold. It was done.

Jane was pointing eagerly at a pie stall near the busy market cross. Bridget decided it would be a ha'penny well spent. As they neared the stall, a crier arrived at the cross. He took up his position on a box, and people began to drift in around to hear his announcements. Bridget listened with only half an ear, until the final announcement, which caught all her attention. The crier proclaimed of a burning to take place in three days' time at Smithfield. A wicked heretic was to be punished, he declared, both for the edification of the populace and for the hopeful recantation of the heretic herself. The name the crier called out was Honor's.

Bridget Sydenham was surprised. Not that Honor had been captured; it was only too like her to have returned to England for some reason of her own. Bridget was surprised, rather, because she knew that Honor had never been a wholehearted believer in their cause. Yet there it was; Honor was going to burn rather than recant. The Lord's love must have finally reached her after all.

Bridget closed her eyes. She thought of Humphrey, and imagined him, as she always did, sitting at the feet of God. She said a silent prayer that Honor's soul would soon find such sweet repose as well.

"Dear Lord," she whispered, "accept another martyr for Thy dear name."

❧ 38 ❧

Smithfield

Honor's ankle chains clanged over the worn flagstones of St. Paul's. She had just emerged with her escort from the Lollard's Tower in the corner of the cathedral. Led by Bastwick and followed by three officers, she walked barefoot down the nave toward the main doors. She wore a rough homespun tunic and her head was bare, for the clothes she had arrived in she had sold to her jailer for food; the homespun dress was one of his wife's castoffs.

The cathedral doors opened. Sunlight streamed in, dissolving the gloom. Honor stepped outside and squinted in the strong light. She paused for a moment on the step and felt the sun-heated stone warming her feet. She inhaled deeply, then coughed, for the freshness of the air was startling. For two weeks she had been breathing the stuffiness of her cell. The morning air tasted inexpressibly sweet.

An officer bent to unlock her ankle fetters, then nudged her down the stairs. A workhorse stood ready with a hurdle harnessed behind it. Honor lay on her back on the hurdle and the officers strapped her down. The leather restraining thongs cut into her wrists. Bastwick and his men swung onto their mounts, two ahead of her and two behind. One tugged the workhorse's lead. It shook its harness and the small procession started out of the churchyard. Every thud of the hurdle over the cobbles jolted Honor's bones.

People cleared a path as the execution party passed under Newgate. Boys cavorted in its wake. Honor knew there must be a din of voices around her, but she heard nothing but her own heartbeats and her own breaths, slow and deep. Under the baked, blue sky the city outlines drifted past the borders of her vision: peaked roofs, church belfries, tavern signs, and lazy banners, their colors achingly bright.

Nearing Smithfield the hurdle passed slowly under a house-sized chestnut tree, and Honor gazed up entranced at the myriad shades of green in its leafy depths. The scent of its heavy flowers shook a bouquet of memories down on her—the sweetness of the summer hay in Bridget Sydenham's attic where she and Thornleigh had last made love; the fragrance of her baby's hair; the blossoms of speedwells in spring. She pulled the perfume into her lungs and felt it turn liquid inside her, like rising sap. As she moved under the tree, sunlight shot out through the leaves, then hid, then darted out again, its warmth sprinkling her face like a lover's kisses. The beauty of the world swirled around her, beloved and immense. She closed her eyes to resist its seduction, its pull that was draining her resolve. She was ready to die, she was not afraid to die, but this barrage of beauty reminding her of all she must leave behind suddenly seemed too cruel.

More cruel even than Bastwick.

"Do you recant your erroneous beliefs?" he had asked.

He had sat at the head of a committee of three churchmen during her interrogation in St. Paul's. She had answered willingly "Yes," for she longed to live.

And answered truthfully, too, for until that point all their questions had concerned opinions she no longer held, if indeed she ever had. She had almost smiled, in fact, for the two other priests had flailed at her from their rut of anti-Lutheranism, accusing her of only the standard heresies. Unaware of how much beyond the limits of common unorthodoxy her thinking had flown, they probed no deeper. Atheism was beyond their comprehension.

But though they were satisfied, Jerome Bastwick was not, and to his outright demand for her beliefs she had finally lied. The words tasted as bitter as wormwood in her mouth, but lies were all a tyrant deserved; she would not hand him her life.

Bastwick had no choice then but to release her. She stepped outside, a free woman. She walked through the churchyard, stunned, and was pushing through Little Gate into the crowded street when Bastwick's clerk snatched her elbow. He brought her back before the committee as a relapsed heretic. If they found her guilty again, a second recantation would not be permitted.

Bastwick's colleagues expressed some concern that two interrogations of the same suspect within one day was highly unusual. But in the face of his aggressive zeal, the two—a timid vicar and an ambitious young archdeacon—demurred. Bastwick then brought forth a couple of Cromwell's former servants to testify. In the end, it was Honor's own writings held high in Bastwick's hands—the pamphlets commissioned by Cromwell and sworn to by the witnesses as Honor's work—that had condemned her.

The workhorse and hurdle lurched to a stop before the pit at Smithfield. A young groom no more than ten years old ran forward. Bastwick and his men dismounted and handed their horses to the boy. Bastwick strode to the dignitaries' stands. He still limped slightly from the wound Honor had inflicted on London Bridge. He climbed up the stands and took his place.

Dust swirled up to Honor's mouth as people shuffled closer to the rope barrier. The news of her trial and sentence had spread quickly, exciting the city, for the burning of a woman was a rare event. The officers stationed around the pit jabbed a shoulder here and uttered a curse there to keep individuals in line, but the crowd was more fascinated than unruly.

One of the officers cut Honor's leather straps, freeing her from the hurdle. She stood. She was facing away from the pit. Her legs wobbled for a moment, her muscles weak, her brain fogged, for all her energies of body and mind were concentrated in an effort of will to remain strong enough to bear the ordeal to come.

"Turn 'round, mistress!" someone shouted. "The show's this way!"

There was laughter. An officer's hands clamped her shoulders and twisted her around. She looked at the pit straight ahead. A single stake thrust out of the sand. Sticks lay scattered at its base, like bones. Several yards from it, just inside the rope barricade, stood a wagon heaped with straw for extra fuel. Honor looked behind the stake, across the pit. The sun was creeping up the back of the lantern tower of St. Bartholomew's Church. Suddenly, its rays blazed full in her face. She began to lift her hand as a shield, but her muscles would not respond quickly. The motion seemed to take forever. She stood blinking—even her eyelids moved slowly—as the sun bleached her field of vision.

She heard a small voice whisper, "Mistress Larke!"

She turned her head to the right. There were only gaping strangers.

"Over here!" the voice whispered again.

Honor looked to the left. A young woman was leaning forward over the rope, holding out a small wooden cross, offering it. Honor stared at the face. It seemed vaguely familiar.

"Take it, mistress," the young woman entreated with bright eyes, thrusting out the cross. "And take heart! Believe in the Lord Jesus Christ and you will be saved!"

The dull words clanged through the stupor in Honor's brain. The platitude seemed grotesque. *Must I bear this, too?* she thought. *Are these whimpers about God to dog me to the last moment of my life? Are mindless pieties to be the last words I'll ever hear?* It seemed the final humiliation.

The crowd hushed. At the edge of the circle the executioner was striding forward with his flaring torch. Its smoke snaked up into the still air. Two officers flanked Honor and grabbed her elbows. She took a step, but her legs seemed dead as logs already.

A bunch of violets fell at her feet. She looked to the right. Samuel Jinner's leathered face stared across the rope. Tears glistened in his eyes. Honor gasped as if wounded, for the sight of him brought Thornleigh's face blazing into her mind, and then Isabel's, the rosebud mouth sucking at her breast. The images unstopped a violent surge of regret, a torment that drained more of the precious energy she was clinging to for strength. It was not dying she feared. She had died once before, in the hold of the *Dorothy Beale*, and she knew that death was no more than a stopping of her body's motions. But this torture of regret, of loss, of beloved faces she would never see again was overwhelming. Her body slumped. The officers had to drag her the last few feet to the stake.

A priest came to her side and began a sermon. "Though our pious King strives to burn heresy from his realm . . ."

"Step up!" An officer was prodding her. She realized he wanted her to go up onto a narrow, wooden shelf tacked to the base of the stake. It would hold her higher so that all the onlookers would have a clear view.

She stepped up. The shelf was cut from rough lumber. A splinter gouged the skin between her toes.

"Yet still," the preacher went on, "the heretics run under the fouled skirts of Luther, or to the bosom of the painted whore of Rome . . ."

A young guard strode toward Honor carrying a heavy chain. It was black with soot. Soot streaked his sleeve. He took his place behind her at the stake and waited while the officer tied her hands behind her back with twine.

Honor's eyes blurred over the heads of the crowd, then focused on one. The face was staring straight into her own eyes, as still as a rock—a woman, tall and stern, with iron gray hair under a starched cap and a face of fretted bone. Bridget Sydenham.

Again, regret stabbed Honor's heart. This woman's sweet-natured husband she could not save, and her friend, Brother Frish, she had lured home to his death. In so much, she had failed. Yet on Mrs. Sydenham's solemn, unmoving face she read no blame. In fact, at the corners of her mouth there was the slightest motion— was there not?—yes, the merest smile was forming on those thin lips. It was a smile that spoke of understanding, of respect, even of love. Honor's tears spilled, grateful for this final, generous gift.

". . . in the name of the Father, and of the Son, and of the Holy Ghost . . ."

The priest was fidgeting the sign of the cross over her. When he had finished he walked away. The officers who had brought Honor to the stake left, too. From behind her, the young guard's sooted hands thrust out the chain. His hands met in front of her waist to pass the chain around her body and the stake.

There was an explosion. Honor knew it must be in her head— her own mind screaming, or letting go. But then she heard a woman cry out. And she saw the chain slump into the soldier's right hand, unfastened.

There was a second blast. Another scream. The sound of fear eddied through the crowd like wind riding through a forest.

"It's St. Bartholomew's!" someone cried. "Look! Up there!"

All heads turned to the church, Honor's as well. People were pointing up to the lantern tower. A cloud of black smoke was boiling along its flat top. From its billowing center a form sprang out.

"A devil!" a woman screamed.

And so it was. A black-furred monster like an ape. Its grotesque face was as bleached as a skeleton except for coal-red eyes. Its skull sprouted massive antlers, and under them long, black witch's hair streamed. The creature danced and leapt on the tower, its scarlet cloak flashing like flame. Its claws, like long knives, lashed at the smoky air. When it flung wide its arms, fire erupted at its feet, fire as white as the sun that blazed at its back.

"Satan himself!" a man bleated. "He's come for the heretic! Come to claim his own!" He thrashed his way out of the crowd. Several women fell to their knees. People crossed themselves or buried their faces in their hands.

The Devil shrilled a long, blood-freezing wail. When its beastly arms jerked out again, a ball of fire hurtled down from the tower. It exploded at the feet of some people, sparking skirts, igniting fear. The creature cast out more missiles—some were tarry globs of flame, some were sulfurous blasts. They flared inside the pit. One hit the fuel wagon. The straw roared into flames.

Panic swept the crowd. The wagon was close to the rope around the pit, and people standing in the front ranks whirled and tried to push their way out, but the ones behind stood dumbly gaping up at the monster, blocking the way. The frenzied front ranks turned back and crashed through the rope and stampeded across the pit. Monks were now streaming from the church doors, craning up at the fire-throwing demon on their tower. The mayor and aldermen were on their feet in the stands, shouting. Some were clambering down the tiers. Under the Devil's hail of fireballs the square soon seethed with fleeing men and women, monks and children, all zigzagging around the growing pools of flame.

A cold hand snatched Honor's arm. She gasped at the creature before her—a man's body with a fox's face. He drew a dagger. She froze as it whipped by her throat. But he bent and slit the twine binding her wrists. As people rushed past, screaming, two more demi-humans appeared at Honor's side. These were women's forms, one with the face of a horned goat, the other a hawk, tall and fierce. They sprang at the guard behind the stake and knocked him to the ground. The chain clattered from his hands.

The fox-man yanked Honor from her death-perch.

"Flee!" the hawk-woman commanded. And in the wildness of the moment Honor thought it was the voice of Bridget Sydenham.

Two officers were running toward Honor. Suddenly, white-faced devils appeared and danced like savage monkeys in front of the officers, barring their way.

The fox-man seized Honor's hand. Disoriented, she stumbled after him. No one stopped them; even in the mindless swirl of panic, people were staying clear of his swiping dagger. He and Honor reached the trampled rope. A horse and rider appeared. The fox-man threw his cloak around Honor, then hoisted her up behind the rider—another apparition, this one a man with the head of a lion. With Honor barely aboard he whipped the frightened horse into the sea of scattering men and women. He was heading east toward the dignitaries' stands.

Honor saw Bastwick hurrying down the last steps. He was pointing at her, his face red with fury. "Stop her!" he screamed.

His officers were already at their horses, shouting at the young grooms, but there was confusion there—a jumble of children around the horses—and Honor saw that none of the men were mounting.

The Devil atop the church kept up its hail of fire, but Bastwick ignored it. He was striding straight for Honor, lurching with his limp but closing the gap, for the horse was making little headway

in the crowd. With eyes fixed on her he moved through the panicked people like a rolling prow splitting waves. The lion-headed
horseman could not break free of the melee.

Bastwick burst through and reached the horse. He snatched the
bridle. The horse danced on the spot. A fireball spewed down from
the tower onto Bastwick's back. He gasped and let go the bridle
and clawed over his shoulder. But the flaming tar stuck to him.
Fire swept across his back and jumped to his hair. Screaming, he
dove to the ground and rolled. People staggered back, opening a
space. The horse, sensing escape, whinnied and strained. The
horseman gave it its head, and they bolted forward.

Honor glanced back. A wave of running people had reached
Bastwick. In their terror to escape, they were trampling him.

As the horse capered past the stands, the horseman jerked his
lion's mask up onto his forehead. Its gold mane tumbled down his
shoulders over his own long, silvery-black hair.

"You don't recall me, mistress!" he shouted exuberantly back at
her. "Legge's the name. You offered to do me a kindness once. Remember?"

"Bastwick's man!" she cried. She let go of his coat and prepared
to jump.

But Legge was a hardened soldier, and it was a strong hand that
whipped backwards around her waist and held her tight, even as
the horse galloped on. "*Was* his man, but no longer," Legge said,
and Honor suddenly recalled how in those moments of crisis on
London Bridge Legge had given her his fast horse. He released
her and grappled the reins again with both hands. They were at
the edge of the square.

Clutching Legge's coat, Honor turned for a last look at the monster atop the lantern tower. Shouting monks were hurling stones at
it, but even as it held up its arms to deflect the blows it lurched to
the edge as if to watch her go, and she saw, as it came forward, that
one of its feet turned inward. Her breath stopped. Her heart recognized that awkwardly lovable gait before her mind could grasp
the truth.

"It's Richard!"

"None other," Legge cried. "For a year and more I've served

him. No, don't faint away, my lady, for I promise you it's God's truth!"

Richard's alive! "But how—?"

"Later! I'm sworn to him to get you safe away. Hold on!" He bent over the horse's neck and dug his heels into its flanks.

They cannoned into an alley, sending pigs squealing, then galloped down narrow streets, zig-zagging into one after another until Honor was as lost as in a labyrinth. Legge's riding was sure and swift, as if he had had much practice in evading the law.

They gained Cheapside and quickly merged with the bustle of the thoroughfare. Honor could hold back no longer. "But on London Bridge I saw Bastwick's archers kill him. I saw him plunge into the river. How—?"

"Oh, the arrows hit him alright," Legge said. "And he plunged alright. From the downstream shore I watched him bob over the rapids like a speared perch. But when the priest's men rode into Southwark after you, I scrambled down the bank and fished him out. For many a week he lay in my house, and my wife swore that with all those wounds he'd sink again, and that would be into his final sleep. But Master Thornleigh's a tough bugger. Ha! I knew as much that night at Mrs. Sydenham's when he told you to watch out for *me*!"

Honor could not speak. To have life and love handed back in the same heartbeat was almost too much joy. Then, suddenly, questions burst from her. "But how has he managed this? And who were those others?"

"Did you not know Sam Jinner when he snatched you?"

"The fox-man!" she cried.

"He insisted he'd have none other take the job of plucking you away."

"And the hawk-woman? Was that really Bridget Sydenham?"

"Aye. And with her, a game young widow—"

"Alwyn! I knew I'd seen that face before! She and her grandfather, old Master Paycocke, were on the *Speedwell*'s maiden voyage. But she lives in Amsterdam—"

"She came home when the old man died. Said she couldn't change to foreign ways."

Honor was trying to digest the flurry of information. "And the others?"

"All those silly, painted devils? More of your friends. Some of them started the show by shouting, 'Look! The Devil!'" He shook his head as if amazed by the success of the rescue. "Can you credit the fear of folks?"

"Friends?" she asked, at a loss.

"Some, men you've saved. Mostly, relatives of men you've saved. All mustered gladly at Master Thornleigh's call, for he'd arrived at Mrs. Sydenham's just after she heard of your fate."

Honor was overcome. Her brain was smothered under the avalanche of shocks. "But, he'll . . . they'll all be in danger now."

"No. They'll slip off the masks and no one will be the wiser in that mad crowd. Even if one or two are nabbed, well, what's the crime in a body being in possession of a fool's mask?"

"But, Sam stabbed at an officer—"

"Oh, Jinner'll make it away, never fear. To collect his wager from me, if for nothing else. He was proud as a peacock about that fox get-up of his, so just to rile him I bet him a shilling that you'd know him straight away. But," he growled, "it's clear you didn't." He glanced back at her and his gravelly voice softened. "You wouldn't consider telling him a small mistruth, my lady?"

She laughed. "Master Legge, I have done forever with lies and deception!"

She glanced back at the normal bustle of the street behind them. "It's incredible. No one has followed us."

Legge chuckled. "The children saw to that."

"Children?" The tale was becoming more fantastic at every turn.

"Aye. When we heard your fate three days ago, Mistress Sydenham sent her little granddaughter, Jane, to skip out to Smithfield and make a friend of the boy who grooms there. When we saw you drawn up to the pit, that imp and her band of cousins set about their work. Some of the officers' horses they hobbled. Some they fed horse-bane. So when the men went to mount 'em, they came upon swooning, useless beasts. All I needed was a head-start."

Honor threw her head back and laughed. Bastwick had been outwitted by a pack of children!

They were trotting into Thames Street, and Honor smelled the river and glimpsed the traffic of ferries plying around the wharves. She had already guessed that the river would be their destination.

"Now, Master Legge, tell me of your master. Tell me all. I am hungry to hear of him. What is his plan for escaping from the Smithfield tower?"

Legge edged the horse towards Paul's Wharf. "My wife's brother's a fishmonger," he said brightly. "He has a barge waiting."

This was no answer. Honor tensed. "Master Legge, tell me."

He sighed. "I warn you now, my lady. Master Thornleigh may have a rough time getting quit at Smithfield."

They had reached the wharf and had to trot in silence past a handful of ferrymen and lounging customers. Legge halted the horse, swung his leg over its neck, jumped down and tethered it. He turned to help Honor, but she was already sliding off on her belly, her bare feet stretching for the ground. Legge grabbed her elbow and spoke in a gruff whisper. "His orders were we should not wait for him above a quarter hour." He saw her blanch, but without waiting for a reply he hustled her towards the barge.

It was a grimy, patched affair, with two shipped sets of splintered oars. A low cabin of woven-reed mats tacked onto a wooden frame took up half its stern, and a flap of sack-cloth was slung across the cabin's entrance. As they approached, the craft appeared deserted. Then, a hand threw up the flap and a dark, tousled head popped out.

"Adam!" Honor cried, and covered her mouth too late. One or two of the men on the wharf glanced over. But Honor noticed nothing but Thornleigh's bright-eyed son beaming out at her.

Legge pushed the two inside the cabin, then followed. As Honor and Adam embraced, Legge flopped down on a heap of nets and peered out through a puncture in the reed walls. "Now, we wait," he growled. It was clearly the part of the plan he loathed and mistrusted.

The other two could not speak fast enough. Clasping hands, they breathlessly compared stories.

"And so," Adam finished, "my aunt Joan and her husband have had the care of my father's business all the while he searched for you."

"Searching abroad all these months!"

"We feared you were dead."

"I thought it safer for you to think so. I was so sure that *he* was dead."

"He wrote us that he'd followed your trail to Amsterdam, then lost it. He kept searching southward. He even went to France. In a hill-town there he had to fight a highwayman who almost stole his horse."

"And all the while I was safe in Freiburg."

"The name of Erasmus never crossed our minds."

"Of course not. Why should it? An old scholar I had never even met."

"Finally," Adam said, "Father found friends of the people who had taken you to Münster, and he said he knew then that you must be inside that place, a prisoner. And then, just weeks ago, he wrote us again from Münster. The Prince-Bishop's army had routed the city, and all the inhabitants were killed. My father wrote us he was coming home."

Honor felt a pang for the poor Deurvorsts. Then her eyes darted to Legge. He was still peering out between the reed mats. Where was Thornleigh?

Legge got up. Adam took the cue. His young face settled instantly into that of a man of action. He pulled his hands from Honor's. "Pardon me, madam," he said, "I must see to the charts."

She gazed at the boy, now a sturdy thirteen-year-old, and for his sake she forced down her fears. There was time yet, she told herself, for Thornleigh to reach the barge.

Adam busied himself with the charts. Legge prowled the small cabin, his fighting hand twitching near his sword. The nearby bells of Blackfriars and St. Paul's clanged in angry discord.

"That's it," Legge growled. "I'm sorry, my lady, but we must be gone if any of us is to see another day."

"No!" she begged. "We cannot leave him. Another quarter hour, please!"

Legge set his jaw, uttered a low oath, then paced again. The quarter hour passed.

Outside, there came the thudding of horse's hooves.

"Richard!" Honor's hands flew to her mouth to muffle the cry of happiness. But when she caught the gleam of Legge's drawn sword and the dagger that quivered in Adam's hand she realized that it was not Thornleigh they expected.

The hooves halted. Footsteps, solid and hurried, thudded in their place. The three in the cabin watched the swaying sackcloth flap. No one dared to breathe.

The flap was wrenched up.

"Sam!"

Honor embraced him. A young man ducked in after Jinner. His forehead was gashed, bright with blood. "You helped his brother to Antwerp, my lady," Jinner said quickly by way of introduction. "He's off to join him, if you'll agree."

She thanked them both profusely. And then they all sat down to wait.

Finally, Legge's nervousness burst out. "No more, my lady. It's well past time. The first place they'll check is the wharves. We must be off!"

She looked from face to face. Each one stared back at her, waiting for her to give the word. They were brave men who had already proved their courage in her rescue, and she knew that they would wait longer, wait an hour even, if she begged it. But she also saw in each man's eyes an ache to be gone, a craving to be out of harm's reach. She looked at Adam, so gallantly steadfast, so bravely ready to carry out his father's wishes. One of those wishes, she knew, would be to have his son safe. How could she forsake such a duty? Accepting it, her shoulders sagged. She nodded to Legge.

"Cast off!" he cried, springing past her. "Man the oars!" The other three dashed out behind him. Slowly, Honor followed.

She crouched on deck, afraid of being seen yet unable to tear her eyes from the wharf. She searched the moving forms for Thornleigh's. But he was not there.

The water was calm and the barge slipped out into the river traffic, leaving Paul's wharf behind. They passed the Steelyard Wharf. London Bridge loomed dead ahead. Once through the turbulence under its arches they would have smooth going to Gravesend. And at Gravesend, Adam had said, the *Speedwell* waited at anchor.

Honor watched Paul's wharf dwindle in the distance. She felt suddenly cold. She lifted the flap to go back into the cabin. The faint sound of splashing made her glance over her shoulder.

The flap fell from her hand. In the water, between the barge and the Steelyard Wharf, someone was swimming toward them.

"Stop!" she cried to the rowers.

Legge and Jinner shipped their oars. "Good Christ, he's made it!" Jinner croaked. He clambered to the side.

Honor was already leaning out, stretching her hands out to the flailing arms blurred behind spray.

They pulled Thornleigh aboard and he flopped onto the deck. He was naked to the waist, his devil's costume abandoned, and he sat with his head between his drawn-up knees, sputtering and fighting for air. Red and black lines of scarlet paint and charcoal ran down the tendons of his neck. He flung his head up, and water drops flew from his hair. He turned his face to Honor. She gasped. A sodden leather patch covered his left eye.

She threw an arm under him and with her help he struggled to his feet, his chest still heaving for air. They stood for one charmed moment face-to-face.

She was the first to speak. "You take too many risks, my love."

He threw his head back with a laugh. "And you," he said, taking her face in his hands and gazing at her, "you take my breath away."

"You have a daughter," she said softly. And when she saw tears spring into the one eye that, all alone, beamed as blue as the summer sky, she fell against him and they kissed with all the hunger of four hundred days and nights of longing.

"Bridge ahead!" Jinner shouted. Thornleigh and the other men leaped to the oars to manage the sudden swell of the river. Compressed between the stone arches, the angry water frothed and roared.

Honor and Adam held tight to the gunwales as the barge shuddered through the rapids. Above, at the entrance to the bridge, a grisly array of heads pinned on pikes leered down at them. Sunlight glanced off the head of Sir Thomas More. Its eyes were wide and staring, but blind in death. As he was blind to so much in life, Honor thought. Now, blind for all eternity.

The barge passed safely under the arch. The river calmed. Thornleigh left the other two men to row, and came back and slipped his arm around Honor.

She smiled up at him and wiped a smear of charcoal from his cheek. "My husband, the Devil." She shook her head in amazement. "But how could you know it would work?"

He grinned. "People believe what they want to believe."

She hugged him, then looked back at More's head atop the bridge. Adam followed her gaze. "That man must have been a terrible traitor," he said with a shiver.

"Only to himself," she murmured. A thought struck. "Once we're safe across the Channel, Adam, there's a book I'll buy for you. It's called *Utopia*. I want you to have it." She searched the boy's face for a fragment of her past, a moment long ago when a stranger had placed in her hands a book she could not read.

She looked up again and watched the head become a small, featureless blot against the sunny sky. "*Utopia*," she said. "As long as it speaks to the living, its author will never die. There lies Sir Thomas More's immortality."

AUTHOR'S NOTES

Historical facts are the core of historical fiction. In writing about people who actually lived, I have taken care, when setting a scene, not to deviate from the historical record. King Henry and Queen Catherine, Anne Boleyn, Cardinals Wolsey and Campeggio, Cromwell, Holbein, Erasmus, and the fascinatingly complex Sir Thomas More—even "King" Jan of Münster and his several wives—all are placed, whenever possible, in the actual locations of the events they participated in, and at the actual times. (The London apprentices did riot on May Day, 1517, when Thomas More was Undersheriff; Queen Catherine did beg Henry on her knees at the Blackfriars trial; More did wear a hair shirt and indulge in self-flagellation; and Anabaptists in Münster did institute mass baptisms, mass executions, and polygamy.) While the words and thoughts of the historical figures in the novel are my speculation, their actions are authentic.

There are two exceptions, both temporal in nature. Sir Thomas More resigned the chancellorship in May 1532, but for the dramatic purposes of my story, I have set the scene of his resignation six months later. The second exception regards Cuthbert Tunstall, More's friend, who was Bishop of London from 1522. In 1530 he was transferred to the see of Durham, and John Stokesley became Bishop of London. However, to reduce confusion for the reader, I have retained Tunstall as Bishop of London throughout 1532.

As for the characters I have invented—Honor Larke and Richard Thornleigh, Ralph Pepperton, Bastwick, Frish, the Sydenhams, the Deurvorsts, and Pieter—they "live" only in that best of all possible worlds, the reader's imagination.

A note about Sir Thomas More's family. While I have invented Honor, and, consequently, her position as More's ward, More did in fact have three wards, two female and one male. He married two of them to his children, Cecily and John. The marriages appear to have been happy ones.

It seems cruel to leave any reader in ignorance of the fate of the passionate and tenacious historical figures who appear in the novel, so I include here some notes about their various destinies after July 1535, when the book closes.

In January 1536, Catherine of Aragon, still avowing her love for Henry, died in her bed from natural causes.

The summer that More was executed, Erasmus went back to Basle. The following year, while still working on his *Ecclesiastes* in old Froben's printing shop, Erasmus died—a "preacher of that general kindness which the world still so urgently needs." (Huizinga)

On May 19, 1536, Anne Boleyn was beheaded. She had failed to produce a male heir, and Henry instructed Cromwell to find a way out of the marriage. Cromwell's commissioners quickly brought charges against Anne of adultery with several courtiers—including her own brother—and, using a gross interpretation of the law, they called the adultery "treason." For good measure, Henry once again exploited the rules against consanguinity in canon law, for, as J. J. Scarisbrick tells us: "Two days before Anne died, a court presided over by Archbishop Cranmer at Lambeth reached the astounding conclusion that Henry's earlier adultery with her sister, Mary, had rendered the marriage void from the start."

The day after Anne's execution, Henry was betrothed to Jane Seymour, one of Anne's ladies-in-waiting, and on May 30 he married her. In 1537 Jane gave birth by Cesarean section to the son Henry craved, Prince Edward. Twelve days later, "a victim of that terrifying thing, Tudor medicine," Jane was dead.

Cromwell urged Henry to take Anne of Cleves for his next wife—a political union, for Henry did not lay eyes on the German lady until just days before the marriage in 1540. When he finally did see her he was physically repulsed by the "Flanders mare," did not consummate the marriage, and had it declared null. Humiliated and furious after the ordeal, Henry ordered Cromwell arrested. On July 28, 1540, Thomas Cromwell was beheaded. (A century later, his nephew's great-grandson, the Puritan Oliver Cromwell, ruled England under the Commonwealth.)

Henry immediately took, for his fifth wife, a sensuous nineteen-year-old, Catherine Howard. A year and a half later, maddened by her adulteries, he had her beheaded. His final marriage was to an intelligent, good-natured widow, Catherine Parr. She outlived Henry.

On January 28, 1547, Henry VIII's corpulent body released its hold on life. His nine-year-old son took the throne as Edward VI, made the country officially Protestant, and six years later died of tuberculosis. At the age of thirty-seven, Henry's daughter by Catherine of Aragon became Queen Mary I—"Bloody Mary." She wrenched the country back to Catholicism, burned some three hundred Protestants at the stake, married Philip II of Spain, and died childless after five years on the throne. Henry's daughter by Anne Boleyn was then crowned Elizabeth I at age twenty-five. She kept a tight leash on both Catholic and Protestant extremists, made the sea lanes safe for pirating English seamen (and claimed a Queen's share of their plunder), beat the "invincible" Spanish armada, never married, and ruled a prosperous England for forty-five years.

In 1536 William Tyndale, the English exile, was burned at the stake in Antwerp. Though only a name in the novel and not a character who makes an appearance, Tyndale had a profound impact on his world, and ours. The English Church had fought hard to suppress any vernacular Bible and burned all the copies of Tyndale's translation it could seize. Yet when an English version of Scripture was eventually authorized, the committee turned to this "heretic's" work as its cornerstone; a large percentage of the King James Version of the Bible is Tyndale's sublime prose.

The odious Richard Riche, after satisfying Cromwell by delivering the perjured testimony that doomed Sir Thomas More, went on to give evidence against Cromwell five years later. Riche was Lord Chancellor from 1547 to 1551 and was made a baron. He enforced the persecution against Catholics under Edward VI (including turning out the monks of the Church of St. Bartholomew at

Smithfield and making it into a house for his own use); then helped burn Protestants in the reign of Mary. He died in 1567, a respected justice of the peace and landowner in Essex.

In 1945, in Rome, Sir Thomas More was declared a saint of the Catholic Church.